DWARFS

BENEATH THE MOUNTAINS of the Old World lies the great realm of the dwarfs. Miners and smiths beyond compare, the dwarfs are renowned for their appetite for battle, thirst for ale and lust for gold. Fighting a constant struggle for survival against goblins, skaven and other creatures of the deeps, they strive to restore their realm to the glory of ancient days.

This omnibus edition collects three novels and a short story featuring tales of broken honour, desperate vengeance and mighty battles against impossible odds. It also includes *Grudgelore*, epic tales from dwarf history of the grudges they hold against their most hated foes.

Grudge Bearer – Barundin, the newly-crowned king of Zhufbar, embarks upon a desperate quest to avenge the treachery that led to his father's death. When he uncovers a grave threat to his people, Barundin must choose between duty and vengeance in this epic tale that spans centuries.

Oathbreaker – When Karak Varn is overrun by the skaven, Uthor Algrimson makes a rash vow to reconquer the hold from the verminous ratmen, or die in the attempt. He and his band of brave and stalwart dwarfs face goblins, trolls and worse as they battle to reclaim the hold, little realising that their bold endeavour is doomed.

Honourkeeper – King Bagrik's son is dead, slain by Chaos marauders. Overcome with grief, the king forges an alliance with Prince Ithalred of the elves to exact revenge. Beset by enemies, secrets threaten to tear the allies apart and lead them all to destruction.

Grudgelore recounts great deeds from the long history of the dwarfs. Epic battles against barbarous greenskins, verminous skaven and treacherous elves shed new light on the culture of the sons of Grungni – and no one holds a grudge like a dwarf.

By Nick Kyme

· WARHAMMER ·

GRIMBLADES – An Empire Army novel

· WARHAMMER 40,000 ·

The Tome of Fire trilogy

Book 1 – SALAMANDER
Book 2 – FIREDRAKE
Book 3 – NOCTURNE (November 2011)
FIREBORN (Audio drama)

FALL OF DAMNOS – A Space Marine Battles novel

THUNDER FROM FENRIS (Audio drama)

By Gav Thorpe

· WARHAMMER ·

Time of Legends: The Sundering

Book 1 – MALEKITH
Book 2 – SHADOW KING
Book 3 – CALEDOR
AENARION (Audio drama)

· WARHAMMER 40,000 ·

The Eldar Path series

Book 1 – PATH OF THE WARRIOR
Book 2 – PATH OF THE SEER (September 2011)

THE PURGING OF KADILLUS – A Space Marine
Battles novel

THE LAST CHANCERS OMNIBUS
(Contains the novels *13th Legion*, *Kill Team* and
Annihilation Squad)

· THE HORUS HERESY ·

RAVEN'S FLIGHT (Audio drama)

DWARFS

Nick Kyme & Gav Thorpe

BLACK LIBRARY

A Black Library Publication

Grudge Bearer copyright © 2005, Games Workshop Ltd.
Oathbreaker and *Grudgelore* copyright © 2008, Games Workshop Ltd.
Honourkeeper copyright © 2009, Games Workshop Ltd.
Ancestral Honour first published in *Inferno!* magazine,
copyright © 2001, Games Workshop Ltd.
All rights reserved.

This omnibus edition published in Great Britain in 2011 by
The Black Library,
Games Workshop Ltd.,
Willow Road,
Nottingham, NG7 2WS, UK.

10 9 8 7 6 5 4 3 2 1

Map by Nuala Kinrade

Grudgelore illustrations by Alex Boyd, Paul Dainton, Wayne England, David Gallagher,
Mark Gibbons, John Gravato, Des Hanley, Paul (Prof) Herbert, Quinton Hoover, Jeremy
Jarvis, Veronica Jones, Jeff Johnson, Karl Kopinski, Andrew Law, Michael Phillippi,
Duane Redhead, Wayne Reynolds, Adrian Smith, Geoff Taylor, Tiernen Trevallion, Andrea
Uderzo, John Wigley and Sam Wood.

A CIP record for this book is available from the British Library.

UK ISBN13: 978 1 84970 048 1
US ISBN13: 978 1 84970 049 8

See the Black Library on the internet at

www.blacklibrary.com

Find out more about Games Workshop
and the world of Warhammer at

www.games-workshop.com

Printed and bound in the UK.

CENTURIES BEFORE SIGMAR united the tribes of man and forged the Empire, dwarfs and elves held sway over the Old World.

Beneath the mountains of this land lies the great realm of the dwarfs. A proud and venerable race, dwarfs have ruled over their subterranean holds for thousands of years. Their kingdom stretches the length and breadth of the Old World and the majesty of their artifice stands boldly for all to see, hewn into the very earth itself.

Miners and engineers beyond compare, dwarfs are expert craftsmen who share a great love of gold, but so do other creatures. Greenskins, ratmen and still deadlier beasts that dwell in the darkest depths of the world regard the riches of the dwarfs with envious eyes.

At the height of their Golden Age, the dwarfs enjoyed dominion over all that they surveyed but bitter war against the elves and the ravages of earthquakes put paid to this halcyon era. Ruled over by the High King of Karaz-a-Karak, the greatest of their holds, the dwarfs now nurse the bitter memories of defeat, clinging desperately to the last vestiges of their once proud kingdom, striving to protect their rocky borders from enemies above and below the earth.

CONTENTS

INTRODUCTION

by Gav Thorpe

HANDS UP IF you think Gimli is way cooler than Legolas? Chances are that you are now holding this book in one hand, otherwise why did you buy a book full of stories about dwarfs? Let's face it, everyone knows Gotrek could take down Teclis. Though of late my foray into all things elfy in The Sundering has perhaps led me astray, my Warhammer heart has always been, first and foremost, for those bearded underground dwellers (and I don't mean Great Uncle Bulgaria from the Wombles).

I've had a soft spot, underneath a suitably craggy exterior, for Warhammer dwarfs for a long, long time. You have to admire their dependability and stubbornness, and an attitude to craftsmanship we should all aspire to. From the grumbling longbeards to the fatalistic slayers, dwarf society is rich in character, pathos and humour that we can all relate to. There is also a certain kind of self-denial about the dwarfs that endears me to them; a race of folk who take their word so seriously they can actually die of shame while at the same time harbouring all manner of secret ambitions and desires.

It's perhaps a very British (nay, English) mindset to confront monstrous dragons and the delicate rituals of courtship with an equally stiff upper lip, concluding both encounters with a gruff harrumph and getting on with normal life. Indefatigable perhaps describes the dwarfs best; a slow but relentless determination to overcome with no regard to the odds of a good outcome.

11

The dwarfs are the people of the mountains not just in geography but also in outlook and culture. Yielding only slowly to change, yet helpless against the constant erosion that is existence. As solid and predictable as an everlasting peak, yet prone to occasional ferocious tempests that sweep away all in their path. Simple and serene from a distance, yet hiding highly complex ways that are dangerous to navigate. The dwarfs are born of the mountains, and from the mountains they take their strength.

Grudgebearer still remains one of my favourite novels. Not only was it the first book I wrote that attempted to tell a tale that lasted for centuries, it gave me an unprecedented opportunity to delve into that most intricate of dwarf constructions – the grudge. A thing that has a life of its own, living beyond generations, hungering to be answered, nagging at the minds of those whose shoulders it falls upon. The grudge is dwarfishness incarnate, and nothing encompasses better the huge weight of dwarf belief and law. Plus who would pass up the chance to write a few, ahem, bawdy dwarf songs (with thanks to generations of Rugby players that inspired them)?

Following the grudge theme, it was also an immense pleasure to pen *Grudgelore* with Nick. We spent much time together amusing ourselves with endless conversations on the minutiae of dwarf culture and technology, throwing back and forth any and every idea that came to us. It is something of a credit to the enduring quality of the Warhammer dwarfs that we could have filled many more volumes with the stuff we came up with, but the select amount presented in this book will have to suffice. I hope you enjoy my and Nick's efforts as much as we enjoyed producing them.

Now, sing along everyone...
Gold, gold, gold, gold... Gold, gold, gold, gold...

Gav Thorpe

INTRODUCTION

by Nick Kyme

IT WAS ABOUT twenty years ago (man, that sounds like a long time – it's two-thirds of my entire life!) when I wandered into my local hobby shop D. Hewings and bought two blister packs of dwarf models. My eldest brother Richard got me into Games Workshop in the first place, and it was when I was flicking through one of his *White Dwarf* magazines that I came across a page of dwarfs. Back then they were made by Marauder miniatures (before it all became one sculpting house) and I *loved* them – the stout armour, the gruff expressions, meaty weapons and bushy beards – they were the race for me.

I didn't play Warhammer then, instead I used the old Citadel Combat Cards to make up game rules and stats so my dwarfs could batter the living Grimnir out of each other – at least, in my imagination.

My blister pack of hammerers and longbeards (the ones I bought from the model shop – we didn't have a GW in Grimsby back then) were soon joined by monsters, beasts, undead but more importantly more dwarfs. And I can honestly say, twenty years and a vast horde of the little blighters on, the dwarfs are still my favourite of all the Warhammer races. I've been lucky: I've got to play them in a battle report for *White Dwarf*, write background articles for them (anyone remember 'Bugman's Lament'?) and interview designers (esteemed chaps like Gav, who I share this sturdy volume with) about them, I've even penned two and a half novels about the sons of Grungni, which leads me neatly to this omnibus.

Within you'll find three grudge-filled, orc-slaying, elf-hating,

13

gold-loving, stubborn-as-stone novels about the dwarfs and some shiny extra material fit for the treasure vault of any thane. I'm pretty sure almost all of the archetypes are covered – I made especially sure to include a hammerer and a longbeard in my first ever Warhammer novel, *Oathbreaker*. Let's just say the characters of Gromrund and Halgar were in homage to those first miniatures I bought. You'll also find slayers, runesmiths, ironbreakers, thanes, quarrellers, engineers, princesses, reckoners and even thieves amongst the sprawling cast.

Not only *Oathbreaker*, but from my rune-scribe's fingers you'll also get *Honourkeeper*. Incidentally, the two aren't related, other than the fact there's a lot of dwarfs and dwarf culture in them. There's actually a fair few years in-between the novels with *Honourkeeper* being the earliest, set just before the War of Vengeance. Together with Gav's seminal *Grudge Bearer* and an abridged version of the background book we both worked on, *Grudgelore*, you'll have about as complete a volume about the hardy race of the dwarfs as you could possibly want.

Looking back, misty-eyed, through the twenty years since I picked up my very first dwarf hammerer I can honestly say I never expected to be here, doing this. I feel as proud as a son of Grungni to have my name on this volume and I reckon it'll always be that little bit special for me. Times have changed, grudges have been written and struck out again, battles won and lost, but one thing always stays the same: never trust an elf...

Nick Kyme

GRUDGE BEARER

Gav Thorpe

GRUDGE ONE

Hard as Stone

The twisted, baying creatures came on in a great mass, howling and scream-ing at the darkening sky. Some shambled forwards on all fours like dogs and bears, others ran upright with long, loping strides. Each was an unholy hybrid of man and beast, some with canine faces and human bodies, others with the hindquarters of a goat or cat. Bird-faced creatures with bat-like wings sprouting from their backs swept forwards in swooping leaps alongside gigantic mon-strosities made of flailing limbs and screeching faces.

As the sun glittered off the peaks of the mountains around them, the host of elves and dwarfs stood grimly watching the fresh wave of warped horrors sweep down the valley. For five long days they had stood against the horde pouring from the north. The sky seethed with magical energy above them, pulsing with unnatural vigour. Storm clouds tinged with blue and purple roiled in the air above the dark host.

At the head of the dwarf army stood the high king, Snorri Whitebeard. His beard was stained with dirt and blood, and he held his glimmering rune axe heavily in his hand. Around him his guards picked up their shields, axes and hammers and closed around the king, preparing to face the fresh onslaught. It was the dwarf standing to Snorri's left, Godri Stonehewer, who broke the grim silence.

'Do you think there'll be many more of them?' he asked, hefting his hammer in his right hand. 'Only, I haven't had a beer in three days.'

Snorri chuckled and looked across towards Godri. 'Where did you find beer three days ago?' the high king said. 'I haven't had a drop since the first day.'

'Well,' replied Godri, avoiding the king's gaze, 'there may have been a barrel

17

or two that were missed when we were doling out the rations.'

'Godri!' snapped Snorri, genuinely angry. 'There's good fighters back there with blood in their mouths that have had to put up with that elf-spit for three days, and you had your own beer? If I survive this we'll be having words!'

Godri didn't reply, but shuffled his feet and kept his gaze firmly on the ground.

'Heads up,' someone called from further down the line, and Snorri turned to see four dark shapes in the sky above, barely visible amongst the clouds. One detached itself from the group and spiralled downwards.

As it came closer, the shape was revealed to be a dragon, its large white scales glinting in the magical storm. Perched at the base of its long, serpentine neck was a figure swathed in a light blue cloak, his silvered armour shining through the flapping folds. His face was hidden behind a tall helm decorated with two golden wings that arched into the air.

The dragon landed in front of Snorri and folded its wings. A tall, lean figure leapt gracefully to the ground from its saddle and strode towards Snorri, his long cloak flowing just above the muddy ground. As he approached, he removed his helm, revealing a slender face and wide, bright eyes. His skin was fair and dark hair fell loosely around his shoulders.

'Made it back then?' said Snorri as the elf stopped in front of him.

'Of course,' the elf replied with a distasteful look. 'Were you expecting me to perish?'

'Hey now, Malekith, don't take on so,' said Snorri with a growl. 'It was a simple greeting.'

The elf prince did not reply. He surveyed the oncoming horde. When he spoke, his gaze was still fixed to the north.

'This is the last of them for many, many leagues,' said Malekith. "When they are all destroyed, we shall turn westwards to the hordes that threaten the cities of my people.'

'That was the deal, yes,' said Snorri, pulling off his helmet and dragging a hand through his knotted, sweat-soaked hair. 'We swore oaths, remember?'

Malekith turned and looked at Snorri. 'Yes, oaths,' the elf prince said. 'Your word is your bond, that is how it is with you dwarfs, is it not?'

'As it should be with all civilised folk,' said Snorri, ramming his helmet back on. 'You've kept your word, we'll keep ours.'

The elf nodded and walked away. With a graceful leap he was in the dragon's saddle, and a moment later, with a thunderous flapping of wings, the beast soared into the air and was soon lost against the clouds.

'They're a funny folk, those elves,' remarked Godri. 'Speak odd, too.'

'They're a strange breed, right enough,' agreed the dwarf king. 'Living with dragons, can't take their ale, and I'm sure they spend too much time in the sun. Still, anyone who can swing a sword and will stand beside me is friend enough in these dark times.'

'Right enough,' said Godri with a nod.

The dwarf throng was silent as the beasts of Chaos approached, and above

*the baying and howling of the twisted monsters, the clear trumpet calls of the
elves could be heard, marshalling their line.*

*The unnatural tide of mutated flesh was now only some five hundred yards
away and Snorri could smell their disgusting stench. In the dim light, a storm
of white-shafted arrows lifted into the air from the elves and fell down amongst
the horde, punching through furred hide and leathery skin. Another volley
followed swiftly after, then another and another. The ground of the valley was
littered with the dead and the dying, dozens of arrow-pierced corpses strewn
across the slope in front of Snorri and his army. Still the beasts rushed on, heedless of their casualties. They were now only two hundred yards away.*

Three arrows burning with blue fire arced high into the air.

*'Right, that's us,' said Snorri. He gave a nod to Thundir to his right. The
dwarf lifted his curling horn to his lips and blew a long blast that resounded
off the valley walls.*

*The noise gradually increased as the dwarfs marched forwards, the echoes
of the horn call and the roaring of the Chaos beasts now drowned out by the
tramp of iron-shod feet, the clinking of chainmail and the thump of hammers
and axes on shields.*

*Like a wall of iron, the dwarf line advanced down the slope as another salvo
of arrows whistled over their heads. The scattered groups of fanged, clawed
monsters crashed into the shieldwall. Growling, howling and screeching, their
wordless challenges met with gruff battle cries and shouted oaths.*

*'Grungni guide my hand!' bellowed Snorri as a creature with the head of a
wolf, the body of a man and the legs of a lizard jumped at him, slashing with
long talons. Snorri swept his axe from right to left in a low arc, the gleaming
blade shearing off the beast's legs just below the waist.*

*As the dismembered corpse tumbled down the hill, Snorri stepped forward
and brought his axe back in a return blow, ripping the head from a bear-like
creature with a lashing snake for a tail. Thick blood that stank of rotten fish
fountained over the king, sticking to the plates of his iron armour. Gobbets
caught in his matted beard, making him gag.*

It was going to be a long day.

THE THRONE ROOM of Zhufbar echoed gently with the hubbub of the
milling dwarfs. A hundred lanterns shone a golden light down onto
the throng as King Throndin looked out over his court. Representatives
of most of the clans were here, and amongst the crowd he spied the
familiar face of his son Barundin. The young dwarf was in conversation
with the runelord, Arbrek Silverfingers. Throndin chuckled quietly to
himself as he imagined the topic of conversation: undoubtedly his son
would be saying something rash and ill-considered, and Arbrek would
be cursing him softly with an amused twinkle in his eye.

Movement at the great doors caught the king's attention. The background noise dropped down as a human emissary entered, escorted by
Hengrid Dragonfoe, the hold's gatewarden. The manling was tall, even

for one of his kind, and behind him came two other men carrying a large iron-bound wooden chest. The messenger was clearly taking slow, deliberate strides so as not to outpace his shorter-legged escort, while the two carrying the chest were visibly tiring. A gap opened up in the assembled throng, a pathway to the foot of Throndin's throne appearing out of the crowd.

He sat with his arms crossed as he watched the small deputation make its way up the thirty steps to the dais on which his throne stood. The messenger bowed low, his left hand extended to the side with a flourish, and then looked up at the king.

'My lord, King Throndin of Zhufbar, I bring tidings from Baron Silas Vessal of Averland,' the emissary said. He was speaking slowly, for which Throndin was grateful, as it had been many long years since he had needed to understand the Reikspiel of the Empire.

The king said nothing for a moment, and then noticed the manling's unease at the ensuing silence. He dredged up the right words from his memory. 'And you are?' asked Throndin.

'I am Marechal Heinlin Kulft, cousin and herald to Baron Vessal,' the man replied.

'Cousin, eh?' said Throndin with an approving nod. At least this manling lord had sent one of his own family to parley with the king. In his three hundred years, Throndin had come to think of humans as rash, flighty and inconsiderate. Almost as bad as elves, he thought to himself.

'Yes, my lord,' replied Kulft. 'On his father's side,' he added, feeling perhaps that the explanation would fill the silence that had descended on the wide, long chamber. He was acutely aware of hundreds of dwarfs' eyes boring into his back and hundreds of dwarfs' ears listening to his every word.

'So, you have a message?' said Throndin, tilting his head slightly to one side.

'I have two, my lord,' said Kulft. 'I bring both grievous news and a request from Baron Vessal.'

'You want help, then?' said Throndin. 'What do you want?'

The herald was momentarily taken aback by the king's forthright manner, but gathered himself quickly. 'Orcs, my lord,' said Kulft, and at the mention of the hated greenskins an angry buzzing filled the chamber. The noise quieted as Throndin waved the assembled court to silence. He gestured for Kulft to continue.

'From north of the baron's lands, the orcs have come,' he said. 'Three farms have been destroyed already, and we believe they are growing in number. The baron's armies are well equipped but small, and he fears that should we not respond quickly, the orcs will only grow bolder.'

'Then ask your count or your emperor for more men,' said Throndin. 'What concern is it of mine?'

'The orcs have crossed your lands as well,' replied Kulft quickly, obviously prepared for such a question. 'Not only this year, but last year at about the same time.'

'Have you a description of these creatures?' demanded Throndin, his eyes narrowing to slits.

'They are said to carry shields emblazoned with the crude image of a face with two long fangs, and they paint their bodies with strange designs in black paint,' said Kulft. This time the reaction from the throng was even louder.

Throndin sat in silence, but the knuckles of his clenched fists were white and his beard quivered. Kulft gestured to the two men that had gratefully placed the chest on the throne tier, and they opened it up. The light of a hundred lanterns glittered off the contents – a few gems, many, many silver coins and several bars of gold. The anger in Throndin's eyes was rapidly replaced with an acquisitive gleam.

'The baron would not wish you to endure any expense on his account,' explained Kulft, gesturing to the treasure chest. 'He would ask that you accept this gesture of his good will in offsetting any cost that your expedition might incur.'

'Hmm, gift?' said Throndin, tearing his eyes away from the gold bars. They were of a particular quality, originally dwarf-gold if his experienced eye was not mistaken. 'For me?'

Kulft nodded. The dwarf king looked back at the chest and then glowered at the few dwarfs that had taken hesitant steps up the stairway towards the chest. Kulft gestured for his companions to close the lid before any trouble started. He had heard of the dwarf lust for gold, but had mistaken it merely for greed. The reaction had been something else entirely, a desire for the precious metal that bordered on physical need, like a man finding water in the desert.

'While I accept this generous gift, it is not for gold that the King of Zhufbar shall march forth,' said Throndin, standing up. 'We know of these orcs. Indeed, last year they were met in battle by dwarfs of my own clan, and the vile creatures took the life of my eldest son.'

Throndin paced forwards, his balled fists by his side, and stood at the top of the steps. When he next spoke, his voice echoed from the far walls of the chamber. He turned to Kulft. 'These orcs owe us dear,' snarled the king. 'The life of a Zhufbar prince stains their lives and they have been entered onto the list of wrongs done against my hold and my people. I declare grudge against these orcs! Their lives are forfeit, and with axe and hammer we shall make them pay the price they owe. Ride to your lord, tell him to prepare for war, and tell him that King Throndin Stoneheart of Zhufbar will fight beside him!'

THE TRAMPING OF dwarf boots rang from the mountainsides as the gates of Zhufbar were swung open and the host of King Throndin marched out. Rank after rank of bearded warriors advanced between the two great statues of Grungni and Grimnir that flanked the gateway, carved from the rock of the mountain. Above the dwarf army swayed a forest of standards of gold and silver wrought into the faces of revered ancestors, clan runes and guild symbols.

The thud of boots was joined by the rumbling of wheels and the wheezing and coughing of a steam engine. At the rear of the dwarf column, a steamdozer puffed into view, its spoked, iron-rimmed wheels grinding along the cracked and pitted roadway. Billows of grey smoke rose into the air from the fluted funnel as the traction engine growled forwards, pulling behind it a chain of four wagons laden with baggage and covered by heavy, cable-bound, waterproof sacking.

The autumn sky above the Worlds Edge Mountains was low and grey, threatening rain, yet Throndin was in high spirits. He walked at the head of his army, with Barundin to his left carrying the king's own standard, and marching to his right, the Runelord Arbrek.

'War was never a happy occasion in your father's day,' said Arbrek, noticing the smile on the king's lips.

The smile faded as Throndin turned his head to look at the runelord. 'My father never had cause to avenge a fallen son,' the king said darkly, his eyes bright in the shadow of his gold-inlaid helmet. 'I thank him and the fathers before him that I have been granted the opportunity to right this wrong.'

'Besides, it is too long since you last took up your axe other than to polish it!' said Barundin with a short laugh. 'Are you sure you still remember what to do?'

'Listen to the beardling!' laughed Throndin. 'Barely fifty winters old and already an expert on war. Listen, laddie, I was swinging this axe at orcs long before you were born. Let's just see which of us accounts for more, eh?'

'This'll be the first time your father has had a chance to see your mettle,' added Arbrek with a wink. 'Stories when the ale is flowing are right enough, but there's nothing like seeing it firsthand to make a father proud.'

'Aye,' agreed Throndin, patting Barundin on the arm. 'You're my only son now. The honour of the clan will be yours when I go to meet the ancestors. You'll make me proud, I know you will.'

'You'll see that Barundin Throndinsson is worthy of becoming king,' the youth said with a fierce nod that set his beard waggling. 'You'll be proud, right enough.'

They marched westwards towards the Empire until noon, the towering ramparts and bastions of Zhufbar disappearing behind them, the mountain peak that held the king's throne room obscured by low cloud.

At midday, Throndin called a halt and the air was filled with the noise of five thousand dwarfs eating sandwiches, drinking ale and arguing loudly, as was their wont when on campaign. After the eating was done the air was thick with pipe smoke, which hung like a cloud over the host.

Throndin sat on a rock, legs splayed in front of him, admiring the scenery. High up on the mountains, he could see for many miles, league after league of hard rock and sparse trees and bushes. Beyond, he could just about make out the greener lands of the Empire. As he puffed his pipe, a tap on his shoulder caused him to turn. It was Hengrid, and with him was an old-looking dwarf with a long white beard tucked into a simple rope belt. The stranger wore a hooded cloak of rough-spun wool that had been dyed blue and he held a whetstone in his cracked, gnarled hands.

'Grungni's honour be with you, King Throndin,' said the dwarf with a short bow. 'I am but a simple traveller, who earns a coin or two with my whetstone and my wits. Allow me the honour of sharpening your axe and perhaps passing on a wise word or two.'

'My axe is rune-sharp,' said Throndin, turning away.

'Hold now, king,' said the old dwarf. 'There was a time when any dwarf, be he lowly or kingly, would spare an ear for one of age and learning.'

'Let him speak, Throndin,' called Arbrek from across the other side of the roadway. 'He's old enough to even be my father – show a little respect.'

Throndin turned back to the stranger and gave a grudging nod. The peddler nodded thankfully, pulling off his pack and setting it down by the roadside. It looked very heavy and Throndin noticed an axe-shaped bundle swathed in rags stuffed between the folds of the dwarf's cloak. With a huff of expelled breath, the dwarf sat down on the pack.

'Orcs, is it?' the peddler said, pulling an ornate pipe from the folds of his robe.

'Yes,' said Throndin, taken aback. 'Have you seen them?'

The dwarf did not answer immediately. Instead he took a pouch from his belt and began filling his pipe with weed. Taking a long match from the pouch, he struck it on the hard surface of the roadway and lit the pipe, puffing contentedly several times before turning his attention back to the king.

'Aye, I seen them,' said the dwarf. 'Not for a while now, but I seen them. A vicious bunch and no mistake.'

'They'll be a dead bunch when I catch them,' snorted Throndin. 'When did you see them?'

'Oh, a while back, a year or thereabouts,' said the stranger.

'Last year?' said Barundin, moving to stand beside his father. 'That was when they slew Dorthin!'

The king scowled at his son, who felt silent.

'Aye, that is right,' said the peddler. 'It was no more than a day's march from here, where Prince Dorthin fell.'

'You saw the battle?' asked Throndin.

'I wish that I had,' said the stranger. 'My axe would have tasted orc flesh that day. But alas, I came upon the field of battle too late and the orcs were gone.'

'Well, this time the warriors of Zhufbar shall settle the matter,' said Barundin, putting his hand to the axe at his belt. 'Not only that, but a baron of the Empire fights with us."

'Pah, a manling?' spat the peddler. 'What worth has a manling in battle? Not since young Sigmar has their race bred a warrior worthy of the title.'

'Baron Vessal is a person of means, and that is no mean feat for a manling,' said Hengrid. 'He has dwarf gold, even.'

'Gold is but one way to judge the worth of a person,' said the stranger. 'When axes are raised and blood flows, it is not wealth but temper that is most valued.'

'What would you know?' said Throndin with a dismissive wave. 'I'd wager you have barely two coins to rub together. I'll not have a nameless, penniless wattock show disrespect for my ally. Thank you for your company, but I have enjoyed it enough. Hengrid!'

The burly dwarf veteran stepped forward and with an apologetic look gestured for the old peddler to stand. With a final puff on his pipe, the wanderer pushed himself to his feet and hauled on his pack.

'It is a day to be rued when the words of the old fall on deaf ears,' said the stranger as he turned away.

'I am no beardling!' Throndin called after him.

They watched the dwarf walk slowly down the road until he disappeared from view between two tall rocks. Throndin noticed Arbrek watching the path intently, as if he could still see the stranger.

'Empty warnings to go with his empty purse,' said Throndin, waving a dismissive hand in the peddler's direction.

Arbrek turned with a frown on his face. 'Since when did the kings of Zhufbar count wisdom in coins?' asked the runelord. Throndin made to answer, but Arbrek had turned away and was stomping off through the army.

The solemn beating of drums could be heard echoing along the halls and corridors of Karaz-a-Karak. The small chamber was empty save for two figures. His face as pale as his beard, King Snorri lay on the low, wide bed, his eyes closed. Kneeling next to the bed, a hand on the dwarf's chest, was Prince Malekith of Ulthuan, once general of the Phoenix King's armies and now ambassador to the dwarf empire.

The rest of the room was hung with heavy tapestries depicting the battles the two had fought together, suitably aggrandising Snorri's role. Malekith did not begrudge the king his glories, for was not his own name sung loudly in Ulthuan while the name of Snorri Whitebeard was barely a whisper? Each people to their own kind, the elf prince thought.

Snorri's eyelids fluttered open to reveal cloudy, pale blue eyes. His lips twisted into a smile and a fumbling hand found Malekith's arm.

'Would that dwarf lives were measured as those of the elves,' said Snorri. 'Then my reign would last another thousand years.'

'But even so, we still die,' said Malekith. 'Our measure is made by what we do when we live and the legacy that we leave to our kin, as any other. A lifetime of millennia is worthless if its works come to nought after it has ended.'

'True, true,' said Snorri with a nod, his smile fading. 'What we have built is worthy of legend, isn't it? Our two great realms have driven back the beasts and the daemons and the lands are safe for our people. Trade has never been better, and the holds grow with every year.'

'Your reign has indeed been glorious, Snorri,' said Malekith. 'Your line is strong; your son will uphold the great things that you have done.'

'And perhaps even build on them,' said Snorri.

'Perhaps, if the gods will it,' said Malekith.

'And why should they not?' asked Snorri. He coughed as he pushed himself to a sitting position, his shoulders sinking into thick, gold-embroidered white pillows. 'Though my breath comes short and my body is infirm, my will is as hard as the stone that these walls are carved from. I am a dwarf, and like all my people, I have within me the strength of the mountains. Though this body is now weak, my spirit shall go to the Halls of the Ancestors.'

'It will be welcomed there, by Grungni and Valaya and Grimnir,' said Malekith. 'You shall take your place with pride.'

'I'm not done,' said Snorri with a frown. His expression grim, the king continued. 'Hear this oath, Malekith of the elves, comrade on the battlefield, friend at the hearth. I, Snorri Whitebeard, high king of the dwarfs, bequeath my title and rights to my eldest son. Though I pass through the gateway to the Halls of the Ancestors, my eyes shall remain upon my empire. Let it be known to our allies and our enemies that death is not the end of my guardianship.'

The dwarf broke into a wracking cough, blood flecking his lips. His lined faced was stern as he looked at Malekith. The elf steadily returned his gaze.

'Vengeance shall be mine,' swore Snorri. 'When our foes are great, I shall return to my people. When the foul creatures of this world bay at the doors to Karaz-a-Karak, I shall take up my axe once more and my ire shall rock the mountains. Heed my words, Malekith of Ulthuan, and heed them well. Great have been our deeds, and great is the legacy that I leave to you, my closest confidant, my finest comrade in arms. Swear to me now, as my dying breaths fill my lungs, that my oath has been heard. Swear to it on my own grave, on my spirit, that you shall remain true to the ideals we have both striven for these many years. And know this, that there is nothing so foul in the world as an oath-breaker.'

Malekith took the king's hand from his arm and squeezed it tight. 'I swear it,' the elf prince said. 'Upon the grave of high king Snorri Whitebeard, leader of the dwarfs and friend of the elves, I give my oath.'

Snorri's eyes were glazed and his chest no longer rose and fell. The keen hearing of the elf could detect no sign of life, and he did not know whether his words had been heard. Releasing Snorri's hand, he folded the king's arms *across his chest and with a delicate touch from his long fingers, Malekith closed Snorri's eyes.*

Standing, Malekith spared one last glance at the dead king and then walked from the chamber. Outside, Snorri's son Throndik stood along with several dozen other dwarfs.

'The high king has passed on,' Malekith said, his gaze passing over the heads of the assembled dwarfs and across the throne room. He looked down at Throndik. 'You are now high king.'

Without further word, the elf prince walked gracefully through the crowd and out across the nearly empty throne chamber. Word was passed by some secret means throughout the hold and soon the drums stopped. With Throndik at their head, the dwarfs entered the chamber and lifted the king from his deathbed. Bearing Snorri's body aloft on their broad shoulders, the dwarfs marched slowly across the throne chamber to a stone bier that had been set before the throne itself. They lay the king upon the stone and turned away.

The doors to the throne room were barred for three days while the remaining preparations for the funeral were made. Throndik was still prince and would not become king until his father had been buried, so he busied himself with sending messengers to the other holds to bear the news of the king's death.

At the appointed hour, the throne room was opened once more by an honour guard led by Throndik Snorrisson and Godri Stonehewer. As once more the solemn drums echoed through the hold, the funeral procession bore the high king to his final resting place deep within Karaz-a-Karak. There were no eulogies, there was no weeping, for Snorri's exploits were there for all to see in the carvings upon the stone casket within his tomb. His life had been well spent and there was no cause to mourn his passing.

On Snorri's instructions, the casket had been carved with dire runes of vengeance and grudge-bearing by the most powerful runelords in the hold. Inlaid with gold, the symbols glowed with magical light as Snorri was lowered into the sarcophagus. The lid was then placed on the stone coffin and bound with golden bands. The runelords, chanting in unison, struck their final sigils onto the bands, warding away foul magic and consigning Snorri's spirit to the Halls of the Ancestors. There was a final crescendo of drums rolling in long echoes along the halls and corridors over the heads of the silent dwarfs that had lined the procession route.

Throndik performed the last rite. Taking up a small keg of beer, he filled a tankard with the foaming ale and took a sip. With a nod of approval, he reverently placed the tankard on top of the carved stone casket.

'Drink deep in the Halls of the Ancestors,' intoned Throndik. 'Raise this tankard to those who have passed before you, so that they might remember those that still walk upon the world.'

* * *

BY MID-MORNING THE following day, the dwarf army had left the Worlds Edge Mountains and was in the foothills that surrounded the Zhufdurak, known by men as the River Aver Reach. The thudding of the cargo-loco's steam pistons echoed from the hillsides over the babbling of the river, while the deep murmuring of dwarfs in conversation droned constantly.

At the head of the column, Throndin marched with Barundin and Arbrek. The king had been in a silent mood since the encounter with the peddler the day before. Whether he was deep in thought or sulking because of Arbrek's soft admonishment, Barundin didn't know, but he was not going to intrude on his father's thoughts at this time.

A distant buzzing from the sky caused the dwarfs to lift their heads and gaze into the low cloud. A speck of darkness from the west grew closer, bobbing up and down ever so slightly in an erratic course. The puttering of a gyrocopter's engine grew louder as the aircraft approached and there were pointed fingers and a louder commotion as the pilot pushed his craft into a dive and swooped over the column. Almost carving a furrow in a hilltop with the whirling rotors of the gyrocopter as he dipped toward the ground, the pilot swung his machine around and then passed above the convoy more sedately. About half a mile ahead, a great trailing of dust that rose as a cloud into the air marked the pilot's landing.

As they neared, Barundin could see the pilot more clearly. His beard and face were soot-stained, two pale rings around his eyes from where his goggles had been. Those goggles dangled from a strap attached to the side of the dwarf's winged helm, hanging down over his shoulder. Over a long chainmail shirt, the pilot wore a set of heavy leather overalls, much darned and patched.

The pilot regarded the king and his retinue with a pronounced squint as he watched them approach.

'Is that you, Rimbal Wanazaki?' said Barundin.

The pilot gave a nod and a grin, displaying broken, yellowing, uneven teeth. 'Right you are, lad,' said Wanazaki.

'We thought you were dead!' said Throndin. 'Some nonsense about a troll lair.'

'Aye, there's a lot of it about,' replied Wanazaki. 'But I'm not dead, as you can see for yourself.'

'More's the bloody pity,' said Throndin. 'I meant what I said. You're no longer welcome in my halls.'

'You're still mad about that little explosion?' said Wanazaki with a disconsolate shake of the head. 'You're a hard king, Throndin, a hard king.'

'Get gone,' said Throndin, thrusting a thumb over his shoulder. 'I shouldn't even be talking to you.'

'Well, you're not in your halls now, your kingship, so you can listen and you don't have to say a word,' said Wanazaki.

'Well, what have you got to say for yourself?' said the king. 'I haven't got the time to waste with you.'

The pilot held up one hand to quiet the king. Reaching into his belt, he pulled out a delicate-looking tankard, no bigger than twice the size of a thimble, so small that only one finger would fit into its narrow handle. Turning to the gyrocopter engine, which was still making the odd coughing and spluttering noise, he turned a small tap on the side of one tank. Clear liquid dripped out into the small mug, which the pilot filled almost to the rim. Barundin's eyes began to moisten as the vapours from the fuel-alcohol stung them.

With a wink at the king, the disgraced engineer knocked back the liquid. For a moment he stood there, doing nothing. Wanazaki then gave a small cough and Barundin could see his hands trembling. Thumping a fist against his chest, the pilot coughed again, much louder, then stamped his foot. Eyes slightly glazed, he leaned forwards and squinted at the king.

'It's orcs you're after, am I right?' said Wanazaki. The king did not reply immediately, still taken aback by the engineer's curious drinking habit.

'Yes,' Throndin said eventually.

'I've seen them,' said Wanazaki. 'About thirty, maybe thirty-five miles south of here. Day's march, no more, if it's a step.'

'Within a day's march?' exclaimed Barundin. 'Are you sure? Which way are they heading?'

'Course he's not sure,' said Throndin. 'This grog-swiller probably doesn't know a mile from a step.'

'A day's march, I'm telling you,' insisted Wanazaki. 'You'd be there by midday tomorrow if you turn south now. They were camped, all drunk and fat by the looks of it. I seen smoke to the west, reckon they've been having some fun.'

'If we go now, we could catch them before they sober up, take them in their camp,' said Barundin. 'It'd be an easy runk and no mistake.'

'We don't need some gangly manlings – we can take them,' said Ferginal, one of Throndin's stonebearers and a cousin of Barundin on his dead mother's side. The comment was met with a general shout of encouragement from the younger members of the entourage.

'Pah!' snorted Arbrek, turning with a scowl to the boisterous dwarfs. 'Listen to the beardlings! All eager for war, are you? Ready to march for a day and a night and fight a battle? Made of mountain stone, are you? Barely a full beard between you and all ready to rush off to battle against the greenskins. Foolhardy, that's what they'd call you if you lived long enough to have sons of your own.'

'We're not scared!' came a shouted reply. The dwarf that had spoken up quickly ducked behind his comrades as Arbrek's withering stare was brought to bear.

'Fie to scared – you'll be dead!' snarled the runelord. 'Get another thousand miles under them legs of yours and you might be ready to force march straight into battle. How are you going to swing an axe or hammer without no puff, eh?'

'What do you say, father?' said Barundin, turning to the king.

'I'm as eager to settle this grudge as any of you,' Throndin, and there was a roaring cheer. It quieted as he raised his hands. 'But it'd be rash to chase off after these orcs on the words of a drunken outcast.'

Wanazaki gave a grin and a thumbs up at being mentioned.

Throndin shook his head in disgust. 'Besides, even if the old wazzock is right, there's no guarantee the orcs would still be around when we got there,' the king continued. There was a rumble of disappointment from the throng. 'Most importantly,' Throndin added, raising his voice above the disgruntled grumbling, 'I made a promise to Baron Vessal to meet him, and who here would have their king break his promise?'

As THEY MARCHED westwards to their rendezvous with the men of Baron Vessal, the dwarf army crossed the advance of the orcs. The signs were unmistakable: the ground was trampled and littered with discarded scraps and even the air itself still was filled with their taint, emanating from indiscriminate piles of orc dung. The most veteran orc-fighters inspected the spoor and tracks and estimated there to be over a thousand greenskins. Even with just eight hundred warriors, all that duty would spare from the guarding of Zhufbar, Throndin felt confident. Even if Vessal had only a handful of men, the army would be more than a match for the greenskins.

As the evening twilight began to spill across the hills, several campfires could be seen in the distance along a line of hills.

About a mile from the camp, the leading elements of the dwarf army encountered two men on the trail. Two horses were tethered to a tree and a small fire with a steaming pot was set to one side of the road. They were dressed in long studded coats and bore bulky harquebuses. Throndin could smell ale. They looked nervously at each other and then one stepped forward.

'Ware!' he shouted. 'Who would pass into the lands of Baron Vessal of Averland?'

'I bloody would,' shouted Throndin, stomping forward.

'And you are?' asked the sentry, his voice wavering.

'This is King Throndin of Zhufbar, ally to your master,' said Barundin, carrying his father's standard to the king's side. 'Who addresses the king?'

'Well,' said the man with a glance behind him at his companion, who was busily studying his feet, 'Gustav Feldenhoffen, that's me. Road warden. We's road wardens for the baron. He said to challenge anyone on the road, like.'

'A credit to your profession,' said Throndin, giving the man a comforting pat on the arm. 'Dedicated to your duty, I see. Where's the baron?'

Feldenhoffen relaxed with a sigh and waved towards a large tent near one of the fires. 'The baron's in the centre of the camp, your, er, kingliness,' said the road warden. 'I can take you, if you'd like.'

'Don't worry, I'll find him right enough,' said Throndin. 'Wouldn't want you leaving your post.'

'Yes, you're right,' said Feldenhoffen. 'Well, take care. Erm, see you at the battle.'

The king grunted as the road warden stepped aside. Throndin waved the army forwards again and passed the word to his thanes to organise the camp while he sought out the baron. Tomorrow they would march to battle, and he was looking for a good night's sleep before all the exertion.

THE SUN WAS barely over the horizon and Baron Vessal looked none too pleased about a visit from his dwarf ally. For his part, Throndin was dressed in full battle armour, his massive double-bladed axe propped up against his leg as he sat on the oversized stool, and he seemed eager to get going. Vessal, on the other hand, was still in his purple bed robes, scratching at his stubbled chin as he listened to the dwarf king.

'So I suggest you use your horsey men to go ahead and look for the orcs,' Throndin was saying. 'When you've found them, we can get after them.'

'Get after them?' said the baron, eyes widening. He smoothed back the straggling black hair that was hanging down around his shoulders, revealing a thin, almost haggard face. 'Not to be indelicate, but how do you propose you'll catch them? Your army is not built for speed, is it?'

'They're orcs, they'll come to us,' Throndin assured him. 'We'll pick somewhere good, send a bit of bait forward – you for example – and then draw them in and finish them.'

'And where do you propose to make this stand?' asked Vessal with a sigh. He had drunk more wine than he was used to the night before and the early hour was not helping his headache.

'Where have the orcs been lately?' Throndin asked.

'Up and down the Aver Reach, heading westwards,' replied Vessal. 'Why?'

'Well, we'll set up somewhere west of where they last attacked and wait for them,' said Throndin. The king scowled as the sound of the first pattering of rain trembled across the canvas of the tent.

'Surely such hardened warriors are not troubled by marching in a little rain?' said Vessal, raising his eyebrows.

'Don't rain much under a mountain,' said Throndin with a grimace. 'Makes your pipe weed soggy, and your beard all wet. Rain's no good for a well-crafted cannon, nor the black powder needed to fire it. Some of them engineers are clever, but I still haven't met the one who'd invented black powder that'll burn when it's wet.'

'So we stay in camp today?' suggested Vessal, his enthusiasm for the idea plain to see.

'It's your folk getting killed and robbed,' Throndin pointed out. 'We can kill orcs whenever we like. We're in no hurry.'

'Yes, I suppose you're right,' agreed the baron. 'My tenants tend to get argumentative about taxes when there's orcs or bandits on the loose. The sooner it is settled the quicker things can return to normal.'

'So, get your army ready to march and we'll head west as soon as you like,' said Throndin, slapping himself on the thighs as he stood up. He grabbed his axe and swung it over his shoulder as he turned.

'West?' said Vessal as the dwarf king was heading for the flaps of the door. 'That'll take us into the Moot.'

'Where?' said Throndin, turning around.

'Mootland, the halfling realm,' Vessal told him.

'Oh, the grombolgi-kazan,' said Throndin with a grin. 'What's the matter with that?'

'Well, they're not my lands, for a start,' said Vessal, standing up. 'And there'll be halflings there.'

'So?' asked Throndin, scratching his beard and shaking his head.

'Well…' began Vessal before shaking his head as well. 'I'm sure it will be fine. My men will be ready to march within the hour.'

Throndin gave a nod of approval and walked out of the tent. Vessal slumped back into his padded chair with a heavy sigh. He glanced towards the table where he had been dining with his advisors and saw the piles of half-eaten chicken and the nearly empty goblets of wine. The thought of the excess the night before made his stomach heave and he shouted for his servants to attend him.

By the time the baron was ready, dressed in his full plate armour and mounted atop his grey stallion, the dwarfs were already lined up along the trail. The rain rattled from their armour and metal standards like hundreds of tiny dancers on a metal stage, jarring every hangover-heightened nerve in Vessal's body. He gritted his teeth as Throndin gave him a cheery wave from the front of the column and raised his hand in return.

'The sooner this is over with, the better,' the baron said between gritted teeth.

'Would you rather we did this alone?' asked Captain Kurgereich, the baron's most experienced soldier and head of his personal guard.

'Not after sending them all of my bloody money,' snarled Vessal. 'I thought they'd be only too happy for some help killing the orcs that slew the king's heir. They were meant to send back my gift.'

'Never show a dwarf gold, my old grandmother used to say,' replied Kurgereich.

'Well the old hag was a very wise woman indeed,' growled Vessal. 'Send out the scouts and then leave me in peace. All this, and bloody halflings as well.'

Kurgereich turned his horse away to hide his smirk and cantered off to find the outriders. Within minutes the light cavalry had ridden off and soon some fifty knights and the baron's two hundred infantry were trudging along the road, which had started to resemble a shallow stream in the continuing downpour.

Over the tramping of feet, a bass tone rose in volume as Throndin led his host in a marching song. Soon eight hundred dwarfs in full voice made the banks of the Aver tremble as they advanced to the rhythm of the tune. At the end of each couplet the dwarfs crashed their weapons on their shields, the sound reverberating along the line. As they fell in behind the baron's men, the dwarfs' war horn joined the chorus, its long blasts punctuating every verse.

It was mid-afternoon when they sighted smoke on the horizon, and within two miles they came across a halfling village. Across the rolling hills, low, sprawling houses were spread between dirt tracks next to a wide lake. As they came closer, they could see uneven windows and doors carved into the turf of the hills themselves, surrounded by hedged gardens over which tall plants could be seen waving in the rain-flecked breeze.

Baron Vessal called a halt and dismounted, waiting for Throndin to join him. Heinlein Kulft stood beside him, holding the sodden banner of his lord. Barundin accompanied his father, proudly hefting the standard of Zhufbar and exchanging a glance with Kulft. A reedy voice drifted out of the bushes that lined the road.

'Dwarf and tall folk in Midgwater, by my old uncle, I wouldn't believe it hadn't I seen it with me own eyes,' the voice said.

Turning, Barundin saw a small figure, shorter even than he, with a thick mop of hair and side burns that reached almost to his mouth. The halfling was dressed in a thick green shirt that was dripping with rain. His leather breeches were around his ankles and he glanced down and then tugged them back up, tying them at his waist with a thin rope belt.

'You caught me unawares,' the halfling said, jutting out his chin and puffing out his chest.

'Who is your elder?' asked Kulft. 'We must speak with him.'

'He's a she, not a he,' said the halfling. 'Melderberry Weatherbrook, lives in the burrow on the other side of the lake. She'll be having tea 'bout now, I would say.'

'Then we'll be on our way, and leave you to your…' Kulft's voice trailed off at the stare from the halfling. 'Whatever it is you're doing.'

'You after them orcs?' the halfling asked.

Throndin and Vessal both looked sharply at the halfling but it was Barundin who spoke first.

'What do you know, little one?' the king's son asked.

'Little one?' snapped the halfling. 'I'm quite tall. My whole family is, 'cept for my third cousin Tobarias, who's a little on the short side. Anyways, the orcs. My uncle Fredebore, the one on my grandfather's side, was out fishing on the river with some friends and they saw them. Rowed back sharpish they did, 'bout lunchtime. Them orcs is heading this way they reckons.'

Vessal absorbed this news in silence, while Throndin turned to Arbrek, who had joined them. 'What do you think?' the king asked his runelord.

'If they're coming here, no point in marching when we don't have to,' Arbrek replied. 'Good hills for the cannons, plenty of food and ale, if the tales of the grombolgi are true. Could be worse.'

Throndin nodded and turned to the halfling. 'Is there somewhere we can camp, close by to the lake?' he asked.

'Stick yourselves in old farmer Wormfurrow's field,' the halfling told them. 'He died last week and his missus won't be complaining, not with her being up at farmer Wurtwither's place these days. No one's seen her since the funeral, four days ago.'

'Right then,' said Throndin. 'I'll go see Elder Weatherbrook, everyone else make camp in the fields.'

'I'll come with you,' said Vessal. 'My lands border the Moot, I know these folk a little better than you.'

'I'll be glad of the company,' said Throndin with a glance at Barundin. 'Help with the camp, lad. I don't think waving standards around is going to impress anyone around these parts.'

Barundin nodded and started walking back towards the other dwarfs. Kulft looked to the baron, who waved him away with barely a glance.

'Shall we go?' the king asked. Vessal nodded. As they began to walk up the road, Throndin stopped and patted his belt. With a frown, he turned back down the road but the halfling was nowhere to be seen.

'The little kruti's had it away with my pipe,' the king exclaimed.

'I did try to warn you,' said Vessal. 'I'm sure you'll get it back soon enough, just don't accuse anyone of thieving – they don't take to it in the Moot.'

'But he stole my pipe!' growled Throndin. 'Theft's theft! I'm going to be bringing this up with the elder when we see her.'

'It won't help,' said Vessal, motioning with his head for them to continue up the road. 'They just don't understand. You'll see.'

The white stone of the city's walls was marked with soot as flames and smoke poured across the sky from the burning buildings inside the elven settlement of Tor Alessi. Tall spires, their peaks glittering with silver and gold, disappeared in the thick clouds, towering many hundreds of feet into the smoke-choked heavens.

A double gateway protected by three slender towers was battered and scorched, and stone blocks fell to the ground as boulders, hurled through the sky, crashed into them. By the gates themselves, short armoured figures hauled an iron-shafted battering ram forward.

Flocks of white arrows dove down onto the dwarf army from the cracked

battlements above, punching through raised shields and oiled chainmail.
Withering fire from repeating bolt throwers hurled branch-like missiles into the
ranks of the assembled throng, cutting down a dozen dwarfs at a time, ripping
holes through the packed mass pressing towards the beleaguered gate towers.

Above the dwarfs the barrage of rocks from the siege catapults contin-
ued, as armoured warriors surged forwards to take the places of the fallen.
With a resounding crash, the battering ram slammed into the thick white
timbers of the right-hand gate, sending splinters and shards of metal into
the air. With a bellowed order, the dwarfs hauled the ram back, some of
them dragging aside the dead to make way for the iron-rimmed wheels of
the war machine.

With a collective grunt that could be heard above the crackle of flames and
the shouts of the wounded and dying, the dwarfs pushed forwards once more,
the serrated spike of the ram again biting into the wood, ripping between the
planks of the gate and shearing through the bars beyond. With a triumphant
roar the dwarfs stormed forwards, throwing their weight against the ram and
forcing the breach in the gate even wider. Drawing their axes, the dwarfs
continued to hack at the planks until there was enough room to force their
way through.

A storm of arrows swept through the gateway, embedding themselves into
helmeted heads and piercing iron rings of mail shirts. At the centre of the
dwarfs' charge was a figure decked in ornate plate armour and shining mail,
a purple cloak flowing from his shoulders. His face was hidden behind the
metal ancestor mask of his helm, his long white beard flowing from beneath it,
clasped with golden bands.

The warrior's armour glowed with runes, and the sigils upon his great two-
handed axe pulsed with magical energies as he thundered into the elf line, the
arcane blade slicing through armour, flesh and bone with ease.

None of the other dwarfs knew who the mysterious warrior was or where
he came from, and over the long years of fighting none could recall when
he had first appeared. Like an avenging spirit he had turned up at the
first battle against the elves, when the ancient alliance had been shattered
with discord. As tales of the fighter's prowess spread, he was given a simple
name, but one that now conjured up images of bloodshed and vengeance –
the White Dwarf.

BARUNDIN SCOWLED AND rounded on the halfling barmaid stood behind
him.

'If you pinch my backside one more time…' he growled. But Shella
Heartyflanks was unconcerned. With a leer and a wink, she turned away
and swept between the tables of the small inn, enthusiastically waving
her jugs at the dwarfs that had taken up residence for the evening.

All day Barundin had been pestered by complaints from the other
dwarfs. His father, in his wisdom, had immediately deferred all halfling-
related matters to the prince and closeted himself away with Arbrek and

his other advisors. Since then, Barundin had not had a moment's peace.

He'd been forced to set up a standing guard around the baggage train after reports that the light-fingered Mootfolk had been helping themselves to ale, tobacco, bed sheets, black powder and all manner of sundry items. His father had told him not to hurt any of the halflings, but to gently but insistently keep them at arm's length.

Then there had been the episode with the two young halflings that had been found in an act of intimacy under Norbred Sterneye's wagon, and Barundin had been forced to resort to a bucket of water to resolve the situation before some of the older dwarfs exploded with indignation.

Just as he had been losing the will to live, the invitation had been passed around that the Red Dragon Inn was willing to provide free ale and food to the bold protectors of Midgwater. Barundin, while thankful for the show of generosity, had then been engaged in a long and complicated process of planning how to get eight hundred thirsty dwarfs into an inn no bigger than a forge fire, whilst making sure there were enough bodies left behind to protect the camp from the acquisitive attentions of the halflings.

When he had finally managed to enjoy the tavern's hospitality himself, late into the night after many others had retired to bed, he had been less than thrilled to find that the old halfling, Shella, had taken a fancy to him. He was sure his buttocks would be black and blue all over from her playful yet painful signs of affection.

It was with some relief then that a table near to the nook was vacated and Barundin hurriedly occupied the space with a sigh. The relief was short-lived though, as the doors opened and his father strode in, bellowing for a mug of the finest ale. Baron Vessal stooped through the low doorway behind him, followed by his marechal, Kulft.

The trio saw Barundin and headed across the inn towards him, the manlings bent at the waist to avoid the beams across the ceiling. Barundin pushed himself to his feet to make space for the new arrivals, as Shella brought over three foaming tankards and slammed them onto the table. She reached across to ostensibly wipe at a spillage, and Barundin tried to squeeze himself into the bricks of the wall as the halfling pressed herself against him in an attempt to push past.

When she was gone, they settled down, and Barundin managed to clear his mind and concentrate on his beer, blocking out the occasional conversation that passed between the others. He vaguely heard the rusted hinges of the doors squeaking again and felt his father tense next to him.

'By Grungni's flowing beard…' muttered Throndin, and Barundin looked up to see what was happening.

In front of the door stood the peddler, still swathed in his ragged travelling cloak, his heavy pack across his shoulders. He glanced around the inn for a moment, until his eyes lingered on Throndin. As he crossed the room, the peddler pulled his pipe from his belt and began stuffing it with tobacco. By the time he had reached their table, he was busily puffing away on the pipe.

'Hail, King Throndin of Zhufbar,' the dwarf said with a short bow.

'Is this a friend of yours?' said Vessal, eyeing the newcomer suspiciously.

'Not at all,' growled Throndin. 'I believe he was just leaving.'

'It is by the hospitality of the grombolgi that I stay, not by the invite of the King of Zhufbar,' the pedlar replied as he worked his way onto the end of a bench, shoving Kulft into the baron.

The king said nothing and an uneasy quiet descended, broken only by the crackling fire nearby and the murmuring from the other tables.

'So, you'll be fighting tomorrow then?' said the stranger.

'Aye,' replied Throndin, staring into his mug of ale.

'It's a fine body of warriors you've got here,' the stranger said. 'Are you sure it'll be enough though?'

'I think we can handle a few orcs,' said Barundin. 'We also have the baron's men. Why, do you know something?'

'I know many things, beardling,' said the pedlar before pausing to blow a trio of smoke rings that floated around Kulft's head. The baron's companion coughed loudly and swept them away with his hand.

The stranger looked at Throndin. 'I know that he who is as hard as stone, shall break as stone,' the pedlar said, looking at the baron. 'And he who is as hard as wood, shall break as wood.'

'Look here, vagabond, I don't like your tone at all!' replied Vessal. He looked at Throndin. 'Can't you control your people, casting aspersions all over the place like that?'

'He's not one of mine,' said Throndin with a grunt.

'Well, it seems that nothing can change in a day,' the stranger said, packing away his pipe and standing up. 'Even an old fool like me can tell when he's welcome, and when his wisdom falls on deaf ears. But you'll remember this, in a time to come, and then you'll know.'

They watched as he turned away and walked back towards the door.

'Know what?' Barundin called after him, but the stranger did not reply, and left the inn without a backward glance.

A PARTY OF halfling hunters returned in the early hours the next morning, warning that their predictions had been correct. The orcs were moving in force down the Aver, straight towards Midgwater.

Throndin was unconcerned, as this was exactly what he had hoped would happen. He walked out of the halfling village, ignoring the stray dogs running beside him, and looked across the fields to the east of the town where his army and the baron's men were readying themselves for battle.

The dwarfs held the northernmost fields, their flank secured by the rushing waters of the River Aver. Behind the dwarf army, atop a line of hills that had recently been home to several halfling families, now evicted for their own safety and Throndin's sanity, sat the four cannons that had been brought with them. The steam loco sat like a silent shadow behind them, its small cannon not yet fired up. The morning sun gleamed with a golden light from polished iron barrels and gilded ancestor faces, and Throndin paused for a moment to enjoy the sight.

In a staggered line, his warriors were spread across the field, groups of thunderers armed with handguns taking up positions behind fences and hedges, his crossbow-armed quarrellers on the slopes of the hills in front of the cannons. At the centre stood Barundin with the standard of Zhufbar, protected by the hold's hammerers – Throndin's own bodyguard.

At the very end of the line was a mess of halflings, carrying bows, hunting spears and other weaponry. They had arrived at dawn, declaring their intent to fight for themselves, and Throndin had not had the heart to send them on their way. They had looked so eager, and many of them had a dangerous glint in their eyes that had caused the dwarf king to pause for a moment. He had concluded that they were far better on the battlefield where he could see them than causing trouble somewhere else.

In consultation with Captain Kurgereich, Throndin had arranged for the halflings to be positioned between Throndin's axe-wielding hearth guard and the bodyguard of the baron, in an effort to keep them out of harm's way as much as possible,

To the south were arranged the baron's spearmen and halberdiers, with his knights held in reserve behind them, ready to counter attack. The basic plan was to shelter under the cannonade for as long as possible, before the dwarfs marched forwards to finish the battle toe-to-toe. The baron was to ensure no swift-moving wolf riders or chariots swept around the end of the dwarf line and attacked them from behind. It was simple, and both Throndin and Krugereich had agreed that was for the best.

The waiting went on for several hours, through lunchtime (both elevenses and lunchtime in the case of the halflings), and into the afternoon. Throndin began to fear that the orcs would not reach Midgwater in the daylight hours, but the doubts had only begun to form when he noticed a dust cloud on the horizon. Soon after, the easterly breeze brought the stench of the orc horde wafting over the army, causing the horses to stamp and whinny and the halflings to choke.

At the merest hint of the orc smell, a strange mood came over the dwarfs, a race memory of holds being destroyed and ancestors being slain. They began a mournful dirge, which rippled along the line and gathered in strength, as Throndin walked out from his hammerers to stare at the approaching horde. The low blast of war horns accompanied the sombre hymn, echoing from the hills around the battlefield.

There were gasps of dismay from the manlings as the orcs came into view. There were many more than anyone had expected – several thousand brutal green-skinned savages. The horde stretched out from the riverbanks for a mile, their tattered banners and skull totems bobbing up and down above the green mass as they advanced.

Throndin could see their warboss, a broad warrior that stood over a head taller than the orcs around him, his face daubed in black war paint with only his evil-red eyes showing through. He wore a great horned helm and carried a cleaver as long as a halfling was tall in each hand, their serrated blades glinting in the afternoon sun.

Upon seeing their foes, the orcs gave up a great clamour of shouting, and beat their weapons upon the fanged faces daubed onto their shields. Their harsh voices cut the air, the cacophony of bellowing drowning out the deep song of the dwarf army. Brassy horns and erratic drumbeats signalled the advance to begin anew and the orcs came pouring forward, waving weapons and shields in the air.

Throndin gestured for his stonebearers and they came forward, carrying between them a lump of granite, hewn into a long flat step carved with runes. Lowering it to the ground by the iron rings driven into its ends, they placed the grudgestone in front of the king. He gave them a nod and then turned to face his army, who fell silent.

'Here I place the grudgestone of Zhufbar, and here we shall stand,' he called out, his voice clear above the tumult of the orcs. 'I shall be victorious standing upon this grudgestone, or I shall be buried beneath it. No dwarf takes a step back from this line. Death or victory!'

With great ceremony Throndin took a step up onto the stone and unslung his broad-bladed axe. He hefted it above his head and a great cheer went up from the dwarfs. At his signal, the battle began.

With a loud roar, the first cannon opened fire and its ball went sailing over the heads of the dwarfs. Pitching off the turf in a great explosion of mud and grass, the ball skidded forwards and slammed through the orc line, ripping limbs from bodies and smashing bones. A great cheer went up from the men of the baron, while the dwarfs resumed their mournful hymn to Grimnir.

A succession of three loud reports signalled the start of the bombardment as the other cannons opened fire. Unconcerned by the mounting casualties, the orcs continued forward, screaming and cavorting in their excitement. The swish of crossbow quarrels and the rattle of handgun fire added to the noise of battle as the other dwarf troops loosed their weapons upon the charging greenskins.

Fully a third of the orc host had been wounded or killed by the time it crashed into the dwarf line. Fanged faces bellowing battle cries met stubborn bearded visages set with grim intensity.

The cleavers and mauls of the orcs clanged off mail and plate armour, while the axes and hammers of the dwarfs cleaved through flesh and pulverised bone. Despite their losses, the orcs pushed onwards, their numbers beginning to tell against the thin dwarf line. Thunderers wielded their guns like clubs while Throndin's axe sang through the air as he cleaved apart his foes.

The ground shook with a great pounding, and Throndin felt the thundering of many hooves. He turned to his right and glanced over the heads of his comrades, expecting to see Vessal's knights charging forwards to counter some move by the orcs to surround the dwarfs. To his dismay, he saw a wall of boar-mounted greenskins charging through the halflings, crushing them beneath their trotters and spitting them on crude spears.

'The baron, he has abandoned us!' cried Barundin, standing next to the king. The prince pointed over his shoulder and Throndin turned to see the humans retreating from the field. The orcs were advancing quickly across the now open field.

'The oathbreaker!' shouted Throndin, almost falling off his grudgestone.

The squealing of gigantic boars mingled with the crude shouts of the charging orcs drowned out Throndin's curses. Spears lowered, the boar riders smashed into Throndin's hammerers like a thunderbolt.

Crude iron speartips crashed against dwarf-forged steel armour while the boars trampled and gored anything in front of them. The hammerers swung their heavy mattocks in wide arcs, smashing riders from their porcine steeds and breaking bones. In the midst of the fighting, Throndin stood upon his grudgestone lopping off heads and limbs with his rune axe, bellowing the names of his ancestors as he did so.

A particularly large and brutal orc came charging through the mass, his heavy spear held above his head. Throndin turned and raised his axe to parry the blow but was too slow. The serrated point of the spear slid between the overlapping plates protecting his left shoulder and bit deep into royal flesh. With a roar of pain, Throndin brought his axe down, carving the orc's arm from its body. The spear was still embedded in the king's chest, with arm attached, as he took a step backwards, the world spinning around him. His foot slipped from the back of the grudgestone and he toppled to the muddy ground with a crash.

Hengrid Dragonfoe gave a shout to his fellow hammerers and they surged forward around the king as more orcs poured into the fray, joining the boar riders. Barundin was caught up in the swirling melee, his axe cutting left and right as he fought to stand beside his father. The king's face was pale and deep red was spilled across his armour from the grievous wound. Throndin's eyes were still open though, and they turned to Barundin.

Feeling his father's gaze upon him, Barundin planted the standard into the dirt, driving it down through the turf of the field. He hefted his axe and lunged forward to meet the oncoming greenskins.

'For Zhufbar!' he shouted. 'For King Throndin!'

The goblins scattered as the lone figure approached, abandoning their loot-ing of the corpses strewn across the narrow mountain valley. Dead orcs and goblins were piled five deep in places, around the bodies of the dwarfs they had ambushed, who had fought to the very end. The goblins backed away to the far end of the valley, fearful of the powerful aura that surrounded the newly arrived dwarf.

He was dressed in rune-encrusted armour, a purple cloak hanging from his shoulders. His long white beard was banded with golden clasps as it spilled from his helm to his knees. The White Dwarf picked his way through the piles of the slain, his gaze sweeping left and right. Seeing the object of his search, he cut right, pushing his way past a mound of dismembered orc bodies. Within the circle of dead greenskins lay four dwarfs, amongst them a battered metal standard driven into the earth of the valley floor.

One of the dwarfs was sitting upright, his back to the standard, blood drying in his greying beard, his face a crimson mask. The dwarf's eyes fluttered opened at the approach of the White Dwarf and then widened in awe.

'Grombindal!' he wheezed, his voice cracked with pain.

'Aye, Prince Dorthin, it's me,' the White Dwarf replied, kneeling beside the fallen warrior and placing his axe on the ground. He gently laid a hand on the prince's shoulders. 'I wish I had arrived earlier.'

'There were too many of them,' the prince said, trying to pull himself up. Blood bubbled from a massive cut to his temple and he collapsed back again.

Dorthin looked up at the White Dwarf, his face twisted with pain. 'I'm dying, aren't I?'

'Yes,' the White Dwarf replied. 'You fought bravely, but this is your last battle.'

'They say you have come from the Halls of the Ancestors,' said Dorthin, one eye now clotted with fresh blood. 'Will they welcome me there?'

'Grungni and Valaya and Grimnir and your ancestors will more than wel-come you,' said the White Dwarf. 'They will honour you!'

'My father...' said Dorthin.

'Will be very proud and aggrieved,' the White Dwarf interrupted him with a raised hand.

'He will declare a grudge against the orcs,' said Dorthin.

'He will,' said the White Dwarf with a nod.

'Will you help him avenge me?' asked the prince, his eyes now closed. His breath rattled in his throat, and with one final effort he forced himself to look at the White Dwarf. 'Will you avenge me?'

'I will be there for your father, because I could not be here for his son,' the White Dwarf promised. 'You have the oath of Grombrindal.'

'And we know that your oath is as hard as stone,' said the prince with a smile.

His eyes closed once more and his body slumped as death took him.

The White Dwarf stood and looked across the battlefield before turning his gaze back to the fallen prince. He reached into his pack, unfolded a broad-headed shovel, and drove it into the ground.

'Aye, laddie,' he said as he started digging the first of many graves. 'Hard as stone, that's me.'

BARUNDIN'S ARM WAS beginning to ache as he chopped his axe into another orc head. His armour was dented and scratched from numerous blows, and he could feel broken ribs grinding inside him. Every time he breathed in, new pain flared through his chest.

It seemed hopeless. The orcs were all around them now, and the hammerers were virtually fighting back to back. Barundin glanced at his father, and saw blood frothing on his lips. At least the king was still alive, if only just.

A crude cleaver slammed into Barundin's helmet, dazing him for a second. He swung his axe in instinct, feeling it bite home. As he recovered his senses he saw an orc on the ground in front of him, cradling the stump of its left leg. He drove his axe into its chest, and the blade stuck.

As he tried to wrench the weapon free, another orc, almost twice as tall as Barundin, loomed out of the press, each hand grasping a wicked-looking scimitar. The orc grinned cruelly and swung the blade in its right hand at Barundin's chest, forcing the dwarf prince to duck. With a yell, Barundin yanked his axe free and brought it up, ready to deflect the next blow.

It never came.

A dwarf in shining rune armour crashed out of the orc ranks, his glittering axe hewing down foes in twos and threes with every swing. Orc blood stained his purple cloak and his flowing white beard was muddy and bloodied. With another mighty blow he cleaved the scimitar-armed orc from neck to waist.

Barundin stepped back in shock as the White Dwarf continued the assault, his axe a whirling, glowing arc of death for the orcs. Their clumsy blows rebounded harmlessly from his armour or missed entirely as the legendary warrior ducked and weaved through the melee, his every stroke disembowelling, severing and crushing.

Out of the corner of his eye, Barundin saw something moving, a golden light, and he turned to see the runelord, Arbrek Silverfingers. He had a golden horn in his hand, glowing with inner light. The runelord raised the instrument to his lips and blew a long, clear blast.

The deep blow reverberated across the battlefield, causing the ground itself to tremble. The note seemed to echo down from the clouds and rise up from the earth, filling the air with thunderous noise. The runelord took a deep breath and blew again, and this time Barundin felt the earth shaking beneath his boots. The shuddering grew in intensity and gaping cracks began to emerge in the tortured ground. Orcs and goblins toppled into the newly formed crevasses.

'Come on lad, don't just stand and gawp!' cried Hengrid raising his hammer above his head. Looking around, Barundin saw that the orcs were stunned, many of them on the ground clasping their ears, others pulling themselves out of holes and cracks.

Barundin snatched up the standard of Zhufbar in his left hand and charged forward with the hammerers, like the tail of a destructive comet behind the White Dwarf. Hammers rose and fell onto orc skulls, while Barundin's axe bit into flesh and shattered bone. Within minutes, the orcs were broken, the tattered remnants of the horde fleeing faster than the dwarfs could follow.

The enemy vanquished, Barundin felt exhaustion sweep through his body and his legs weaken. He stumbled and then righted himself, aware that he was in front of his fellow dwarfs and needed to be strong.

He remembered his father and with a curse turned and ran back across the corpse-laden field to where the king still lay. Arbrek was beside Throndin, cradling his head and holding a tankard to the king's lips. Throndin spluttered, swallowed the beer, and heaved himself onto one arm.

'Father!' gasped Barundin as he came to a stop and leaned on the standard for support.

'Son,' croaked Throndin. 'I'm afraid I'm all done in.'

Barundin turned to Arbrek for some form of denial, but the runelord simply shook his head. The dwarf prince turned as he felt a presence behind him. It was the White Dwarf. With gauntleted hands, he removed his helm, his bushy beard gushing out like a waterfall. Barundin gave another gasp. The face that looked at him was that of the old pedlar.

The White Dwarf gave him a nod and then stepped past and knelt beside the king. 'We meet again, King Throndin of Zhufbar,' he said in a gruff tone.

'Grombrindal...' the king wheezed. He coughed and shook his head. 'I should have seen, but I refused to. It is not in our nature to forgive, so I can only offer my thanks.'

'It is not for gratitude that I am here,' replied the White Dwarf. 'My oath is as hard as stone, and cannot be broken. I only regret that the leader of the orcs escaped my axe, but I will find him again.'

'Everything would have been lost without you,' said Barundin. 'That oathbreaker Vessal must be held to account.'

'Manlings are weak by nature,' said the White Dwarf. 'Their time is so short, they fear to lose everything. Not for them the comfort of the Hall of Ancestors, and so each must make what he can of his short life and hold that life dearly.'

'He forsook his allies. He is nothing more than a coward,' growled Barundin.

The White Dwarf nodded, his gaze on Throndin. He stood and stepped up to Barundin, looking him in the eye. 'The King of Zhufbar is dead. You are now king,' the White Dwarf said. Barundin glanced over Grombrindal's shoulder and saw that it was true.

'King Barundin Throndinsson,' said Arbrek, also standing. 'What is your will?'

'We shall return to Zhufbar and bury our honoured dead,' said Barundin. 'I shall then take up the Book of Grudges and enter into it the name of Baron Silas Vessal of Uderstir. I shall right the wrong that has been done to us today.'

Barundin then looked at the White Dwarf. 'I swear an oath that it shall be so,' he said. 'Will you swear with me?'

'I cannot make that promise,' said the White Dwarf. 'The slayer of your brother still lives, and while he does, I must avenge Dorthin. In time, however, you may yet see me again. Look for me in the unseen places. Look for me when the world is at its darkest and when victory seems far away. I am Grombrindal, the White Dwarf, the grudgekeeper and the reckoner, and my watch is eternal.'

GRAMMAR

GRUDGE TWO

The Grudgesworn

THE DWARFS STOOD in a quiet group, King Barundin at their head, looking out over the battlefield. The pyres of orc bodies were now no more than dark patches in the mud and grass, and the grey sky was tinged with smoke from the halfling hearths around the battlefield.

Upon a bier decorated with golden knotwork and the stylised faces of hanging ancestor badges lay the body of King Throndin, held aloft by Ferginal and Durak. The king's stonebearers in life were now the carriers of his body in death. Beyond them, a large knot of halflings stood watching the ceremony, many of them weeping. Their scabrous little dogs even felt the mood, lying on the ground whining and yapping. For their part, the honour guard of dwarfs stood in stoic silence, their glimmering mail and long beards frosted by the cold air.

Arbrek stepped up to Barundin and gave a nod. The new King of Zhufbar cleared his throat and turned to the assembled mourners.

'In life, King Throndin was everything that a dwarf should be,' said Barundin. His gruff voice was deep and strong, the words well-rehearsed. 'Never one to forget a vow, his life was dedicated to Zhufbar and our clans. Now, as he looks upon us from the Hall of Ancestors, we give thanks for his sacrifice. I must now take up the burden that he carried upon his shoulders for those many long years.'

Barundin walked across to the shroud-covered body of the dead king. His face, pale and sunken in death, was framed by a shock of greying hair. Throndin's beard had been intricately braided into funerary knots, the better for him to look in the Halls of the Ancestors.

Throndin laid a hand upon his father's unmoving chest and looked eastwards, where the Worlds Edge Mountains reared up from beyond the horizon, disappearing into the low clouds.

'From stone we came and to stone we return,' said Barundin, his gaze focussed on the mountains in the distance. 'On this very field, a year ago, King Throndin gave his life. He died not in vain, for his life was taken avenging the death of his son and fulfilling his last oath.'

Barundin then looked at the dwarfs and pointed to the ground a short distance away. A hole had been dug, lined with carved stone tablets, and to one side on a small stand was Throndin's oathstone.

'Here my father took his last breath, to swear never to take a step back, never to surrender to our foes,' continued Barundin. 'He was true to his word and was struck down on this spot. As he swore then, so shall we obey his will. We have returned here from Zhufbar to see his wish carried out, after a due period of state and my true investiture as king. The clanhave paid their respects, we have received messages of courage from my fellow kings in the other holds, and my father has lay in state as appropriate to his station. Now it is time for us to wish him well on his journey to the Halls of the Ancestors.'

The bier-bearers marched forward with the body of the king, Barundin and Arbrek following them, and stood beside the open grave. Hengrid Dragonfoe joined them, a foaming mug of ale in his hand. It was half-ling ale, nowhere near as good as dwarf ale, but the Elder of the village had been so adamant and sincere that Barundin had wilted under her impassioned request to provide the final pint. Arbrek had assured the king that his father would have been grateful for the gesture from the people he had died fighting to protect.

Hengrid handed him the mug and Barundin took a swig before placing the tankard on his father's chest. With great care Throndin's body was lowered into the grave until it rested on a stone plinth at its bottom. A covering stone, inlaid with silver runes of protection by Arbrek, was then lifted over the tomb, completing the blocky sarcophagus. Barundin took a proffered shovel and began to pile the earth from the grave onto the coffin of his father. When the funeral mound was complete, Ferginal and Durak took up the king's oathstone and placed it at the top of the mound, marking the grave for all eternity.

'Stone to stone,' said Barundin.

'Stone to stone,' echoed the dwarfs around him.

'Rock to rock,' intoned the king.

'Rock to rock,' murmured the throng.

They stood in silence for a few moments, broken only by the yelps of dogs and the sniffling of the halflings themselves, each dwarf paying his last respects to the fallen king.

Finally, Barundin turned and faced the crowd of dwarfs. 'We return to Zhufbar,' the king said. 'There are fell deeds to be done, grudges to be written and oaths to be sworn. On this, the day of my father's end, I swear again that the name of Baron Silas Vessal of Uderstir is worth less than dirt, and his life is forfeit for his betrayal. I shall right the wrong that has been done to us by his treachery.'

BARUNDIN LED THE small host eastwards into the Worlds Edge Mountains and they took the southerly route towards Zhufbar, passing close to the ancient hold of Karak Varn. The dwarfs proceeded cautiously as they neared the fallen stronghold, keeping their axes and hammers loose in their belts. Small groups of rangers preceded them, wary of orcs and goblins and other foes who would look to attack them. On the afternoon of the second day, they reached the shores of Varn Drazh – Blackwater – a vast mountain lake that filled a crater smashed into the mountains millennia before.

The name was well earned, for the lake was still and dark, its surface rippled only by the strong mountain winds. As they marched along the shoreline, the dwarfs were quiet, wary of the creatures that were known to lurk in the depths of the water. Their unease grew as their course took them around Karaz Khrumbar, the tallest mountain surrounding the lake and site of the ancient beacon tower of Karak Varn. The blackened, tumbled stones of the outpost could still be seen littering the mountainside, gutted by fire nearly four thousand years earlier as orcs had attacked Karak Varn.

The fallen hold itself lay at the south-western edge of the lake, and the cliff face from which it had been delved could be seen rearing out of the mountain mists in the distance. Looking upon it, Barundin felt a tremor of emotion for his lost kinsmen. He could imagine the scene as vividly as if he'd been there four millennia ago, for the tale of the fall of Karak Varn had been a bedtime tale for him as a young dwarf, along with the stories of all the other dwarf holds.

The king could almost hear the sound of warning horns and drums echoing across the lake as the green skinned hordes had assaulted the small towers atop Karaz Khrumbar. They called in vain, for Karak Varn was already doomed. The mountains had shook with a ferocity never known and the great cliff had been rent in two, smashing aside the gates and allowing the cold waters of the Varn Drazh to pour into the hold, drowning thousands of dwarfs. Sensing the dwarfs' weakness, their enemies had gathered.

From below, in tunnels gnawed from the bedrock of the mountains, the rat-things had come, silently in the darkness, slitting throats and stealing away newborns. The dwarfs of Karak Varn had mustered what might they could against this skulking foe, but they'd been unprepared when the orcs and goblins had come from above.

The dwarfs of Karak Varn had fought valiantly, and their king refused to leave, but some clans realised their doom and managed to escape the trap before it fully closed. Some of those clans still wandered the hills,

Dwarfs

dispossessed until their lines died out or were absorbed by one of the hold clans. Others had sought shelter in Zhufbar or gone west to the Grey Mountains. None of the dwarfs that had remained in the hold had survived.

Now majestic Karak Varn was no more. Called Crag Mere, it was a desolate place, full of shadows and ancient memories. Barundin looked out across the water and knew that beneath the rock and water lay the treasures of Karak Varn alongside the skeletons of his forefathers' kin. Occasionally the engineers of Zhufbar would construct diving machines to explore the sunken depths of the hold, but few of these expeditions returned. Those who did spoke of troll infestations, goblin tribes and the vile ratmen clawing an existence out of the ruined hold. There was the odd treasure chest recovered, or an ancient rune hammer or some other valuable, enough to keep the stories fuelled and spark the imagination of others adventurous or foolhardy enough to dare the dangers of the Crag Mere.

Blackwater's name had taken on new meaning, and had become the site of many a battle between dwarfs and goblinkind. It had been here that the Runelord Kadrin Redmane had stood upon the shores, protecting his carts of gromril ore against an orc ambush. Seeing that his force was doomed, his final act had been to throw his rune hammer into the depths so that it would not fall into greenskins' hands. Many an expedition had sought to recover it, but it still lay in the murky waters.

It was on these bleak shores that the dwarfs finally slew Urgok Beard Burner, the orc warboss that had assailed the city of Karaz-a-Karak over two and a half thousand years before in retaliation for the capture of their high king.

And so the history of Blackwater went on, skirmishes and battles punctuating short periods of peace. The latest had been the Battle of Black Falls, when the high king had led the army of Karaz-a-Karak against a goblin host. At the culmination of the battle High King Alrik was dragged over the falls into Karak Varn by the mortally wounded goblin chieftain Gorkil Eye Gouger.

Yes, mused Barundin, Blackwater has become an accursed place for the dwarfs.

AS NIGHT CLOSED in, they set camp near the northern tip of Blackwater. Barundin was in two minds about whether to set fires or not, and consulted with Arbrek. The runelord and king stood at the water's edge, tossing stones into its unmoving darkness.

'If we light fires, it will keep wild animals and trolls at bay,' said Barundin. 'But they might attract the attention of a more dangerous foe.'

Arbrek looked at him, his eyes glittering in the dying light. He did not reply immediately, but laid a hand on Barundin's shoulder. Arbrek smiled, surprising Barundin.

'If this is the most difficult decision of your kinghood, then your reign will have been blessed by the ancestors,' said the runelord. His smile faded. 'Light the fires, for if a foe is to come upon us, better that we have more than just starlight to watch for their coming.'

'I'll set double guard, to be on the safe side,' replied Barundin.

'Yes, better to be on the safe side,' agreed Arbrek.

As night settled, the winds calmed and turned northerly. Over the crackling of the flames of the half dozen fires, Barundin could hear another noise, distant and more comforting. It was a dim, barely audible sound like a bass roaring and rattling from the north. He slept fitfully and when he awoke, his eyes were drawn to the still menace of the lake, his spine tingling with the sensation of being watched. He turned his eyes northward and saw the faintest of glows in the darkness beyond the nearest mountains, a dull, ruddy aura from the forges of Zhufbar. With happier thoughts, he fell asleep again.

The night passed without incident and as the sun crept over the eastern peaks, the dwarfs finished their breakfast and readied for the march. Gorhunk Silverbeard, one of Barundin's hammerer bodyguards, sought out the king as he brushed and plaited his beard. The veteran warrior wore the tanned hide of a bear across his shoulders, suitably tailored for his frame. If the stories were to be believed, he had killed the bear with only a small wooden hatchet when he was a beardling. Gorhunk had never confirmed or denied this, though he seemed happy with the reputation. That he was an accomplished and experienced fighter was obvious just from the two ragged scars that ran the length of his right cheek, turning his beard white in two stripes.

'The rangers have returned,' Gorhunk told his king. 'The path to the north is clear of foes, though they found spoor of wolf riders, a few days old.'

'Pfah! Wolf riders are nothing but scavengers and cowards,' spat Barundin. 'They'll give us no trouble.'

'That's true, but they can also fetch help,' warned Gorhunk. 'Where there are wolf riders, there'll be others. This place is crawling with grobi scum.'

'We'll set off as soon as is convenient,' said the king. 'Send the rangers out again. There's no harm in being forewarned.'

'Aye,' said Gorhunk with a nod. The hammerer turned and strode off into the camp, leaving Barundin to his thoughts.

With the fall of Karak Varn, Zhufbar had been left partially isolated from the rest of the old dwarf empire. Now they were surrounded by hostile orc and goblin tribes, while the ratmen were never too far away. It was a constant battle, and on a handful of occasions the hold had been seriously threatened with invasion. But they had survived these attempts, and the mettle of Zhufbar was as strong as ever. Barundin, as new king, was determined that his hold would not fail during his reign.

* * *

NOT LONG AFTER the sun had reached noon, the dwarfs passed into the chasm at the north end of Blackwater. Here the dark waters rushed over the edge of the cliff in a gushing waterfall, the mountainsides echoing with the roaring, foaming torrent. Behind the noise was another, more artificial sound: the pounding and clanking of machinery.

The walls of the waterfall were lined with scores of waterwheels, some of them massive. Gears, pulleys and chains creaked and groaned in constant motion, driving distant forge hammers and ore crushers. Stone viaducts and culverts redirected the waters into cooling tanks and smelters. Amongst the spume and spray, gantries of iron and bulwarks of stone dotted the landscape, the muzzles of cannons protruding menacingly from embrasures, watching over this vulnerable entrance into Zhufbar.

Steam and smoke from the furnaces was lifted high above the vale, gathering in a pall overhead. The air was thick with moisture and droplets formed on Barundin's beard and armour as they began their descent. The path wound back and forth along the chasm's southern face, in places curving down spiral steps hewn through the rock, in others crossing cracks and fissures over arcing bridges with low parapets. Beneath them, the glow of Zhufbar's forges tinged the watery air with a glinting red hue.

At the foot of the chasm, the road took a long spiral turn northwards to the main gate, overlooked by more fortifications. As the group neared, word was passed from watchtowers to the gate wardens. A deep rumbling made the ground reverberate underfoot, as water was redirected from the flow through the gate locks. Heavy iron bars and granite lockstones were separated from one another, and the gates swung open, driven by large gears and chains machined into the rock on either side of the gateway.

A lone dwarf stood in the gaping opening, which stretched five times his height. He planted his hammer at his feet and barred their passage. Barundin walked forward to initiate the ritual of entry.

'Who approaches Zhufbar?' the door warden demanded gruffly.

'Barundin, King of Zhufbar,' Barundin replied.

'Enter your hold, Barundin, King of Zhufbar,' the gatekeeper said, stepping aside.

As the dwarfs entered, they passed beneath a lintel stone as thick as a dwarf is tall, carved with runes and ancestor faces. It was the oldest stone in the hold, as near as could be reckoned from the ancient stories, and local tradition held that should a person pass beneath it without permission, it would crack and break, bringing the rocks down onto his head and sealing the entrance to the hold. Barundin was glad that the tale had never been tested.

Inside, the dwarfs passed into the entrance chamber. It was low and long, lit by lanterns set into alcoves every few feet. The walls were hewn into the shape of castellations, three tiers on each side, and dwarfs with handguns – the fabled thunderers – patrolled its length. Cannons and other war machines overlooked the entrance, ready to unleash lethal metal at any foe that managed to breach the gate. It could never be said that the dwarfs would be caught unprepared.

From the entrance chamber, Zhufbar spread out, north, east and south, up and down, in a maze of tunnels. Here, at the heart of the underground city, the walls were straight and true, decorated with runes and carved pictures telling the stories of the ancestor gods. In places it opened out into wide galleries overlooking eating halls and armouries, audience chambers and forge-halls. Armoured doors of stone and grom-ril protected treasuries containing wealth equivalent to that of entire human nations.

Dismissed by Barundin, the dwarf throng quickly dispersed, returning to their clan-halls and families. Barundin made his way to the chambers above the main hall, where the kings of Zhufbar had lived for seven generations. He swiftly undressed and washed in his chambers, hanging his mail coat on its stand next to his bed. Putting on a heavy robe of dark red cloth, he brushed his beard, using the troll-bone comb that had belonged to his mother. Taking golden clasps from a locked chest beneath the bed, he plaited his beard into two long braids and swept his hair back into a ponytail. Feeling more refreshed, he left and walked to the whispering chamber a short way from his bedroom.

Named for its amazing acoustics, the whispering chamber had a low, domed ceiling that echoed sound to every corner, allowing a large number of dwarfs to converse with each other without ever raising their voices. It was empty now except for a solitary figure. Seated at the near end of the long table was Harlgrim, thane of the Bryngromdal clan, second in size and wealth to Barundin's own clan, the Kronrikstok.

'Hail, Harlgrim Bryngromdal,' said Barundin, taking a seat a little way from the thane.

'Welcome back, King Barundin,' said Harlgrim. 'I take it that the funeral went without hindrance?'

'Aye,' said Barundin. He paused as a young dwarf maid entered, dressed in a heavy apron and carrying a platter of cold meat cuts and piles of cave mushrooms. She placed the food between the two dwarf nobles and withdrew with a smile. A moment later, a young beardling brought in a keg of ale and two mugs.

'We've received more messages from Nuln,' said Harlgrim as he stood and poured out two pints of beer.

Barundin pulled the platter towards him and began nibbling at a piece of ham. 'I take it that all is well?'

'It appears so, though it's hard to tell with manlings,' said Harlgrim. He took a swig of beer and grimaced. 'I miss real beer.'

'How is work on the brewery?' asked Barundin, tentatively sipping his ale. It wasn't that it was bad as such. It was still dwarf ale, after all. It just wasn't *good*.

'The engineers assure me that it is proceeding to schedule,' said Harlgrim. 'Can't work fast enough if you ask me.'

'So, is the Emperor still this Magnus fellow?' said the king, bringing the conversation back on topic.

'Seems so, though he must be getting on a bit for a manling,' said Harlgrim. He plucked a leg of meat from the platter and bit into it, the juices dribbling into his thick black beard. 'Apparently, the elves are helping him.'

'Elves?' said Barundin, his eyes narrowing instinctively. 'That's typical of elves, that is. They bugger off for four thousand years with nary a word, and then they're back, meddling again.'

'They did fight alongside the high king against the northern hordes,' said Harlgrim. 'Apparently, some prince, Teclis he's called, is helping the manlings with their wizards, or some such nonsense.'

'Elves and manling wizards?' growled Barundin. 'No good will come of it, mark my words. They shouldn't be teaching them that magic they're so proud of, it'll end in tears. Humans can't do runework, can barely brew a pint or lay a brick. I can't see any good coming from manlings having truck with elves. Perhaps I should send a message to Emperor Magnus. You know, warn him about them.'

'I don't think he'll listen,' said Harlgrim.

Barundin grunted and started on a piece of ham. 'What's in it for them?' the king asked between mouthfuls. 'They must be after something.'

'I've always considered it good sense not to think too long about the counsel of elves,' suggested the thane. 'You'll tie yourself in knots, worrying about that sort of thing. Anyway, it's not just elves he's looking to make friends with. This Magnus is setting up a foundry in Nuln, calling it the Imperial Gunnery School, according to his message. He's been told, rightly so, that the best engineers in the world live in Zhufbar, and he wants to hire their services.'

'What does the guild reckon?' asked Barundin, putting aside his food and concentrating for the first time. 'What's Magnus offering?'

'Well, the Engineers Guild hasn't met to formally discuss it, but they're going to bring it up at the next general council. They've already assured me that any extra commitment they undertake won't affect work here, especially on the brewery. Magnus's offer is very vague at the moment, but the language he uses sounds generous and encouraging. The poor souls have only just finished squabbling amongst themselves again. They're looking for a bit of stability.'

'Sounds like good sense to me,' said Barundin. 'These past few centuries have been troublesome indeed, with them fighting amongst themselves, allowing orcs to grow in numbers. Do you think it's worth sending someone to Nuln to have a proper talk with this fellow?'

'I believe the high king himself travelled to Nuln only five years ago,' said Harlgrim. 'I can't think of anything to add to whatever he might have said – he's a sensible dwarf.'

'Well, let's wait and see what they have to offer,' said Barundin. 'There's more pressing business.'

'The new grudge?' asked Harlgrim.

Barundin nodded. 'I need the thanes assembled so that we can enter it into the book and send word to Karaz-a-Karak,' said the king.

'The Feast of Grungni is almost upon us. It would seem right that we do it then,' suggested Harlgrim.

'That'd suit,' said Barundin, standing up and finishing his beer.

He wiped the froth from his moustache and beard and nodded farewell.

Harlgrim watched his king leave, seeing already the weight of rulership on his friend's shoulders. With a grunt, he also stood. He had things to do.

HAD THE LONG tables not been sturdily dwarf-built, they would have been sagging with the weight of food and ale barrels. The air rang with the shouts of the assembled thanes, the glugging of beer into tankards, raucous laughter and the trample of serving wenches hurrying to and from the king's kitchens.

They were seated in three rows at the centre of the shrine to Grungni, greatest of the ancestor gods and lord of mining. Behind Barundin, sitting on his throne at the head of the centre table, a great stylised stone mask glowered down at the assembled throng. It was the face of Grungni himself, his eyes and beard picked out in thick gold leaf, his helm crafted from glinting silver. Above the diners, great mine lanterns hung from the high ceiling, spilling a deep yellow light onto the sweating gathering below.

All across Zhufbar other dwarfs were holding their own celebrations, and beyond the great open doors of the shrine, the sounds of merriment and drunken dwarfs echoed along the corridors and chambers, down to the deepest mines.

Refilling his golden tankard, Barundin stood up on the seat of his throne and held the beer aloft. Silence rippled outwards as the thanes turned to look at their king. Dressed in heavy robes, his war crown on his head was studded with jewels, at the centre of which was a multi-faceted brynduraz, brightstone, a blue gem more rare than diamond. A golden chain of office hung around the king's neck, studded with gromril rivets and pieces of amethyst. His beard was plaited into three long braids, woven with golden thread and tipped with silver ancestor badges depicting Grungni.

As quiet descended, broken by the occasional belch, loud gulp or cracking of a bone, Barundin lowered his pint. He turned and faced the image of Grungni.

'Oldest and greatest of our kind,' he began. 'We thank you for the gifts that you have left us. We praise you for the secrets of delving and digging.'

'Delving and digging!' chorused the thanes.

'We praise you for bringing us gromril and diamonds, silver and sapphires, bronze and rubies,' said Barundin.

'Gromril and diamonds!' shouted the dwarfs. 'Silver and sapphires! Bronze and rubies!'

'We thank you for watching over us, for keeping our mines secure and for guiding us to the richest veins,' chanted Barundin.

'The richest veins!' roared the dwarfs, who were now standing on the benches, waving their mugs in the air.

'And we give greatest thanks for your best gift to us,' Barundin intoned, turning to the thanes, a grin splitting his face. 'Gold!'

'Gold!' bellowed the thanes, the outburst of noise causing the lanterns to sway and flicker. 'Gold, gold, gold, gold! Gold, gold, gold, gold!'

The chanting went on for several minutes, rising and falling in volume as varying numbers of dwarfs emptied their tankards and refilled them. The hall reverberated with the sound, shaking the throne beneath Barundin's feet, though he did not notice for he was too busy shouting himself. Several of the older thanes were running out of breath and eventually the hubbub died down.

Barundin signalled to Arbrek, who was seated to the king's left. The runelord took a keg of beer and carried it to the stone table in front of the face of Grungni. Barundin took up his axe, which had been propped up against the side of his throne, and followed the runelord.

'Drink deep, my ancestor, drink deep,' Barundin said, smashing in the top of the keg with his axe. With a push, he toppled the barrel so that the beer flowed out, spilling across the table and running into narrow channels carved into its surface. From here, the ale flowed down into the ground, through narrow culverts and channels, into the depths of the mountains themselves. Nobody now knew, if anyone ever had, where they ended, except that it was supposedly in the Hall of the Ancestors, where Grungni himself awaited those that died. From all across the dwarfs' empire, the tankard of Grungni was being filled this night.

With his duty done, Barundin turned and nodded to Harlgrim, who had been sitting at his right-hand side. The mood in the hall changed rapidly as the leader of the Bryngromdals unwrapped the thick leather covers of Zhufbar's book of grudges.

Barundin took the tome from Harlgrim, his face solemn. The book itself was almost half as tall as Barundin, and several inches thick. Its cover was made from thin sheets of stone bound with gromril and gold, and a heavy clasp decorated with a single large diamond held it shut.

Placing the book on the table in front of him, Barundin opened it. Ancient parchment pages crackled, bound with goblin sinew. As each page turned, the dwarfs in the hall murmured louder and louder, growling and grunting as seven thousand years of wrongs against them turned before their eyes. Finding the first blank page, Barundin took up his writing chisel and dipped the tip of the steel and leather writing implement into an inkpot proffered by Harlgrim. The king spoke as he wrote.

'Let it be known that I, King Barundin of Zhufbar, record this grudge in front of my people,' Barundin said, his hand rapidly dabbing the writing-chisel onto the pages to form the angular runes of khazalid, the dwarf tongue. 'I name myself grudgesworn against Baron Silas Vessal of Uderstir, a traitor, a weakling and a coward. By his treacherous act, Baron Vessal did endanger the army of Zhufbar, and through his actions brought about the death of King Throndin of Zhufbar, my father. Recompense must be in blood, for death can only be met with death. No gold, no apology can atone for this betrayal. Before the thanes of Zhufbar and with Grungni as my witness, I swear this oath.'

Barundin looked out at the sea of bearded faces, seeing nods of approval. He passed the writing-chisel to Harlgrim, blew gently on the book of grudges to dry the ink, and then closed it with a heavy thud.

'Reparation will be made,' the king said slowly.

THE NEXT DAY, Barundin's loremaster, the king's librarian and scribe, penned a message to Baron Silas Vessal, urging him to travel to Zhufbar and present himself for Barundin's judgement. The dwarfs knew full well that no manling would ever be so honourable as to do such a thing, but form and tradition had to be followed. After all, there was a centuries-long alliance between the dwarfs and the men of the Empire, and Barundin was not about to wage war upon one of the Empire's nobles without having his house in order.

None of the wisest heads in the hold could determine where Uderstir actually was, and so it was decided to send a contingent of rangers into the Empire to locate it. While preparations were being made for this expedition, another group of dwarfs was sent on the long, dangerous march south to Karaz-a-Karak. With them they carried a copy of Barundin's new grudge to present to High King Thorgrim Grudgebearer, so that it might be recorded in the Dammaz Kron, the mighty book of grudges that contained every slight and betrayal against the whole dwarf race. The Dammaz Kron's first grudge, now illegible with age and wear, had supposedly been written by the first high king, Snorri Whitebeard, against the foul creatures of the Dark Gods. Seven thousand years of history were recorded in the Dammaz Kron, a written embodiment of the dwarfs' defiance and honour.

For many days, as he awaited the return of the travelling bands, Barundin busied himself with the day-to-day affairs of the hold. A new seam of iron ore had been discovered south of the hold, and two clans staked rival claims to it. There were many laborious hours spent with the hold's records and Loremaster Thagri to reconcile the two claims and work out who held ownership of the new mine.

Barundin spent a day inspecting the work on the new brewery. The vats and mechanisms of the old brewery that had been salvaged had been carefully restored, while new pipes, bellows, fire grates and oast houses were being erected on the site of the old brewery. Engineers and their apprentices were gathered in groups, discussing the finer points of brewery construction, and arguing over valves and sluices with beermasters and keglords.

While work was still ongoing, and had been for several years, crude measures had been taken to supply the hold with sufficient beer. Part of the king's own chambers had been turned into a storehouse to allow the beer to mature, while many of the other clans had donated halls and rooms to the endeavour. However, the result was, by dwarf standards, thin and weak, and lacked the real body and froth of proper dwarf ale. Without exception, the new brewery was the single most observed engineering project the hold had seen since the first waterwheels were built thousands of years earlier.

Six days after they had set out, the messengers to Uderstir returned. As expected, their news was grim. It had taken them four days to find Uderstir, and upon arrival in the early evening of the fourth day, had found themselves unwelcome. They had called for Silas Vessal and he had come to the gatehouse to parley. They had politely explained the terms of Barundin's grudge and requested that the baron accompany them back to Zhufbar. They assured him that he was in their safeguard and no harm would come to him until the king's judgement.

The baron had refused them admittance, cursed them for fools, and had even had his men pelt the dwarfs with stones and rotten fruit from the ramparts of his castle. As instructed, the dwarfs had left a copy of the grudge nailed to the castle gate, translated as well as possible into the Reikspiel spoken by most of the Empire, and had departed.

When he heard the news, Barundin was incensed. He had not expected Vessal to comply with his demand that he travel to Zhufbar, but to act with such brazen cowardice and insult made the king's blood boil. The next day, he brooded in his audience chamber with Arbrek, Harlgrim and several of the other most important thanes.

The king sat in his throne, with his council on high-backed seats in a semi-circle in front of him.

'I do not wish a war,' growled Barundin, 'but war we must have for this despicable behaviour.'

'I do not wish for war, either,' said Thane Godri, head of the Ongurbazum clan.

Godri's interest was well known, for it had been the Ongurbazum that had been the first to send emissaries back into the Empire after the Great War against Chaos and the election of Magnus as Emperor. They were amongst the foremost traders in the hold and had recently negotiated several contracts with the Imperial court. It was they who had brought news of the new Gunnery School in Nuln, and the profit to be made.

'This Magnus seems a sensible enough fellow,' continued Godri, 'but we can't say for sure how he will react to us attacking one of his nobles.'

'Doesn't the insult done to us merit a response?' asked Harlgrim. 'Does not the late king demand that honour be restored?'

'My father died fighting with a coward,' said Barundin, thumping a fist onto the arm of his throne.

Arbrek cleared his throat and the others looked at him. He was by far the oldest dwarf in Zhufbar, over seven hundred years old and still going strong, and his counsel was rarely wrong. 'Your father died trying to avenge a fallen son,' said the runelord. 'It would honour him not to be hasty, lest his other son join him too swiftly in the Halls of the Ancestors.'

They pondered this in silence until Arbrek spoke again, with a glance at Godri. 'The thane of the Ongurbazum has a point. Your father would also not thank you for emptying the coffers of Zhufbar when we could be filling them.'

'What would you have me do?' growled Barundin. 'I have declared the grudge, it is written in the book. You would have me ignore this manling and pretend that he did not contribute to my father's death and slight my hold?'

'I would have no such thing,' said Arbrek, drawing a deep breath, his beard bristling, eyes glinting angrily under his bushy eyebrows. 'Do not put words in my mouth, King Barundin.'

Barundin sighed heavily and raked his fingers through his beard, looking at the others around the table. Straightening in his throne, he clasped his hands together and leaned forward. When he spoke, Barundin's voice was quiet but determined.

'I will not be known as an oathbreaker,' the king said. 'For less than a year I have ruled Zhufbar. I shall not have my reign begin with an unfulfilled grudge. Whatever the consequences, if war it must be, then war we shall have.'

Godri opened his mouth to retort, but said nothing as the doors to the chamber opened, letting in the hubbub of the corridor outside. Thagri the loremaster entered, carrying with him a small book in one hand, and the book of grudges under his arm. He had excused himself from the debate on the grounds that he had research to do that might have a bearing on the subject. The king, runelord and thanes watched expectantly as the loremaster closed the doors behind him and walked across the hall and up the steps. He sat down in the empty chair that had been left for him.

He looked around the group as if noticing their stares for the first time. 'My noble kinsmen,' he began, his white beard wagging as he spoke. 'I believe I have discovered something of import.'

They waited for him to continue.

'Well, what is it?' asked Thane Snorbi of the Drektrommi, a stout warrior even for a dwarf, known for his somewhat heated temper. 'Don't keep us waiting like a bunch of idiots.'

'Ah, sorry, yes,' said Thagri. 'Well, it appears that my predecessor, Loremaster Ongrik, was slightly amiss in his book-keeping. Your father, I have just found, recorded a last grudge several years ago. It was in his journal, but Ongrik witnessed it, which is why it wasn't with all the other documents.' He waved the smaller book he was carrying.

'Last grudge?' asked Godri, one of the youngest thanes present.

'It's an old tradition, not used much in recent centuries,' explained Thagri with a wistful smile. 'Your father was very much a traditionalist in that regard. Anyway, the last grudge was recorded by a dwarf as a vow to settle it before his death, or if he could not do so, then to bequeath the settlement of that particular grudge to his heir. It started during a bit of wrangling many, many centuries ago during the Time of the Goblin Wars, to avoid breaking an oath because of an untimely death during all the fighting with the grobi scum.'

'Are you suggesting that I record this grudge as a last grudge and avoid my responsibilities?' asked Barundin, eyes narrowing.

'Of course not!' spluttered Thagri, truly indignant. 'Besides, a king can't record a last grudge until he's been in power for a hundred and one years. If we let kings have last grudges all over the place, the system would become a complete joke.'

'So what does it have to do with this debate?' asked Harlgrim.

'The last grudge is the first grudge that the heir must try to right,' said Arbrek, speaking as if he had just remembered something. He looked at Thagri, who nodded in confirmation. 'Before you do anything else, you must avenge your father's last grudge or dishonour his wishes.'

'Why didn't he tell me he had done such a thing?' asked Barundin. 'Why did he only write it in his journal?'

Thagri avoided the king's gaze and fiddled with the clasp of the book of grudges.

'Well?' demanded Barundin with a fierce stare.

'He was drunk!' blurted Thagri with a desperate look in his eyes.

'Drunk?' said Barundin.

'Yes,' said the loremaster. 'Your father and Ongrik were close friends, and as I've read this very morning in my late master's own diary, the two of them drank with each other frequently. It appears that the pair of them, this particular day, had drunk rather more than was normal even for them and had begun reminiscing about the Time of the Goblin Wars and how they wished they had been there to give the grobi a solid runking. Well, one thing led to another. Ongrik mentioned the last grudge tradition and your father ended up writing it in his journal, swearing to avenge the depredations against Zhufbar.'

'What, precisely, did my father swear?' asked Barundin, his heart heavy with foreboding. 'He didn't vow to retake Karak Varn or something like that?'

'Oh no,' said Thagri with a shake of his head and a smile. 'Nothing quite that grand. No, not that grand at all.'

'Then what was his grudge?' asked Harlgrim.

'Well, a last grudge is not a new grudge at all,' explained Thagri, placing the journal on the floor at his feet and opening the book of grudges. 'It's an oath to fulfil an existing grudge. There was one in particular that your father was always annoyed by, particularly when he was in his cups.'

The loremaster fell silent and the others were quiet as they saw a pained expression twist Barundin's face.

The king wiped a hand over his lips. 'Grungankor Stokril,' he said, his voice barely a whisper.

'Grunga…' said Harlgrim. 'The old mines to the east? They've been overrun by goblins for nearly two thousand years.' He fell silent as he saw Barundin's look, as did the others except one.

'Dukankor Grobkaz-a-Gazan?' asked Snorbi. 'That's connected to Mount Gunbad now. Thousands, tens of thousands of grobi there. What did King Throndin want with that doomed place?'

The thane looked at the pale expressions on the other dwarfs and then stared at Thagri. 'There's a mistake,' insisted Snorbi.

The loremaster shook his head and handed Snorbi the book of grudges, pointing to the relevant passage. The thane read it and shook his head in disbelief.

'We have a war to prepare for,' said Barundin, standing. There was a fell light in his eyes, almost feverish. 'War against the grobi. Call the clans, sound the horns, sharpen the axes! Zhufbar marches once again!'

GRUDGE THREE

The Rat Grudge

THE HALLS AND corridors of Zhufbar rang constantly with the pounding of forge hammers, the hiss of steam, the roar of furnaces and the tramp of dwarf boots. To Barundin, it was a symphony of craftsmanship, suffused with the melody of common purpose and kept in beat by the rhythm of industry. It was the sound of a dwarf hold bent to a single goal: war.

The armouries had been opened and the great rune weapons of the ancestors brought forth once more. Axes with glimmering blades and fiery runes were polished; shields and mail of gromril carved with the images of the clans' ancestors were hefted once more. Hammers graven with gold and silver hung upon the walls. Battle helms decorated with wings and horns and anvils sat upon bedside tables, awaiting their owners.

The engineers were bent to their craft as the forges billowed with fire and smoke. Keg upon keg of black powder was made in the strong rooms, while artisans of all types turned their minds to great war machines, weapons and armour. Cannons were pulled from the foundries and lovingly awakened from their slumber with polish and cloth. Flame cannons, organ guns, bolt throwers and grudgethrowers were assembled and inscribed with oaths of vengeance and courage.

This was no mere expedition, no foray into the wilds for a skirmish. This was dwarf war, grudge-born and fierce. This was the righteous anger that burned within the heart of every dwarf, young and old alike. This was the power of the ancients and the wisdom of generations set on a single course of destruction.

Barundin could feel it flowing through his veins, even as the spirits of seventy generations looked upon him from the Halls of the Ancestors. Never had he felt so sure of his mind; never had his being been set on something so singular and yet so worthy. Although at first the thought of reclaiming Grungankor Stokril had filled the king with apprehension, it had taken but a few moments thought to reconsider the idea.

Though it had begun as a necessity so that he might pursue his own goals, Barundin had become wedded to the idea of the purge of Dukankor Grobkaz-a-Gazan – the Warren of Goblin Ruin. It would be a fitting way to start his kingship, and would set the minds of his people for his whole reign. A conquest to reclaim the ancient mines would launch Zhufbar into a new period of endeavour and prosperity. It was more than a simple battle, a stepping-stone to his own needs. The destruction of the goblin kingdom in distant lands would herald his ascendancy to the throne of Zhufbar.

Though the war would be terrible, and the dwarfs implacable in the conflict, life in a dwarf hold did not turn quickly. The preparations for Barundin's march forth against the goblins had been going on for five years. Such an undertaking could not begin lightly, and no dwarf worth his gold would do so in a hasty, unprepared fashion.

While the engineers and axe-smiths, armourers and foundry workers had laboured, so too had Barundin, the thanes and the loremaster. From the depths of the libraries, the old plans of the mine workings of Grungakor Strokril had been brought into the light for the first time in a millennium and a half. With his advisors, Barundin pored for long weeks and months over the detailed maps. They postulated where the goblins would have dug their own tunnels, and where they might be trapped.

Rangers were sent into the tunnels eastwards, to gauge the numbers of the goblins and their whereabouts. Ironbreakers, veteran warriors of tunnel-fighting, spent time teaching their ways of war to young beardlings, tutoring them in axe-craft and shield-skill. The oldest of the Zhufbar throng taught the youngest the ways of grobkul, the ancient art of goblin-stalking. Miners were tasked with practising demolition as well as tunnel building, so that the goblin holes might be filled and reinforcements waylaid.

Amid all of this, the hold tried its best to continue life as normal. Barundin was assured that work was continuing apace on the brewery, and with no effect from the stronghold's new war footing. There were still trade agreements to be fulfilled, mines to be dug, ore to be smelted and gems to be cut and polished.

Despite the length of time it had taken so far, Barundin knew that soon his army would be ready. It would be a force the like of which Zhufbar had not seen in five generations. Of course, Abrek cautioned, such armies as those that had fought during the War of Vengeance against the elves, or had valiantly defended Zhufbar during the Time of the Goblin Wars, would never be seen again. Dwarfs no longer had such numbers, nor the ancient knowledge and weapons of those times. He warned against underestimating the threat of the goblins. However, the ancient runelord's pessimism did little to dent Barundin's growing hunger for the coming battles.

It was then, perhaps only weeks from the date the army was due to march forth, that troubling news was brought to Barundin's ears. It was from Tharonin Grungrik, thane of one of the largest mining clans, as Barundin held his monthly war council.

'I don't know what it is, but we've stirred something up,' Tharonin told them. 'Perhaps it's grobi, perhaps something else. There's always a young beardling or two goes missing now and then, lost their way most likely. These past few months, there's been more not coming back than in the ten years before. Seventeen went down and never returned.'

'You think it's the grobi?' asked Barundin, reaching for his alepot.

'Maybe, maybe not,' Tharonin told him. 'Perhaps some of them followed the rangers back from the east. Perhaps they found their own way through the tunnels. Who knows where they've been digging?'

'All the more reason why we have to press on with our preparations,' snorted Harlgrim. 'Once we're through with them, the grobi won't dare set foot within fifty leagues of Zhufbar.'

'There's been bodies found,' said Tharonin, his deep voice ominous. 'Not hacked up, not a shred of cloth nor a ring or trinket taken. That doesn't come across as grobi work to me.'

'Stabbed?' said Arbrek, stirring and opening his eyes. The other dwarfs had assumed he was asleep. Apparently he had been deep in thought.

'In the back,' said Tharonin. 'Just the once, right through the spine.'

'I'll wager a fist of bryn that it wasn't no grobi did that,' said Harlgrim.

'Thaggoraki?' suggested Barundin. 'The ratmen are back, do you think?'

The others nodded. Along with orcs and goblins, trolls and dragons, the thaggoraki, mutant ratmen also known as skaven, had contributed to the downfall of several of the ancient dwarf holds during the Time of the Goblin Wars. Twisted, cursed scavengers, the skaven were a constant menace, digging their own tunnels in the dark of the world, unseen by man or dwarf. It had been many centuries since Zhufbar had been troubled by them, the last of the skaven having been driven south by the goblins.

'We've laboured too long to be put off by guessing and hearsay,' said Barundin, breaking the gloomy silence. 'If it is the walking rats, we need to be sure. Perhaps it's just some grobi that've followed the expeditions back, like Tharonin says. Send parties into the mines, open up the closed, barren seams and see what's down there.'

'It'll be good practice for the beardlings,' said Arbrek with a grim smile. 'If they can catch themselves some thaggoraki, grobi will be no problem.'

'I'll talk to the other mining clans,' offered Tharonin. 'We'll split the job between us, send guides for those parties that don't know the workings out eastward. We'll delve into every tunnel, root them out.'

'Good,' said Barundin. 'Do what you must to keep safe, but find me proof of what's happening. It'll take more than a few rats in the dark to turn me from this path.'

A STRANGE ATMOSPHERE settled over Zhufbar as news of the mysterious disappearances spread. Speculation was rife, particularly amongst the older dwarfs, who cited tales from their past, or their father's past, or their grandfather's past. The old stories resurfaced – sagas of ancient dwarf heroes who had fought the grobi and thaggoraki.

In meticulous detail, the wisest oldbeards spoke of Karak Eight Peaks, the hold that had fallen to both of these vile forces. Surrounded by eight daunting mountains – Karag Zilfin, Karag Yar, Karag Mhonar, Karagril, Karag Lhune, Karag Nar and Kvinn-wyr – the dwarfs of the hold had thought they were protected by a natural barrier as sure against attack as any wall. In its glory days, Karak Eight Peaks was known as the Queen of the Silver Depths, Vala-Azrilungol, and its glory and magnificence were surpassed only by the splendour of Karaz-a-Karak, the capital.

But the earthquakes and volcanic eruptions that preceded the Time of the Goblin War rent the Eight Peaks and threw down many of the walls and towers that had been erected there by the dwarfs. For nearly a hundred years, orcs and goblins attacked the hold from above. The beleaguered dwarfs were already under threat from below by the skaven, and gradually they were pushed towards the centre of the hold, assaulted from above and below.

The final, vile blow came when the skaven, arcane engineers and manipulators of the raw stuff of Chaos, warpstone, unleashed poisons and plagues onto the besieged dwarfs. Sensing that their doom was nigh, King Lunn ordered the treasuries and armouries locked and buried, and led his clans from the hold, fighting through the greenskins to the surface. To this day, short-lived expeditions ventured into Karak Eight Peaks in attempts to recover the treasures of King Lunn, but the warring night goblin tribes and skaven clans had destroyed or turned back any attempt to penetrate the hold's depths.

Such talk did nothing but darken the mood of Barundin. Though none had yet brought it up, he could sense the mood of the thanes was changing. They were preparing to dig in, as the dwarfs had always done, to fight off the skaven threat. It was a matter of days before the first real evidence that the skaven were close by in any numbers would be found, and then the thanes would suggest that the march against Dukankor Grobkaz-a-Gazan be postponed. They would have good reason, Barundin knew well, and he had his own doubts. His greatest fear, though, was that the impetus that had begun to stir the hold would be lost again.

Barundin was young in dwarf terms, less than one hundred and fifty, and older heads than his would call him impetuous, rash even. His growing dream of conquering the lost mines, avenging his father, and leading his hold boldly into the future would slowly wither away. His centuries, such as the ancestors granted him, would be bound to Zhufbar, watching the world outside fall into the grip of the orcs, his people afraid to venture forth over what were once their lands, their mountains.

These thoughts stirred a deep anger in Barundin, the latent ire that lay dormant within every dwarf. Where the greyhairs would wag their beards, growl into their cups and speak of the lost glories of the past, Barundin felt the need to seek reparation, to act rather than talk.

So it was that the King of Zhufbar waited with growing trepidation for every report from the mines. Tharonin Gungrik had assumed authority over the investigations, being the oldest and most respected of the mine-thanes. Each day, he would send a summary to Barundin, or report in person when his many duties allowed.

Each account made Barundin's heart sink. There were tales of strange smells in the depths, of fur and filth. The most experienced miners spoke of weird breezes from the deeps, odd odours that no dwarf-dug tunnel contained. With senses borne of generations of accumulated wisdom, the miners reported odd echoes, subtle reverberations that did not bear any relationship to the dwarfs' own digging. There were scratching noises at the edge of hearing, and odd susurrations that fell quiet as soon as one began listening for them.

Even more disturbing were the tales of peculiar shadows in the darkness, blacker patches in the gloom that disappeared in the light of a lantern. No dwarf could swear by it, but many thought they had half-glimpsed red eyes peering at them, and a growing sense of being watched pervaded the lower halls and galleries.

The disappearances were becoming more frequent too. Whole parties had gone missing, the only evidence of their abduction being their absence from the halls at mealtimes. Neither Tharonin, nor Barundin or any of the other council members could discern a pattern in the disappearances. The current mine workings covered many miles east, north and west, and the older mines covered several leagues.

IT WAS A disconcerted Tharonin that addressed Barundin's council when they were next gathered. The thane had come to the king's audience chamber directly from the mines, and he still wore a long shirt of gromril mail and his gold-chased helm. His beard was spotted with rock dust and his face grimy.

'It is bad news, very bad news,' said Tharonin before taking a deep gulp of ale. His face twisted into a sour expression, though whether this was because of the beer or the news that he bore was unclear.

'Tell me everything,' said Barundin. The king leaned forward with his elbows on the table, his bearded chin in his hands.

'There's new tunnels, without a doubt,' said Tharonin with a shake of the head.

'Skaven tunnels?' asked Harlgrim.

'For certain. They have the rat reek about them, and there's been spoor found. We've started finding bodies too, many of them, some of them little more than skeletons, picked clean by vermin.'

'How many tunnels?' asked Barundin.

'Seven so far,' said Tharonin. 'Seven that we've managed to find. There could be more. In fact, I'd wager there are definitely more that we don't know about yet.'

'Seven tunnels…' muttered Arbrek. He stirred the froth of his ale with a finger as he considered his words. He looked up, feeling the gazes of the others on him. 'Seven tunnels – this is no small number of foes.'

Barundin looked at the faces of the council members, wondering which of them was going to be the first to mention the planned war against the goblins. They looked back at him in silence, until Snorbi Threktrommi cleared his throat.

'Someone's got to say it,' said Snorbi. 'We can't march against the grobi while there's an enemy at our doorstep. We must move against the skaven before we can deal with the grobi.'

There was a chorus of grunted approvals, and Barundin could tell by the looks on their faces that they were expecting his reply and were ready with their arguments. Instead, he nodded slowly.

'Aye,' said the king. 'My saga will not begin with a tale of foolish stubbornness. Though it pains me beyond anything, I will postpone the war against Dukankor Grobkaz-a-Gazan. I will not be remembered as the king who reclaimed our distant realm and lost his hold in doing so. The throng that has been mustered for the march must be sent to the mines, and we shall root these vile creatures from our midst. Tomorrow morning, I want companies of warriors to go with the miners into the tunnels that have been found. We shall seek out their lair and destroy it.'

'It is a wise king that listens to counsel,' said Arbrek, patting Barundin on the arm.

Barundin looked over at Thagri, the loremaster, who was taking notes in his journal.

'Write this,' said the king. 'I said the war on the grobi was postponed, but I swear that when our halls are safe, the army will march forth to reclaim that which was taken from us.'

'You'll get no argument from me,' said Harlgrim, raising his tankard. There were similar words of affirmation from the others.

From the hall, word was passed around the hold to the thanes of the clans. In the morning they would assemble their throngs in the High Hall, to be addressed by the king. There was much more planning and wrangling to be done, which lasted past midnight. With even his considerable dwarf constitution waning, it was a weary Barundin who left the audience chamber and walked back to his bedchambers.

The king could feel the mood of the hold as he walked along the lantern-lit corridors. It was subdued and tense, and each little creak and scratch drew his attention, suspecting some vile thing to be hidden in the shadows. Like the ominous oppression before a cave-in, Zhufbar was poised, laden with potential catastrophe. After the long weeks of preparation for war, the tunnels and halls were eerily quiet and still.

Barundin reached his chambers and sat wearily on his bed. He removed his crown and unlocked the chest beside the bed, placing the crown into the padded velvet bag inside. One by one, he removed the seven golden clasps in his beard, wrapped them and placed them next to the crown. Taking a troll-bone comb from his bedside table, he began to straighten his beard, working out the knots that had gathered during his fidgeting through the day. He untied his ponytail and brushed his hair, before taking up three strands of thin leather and tying his beard. He stripped off his robes and folded them neatly into a pile on top of the chest, and then grabbed his nightgown and cap from the bed and donned them.

He stood and crossed the chamber to throw a shovel of coal onto the dying fire in the grate at the foot of the bed. As it caught, the flames grew and smoke billowed, disappearing up the chimney, which was dug down hundreds of feet from the mountainside above, barred by mesh and grates to prevent anything entering, accidentally or otherwise. He poured water from the ewer beside his bed and washed behind his ears. Lastly, he opened the window on the lantern above his bed and blew out the candle, plunging the room into the ruddy glow of the fire. His preparations complete, Barundin flopped back on to the bed, too tired to crawl beneath the covers.

Despite his fatigue, sleep did not come easily, and Barundin lay fitfully on the bed, turning this way and that. His mind was full of thoughts, of the discussions of the day and the fell deeds that had to be done the next. As his weariness finally overcame him, Barundin sunk into a disturbing dream, filled with fanged, rat-like faces. He imagined himself surrounded by a swarm of vermin, scratching and biting, gnawing at his lifeless fingers. There were eyes in the shadows, staring at him with evil intent, waiting to pounce. Scratching echoed in the darkness around him.

Barundin woke and, for a moment, he was unsure where he was, the after-images of the dream lingering in his mind. He was alert, aware that something was not right. It was a few moments before he determined the cause of his unease. The chamber was pitch dark and silent. Not just the gloom of a cloudy night, but the utter dark beneath the world that holds terror for so many creatures. Even the dwarfs, at home in the subterranean depths, filled their holds with fires and torches and lanterns.

Straining his eyes and ears, Barundin sat up, his heart thudding in his chest. He felt as if he was being watched.

The fire was out, though it should have burned through the night.

Moving slowly, he began to slide his legs towards the edge of the bed, ready to stand. It was then that he heard the faintest of noises. It was little more than a tingling at the edge of hearing, but it was there, a scraping, wet noise. In the darkness to his right, beside the dead grate, he caught a flicker of something. It was a pale, sickly green glow, a sliver against the blackness. Looking out of the corner of his eye, he saw a tiny dot drop and hit the ground.

He heard rather than saw the figure move towards him: a fluttering of cloth, the scritch-scratch of claws on the stone floor. Unarmed, he grabbed the first thing to hand, a pillow, and flung it at the approaching shape.

Now, dwarfs are a hardy folk, and are not only able to withstand much discomfort, but take pride in the fact. They eschew the dainty comforts of other races, and their soft furnishings are anything but soft. So it was that the intruder was greeted with a starched canvas bag stuffed with a dozen pounds of finely ground gravel mixed with goat hair.

In the dark, Barundin saw the figure fling up an arm, but to little effect as the dwarf pillow thudded into its shoulder, knocking it backwards, its blade toppling from its grip and clanging to the floor. Barundin was off the bed and running full tilt by the time the foe recovered.

With a hiss, the creature leapt aside from Barundin's mad rush, springing against the wall and hurtling over his head. Barundin tried to turn, but his impetus slammed him shoulder-first into the wall. Underfoot, he felt something snap, and his bare foot stung with pain. With a grunt, he turned to see the assassin dart forward, a knife in one hand. It was fast, so fast that Barundin barely had time to raise a hand before the dagger plunged into his stomach. With a roar, Barundin swept a fist backwards, smashing it against the rat-like muzzle of the creature, knocking it backwards.

'Hammerers!' bellowed Barundin, backing away from the skaven assassin until his spine was against the wall. 'To your king! Hammerers to me!'

Barundin fended off another blow with his left arm, the knife blade scoring the flesh of his hand. He could feel blood soaking into the fabric of his nightshirt and running down onto his legs.

The door burst open, spilling in light from outside, momentarily blinding Barundin. As he squinted he saw Gudnam Stonetooth running into the room, followed by the other bodyguards of the king. The assassin spun on its heel and was met by a crunching blow to the ribs from Gudnam's warhammer, sending it sprawling backwards. In the light, Barundin could now see his attacker clearly.

It was shorter than a manling, though a little taller than a dwarf, hunched and alert, and clad in black rags. A furless, snake-like tail twitched back and forth in agitation, and its verminous face was curled in a snarl. Red eyes glared at the newly arrived dwarfs.

The creature bounded past Gudnam, heading towards the fireplace, but Barundin launched himself forwards, snatching up a poker and bringing it down onto the skaven's back, snapping its spine with a crack. It gave a hideous mewl as it collapsed, legs twitching spasmodically. A hammerer, Kudrik Ironbeater, stepped forward and brought his weapon down onto the assassin's head, crushing its skull and snapping its neck.

'My king, you are hurt.' said Gudnam, rushing to Barundin's side.

Barundin pulled open the ragged tear in the nightshirt and revealed the gash across his stomach. It was long, but not deep, and had barely cut into the solid dwarf muscle beneath the skin. The wound on his arm was similarly minor, painful but not threatening.

Kudrik picked up the broken blade on the ground, gingerly holding it in his gauntleted fist. A thick ichor leaked from the rusted metal of the sword, gathering in dribbling streams along its edge. The poison shimmered with the disturbing un-light of ground warpstone.

'Weeping blade,' the hammerer spat. 'If this had wounded you, things would be more serious.'

'Aye,' said Barundin, glancing around the room. 'Bring me a lantern.'

One of the hammerers went into the antechamber and returned with a glass-cased candle, which he passed to the king. Barundin stooped into the grate and held up the lantern, illuminating the shaft of the chimney. He could see where the assassin had cut its way through the bars blocking the duct.

'There may be others,' said Gudnam, hefting his hammer over one shoulder.

'Send the rangers out to the surface,' said Barundin. 'Have them start with the waterwheels and forge chimneys. Check everything.'

'Yes, King Barundin,' said Gudnam with a nod to one of his warriors, who strode from the chamber. 'The apothecary should have a look at those wounds.'

As Barundin was about to reply, there came a sound from outside, distant but powerful. It was the low call of a horn, blowing long blasts, a mournful echo from the depths.

The king's eyes met the worried look of Gudnam. 'Warning horns from the deeps!' snarled Barundin. 'Find out where.'

'Your wounds?' said Gudnam.

'Grimnir's hairy arse to my wounds – we are under attack!' bellowed the king, causing Gudnam to flinch. 'Rouse the warriors. Sound the horns across Zhufbar. Our foe is upon us!'

THE TUNNEL RANG with the sound of clinking metal and the tramp of booted feet as Barundin and a force of warriors ran down through the hold towards the lower levels. He was still tightening the straps on the gromril plates of his armour and his hair was loosely packed under his crowned helm. Across his left arm, Barundin carried a circular shield of steel inlaid with gromril in the likeness of his great-great-great grandfather, King Korgan, and in his right hand he carried Grobidrungek – the Goblinbeater – a single-bladed runeaxe that had been in his family for eleven generations. Around him, the dwarfs of Zhufbar readied axes and hammers, their bearded faces stern and resolute as they quickly advanced.

Above the din of the assembling throng, shouts and horn blasts from further down the mineshaft could be heard, growing louder as Barundin pounded forward. The low arched tunnel opened out into the Fourth Deeping Hall, the hub of a network of mines and tunnels that delved north of the main chambers of Zhufbar, which branched out from the chamber through open square archways. Here, Tharonin was waiting with the Gungrik clan, armed and armoured for battle. Thanes marched to and fro bellowing orders, assembling the battle line in the wide hall.

'Where?' demanded Barundin as he stepped up next to Tharonin.

'The seventh north tunnel, the eighth north-east passage and the second north passage,' the thane said breathlessly. His face was smeared with grime and sweat beneath his gold-rimmed miner's helm. The candle in the small lantern mounted on its brow guttered but still burned.

'How many?' asked Barundin, stepping aside as handgun-bearing thunderers jogged past, the silver and bronze standard in their midst displaying their allegiance to the Thronnson clan.

'No way of telling,' admitted Tharonin. He pointed to an archway to the left, opposite which the army was gathering. 'Most of them seem to be in the north passages. We've held them in the seventh tunnel for the moment. Perhaps it was just a diversionary attack, or maybe there's more to come.'

'Bugrit!' snapped Barundin, glancing around. There were about five hundred warriors in the hall now, and more were entering with every moment. 'Where're the engineers?'

'No word from them yet,' said Tharonin with a shake of his head that sent motes of dust cascading from his soiled beard.

The hall was roughly oval, seven hundred feet at its widest point and some three hundred feet deep, running east to west. Through a series of low stepped platforms, it sloped down nearly fifty feet to the north and the missile troops of the hold were gathering on the higher steps so that they could shoot over the heads of their kinsdwarfs assembling in shieldwalls halfway across the hall.

With clanking thuds, a traction locomotive puffed into sight from the eastern gateway, pulling with it three limbered war machines. Two were cannons, their polished barrels shining in the light of the hall's gigantic lanterns suspended from the ceiling a dozen feet above the dwarfs' heads. The third was more archaic, consisting of a large central boiler-like body and flared muzzle, surrounded by intricate pipes and valves: a flame cannon.

Engineers clad in armoured aprons, carrying axes and tools, marched alongside the engine, their faces grim. A bass cheer went up upon their arrival. The engine grumbled to a halt and they began unlimbering their machines of destruction on the uppermost step.

'Hammerers, to me!' ordered Barundin, waving his axe towards the archway leading to the north passages. He turned to Tharonin. 'Care for a jaunt into the tunnels to have a look-see?'

Tharonin grinned and signalled to his bodyguards, the Gungrik Longbeards, who fell into step beside the king's hammerers. The two hundred warriors marched across the platforms and down the steps, winding between the gathering regiments. Above the dwarf army, now over a thousand strong, golden icons shone and embroidered pennants fluttered, and the murmuring of deep dwarf voices echoed around the hall.

Ahead, the tunnel was dark and forbidding. Tharonin explained that they had extinguished the lanterns to prevent the retreating warriors from being silhouetted against the light from the hall. Barundin nodded approvingly and they paused for a few moments while warriors were sent to light torches and lanterns to carry into the darkness. Suitably illuminated, they continued forward.

The tunnel was nearly twenty feet wide and just over ten feet high, allowing the dwarfs to advance ten abreast, Tharonin at the front of a five-wide line of longbeards, Barundin leading his hammerers. The sounds of fighting grew even as the noise from the hall behind them receded into the distance. Side tunnels, some no bigger than two dwarfs side by side, branched off from the main passage, and as they reached a fork, Tharonin signalled to the left. The shouts and clash of weapons echoed from the walls in odd ways, sometimes seemingly behind the group, other times quiet and from one side or the other.

It soon became obvious that they were on the right course though, as they started to find dwarf bodies littering the ground. Their jerkins and mail coats were ragged and bloody, but there were piles of dead skaven too. The human-like rats were scabrous things, their fur mangy and matted, their faces balding and scarred. Those that wore any clothing at all were dressed in little more than rags and loincloths, and their broken weapons were crude mauls, and the occassional sharpened hunk of metal, with wooden handles. Most seemed to have been killed as they ran away; vicious axe wounds cut across shoulders and spines, hammer blows marked into the backs of heads and shattered backbones.

'These are just slaves,' said Tharonin. 'Fodder for our weapons.'

Barundin did not reply immediately, but looked around. Skavenslaves were cowardly creatures, herded into battle by the goads and whips of their masters. He knew what little there was to know about the foe, having read several of the old journals of his predecessors and accounts from other holds. If the skaven had intended to break through into the upper reaches, slaves were a poor choice of vanguard, no matter how expendable they were.

Barundin stopped suddenly, the hammerer behind him cannoning into his back and causing him to stumble.

'Halt!' Barundin called out over the apologies of the bodyguard. The king turned to Tharonin with a scowl. 'They're drawing us out. The fools have followed them into the tunnels.'

Tharonin glanced over his shoulder with sudden concern, as if expecting a horde of ratmen to burst upon them from the rear. He tapped his hornblower on the shoulder.

'Sound the retreat,' he told the musician. 'Get them to fall back.'

The hornblower raised his instrument to his lips and blew three short blasts. He repeated the note three more times. After a few moments, it was answered by another call from ahead, repeating the order. Barundin gave a satisfied nod and ordered the small force to turn around and head back to the Fourth Deeping Hall.

AS THEY PASSED back into the hall, Barundin peeled away from his hammerers and waved them on, stopping to admire the sight. The Fourth Deeping Hall was packed with dwarf warriors from each clan and family, standing shoulder to shoulder, gathered about their standards, drummers and hornblowers arrayed along the line. Fierce dwarfs of the Grogstoks with their golden dragon icon above them stood beside Okrhunkhaz clansdwarfs, their green shields emblazoned with silver runes. On and on, from one end of the hall to the other they stretched.

Beyond them waited ranks of thunderers with their handguns and quarreller regiments loading their crossbows. Five deep they stood along three steps of the hall, their weapons directed down towards the north arches.

Beyond them the engineers now had five cannons, and beside them the bulky, menacing shape of the flame cannon. To each flank, five-barrelled organ guns were set close to the walls, their crews tinkering with firing locks, inspecting the piles of cannonballs and stacking parchment bags of black powder charges.

Arbrek had arrived and now stood in the centre of the front line, where the hammerers and other battle-hardened fighters of the clans were assembled. Barundin walked over to the runelord, and as he crossed the gap between the passage and the dwarf line he saw the staffs of several lesser runesmiths amongst the throng.

The aged Arbrek stood stiff-backed, his iron and gold runestaff held in both hands across his thighs, his piercing eyes peering at the approaching king from under the brim of a battered helm glowing with flickering golden runes.

'Good to see you,' said Barundin, stopping beside Arbrek and turning to face the north passages.

'A damned unwelcome sight you are,' growled Arbrek. 'In the name of Valaya, what an uncivilised time for a battle. Truly, these creatures are vile beyond reckoning.'

'It's more than their manners that leaves a lot to be desired,' said Barundin. 'But it is truly shocking that they have no respect for your sleep.'

'Are you mocking me?' said Arbrek with a curled lip. 'I have laboured many long years and I have earned the right to a full night's sleep. I used to miss bed for a whole week when I was casting the Rune of Potency upon this staff. Your forefathers would wag their beards to hear such flippancy, Barundin.'

'No offence was meant,' said Barundin, quickly contrite.

'I should think not,' muttered Arbrek.

Barundin waited in silence, and a quiet descended upon the hall, broken by the shuffling of feet, the clink of armour, the rasp of a whetstone and scatters of conversation. Barundin began to fidget with the leather binding of his axe haft as he waited, teasing at stray threads. From his left, a deep voice started to sing. It was Thane Ungrik, descended from the ancient rulers of Karak Varn, and soon the hall was filled with the ancient dwarf verse resounding from the mouths of his clan.

Beneath a lonely mountain hold
There lay a wealth worth more than gold
In a land with no joy nor mirth
Far from welcome of the hearth

In the dark beneath the world
A place never before beheld
The wealth of kings awaited there
Only found by those that dared

Deep we dug and far we dove
Digging gromril by the drove
No light of star, no light of sun
Hard we toiled, sparing none

But came upon us, green-skinned foes
Our joys were ended, came our woes
No axe nor hammer turned them back
Their blood stained lake and turned it black

King and thanes, a war we spoke
Upon our fists, their armies broke
But from the deep, a fear unspoken

Our fighting had now loudly woken
Up from darkness, our coming fall
A terror beneath us, killing all
With heavy hearts we left our dead
Our hope now broken, turned to dread

Driven from our halls and homes
Forced upon the hills to roam
Forever gone, a loss so dear
Left in the dark of fell Crag Mere

Even as the last verses echoed from the walls and ceiling, noises could be heard from the passage. There was a rush of feet and panicked shouting. Wracking coughs and wet screams could be heard, and an unsettled ripple of muttering spread across the dwarf throng.

A deep fog began to leak from the tunnel entrance, in thin wisps at first but growing in thickness. It was yellow and green, tinged with patches of rotten blackness; a low cloud that seeped across the floor, its edges dusted with flecks of glittering warpstone.

'Poison wind!' a voice cried out, and within moments the hall was filled with a cacophony of shouts, some of dismay, many of defiance.

Barundin could now see shapes in the sickly cloud, floundering shadows of dwarfs running and stumbling. Alone and in twos and threes they burst from the mist, hacking and coughing. Some fell, their bodies twitching, others clasped hands to their faces, howling with pain, falling to their knees and pounding their fists on the stone ground.

One beardling, his blond hair falling in clumps through his fingers as he clawed at his head, staggered forward and collapsed a few yards in front of Barundin. The king stepped forward and knelt, turning the lad over and resting his head against his knees. The king had to fight back the heaving of his stomach.

The dwarf's face was a wretched sight, blistered and red, his eyes bleeding. His lips and beard were stained with blood and vomit, and he flailed his arms blindly, clutching at Barundin's mailed shirt.

'Steady there,' said the king, and the beardling's floundering subsided.

'My king?' he croaked.

'Aye lad, it is,' said Barundin, dropping his shield to one side and laying a hand on the dwarf's head. Arbrek appeared next to them as other dwarfs rushed forward to help their fellows.

'We fought bravely,' the lad rasped. 'We heard the retreat, but did not want to run.'

'You did well, lad, you did well,' said Arbrek.

'They came upon us as our backs were turned,' the beardling said, his chest rising and falling unsteadily, every breath contorting his face with pain. 'We tried to fight, but we couldn't. I choked and ran…'

'You fought with honour,' said Barundin. 'Your ancestors will welcome you to their halls.'

'They will?' the lad said, his desperation replaced with hope. 'What are the Halls of the Ancestors like?'

'They are the finest place in the world,' said Arbrek, and as Barundin looked up at the runelord he saw that his gaze was distant, drawn to some place that nobody living had seen. 'The beer is the finest you will ever taste, better even than Bugman's. There is roast fowl on the tables, and the greatest hams you will ever see. And the gold! Every type of gold under the mountains can be found there. Golden cups and plates, and golden knives and spoons. The greatest of us dwell there, and you will hear their stories, of fell deeds and brave acts, of foul foes and courageous warriors. Every dwarf lives better than a king in the Halls of the Ancestors. You shall want for nothing, and you can rest with no more burden upon your shoulders.'

The beardling did not reply, and when Barundin looked down he saw that he was dead. He hefted the boy over his shoulder and picked up his shield. Carrying him back to the dwarf line, he handed the corpse over to one of his warriors.

'See that they are interred with the honoured dead,' said Barundin. 'All of them.'

As he turned back, Barundin saw that the poison wind was dispersing into the hall. It stung his eyes and caused his skin to itch and every breath felt heavy in his chest, but it was thinning now and not so potent as it had been in the confines of the mine tunnels.

Other figures appeared in the mist, hunched and swift. As they came into sight, Barundin saw that they were skaven, clad in robes of thick leather, their faces covered with heavy masks pierced with dark goggles. As they scuttled forward they threw glass orbs high into the air, which shattered upon the ground, releasing new clouds of poison wind. As the dwarfs pushed and pulled at each other get away from this attack, more skaven marched through the dank cloud. Some succumbed to the poison and fell twitching to the ground, but those that survived pressed on without regard for their dead. They wore heavy armour, made from scraps of metal and rigid hide, painted with markings like claw scratches, and tattered triangular red banners were carried at their fore.

There was a bellowed shout from behind Barundin as one of the thanes gave an order, and a moment later the chamber rang with the thunder of handguns. Metal bullets whirred over the king's head, plucking the skaven from their feet, smashing through their armour.

The rippling salvo continued from east to west, punctuated by the twang and swish of crossbow bolts from the quarrellers. A hundred dead skaven littered the floor around the passage entrance and still they pressed forwards. From behind them, a nightmarish host spread out into the hall, running swiftly.

The skaven swarm advanced, chittering and screeching, the rat warriors bounding forward with crude blades and clubs in their clawed hands. A cannon roar drowned out their noise for a moment and the iron ball, wreathed in magical blue flame, tore through them, smashing bodies asunder and hurling dismembered corpses into the air. As more cannonballs crashed into the press of bodies, the skaven advance slowed and some tried to turn back. Another solid fusillade of handgun fire tore a swathe through the swarming horde as some skaven attempted to retreat, others pushed forwards, and even more tried to advance out of the confines of the tunnel, clambering over the corpse-piles.

The crossfire of thunderers and quarrellers turned the mouth of the tunnel into a killing ground, forcing those skaven that managed to scuttle through the opening to dart to the left and right, circling around the devastation. Barundin watched warily as they began to gather in numbers again, clinging to the shadows in the northern corners of the Deeping Hall. From amongst them, weapon teams began to advance on the dwarf line, partially obscured from attack by the ranks of clanrat warriors around them.

Consisting of a gunner and a loader, the weapon teams sported a variety of arcane and obscene armaments. Hidden behind shield bearers, engineers fired long, wide-bored jezzails into the dwarf throng, their warpstone-laced bullets smashing through chainmail and steel plates with ease. The thundering fusillade smashed aside a rank of quarrellers on the third step, killing and wounding over a dozen dwarfs in one salvo.

Ahead of the jezzails, gun teams worked their way forward. One pair stopped just a couple dozen feet from Barundin. The gunner lowered a multi-barrelled gun towards the dwarf line and began to crank a handle on the side of the mechanism. A belt carried in a barrel on the back of the loader was dragged into the breach and a moment later the gun erupted with a torrent of flame and whizzing bullets, ripping into the hammerers. Small shells screamed and clattered around Barundin, and beside him Arbrek gave a grunt as a bullet buried itself in his left shoulder, knocking the runelord to one knee. Wisps of dark energy dribbled from the wound.

The skaven was turning the handle faster and faster with growing excitement, the rate of fire increasing as it did so. Green-tinged steam leaked from the heavy gun and oil spattered the creature's fur from the spinning gears, chains and belts.

With a detonation that flung green flames ten feet in every direction, the gun jammed and exploded, hurling chunks of scorched, furred flesh into the air and scything through the skaven with shrapnel and pieces of exploding ammunition. As they moved away from the explosion, the skaven strayed into range of the flame cannon on the east flank of the hall.

Helping Arbrek to his feet, Barundin watched as the engineers pumped bellows, wound gears, adjusted the elevations of the war machine and twirled with valves and nozzles to balance the pressure building inside the fire-thrower. At a signal from the master engineer standing on the footplate of the war machine, one of the apprentices threw down a lever and unleashed the might of the flame cannon.

A gout of burning oil and naphtha arced high over the heads of the dwarfs in front, dripping fiery rain onto them. Splashing like waves against a cliff, the flaming concoction burst over the nearest skaven, setting fur alight, searing flesh and seeping through armour. Doused in burning oil, the creatures wailed and flailed, rolling on the ground and setting their kin alight with their wild thrashing. Their panicked screams echoed around the hall, along with the cheers of the dwarfs.

Terrified by this attack, a swathe of skaven broke and fled, fearing another burst of deadly flame. Bullets and crossbow bolts followed them, punching into their backs, ripping at fur and flesh as they ran for the tunnel, accompanied by the jeers of the army of Zhufbar.

Despite this triumph, the fighting had become hand-to-hand in many places, the steel-clad dwarfs holding the line against a tide of viciously fanged and clawed furry beasts. With pockets of bitter combat breaking out across the hall, the war machines and guns of the skaven were finding fewer and fewer targets to attack, and the sound of black powder igniting and the thwip of crossbow quarrels was replaced with the ringing of rusted iron on gromril and steel biting into flesh.

Barundin bellowed for the line to push forward in the hope of forcing the skaven back into the tunnels where their numbers would be no advantage. Inch by inch, step by step, the dwarfs advanced, their axes and hammers rising and falling against the brown deluge rushing upon them.

Barundin turned and cast a glance at the wound in Arbrek's shoulder. Already the vile poison of the warpstone was hissing and melting the flesh and gromril mail around the puckered hole in his flesh.

'You need to get that cleaned up and taken out,' the king said.

'Later,' replied Arbrek, his teeth gritted. He pointed towards the tunnel. 'I think I shall be needed here for the moment.'

Barundin looked out across the hall, over the heads of the dwarfs in front battling against the skaven horde. In the gloom of the passage entrance he could see a glow: the unearthly aura of warpstone. In that flickering, dismal light he saw several skaven hunched beneath large backpacks. Their faces were coiled with thick wires, their arms pierced with nails and bolts.

'Warlocks,' the king murmured.

As the skaven spellcasters advanced, they gripped long spear-like weapons, connected to the whirling globes and hissing valves of their backpacks with thick, sparking wires. Motes of energy played around the

jaggedly pronged tips of the warp-conductors, gathering in tiny lightning storms of magical energy.

Their grimacing, twisted faces were thrown into stark contrast as they
unleashed the energies of their warp-packs; bolts of green and black
energy splayed across dwarfs and skaven alike, charring flesh, exploding
off armour and burning hair. Arcs of warp lightning leaped from figure
to figure, their smouldering corpses contorting with conducted energy,
glowing faintly from within, smoke billowing from blackened holes in
skin and ruined eye sockets.

Here and there, the magical assault was countered by the runesmiths
harmlessly grounding the arcs of devastating warp energy with their
runestaffs. Beside Barundin, Arbrek was muttering under his breath and
stroking a hand along his staff, the runes along its length flaring into life
at the caress of his gnarled hands.

Behind the advancing warlocks, another figure appeared, swathed in
robes, its hood thrown back to reveal light grey fur and piercing red eyes.
Twisted horns curled around its ears as it turned its head from side to side,
surveying the carnage being wrought by both sides. A nimbus of dark energy
surrounded the Grey Seer as it drew in magical power from the surrounding
air and rocks.

It raised its crooked staff above its head, the bones and skulls hanging from its tip swaying and clattering. A shadow grew in the tunnel
behind the skaven wizard and Barundin strained his eyes to see what
was within. Brief lulls in the fighting brought a distant noise, a far-off
scratching and chittering that grew in volume, echoing along the north
passage.

In a cloud of teeth, claws and beady eyes, hundreds upon hundreds
of rats burst into the Deeping Hall, pouring around the Grey Seer. In a
packed mass of verminous filth, the rats spewed forth from the passageway, scuttling across the ground and spilling over the skaven. Onwards
came the swarm until it reached the dwarf line. Barundin's warriors
struck out with hammers and axes, but against the tide of creatures,
there was little they could do.

Dwarfs flailed with dozens of rats scrabbling into their armour, biting and scratching, clawing at their faces, tangling in their beards, their
claws and fangs lacerating and piercing tough dwarf skin. Though each
bite was little more than a pinprick, more and more dwarfs began to fall
to the sheer number of the rodents, their bites laced with vile poison.

Barundin took a step forward to join the fray but was stopped by
Arbrek's hand on his shoulder. 'This is sorcery,' said the runelord, his
face set. 'I shall deal with it.'

Chanting in khazalid, the runelord held his staff in front of him, its
runes growing brighter and brighter. With a final roar, he thrust the tip
of the staff towards the immense rat pack spilling up the steps, and
white light flared out. As the magical glow spread and touched the rats,

they burst into flames, ignited by the mystical energy unleashed from the runes. In a wave spreading out from Arbrek, the white fire blazed through the tide of vermin, driving them back, destroying those touched by its ghostly flames.

The counter-spell dissipated as the Grey Seer extended his own magical powers, but it was too late. The few dozen rats that remained were scurrying back into the darkness of the passageway. With a hiss and a wave of its staff, the Grey Seer urged its warriors on, and the skaven threw themselves once more against the dwarf line.

'Come on, time to fight!' Barundin called to his hammerers.

They marched forward as a solid block, driving into the skaven horde. Barundin led the charge, his axe chopping into furred flesh, the blades and mauls of the skaven bouncing harmlessly from his armour and shield. Around him, the hammerers gripped their mattocks tightly, crushing bones and flinging aside their foes with wide sweeping attacks. The king and his veterans pushed on through the melee, driving towards the Grey Seer.

More skaven were still emerging from the passageway in a seemingly unending stream. Barundin found himself facing a rag-tag band swathed in tattered, dirty robes, bearing wickedly spiked flails and serrated daggers. Their fur was balding in places, their skin pocked with buboes and lesions. The ratmen frothed at the mouth, their eyes rheumy yet manic, their ears twitching with frenzied energy, they launched themselves headlong at the dwarfs.

There were those amongst their number whirling large barbed censers around their heads, thick dribbles of warp-gas seeping from their weapons. As the choking cloud enveloped Barundin, he felt the poisonous vapours stinging his eyes and burning his throat. Coughing and blinking through tear-filled eyes, he saw the rat-things leaping towards him and raised his shield barely in time to ward off a vicious blow from a flail.

Knocked sideways by the force of the jolt, Barundin only had time to steady his footing before another swipe rang against the side of his helm, stunning him for a moment. Ignoring the rushing of blood in his ears and the cloying smoke, the king struck out blindly with his axe, hewing left and right. He felt the blade bite on more than one occasion and gave a roar of satisfaction.

'Drive the filth back to their dirty holes!' he urged his fellow dwarfs, and he could feel his hammerers pressing forward around him.

His eyes clearing slightly, Barundin continued his advance, surrounded by the swirl and cacophony of battle. He struck the head from a skaven that had launched itself at him with two daggers in its hands, its tongue lolling from its fanged mouth. Goblinbeater proved equally good at killing skaven as again and again, Barundin buried the axe's head into chests, lopped off limbs and caved in skulls.

As he wrenched the runeaxe from the twitching corpse of yet another dirt-encrusted invader, Barundin felt a pause in the advance around him and caught a murmur of dismay spreading through the warriors close by. Battering aside another foe with the flat of his axe blade, the king caught a glimpse of the passageway ahead.

From the gloom loomed four massive shapes, each at least thrice the height of a dwarf. Their bodies were distended and bulged with unnatural muscle, in places bracketed with strips of rusted iron and pierced with metal bolts. Tails tipped with blades lashed back and forth as the creatures were driven on by the barbed whips of their handlers.

One of the rat ogres, as they had been named in the old journals, charged straight at Barundin. The skin and flesh of its face hung off in places, revealing the bone beneath, and its left hand had been sawn away and replaced with a heavy blade nailed into the stump. In its other hand the creature held a length of chain attached to a manacle around its wrist, scything left and right with the heavy links and scattering dwarfs all around.

Barundin raised his shield and broke into a run, countering the beast's impetus with his own charge. The chain glanced off the king's shield in a shower of sparks, and he ducked beneath a vicious swipe of the rat ogre's blade. With a grunt, Barundin brought Goblinbeater up, the blade biting into the inner thigh of the creature's leg.

It gave a howl and lashed out, its swipe crashing into Barundin's shield with the force of a forge hammer, hurling him backwards and forcing him to lose his grip on Goblinbeater. Pulling himself to his feet, Barundin ducked behind his shield once more as the chain whirled around the head of the rat ogre and crashed down, splintering the stone floor.

His short legs driving him forward, Barundin launched himself at the rat ogre and smashed the rim of his shield into its midriff, wincing as the impact jarred his shoulder. With the brief moments this desperate act bought him, Barundin snatched at the handle of Goblinbeater and ripped it free, dark blood spouting from the wound in the mutated monstrosity's leg.

With a backwards slash, Barundin brought the blade of the runeaxe down and through the knee of the rat ogre, slicing through flesh and shattering bone. With a mournful yelp the rat ogre collapsed to the floor, lashing out with its blade-hand and scoring a groove across the chest plate of Barundin's armour. Using his shield to bat aside the return blow, the king stepped forward and hewed into the creature's chest with Goblinbeater, the blade slicing through wooden splints and pallid, fur-patched flesh.

Again and again, Barundin pulled the axe free and swung it home, until the rat ogre's thrashing subsided. Panting with the effort, Barundin glanced up to see the other beasts fighting against the embattled hammerers. More skaven were pouring from the tunnel and the dwarf line was buckling under the weight of the attack, being driven back simply by the numbers of the horde.

The crackle of gunfire and the boom of the occasional cannon shot echoed around the Fourth Deeping Hall. Flares of warp lightning and the glow of runes highlighted bearded faces shouting battle oaths and ratmen features twisted in snarls. A horn blast joined the tumult and a silvery knot of dwarf warriors pushed through the tumult, their weapons cutting a swathe through the skaven mass.

Tharonin's ironbreakers surged forward to the king, their rune-carved gromril armour glowing in the light of lanterns and magical energies. Virtually impervious to the attacks of their foes, the veteran tunnel-fighters tore into the skaven army like a pickaxe through stone, smashing aside their enemies and marching over their hewn corpses.

Heartened by this counter attack, the dwarfs, Barundin amongst them, surged forward once more, ignoring their casualties, shrugging off their wounds to drive the skaven back into the tunnel. As he fought, Barundin saw that the Grey Seer was no longer in view, and could sense that victory was close. In growing numbers, the skaven began to break from the bloody combat, their nerve shattered. In their dozens and then their hundreds they bolted and fled, hacking at each other in their attempts to escape and reach the passageway.

GRUDGE FOUR

The Beer Grudge

UNLIKE THE NEAT, geometric construction and straight lines of the dwarf mines, the skaven tunnels were little more than animal holes dug through dirt and laboriously clawed through hard rock. Linking together natural caves, underground rivers and dark fissures, they extended down into the depths of the mountain in every direction.

The subterranean warren had no planning, no sense or reason behind its layout. Some tunnels would simply end, others double-backed frequently as they sought easier routes through the rock of the Worlds Edge Mountains. Some were broad and straight, others so small that even a dwarf was forced down to his hands and knees to navigate them.

The walls were slicked with the passing of the creatures, their oily, furry bodies wearing the rock smooth in places over many years. The stench of their musk was like a cloud that constantly hung over the hunting parties of Zhufbar as they tried to track down the skaven and map their lair. The task was all but impossible, made more difficult by the fear of ambush and the sporadic fighting that still broke out.

Most of the expeditions were led by detachments of ironbreakers, whose skill and armour were invaluable in such close confines. As they descended into the dank maze of burrows, they took with them signalling lanterns, and left small sentry groups at junctions and corners. By keeping track of the beacon lights in this way, the various parties could communicate with each other, albeit over relatively short distances. The tunnels themselves made navigating by noise all but impossible, with odd echoes and breaks in the walls through unseen crevasses making any sound seem closer or further away than it was, or coming from a different direction.

The lantern-lines at least allowed the dwarfs to signal for help, to send warnings and sometimes simply to find their way back to the outer workings of the north Zhufbar mines.

Barundin was accompanying one of the delving bands, as they had come to be called, searching through the rat-infested caverns north-east of Zhufbar, several miles from the hold. There had been quite a lot of fighting in the area over the previous days, and the opinion of several of the team leaders was that they had broken a considerable concentration of the skaven in the region.

It was cold, depressing work: clambering over piles of scree, scraping through narrow bolt-holes, kicking the vermin from underfoot. These were the evil places of the mountainscape, crawling with beetles and maggots, writhing with rat swarms, and made all the more awful by the stench of the skaven and pockets of choking gas.

As far as Barundin could judge this far underground, it was the middle of the afternoon. They had laboured through the tunnels since an early breakfast that morning, and his back was almost bent from frequent stooping and crawling. They tried to move as quietly as possible so as not to alert any ratmen that might be nearby, but it was a vain effort. Dwarf mail chinked against every stone, their hobnailed boots and steel-shod toecaps clumping on rock and crunching through dirt and gravel.

'We're getting close to something,' whispered Grundin Stoutlegs, the leader of the group.

Grundin pointed to the ground and Barundin saw bones in the dirt and spoil of digging – bones picked clean of flesh. There were scraps of cloth and tufts of fur, as well as skaven droppings littering the floor. Grundin waved the group to a stop and they settled. Silence descended.

A strange mewling sound could be heard from ahead, distorted by the winding, uneven walls of the tunnel. There were other noises: scratching, chittering and a wet sucking sound. Now that they were still, Barundin could feel the ground throbbing gently through the thick soles of his boots, and he pulled off a gauntlet and touched his hand to the slimy wall, ignoring the wetness on his finger tips. He could definitely feel a pulsing vibration, and as they adjusted, his ears picked up a humming noise from ahead. Wiping the filth from his hand as best he could, he pulled his gauntlet back on with a grimace.

Grundin slipped his shield from his back and pulled his axe from his belt, and the other ironbreakers followed his example and readied themselves. Barundin was carrying a single-handed hammer, stocky and heavy, ideal for tunnel-work, and he pulled his shield onto his left arm and nodded his readiness to Grundin.

They set off even more cautiously than before. Barundin could feel the bones and filth slipping and shifting underfoot, and he cursed silently to himself every time there was a scrape or clatter. Ahead, in a growing glow from some distant light, he could see the tunnel branching off through several low openings.

Reaching the junction, it was clear that the tunnels all led by different paths to some larger chamber ahead; the flickering light that could be seen in each of them was the same quality. Grundin split the group into three smaller bands, each about a dozen strong, sending one to the left, one to the right, and taking the centre group himself. Barundin found himself directed to the right by a nod from Grundin. The king took the order without a word. In the halls of Zhufbar he was beyond command, but in these grim environs he would not dare to question the grizzled tunnel fighter.

One of the ironbreakers, recognisable as Lokrin Rammelsson only by the dragon-head crest moulded from the brow of his full face helm, gave Barundin a thumbs up and waved the king into the tunnel, following behind with several more of the ironbreakers. Rats shrieked and fled down the passageway as the dwarfs advanced, following the tunnel as first it wound to the right and then banked back of itself, dropping down to the left. It widened rapidly and Barundin saw the group ahead gathering at the edge of whatever lay beyond. He pushed his way between two of them to see what had halted their advance, and then stopped.

THEY STOOD ON on the edge of a wide, oval-shaped cave, which sloped down away from them and arched high overhead. It was at least fifty feet high, the walls dotted with crude torches, bathing the scene in a fiery red glow. Other openings all around the chamber led off in every direction, some of them almost impossibly high up the walls, which could have only been reached by the most nimble of creatures were it not for the rickety gantries and scaffolds that ran haphazardly around the chamber, connected by bridges, ladders and swaying walkways. Here and there Barundin recognised scavenged pieces of dwarf-hewn timber or metalwork, bastardised into new purpose by the skaven.

The floor of the chamber was a writhing mass of life, filled with small bodies in constant motion, some pink and bald, others with patches of fur growing on them. Like a living carpet, the skavenspawn spread from one end of the cavern to the other, crawling over each other, fighting and gnawing, biting and clawing in heaving piles. Mewing and crying, they blindly slithered and scuttled to and fro, littering the floor with droppings and the corpses of the weakest runts.

Amongst them hurried naked slaves, their fur marked with burns from branding irons and the scores of whips. They pushed their way through the morass of wriggling flesh, picking out the largest offspring and taking them away. Several dozen guards dressed in crude armour stood watch with rusted blades, while pack masters cracked their whips on slaves and skavenspawn alike, chittering orders in their harsh language.

At the centre of the nightmarish heap were three pale, bloated shapes, many times larger than any of the other skaven. They lay on their sides, their tiny heads barely visible amongst the fleshy mass of their offspring and the arcane machineries they were connected to. The skavenspawn were all the more vicious here, biting and tearing in a frenzy to get at the food, the older ones feeding upon the dead runt corpses instead of the greenish-grey spew coursing from the distended, pulsating udders of the skaven females.

Barundin felt the contents of his stomach lurch and swallowed heavily to avoid vomiting. The stench was unbelievable: a mix of acrid urine, rotting flesh and sour milk. One of the ironbreakers lifted his gold-chased mask, revealing the scarred face of Fengrim Dourscowl, one of Barundin's distant nephews.

'We've not found one of these for quite a while,' Fengrim said to Barundin.

'There must be hundreds of them,' said Barundin after a moment, still staring in disbelief. He had heard stories of these brood chambers, but nothing could have prepared him for this awful vision of sprawling, noxious life.

'Thousands,' spat Fengrim. 'We have to kill them all and seal the chamber.'

A sound from behind caused them to turn quickly, weapons raised, but it was another ironbreaker.

'Grundin has sent a signal to bring up the miners and engineers,' the ironbreaker told them, his voice metallic from inside his helm. 'We have to secure the chamber for their arrival.'

Looking back out into the brood-chamber, Barundin saw two knots of dwarfs advancing from other entrances, crushing the skavenspawn underfoot. Slaves were shrieking in panic and fleeing while the guards, alerted to the attack, were gathering quickly under one of the soaring gantries.

'Come on then, let's be about it!' said Barundin, hefting his hammer and marching out of the tunnel mouth.

His footing was unsure as he waded through the carpet of skaven offspring, his heavy boots snapping bones and squashing flesh. He could not feel anything through the heavy armour he was wearing, but as he looked down at his feet he saw the skavenspawn squirming and clawing, scraping ineffectually at the gromril plates or pulling themselves sluggishly away. With a snarl, he brought his foot down onto the back of one particularly loathsome specimen, its beady eyes flecked with bloodspots, snapping its spine.

Advanced upon from three directions, and realising they were outnumbered, the guards quickly fled without a fight, stampeding over the bodies of their own children in an effort to escape the advancing, vengeful dwarfs.

Barundin kicked and battered his way through the filth, sometimes thigh-deep in writhing skavenspawn, caving in heads with the edge of his shield, smashing small bodies against the rock with his hammer. Eventually he stood a short way from one of the broodmothers. Its eyes were almost lifeless with no flicker of intelligence or recognition and its artificially fattened bulk several times his height. Its entire body was riddled with blue veins and coarse with spots and blisters. The feeding spawn did not even react to his presence, so intent was it on its unwholesome nourishment.

'This is axe work, my king,' said Fengrim, who had followed Barundin to the nearest female.

Raising his axe, Fengrim brought the blade up and over his head and then into a downward stroke, as one might chop wood. The razor-sharp blade sliced through bloated flesh, peeling away the skin and revealing a thick layer of fat beneath. Another stroke opened the wound to the flesh and bone, spilling dark blood and globules of fatty tissue onto the crawling carpet of skavenspawn.

A wave of stench hit Barundin and he turned away, gagging heavily. Although he could no longer see it, he still felt sickened by the wet chopping noise of Fengrim's bloody work. A spouting wave of fluids splashed over the king's legs; deep red and pale green life fluids stained the once-polished gromril of his greaves.

Barundin raised his hammer and began sweeping it through the morass of squirming creatures around him, the slaughter of the vile skavenkin distracting him from the noisome sounds and smells of the broodmother's grisly execution.

THE SKAVEN ATTACKED the brood chamber twice over the next day, but the dwarfs had moved up in strength and the ratmen were easily pushed back. Barundin agreed with Grundin that it seemed the skaven's strength in the area had been thoroughly broken. With their breeding grounds taken, they would not be a threat from this quarter for many years.

Engineers with casks of oil and kegs of black powder were brought in, and aided by dwarf miners prepared for the demolition of the many tunnels leading from the brood chamber. Already a pyre of burning skaven bodies was piled in the centre of the cavern, the oily smoke from the flaming carcasses filling the air with a choking fume.

Miners dug holes into the sides of the access tunnels for charges to be placed, while the engineers measured and drew up plans, arguing about where to place the explosives, where to dig out the tunnels and burn away supports to bring the roofs down. As teams of dwarfs dismantled the ramshackle walkways and towers of the skaven, reclaiming what had been taken from them, Barundin toiled alongside them, cutting through planks and ropes, smashing apart timbers and poles to fuel the demolition work.

Amongst the debris, Barundin found a stone ancestor face, looted from one of the miners' halls. It was Grungni, ancestor god of mining, his beard chipped and mould-covered, his horned helm cut with crude skaven marks. Wiping away the filth with his fingers, Barundin realised that it had been seventeen long years since the battle of the Fourth Deeping Hall.

Since their first victory, the dwarfs had been hard-pressed for many years, losing many of the mine-workings to the innumerable skaven assaults. Time and again they had been driven back, sometimes within sight of the central hold itself. Always Barundin's resolution had held firm, and he would not give an inch of ground to the invaders without a fight. It would have been easy to abandon the northern passages and mines, to seal the gates and bar them with steel and runes, but Barundin, like all his kind, was stubborn and loathe to retreat.

Losing the war of attrition, outnumbered by many thousands of rat-men, Barundin and his council had devised a plan. New workings had been dug to the east, where the skaven seemed fewer, perhaps wary of the goblins of Mount Gunbad that lay in that direction. Using these new tunnels, Barundin and his warriors had sallied forth several times, trapping the skaven between them and armies issuing from Zhufbar itself.

Month by month, year by year, the skaven had been pushed back once more, into the Second Deep, then the Third and the Fourth. Six years ago, the Fourth Deeping Hall had been reclaimed and Barundin had allowed a month's respite to celebrate the victory and for his host to rest and regain its strength. Young beardlings were now hardened warriors, and hundreds of new tombs had been dug in the clan chambers across the hold to house the dead the bitter fighting had claimed.

Three years ago they had been able to first venture into the skaven tunnels, bringing death and fire to cleanse the verminous creatures from the mountain depths around Zhufbar. For the last year, the fighting had been sporadic and little more than skirmishes. Barundin was in no doubt that the skaven would gather their numbers again and return, but not for many years. Just as it had been over a century since the last skaven assault of Zhufbar, the king hoped that it would be decades before they came again.

For three more days the dwarfs toiled, preparing for the destruction of the brood chamber. When it was done, slow fuses hanging from supports in the walls, fires flickering in cracks and holes dug into the tunnels walls, the engineers ordered the other dwarfs to return to Zhufbar. Barundin was allowed to watch, and was even given the privilege of lighting one of the touch-fuses.

The dwarf mines shook with the detonations which rumbled on for many hours as caves and tunnels collapsed. There was no cheering, no celebration from the dwarfs. Seventeen years of desperate war had left them ruing the evils of the world and feeling sombre for the fallen.

It was the first time Barundin truly understood himself and his people; the long march of centuries eroded their lives and culture. There could be little joy in the victory, not only for its cost, but for the fact that it was nothing more than a respite, a pause of breath in the unending saga of bloodshed that had become the lot of the dwarfs for four thousand years.

The golden age of the ancestor-kings had passed, the silver-age of the mountain realm had been swallowed by the earthquakes and the green-skins. Now Barundin and his people clung to their existence, their hold half-filled and full of empty halls, the ghostly silence of their ancestors' shades wandering the corridors and galleries, mourning for the glories of the past.

But though he understood better the plight of his race, Barundin was not without hope. While those older and greyer than he were content to grumble into their beer and sigh at the merest mention of the old times, Barundin knew that there was still much that could be done.

First and foremost, he resolved as he lay that night in his chambers, he would lead Zhufbar to the conquest of Dukankor Grobkaz-a-Gazan, destroying the grobi as they had vanquished the skaven. It would take a while to rebuild, but within twenty years, perhaps thirty, the halls of Grungankor Stokril would again be filled with good, honest dwarf lights, and the gruff laughter of his people.

IT WAS WITH some surprise that Barundin received a message from the Engineers Guild the next day. He had not yet sent word to them to continue on their war production so that the army might be rebuilt for the invasion of Dukankor Grobkaz-a-Gazan. He was, the message told him, politely invited to attend a meeting of the Engineers Guild High Council that night. It was worded as a request, as befitted the king, but not even the king refused the Engineers Guild in Zhufbar. He ruled, if not by their consent, then at least by their acceptance. Larger than any of the clans, and essential to the running of the hold, the Engineers Guild wielded its power lightly, but it wielded it nonetheless.

Barundin spent the day overseeing the withdrawal of warriors from the north passages, and spent much time with Tharonin, discussing the reopening of the mine workings so that ore and coal could be sent to the smelters again, which had run low on many supplies during periods of fighting with the skaven.

So it was armed with this good news, and a light heart, that Barundin dressed that evening. A guild meeting was a formal occasion, part committee meeting, part celebration dedicated to Grungni and the other ancestor gods. Barundin decided to leave his armour upon its stand. This was perhaps only the third or fourth time he had not worn it in seventeen years. It would be a good sign to his people, their king walking through Zhufbar unarmed, safe in his own hold.

He dressed in dark blue leggings and a padded jerkin of purple, tied with a wide belt. To say that the years of war had made him lean would have not been entirely true, for all dwarfs have considerable girth even when starved, but his belt was certainly a few notches tighter than it had been when he had taken to the throne of Zhufbar. His beard was longer and now hung to his belt, a source of private pride for the king. He knew that he was young for his position, too young in the eyes of some of his advisors, he suspected, but soon he would be able to use belt-clasps to secure his beard, a sure sign of growing age and wisdom. By the time the grobi of Dukankor Grobkaz-a-Gazan had been sent running back to their holes in Mount Gunbad, he would have the respect of them all.

Warriors from the guild, bearing shields with the anvil motif of the Master Engineers, came for Barundin in the early evening, to provide escort. He knew the way, of course, but the formality of the invitation had to be respected, and due ceremony observed.

They led him down to the forges powered by Zhufbar's waterwheels, which had continued their slow turns all through the fighting, never once stopping, the lights of the furnaces never dimming. It was a credit to the engineers that they had done so much with so little for those seventeen years, and Barundin decided to make a point of complimenting them to this effect. He was about to ask them for just as much effort for another potentially long war, and a little flattery would never harm his cause.

Having passed through the foundries, they came to the workshops, hall upon hall of benches and machinery, from the finest clockwork mechanism to the mighty casting cranes of the cannon-makers. Even at this hour, it was alive with activity – the clinking of hammers, the buzz of heated conversations, the whirr and grind of whetstones and lathes.

At the far end of the workshops was a small stone door, no taller than a dwarf and wide enough for two to enter abreast. The lintel stone above it was heavy and carved with shallow runes in the secret language of the engineers. A brass boar's-head knocker was set into the stone of the door; below it was a metal plate worn thin with centuries of use. One of Barundin's guides took the knocker in his hand and rapped it onto the plate in a succession of rapid knocks. Answering taps resounded from the other side, to which the engineer replied with more raps of his own.

A few moments passed and then, with a grinding sound from within the walls, the door slid to one side, dark and forbidding. The dwarf guards gestured for Barundin to enter and he did so with a nod, stepping through into the smoky gloom beyond. Another guard on the far side of the door nodded in welcome as the portal closed, rolling back into place on hidden gears.

He was in the antechamber to the guildhall and could hear raised voices from the closed double doors ahead of him. A few small candles did little to light the darkness, but his eyes soon adjusted and he could make out the wheel-gears of the door locks mounted into the walls around him. Like all the work of the engineers, it was not only functional but a piece of artistic beauty. The gears were chased with golden knotwork and a thick bolt decorated with an ancestor head pinioned each cog. The chains glistened in the candlelight with oil and polish.

'They're ready for you,' said the dwarf, walking across the room and laying his hands upon the door handles, giving Barundin a moment to collect himself. The king straightened his jerkin, smoothed the plaits of his beard across his chest and belly and gave the guard a thumbs up.

Thrusting open the doors, the guard strode into the room. 'Barundin, Son of Throndin, King of Zhufbar!' bellowed the guard-turned-herald.

Barundin walked past him into the great Guild Hall and stopped while the doors were closed behind him. The engineers were not so proud that they would try to outshine their king, and so their guild hall was smaller than Barundin's own audience chamber, though not by much. No pillars supported the rock above their heads. Instead the ceiling was vaulted with thick girders crossing each other in intricate patterns, their foundations set within the walls of the hall itself. Gold-headed rivets sparkled in the glow of hundreds of lanterns, though the size of the hall meant that the furthest reaches were still swathed in shadow.

In an island of light in the centre of the vast hall, around a fire pit blazing with flames, was the guild table. It was circular, and large enough for two dozen dwarfs to sit in comfort, although only half that number were now there; they were the twelve thanes of the guild clans, twelve of the most powerful dwarfs in Zhufbar. Each held office as the high engineer for five years, although this was regarded as a position of first amongst equals, a spokesman, not a ruler, hence the circular meeting table.

The current incumbent was Darbran Rikbolg, whose clan in times past had been granted the title kingmakers for their efforts in supporting Barundin's ancestors' accession to the throne of Zhufbar. Before him was a large sceptre of steel, its head shaped like a spanner, holding a bolt carved from a sapphire as big as two clasped fists. The guildmasters, as the thanes were known, were dressed in identical robes of deep blue, trimmed with chainmail and fur. Their beards were splendidly trimmed and knotted, clasped with steel designs and imbedded with sapphires.

'Welcome, Barundin, welcome,' said Darbran, standing up. His smile seemed genuine enough.

Barundin crossed the hall, the guildmasters' eyes upon him, and shook hands with the high engineer. Darbran gestured to a seat at his right that stood empty, and Barundin sat down, exchanging nods with the guildmasters. The remains of a meal lay scattered about the table, as did several half-full flagons of ale.

Catching the king's gaze, Darbran grinned. 'Please, help yourself. There's plenty to go around, right?' he said, grabbing a spare cup and emptying a flagon into it, handing the frothing ale to the king.

'Aye, plenty of ale for all,' echoed Borin Brassbreeks, thane of the Gundersson clan. 'The guild would not have it said we offer a poor welcome to the king, would we?'

There was much naying and shaking of heads, and Barundin realised that the aging dwarfs were already well into their cups. He wasn't sure whether this was a bad thing; as when dwarfs get more drunk they are more susceptible to flattery and bribery, but their stubborn streak widens considerably and their ears tend to close. All in all, the king considered, what he was going to propose was more likely to fall better on drunk ears than sober ones.

'It's no secret the war with the skaven is all but over,' said Darbran, sitting down heavily. He raised his tankard, spilling beer onto the stone floor. 'Well done, Barundin, well done!'

There was a chorus of hurrahs and a few of the thanes slapped the table with calloused hands in appreciation.

'Thank you, thank you very much,' said Barundin. He was about to continue but he was interrupted.

'We showed 'em, didn't we?' laughed Borin.

'Yes, we showed them,' said Barundin, taking a gulp of ale. It was a little too bitter for his liking, but not altogether unpleasant.

'Now that we've got all of this nasty business out of the way, things can get back to normal around here,' said another of the thanes, Garrek Silverweaver. He wore a pair of thick spectacles that had slipped down to the end of his pointed nose, making it look as if he had four eyes.

'Aye, back to normal,' said one of the other thanes.

Barundin gulped another mouthful of ale and smiled weakly. Darbran noticed his expression and scowled.

'The war is won, isn't it?' asked the engineer.

'Oh yes, well as much as it will ever be against that loathsome filth,' said Barundin. 'They'll not trouble us again for many a year.'

'Then why wear a face that would spike a wheel?' asked Darbran. 'You look troubled, my friend.'

'The war with the skaven is over, that is true,' said Barundin slowly. He had been rehearsing this for the whole day between his talks with Tharonin, but now the words jarred in his throat. 'There is, however, the issue of the goblins still to be resolved.'

'The goblins?' said Borin. 'What goblins?'

'You know, Dukankor Grobkaz-a-Gazan,' said the engineer sitting next to Borin, ramming an elbow into his ribs as if this would act as a reminder. 'Barundin's father's dying grudge!'

Barundin was pleased that they had remembered, but his hopes were dashed by Borin's reply.

'Yes, but we decided we can't be having any of that, didn't we?' the old dwarf said. 'That's what we were just saying, wasn't it?'

Barundin turned his inquisitive glare to Darbran, who, to his credit, looked genuinely guilty and nonplussed. 'We knew you would want to discuss this, and so made it one of our items of business for today's meeting,' explained Darbran. 'We can't support another war, not now.'

'No, not now, not ever,' growled Borin, who had only recently handed over the role of high engineer and was quite clearly not out of the habit. 'For Grungni's sake, there's barely an ounce of iron or steel left. We can't forge from the bones of dead ratmen, can we? It's out of the question!'

'The mines are reopened even as we speak,' said Barundin, leaning forward and looking at the assembled guildmasters. 'I have spoken to Tharonin and he assures me there will be ore aplenty within a few weeks. We'll not let your furnaces grow cold.'

'We know about your talks with Tharonin,' said Darbran. 'He might have promised his own mines, but there's no guarantee the other clans will be back to work straight away. They've been fighting those bloody skaven for seventeen years, lad. That's a fair time in anybody's book. You don't run from one war into another.'

Barundin turned to the others, mouth open, but it was Gundaban Redbeard, youngest of the guildmasters at just over three hundred years old, who spoke first.

'We know you have to fulfil your father's dying grudge before you can go after that toad Vessal,' said Redbeard. 'But wait awhile. Let everyone catch their breath, so to speak. The clans are tired. We're tired.'

'Vessal's a manling, he'll not live forever,' snapped Barundin, earning him scowls from the eldest members of the guild council. 'Next year or a hundred years, the war with the grobi is going to be hard and long. Sooner started, sooner finished, isn't that right? If we stop now, it will take us years to get going again.'

His plea was met by blank expressions. They were not going to cooperate. Barundin took a deep breath and another swig of beer. He had hoped it wouldn't come to this, but he had one last bargaining chip.

'You're right, you're right,' said Barundin, sitting back in his chair. He waited a moment, then raised his tankard and said, almost conversationally, 'How's work on the brewery?'

There was much angry muttering and shaking of beards.

'We're far behind schedule,' admitted Darbran with a grimace. 'Behind schedule! Can you imagine? I tell you, some proper ale would soon give the clans some backbone again.'

'Curse that Wanazaki,' grumbled Borin. 'Him and his new-fangled ideas.'

'Look, Borin, we agreed,' said Redbeard. 'He was stupid not to have tested his automatic kegger, but the principles were sound. He just got his pressures mixed up.'

'Yes, but he burned all of his notes, didn't he?' said Barundin, and the engineers turned as one and glared at him.

'The coward,' said Borin. 'Running away like that. Showed a lot of promise that lad, but then to go and flit off like some manling...'

'I can get him back,' said Barundin. His statement was met with blank stares. 'I'll organise an expedition, to go and find him and bring him back.'

'What makes you think we want that oath-breaker back?' snarled Darbran.

'Well, to bring him to book, at the very least,' said Barundin. 'Surely he has to make account for himself. Besides which, if you can get him back, there's a chance he'll repent and try to make good.'

'If we wanted him, what makes you think we couldn't go and get him ourselves?' asked Redbeard.

'We all know he would make another run as soon as he saw a flag or sigil of the guild,' said Barundin. 'He's in terror of what punishment might be meted out on him.'

'And why do you think he'll stay around for you?' asked Darbran.

'I've already met him once,' said Barundin. 'When my father marched out to meet Vessal, remember? He didn't seem at all coy then.'

The engineers looked at each other and then at Barundin.

'We'll table the topic for a meeting,' said Darbran. 'We need to talk it over.'

'Of course you do,' said Barundin.

'We'll let you know our decision as soon as it's made,' the high engineer assured him.

'I'm sure you will,' said the king, standing. He downed the dregs of his ale. 'In fact, why don't I leave you learned folk to continue your meeting without me? I am weary, and I am sure you still have many other things to talk about, my proposition notwithstanding.'

'Aye, many things,' said Borin, his eyebrows waggling furiously.

'Then I bid you good night,' said Barundin.

He could feel their anxious stares on his back as he turned and walked away, and had to suppress a smile. Yes, he thought contentedly, he had given them plenty to talk about. A knock on the doors opened them and as the warden closed them behind him, he could already hear the guildmasters' voices rising.

THE LAST CHILLS of winter still lingered over the mountain, and the sky above was clear and blue. Barundin had spent those winter months preparing for the expedition, knowing that the snows would make any travelling almost impossible before the first spring thaws. While the mountain passes had remained navigable, he had sent rangers south and west, seeking for some news of Wanazaki. As the snows had closed in, a few brave bands had used the underway towards Karak Varn, though in places it was flooded and collapsed. Though none had found the mentally unstable engineer, there were several sightings of his gyro-copter in the lands to the south.

So it was that Barundin found himself leading a party of twenty dwarfs around the shore of Karak Varn. Both Tharonin and Arbrek had argued against the king accompanying the expedition, saying that it was too dangerous. Barundin had ignored their council, much to the older dwarfs' annoyance, and enlisted the services of Dran the Reckoner, one of the less respectable thanes of Zhufbar. Dran had a good reputation with the rangers, and knew the lands between Karak Varn and the Black Mountains, where Wanazaki was now reputedly living.

Barundin was in a fair mood. Though the heart of every dwarf is for solid stone and deep tunnels, there was also something about a crisp morning on a mountainside that stirred his soul. They had skirted west of Blackwater the night before and camped in a small hollow not far from the lake. Now, as they looked across the dark, still waters, the peaks of the mountains beyond could clearly be seen. Highest amongst them was Karaz Brindal, atop whose summit was one of the greatest watch towers of the dwarf realm, though now abandoned and infested with stone trolls. It was said that a dwarf upon Karaz Brindal could see all the way to Mount Gunbad, and that when the city had fallen, the sentries of the keep had bricked up the eastern windows so that they did not have to look upon the sight of their ancient hold despoiled by goblins.

On a ridged shoulder of Karaz Brindal was the sprawling open mine of the Naggrundzorn, now also flooded by the same waters that had burst open Karak Varn. It was there that Barundin's great-great-great-great-great grandfather had met his doom, fighting wolf riders from Mount Gunbad whilst protecting an ore caravan taking tribute to the high king at Karaz-a-Karak. A king's ransom it was called at the time, although perhaps in these years it would have been half the wealth of all Zhufbar. The days when the Silver Road to Mount Silverspear had been decorated with real silver had long passed, and the pillaging of the dwarfs' wealth for four millennia was just one more reason to berate the world for its shortcomings.

Snow still lay far down the mountain slopes, and Barundin wore a heavy woollen cloak over his chainmail and gromril armour. He wore a new pair of stout walking boots, which still needed breaking in, and his left heel was badly blistered from the march of the day before. Ignoring the pain, he pulled on his boots, as Dran filled his canteen from a thin rill of water running off the lake and down the mountainside.

'How far to Karak Varn?' asked Barundin.

The ranger looked over his shoulder at the king and grinned. The expression twisted the scar that ran from his chin to his right eye, leaving a bald slash through Dran's beard. Nobody knew how he had got the scar, and the dispossessed thane certainly wasn't telling.

'We'll be there by midday tomorrow,' said Dran, stoppering his water bottle as he walked back. 'From there it's three, maybe four, days to Black Fire Pass.'

'How can you be sure that Wanazaki has headed towards the Black Mountains?' asked the king, standing up and grabbing his pack. 'He might have headed south-east.'

'Towards Karaz-a-Karak?' said Dran with a snort. 'Not a chance. The guild will have sent word to their members there. Wanazaki knows that. No, he'll not go within a dozen leagues of Karaz-a-Karak.'

'I don't intend to walk all the way to Karak Hirn, only to find there's no sign of him,' said Barundin, shouldering his pack.

Dran tapped his nose. 'I make my money doing this, your highness,' said the Reckoner. 'I know how to find folk, and Wanazaki's no different. Mark my words, he doesn't know much, but he's clever enough to stick to the old North Road.'

'It's been nearly twenty years since I last saw him,' said Barundin as Dran waved to the other rangers to assemble. 'He could be in Nuln by now.'

'Well, you've got a choice then, haven't you?' said Dran. 'Turn back now before we've walked too far, and forget about Dukankor Grobkaz-a-Gazan and Vessal, or we can get going.'

'Lead on,' said the king.

THE GATES OF Karak Varn were a pitiable sight. Gaping into the darkness beyond, the great portal was thrown open, half sunk in the water. The ancient faces of the kings of Karak Varn carved into the stone had been worn away, leaving only the faintest of marks, which could barely be seen from the shore.

The entire lakeside around the area was littered with the spoor of grobi and other creatures, though none of it recent by the estimate of Dran. Just like most living things, even greenskins preferred not to venture too far abroad in the winter, and they would be in the dark places of the fallen hold away from the harsh light.

The dwarfs turned away from the depressing view, skirting the hold to the west, looking down upon the foothills of the Worlds Edge Mountains. To the west, these rugged, rock-strewn hills gave way to the meadows and pastures of the Empire, and on the edge of vision at the horizon, the dark swathe of the forests that swept across most of the manling realm.

South and west they travelled, leaving behind the bleak shores of Blackwater, passing the desolate, ruined towers that had once been the outlying settlements of Karak Varn. Now they were overgrown and barely visible; they were the dens of wolves and bears, and other, more wicked, creatures.

The mountains shallowed as they neared the Black Fire Pass, though their route took them across steep ridges and amongst the broad shoulders of the Worlds Edge Mountains, as if cutting across the grain of the mountain range. Dran led them on without pause or doubt, finding caves and hollows when the weather turned foul, which it did often. Usually they pressed on, even into the last flurries of snow and the gales that howled up the valleys from the Border Princes and Badlands to the south.

On the seventeenth day after leaving Zhufbar, having covered some two hundred and twenty miles as the crow flies, they came upon the mountainside of Karag Kazak. Below them, the slope fell steeply to the floor of the pass, dotted with pines and large boulders. Though it was just before noon and there were many hours left in the day, Dran made camp. By the light of the noon sun, he led them a short way from the dell where their packs were left. Storm clouds glowered in the eastern sky, dark and menacing, coming towards them on a strong wind.

The Reckoner took them to a shoulder of rock which jutted from Karag Kazak for a half a mile. Barundin was astounded, for the area was littered with cairns, each adorned by an ancient oathstone, so time-worn many were little more than hillocks identified only by the rings of bronze occasionally spied amongst the tufts of hardy grass and heaps of soil. There were dozens of them, perhaps hundreds; the last resting places of a great many fallen dwarf warriors who chose to stand and die in the pass rather than retreat.

Further down the slope there was a large gathering of manlings: men, women and children were clustered around a tall statue of a large, bearded man holding a hammer aloft. Some were dressed in little more than rags, while others wore the pale robes Barundin had seen worn by manling priests.

'This is where they fought, isn't it?' said the king.

'Aye,' said Dran with a solemn nod. 'Here was arrayed the host of High King Kurgan, and down there Sigmar and his warlords made their stand.'

'Who are these manlings?' asked one of the rangers.

'Pilgrims,' said Dran. 'They consider it a sacred site, and travel for months even to tread upon the same ground where Sigmar fought alongside us. Some come here to pray to him, others to give thanks.'

'Are they not afraid of the greenskins?' asked Barundin. 'I see no garrison, no soldiers.'

'Even the orcs remember this place,' said Dran. 'Don't ask me how, but they do. They know that thousands of their kind were slaughtered here, upon these rocks, and most give it a wide berth. Of course, warbands still pass along here, and the odd army, but the manlings have a small keep away to the east beyond that ridge, and a much larger castle at the western end. Warning can be sent and the pilgrims can find refuge in plenty of time if there are greenskins on the move.'

'We could ask them if they have heard news of a dwarf engineer around these parts,' said Barundin.

'Aye, that was my purpose,' said Dran. 'As well as letting you see this, of course. I'll go down to their camp this evening. It's probably best that they not know one of our kings is abroad.'

'Why so?' asked Barundin.

'Some of them are a little, let's say, unhinged,' said Dran with a look of distaste. 'Dwarf worshippers.'

'Dwarf worshippers?' said Barundin, looking with sudden suspicion at the gathering below them.

'Sigmar's alliance and all that,' said Dran. 'It was very important to them, the battle here, and they see our part in it as almost divine. Crazy, the lot of them.'

They did not speak as they made their way back up the slope, out of sight of the manling pilgrims. Barundin mused upon Dran's words, and the strange beliefs of the manlings. The Battle of Black Fire Pass had been important to the dwarfs too, and the alliance with the fledgling Empire of Sigmar no less significant at the time. It had signalled the end of the Time of the Goblin Wars, when a great host of orcs and grobi had been crushed along this pass, having been driven from the west and down out of the mountains by men and dwarfs. Not for many centuries had the greenskins returned in any numbers, and never again in the numberless hordes that had ravaged the lands since the fall of Karak Ungor some fifteen hundred years before.

Barundin passed the afternoon reading his father's journal which he had brought with him. He had read it many times since the old king's death, trying to find inspiration and meaning in his father's words. At times the runic script was heavy and clumsy and his language more colourful. Barundin guessed these to be the nights on which he had gotten drunk with the loremaster, Ongrik. Time and again he felt himself drawn to the pages on which Throndin had scrawled his dying grudge, and the two signatures beneath it. The page was almost falling out, the edges well thumbed.

Never once had it crossed Barundin's mind that it was too much to ask. He had never contemplated abandoning the grudge against Baron Vessal, no matter what obstacles were in his path. It was not in his nature to accept defeat, just as it was not in the nature of the whole dwarf race to accept that their time as a power in the world had long since passed.

Barundin would take his people through war and fire to avenge his father, for the death of a king was beyond any counting of value, worth more than any amount of effort. Not only did his father expect nothing less from Barundin, but also all his ancestors, back to Grimnir, Grungni and Valaya themselves. Not once did the burden feel too heavy, though, for from those same ancestors he knew he had the strength and the will he needed to persevere and to triumph. To countenance anything other than success was unthinkable to the king.

Dran returned from the manling gathering after dark, having spent several hours amongst them. He had a certain self-satisfaction about him that told Barundin the Reckoner had been right. Indeed, Dran confirmed, the half-mad engineer had taken employment in a manling town not far from the western approach to the pass. It would be two days' travel, three if the weather turned foul, as it seemed it would. The news bolstered Barundin's confidence further, knowing that Wanazaki's return would bring the Engineers Guild into his camp, and with that the hold would be willing to embark on another war, this time against the grobi of Dukankor Grobkaz-a-Gazan.

'DWARF-BUILT FOR SURE,' said Barundin, looking down at the keep at the foot of the pass. 'Oh, the manlings have put all sorts of nonsense on top, like those roofs, but that's dwarf masonry down at the bottom.'

'Yes, our forefathers helped build this place,' said Dran, leading them down a track that wound between thin trees and scattered boulders. 'If you'd travelled as much as I have, you'd have seen the cut of dwarf chisel all across the Empire. The manlings might have driven out the orcs, but their castles and cities were built with dwarf hands.'

'And Wanazaki is in there?' said Fundbin, a ranger swathed in a deep red cloak, little more than his beard and the tip of his nose protruding from the hood. The bitter wind blowing from the east along Black Fire Pass had chilled even the hardy dwarfs.

'Oh, he's here all right,' said Dran.

Dran pointed to a tower on the north wall, a thick chimney protruding from its stones. Its iron-crowned tip belched grey smoke that gathered in clouds, shrouding the mountainside. Looking down over the walls from the slope of the pass, they could see two massive pistons moving up and down near the base of the tower, though their purpose was unclear. Part of the wall next to the tower had been extended over the courtyard with a wooden gantry and steel platform, and atop the platform sat a gyrocopter, its blades taken off and stacked neatly next to the flying machine.

There were few people on the road as they reached the floor of the pass. Scattered groups of travellers, most walking, a few with horse and wagon, gave them long looks as they passed. Some stared openly in disbelief at the large group of dwarfs, and some had a look of awe that sent a nervous shiver through Barundin. Dran's talk of dwarf worshippers had unsettled him considerably.

It was late afternoon and the shadow of the tall castle lay long across the road. A ravine, nearly two hundred feet deep and thirty feet wide, was dug around the base of the castle on three sides, which was itself built out of the rock of the pass itself, its foundations were the feet of the Worlds Edge Mountains. The walls were some fifty feet high, studded with two gate towers and protected by blocky fortifications at each corner.

The dwarfs passed over a wooden bridge laid across the ravine, and noted the heavy chains and gear mechanisms that would allow the bridge to be toppled into the chasm with the pull of a couple of levers. The only way to storm the castle was from the mountainside itself, and looking up the slope, Barundin could see entrenchments and revetments dug into the rock. They were empty now, and the dwarf king could see few soldiers on the walls. He wondered if perhaps the watch of the man-lings had grown lax in the recent years of peace and prosperity they had enjoyed since the Great War.

There was a cluster of guards at the gate, over a dozen, and their cap-tain approached the party as they came off the bridge. He was dressed in the same black and yellow livery as his men, his slashed doublet obscured by a steel breastplate wrought with a rearing griffon holding a sword. His sallet helm sported two plumed feathers, both red, and he held a demi-halberd across his chest as he walked toward the dwarfs. His expression was friendly, a slight smile upon his lips.

'Welcome to Siggurdfort,' the manling said, stopping just in front of Dran, who stood ahead of Barundin. 'At first I thought I had misheard when news came of twenty-one dwarfs travelling the pass, but now I see the truth of it. Please, enter and enjoy what comforts we have to offer.'

'I'm Dran the Reckoner,' said Dran, speaking fluently in the mannish tongue. 'It's not our custom to accept invitation from unnamed strang-ers.'

'Of course, my apologies,' said the manling. 'I am Captain Dewircht, commander of the garrison, soldier of the Count of Averland. We have someone who might be very pleased to meet you, one of your own.'

'We know,' said Dran, his voice betraying no hint of the dwarfs' intent. 'We want to see him, if you could send word.'

'He is fixing the ovens in the kitchen at the moment,' said Dewircht. 'I say fixing, but actually he's fitting a new redraft chimney, which he tells us means we'll have to burn only half as much wood. I'll send him word to meet you in the main hall.'

Dewircht stood aside and the dwarfs passed into the shadow of the gatehouse, feeling the stares of the guards upon them. Inside the castle, the courtyard was filled with small huts and wooden structures, with roofs made of hides and slate. The ground was little more than packed dirt, potholed and muddy, and the dwarfs hurried through the ramshackle buildings, ignoring the dogs and cats running stray and the pockets of whispering people.

Smoke from cooking fires was blown by gusts of wind into eddies, and the sounds of clattering pans and muffled conversation could be heard from within the huts as the folk of the keep readied their evening meals.

Coming to the rear of the castle, they found the main hall. It was built into the foundations of the wall and from the same huge stone blocks. It was roofed with red-painted tiles, chipped and worn and slicked with moss. A great double door stood open at the near end, the gloomy fire-light of the inside barely visible within. Laughter and singing could be heard.

Entering, they found that the hall was much longer than it appeared, burrowing under the wall and into the roots of the mountain beyond. Along the length of the walls were four huge fireplaces, two on each side, the smoke from the fires disappearing up flues that had been dug through the wall and the mountain slope. The room was full of tables and benches, and there were several dozen people inside, many in the uniforms of the garrison, some dressed in the manner of the pilgrims the dwarfs had seen in the pass the last two days.

There was an empty bench near the far end, close to one of the fires, and a stone counter that ran nearly the whole width of the hall. Small grates were built into the counter, over which pots boiled and shanks of meat on spits roasted gently. The aroma made Barundin's mouth water and he realised that it had been a while since he had really filled his stomach, having had nothing more than trail rations and what game the rangers had caught whilst on the journey south.

'Hungry?' said Dran.

Barundin nodded enthusiastically. 'And some beer!' the king said, and there were grunts of agreement from the other dwarfs. 'We'll need plenty of it, I bet. Manling beer is little more than coloured water.'

'We need to pay,' said Dran, with a pointed look at the king.

'I'll come with you,' Barundin agreed with a sigh.

As the rangers took places around the table, looking slightly ridiculous on the manling benches, their feet dangling above the ground, Dran and Barundin walked to the counter. There was a man and a woman behind it, arguing. The woman saw the two dwarfs approach and broke off the conversation.

'You'll be wanting a hearty meal after your travels, I'll warrant,' she said. 'I'm Bertha Felbren, and if there's anything you'll be wanting, just shout for me. Or my lazy oaf of a husband, Viktor, if you can't find me.'

'We have twenty-one hungry stomachs to fill,' said Dran with a nod to the table full of dwarfs. 'Bread, meat, broth, whatever you have, we'll take.'

'And your best ale,' added Barundin. 'Lots of it, and often!'

'We'll bring it over,' said Bertha. 'If you're wanting rooms, I'll ask around for you. Most folk that come through here camp in the pass, but we'll be able to find enough beds if you wish.'

'That would be grand,' said Dran. The Reckoner looked at Barundin and gestured with his head towards Bertha. Barundin didn't responded and Dran repeated the gesture, this time with a scowl.

'Oh,' said Barundin with a sheepish grin. 'You'll want paying.'

Sweeping back his cloak, Barundin lifted up the chainmail sleeve of his armour and slipped the gold torque from around his upper arm. He took a small chisel from his belt, carried for just such a purpose, and chipped off three slivers of shining metal. He pushed them across the counter to Bertha, who looked at the dwarf with wide-eyed surprise.

'Not enough?' said Barundin, turning to Dran for guidance. 'How much?'

'I think you've just paid them enough for a week,' said Dran with a grin.

Barundin fought the urge to grab the gold back, his fingers twitching as Bertha swept up the shards of precious metal, quickly depositing them out of sight.

'Yes, whatever you want, just give Bertha a shout, any time, day or night,' she said breathlessly, turning away. 'Viktor, you worthless donkey, get out the Bugman's for these guests.'

'Bugman's?' said Dran and Barundin together, looking at each other in amazement.

'You have Bugman's ale here?' said Barundin.

'Aye, we do,' said Viktor, walking over to the counter, wiping his hands on a cloth. 'Not much, perhaps a tankard each, I'm afraid.'

'It's not Bugman XXXXXX, is it?' asked Dran, his voice dropping to a reverential whisper.

'No, no,' laughed Viktor. 'Do you think I'd be stuck out here with this hag of a wife if I had a barrel of XXXXXX? It's not even Troll Brew, I'm sorry to say. It's Beardling's Best Effort. Nothing fancy for you folk, I'm sure, but much more to your taste than our own brew.'

'Beardling's Best Effort?' said Barundin. 'Never heard of it. Are you sure it's Bugman's?'

'You can inspect the cask yourself, if you don't believe me,' said Viktor. 'I'll bring it to the table with some mugs for you.'

'Aye, thanks,' said Dran, nudging Barundin in the side and signalling for them to return to the table.

THE MEAL WAS pleasant enough, consisting of tough stewed goat's meat broth, roast lamb and boiled potatoes. There was plenty of bread and goat's cheese with which the dwarfs could vanquish the last vestiges of their appetites, in anticipation of the ale to come.

Although it was by no means the quality associated with most of the beer from the Bugman brewery, it was certainly finer than the manlings' own brew. Having been starved of proper dwarf beer even at home for nearly twenty years, the dwarfs supped the Beardling's Best Effort in a cautious manner. Each mouthful was greeted with much contented umming and aahing.

In the convivial atmosphere, the dwarfs began to relax. As night fell outside, Bertha built up the fires and lit more candles, and the hall was awash with a warm glow and the gentle hubbub of voices as more folk of the castle, soldiers and visitors, entered. Maids came in, young lasses from the soldiers' families, to serve the growing crowd, and in one corner a minstrel broke out a fiddle and began to play quietly to himself. The dwarfs were left to their own devices for the most part, disturbed only by the enquiries of Bertha and Viktor checking that they were well served.

Barundin was nudged by Dran, tearing him away from the silent contemplation of his pint, and he looked up to see the gathered patrons parting to allow Rimbal Wanazaki to pass through. The engineer looked much the same as he had when Barundin saw him in the foothills west of Black Water; his beard was longer, his eyes red-rimmed through the grime and soot that stained his tanned skin. He held a lump hammer in one hand and an oil can in the other.

'Evening, lads, nice of...' The engineer's voice trailed off as he caught sight of Barundin, sitting with a stern expression on his face, his arms crossed tightly. 'Well, blow me!'

'Sit down, Rimbal,' said Dran, standing up on the bench to reach for the tankard of ale they had kept aside for the engineer. 'Have yourself a drink.'

Wanazaki cautiously wormed his way between the Reckoner and Barundin, and took the ale with a grin.

'You're not here to check on my health, are you?' said Wanazaki, and Barundin noticed that his tic was very pronounced now, his whole body twitching occasionally. 'You'd think that after all that happened, you'd be the last people I'd want to see, but bless my mail, you are a welcome sight! These manlings are fine enough folk once you know them, but they're so difficult to get to know, so flighty. One year they're a youngster you can bob up and down on your knee, a few years later, they're married and leaving. There's no time to enjoy their company. They're always in such a rush to get things done.'

'You're coming back with us,' said Dran, laying a hand on Wanazaki's shoulder. 'Plenty of good company back in Zhufbar.'

A panicked expression fixed on the engineer's face and he shrugged off Dran's hand and stood up, backing away from the group. 'Well, it's nice of you to visit me and everything, but I don't think that's a good idea,' said Wanazaki, his voice rising in volume with the level of his fear. 'The guild... I can't... I'm not going back!'

This last was a shout in the Reikspiel of the manlings, which turned the heads of the others in the hall. There were angry murmurings and a crowd began to gather around the dwarfs.

Captain Dewircht pushed his way through the growing group and stood at the end of the table, his demi-halberd gripped in his right hand.

'What's the commotion here?' he demanded. 'What's going on?'

'Rimbal is coming back with us to Zhufbar,' said Dran, his voice emotionless.

'It seems that he isn't so keen on the idea,' said Dewircht as a knot of soldiers closed around him, more forcing their way through the crowd. 'Maybe you should think about returning without him.'

'Yeah!' said another man, faceless in the throng. 'Old Rimbal here doesn't need to be going nowhere. He's good enough right here.'

'He must return to Zhufbar to account for himself,' said Dran. 'I am the Reckoner, and I do not come back empty-handed.'

'He lives in lands that are free to him, to do as he pleases,' said Dewircht. 'It is his choice whether he comes or goes, not yours.'

'No, it is mine,' growled Barundin. 'He is my vassal, oath-sworn and honoured, and I command him.'

'And who would you be?' said Dewircht. 'Who would dare issue commands in a fortress of the Emperor, in from the wilds and nameless?'

Barundin stood up and jumped onto the table, unclasping his cloak and tossing it aside to reveal his silver and gold inlaid armour, glowing subtly with rune power. He pulled forth his axe and held it in front of him. Awe and surprise swept across the hall.

'Who am I?' he roared. 'I am Barundin, son of Throndin, King of Zhufbar. Do not tell me of rights! What right have you to deny me, who sit and feast in a hall hewn from the rock by dwarfish hands? What right have you to deny me, who stand guard upon walls laid by dwarfish masons? What right have you to deny me, who keep these lands only by the unseen might of dwarf axes, whose lands were once those ruled over by my ancestors?'

'A king?' laughed Dewircht, astounded. 'A king of the dwarfs comes here? And if we still deny you, what then? Will you declare war on the whole Empire?'

At their captain's words, a few soldiers drew their weapons and some raised crossbows, pointing at Barundin. Quicker than one would expect from a dwarf, Dran was stood on the bench, a throwing axe in one hand. He stared at Dewircht and the soldiers.

'Your captain dies the moment one of you moves against my king,' the Reckoner warned, his scarred face crumpled in a menacing scowl.

Barundin looked at Dewircht then lowered his axe and hung it on his belt again. 'There will be no fighting here, today,' said the dwarf king. 'No, it would not be so simple for you. If you do not surrender up the renegade engineer to me, I shall return to Zhufbar. There I shall call for the loremaster to bring forth our book of grudges. Within its many pages shall be recorded the place of Siggurdfort, and the name of Captain Dewircht.'

The king turned on the rest of the crowd, his eyes ablaze with anger. 'With an army I shall return,' said Barundin. 'While you protect Wanazaki from his judgement, the grudge will stand. We shall tear down the walls that we built, and we shall kill every man inside, and we shall take your watery beer and pour it into the dirt, and we shall burn down the wooden hovels you have spoiled our stones with, and we shall take your gold as recompense for our trouble, and the engineer will still return with us. And if not I, then my heir, or his heir, until the lives of your grandfathers have passed, your names shall still be written in that book, the wrong you do us unavenged. Do not treat the ire of the dwarfs lightly, for there may come a day when your people again look to us as allies, and we might then open our books and see the account you have made for yourselves. In this place, upon the very slopes where our ancestors fought and died together in an age past, you would deny me for the sake of this rogue?'

The speech was followed by a deep, still silence across the hall. Dewircht looked between Barundin and Dran, and then his gaze fell upon Rimbal Wanazaki.

The engineer looked worried, and glanced up at the king. He walked forward and stood in front of the captain. 'Put down your weapons,' said Rimbal. 'He is right, everything he says.' He turned to the king. 'I do not want this, but even more I do not want what you will surely do. I shall fetch my things. What of my gyrocopter?'

'If you give me your word to stay with me until Zhufbar, then you may fly it back,' said Barundin.

'My word?' said Wanazaki. 'You would take the word of an oath-breaker?'

'You are not yet oathbreaker, Rimbal,' said Barundin, his expression softening. 'You never were, and I do not think you will be one now. Come home, Rimbal. Come back to your people.'

Rimbal nodded and turned back to Captain Dewircht. He shook the manling's free hand with a nod, and the people in the hall parted again to allow him to leave, his head held proudly, his steps brisk and firm.

GRUDGE FIVE

The Goblin Grudge

STEAM AND SMOKE billowed from the chimneys of the brewery, swiftly appearing from gold-edged flues and out into the mountain sky. The great oast towers glistened in the light of the morning sun, and miles of glinting copper piping sprouted from the stone walls and coiled about each other.

The brewery had been built on top of the foundations of the original site, extending out from the southern side of the hold, high up the mountain overlooking Black Water. From the cavernous interior of Zhufbar, the building spilled across the mountainside, a massive edifice of grey stone, red brick and metalwork. A narrow, fast torrent of water spilled down from the mountainside above, disappearing into the depths of the brewery, for the dwarfs only used the freshest spring water in their beer-making.

As the construction had neared completion, the master brewers and their clans had read their old recipe books and orders for the finest ingredients had been sent to the other holds and the lands of the empire. The vast storehouses of the brewery were now brimming with barrels of different malts and barleys, yeast and honey, and sundry other ingredients, some of them clan secrets for many generations.

Barundin stood atop a stage made from empty barrels, a great host of dwarfs around him, in front of the brewery entrance. Beside him stood the brewmasters and the engineers, Wanazaki amongst them. The itinerant dwarf had renewed his oaths with the Guild and, in an act of clemency, they had spared him the humiliation of the Trouser Leg Ritual and banishment. Instead he had agreed to work on the rebuilding of the brewery for free, an act that would quell the acts of even the most rebellious dwarfs. With Wanazaki's aid, work had progressed apace and now, only three years since his return, the brewery was finished.

In his hand, the king held grains of barley, which he scrunched nervously in his palm as he waited for the crowd to settle. The sun was warm on his face, even this early in the morning, and he was sweating heavily. As quiet descended, Barundin cleared his throat.

'Today is a great day for Zhufbar,' the king began. 'A proud day. It is a day when we can once again make a claim to our ancestral heritage.'

Barundin held up his hand and allowed the grains to dribble through his fingers, pattering against the wooden barrel beneath his feet.

'A simple seed, some might think,' he continued, gazing up above the crowd to the mountains beyond. 'But not us, not those that know the real secrets of beer-making. These simple seeds contain within them the essence of beer, and in that the essence of ourselves. It is in beer that we might judge our finest qualities, for it requires knowledge, skill and patience. Beer is more than a drink, more than something to quench a thirst. It is our right, its making passed down to us from our oldest ancestors. It is the lifeblood of our people, our hold. The ale that we shall drink will have been long in the making, tested for its qualities, proven in the taverns.'

Barundin flicked the last few grains from his hand and turned his gaze to the assembled dwarfs, his expression fierce.

'And just as an ale must pass the test for it to prove its qualities, so too must our warriors,' Barundin told them. 'The skaven have been crushed, their menace to us passed. Our brewery is rebuilt and this very day the first pints of fine ale shall begin their lives. These tasks are done, but there is one great task that yet remains unfulfilled, an oath yet to be met.'

Barundin turned to the east and waved his hand across the view, his gesture encompassing the rising peaks of the Worlds Edge mountains and the clear blue sky.

'These are my lands,' he said, his voice rising. 'These are your lands! From ages past we have lived upon and within these peaks, and unto the ending of the world itself, here we shall remain, as steady as the mountains from which our spirits were hewn. But we shall never know peace again, not while there is a vile taint upon our lands that we dare not face. East of here, the vile, disgusting grobi have plundered our mines, stolen our halls, desecrated our tunnels with their presence. For a score of generations they have been interlopers upon our realms, their stench filling the taverns and drinking dens of our forefathers, their black throats breathing the air once breathed by our kin.'

Again Barundin turned his gaze back to the throng, who were murmuring loudly now, their anger roused by his words.

'No more!' bellowed Barundin. 'No more will we stand idly by while these pieces of filth live and breed in our homes. No more shall we whisper the name of Dukankor Grobkaz-a-Gazan. No more shall we stare into our ale and ignore the creatures that knock upon our door. No more will the grobi feel themselves safe from our wrath.'

'Kill the grobi!' someone shouted from the crowd, and the chant was taken up by many dozens of throats.

'Yes!' shouted Barundin. 'We shall march forth and slay them in their lair. Once more we shall build Grungankor Stokril, and it will be filled with the light of our lanterns, not the darkness of the grobi; it will resound to the hearty laughs of our warriors and not the snickering cackles of greenskins.'

Barundin began to pace up and down the stage, spittle flying from his lips as he ranted. He pointed south across across Black Water.

'Within two days' march of here, they lie in their rags and filth,' he said. 'Karak Varn, taken by them scant years after Karak Ungor fell to the wicked-eyed thieves. Then, to the east, Mount Gunbad was taken, and from there came the creatures that invaded our lands. There they looted the wonderful brynduraz from Gunbad and spoiled it with their pawing hands, destroying the most beautiful stones to be found beneath the world. Not content, they assailed Mount Silverspear, and it is now a dark place filled with their grime, a toilet for grobi! Where once a king sat, a hateful greenskin now squats! In this way, the east was taken from us.'

Barundin's roaring now could be barely heard above the tumult of the throng, their angry chanting resounding from the mountainside.

'South, far south, the greenskins came for our gold,' he continued. 'In Karak Eight Peaks, they slew our kin, in wretched alliance with the ratmen. Not content, their invasions continued, until Karak Azgal and Karak Drazh were swarming with their litters. They even tried to beat upon the gates of Karaz-a-Karak!

'Well, no more! Now only seven holds remain. Seven fortresses against this horde. But we shall make them know that there is still strength left in the arms of the dwarfs. Though we might not reclaim the holds of our ancestors from their clutches, we can yet show them that our lands are our own still, and that trespassers are not welcome. The grobi may have forgotten to fear dwarf steel and gromril, but they shall come to dread it again. We shall drive them forth, cleanse the old tunnels of their disgusting spoor, and hound them back to the halls of Gunbad itself. Though it might take a generation, I swear upon my father's tomb and upon the spirits of my ancestors that I shall not rest while one greenskins still treads upon the flagstones of Grungankor Stokril!'

Barundin stormed to the front of the stage and raised his hands above his head, his fists trembling mightily.

'Who shall swear with me?' he called out.

The bellow from the crowd was such that the clanking of the water-wheels, the hissing of the brewery pipes and even the steam hammers of the forges were drowned out by the wall of noise.

'We swear!'

THE TRAMPING OF feet, hornblows and drums kept a steady rhythm as the Zhufbar army marched eastwards. The steel-clad host passed out through the eastern deep gates into the mighty underground highway that once led eastwards to Mount Gunbad. Part of the Ungdrim Ankor, the massive network of tunnels that once linked all the dwarf holds together, the highway was wide enough for ten dwarfs to march abreast. Above the clinking of mail and the clump of boots, Barundin led the several thousands warriors in a marching song, their deep voices echoing ahead of them along the tunnel.

Let no warrior mine now refuse
To march out and reclaim his dues,
For now he's one of mine to pay
Under the Hills and far away.

Under the Hills and o'er the moor,
To Azul, Gunbad and bright Ungor,
The king commands and we'll obey
Under the hills and far away.

I shall keep more happy tracks
With gleaming armour and shining axe
That cut and cleave both night and day
Under the Hills and far away.

Under the Hills and o'er the moor,
To Azul, Gunbad and bright Ungor,
The king commands and we'll obey
Under the hills and far away.

Courage, lads, 'tis one to a tun,
But we'll stay the fight til it is done
All warriors bold on every day,
Under the Hills and far away.

Under the Hills and o'er the moor,
To Azul, Gunbad and bright Ungor,
The king commands and we'll obey
Under the hills and far away.

In the vanguard of the host marched the ironbreakers, whose regular duties included patrolling the Ungdrin to hunt down interloping grobi and other creatures. The going was slow at times, for the walls and some-times the ceiling had collapsed in places. Teams of miners worked hard to clear piles of debris, toiling ceaselessly for hours on end until there was room to pass. In this way, their hundreds of lanterns lighting the ancient flagstones and statues that lined the highway, the dwarfs trav-elled eastwards towards their long-lost outpost.

It was after two days of travel and much backbreaking labour by the caravan that they came upon the tunnels beneath Grungankor Stokril. There was grobi-sign everywhere. Old stairwells were choked with filth and debris, bones littered amongst them and dried dung piled in heaps.

Barundin felt his ire rising once more as he looked upon the scars left by the goblins. Statues of the ancestors lay ruined and defaced with blood and grime, and the ornate mosaics that had once decorated the walls had been torn down in many places, the bright squares of stone taken as baubles by the greenskins. Here and there they found the body of a dwarf; ages-dead carcasses that were little more than piles of dust and rust, identified only by the odd scrap of cloth. Anything of value had been looted long ago and not a shred of steel, silver or gold remained. Barundin ordered these remains to be gathered up in sealed boxes and sent back to Zhufbar for a proper burial.

Though it was dark both night and day, it was in the shadow-shrouded early hours of one morning, when the dwarfs had doused most of their lanterns to get some sleep, that the first grobi foray attacked. The assault was short-lived, for the ironbreakers were swift in their response and the sentries wary, so close to the lair of the enemy. Shrieking and crying, the grobi were sent fleeing back into the depths.

The next morning, Barundin met with many of the thanes and his best advisors. They decided to launch an expeditionary attack into the south vaults, a series of mines and halls less than a mile from where they were camped. In an effort to establish some form of presence in the tunnels away from the Ungdrin, Barundin would lead half the army south and try to take one of the larger halls. From here he could make more raids on the grobi holes, while Hengrid Dragonfoe would lead a third of the army north the next day and attempt to cut the grobi off from the much larger settlement of Mount Gunbad, which lay some two hundred miles to the east. Hengrid, once gatewarden and leader of the hammerers, had proved himself an able general in the fighting against the skaven and, upon the death of his uncle had become Thane of his clan. They were counted amongst the fiercest fighters in the hold now, and if anyone would be able to stop more grobi coming from the east, it would be Hengrid and his warriors.

The remaining part of the force was to stay in the Ungdrin to act as a rearguard or a reserve as necessary. The youngest and quickest warriors were designated as runners, and they spent several hours with the iron-breakers, learning the quickest routes around the Ungdrin and nearby tunnels. It would be dangerous work, travelling alone and in the dark, but Barundin gave the beardlings a stirring speech to bolster their courage, and impressed upon them the necessity of the messengers' task; the dwarfs were massively outnumbered, and if they were to prevail they would need to be disciplined, resolute and, most of all, coordinated.

The plan thus devised, Barundin gave the command for the army to march forth just before noon. Afraid of the bright light of the sun, the grobi would be in their holes during the day, which had earned them the name of night goblins over the many centuries of enmity between their kind and the dwarfs. Barundin hoped that by attacking during daylight hours he would have a better idea of the enemy's numbers. With luck, he chuckled to his hammerers, many of them would be asleep and easy targets.

THE INITIAL ADVANCE went well, with the ironbreakers in the fore, leading the way and meeting little resistance. As the army wound its way up a large staircase into the halls above, the grobi were waking to the threat. Gongs and bells began to clamour, echoing down to the dwarfs. Here and there, small bands of greenskins were trying to organise themselves, but they were little match for the stout dwarf warriors that fell upon them, and most of the grobi fled deeper into their lair.

Splitting his force into three, Barundin spread out his army, herding the grobi eastwards and southwards. Through the corridors, the dwarfs pushed on. In the close confines, the diminutive greenskins were outclassed by the skill and weapons of the dwarfs, and unable to bring their numbers to bear.

After three hours of fighting, Barundin was on the second level of the mine-workings, only one level down from the main hall of the south vaults. He was taking a brief rest and wiping the dark goblin blood from the blade of his axe. He stared with contempt at the pile of bodies that littered the floor. The grobi were scrawny creatures, a head shorter than a dwarf and far skinnier. They wore ragged robes of black and dark blue, trimmed with stones and bits of bone, and with long hoods to shield themselves from the light that occasionally trickled through the millennia-old grime that stained the high windows of their lair.

The green of their skin was pallid and sickly, even lighter along their pointed ears and thin, grasping fingers. Shards of sharp, small fangs and broken claws were scattered across the bodies from the blows of Barundin's hammerers, stained and filthy. Barundin kicked at one of the corpses, smashing it against the wall, feeling that death was not near enough punishment for the thieving little fiends that had despoiled the fine halls of his ancestors.

Giving a satisfied grunt, he turned to his hammerers, who were resting further along the corridor, some munching on food they had brought with them and swigging from their flasks. Barundin saw Durak, once stonebearer to the dead king and now the new gatekeeper. The weathered face of Durak looked back at him and the veteran gave his king a thumbs up. Barundin nodded in return.

'Been a while, eh?' said Durak, reaching into his belt and pulling out a pipe.

'Since what?' asked Barundin, declining the gatekeeper's offer of pipe weed with a shake of his head.

'Since I carried your father's stone to the battle where he fell,' said Durak. 'Who could have guessed then that it would lead us here, eh?'

'Aye,' said Barundin. 'It's been a while, for sure.'

'Worth it, though, I reckon,' said Durak. 'All the fighting, I mean. Always feels good to smash a grobi skull, eh?'

'Let's smash some more, shall we?' suggested Barundin.

'Aye, let's,' said Durak with a grin.

ONWARDS THE DWARF host advanced, until they reached a wide stairway leading up to the gates of the Great South Hall. From the end of the tunnel the steps fanned outwards onto a wide platform, easily large enough for several hundred dwarfs to stand upon at the same time. Dirt and mould slicked the stairs, obscuring the veins of the marble with filth. The huge gates themselves had been torn off their hinges long ago and the remains lay across the upper steps. The great bands of iron were rusted and looted in places, the nails torn from the thick oak beams that made up the doors. Scraps of torn cloth were caught on rusted rivets, and the goblin spoor was heaped around the gateway in piles taller than a dwarf. The stench that wafted from the hall beyond stuck in Barundin's throat.

'By Grimnir's tattooed arse, they'll pay for this,' the king muttered.

'Bring up the firepots,' shouted Durak, waving to some of the engineers that accompanied the army. 'We'll burn them out.'

'Wait!' said Barundin, holding up a hand to halt the dwarfs pushing their way to the front of the line. 'Enough destruction has been heaped upon our ancient homes here. First we'll drive them out with axe and hammer, and then we'll burn the filth.'

A horde of greenskins awaited them on the stairs, more and more pouring through the ruined doorway as the dwarfs advanced. Barundin led the charge with his hammerers, flanked by ironbreakers and miners. Like a mailed fist crashing into soft flesh, the dwarf warriors battered into the goblins, scattering them quickly and driving them back into the hall.

Caught up in the fighting, Barundin hewed left and right with his axe, felling a score of goblins before gaining the gateway. Here he paused to catch a breath, as the goblins retreated from his wrathful attack.

He stopped in his stride, eyes narrowing in anger as he saw what had become of the Great South Hall.

The large chamber had once been the focal point of the mine workings, the audience chamber and throne room of the clan that had delved for ore beneath the mountain. Though not as grand as the halls of Zhufbar proper, it was still a large space. Columns as thick as tree trunks supported the vaulted roof, and to Barundin's right a large area, where once the thane's throne had sat, was raised up a dozen feet above the rest of the chamber, reached by a sweeping stair.

The detritus of the grobi was everywhere. Glowing fungal growths sprawled across the floor and walls, with towering toadstools erupting from the fronds and spore clouds. The statues that had once formed a colonnade leading towards the throne had been toppled, daubed in disgusting glyphs with unidentifiable filth. Small fires blazed everywhere, filling the chamber with acrid smoke and a ruddy glow.

The place was crawling with night goblins, hastily grouping together around crude standards of beaten copper shaped like stars and moons, the shrieking bawls of their masters attempting to instil order upon the chaos. Strange creatures, little more than round, fanged faces with legs, gibbered and screeched amongst the throng, held in check with whips and barbed prongs.

Here and there, leaders bedecked in more ornate robes moved to and fro, carrying wickedly serrated blades or leaning upon staffs hung with bones and fetishes. Upon the dais several rickety war machines had been hastily drawn up; bolt throwers and rock lobbers capable of skewering and crushing a dozen dwarfs at a time.

As Barundin led his army through the gateway, the goblins responded, streaming forward in a dark wave. Clouds of black-feathered arrows sailed above the onrushing horde, loosed from the short, crude bows of the night goblins. As Barundin and his hammerers worked their way to the right, allowing more dwarfs through the gate, they raised their shields to ward away the iron-tipped volley falling towards them. Thin arrows splintered and ricocheted off the steel wall of shields, although an unlucky dwarf fell, the shaft of an arrow protruding from his exposed cheek, blood spilling into his beard.

Ahead of Barundin, night goblin herders goaded their charges forward, unleashing a drove of betoothed monstrosities that bounded forward, gnashing and growling. Barundin knew the creatures well: cave squigs. The tanned hide of the creatures worked well as rough bindings, and their guts, suitably treated, made for hardwearing laces.

From amongst the orange-skinned beasts, riders emerged, haphazardly mounted atop several of the strange creatures, clinging on with little control over their outlandish steeds. Waving spiked clubs and short swords, the riders were carried forwards by the springing hops of their beasts, and one leaped high into the air, over the front of the shieldwall raised by the hammerers.

The rider brought his club down atop the helmet of a dwarf with a resounding clang, while the squig snapped its massive jaws shut around the poor hammerer's arm, ripping it from the shoulder. Another beast launched itself straight at the row of shields, it's unnaturally powerful legs smashing it through the wall of metal and hurling a handful of dwarfs to the ground. It scratched and bit at the fallen until driven away in another bounding leap by the attacks of the other hammerers.

Several hundred dwarfs had now made it into the hall and a line formed and began to slowly advance towards the approaching grobi. Spears with barbed tips were launched across the cavern from the two bolt throwers atop the dais, one arcing high over the dwarfs' heads to smash uselessly against the wall. The other found its mark, however, punching through armour and flesh and scything through the dwarf ranks, leaving a line of dead and maimed warriors in its trail.

Barundin watched with apprehension as the goblins pulled back the arm of a mighty catapult and loaded its sling with a large rock. As the crew hastily backed away, their captain pulled a lever. Nothing happened. The crew cautiously returned to their machine, prodding and poking, shouting at each other. Suddenly the strands of one of the ropes holding the machine together parted, and with a crack that could be heard over the cacophony of the goblins horde, the arm snapped forward. In a shower of rusted nails and splintered rotten wood, the catapult disintegrated, shards of metal and chunks of rock exploding outwards, cutting down the goblins in a cloud of dust, tattered rags and dark blood. Barundin noticed the crews of the other machines pointing and laughing at the remains of their unfortunate comrades.

Barundin bellowed to his quarrellers, who turned their crossbows towards the war machines. With a steady staggered volley, the quarrellers loosed a storm of bolts at the engines, most of the missiles missing or breaking harmless against the machines themselves. However, a few robed bodies, pinned with crossbow bolts, littered the bloodstained stones after the salvo.

With the war machine crews reloading their engines, the goblins surged forwards again under another storm of arrows. To Barundin's right, the hammerers were still fighting against a swarm of cave squigs, and many of their number lay dead amongst the corpses of the savage beasts heaped in front of their line.

The goblins advanced as a sea of spiteful green faces poking from beneath their black hoods, spitting and snarling. The horde advanced haphazardly as fights broke out amongst the ranks of unruly fighters; their chiefs cracked heads together and shouted shrill commands to keep the tide of grobi moving. The light from dozens of fires glinted cruelly from serrated short swords and barbed speartips, a constellation of fiery stars in the fumes and shadows.

Bursts of green energy erupted from the advancing line as cavorting shamans gathered their magical powers and unleashed them, spewing forth vomits of destruction and blasts from their staffs. Axe and hammer-wielding warriors to Barundin's left were hurled from their feet by the sorcerous attacks, green flames licking up from their shattered bodies.

A particularly ostentatious-looking shaman stood near the centre of the approaching horde, his tall hood bedecked with bones and crudely shaped precious stones, delved a hand into a pouch hung from his crude rope belt and pulled forth a fistful of luminous fungus. Devouring these, he began to hop from one foot to the other, cackling and yelping, swinging his staff around his head. Sickly green tendrils of energy began to leak from his mouth and from under his hood, rising up like a mist around the grobi. Green sparks leaped from hood tip to hood tip, until a mass of warriors in front of the shaman were swathed in a flowing green cloud of energy. Invigorated by these conjurations, the goblins surged forwards ever more quickly, the tramping of their feet echoing from the high walls.

A detonation to Barundin's right attracted the dwarf king's attention and he turned just in time to see a shaman bursting from the ranks, bathed in crackling green force. With manic energy, the shaman fell to the ground, flailing madly, legs and arms jerking spasmodically. The creature began to glow from within and then, after a few moments, exploded in a cloud of green-tinged arcs of lightning, striking down a handful of his fellows stood too close.

'Brace yourselves!' bellowed Barundin, setting his shield and getting a firm grip on his axe.

The foremost goblins were now less than two dozen yards away and charging fast. As they closed the gap, their ranks parted to unleash a new terror. Frothing at the mouth, their eyes glazed, goblins wielding immense balls on lengths of chain burst from the goblin horde. Intoxicated by strange mushrooms and toadstools, imbued with narcotic strength, the fanatics began to spin madly, their heavy weapons whirling around with deadly speed. Some careened off dizzily, smashing into one another in bloody tangles of metal, while others spun back into the grobi army, cutting a devastating swathe through the night goblins, who advanced onwards, unconcerned with their losses.

Several of the fanatics fell or tripped before they reached the dwarf line, crushing their own heads and bodies with their heavy iron balls, but a handful made it as far as the dwarfs. The carnage was instant, shields and mail no protection against the crushing blows of the twirling lunatics. A score of dwarfs were reduced to bloody pulps by the first impact, and as the fanatics bounced back and forth, ricocheting from one dwarf to another, they left a trail of mangled bodies in their wake.

A great groan rose up from the dwarf line and they began to edge away from the fanatics, pushing and shoving at each other to get away from the demented goblins. Even as the line buckled under the onslaught, the goblin charge hit home.

Their shieldwall broken in places by the fanatics, the dwarfs were unprepared for the grobi and many fell to jabbing swords and wild spear thrusts as they attempted to reform the line. As they weathered the initial assault, the dwarfs locked their shields together and pushed back, hewing down the goblins with their axes and hammers, smashing helmeted heads into the faces of their foes and breaking bones with their steel shields.

A score of centuries of hatred boiled up from within the dwarf army and they lashed out vengefully. The explosion of violent anger erupted along the dwarf line, engulfing Barundin, who threw himself forward, axe raised.

'For Zhufbar!' he shouted, bringing his axe down into the hooded head of a goblin, shearing through its skull with a single blow. 'For Grimnir!'

Hacking to his right, he chopped through the upraised arm of another foe, and the return blow sheared the head from the shoulders of another. The rune axe blazed with power, trailing droplets of dark grobi blood that spattered into the king's beard. He did not notice it, for the battle rage was upon him. As the goblins closed in on him, Barundin's rune armour and shield rang with blows, although the gromril plates remained true and he felt nothing. Another wide swing of his axe tore down another two goblins, a bloody furrow carved across their chests, their tattered robes flung into the air.

Growling and panting, Barundin slashed again and again, his arm strengthening with every corpse hurled to the ground. All around him was bedlam as dwarf weapons cut through flesh and bone and goblin spears and swords broke upon dwarf-forged steel. The clattering of metal and wood, the bellowing of dwarf curses and the panicked shrieks of the grobi filled the cavern, resounding back off the walls, growing in volume.

Step-by-step, the dwarfs advanced into the hall, trampling over countless bodies of the goblins they had slain, spitting vengeful oaths at their hated foes. Their beards and armour doused with goblin blood, they were a horrific sight, their eyes fixed with the madness that only millennia of enmity can create. With every axe blow, with every hammer strike, the dwarfs repaid the goblins for each and every dwarf death at their hands, for every mine they had taken, for each hold they had overrun.

There was a purity in Barundin's fury; he felt a keen sense of satisfaction with each goblin death. The righteousness of his anger filled him with purpose and he easily ignored the soft, clumsy blows of his enemies, his axe hewing death all around him.

He was broken from his destructive reverie by panicked shouts to his left. Cutting down another handful of goblins, he broke free from the knot of grobi that had surrounded him and saw the cause of his kinsmen's dismay.

Towering above both dwarfs and grobi, eight gigantic trolls strode through the goblins' line, pushing and kicking aside their small masters. Each three times the height of a man, the stone trolls were lanky, their limbs taut with whipcord muscle, their fat bellies gawky and distended. As the trolls lumbered forwards, their blunt faces regarded the dwarfs stupidly, and they scratched idly at their ragged, pointed ears and swollen bellies, or dug clawed fingers into their bulbous noses. Their greyish-blue skin was thick and nobbled, and had a cracked appearance like old granite. One of the trolls stopped and looked around in dazed confusion, moaning loudly into the air, the goblins around it trying to urge it forwards with shouts and the hafts of their spears. The other trolls loped forward and broke into a long-strided run that covered the ground with surprising speed, dragging rocks and crude wooden clubs behind them.

As it reached the dwarf line, the foremost troll raised a massive fist above its head and brought it down upon the helm of one of the dwarfs, crushing it with a single blow and snapping the warrior's back. A backhanded smash crumpled the shield of another, driving shards of steel into the bearer's ribs. Another troll, a rock gripped between its hands, flattened another dwarf with its improvised weapon, and then stopped and bent over to peer dumbly at the twitching corpse.

Their momentum suddenly halted by the stone trolls, the dwarfs found themselves on the back foot. More and more goblins were swarming forwards, circling left and right, avoiding the left of the dwarf line where the trolls were wreaking horrendous damage on the dwarfs around them.

'My king!' called Durak, pounding his hammer into the chest of a goblin and pushing past the falling corpse. The gatekeeper turned and pointed behind him.

Turning to look, Barundin daw that the dwarfs had advanced away from the doorway into the hall, and there was a growing number of goblins gathering behind them.

'We'll be cut off,' said Durak.

'Not if we're victorious!' Barundin replied, catching a sword on his shield and then swinging his axe to decapitate the greenskin attacker.

'There's too many of them,' Durak yelled as a handful of goblins rushed forward to attack him.

Barundin grunted as he cut down another goblin, and risked a glance around. The fanatics and trolls had carved a bloody hole in the left flank of his host, and the warriors and quarrellers holding that side were in danger of being surrounded. His hammerers held the right and the cave squigs had all been slain, but they were being hard-pressed by the sheer numbers of the grobi. Every fibre in his body and soul urged him to keep fighting, but he mastered his natural hatred and realised that it would be folly to stay. Nothing would be achieved if they were cut off from their route back to the Ungdrin. He spied a hornblower not far away and hacked his way through half a dozen goblins to reach the dwarf's side.

'Sound the retreat,' Barundin said, spitting out the words with distaste.

'My king?' replied the hornblower, eyes widening.

'I said sound the retreat,' snarled Barundin.

As the king fended off more goblins, the hornblower raised his instrument to his lips and blew the notes. The horn blast echoed dully over the clash of weapons, the angry shouts of the dwarfs, the low moaning of the trolls and the screeches of dying goblins. It was picked up by other musicians along the line, and soon the dwarf army was reluctantly stepping back.

In a fighting withdrawal, falling back in small groups of a dozen or so warriors, the dwarfs made their way back to the edge of the hall and their line reformed into a semi-circle around the doorway. Barundin and his hammerers held the apex of the arc, the ironbreakers to his left and right, as the other dwarf warriors retreated back down the steps.

With a shout full of wrath and disappointment, Barundin sheared his axe through the gut of a troll, spilling out the noxious guts, the air filled with the acrid reek of its powerful stomach juices. As the goblins backed away from the spray of filth, Barundin and his rearguard broke from the fighting, quickly backing away through the gateway and onto the steps.

'Keep going!' he roared over his shoulder as he saw some of his warriors hesitating, thinking of turning back to aid their king. 'Secure the tunnels back to the Ungdrin!'

As STEADILY AND methodically as they had advanced, the dwarfs withdrew from the Great South Hall. At junctions and stairways, the ironbreakers and hammerers paused, holding the corridors and chambers against the goblin attacks while the rest of the army fell back towards the underway, taking up positions to defend. Covered by volleys from the quarrellers and thunderers, the king and his elite fighters broke away from the goblins and trolls.

For several more hours the dwarfs fought on, making the goblins pay a heavy price for their pursuit. In places, the tunnels were literally filled with the dead, as the dwarfs heaped the bodies of the grobi to make barricades to defend, or set fire to piles of corpses to block the goblins' advance. The two engineers that had accompanied Barundin made small charges of black powder and rigged traps that triggered rock falls and cave-ins on the heads of the following goblin horde, sealing off tunnels or choking them with the slain.

With the black-feathered arrows of the goblins skittering off the walls and ceiling around them, Barundin and his hammerers were the last to set foot on the stairwell winding back down to the Ungdrin. Barundin gave a last, sour look at the realm of Dukankor Grobkaz-a-Gazan, before turning and running down the steps.

He could hear the thundering of hundreds of feet not far behind him as the goblins poured down the stairs after the retreating dwarfs. Their harsh cackles and the flickering flames of their torches followed him.

Bursting out onto the highway from under the wide arched stairwell, Barundin was pleased to see that his host had organised themselves into something resembling an army, and stood waiting not far from the entranceway.

In particular, he saw the four barrels of an organ gun to his right, pointed directly at the stairway. Behind it he saw Garrek Silverweaver, one of the thane-engineers, holding a long lanyard. The engineer gave him a thumbs up as the king marched across the flags to take up a position near the centre of the line that stretched out, awaiting the goblins.

The first grobi burst into view, hurried on by their fellow goblins from behind. They were met by a hail of crossbow bolts and died to a goblin. More followed quickly and were greeted by a thunderous volley of hand-gun fire that tore them to shreds. Still not aware of the danger awaiting them, more goblins stormed into sight, almost tripping over themselves in their excitement.

'Skoff 'em!' Garrek shouted as he pulled the lanyard of the organ gun.

The war machine belched fire and smoke as the barrels fired in quick succession, hurling four fist-sized cannonballs at the mass of goblins. Packed into the confines of the stair entrance, there was no way to avoid the fusillade and the heavy iron balls ripped through the grobi, smashing heads, punching through chests and ripping off limbs. A tangled ruin of green flesh, dark blood and black robes littered the steps.

Aware that they would not catch their prey unprepared, the goblins halted out of sight, although a few came tumbling down the steps, followed by the childish cackling of the goblins that had pushed them. A lull began, and the dwarfs stood in silence, listening to the grating, high-pitched voices of the goblins as they argued amongst themselves about what to do. Now and then a poor volunteer came stumbling down the steps and would have only time to give a panicked shriek before being picked off by a bolt or bullet.

After more than an hour, amid much laughing and shouting, the goblins finally began to withdraw back up the steps. Barundin ordered the ironbreakers to follow a little way behind and ensure that the goblins were not making a false retreat, and to set guards at the top of the long stairway. With that done, he ordered his warriors to get some rest and food.

As the dwarfs broke out water, cheese, cold meats and stonebread from their packs, Barundin sought out Baldrin Gurnisson, the thane that had been left in charge of the reserve. He saw the elderly dwarf in conversation with one of the runners.

'What news from Hengrid?' the king asked as he walked towards the pair.

Both thane and runner turned towards Barundin, their expressions sorrowful.

'Come on, tell me!' snapped Barundin, who was in no mood for niceties. 'How fares Hengrid Dragonfoe and his army?'

'We don't know, my king,' said Baldrin, wringing a gnarled hand through the long braids of his beard.

'I couldn't find them,' explained the runner, the beardling's face a mask of worry. 'I looked and looked, and asked the others, but no one has seen or heard from them since they set out.'

'I did not know whether to march to their aid or not,' said Baldrin, shaking his head woefully. 'I can still go now, if you command it.'

Barundin took off his helmet and dragged his fingers through his matted, sweaty hair. His face was covered in grime and blood, his beard tangled and knotted. His armour was scratched and dented, stained with goblin blood and splashed with troll guts. He dropped his helmet, and in the quiet the clang of its falling rang along the Ungdrin like a death knell.

'No,' the king finally said. 'No, we must accept that they are probably lost to us now.'

'What are we to do?' asked the beardling, his eyes fearful.

Barundin turned away from them and looked at his army, which had lost over a tenth of its number that day. Many were already asleep, using their packs as pillows, while others sat in small groups, silent or talking in hushed whispers. A good number of them turned and looked at Barundin as they noticed the gaze of their king sweeping over them.

'What do we do now?' he said, his voice steadily rising. 'We do what we always do. We keep fighting!'

GRUDGE SIX

Barundin's Grudge

THE EMPTY HALL was disquieting to Barundin. Now scoured of the last of the grobi desecration, it was at least an imitation of its former glory, if not a replica. He stood upon the thane's platform, resting a hand on the arm of the newly carved throne that had been set there. A diamond the size of his fist pierced the top of the back of the chair, glinting in the light of the dwarf lanterns.

Voices echoed from beyond the hall's portal, once again hung with two mighty doors hewed from the thickest oak, and Barundin looked up to see Arbrek. The runelord leaned heavily on his staff, his flowing grey beard knotted to his belt to stop him tripping on it. With him were several of the thanes, Tharonin Grungrik amongst them, and Loremaster Thagri. The small group crossed the hall and walked up the steps. They stopped just before reaching the dais, except for Tharonin who strode up and stood before the king. Thagri had a book and writing chisel in his hands, and sat down upon the seat. He dipped the chisel in his inkwell and looked up at the king expectantly.

'Hail, Tharonin Grungrik, thane of Grungankor Stokril,' said Barundin, his voice stiff with formality.

Tharonin glanced over his shoulder at the other thanes and then looked back at Barundin.

'Some might say usurper,' he said with a wink. There was a tut from Arbrek at the thane's flippancy.

Barundin pressed on. 'Let it be now recorded that I, King Barundin of Zhufbar, hereby and forthwith bestow the halls, corridors, chambers,

123

mineworkings and all associated lands and properties of Grungankor Stokril to the stewardship of Thane Tharonin Grungrik,' said Barundin. 'In recognition for the valorous acts of his clan in the reclaiming of these lands, this deed to him shall be passed on to his descendants forever, or until such time as the thane of the Grungriks breaks oath with the king of Zhufbar.'

'I, Thane Tharonin Grungrik, do solemnly accept the stewardship of the halls, corridors, chambers, mineworkings and all associated lands and properties of Grungankor Stokril,' replied Tharonin. 'I hereby renew my oath of fealty to the King of Zhufbar, Barundin, and that of my clan. These halls we will protect with our lives. These mines we shall work diligently and with due care, and give over not less than one tenth of any such ores, precious metals and valuable stones derived thereof to the king of Zhufbar, in repayment for his protection and patronage.'

Tharonin stood beside the king as Thagri pushed himself to his feet and walked up the steps. He held out the pen chisel to Barundin, who took it and signed his mark underneath the new entry in the Book of Realms. Tharonin did likewise, and then the book was passed around the six other thanes, who each signed witness to the pledges. Finally Arbrek and Thagri countersigned the agreement, and the deal was sealed.

'Thank you, my friend,' said Barundin, laying a hand on Tharonin's shoulder. 'Without you, I don't know if I would have had the strength to keep going.'

'Pah!' snorted Tharonin. 'The blood of our kings is thick in your veins, Barundin. You have a gut of stone, and no mistake.'

The clumping of iron-shod boots and voices raised in laughter echoed around the hall as a group of ironbreakers entered from the western doorway. At their front was Hengrid Dragonfoe, a goblin head in each hand. Droplets of blood dribbled from the creature's severed necks.

'Hoy there, we've just had the floor cleaned!' snapped Tharonin. 'Show some manners!'

'Well, that's gratitude for you,' said Hengrid with a grin, handing the heads to one of his comrades and marching quickly across the dark stone flags to the foot of the steps. 'Here's you accepting your new realm, while I'm out there protecting it for you. And if you don't want your inauguration presents, I'll keep them myself. My cousin, Korri, he's a dab hand at taxidermy. Reckon them two would look good flanking my mantel.'

'Has anybody told you that you're a bloodthirsty thug?' said Tharonin, smiling as he walked down the steps.

Clapping a hand to Tharonin's shoulder, Hengrid walked up the steps, shaking hands and nodded in greeting to the other thanes. He gave a respectful bow to Arbrek, who merely glowered back, and then stepped up in front of Barundin.

'Are the halls of Grungankor Stokril now safe?' the king asked.

'I swear by my grandfather's metal eyeball, there's not a grobi within two days of where we stand,' said Hengrid. 'It's been a long time coming, but I think we can safely say that you can add conqueror of Dukankor Grobkaz-a-Gazan to your list of achievements.'

'They will come again,' warned Arbrek, glaring at Tharonin. 'Keep a sharp watch and a sharper axe close by, lest that name not be consigned to history.'

'It will be a lifetime before the grobi dare come within sight of these halls,' said Barundin. 'As I swore, they have learned to fear us again.'

'A lifetime, aye, it will be,' said Hengrid. He leaned forward and pointed at Barundin's beard. 'Is that a grey hair I see? Have these past forty-two years of war aged the youthful king?'

'It is not age, it is worry,' growled Barundin. 'You could have been the death of me, disappearing for months, years at a time! Retaking the north gate and besieged by goblins for three years – what were you thinking?'

'I got carried away, that's all,' laughed Hengrid. 'Are you going to keep mentioning that every time I see you? It's been forty years, for Grimnir's sake. Let it go.'

'It'll be forty more years before I forgive you,' said Barundin. 'And forty more after that before I can forget the voice of your wife in my ear, accusing me of abandoning you every day for three years. I shudder in my sleep when I think about it.'

'I can't stand around here gossiping, there's preparations to be made,' grumbled Arbrek, turning away.

'Preparations?' asked Hengrid, darting an inquiring glance at the thanes. They shuffled nervously, looking pointedly at the king.

Hengrid shrugged and turned back to Barundin, a look of mock innocence on his face. 'Is there something important happening?'

'You know very well that it is my hundred and seventieth birthday tomorrow,' said Barundin. 'And you better bring something better than a couple of grobi heads. This will be a celebration of your victories as much as my birthday, so make sure you wash that blood from your beard before you come. I hope you have a speech ready.'

'A speech?' said Tharonin with a gasp. 'Grungni's beard, I knew I'd forgotten something!'

They watched as the ageing thane hurried down the steps and disappeared from the hall.

Barundin laid an arm across Hengrid's shoulders and walked him down the steps. 'And you're not to get drunk and sing that damnable song again,' he warned.

HENGRID SWAYED FROM side to side in beat to the clapping and the thumping of tankards on tables. As he walked along the table he stumbled over ale jugs and plates covered with bones and others remains of the feast. Beer swilled from the mug in his hand, spilling down the front of his jerkin and sticking in his beard. With a roar, he upended the tankard over his face, and then spluttered for a moment before his voice boomed out in song. Barundin covered his face and looked away.

A lusty young lad at his anvil stood beating,
Lathered in sweat and all covered in mucket.
When in came a rough lass, all smiles and good greeting,
And asked if he could see to her rusty old bucket.

'I can,' cried the lad, and they went off together,
Along to the lass's halls they did go.
He stripped off his apron, 'twas hot work in thick leather,
The fire was kindled and he soon had to blow.

Her fellow, she said, was no good for such banging,
His hammer and his arms were spent long ago.
The lad said, 'Well mine now, we won't leave you hanging,
As I'm sure you'll no doubt all very soon know.'

Many times did his mallet, by vigorous heating,
Grow too soft to work on such an old pail,
But when it was cooled he kept on a-beating,
And he worked on it quickly, his strength not to fail.

When the lad was all done, the lass was all tearful:
'Oh, what would I give could my fellow do so.
Good lad with your hammer, I'm ever so fearful,
I ask could you use it once more ere you go?'

Even Barundin was laughing uproariously by the time Hengrid had finished, and laughed even more heartily when the thane, on attempting to clamber down from the table, slipped and fell headlong to the floor with a crash and a curse. Still chuckling, Barundin pulled himself up on to the table and raised his hands. Quiet descended, of a sort, punctuated by snorts and belches, the glug of beer taps and numerous other sounds made by any group of drunken dwarfs.

'My wonderful friends and kin!' he began, to an uproarious shout of approval. 'My people of wonderful Zhufbar, you have my thanks. There is no prouder day for a king to be amongst such wonderful company. We have wonderful beer to drink in plentiful amounts, wonderful food and wonderful song.'

His face took on a sincere expression and he looked down sternly at the still-prostrate form of Hengrid.

'Well, perhaps not such wonderful song,' he said, to much clapping and laughter. 'There have been many speeches, fine oratory from my great friends and allies, but there is one more that you must listen to.'

There were groans from some of the younger members of the crowd, and cheers from the older ones.

In the short silence before Barundin spoke, the distinctive sound of snoring could be heard, and Barundin turned to look in its direction. Arbrek was at the foot of the table, his head against his chest. With a snort, the runelord jerked awake, and sensing the king's gaze stood up and raised his tankard.

'Bravo!' he cried. 'Hail to King Barundin!'

'King Barundin!' the crowd echoed enthusiastically. Arbrek slumped down and his head began to nod toward his chest once more.

'As I was saying,' said Barundin, pacing up the table. 'We are here to celebrate my one hundred and seventieth birthday.'

There was much cheering, and cries of, 'Good Old Barundin', and, 'Just a beardling!'

'I was little over a hundred years old when I became king,' said Barundin, his voice solemn, his sudden serious mood quieting the boisterous feasters. 'My father was cut down in battle, betrayed by a weak manling. For nearly seventy years I have toiled and fought, and for nearly seventy years you have toiled and fought beside me. It has been for one reason, and one reason alone, that we have endured these hardships: retribution! My father now walks the Halls of the Ancestors, but he cannot find peace while his betrayers still have not been brought to book. As I declared that day, so now do I renew my oath, and declare the right of grudge against the Vessals of Stirland. Before the year is out, we will demand apology and recompense for the wrongs they have done against us. My brave and vigorous people, who have kept faith with me through these hard times, what say you now?'

'Avenge King Throndin!' came one shout.

'Grudge!' bellowed a dwarf from the back of the hall. 'Grudge!'

'We'll be with you!' came another cry.

'Sing us a song!' came a slurred voice from behind Barundin, and he turned to see Hengrid slouched across the bench, a full mug of ale in his hand again.

'A song!' demanded a chorus of voices from all over the hall.

'A song about what?' asked Barundin with a grin.

'Grudges!'

'Gold!'

'Beer!'

Barundin thought for a moment, and then bent down and grabbed the shoulder of Hengrid's jerkin, dragging him back to the tabletop.

'Here's one you should all know,' said Barundin. He began to beat out a rhythm with a stamping foot, and soon the hall was shuddering again.

Well it's all for me grog, me jolly, jolly grog
It's all for me beer and tobacco
For I spent all me gold on good maps of old
But me future's looking no better.

Where are me boots, me noggin', noggin' boots?
They're all gone for beer and tobacco
For the heels are worn out and the toes kicked about
And the soles are looking no better.

Where's me shirt, me noggin', noggin' shirt?
It's all gone for beer and tobacco
For the collar's so thin, and the sleeves are done in
And the pockets are looking no better.

Where's me bed, me noggin', noggin' bed?
It's all gone for beer and tobacco
No pillows for a start and now the sheet's torn apart
And the springs are looking no better.

Where's me wench, me noggin', noggin' wench?
She's all gone for beer and tobacco
She's healthy, no doubt, and her bosom's got clout
But her face is looking no better!

THE CELEBRATIONS LASTED for several more days, during which Tharonin finally delivered his speech, thanking Barundin for his kingship and volunteering to act as messenger to the Vessals. After his sterling work in tracking down Wanazaki, Dran the Reckoner was brought in by Barundin to assist Tharonin in his expedition. Dran earned his keep by settling old debts and grudges, but for Barundin's missions, he volunteered his services free of charge.

When pressed by Barundin about this uncharacteristically generous offer, Dran was at first reluctant to discuss his reasons. However, the king's persistent inquiries finally forced the Reckoner to share his motives. They were sitting in the king's chambers, sharing a pitcher of ale by the fireside, and had been discussing Dran's plan to bring the Vessals to justice.

'Proper form must be observed,' insisted Barundin. 'They must be left in no doubt as to the consequences of failing to comply with my demands for restitution.'

'I know how to handle these matters,' Dran assured him. 'I will serve notice to the Vessals, and will warn them of your resolve. What exactly are your demands?'

'A full apology, for a start,' said Barundin. 'The current holder of the barony is to abdicate his position and take exile from his lands. We will take custody of the body of Baron Silas Vessal and dispose of it in a way fitting to such a traitor. Lastly, for the death of a king, there can be no price too high, but I will settle for a full one-half of the wealth of the Vessals and their lands.'

'And if they do not agree to your terms?' asked Dran, taking notes on a small piece of parchment.

'Then I shall be forced to violent resolution,' said Barundin with a scowl. 'I will unseat them from their position, destroy their castle and scatter them. Look, just make them realise I'm in no mood to be bargained with. These manlings will try to get out of it, but they can't. Vessal's despicable behaviour must be atoned for, and if they can't move themselves to make that atonement, I will make them regret it.'

'Seems pretty reasonable,' said Dran with a nod. 'I will have Thagri write a formal declaration of this intent, and Tharonin and I will deliver it to those dogs in Uderstir.'

'They have forty days to reply,' added Barundin. 'I want them to know that I'm not messing about. Forty days, and then they'll have the army of Zhufbar at their gate.'

'It's my job to make sure it doesn't come to that,' said Dran, folding the parchment into a small packet and placing it in a pouch at his belt. 'But if it does, I'll be standing there beside you.'

'Yes, and for no gain as far as I can tell,' said Barundin, offering more ale. 'What's in this for you?'

'Why does there have to be something for me in the deal?' asked Dran, proffering his mug. 'Can't I offer my services to a just cause?'

'You?' snorted Barundin. 'You would ask for gold just to visit your grandmother. Tell me, why are you helping with this? If you don't answer, consider your services not needed.'

Dran did not reply for a while, but sat in silence, sipping his beer. Barundin continued to stare intently at the Reckoner, until finally Dran put his mug down with a sigh and looked at the king.

'I've amassed a good deal of gold over the years,' said Dran. 'More even than most folk think I have. But I'm getting older, and I'm tiring of the road. I want to take a wife and raise a family.'

'You want to settle down?' said Barundin. 'A great wanderer like you?'

'I started because I wanted to see justice done,' said Dran. 'Then I did it for the money. Nowadays? Nowadays, I don't know why I do it. There's easier ways to earn gold. Perhaps have some sons and teach them my craft, who knows?'

'What's that got to do with the Vessals and my grudge?' asked Barundin. 'It's not like you're after a single last payoff to set yourself up.'

'I want a good wife,' said Dran, staring down into his cup. 'For all my success, I'm not that widely regarded. Being a Reckoner doesn't get you many friends, or much recognition. I'll be moving on, perhaps to Karak Norn or Karak Hirn. But for all my wealth, I don't have much to offer for a wife, and that's where you come in.'

'Go on,' said Barundin, filling his own mug and taking a gulp of frothy ale.

'I want to be a thane,' said Dran, looking deep into the king's eyes. 'If

I arrive as Thane Dran of Zhufbar to go with my chests of gold, I'll be beating them off with a hammer.'

'Why didn't you mention this before?' asked Barundin.

'I didn't want to do it this way,' said Dran with a shrug. 'I hoped that if I helped you with this, and perhaps if you wanted to show a mark of your gratitude, I could ask for it then. I didn't want it to sound like naming a price by different means.'

'Well, I'm sorry then that I forced you to answer,' said Barundin. 'Don't worry too much about it. I remember that you were the first on his feet to protect me when we found Wanazaki, and a king's memory does not fade quickly. Do your job well with this matter, and I'll think of some way to reward you.'

Barundin raised his mug and held it towards Dran. The Reckoner hesitated for a moment and then raised his own cup and clinked it against the king's.

'Here's to a good king,' said Dran.

'Here's to justice,' replied Barundin.

IT WAS SEVERAL more days before Tharonin and Dran set out, the formalities of the grudge and reparations having been arranged with Thagri, and preparations for the expedition made. The aim of the journey was not war, so Tharonin took only his personal guard, some hundred and twenty longbeards, whose axes had made much fell work during the wars against the skaven and grobi. Dran mustered a few dozen rangers to act as his entourage, more for company than any other reason.

It was a solemn occasion as the group set out. Barundin bade them farewell from the main gate of Zhufbar, and watched for several hours until they were out of sight. He returned to his chambers, where he found Arbrek waiting for him.

The runelord was napping in a deep armchair near the fire, snoring loudly. Barundin sat down next to Arbrek, and was deep in thought for a long time, not wishing to waken the runelord from his rest.

Barundin pondered what might happen over the coming days. There was a chance, albeit slim to his mind that, Tharonin's expedition would come under attack from the Vessals and their warriors. If that happened, he would march straight away to Uderstir and raze their keep to the ground. More likely would be refusal. The thought of waging war against men of the Empire genuinely pained him, for they and the dwarfs had a long history together, and few conflicts. Despite the ancestral bonds between his kind and the Empire, Barundin knew he would not balk at doing his duty.

Eventually Arbrek roused himself with a snort, and spent a moment gazing around the room in slight confusion. Finally, his eyes focussed on Barundin, their harsh glare not at all dulled by his age.

'Ah, there you are,' said the runelord, straightening in the chair. 'I've been waiting for you. Where have you been?'

Barundin bit back his first retort, remembering not to be disrespectful of the aged runelord. 'I was seeing Tharonin off,' he explained. 'Nobody sent word that you wanted to see me, or I would have come quicker.'

'Nobody sent word, because I gave no word to send,' said Arbrek. The runelord leaned forward, resting his elbows on his knees. 'I'm getting old.'

'There's still years left in your boiler,' said Barundin, the reply made without hesitation.

'No,' said Arbrek, shaking his head. 'No, there is not.'

'What are you saying?' said Barundin, concerned.

'You have been a fine king,' said Arbrek. 'Your forefathers will be proud. Your mother will be proud.'

'Thank you,' said Barundin, not sure what else to say to such unexpected praise. Arbrek was as traditional as they got, and so expected anyone younger than him to be unsteady and somewhat worthless.

'I mean it,' said the runelord. 'You've a heart and a wisdom beyond your years. You've led your people on a dangerous path, taken them into war. If, for a moment, I thought this vain ambition on your part, I would have spoken out, turned the council against you.'

'Well, I'm glad I had your support,' said Barundin. 'Without it, I think many more of the thanes would have been difficult to win over to my cause.'

'I did not do it for you,' said Arbrek, sitting up. 'I did it for the same reasons you did. It was for your father, not for you.'

'Of course,' said Barundin. 'These long years, it has always been for my father, to settle the grudge I declared the day that he died.'

'And now that is almost over,' said Arbrek. 'Soon you will have settled it.'

'Yes,' said Barundin with a smile. 'Within weeks, the grudge will be no more, one way or another.'

'And then what will you do?' asked Arbrek, studying the king's face intently.

'What do you mean?' said Barundin, standing. 'Beer?'

Arbrek nodded and did not speak while Barundin walked to the door and called to his servants for a small cask of ale. As he sat down again, he glanced at the runelord. His penetrating gaze had not wavered.

'I don't understand. What do you mean,' said Barundin. 'What will I do?'

'This grudge of yours, it has been everything to you,' said Arbrek. 'As much as you were dedicated, devoted to your father in life, avenging his death has become your driving force, the steam within the engine of your heart. What will drive you when it is done? What will you do now?'

'I hadn't really thought about it,' said Barundin, scratching at his beard.

'It has been so long… I sometimes thought there would never be a time without the grudge.'

'And that is what concerns me,' said Arbrek. 'You have done well as king until now. The true test of your reign, though, will be what you do next.'

'I will rule my people as best I can,' said Barundin, confused by the intent of Arbrek's questioning. 'With luck, in peace.'

'Peace?' said Barundin. 'Pah! Our people have not known peace for thousands of years. Perhaps you are not as wise as you seem.'

'Surely a king does not court war and strife for his people?' said Barundin.

'No, he does not.' replied Arbrek.

He paused as one of the king's servants entered, carrying a silver tray with two tankards upon it. He was followed by one of the maids from the brewery, carrying a small keg. She set it on the table and then left.

Barundin took a tankard and leaned over to put it under the tap. Arbrek laid a hand on his arm and stopped him.

'Why so hasty?' said the runelord. 'Let it settle awhile. There is no rush.'

Barundin sat back, toying with the tankard, turning it over in his fingers, looking at the way the firelight glimmered off the gold thread inlaid into the thick clay cup. He risked a glance at Arbrek, who was contemplating the keg. Barundin knew better than to speak; to do so would risk the runelord's ire for hastiness.

'You are shrewd, and you have a good fighting arm,' Arbrek said eventually, still looking at the firkin. 'Your people admire and respect you. Do not let peace lull you into idleness, for it will dull your mind as much as battle dulls a poor blade. Do not seek war, you are right, but do not run from it. Hard times are not always of our own making.'

Barundin said nothing, but simply nodded. With an unusually spry push, Arbrek was on his feet. He took a step towards the door, and then looked back. He smiled at Barundin's perplexed expression.

'I have made a decision,' said Arbrek.

'You have?' said Barundin. 'What about?'

'Come with me. There is something I want you to see,' said Arbrek. There was a twinkle in the runelord's eye that excited Barundin and he stood swiftly and followed him out the door.

Arbrek led Barundin through the hold, taking him through the chambers and halls towards his smithy which lay within the highest levels. In all his years, Barundin had never been in this part of the hold, for it was the domain of the runesmiths. It did not seem any different from most of the rest of Zhufbar, although the sound of hammering echoed more loudly from behind the closed doors.

At the end of a particular corridor, the king found himself in a dead end. He was about to ask Arbrek what he was up to, but before he could the runelord had raised a finger to his lips with a wink. With careful ceremony, Arbrek reached into his robes and pulled a small silver key from its depths. Barundin looked around but could see no lock.

'If dwarf locks were so easy to find, they would not be secret, would they?' said Arbrek with a chuckle. 'Watch carefully, for very few of our folk have ever seen this.'

The runelord held the key just in front of his lips, and appeared to be blowing on it. However, as Barundin looked on, he saw that Arbrek was whispering, ever so softly. For several minutes he spoke to the key, occasionally running a loving finger along its length. In the silver, the king saw thin lines appear, narrower than a hair. They glowed with a soft blue light, just enough to highlight the runelord's features in azure tints.

Barundin realised that he had been concentrating so hard on the key, that he had not noticed anything else. With a start, he snapped his attention away from the runelord and glanced around. They were still in a dead-end tunnel, but where the end had been to his left a moment ago, it was now to his right. The walls emitted a golden aura and he saw that there were no lanterns, but more of the thin traceries of runes that had been on the key, covering the walls and providing the illumination.

'These chambers were built by the greatest of the runelords of Zhufbar,' said Arbrek, closing a gnarled hand around the key and deftly hiding it within the folds of his cloak. He took the king by the arm and started to lead him along the corridor. 'They were first dug under the instructions of Durlok Ringbinder, in the days when the mountains were still young, and Valaya herself was said to have taught him the secrets he used. During the Time of the Goblin Wars, they were sealed for centuries, and it was thought that all knowledge of them was lost, for no runelord had ever committed their secrets to written lore. But it was not so, for in distant Karaz-a-Karak, the runelord Skargim lived, but he had not been born there. He was born and raised in Zhufbar, and upon being released from his duties by the high king, he returned and unearthed these chambers. He was the grandfather of my tutor, Fengil Silverbeard.'

'They're beautiful,' said Barundin, gazing around.

'Yes they are,' said Arbrek with a smile. 'But these are just tunnels. Wait until you see my workshop.'

The room to which Barundin was led was not large, although the ceiling was quite high, three times his height. It was simply furnished, with a grate, an armchair and small workbench. Upon the bench was a miniature anvil, no larger than a fist, and small mallets, pincers and other tools. By the fire was a clockwork bellows and many pails of coal. The wall opposite was decorated with a breath-taking mural of the mountains swathed in clouds.

And then movement caught Barundin's eye. One of the clouds in the painting had definitely moved. He staggered, amazed, across the room, Arbrek following close behind. As he stood a few paces from the wall, he could see downwards, along the mountainside of Zhufbar itself.

Hesitantly, he stretched out an arm, and felt nothing. He felt dizzy and started to topple forward. Arbrek grabbed his belt and hauled him back.

'It's a window,' said Barundin, dazed by the magnificence of the sight.

'More than a window,' said Arbrek. 'And yet, oddly, less. It's just a hole, cut through the hard rock. There are runes carved into the ground outside that we cannot see from here. They ward away the elements, surer than any glass.'

'It is a wonderful sight,' said Barundin, gathering himself. From this high in the mountain, he could see far out across Black Water, the lake itself hidden by mist, and the mountains beyond. 'Thank you for showing it to me.'

'This isn't what I wanted to show you,' said Arbrek with a scowl. 'No, the view is nice enough, but a good view does not make a good king.'

The runelord walked to the corner of his room and took a bundle wrapped in dark sack cloth. 'This is what I wanted you to see,' he said, handing the package to Barundin. 'Open it, have a look.'

Barundin took the sacking, and there was almost no weight to it at all. He pulled away the cloth, revealing a metal haft, and then a single-bladed axe head. Tossing the sacking aside, he hefted the axe in one hand. His arm moved as freely as if it were carrying nothing more than a feather. There were several runes etched into the blade of the axe, which glittered with the same magical light as the tunnels outside.

'My last and finest work,' said Arbrek. 'Your father commissioned it from me the day that you were born.'

'One hundred and seventy years?' said Barundin. 'You've kept it that long?'

'No, no, no,' said Arbrek, taking the axe from Barundin. 'I have only just finished it! It has my own master rune upon it, the only weapon in the world. That alone took me twenty years to devise and another fifty before it was finished. These other runes are not easy to craft either: the Rune of Swift Slaying, the Rune of Severing, and particularly the Rune of Ice.'

'It is a wondrous gift,' said Barundin. 'I cannot thank you enough.'

'Thank your father, he paid for it,' said Arbrek gruffly, handing the axe back to Barundin. 'And thank me by wielding it well when you need to.'

'Does it have a name?' asked Barundin, stroking a hand across the flat of the polished blade.

'No,' said Arbrek, looking away and gazing out across the mountains. 'I thought I would leave that to you.'

'I have never had to name anything before,' said Barundin.

'Then do not try to do it quickly,' said Arbrek. 'Think on it, and the right name will come. A name that will last for generations.'

IT WAS SEVERAL days later when Tharonin and Dran returned. They had travelled to Uderstir and delivered the king's demands. Silas Vessal had been dead for over a hundred and fifty years and his great-grandson, Obious Vessal, was now baron, and an old man himself. He had pleaded with Dran to send his profuse apologies to the king for his forefather's damnable actions. However, upon the matter of his great-grandfather's body and the monies to be paid, he had given no answer.

It was the opinion of Dran that the new baron would renege on any deal that he struck, and that he could not be trusted. Tharonin, although he agreed in part with the Reckoner's view, urged Barundin to give the baron every chance to make recompense. For a manling, he had seemed sincere, or if not sincere, then suitably afraid of the consequences of inaction.

'Forty days I give him,' said Barundin to his council of advisors. 'Forty days I said, and forty days he shall have.'

Troubling news came only a few days later. There were shortages in the furnace rooms. The timber that was usually sent each month by ancient trade agreement from the Empire town of Konlach had not arrived. Although there was still coal aplenty, many of the engineers regarded using coal as a waste for many of their projects, since there were usually so many spare trees to cut down instead.

It was Godri Ongurbazum who had the most concerns. It was his clan that was responsible for the agreement, one that had been nearly unbroken for centuries, incomplete only during the dark times of the Great War against Chaos. There was no good reason, as far as Godri could discern, for the men of Konlach to break faith.

In one council meeting the thane of the Ongurbazumi argued against Barundin setting off with the army to remonstrate with Obious Vessal. He brought the argument that the trouble with Konlach was more urgent, for if no other supply of timber could be secured, the forges might have to stand cold for want of fuel.

Barundin would have none of it. When the forty days were up, the army of Zhufbar would go and take by force what the king was owed. The debate raged for several nights, with Godri and his allies arguing that after so long, an extra month or two would not be amiss. Barundin countered that it was because it had taken so long to resolve the grudge that he wanted to act as swiftly as possible and have it done with.

In the end, Barundin, losing his temper completely with the trade clan's leader, shouted him out of the audience chamber, and then dismissed the rest of the council. For three days he sat upon his throne and fumed. On the fourth day, he called them back.

'I will have no more argument against my course of action,' Barundin told the assembled thanes.

Arbrek arrived, mumbling about lack of sleep, but Barundin assured him that what he had to say was worth the runelord being disturbed. He drew out the rune axe that had been given to him, much to the awe and interest of the thanes. They looked at the craftsmanship of the blade, passing it amongst themselves, cooing delightedly and praising Arbrek.

'Fie to timber contracts!' said Barundin. 'Skaven and grobi have not stood in our way, and I'll not let a few damn trees halt us now. I have gathered you here to witness the naming of my new axe, and to assure you that if they do not comply with my demands, the first enemies to taste its wrath will be the Vessals of Uderstir.'

He took back the enchanted weapon and held it out in front of him. The lantern light shimmered in the aura surrounding the blade.

'I name it Grudgesettler.'

THERE WAS NO improvement in the timber situation and for the forty days until the Vessals' deadline, Barundin was under constant pressure from the trading clans and the engineers to put his grudge on hold once more to resolve the issue with Konlach. Although he was always polite about the matter, he made it clear that he would brook no more delays and no more disagreement.

On the eve before the ultimatum expired, Barundin addressed the warriors of the hold. He explained to them that the hour of their vengeance was almost at hand. He warned that they might be called upon to perform fell deeds in the name of his father, and to this they responded with a roar of approval. Many of them had fought beside King Throndin when he fell, or lost clan members to the orcs when Silas Vessal had quit the field without fighting. They were as eager as Barundin to make the noble family of the Empire atone for their forefather's cowardice.

It was a cold morning that saw the dwarf army setting out, heading westwards into Stirland. Autumn was fast approaching, and in the high peaks snow was gathering, frosting the highest reaches of the scattered pine woods that dotted the mountains around Zhufbar

They made swift progress, but did not force the march. Barundin wanted his army to arrive eager and full of strength. With them came a chugging locomotive of the Engineers Guild, towing three cannons behind it. Where once the machine had been a source of wonder and awe to the soldiers of Uderstir, it would become a symbol of dread should they choose to resist Barundin's demands again.

On the fourth day they arrived at the castle, the tops of its walls visible over a line of low hills some miles in the distance. It was not a large fortress, barely a keep with a low curtain wall. A green banner adorned with a griffon holding an axe fluttered madly from the flag pole of the central tower.

Smoke filled the air, and occasionally there was a distant reverberating thump, as of a cannon firing. As the head of the dwarf army crossed the crest of the line of hills, Barundin and the others were greeted by an unexpected sight.

An army encircled Uderstir. Under banners of green, yellow and black, regiments of halberdiers and spearmen stood behind makeshift siege workings, avoiding the desultory fire of handguns and crossbows from the castle walls. The noise had indeed been a cannon, ensconced in a revetment built of mud and reinforced with gabions made from woven wood and filled with rocks. The nearest tower was heavily damaged, its upper parts having fallen away under the bombardment, leaving a pile of debris at the base of the wall. Bowmen unleashed tired volleys against the walls whenever a head appeared, their arrows clattering uselessly from the old, moss-covered stones.

Several dozen horses were corralled out of range of the walls, and the armoured figures of knights could be seen walking about the camp or sitting in groups around the fires. It was immediately obvious that the siege had been going on for some time now, and that dreary routine had become the norm. Whoever was leading the attacking army was in no hurry to assault the strong walls of Uderstir.

Barundin gave the order for his army to form up from their column of march, even as the dwarfs were spied and the camp below was suddenly filled with furious activity. As the war machines of the dwarfs were unlimbered and brought forward, a group of five riders mounted up and rode quickly in their direction.

Barundin marched forward with his hammerers, flanked to the left by Arbrek and to the right by Hengrid Dragonfoe, who held aloft the ornate silver and gold standard of Zhufbar. They stopped just as the slope away down the hill began to grow steeper, and awaited the riders. To their left, Dran and the hold's rangers began to make their way down the slope, following the channel of a narrow stream, out of sight of the enemy camp.

The riders came up at a gallop, riding beneath a banner that was split with horizontal lines of green and black, with a lion rampant picked out in gold, standing atop a bridge. On an embroidered scroll beneath the device was the name 'Konlach'.

The riders stopped a little way off, perhaps fifty yards, and eyed the dwarfs suspiciously, their horses trotting back and forth. Barundin could see that they carried long spears, and carried heavy pistols in holsters upon their belts, in their boots and on their saddles.

'Who approaches King Barundin of Zhufbar?' shouted Hengrid, planting the standard firmly in the ground and pulling his single-bladed axe from its sheath.

One of the riders came forward to within a spear's throw of the king. He was dressed in a heavy coat, with puffed and slashed sleeves, showing green material beneath its black leather. He wore a helmet decorated with two feathers, one green and one black, and its visor was pulled down, shaped in the snarling face of a lion. He raised a hand and lifted his visor, revealing a surprisingly young face.

'I am Theoland, herald to Baron Gerhadricht of Konlach,' he said, his voice clear and loud. 'Are you friend to Uderstir? Have you come to lift our siege?'

'I most certainly am not a friend of Uderstir!' bellowed Barundin, stepping forward. 'Those thieves and cowards are my enemies through and through.'

'Then you are friends with Baron Gerhadricht,' Theoland said. He waved a hand to a large green and yellow pavilion at the centre of the camp. 'Please, come with me. My lord awaits you in his tent. He offers his word that no harm will come to you.'

'The words of manlings are meaningless,' said Hengrid, brandishing his axe fiercely. 'That is why we are here!'

Theoland did not flinch. 'If you would but come with me, this can all be settled quickly, I am sure,' said the herald, turning his horse. He looked over his shoulder at the dwarfs. 'Bring as many retainers as you feel comfortable with. You will not find our hospitality lacking.'

As the riders cantered away, Barundin looked to Hengrid and Arbrek. The old runelord simply shrugged and grunted.

Hengrid gave a nod towards the camp. 'They'll not try anything daft with another army arrayed on their flank,' said the thane. 'I'll come with you if you like.'

'No, I want you to stay and keep command of the army should I not return,' said Barundin. 'I'll go alone. Let's not show these manlings too much respect.'

'Fair enough,' said Hengrid.

Barundin took a deep breath and walked down the hill, following in the hoof prints left by the riders. He ignored the stares of the soldiers and peasants as he strode purposefully through the camp, his gilded armour gleaming in the autumn sun, which peeked occasionally from behind the low clouds.

He came to the tent of the baron and found Theoland and his guard of honour waiting outside. The baron's flag fluttered from a pole next to the pavilion. Without a word, Theoland bowed and held open the tent flap for Barundin to enter.

The material of the tent was thick and did not allow much light inside. Instead, two braziers, fuming and sputtering, illuminated the interior. The floor was covered with scattered rugs, hides and furs, and low chairs were arranged in a circle around the near end of the pavilion. The remainder was hidden behind heavy velvet drapes.

The tent was empty except for Barundin and a solitary man, wizened with age, who sat crooked upon one of the chairs, his eyes peering at the newly arrived dwarf. He raised a palsied hand and gestured to a small table to one side, on which stood a ewer and some crystal glasses.

'Wine?' said the man.

'No thanks, I'm not staying long,' said Barundin.

The man nodded slowly, and seemed to drift away again.

'Are you Baron Gerhadricht?' asked Barundin, walking forward and standing in the middle of the rugs.

'I am,' replied the baron. 'What business does a dwarf king seek in Uderstir?'

'Well, first off, I've a matter to bring to you,' said Barundin. 'You're from Konlach, right?'

'I am the Baron of Konlach, that is correct,' said Gerhadricht.

'Then where's our timber?' said Barundin, crossing his arms.

'You've come all this way with an army for some timber?' said the baron with a laugh. 'Timber? Can't you see we've got a war to fight? We don't have any spare timber!'

'We have an agreement,' insisted Barundin. 'I don't care about your wars. We have a contract between us.'

'Once Uderstir is mine, we shall make up the deficit, I assure you,' said the baron. 'Now, is that all?'

'One does not dismiss a dwarf king so easily!' snarled Barundin. 'I'm not here for your timber. I'm here for those bloody cowards, the Vessals. I mean to storm Uderstir and take what is mine by right of grudge.'

'What is yours?' said Gerhadricht with a hiss. 'What claim do you have to Uderstir? Mine goes back many generations, to the alignment of Konlach and Uderstir by my great-great-great uncle. Uderstir is mine by right, usurped by Silas Vessal with bribery and murder.'

The tent flap opened and Theoland entered. 'I heard raised voices,' he said, looking between the baron and Barundin. 'What are you arguing about?'

'Your inheritance, dear boy,' said Gerhadricht. He looked at Barundin. 'My youngest nephew, Theoland. My only surviving kin. Can you believe that?'

'He looks a fine enough lad for a manling,' said Barundin, eyeing up the baron's herald. 'So you think you have a claim to Uderstir?'

'My great-great-great grandfather was once baron here,' said Theoland. 'It is mine by right of inheritance through my uncle and his marriage.'

'Well, you can have whatever's left of Uderstir once I'm through with the Vessals,' said Barundin. 'I have declared right of grudge, and that's far more important than your manling titles and inheritances. Baron Silas Vessal betrayed my father, leaving him on the field of battle to be killed by orcs. I demand recompense and recompense I shall get!'

'Grudge?' said the baron with scorn. 'What about rights of law? You are a dwarf, and you are in the lands of the Empire. Your wishes are of no concern to me. If you agree to assist me in the shortening of this siege, I will gladly hand over the Vessals to your justice.'

'And one half of the coffers of Uderstir,' said Barundin.

'Ridiculous!' snapped Gerhadricht. 'You would have my nephew be a pauper baron, like one of those scrabbling wretches of the Border Princes or Estalia? Ridiculous!'

'Uncle, perhaps...' started Theoland, but he was cut off by the baron.

'There will be no more bargaining,' said Gerhadricht. 'That's my best offer.'

Barundin bristled and looked at Theoland, who shrugged helplessly. Baron Gerhadricht appeared to be contemplating the worn designs of one of the rugs.

'I intend to assault Uderstir, baron,' said Barundin, and his voice was low and calm, on the far edge of anger that is the icy cold of genuine ire rather than the tantrum that most people mistake for rage. 'Your army can stand aside, or stand betwixt me and my foe. It would not go well for you, should you be in my road.'

Without waiting for a reply, Barundin turned on his heel and marched out of the tent.

Footsteps behind him caused him to turn, and he saw Theoland striding after him.

'King Barundin!' the herald called out, and the king stopped, bristling with anger, his hands pale fists by his side. 'Please, let me talk to my uncle.'

'My attack begins as soon as I get back to my army,' growled Barundin. 'You have that long to convince him of his folly.'

'Please, I don't want more blood shed than is necessary,' said Theoland, stooping to one knee in front of the king.

'Remind your uncle that he has broken oath with us on the trade agreement,' said Barundin. 'Remind him that he will be lucky to have half the coffers of Uderstir for your inheritance. And remind him that should he attempt to stand in my way, it will not be just the lives of his men that are forfeit, but also his own.'

With nothing more to say, Barundin stepped around the distraught young noble and marched up the hill.

The dwarf army was now lined up in front of him, flanked to the north by two cannons, and by the third cannon to the south. The clans were gathered around their hornblowers and standard bearers: a row of grim-faced hammer- and axe-wielding warriors that stretched for nearly three hundred yards.

As he approached the army, Barundin pulled forth Grudgesettler and held the weapon aloft. The air shimmered as weapons were raised in return, glinting with the pale sunlight, and a throaty grumbling began to reverberate across the army.

Loremaster Thagri stood ready with the Zhufbar book of grudges open in his hands. Barundin took it from him and addressed his army, reading from the open page.

'Let it be known that I, King Barundin of Zhufbar, record this grudge in front of my people,' Barundin said, his voice loud and belligerent now that the time of reckoning was at hand. 'I name myself grudgesworn against Baron Silas Vessal of Uderstir, a traitor, a weakling and a coward. By his treacherous act, Baron Vessal did endanger the army of Zhufbar, and through his actions brought about the death of King Throndin of Zhufbar, my father. Recompense must be in blood, for death can only be met with death. No gold, no apology can atone for this betrayal. Before the thanes of Zhufbar and with Grungni as my witness, I swear this oath!

'I declare grudge upon the Vessals of Uderstir. Leave no stone upon another while they still cower from justice! Leave no man between us and vengeance! Let none that resist us be punished other than by death! Kazak un uzkul!'

Kazak un uzkul: battle and death. The dwarfs took up the cry, and the horns sounded long and hard from the hilltop.

'Kazak un uzkul! Kazak un uzkul! Kazak un uzkul! Kazak un uzkul! Kazak un uzkul!! Kazak un uzkul!'

The hills resounded with the war cry and all eyes in the shallow valley below were turned to them as the dwarfs began to march forward, beating their weapons on their shields, their armoured boots making the ground shake as they advanced.

The boom of the cannons accompanied the advance, hurling their shot high over the heads of the approaching dwarf army. Although smaller than the great cannons of the Empire, the cannons of Zhufbar were inscribed with magical runes by the runesmiths, their ammunition carved with dire symbols of penetrating and destruction. The cannonballs trailed magical fire and smoke, hissing with mystical energy.

The salvo struck the already-weakened tower, shattering it with three mighty blasts that shook the ground. A fountain of ruptured stone was flung high into the air, raining down blocks of rock and pulverised dust. The walls beside the now ruined tower, unsupported by its strength, buckled and began to crumble. Shouts of alarm and wails of pain echoed from within the walls.

Barundin aimed straight for the growing breach, some two hundred yards away, advancing steadily over the broken ground. The odd whine of a bullet and the hiss of an arrow went past, but the fire from the castle was lacklustre in the extreme and not a single dwarf fell.

The men of Konlach parted in front of the dwarf throng like wheat to a scythe, pushing and hurrying each other in their eagerness to be out of the line of march. Grunting and puffing, the dwarfs pulled themselves over the siege defences created by Baron Gerhadricht's men and poured through the gaps in the earth walls and shallow trenches, reforming on the other side.

Another salvo from the cannons roared out, and the south wall cracked and shuddered, toppling stones the size of men onto the ground, making the battlements jagged like the broken teeth of an impoverished vagrant.

Now only a hundred yards away, the dwarfs raised their shields in front of them, as arrows and bullets came at them with greater frequency and accuracy. Most of the missiles bounced harmlessly away from the shields and armour of the dwarfs, but here and there along the line a dwarf faltered, dead or wounded.

To the left, the gate opened and a troop of several dozen knights sallied forth. They quickly formed their line, lances levelled for the charge. Hengrid left Barundin's side and commanded several of the handgun-armed Thunderer regiments to wheel to the left, facing this new threat. The king forged onward, now only fifty yards from the walls, as another cannonball struck the castle, its cataclysmic impact tearing a hole several yards wide to the foundations of the wall. The king saw spearmen gathering in the breach, preparing to defend the gaping hole.

The thundering of hooves to the left announced the cavalry charge, met with the crackle of handgun fire. Barundin glanced in their direction and saw the knights bearing down on the thunderers, who had not bothered to reload, but instead drew hammers and axes ready for the attack.

It never came.

On the flank of the knights emerged Dran and his rangers, stepping out from the reeds and scattered bushes of the stream's bank. With crossbows levelled, they formed a hasty line and fired, unable to miss at such close range. A quarter of the knights were toppled by the volley, and others fell as their horses tripped on falling bodies and crashed into each other.

Without pause, the rangers slung their crossbows, drew large double-handed hunting axes and stormed forwards. Their charge disrupted, their impetus lost, the knights tried to wheel to face this threat, but they were too disorganised and few of them had their lances at full tilt or were moving at any speed when the dwarf rangers hit. With Hengrid leading them, the thunderers shouldered their weapons and moved forward to join the melee.

Barundin was the first into the breach, bellowing and swinging his axe. Spear points glanced harmlessly off his rune-encrusted gromril armour, their points sheared away by a sweep of Grudgesettler. As the hammerers pressed in beside him, he leapt forward from the tangle of rock and wood within the breach, crashing like a metal comet into the ranks of the spearmen, knocking them over. Grudgesettler blazed as limbs and heads were severed by a mighty swing from the dwarf king, and as the hammerers pressed forward, their deadly war-mattocks smashing and crushing, the spearmen's nerve broke and they fled the vengeful dwarfs.

Once inside the castle, the dwarfs made short work of the fighting. Dozens of manlings had been slain by the collapse of the tower and wall, and those who remained were shocked and no match for the heavily armoured, angry host that poured through the gap in the wall. Many threw up their hands and dropped their weapons in surrender, but the dwarfs showed no mercy. This was not war, this was grudge killing, and no quarter would be given.

Hengrid breached the gates with Dran, having routed the knights, and the defenders gave themselves up in greater numbers. Swarms of women and children huddled in the crude huts inside the walls, shrieking and praying to Sigmar for deliverance. The dwarf army surrounded them, weapons drawn. Barundin was about to give the signal for the execution to begin when a shout rang out from the broken gateway.

'Hold your arms!' the voice commanded, and Barundin turned to see Theoland mounted upon his warhorse, a pistol in each hand, his visor lowered. 'The battle is won, put up your weapons!'

'You dare command King Barundin of Zhufbar?' bellowed Barundin, forcing his way through the dwarf throng towards the young noble.

Theoland aimed a pistol at the approaching king, his arm as steady as a rock. 'The body of Baron Obius Vessal lies outside these walls,' he said. 'These are my people now, my subjects to protect.'

'Stand against me and your life is forfeit,' snarled Barundin, hefting Grudgesettler, whose blade was slicked with blood, the runes inscribed in the metal smoking and hissing.

'If I do not, then my honour is forfeit,' said Theoland. 'What leader of men would I be, to allow the slaughter of women and children? I would rather die than stand by and allow such base murder.'

Barundin was about to reply, but there was something in the boy's voice that caused him to pause. There was pride, but it was tinged with doubt and fear. Despite the steadiness of his aim, Barundin could tell that Theoland was frightened, terrified in fact. The lad's courage struck Barundin heavily, and he glanced back to see the wailing women and children, huddled under the shadow of the north wall, the bodies of their fathers and husbands around them. In that moment, his anger drained away.

'You are a brave manling, Theoland,' said Barundin. 'But you are not yet commander of the armies of Konlach. You stand alone and yet you would confound me.'

'I am Baron of Konlach,' replied Theoland. 'My uncle lies dead, slain by my sword.'

'You would kill your own kin?' said Barundin, his anger beginning to rise again. There were few crimes more serious to the dwarfs.

'He was going to command the army to attack you,' explained Theoland. 'He wanted to destroy you once you had breached Uderstir. I said it would be folly and the death of us all, but he would not listen. We struggled and I drew my sword and cut him down. He was not a good ruler.'

Barundin did not know how to reply. That he owed the lad a debt now, for saving dwarf lives, was beyond question, but he was an enemy and a kin-slayer. Mixed emotion played across the king's face. Eventually he lowered Grudgesettler and glared up at the young baron.

'You would honour the debt of the Vessals?' the king asked. 'One half of the contents of the coffers, and the body of Silas Vessal to be turned over to me?'

Theoland holstered his pistols and dismounted. He flicked up the visor of his lion helm and extended a hand.

'I would honour their debt, as you would honour the people you can spare,' said Theoland.

Barundin gave the order for the army to allow the women and children to leave the castle, and they did so quickly, crying and screaming, pointing at fallen loved ones, some running to give one last hug or kiss to a dead father, son or brother. Soon the castle was empty but for the dwarfs and Theoland.

Another rider came in, bearing a corpse across the saddle of his horse. He flung it down at Barundin's feet.

'Obious Vessal,' said Theoland, kicking the body onto its back. The man was middle-aged, his black hair peppered with grey. His chest plate had been torn nearly in half by an axe blow, exposing shattered ribs and torn lungs. 'Silas Vessal will be in a tomb in the vaults beneath the keep. There too, we will find the treasury, and your precious gold.'

'Take me to it,' ordered Barundin.

The two of them entered a side gate of the keep, and taking a torch from the wall, Theoland led the dwarf king down a winding flight of stairs into the bowels of the castle, passing wine cellars and armouries. This was his ancestral home, denied his family for many generations, and he knew its secrets well. He located the hidden door to the treasury, clumsily hidden to Barundin's eye; he had seen the weaker joins in the stone walls immediately upon entering the arched cellar.

The treasury itself was small and barely high enough for Barundin to stand up in. In the light of the torch, half a dozen chests could be seen. Barundin dragged one out into the open, and sheared through the lock with the blade of Grudgesettler. Wrenching the lid open, he saw silver, but there were also gold coins, marked with the Stirland crown. He picked up a coin and smelled it, then gave it a taste with the tip of his tongue. There was no mistaking, this was dwarf gold, the same as had entranced his father so long ago. He picked up a handful of the coins and let them run through his fingers, a smile upon his lips.

GRUDGE SEVEN

The Gold Grudge

A SINGLE LANTERN illuminated the chamber, its yellow glow reflecting off the contents of Barundin's treasure store. Mail coats and gromril breastplates hung from the wall, shining with silver and dull grey. The gold-embossed axes and hammers, belt buckles and helms glimmered with rich warmth, bathing the king in an aura of wealth.

He sat at his counting desk, ticking off the contents of the fifteenth chest of treasure owned by the king. He picked up a coin and sniffed it, luxuriating in the scent of the gold. He remembered these coins well. Though they now bore the rune of the king, they had once been Imperial crowns, taken from the coffers of the Vessals of Uderstir. Re-smelted and purified by the goldsmiths of Zhufbar, they were now Barundin's favourites amongst all his vast wealth. They were a reminder of the heavy price paid for the betrayal of his father, and a token of his victory and the settling of the grudge.

He twirled the coin expertly through his fingers, enjoying its weight, the grooves around its edge, every little detail. It was intoxicating, the presence of so much gold in one place, and the thought of it made Barundin giddy with joy.

Like all dwarfs, his desire for gold went beyond mere avarice; it was a holy metal to his people, dug from the deepest mines, given to the dwarfs by the Ancestor God Grungni. No single dwarf knew all of the names for the different kinds of gold, for there were many types. It was a common pastime in the drinking halls to name as many different kinds of gold as possible, or even invent new words, and the dwarf that could name the most would win. Such competitions could last for hours, depending on the age, memory and inventiveness of the dwarfs in question.

This gold Barundin had dubbed 'dammazgromthiumgigalaz', which meant gold that he found particularly pleasing and beautiful because it was from the man grudge. He kept it all in a single chest, bound with many steel bands and made from the heaviest iron. In other chests he kept his lucky gold, his reddish gold, his moonlit and sort of silvery gold, his watergold – taken from beneath Black Water – and many others besides. A shiver of pleasure travelled down the dwarf king's spine as he placed the coin on the pile to his left and ticked it off the long list in front of him.

He took the next coin and ran a loving finger around its circumference, his light touch detecting a slight nick. This had been the last coin minted from the Vessals' gold, and he had scored it ever so slightly with the edge of Grudgesettler, as part of the ceremony during which he had crossed out the Vessals' name from the book of grudges.

To the manlings, the affair would be just a distant memory, but to Barundin it felt as if it had only happened yesterday, though over a hundred years had passed. Arbrek had still been alive then, and it had been before Tharonin's disappearance in the mines of Grungankor Stokril. He wondered idly what had become of Theoland. He had last seen him in his middle years, lord of two baronies and becoming an important member of the Count of Stirland's court. But then time had passed by and old age had claimed him before Barundin had the chance to visit him again. Such was the trouble with making friendships with manlings; they lasted such a short time, it was almost not worth the effort.

The memories continued, of Dran's wedding to Thrudmila of Karak Norn, when Barundin had sent the old Reckoner a silver letter-opener in the shape of Dran's favourite axe, with a reminder to keep in touch. Dran was now at the ripe old age of five hundred, and had fathered two daughters. From his last letter, he was apparently trying hard for a son, and enjoying being pestered by the women in his life.

Barundin smiled wryly. His mother had died not long after he had been born, and he had been raised by the other dwarf lords, amongst them his older brother, Dorthin, and the Runelord Arbrek. Now the closest thing to family that Barundin had was Hengrid Dragonfoe, who he spent much time with, drinking and reminiscing about the skaven and grobi wars.

A melancholy settled upon Barundin that even his gold could not cheer, and he packed away the remaining coins, uncounted. As he used his seven secret keys to lock the door to his vault, he came to a decision. Emerging from the hidden passage leading to his treasury, he called for a servant to send word to the thanes. He would be holding a dinner that night in honour of the fiftieth anniversary of Arbrek's death, and they were all to attend, for he had an important announcement to make.

* * *

THE AUDIENCE HALL blazed with hundreds of candles and lanterns, illuminating the platters of sizzling pork and trestled troughs creaking with chickens, bowls filled with mountains of roasted, boiled and mashed potatoes, and all manner of other solid but tasty fare that the dwarfs liked to banquet on. The beer had been flowing well, but not recklessly, for the dwarfs present knew that they were gathered for a solemn occasion. Barundin wore a likeness of Arbrek – an ancestor badge – on a gold chain around his neck as a mark of respect and memory. Many others were also wearing his badge, on necklaces and brooches or hanging from their belts or as beard clasps.

When news of the king's banquet had gone through the hold, it had been accompanied by much rumour and gossip, for he had not thrown such a feast for many years, not since his two hundred and eightieth birthday. Some thought that perhaps he was going to announce a new war, as had been his custom in the past, or that a new grudge had arisen. Others said that the king was past such foolish displays, and would not risk the relative peace that they had enjoyed for the best part of a century.

Still, the dark mutterings persisted, even as the cooks and serving wenches of the royal kitchens grumbled about such short notice, and the trade clans rubbed their hands and negotiated with the king's agents for the best prices for their meat, bread and other produce they made or bought from the manlings.

They claimed that the grobi were returning, that Grungankor Stokril had been attacked in recent months. Word came less regularly from the distant mines and the disappearance of Tharonin had caused a stir for several weeks. His clan had denied that he was dead, and were not at all keen to discuss the matter, and so the idle speculation continued.

Others, who claimed to be better informed, said that armies had been gathering in the north: the dark armies of Chaos. There was said to be an evil host assembling, the likes of which had not been seen since the Great War against Kislev, and their alliance with Emperor Magnus. News from the distant hold in Norsca, Kraka Drak, seemed to confirm this, for the Norse were on the move in large numbers, and gathering their war parties.

Such murmurings were commonplace in a dwarf hold, but when there started to come tales from the east, those who would normally ignore such prattling began to take notice. Manling warriors, fierce and courageous, had been seen fighting amongst themselves across the frozen, desolate lands of Zorn Uzkul, east of the High Pass; some claimed to select their strongest leaders for a coming invasion.

The greatest fuel to the fires of rumour, though, were accounts from Zharr Naggrund, the barren plains far across the Dark Lands, where the Zharri–dum dwelt. Their furnaces were said to be filling the sky with a great pall of smoke, day after day, month after month. Such news was greeted with dismay by young and old alike, for it had been many years since the dwarfs had fought against their distant, twisted kin.

It was with some expectation, then, that the dwarf thanes gathered in the audience chamber and feasted on roast duck and grilled venison, quaffing tankards of ale and swapping their theories concerning Barundin's announcement.

The king let all of the idle chatter wash over him as he sat at the high table, surrounded by his closest advisors. Dromki Quickbeard, the new runelord, sat on one side of him, Hengrid on the other. Rimbal Wanazaki was there also, now one of the advisors to the Engineers Guild steam engine council. Thagri sat a little way down the table, with two of the more important thanes between him and the king, and the rest of the table was filled with various cousins and nephews. All except one chair, which stood empty. Barundin looked at the chair with a heavy heart, ignoring the chatter around him. Filling his tankard, he stood, and the hall hushed quietly, the hubbub of feasting replaced with the occasional murmur and whisper of expectancy.

'My friends and kin,' began Barundin, holding up his tankard. 'I thank you all for coming this day, and on such short notice. We are gathered here to pay respects to the spirit of Arbrek Silverfingers. He dwells now in the Halls of the Ancestors, where I am sure his advice is as pointed and appreciated as it was here.'

Barundin cleared his throat and lowered his mug to his chest, clasping it in both hands. Those around the table stifled their groans, for they knew this was Barundin's 'speaking pose', and it was a sign that he was likely to talk for quite some time.

'As you know, Arbrek was like a second father to me,' said Barundin. 'And after my father's death, perhaps the closest thing I had to family. Over the years that I knew him, and they were too few, he was never shy of correcting me or disagreeing with my opinion. Like any proper dwarf, he spoke little, but spoke his mind. Every word from his lips was as crafted and considered as the runes that he created, and certainly just as valuable.

'And though the worth of a life such as his cannot be easily measured, I would say that his greatest gift to me was my axe, Grudgesettler. It was forged with purpose over a great many years. So to did Arbrek forge my purpose for all the years that I knew him. Without his firm guidance, his looks of disapproval, and those odd moments of praise, I might have never succeeded as king. Though my companions and advisors are a comfort to me, and their wisdom always heeded, it is the words of Arbrek Silverfingers that I now greatly miss.

'And so I ask you, the leaders of Zhufbar, to raise your cups in thanks to Arbrek and his deeds in life, and to his memory now that he has passed on.'

There were no raucous cheers, no grandiose declarations. The company rose to their feet, lifting their tankards above their heads, and as one, they declared:

'To Arbrek!'

Barundin took a gulp of his ale, as much to fortify himself as to toast the memory of the dead runelord. While the other dwarfs seated themselves, he remained standing, once again assuming his stance with his mug held tightly in front of him.

'I have been king of Zhufbar through tough times,' he told the throng. 'We have fought wars and battled vile enemies, to protect our realm and to protect our honour. I am proud to be your king, and we have achieved much together.'

He stood silent for a moment. He was unsure about the next part of his speech, though he had practised it many times. Finally he took a deep breath and then spoke again.

'But there is one duty of a king that I have not fulfilled,' Barundin said, to the obvious puzzlement of his guests. 'I am healthy and in the prime of my life, and though I would like nothing better than to be your king for centuries to come, there is a time when one must face their own future.'

By now the dwarfs were thoroughly confused, and looked at each other with quizzical expressions, whispering to one another and raising their eyebrows. Some scowled in disapproval of the king's teasing speech.

'I am of a mind that Zhufbar needs an heir,' said Barundin, to a mixture of gasps, sighs and claps. 'I shall take a wife, and provide Zhufbar with a king to be, or a queen as nature sees fit.'

'I accept!' declared a voice from the back of the hall.

The dwarfs turned to see Thilda Stoutarm standing upon her bench. Her offer was greeted with laughter, including her own. Thilda was nearly eight hundred years old, had seven children of her own and owned not one of her original teeth, although her mouth was filled with gilded replacements. Now thane of the Dourskinsson clan after the death of her husband over seventy years ago, she was the terror of the bachelor thanes.

'Your offer, I must gratefully but politely decline,' said Barundin with a grin.

'Suit yourself,' said Thilda, downing the contents of her mug and sitting down again.

'I decline not on personal grounds, but on principal,' Barundin continued. 'I intend to wed a bride not of Zhufbar, to strengthen our ancestral bonds with another hold. For all of my reign, we have for the most part battled alone, for they have been our wars to fight. However, times are not comfortable, bad news increases by the month. I fear a time when the strength of Zhufbar alone will not hold back the enemies that will come against us, and for this reason I seek alliance with one of the other great clans, to bind their future with that of mine, and through that to secure Zhufbar for future generations.'

Though there were a few moans of disappointment from thanes that had perhaps hoped Barundin would choose a wife from amongst their clan, for the most part this announcement was greeted with claps of approval. It was a long tradition of the dwarfs to intermarry between clans and holds, to secure trade deals, renew oaths and sometimes, though rarely, even out of love.

'In the morning I shall send forth messengers to the other holds,' declared the king. 'Let it be known all across the dwarf realms that Barundin of Zhufbar seeks a bride!'

There was much cheering and clapping at this, even from those miserable dwarfs who had had their hopes raised, then dashed. If nothing else, a royal wedding would mean visitors, and visitors always brought gold with them.

IT WAS SEVERAL months before the first of the replies came back to Zhufbar. The cousin of the king of Karak Kadrin offered his daughter's hand in marriage, as did several other thanes from the hold. From Karaz-a-Karak, heads of important mining and trade clans offered hefty dowries for Barundin to court their daughters and nieces, while a lone offer from Karak Hirn promised Barundin a mine in the Grey Mountains. Others arrived, week after week, and Barundin put everything in charge of the Loremaster Thagri.

Declarations and histories were sent, extolling the honour and virtues of the prospective clans and brides, and for each one, Thagri searched the records of Zhufbar to find common history with the clans entreating the king. Some were dismissed out of hand, for being too poor, or not the right sort. Others made the second stage of selection, and servants of the king were sent forth to talk directly with the thanes making the propositions, not least to prove the existence of the proposed betrothed.

The accounts of these fact-finding missions began to dribble in, brought by runners and gyrocopter from across the Worlds Edge and Grey Mountains. Some included pictures of the prettiest candidates, drawn by Barundin's agents to help the king make his choice.

It was nearly a year after his announcement when Barundin had narrowed down the field to half a dozen likely looking lasses, and then the real horse-trading began. The question of dowries and wedding expenses were raised, of payment for Barundin's warriors to escort the bride-to-be to Zhufbar, and many other financial details, all of which Barundin and his advisors scrutinised, reread and checked through countless times.

Finally a decision was made, which Barundin announced on the first day of the New Year. He would marry Helda Gorlgrindal, a niece of the king of Karak Kadrin, three times removed. She was said to be of good health, strong of arm, and was only a little younger than Barundin. As a brother-in-law to King Ironfist, her father was considerably wealthy, and also commanded the king's ear on occasion. Barundin had agreed a date for the wedding, to be held on the summer solstice that year.

*   *   *

A LOUD KNOCKING on his chamber doors roused Barundin to a semblance of consciousness. His head pounded, his mouth felt like a rat had crawled into it and died, and his stomach was turning loops. He was sprawled on the covers of his bed, half dressed and covered in flour. The stench of ale permeated the room. He rolled over, ignoring the banging that was surely only inside his head, and came face to face with a plate of fried potatoes on top of which sat a half-eaten sausage. The banging continued, and he covered his head with a pillow. 'Bog off!' he grumbled.

He heard someone calling his name through the door, but diligently put them out of his mind, instead trying not to concentrate on anything because it simply made his head hurt more. He knew it had been a mistake to agree to Hengrid's invitation to organise his boar's night, his final day of celebration of bachelorhood.

Hengrid's plan had been simple: to disguise the king and go roistering through the pubs of Zhufbar. He had dyed the king's beard and, through a judicious use of rouge obtained from a lady of the Empire in some shady deal that Hengrid had not detailed, darkened the king's skin to appear like an old miner.

With several of the others, including Thagri and his cousin Ferginal, they had spent the night carousing in the many taverns of the hold, unfettered by the king's status. Now the ale, of which he had consumed more than he had ever done before, was returning to haunt Barundin.

He felt a hand on his shoulder and he spun over and slapped it away, eyes tightly shut against the light of a lantern held close by.

'I swear if you don't leave me alone, I'll have you banished,' the king growled.

His stomach lurched and the king sat up, eyes wide open. He did not even see who was beside his bed, but simply shoved them out of the way before stumbling to the cold fireplace and throwing up noisily. After several minutes, he was feeling a little better, and drank from the mug of water that had been thrust into his hands some time during the unpleasant proceedings.

Splashing the remainder on his face, he pushed himself to his feet and stood wobbling for a moment. He staggered backwards and sat down heavily on the bed, the mug dropping from his fingers, which felt like a bunch of fat sausages. Blearily, he focussed on the room, and saw a stone, roughly conical in shape, leaning against the wall in one corner. It was etched with several runes and painted red and white. There was a helmet of some kind atop its tip.

'What is that?' he muttered, peering at the strange object.

'It is a warning stone used by miners,' a familiar voice said. 'It is used to block the entrances to unsafe passageways or corridors still under construction. And on top of that, I believe, is the helmet of an ironbreaker.'

Barundin looked around and saw Ottar Urbarbolg, one of the thanes.

Next to him stood Thagri, looking slightly better for wear than the king, but not by much. It was the loremaster who had spoken.

"Where did I get them?' asked Barundin. 'Why are they in my room?'

'Well, last night, you thought the wardstone would be a great gift for your betrothed,' explained Thagri. 'The helmet, well that was Hengrid's idea. Something about a boar's night tradition. Luckily, all the ale had washed the dye from your beard and face, and the ironbreaker from whose head you removed it thought better of lamping the king, though he was undecided for a moment.'

'And my ribs ache,' moaned the king.

'That would be the belly punching competition you had with Snorri Gundarsson,' said Thagri with a wince. 'You insisted since he beat you in a rorkaz.'

'Nothing wrong with a friendly skuf. Anyway, what in the seven peaks of Trollthingaz do you want at this hour?' demanded the king, cradling his head in his hands. 'Can't it wait until tomorrow?'

'It is tomorrow,' said Thagri. 'We tried to wake you yesterday, but you punched Hengrid in the eye without even waking up.'

'Oh,' said Barundin, flapping a hand ineffectually in Thagri's direction.

The loremaster understood the vague gesture, as only someone that had been in the exact same predicament the day before could. He poured another mug of water and passed it to Barundin, who took a sip, retched slightly and then tipped the contents down the back of his shirt. With a yell and a shudder, he was more awake, and turned his attention to Ottar.

'So, what are you doing here?' he demanded.

'Our family records have something that impacts on the wedding, my king,' said Ottar, glancing towards the loremaster for reassurance, who nodded encouragingly.

'What do you mean, "impacts"?' said Barundin, his eyes narrowing.

'I'm afraid you'll have to cancel it,' said Ottar, stepping back as Barundin turned a venomous glare towards him.

'Cancel the wedding?' snapped the king. 'Cancel the bloody wedding? It's only a month away, you idiot, why would I cancel it now?'

'There is an ancient dispute between the Urbarbolgi and the Troggkurioki, the clan of your intended,' said Thagri, stepping in front of Ottar, who was now decidedly pale with fear. 'You know that as king you cannot marry into a clan that is at odds with a clan of Zhufbar.'

'Oh, buggrit,' said Barundin, flopping on to the bed. 'Send for my servants, I need a wash and some clean clothes. And I've got the rutz very badly. I'll attend to this matter this afternoon.'

The two hovered for a moment, until Barundin sat up, the mug in his fist. It looked as if he was going to throw it at the pair, and they fled.

Barundin winced heavily as the door slammed behind them, then pushed himself to his feet. He gazed at the sausage on his bed, picked it up and sniffed it. His stomach growled, so he gave a shrug and took a bite.

'THE WHOLE MATTER revolves around Grungak Lokmakaz,' explained Thagri.

It was in fact evening before Barundin had felt like facing anything except the inside of his water closet. They were sitting in one of Thagri's studies, and the loremaster had a pile of books and documents spread out on the desk in front of him. Ottar sat with his hands clasped in his lap, his face impassive.

'That's a mine up north, isn't it?' said Barundin. 'Not far south of Peak Pass?'

'That's the one, my king,' said Ottar, leaning forward. 'It was dug by my forefathers, an offshoot on my great-uncle's side. Those thieving Troggkurioki stole it from us!'

'But isn't Peak Pass the ancestral lands of Karak Kadrin?' said Barundin, rubbing at his forehead. His head was still sore, although the excruciating pain he had felt for most of the day had been staved off with another couple of pints of beer before the meeting. 'Why is a Zhufbar clan digging around there?'

'That doesn't matter,' said Ottar. 'We found the gold, we registered our claim, and we dug the mine. It's all perfectly accounted for.'

'So what happened?' asked Barundin, turning to Thagri in the hope of a more unbiased account.

'Well, the mine was overrun by trolls and orcs,' said Thagri. 'The clan was all but wiped out, and those who survived fled back here to Zhufbar.'

'Then those damn Troggkurioki took it from us!' said Ottar hotly. 'Jump in our tombs just as quick, I would say.'

'They claimed the mine by right of re-conquest,' explained Thagri, holding up a letter. 'This was also properly registered by the loremaster of Karak Kadrin at the time, who sent a copy of his records to the Urbarbolgi.'

'At the time?' said Barundin, glancing between Ottar and Thagri.

'Yes,' said Thagri, consulting his notes. 'The original claim was made three thousand, four hundred and twenty-six years ago. The re-conquest took place some four hundred and thirty-eight years later.'

'Three thousand years ago?' spluttered Barundin, rounding on Ottar. 'You want me to cancel my wedding because of a dispute you had three thousand years ago?'

'Three thousand years or yesterday, the matter isn't settled,' said Ottar defiantly. 'As thane of the Urbarbolgi, I must dispute your right to marry into the Troggkuriok clan.'

'Can he do that?' asked Barundin, looking at Thagri, who nodded. 'Listen here, Ottar, I'm not happy with this, not happy at all.'

'It's in the book of grudges,' added Thagri. 'As king, it is your duty to see it removed.'

'So, what do you want me to do?' said Barundin.

'It's quite simple,' said Ottar, steepling his fingers to his chin. 'You must renegotiate the dowry to include turning over Grungak Lokmakaz to its rightful owners.'

'But the dowry and expenses have been settled for two months now,' said Barundin with a scowl. 'If I start changing the conditions of the wedding, they might pull out altogether.'

Ottar shrugged expansively, in a manner that suggested that although he understood the nature of the king's dilemma, it was, ultimately, not the thane's problem to deal with. Barundin waved him out of the room and sat growling for a few minutes, chewing the inside of his cheek. He looked at Thagri, who had neatly stacked his documents and sat waiting the king's orders.

'We'll send a messenger to start the negotiations,' said Barundin.

'Already done,' replied the loremaster. 'This matter came to light several weeks ago and, what with you being so busy, I took it upon myself to try to smooth things between the clans without having to bother with you.'

'You did, did you?' said Barundin heavily.

'I have your best interests at heart, Barundin,' said Thagri. The king looked at him sharply, for the loremaster seldom used anybody's first name, especially his. Thagri's expression was earnest, and Barundin realised that he had indeed followed his best intentions.

'Very well. So what has been the reply?' asked the king.

'You must travel to Grungak Lokmakaz yourself,' said Thagri. 'The thane of the mines, an uncle-in-law-to-be, wishes to speak to you personally about the matter and to sign the documents yourself. I think he just wants to have a look at the king that's going to be marrying his niece, because he's got nothing to lose by being connected to the royal family of Zhufbar.'

'Very well, I'll head north for a short trip,' said Barundin. 'Have arrangements made for me to travel three days from now.'

'Actually, the arrangements had already been made,' admitted Thagri with a sheepish look. 'You head off the day after tomorrow.'

'Do I indeed?' said Barundin, anger rising. 'And when did the loremaster inherit the right to order the king's affairs in such a way?'

'When the king decided to get married, but can't organise his way out of his own bedchamber,' replied Thagri with a smile.

IT WAS COLDER, Barundin was sure, than around Zhufbar. He knew that they were only some one hundred and fifty miles from his hold, and that the climate did not change that dramatically, but he knew in his heart that it was colder up north.

The mine itself wasn't much to look at; it was little more than a watch tower over the pit entrance, and a few goat herds straying across the mountainside. He could not see Peak Pass from where he stood, although he knew that it lay just over the next ridgeline. On the northern slopes of the pass lay Karak Kadrin, where his future rinn lived.

'Come on, you ufdi,' called a voice from the tunnel entrance, and he saw Ferginal gesturing for him to follow.

The king passed out of the mountain sun into the lantern-lit twi-light of Grungak Lokmakaz. The entrance to the mineworkings was low and wide, but soon split into several narrower tunnels before opening up into a much larger space: the chamber of the thane.

The hall was thronged with dwarfs, and in their midst, upon a throne of granite, sat Thane Nogrud Kronhunk. Barundin felt rather than saw or heard Ottar beside him, bristling with anger, as he stood between the two thanes. He offered a hand to Nogrud, who shook it ferociously, patting Barundin on the shoulder as he did so.

'Ah, King Barundin,' said Nogrud, with a quick glance at the dwarfs around him. 'So glad that you have come to visit.'

'Always good to meet the family,' said Barundin quietly, keeping a smile fixed on his face, although he was seething inside.

'I trust your journey was uneventful,' continued Nogrud.

'We saw some bears, but that was all,' Barundin told him.

'Ah, good,' said Nogrud, waving the king to sit upon a chair beside his throne. 'I take it you came by way of Karag Klad and Karaz Mingol-khrum?'

'Yes,' said Barundin, suppressing a sigh. Why was it that relatives always wanted to talk about the route you took to get somewhere? 'There have been early snows around Karag Nunka, so we had to take the eastern route.'

'Splendid, splendid,' said Nogrud.

He clapped his hands and a handful of serving wenches brought in pitchers of ale and stools for the king's three companions: Ottar, Ferginal and Thagri. A wave of the hand dismissed the other dwarfs in the room, except for an elderly retainer who sat to one side, a book in his hands.

'This is Bardi Doklok,' the thane introduced the other dwarf. 'He's my bookmaster.'

'You are Thagri?' Bardi asked, looking at the loremaster, who smiled and nodded. 'If we get time before you return to Zhufbar, I would dearly like to talk to you about this word press contraption they have supposedly built down in Karaz-a-Karak.'

'The writing machine?' said Thagri with a scowl. 'Yes, we proba-bly should discuss what we want to do about that. Engineers getting ideas beyond their station, if you ask me.'

'Perhaps,' said Barundin, interrupting the pair. 'However, we have other matters at hand. I want to be away within a few days, because

I still haven't stood for my final measurements on my wedding shirt. These delays are costing me a fortune.'

'Well, let us endeavour to be as quick as possible,' said Nogrud.

'It's simple,' blurted Ottar. 'Relinquish your false claim to these mines, and the matter is settled.'

'False claim?' snarled Nogrud. 'My ancestors bled and died for these mines! That's more than you ungrimi ever did for them!'

'Why you wanazkrutak!' snapped Ottar, standing up and thrusting a finger towards the thane. 'You stole these mines, and you know it! That's my gold you're wearing on your fingers right now!'

'Wanakrutak?' said Nogrud, his voice rising in pitch. 'You big hold thanes think that you can throw your weight around anywhere, don't you? Well, this is my bloody mine, and no stinking elgtrommi clan is going to take it from me.'

'Shut up!' bellowed Barundin, standing up and knocking his chair over. 'The pair of you! We're not here to trade insults; we're here to sort out this bloody mess so that I can get married! Now, sit down, and listen.'

'I have found a precedent,' said Thagri, looking at Bardi more than the two thanes. 'Both clans have equal claim to the mine. That much can be deduced from the original founding and the right of re-conquest. However, since the re-conquest took place less than five hundred years after the abandonment, the Troggkurioki should have offered the Urbarbolgi the right to settle by means of a fighting fee; what you might call expenses of war. They did not do so, and thus they did not legally secure full rights to the mine.'

'And thus, the Troggkurioki owe expenses on one tenth of the mine's profits to the Urbarbolgi?' said Bardi.

'That is correct,' said Thagri with a sly smile.

Bardi scratched his chin and glanced at his thane, before producing a piece of parchment from the inside of his robe.

'Here I have a record that shows, without doubt, the expenses of the re-conquest campaign exceeded the profits of the mine for that first five hundred year period,' said Bardi with a triumphant gleam in his eye. 'That means that no right to settle need be granted, and thus the Urbarbolgi in fact owe the Troggkuri war expenses of not less than one third of their expenditure from the moment they entered the mine to the sealing of the claim by re-conquest.'

Thagri stared open-mouthed at the bookmaster, amazed by the guile of the dwarf. He turned to the others. 'This may take some time,' he said. 'I fear that you may also find it extremely tedious to witness us bandying claim and counter-claim. Might I suggest that you retire to more suitable chambers while your host entertains you in a more convivial fashion?'

'Sounds good,' said Barundin. 'Let's see what beer you've got, eh?'

'Ah,' said Nogrud. 'There we shall certainly find common ground. My brewmaster has a particularly fine red beer just matured two weeks ago. Smooth? I tell you, there's more grip on a snowflake.'

The two book-keepers waited until the group was outside the hall, then looked at each other.

It was Bardi that broke the silence. 'This could take weeks, and neither of us wants that,' he said.

'Look, let's just agree that the Urbarbolgi will pay right of settlement and war expenses in retrospect, and thus entitle them to a ten per cent claim,' suggested Thagri.

'Are you sure that'll be agreed by them?' said Bardi. 'That leaves them out of pocket for several centuries yet.'

'The king will pay,' explained Thagri. 'He's desperate for this wedding to go without a hitch. It's going to cost him more to delay it than to pay the settlement. Your lord gets a one-off payment from Zhufbar, Ottar's clan get an annual payment for the next five hundred years. Only Barundin loses, but he's losing already, so that doesn't really come into it.'

'Fair enough,' said Bardi. 'I've got a keg of Bugman's stowed away in my chambers.'

'XXXXXX?' asked Thagri, eyes alight.

'No, but it is Finest Dirigible, which I am told travels very well,' said Bardi. 'Let us seal the deal over a mug? We'll leave the ufdi to their own devices and tell them what we've agreed this evening.'

'Good idea,' grinned Thagri.

ALTHOUGH IT PAINED him to sign away so much gold in one stroke of the writing chisel, Barundin dragged the parchment towards him and dipped the pen in the inkwell that Bardi had provided.

'This is the only way?' Barundin asked Thagri, as he had already asked many times.

'In the longer term, yes,' sighed Thagri.

'Let's just settle the matter and your wedding will go without a hitch,' said Ottar, who stood to one side, running a finger along the spines of the books that were stacked high on the shelves of Bardi's library.

'That's all right for you to say – you're not paying up front,' said Barundin.

'I hardly call getting one tenth of my own bloody mine a good deal,' said Ottar, turning towards the king. 'There'll be some who think I've signed away our heritage. Look, I've signed, add your mark and we can leave tomorrow and forget the whole thing.'

'Where's Ferginal?' asked Barundin, laying down the pen and earning a scowl from Thagri. 'We need him as a witness from Zhufbar.'

'He went out drinking with some miners,' said Thagri. 'He can sign later.'

'It's not really a witness if they're not present when I sign,' said Barundin heavily. 'That's the point, isn't it?'

'Just a formality, really,' Thagri assured him. 'Nobody doubts the word of a king.'

As Barundin lifted the writing chisel once again, the door opened with a bang and Ferginal rushed in.

'Where've you been?' demanded Barundin. 'We've been waiting for you!'

'Don't sign it!' gasped Ferginal.

'What?' said Barundin.

'The agreement, it's a dirty trick,' said Ferginal. 'There's been no gold in these mines for six centuries!'

'No gold?' said Barundin and Ottar together.

'What do you mean, no gold?' said Thagri, gripping Ferginal by the arms.

'I was talking to some of the miners,' Ferginal breathlessly explained. 'There's plenty of iron ore and coal, but they've not seen a fresh nugget of gold here for over six hundred years.'

'The cheating swine!' roared Barundin, slamming down the pen as he stood. 'They tried to swindle me into buying an empty gold mine!'

'Does this mean the wedding is off?' asked Thagri, pulling a rag from his belt to mop up the ink spilling across the desk.

'By Grungni's beard, it does not!' said Barundin. 'For his elgi tricks, Nogrud is going to sign over this mine to me, lock, stock and every ounce of ore. He'll feel the taste of Grudgesettler if he tries to argue.'

'So it's war again, is it?' sighed Ferginal, leaning against the wall.

At that moment, Bardi entered. Thagri leapt upon him, snatching up the collar of his robe in both hands.

'Try to swindle us, would you?' snarled the loremaster. 'Thought you'd pull the mail over my eyes, did you? I'll see that the Council of Lore Writers has you chased into the hills for this!'

Bardi snatched himself away from the loremaster's angry grip and straightened the front of his robe. 'Nonsense,' he snapped. 'Not once did myself or my lord mention gold in the agreement, merely the profits from the mines.'

'The mine's almost worthless,' said Ottar. 'You've bled it dry.'

'Well, you'll not be wanting it back then,' said Bardi with a hint of smugness.

'Oh, we'll have it back alright,' said Barundin. 'By Grimnir's nose ring, we'll have it back! Just you think on that when our cannons are a-knocking at the doors to your room.'

'I came in to tell you that a messenger from Karak Kadrin has arrived,' said Bardi. 'Before you came we sent word of your coming and the, er, situation, and I expect this is King Ironfist's reply.'

'Like it or not, if he defends what you've done here, he'll face my wrath as well,' said Barundin.

'You would not go to war with another hold, surely?' said Bardi.

'Not if it can be avoided,' replied Barundin.

GRUDGE EIGHT

The First Grudge

WINTER LINGERED LATE in the mountains, and the slopes of Peak Pass were dusted with snow all the way to the bottom of the valley. The pine forests farther up the mountainsides were swathed in snow, barely visible as dark brown patches across the whiteness of the Worlds Edge Mountains.

Just visible to the east, before the pass turned somewhat northward, the silvery flanks of Karaz Byrguz could be seen, and atop it a great fire burned; it was a beacon tower of Karak Kadrin, the hold of King Ungrim Ironfist. Westward was the much smaller mount of Karag Tonk, its foot obscured by boulders and broken trees from recent avalanches.

The pass itself narrowed between the flanks of Karag Krukaz and Karag Rhunrilak; steep-sided and laborious to negotiate as the undulating valley crossed into the western mountains of the tall peaked range.

Just to the west was the summit of Karaz Undok, beneath which lay the gates to Karak Kadrin itself. Although many miles distant, Barundin could just see the great stone faces and battlements carved into the mountain tops surrounding the ancient hold, and the great span of the Skybridge that linked Karak Kadrin with the smaller settlements of Ankor Ekrund.

The wind was fierce, blowing down the valley from the east and north, with a biting edge to it that even the sturdy dwarf king could feel. His cheeks were red and his eyes watered in the early spring air, and he had to keep wiping a hand across his face to clear his vision. He held his helm under one arm, his shield propped up against his left leg as he turned his head to survey his force. The entire strength of Zhufbar had been massed for this battle, from beardlings that were raising their axes for the first time to veterans like himself that had fought in the foetid tunnels of Dukankor Grobkaz-a-Gazan.

Glinting ancestor icons were held aloft beside fluttering standards of deep reds and blues, amongst them the towering banner of Zhufbar held by Hengrid.

They stood on the southern flank of the pass, at the centre of the Zhufbar throng. To their right stood several thousand clansdwarfs, each carrying a sturdy axe or hammer and a steel shield embossed with symbols of dragons and anvils, lightning bolts and ancestor faces, each according to his own taste. Beyond them waited the ironbreakers, formed into small, dense regiments. Little could be seen of the dwarfs themselves under their layers of gromril, rune-encrusted armour: even their beards were protected by articulated steel sheaths.

On the left of the line, Barundin had drawn up the greater strength of his missile troops. Rank upon rank of thunderers and quarrellers stood upon the mountainside, each row far enough back to overlook the lines in front. Behind them were the cannons, bolt shooters and stone lobbers of the engineers, who paced to and fro between their machines, making adjustments, throwing fluttering scraps of cloth in the air to judge wind strength and direction, and generally preparing for the coming battle.

Ramming his helmet onto his head and picking up his shield, Barundin picked his way down the mountainside, heading for his hammerers. As he did so, he looked across to the northern slopes of the pass, and the huge host of Karak Kadrin.

The first thing that caught the eye was its sheer size, nearly twice the number of warriors that Zhufbar could muster. Zhufbar, in its way, was isolated and well protected by the Empire to its west and the impenetrable mountains to the east. Karak Kadrin, on the other hand, held the pass, and here countless invasions of the mountains and the lands beyond had begun and been turned back by the might of the Slayer King and his army.

The slayers themselves were immediately noticeable, and though they stood far to the east, the splash of orange across the dirt and snow could not be missed. Forced to take the Slayer Oath for some real or perceived shame, slayers swore their lives to a glorious death, and for the most part wandered the world alone seeking out trolls, giants and other large monsters to defeat in battle, or die fighting a worthy foe. That was the only way a slayer could atone for his shame. They were dressed in the style that Grimnir himself was said to have done as he marched north at the dawn of time to slay the Chaos hordes that had been unleashed upon the world, and shut the gate that had been opened in the far north. They wore little more than trousers or loincloths, and their bare skin was heavily tattooed or covered in war paint, both with runes of vengeance and punishment, and geometric patterns.

The slayers' hair and beards were dyed bright orange and heavily spiked using lime and other substances, so that their it stood up in great crests, and their beards jutted out in vicious points, often tipped with steel and gromril spikes. Some wore heavy chains piercing their skin, and nose rings and other jewellery. Altogether they were an outlandish lot, and Barundin was glad that their travels rarely took them to Zhufbar – although many passed through now and then – on their way to the flooded caverns of Karak Varn.

The army itself mustered under banners of gold and red and green, and under great scowling faces of Grimnir, most revered of the ancestor gods by the dwarfs of Zhufbar. It was in Karak Kadrin that the greatest shrine to Grimnir had been built, and for this reason, the king was patron to many warriors, and his army was rightly feared and guessed to be second only to the great host of Karaz-a-Karak, serving the high king himself.

For all its size and ferocity, the army of Karak Kadrin could not compare with the army of Zhufbar in one respect: war engines. Zhufbar was renowned for the number and skill of its engineers, and above the mass of Barundin's warriors, gyrocopters buzzed to and fro, landing occasionally then taking off, like gigantic flies. The batteries of cannons behind the king were immaculately kept, and ammunition was in plentiful supply. Such was the demand to be in the Zhufbar Engineers Guild that applicants from across the dwarf empire came to study there, but only the very best were chosen to be admitted to the hold's greatest secrets. Every crew, from the swab-dwarf to the gun captain, was amongst the best gunners in the world, and utterly reliable.

A horn sounded from the east and was taken up by others along the pass, the warning note reverberating along the valley, until a deafening chorus of echoes resounded from both slopes. Barundin looked to his right and saw the slayers heading for the lower slopes, eager to get to grip with their foes.

Behind the horn blast, another sound could now be heard: distant drums. Steadily they pounded, a brisk beat that shook the mountain tops. For such noise, there must be hundreds of them, thought Barundin. The same thought must have occurred to many of the other dwarfs, for mutterings passed along both lines, some of excitement, others of consternation.

It was several minutes of the incessant beating, grinding on Barundin's nerves, until the first attack came. In a great horde they poured along the valley floor, coming from the east, jogging forwards to the beating of the drums.

The army of Vardek Crom, the Conqueror, Herald of Archaon.

The northmen were savages, dressed in crude furs and poorly woven wool. They wore scraps of armour, the occasional breastplate and a few links of mail, and carried vicious-looking axes and shields fitted with spikes and blades.

Horsemen rode at the front of the line, armed with long spears, axes and swords hanging at their belts. Their steeds were not the mighty war-horses of the Empire, but smaller, sturdier steppe ponies, sure-footed and swift. The horsemen peeled away as if part of some pre-arranged plan, allowing the first ranks of infantry to pass between them.

The marauders were arranged in tribal groups, gathered around their ghastly totems of bones and tattered flags, each bearing some mark to identify themselves. One group had hands nailed to their shields, another had helms fashioned from the skulls of rams. Some wore intricate wolf tooth necklaces, while yet another group were covered in bleeding cuts, careful incisions made across their skin, their blood flowing over their naked bodies like a crimson layer of armour.

They were a fearsome sight, although Barundin knew they were just manlings, so their appearance was really the only thing about them that caused any dread. They would be wild and reckless, like all manlings, and easily cut down.

There were an awful lot of them, he thought as he watched the dark mass winding its way around the pass towards him. He could see why King Ironfist had sent for aid to hold back this host. The Slayer King had sworn that he would hold the pass against these incursions from the east, while the Empire mustered their armies to the west and took on the hordes of the dread Archaon that even now were hacking and burning their way through Kislev. If the army of Vardek Crom could not be held in check, they would pour through Peak Pass into the Empire, surrounding the forces of this new Emperor, Karl Franz. Such a thing would be disastrous for the dwarfs' allies, and thus Ungrim Ironfist had led his warriors forth to stand as a bulwark against the tide rising in the east.

The messenger had been well timed, for on the brink of such a war, Barundin had been ready to open hostilities on his own account. The matter of the mine had not been forgotten, but the threat of the northmen gave more common cause than the mine did differences.

The war drummers increased the tempo of their beating and the marauders hastened their pace, coming on now at a run, weapons drawn. Their shouts could be heard, yelling the names of the Dark Gods, swearing their souls away for victory, cursing their foes. As their pace increased, their cohesion began to disintegrate as the more eager or faster warriors broke into headlong charges and sprinted towards the dwarfs.

The slayers headed straight at the line of marauders streaming down the pass, waving their axes and yelling their battle cries. The horsemen rode forward cautiously, hurling javelins and throwing axes at the near-naked dwarfs, before retreating quickly lest the savage, doom-laden warriors catch them.

With a tangle of flesh, metal, bone and orange hair, the two lines of warriors met, as the slayers charged directly into the midst of their foes. The fighting was brutal, with both sides unprotected against the keen blades of their enemies. The marauders outnumbered the slayers by many hundreds of warriors, yet the fearless dwarfs refused to give ground and the barbarians' advance was halted by their attack.

In the valley to the east, the tribes were bunching into a great mass, stalled by the slayers. Already the bottom of the pass was stained with blood and littered with butchered bodies. The slayers, as their numbers dwindled, gradually became surrounded, until a knot of only a few dozen remained, a blot of orange amongst the pale skin and dark hair of the Kurgan tribesmen.

As the fighting continued, Barundin saw the great host further up the valley begin to split. As others saw the new arrivals, a great moan filled the air from the dwarfs. Between the lines of marauders, short, armoured figures marched in deep phalanxes: the Dawi-Zharr, the lost dwarfs of Zharr-Naggrund.

Clad in black and bronze armour, streaming banners of blood red stitched with fell symbols of their bull-god, the Chaos dwarfs advanced. In their midst, titanic engines of destruction were pulled forward by hundreds of slaves: humans, greenskins, trolls and all manner of creatures toiled at the chains, dragging the monstrous cannons and rockets into position.

Their crews bare-skinned, branded and pierced with hooks and spines, the hellcannons, earthshakers and death rockets were pulled up the valley. Once they were in position, ogres came forwards bearing massive hammers, and drove pitons into the ground, nailing down the chains that hung from the immense war engines.

Priests robed in scale coats and wearing daemon-faced iron masks walked amongst the engines, chanting liturgies to the dark god, Hashut. They sprinkled blood onto the swelling barrels of the cannons and dropped burning entrails into their muzzles. With fingers coated in crimson, they scrawled wicked runes onto the rocket batteries and consecrated massive earthshaker shells to their master.

As the rituals were completed, the daemon engines began to wake. Where once there had been inert metal, now unnatural flesh began to writhe and turn, sprouting faces and fangs, claws and tendrils. Bound within the rune-scratched iron of their machines, the daemons possessing the engines began to buck and pull at their chains, and unholy screeches and roars filled the air. Crew dwarfs with smouldering brands prodded their charges into position, while burning skulls were laden into their furnace hearts, the heat shimmer boiling up the valley, melting the snow beneath the engines.

Blood poured forth from horrid maws, while oil dripped from cogs and windlasses. Flaming hammers scalded runes of wrath onto the bound creatures, infuriating them further, while rockets were loaded onto the launch racks and shells fed into the toothy muzzles of the squat earthshakers.

The slayers were now all dead, their bodies mutilated by the victorious marauders. But the Kurgan horde held back now, just out of range of crossbow and handgun. A runner from the cannon battery came to ask Barundin if they should open fire on the barbarians. But he told him no. Instead, he instructed the engineers to move their machines around to target the monstrous creations of the Chaos dwarfs.

Even as the engineers wheeled their cannons and bolt shooters towards this new threat, the first hellcannon opened fire. Its great bronze jaw opened, revealing a sulphurous gullet that squirmed with bound magic. From the depths of its gullet, dark fire churned as it digested the souls trapped within the skulls that had been shovelled into its burning furnace. With a belching roar, the cannon vomited forth a ball of fire that arced high over the marauders, descending towards the army of Karak Kadrin.

The Chaos fire exploded on impact with the ground, consuming dozens of dwarfs within its fiery blast, their ashes scattered to the spring wind within an instant. A gaping hole had been opened in the Karak Kadrin line, as those that had survived the attack retreated from the smouldering crater it had left.

More balls of magical fire stormed towards the dwarfs, and one looped high and began to descend towards Barundin and his hammerers.

'Run!' the king bellowed, and his bodyguard needed no encouragement. As one they turned and hurried up the slope as fast as their short legs could take them, abandoning their formation in their flight.

The blast hit the ground less than two dozen yards behind Barundin, and a moment later he felt a searing wind catch his back, hurling him to the ground. As he lay there dazed, he looked over his shoulder and saw the smoking crater where he had been standing only a few heartbeats earlier. Purple and blue fire still played around its edges, and the ground shifted and melted under the deadly burning.

Rockets screamed skywards, gouting tails of actinic energy, the daemons bound within them steering their explosive bodies towards the enemy. Rippled eruptions spread along the Karak Kadrin army as the death rockets slammed into the mountainside. These were soon followed by the detonations of earthshaker shells, which burrowed into the ground before exploding, hurling up rock and earth and causing the ground to tremble. One exploded not far from Barundin just as he had clambered to his feet, and the violent undulations of the mountainside knocked him down to his knees once more. For almost a minute the tumult continued as pulses of daemonic energy spilled from the impact of the shell.

Now the dwarfs' war machines were sighted on the enemy and

cannonballs screamed back down the valley, crushing Chaos dwarfs and tearing great rents in their arcane machines. Rocks inscribed with ancient grudges and curse runes filled the sky as the stone lobber battery opened fire as one, their ammunition hurtling skywards then crashing down amongst the Chaos dwarf ranks.

Bolt shooters hurled their long harpoons at the marauders, pinioning half a dozen with each hit, ripping off limbs and heads as they sheared through the packed mass of barbaric fighters. The cannons were ready to fire again as the death rockets and hellcannons once more disgorged a hail of destruction from the eastern valley, ripping great swathes in both dwarf lines.

As he gathered his hammerers around him again, converging on the standard still proudly borne aloft by Hengrid who stood shouting defiantly at the twisted cousins of the dwarfs, a cannonball bounced off the earth and sheared through the chains holding down one side of a hellcannon.

With its bonds weakened, the daemonic engine reared backward, its wheels grinding of their own accord, crushing the crew beneath the steel spikes of its treads. As it turned, the remaining chains snapped and tore from the ground and it vomited forth a stream of fire and filth that burned and corroded through the cannon next to it. Attacked by its neighbour, the earthshaker screamed in pain and anger and threw itself at its own chains, ignoring the shouts and prods of its crew.

The freed hellcannon rumbled forward, carving through the Chaos dwarfs and marauders, belching flame and trampling them under its armoured wheels. Malignant energy flared from pores and gashes in its structure and the marauders turned to battle against the creature that attacked them from the rear.

Those warriors that were not fighting the rampaging hellcannon streamed down the valley once more, shields and weapons held high, screaming war cries. Hails of crossbow bolts and handgun bullets that darkened the valley in a thunderous volley greeted them. Scores of barbarians fell to the first onslaught, caught in a crossfire from both sides of Peak Pass. Their tattered flags and icons of bones and metal were raised from amongst the bloody piles and they pressed onwards, more fearful of their dire masters than the weapons of the dwarfs.

It was then that Barundin realised he could not see the horsemen. While the attention of the dwarfs had been on the war machines and marauders, they had slipped out of sight, perhaps disappearing into the woods that grew on the higher reaches of the pass's slopes.

Barundin had no time to worry about them now, as a second volley of fire slashed through hundreds of marauders clambering up the pass through its narrowest reaches. It was because of this choking point that King Ironfist had decided to make his stand here, having sent advance forces to stall and waylay the marauders' approach.

Barely two hundred yards wide, with the mountainsides almost too steep to climb on each side, the narrow area was a killing ground, and the bodies of the marauders lay in heaps. Some fled the fusillade, other groups were wiped out to a man, but still several thousand were pressing forward, accompanied by baying hounds and misshapen creatures that crawled and loped amongst them.

A staccato thundering from behind attracted Barundin's attention, and he turned to look up the slope towards the cannon battery. A pair of multi-barrelled organ guns were unleashing their fire into horsemen pouring from the woods towards the war machines. Barundin smiled grimly, for his trap had worked. Drumki Quickbeard and his runesmiths had worked hard, inscribing runes of invisibility on the short-ranged war engines. Such work was normally difficult; organ guns were a new invention, less than five centuries old, and such runes were not normally intended for the unstable machines. However, the trickery had worked and the horsemen had attacked, unaware that their doom lay just in front of them, hidden from their eyes by the magic of the runes.

Turning his attention back to the valley floor, Barundin saw that most of the marauders had now passed the narrow gap and were flooding into the main part of the pass. There was already hand-to-hand fighting amongst the eastern-most regiments.

A dark mass appeared from behind the dispersing marauders, compact and menacing. Marching in perfect unison, the elite warriors of Zharr-Naggrund advanced, the dreaded immortals of the High Prophet of Hashut. Their armour was painted black, and they wore heavy steel from head to toe. Their curled, piled beards were protected by long sheaths of metal, and parts of their armour were reinforced with solid plates of marble and granite. In their hands they carried large-bladed axes, curved and deadly. Handgun fire and crossbow quarrels rattled off their armour, leaving only a few of them dead, the others quickly filling the holes in their formation.

Gyrocopters buzzed in on attack runs, firing hails of bullets from rapid-firing, steam powered gatlers, while pilots threw makeshift bombs from their seats. Steam cannons venting scalding vapours killed several of the Immortals, but they were undeterred, never once breaking stride, their bull-headed gold standard leading the advance, a great drum made from some monstrous skull calling the step.

Barundin sent word for the ironbreakers to intercept the immortals, and soon his own heavily armoured warriors were marching down to the valley floor, heading directly for their despicable foes. Like two great metal beasts butting each other, the two formations met, the enchanted gromril of the ironbreakers matched against the cursed blades of the immortals.

Barundin had no time to spare to see how his veterans fared, for something else was moving up the valley. It strode forward, a great mechanical giant, belching smoke and fire, the air around it shimmering not just with heat but also diabolical energy. Plated with riveted iron and fashioned in the shape of a great bull-headed man, the infernal machine was rocked back as a cannonball struck it in the midriff, leaving a tearing gate. Oil spilled from the wound like blood, and smashed gears and broken chains could be seen through the rent in its armour.

'A kollossus,' whispered Hengrid, and for the first time ever, Barundin could detect fear in the fierce warrior's voice. Not when they had faced the disgusting rat ogres, the whirling fanatics of the night goblins, the noisome trolls, the crackling energy of the shamans had Hengrid ever shown a moment's hesitation; now his voice quavered, if only slightly.

From firing platforms on the behemoth's shoulders, Chaos dwarfs spewed out gouts of fire, incinerating dwarfs by the handful as the mechanical beast stomped through their lines. Its heavy feet crushed them with every tread, while they tried in vain to pierce its armoured hide with their axes. Bullets whined from its iron plates, while shells chattered forth from a rapid-firing cannon mounted in the mouth of its bull head.

By now the cannon crews were directing all of their fire against the kollossus. One arm was ripped away, spilling burning fuel onto the ground and setting fire to its right leg. A ball trailing magical fire slammed into its knee, buckling the armour and bending the gears. Immaterial shapes began to writhe around the wounded metal beast as they escaped the enchanted machineries that held them to the Chaos dwarfs' bidding.

A gyrocopter swept low, its cannon drilling the head with bullets, and as it lifted its way out of the creature's outstretched hand, Barundin recognised the flying machine as the one that belonged to Rimbal Wanazaki. The king gave a cheer as the mad pilot deftly dived his gyrocopter beneath a swinging metal hand, turning in the air to fire into the exposed innards of the creature's midriff.

Like a creature beset by ants, the immobilised machine was soon swarming with dwarfs, hacking and tearing at the metal plates of its legs, climbing up and firing with pistols into the slits and rents in its armour. Throwing axes scarred its metal skin, and soon there were dwarfs clambering victoriously into the cockpit behind the armoured face of its head. They abandoned its still, metal form, and Barundin signalled to the cannon crews behind him to deal the final blow.

One cannonball struck the metal giant square in the face, tearing the head clean away and hurling it to the ground in an explosion of flames and sparks. Its already damaged leg buckled under another impact, and with a screech of tearing metal and the tormented screams of escaping souls, the kollossus collapsed to its right, shattering upon the ground. A cheer rolled along both lines of dwarfs as the marauders began to fall back.

The immortals, now realising they could be surrounded, broke off from their fighting against the ironbreakers, retreating eastward along the pass. Everywhere, the pass was emptying of enemies, as even the hellcannons were quieted, their magic doused by the priests, teams of slaves coming forward to drag them away from the battle, keeping the valuable machines out of the clutches of the victorious dwarfs.

From the other side of the valley, Barundin saw Ungrim Ironfist raising his fist in triumph and he returned the gesture. The odd cannon shot boomed out as the engineers vented their anger at the retreating horde, punctuating the cheers and jeers that echoed after the defeated host of Chaos.

THE LOSSES OF the dwarfs were comparatively light, most of them coming from the devastation wrought by the Chaos dwarf war machines. There would still be several hundred bodies to take back to the holds' tombs, but compared to the thousands of dead marauders and the hundreds of slain Dawi-Zharr, things could have been a lot worse.

Barundin was on the floor of the pass, sending and receiving messages, organising his army and generally dealing with the aftermath of the battle. He and King Ironfist had decided that a pursuit was risky, as they had no firm idea of the size of the horde that could be waiting further to the east.

Barundin looked up as Hengrid nudged him and nodded to his left. Ungrim Ironfist was striding across the bloodied snow towards him. The king was a strange sight, wearing plates of gromril armour and a dragonscale cloak, with his hair and beard dyed and styled in the manner of a slayer. Barundin felt a strange thrill as he watched the other king approaching. He knew he was king of Zhufbar, and proud of the accomplishments of his reign, but he was in no doubt that he was in the presence of a genuine living legend.

The story of the Slayer King was a long and tragic one, and it began, as most dwarf tales do, hundreds of years ago, when Ungrim's forefather had suffered a terrible loss. Barundin did not know the details, like most dwarfs outside of Karak Kadrin, but knew that it had something to do with the death of King Beragor's son. In a fit of anger and shame, Beragor had taken the Slayer Oath. However, even as he prepared to set forth on his doom quest, his counsellors reminded him that he still had his oaths of kingship to fulfil; that he had sworn to protect and lead his people over all other things.

Unable to reconcile the two oaths, and just as unable to break either, the Slayer King Beragor built a great shrine to Grimnir, and became a patron of the slayer cult. From across the world, slayers travelled to Karak Kadrin to give praise at the shrine, and to take the weapons forged there under the king's instruction. When Beragor died, not only did his oath of kingship pass to his son, but also his slayer oath, for neither could be met. Thus was the line of the Slayer Kings founded, for seven generations.

Ungrim was broad and burly, even for a dwarf, and his armour was resplendent with gold and gems. He raised a hand in greeting as he neared Barundin, and the king of Zhufbar self-consciously waved back limply.

'Hail cousin,' Ungrim boomed out.

'Hello,' said Barundin. He had forgotten that his new wife had been a cousin of the king, and that they were now related. That made him feel better and his confidence grew.

'You'll be heading back to Zhufbar, then,' said Ungrim, his gruff voice making it a statement rather than a question.

'Well, the battle is over,' said Barundin, looking over the corpse-strewn pass.

'It is, it is indeed,' said Ungrim. 'Although my rangers tell me that we have only faced the vanguard.'

'Just a vanguard?' said Barundin. 'There are more?'

'Tens of thousands of the buggers,' said Ungrim, waving a hand eastwards. 'Vardek Crom still holds the strength of his horde in the Dark Lands and the eastern valleys of Peak Pass.'

'Then I must stay,' said Barundin.

'No you bloody won't,' said Ungrim. 'You're to give my cousin a son or daughter before you go risking your neck fighting with me.'

'I swore to come to your aid,' protested Barundin. He flinched as he said the next words, but couldn't stop them coming out. 'I shan't be known as an oath-breaker.'

'Then fulfil your marriage oaths,' said Ungrim, not noticing or choosing to ignore the implicit accusation in Barundin's ill-chosen words. 'The high king has promised me an army, and they march north from Karaz-a-Karak at this very moment. Go home, Barundin, and enjoy your new life for a little while.'

Thagri came over, carrying with him the Zhufbar book of grudges. His face was grim as he handed the volume to Barundin.

'All the names of the dead have been entered,' said the loremaster, handing the king a writing chisel already inked. 'Just put your mark to this page, and they will be entered against the grudges of the northmen and the… the others.'

'That it is a long list,' said Ungrim, peering over Barundin's shoulder as he signed the page. 'I think not in your lifetime will they be all crossed out.'

'No,' said Barundin, blowing the ink dry and flicking through the pages of the heavy book. So many grudges, so few of them drawn through. 'The list is longer than when my father died.'

'Still, plenty of years left in you yet,' said Ungrim with a lopsided smile.

'And plenty of pages still to fill, if need be,' agreed Barundin with a nod, snapping the book shut.

'For me, and for my heir.'

ANCESTRAL HONOUR

Gav Thorpe

THICK, BLUE-GREY PIPE smoke drifted lazily around the low rafters of the tavern, stirred into swirls and eddies by the dwarfs sat at the long benches in the main room. Grimli, known as the Blacktooth to many, hauled another keg of Bugman's Firestarter onto the bar with a grunt. It wasn't even noon and already the tavern's patrons had guzzled their way through four barrels of ale. The thirsty dwarf miners were now banging their tankards in unison as one of their number tried to recite as many different names of beer as he could remember. The record, Grimli knew, was held by Oransson Brakkur and stood at three hundred and seventy-eight all told. The tavern owner, Skorri Weritaz, had a standing wager that if someone named more beers than Oransson they would get a free tankard of each that they named. The miner was already beginning to falter at a hundred and sixty-three, and even Grimli could think of twenty others he had not mentioned yet.

'Stop daydreaming, lad, and serve,' Skorri muttered as he walked past carrying a platter of steaming roast meat almost as large as himself. He saw Dangar, one of the mine overseers, at the far end of the bar gazing around with an empty tankard hanging limply in his hand. Wiping his hands on his apron, Grimli hurried over.

'Mug of Old Reliable's, Dangar?' Grimli offered, plucking the tankard from the other dwarf's grasp.

'I'll wait for Skorri to serve me, if'n you don't mind,' grunted Dangar, snatching back his drinking mug with a fierce scowl. 'Oathbreakers spoil the head.'

175

Skorri appeared at that moment and shooed Grimli away with a waved rag, turning to Dangar and taking the proffered tankard. Grimli wandered back to the Firestarter keg and picked the tapping hammer from his pocket. Placing a tap three fingers' breadth above the lower hoop, he delivered a swift crack with the hammer and the tap drove neatly into the small barrel. Positioning the slops bucket under the keg, he poured off the first half-pint, to make sure there were no splinters and that the beer had started to settle.

As he wandered around the benches, picking up empty plates and discarded bones and wiping the tables with his cloth, Grimli sighed. Not a single dwarf met his eye, and many openly turned their back on him as he approached. Sighing again, he returned to the bar. A shrill steam whistle blew, signalling a change of shift, and as the incumbent miners filed out, a new crowd entered, shouting for ale and food.

And so the afternoon passed, the miners openly shunning Grimli, Skorri bad tempered and Grimli miserable. Just as the last ten years had been. Nothing had changed in all that time. No matter how diligently he worked, how polite and respectful he was, Grimli had been born a Skrundigor, and the stigma of the clan stayed with him. Here, in Karaz-a-Karak, home of the High King himself, Grimli was lucky he was even allowed to stay. He could have been cast out, doomed to wander in foreign lands until he died.

Well, Grimli thought to himself as he washed the dishes in the kitchen at the back of the tavern, perhaps that would be better than the half-life he was leading now. Even Skorri, who was half mad from when a cave-in dropped a tunnel roof on his head, could barely say three words to him, and Grimli considered him the closest thing he had to a friend. In truth, Skorri put up with having the Blacktooth in his bar because no other dwarf would lower themselves to work for the mad old bartender. No one else would listen to his constant muttering day after day, week after week, year after year. No one except Grimli, who had no other choice. He wasn't allowed in the mines because it would bring bad luck, he'd never been taken as an apprentice and so knew nothing of smithying, stonemasonry or carpentry. And as for anything to do with the treasuries and armouries, well no one would let an oathbreaker by birth within three tunnels of those areas. And so, bottle washer and tankard cleaner he was, and bottle washer and tankard cleaner he would stay for the rest of his life, perhaps only two hundred years more if he was lucky.

That thought started a chain of others in Grimli's mind. Dishonoured and desperate for release from this living prison of disdain and hatred, the dwarf's thoughts turned to the Slayer shrine just two levels above his head. He was neither an experienced nor naturally talented fighter. Perhaps if he joined the Slayers, if he swore to seek out an honourable death against the toughest foe he could find, then he would find peace. If not, then his less than ample skills at battle would see him dead within the year, he was sure of it. Grimli had seen a few Slayers; some of them came to Karaz-a-Karak on their journeys and drank in Skorri's tavern. He liked them because they would talk to him, as they knew nothing about his family's past. They would never talk about their own dishonour of course, and Grimli didn't want to hear it; he was still a dwarf after all and such things were for oneself, not open conversation, even with friends and family. But they had talked about the places outside of Karaz-a-Karak, of deadly battles, strange beasts and mighty foes. As a life, it would be better than picking up scraps for a few meagre copper coins.

He was decided. When his shift finished that evening, he would go up to the shrine of Grimnir and swear the Slayer oath.

As HE STEPPED through the large stone archway into the shrine, Grimli steeled himself. For the rest of the day he had questioned his decision, looking at it from every possible angle, seeing if there was some other solution than this desperate measure. But no other answer had come to him, and here he was, reciting the words of the Slayer oath in his mind. He took a deep breath and stared steadily at the massive gold-embossed face of Grimnir, the Ancestor God of Battle. In the stylised form of the shrine's decoration, his beard was long and full, his eyes steely and menacing, his demeanour proud and stern.

I am a dwarf, Grimli recited to himself in his head, *my honour is my life and without it I am nothing*. He took another deep breath. *I shall become a Slayer, I shall seek redemption in the eyes of my ancestors*. The lines came clearly to Grimli's keen mind.

'I shall become as death to my enemies until I face he that takes my life and my shame,' a gravelly voice continued next to him. Turning with a start, Grimli was face-to-face with a Slayer. He had heard no one enter, but perhaps he had been so intent on the oath he had not noticed. He was sure that no one else had been here when he came in.

'How do you know what I'm doing?' asked Grimli suspiciously. 'I might have come here for other reasons.'

'You are Grimli Blacktooth Skrundigor,' the Slayer boomed in his harsh voice. 'You and all your family have been accused of cowardice and cursed by the High King for seventeen generations. You are a serving lad in a tavern. Why else would you come to Grimnir's shrine other than to forsake your previous life and become as I?'

'How do you know so much about me, Slayer?' Grimli eyed the stranger with caution. He looked vaguely familiar, but even if Grimli had once known him, his transformation into a Slayer made him unrecognisable now. The Slayer was just a little taller than he was; though he seemed much more for his hair was spiked with orange-dyed lime and stood another foot higher than Grimli. His beard was long and lustrous, similarly dyed and woven with bronze and gold beads and bands, which sparkled in the lantern light of the shrine. Upon his face were numerous swirling tattoos – runes and patterns of Grungni and Valaya, to ward away evil. In his hand, the Slayer carried a great axe, fully as tall as the Slayer himself. Its head gleamed with a bluish light and even Grimli could recognise rune work when he saw it. The double-headed blade was etched with signs of cutting and cleaving, and Grimli had no doubt that many a troll, orc or skaven had felt its indelicate bite.

'Call me Dammaz,' the Slayer told Grimli, extending a hand in friendship with a grin. Grimli noticed with a quiver of fear that the Slayer's teeth were filed to points, and somewhat reddened. He shuddered when he realised they were bloodstained.

Dammaz, he thought. One of the oldest dwarf words, it meant 'grudge' or 'grievance'. Not such a strange name for a Slayer.

He took the offered hand gingerly and felt his fingers in a fierce grip which almost crushed his hand. Dammaz's forearms and biceps bulged with corded muscles and veins as they shook hands, and it was then Grimli noticed just how broad the other dwarf was. His shoulders were like piles of boulders, honed with many long years of swinging that massive axe. His chest bulged similarly; the harsh white of many scars cut across the deep tan of the Slayer's bare flesh.

'Do you want me to accompany you after I've sworn the oath?' guessed Grimli, wondering why this mighty warrior was taking such an interest in him.

'No, lad,' Dammaz replied, releasing his bone-splintering grip. 'I want you to come with me to Karak Azgal, and see what I have to show you. If, after that, you want to return here and be a Slayer, then you can do so.'

'Why Karak Azgal?' Grimli's suspicions were still roused.

'You of anyone should know that,' Dammaz told him sternly.

'Because that is… was where…' Grimli started, but he found he couldn't say the words. He couldn't talk about it, not here, not with this dwarf whom he had just met. He could barely let the words enter his own head let alone speak them. It was too much to ask, and part of the reason he wanted to become a Slayer.

'Yes, that is why,' nodded Dammaz with a sad smile. 'Easy, lad, you don't have to tell me anything. Just answer yes or no. Will you come with me to Karak Azgal and see what I have to show you?'

Grimli looked into the hard eyes of the Slayer and saw nothing there but tiny reflections of himself.

'I will come,' he said, and for some reason his spirits lifted.

IT WASN'T EXACTLY a fond farewell when Grimli told Skorri that he was leaving. The old dwarf looked him up and down and then took his arm and led him into the small room next to the kitchen which served as the tavern owner's bed chamber, store room and office. He pulled a battered chest from under the bed and opened the lid on creaking hinges. Delving inside, he pulled out a hammer which he laid reverentially on the bed, followed by a glistening coat of chainmail. He then unhooked the shield that hung above the fireplace and added it to the pile.

'Take 'em,' he said gruffly, pointing to the armour and hammer. 'Did me good, killed plenty grobi and such with them, I did. Figure you need 'em more 'n me now, and you do the right thing now. It's good. Maybe you come back, maybe you don't, but you won't come back the same, I reckon.'

Grimli opened his mouth to thank Skorri, but the old dwarf had turned and stomped from the room, muttering to himself again. Grimli stood there for a moment, staring absently out of the door at Skorri's receding back, before turning to the bed. He took off his apron and hung it neatly over the chair by the fire. Lifting the mail coat, he slipped it over his head and shoulders where it settled neatly. It was lighter than he had imagined, and fitted him almost perfectly. The shield had a long strap and he hooked it over one shoulder, settling it across his back.

Finally, he took up the hammer. The haft was bound in worn leather, moulded over the years into a grip that his short fingers could hold comfortably. The weight was good, the balance slightly towards the head but not ungainly. Hefting it in his hand a couple of times, Grimli smiled to himself. Putting the hammer through his belt, he strode out into the busy tavern room. The conversation died immediately and a still calm settled. Everyone was looking at him.

'Goin' somewhere, are ye?' asked a miner from over by the bar. 'Off to fight, perhaps?'

'Perhaps,' agreed Grimli. 'I'm going to Karak Azgal, to find my honour.'

With that he walked slowly, confidently across the room. A few of the dwarfs actually met his gaze, a couple nodded in understanding. As he was about to cross the threshold he heard Dangar call out from behind him.

'When you find it lad, I'll be the first to buy you a drink.'

With a lightness in his step he had never felt before, Grimli walked out of the tavern.

FOR MANY WEEKS the pair travelled south, using the long underway beneath the World's Edge Mountains when possible, climbing to the surface where collapses and disrepair made the underground highway impassable. For the most part they journeyed in silence; Grimli used to keeping his own company, the Slayer unwilling or unable to take part in idle conversation. The night before they were due to enter Karak Azgal they sat camped in the ruins of an old wayhouse just off the main underway. By the firelight, the stone reliefs that adorned the walls and ceiling of the low, wide room flickered in ruddy shadow. Scenes from the great dwarf history surrounded Grimli, and he felt reassured by the weight of the ancient stones around him. He felt a little trepidation about the coming day, for Karak Azgal was one of the fallen Holds, now a nest of goblins, trolls, skaven and many other foul creatures. During the nights they had shared in each other's company, Dammaz had taught him a little of fighting. Grimli was not so much afraid for his own life, he was surprised and gladdened to realise, but that he would fail Dammaz. He had little doubt that the hardened Slayer would not need his help, but he fancied that the old dwarf might do something reckless if he needed protecting and Grimli did not want that on his conscience.

'Worried, lad?' asked Dammaz, appearing out of the gloom. He had disappeared frequently in the last week, returning sometimes with a blood-slicked axe. Grimli knew better than to ask.

'A little,' Grimli admitted with a shrug.

'Take heart then,' Dammaz told him, squatting down on the opposite side of the fire, the flames dancing in bright reflections off his burnished jewellery. 'For fear makes us strong. Use it, lad, and it won't use you. You'll be fine. Remember, strike with confidence and you'll strike with strength. Aim low and keep your head high.'

They sat for a while longer in quiet contemplation. Clearing his throat, Grimli broke the silence.

'We are about to enter Karak Azgal, and I'd like to know something,' Grimli spoke. 'If you don't want to answer, I'll understand but it'll set my mind at rest.'

'Ask away, lad. I can only say no,' Dammaz reassured him.

'What's your interest in me, what do you know about the Skrundigor curse?' Grimli asked before he changed his mind.

Dammaz stayed silent for a long while and Grimli thought he wasn't going to get an answer. The old dwarf eventually looked him in the eye and Grimli met his gaze.

'Your distant forefather Okrinok Skrundigor failed in his duty many centuries ago, for which the High King cursed him and all his line,' Dammaz told him. 'The name of Skrundigor is inscribed into the Dammaz Kron. Until such time as the honour of the clan is restored, the curse will bring great pain, ill fortune and the scorn of others onto Okrinok's entire heritage. This I know. But, do you know why the High King cursed you so?'

'I do,' Grimli replied solemnly. Like Dammaz, he did not speak straight away, but considered his reply before answering. 'Okrinok was a coward. He fled from a fight. He broke his oaths to protect the High King's daughter from harm, and for that he can never be forgiven. His selfishness and betrayal has brought misery to seventeen generations of my clan and I am last of his line. Accidents and mishaps have killed all my kin at early ages. Many left in self-exile, others became Slayers before me.'

'That is right,' agreed Dammaz. 'But do you know exactly what happened, Grimli?'

'For my shame, I do,' Grimli replied. 'Okrinok was sworn to protect Frammi Sunlocks, the High King's daughter, when she travelled to Karak

Azgal to meet her betrothed, Prince Gorgnir. She wished to see something of her new home, and Prince Gorgnir, accompanied by Okrinok and the royal bodyguard, took her to the treasuries, the forges, the armouries and the many other great wonders of Karak Azgal. Being of good dwarf blood, she was interested in the mines. One day they travelled to the depths of the hold so that she could see the miners labouring. It was an ill-chosen day, for that very day vile goblins broke through into the mines. They had been tunnelling for Grungni knows how long, and of all the days that their sprawling den had to meet the wide-hewn corridors of Karak Azgal it was that one which fate decreed.'

Grimli stopped and shook his head with disbelief. A day earlier or a day later, and the entire history of the Skrundigors may have been completely different; a glorious heritage of battles won and loyal service to the High King. But it had not been so.

'The grobi set upon the royal household,' continued Grimli. 'Hard fought was the battle, and bodyguard and miners clashed with a countless horde of greenskins. But there were too many of them, and their wicked knives caught Frammi and Gorgnir and slew them. One of the bodyguards, left for dead by the grobi, survived to recount the tale to the High King and much was the woe of all the dwarf realm. Yet greater still was the hardship for as the survivor told the High King with his dying breath, Okrinok Skrundigor, upon seeing the princess and prince-to-be slain, had fled the fight and his body was never found. Righteous and furious was the High King's anger and we have been cursed since.'

'Told as it has been to each generation of Skrundigor since that day,' Dammaz nodded thoughtfully. 'And was the High King just in his anger?'

'I have thought of it quite a lot, and I reckon he was,' admitted Grimli, poking at the fire as it began to die down. 'Many a king would have had us cast out or even slain for such oathbreaking and so I think he was merciful.'

'We will speak of this again soon,' Dammaz said as he stood up. 'I go to Kargun Skalfson now, to seek permission to enter Karak Azgal come tomorrow.'

With that the Slayer was gone into the gloom once more, leaving Grimli to his dour thoughts.

THE STENCH OF the troll sickened Grimli's stomach as it lurched through the doorway towards him. It gave a guttural bellow as it broke into a loping run. Grimli was rooted to the spot. In his mind's eye he could see himself casually stepping to one side, blocking its claw with his shield as Dammaz had taught him; in reality his muscles were bunched and tense and his arm shook. Then the Slayer was there, between him and the approaching monster. In the darkness, Grimli could clearly see the blazing axe head as it swung towards the troll, cleaving through its midriff, spraying foul blood across the flagged floor as the blade continued on its course and shattered its backbone before swinging clear. Grimli stood in dumbfounded amazement. One blow had sheared the troll cleanly in two. Dammaz stood over the rank corpse and beheaded it with another strike before spitting on the body.

'Can never be too sure with trolls. Always cut the head off, lad,' Dammaz told him matter-of-factly as he strolled back to stand in front of Grimli.

'I'm sorry,' Grimli lowered his head in shame. 'I wanted to fight it, but I couldn't.'

'Calm yourself, lad,' Dammaz laid a comforting hand on his shoulder. 'Next time you'll try harder, won't you?'

'Yes, I will,' Grimli replied, meeting the Slayer's gaze.

FOR TWO DAYS and two nights they had been in Karak Azgal. The night before, Grimli had slain his first troll, crushing its head with his hammer after breaking one of its legs. He had already lost count of the number of goblins whose last vision had been his hammer swinging towards them. Over twenty at least, possibly nearer thirty, he realised. Of course, Dammaz had slain twice, even thrice that number, but Grimli felt comfortable that he was holding his own.

Dammaz had been right, it did get easier. Trolls still scared Grimli, but he had worked out how to turn that fear into anger, imbuing his limbs with extra strength and honing his reflexes. And most of all, it had taught Grimli that it felt good to kill grobi. It was in his blood, by race and by clan, and he now relished each fight, every battle a chance to exact a small measure of revenge on the foul creatures whose kind had ruined his clan so many centuries before.

They were just breaking camp in what used to be the forges, so Dammaz informed him. Everything had been stripped bare by the evacuating dwarfs and centuries of bestial looters and treasure hunters. But the firepits could still clearly be seen, twenty of them in all, spread evenly across the large hall. Grungni, God of Smithing, was represented by a great anvil carved into the floor, his stern but kindly face embossed at its centre. Dammaz told him that the lines of the anvil used to run with molten metal so that its light illuminated the whole chamber with fiery beauty. Grimli would have liked to have seen that, like so many other things from the days when the dwarf realms stretched unbroken from one end of the World's Edge Mountains to the other. Such a great past, so many treasures and wonders, now all lost, perhaps never to be regained and certainly never to be surpassed. Centuries of treachery, volcanoes, earthquakes and the attacks of grobi and skaven had almost brought the dwarfs to their knees. They had survived though; the dwarfs were at their fiercest when hardest pressed. The southern holds may have fallen, but the northern holds still stood strong. In his heart, Grimli knew that the day would come when once more the mountains would resound along their length to the clatter of dwarf boots marching to war and the pound of hammers on dwarfish anvils. Already Karak Eight Peaks was being reclaimed, and others would follow.

'Dreaming of the golden age, lad?' Dammaz asked, and Grimli realised he had been stood staring at the carving of Grugni for several minutes.

'And the glory days to come,' replied Grimli which brought forth a rare smile from the Slayer.

'Aye, that's the spirit, Grimli, that's the spirit,' Dammaz agreed. 'When we're done here, you'll be a new dwarf, I reckon.'

'I'm already...' started Grimli but Dammaz silenced him with a finger raised to his lips. The Slayer tapped his nose and Grimli sniffed deeply. At first he could smell nothing, but as he concentrated, his nostrils detected a whiff of something unclean, something rotten and oily.

'That's the stink of skaven,' whispered Dammaz, his eyes peering into the darkness. Grimli closed his eyes and focused his thoughts on his senses of smell and hearing. There was breeze coming from behind him, where the odour of rats was strongest, and he thought he could hear the odd scratch, as of clawed feet on bare stone, to his right. Opening his eyes he looked in that direction, noting that Dammaz was looking the same way. The Slayer glanced at him and gave a single nod of agreement, and Grimli stepped up beside him, slipping his hammer from his belt and unslinging his shield from his back.

Without warning, the skaven attacked. Humanoid rats, no taller than Grimli, scuttled and ran out of the gloom, their red eyes intent on the two dwarfs. Dammaz did not wait a moment longer, launching himself at the ratmen with a wordless bellow. The first went down with its head lopped from its shoulders; the second was carved from groin to chest by the return blow. One of the skaven managed to dodge aside from Dammaz's attack and ran hissing at Grimli. He felt no fear now; had he not slain a troll single-handedly? He suddenly realised the peril of over-confidence as the skaven lashed out with a crudely sharpened blade, the speed of the attack taking him by surprise so that he had to step back to block the blow with his shield. The skaven were not as strong as trolls, but they were a lot faster.

Grimli batted away the second attack, his shield ringing dully with the clang of metal on metal, and swung his hammer upwards to connect with the skaven's head, but the creature jumped back before the blow landed. Its breath was foetid and its matted fur was balding around open sores in places. Grimli knew that if he was cut, the infection that surrounded the pestilential scavengers might kill him even if the wound did not. He desperately parried another blow, realising that other skaven were circling quickly behind him. He took another step back and then launched himself forward as his foe advanced after him, smashing the ratman to the ground with his shield. He stomped on its chest with his heavy boot, pinning it to the ground as he brought his hammer smashing into its face. Glancing over his shoulder, he saw Dammaz was still fighting, as he'd expected, a growing pile of furry bodies at his feet.

Two skaven then attacked Grimli at once, one thrusting at him with a poorly constructed spear, the other slashing with a wide-bladed knife. He let his shield drop slightly and the skaven with the spear lunged at the opportunity. Prepared for the attack, Grimli deflected the spearhead to his right, stepped forward and smashed his hammer into the skaven's chest, audibly splintering ribs and crushing its internal organs. He spun on the other skaven but not fast enough, its knife thankfully scraping without harm along the links of his chainmail. He slammed the edge of the shield up into the skaven's long jaw, dazing it, and then smashed its legs from underneath it with a wide swing of his hammer. The creature gave a keening, agonised cry as it lay there on the ground and he stoved its head in with a casual backswing.

The air was filled with a musky scent, which stuck in Grimli's nostrils, distracting him, and it was a moment before he realised that the rest of the skaven had fled. Joining Dammaz he counted thirteen skaven corpses on the ground around the Slayer, many of them dismembered or beheaded.

'Skaven are all cowards,' Dammaz told him. He pointed at a darker-furred corpse, both its legs missing. 'Once I killed their leader they had no stomach for the fight.

'Kill the leader, I'll remember that,' Grimli said as he swung his shield back over his shoulder.

FOR THE REST of the day Grimli felt the presence of the skaven shadowing him and the Slayer, but no further attack came. They passed out of the forges and strong rooms down into the mines. The wondrously carved hallways and corridors led them into lower and more basically hewn tunnels, the ceiling supported now by pit props and not pillars engraved with ancient runes. The stench of skaven became stronger for a while, their spoor was littered across the floor or of the mineshafts, but after another hour's travel it faded quickly.

'This is grobi territory, lad. The skaven don't come down these ways,' Dammaz informed Grimli when he commented on this phenomenon.

As they continued their journey Grimli noticed even rougher, smaller tunnels branching off the workings of the dwarfs, and guessed them to be goblin tunnels, dug out after the hold fell. There was a shoddiness about the chips and cuts of the goblin holes that set them apart from the unadorned but neatly hewn walls of dwarf workmanship, even to Grimli's untrained eye. As he absorbed this knowledge, Dammaz led him down a side-tunnel into what was obviously once a chamber of some kind. It was wide, though not high, and seemed similar to the dorm-chambers of Karaz-a-Karak.

'This is where it happened,' Grimli said. It was a statement, not a question. He realised this was where Dammaz had been leading him.

'Aye, that it is, lad,' the Slayer confirmed with a nod that shook his bright crest from side to side. 'This is where Okrinok Skrundigor was ambushed. Here it was that Frammi and Gorgnir were slain by the grobi. How did you know?'

'I'm not sure as I know,' Grimli replied with a frown. 'I can feel what happened here, in my blood, I reckon. It's like it's written in the stone somehow.'

'Aye, the mountain remembers, you can be sure of that,' Dammaz agreed solemnly. 'You can rest here tonight. Tomorrow will be a hard day.'

'What happens tomorrow?' asked Grimli, unburdening himself of his shield and pack.

'Nothing comes to those who hurry, lad, you should know that,' Dammaz warned him with a stern but almost fatherly wag of his finger.

THAT NIGHT, GRIMLI'S dreams were troubled and he tossed and turned beneath his blanket. In his mind he was there, at the betrayal so many centuries before. He could see Frammi and Gorgnir clearly, inspecting the bunks of the wide dormitory, protected by ten bodyguards. Gorgnir was wide of girth, even for a dwarf, and his beard was as black as coal and shone with a deep lustre. His dark eyes were intelligent and keen, but he was quick to laugh at some jest made by Frammi. The princess, to Grimli's sleeping eye at least, was beautiful; her blonde hair tied up in two tresses that flowed down her back to her knees. Her pallor was ruddy and healthy, her hips wide. Clad in a russet gown, a small circlet of gold holding her hair back, she was unmistakably the daughter of a High King.

In his dream-state, Grimli sighed. The lineage of those two would have been fine and strong, he thought glumly, had they but been given the chance to wed. At the thought, the deadly attack happened.

It seemed as if the goblins sprang from nowhere, rushing through the door with wicked cackles and grinning, yellowed teeth. Their pale green skin was tinged yellow in the lamplight, their robes and hoods crudely woven from dark material that seemed to absorb the light. The bodyguards reacted instantly, drawing their hammers and shields, forming a circle around the royal couple. The goblins crashed against the shield-wall like a wave against a cliff, and momentarily they were smashed back by the swings of the bodyguard's hammers, like the tide receding. But the press of goblins was too much and those at the front were forced forward into the determined dwarfs, crushed and battered mercilessly as they fought to get at the prince and princess. Soon they were climbing over their own dead, howling with glee as one, then another and another of the bodyguard fell beneath the endless onslaught. The shield wall broke for a moment, but that was all that was needed. The goblins rushed the gap, pushing the breach wider with their weight of numbers.

This was it, the dark moment of the Skrundigor clan. It was Gorgnir who fell first, bellowing a curse on the grobi even as his axe lodged in one of their skulls and he was swarmed over by the small greenskins. Frammi wrenched the axe free and gutted three of the goblins before she too was overwhelmed; one of her tresses flew through the air as a sword blade slashed across her neck.

Almost as one, the three remaining bodyguards howled with grief and rage, hurling themselves at the goblins with renewed ferocity. One in particular, a massive ruby inset into his hammer's head, smashed a bloody path into the grobi, every blow sweeping one of the tunnel-dwellers off its scampering feet. His helm was chased with swirling designs in bronze and gold and he had the faceplate drawn down, showing a fierce snarling visage of Grimnir in battle. The knives and short swords of the goblins rang harmlessly off his mail and plate armour with a relentless dull chiming, but they could not stop him and he burst clear through the door.

The other two bodyguards fell swiftly, and the goblins descended upon the dead like a pack of wild dogs, stripping them of every item of armour, weapon, jewellery and clothing. They bickered and fought with one another over the spoils, but soon the pillaging was complete and the goblins deserted the room in search of fresh prey. For what seemed an eternity, the looted bodies lay where they had been left, but eventually a low groan resounded across the room and one of the bodies sat up, blood streaming from a dozen wounds across his body. Groggily he stood up, leaning on one of the bunks, and shook his head, causing fresh blood to ooze from a gash across his forehead. He staggered for a moment and then seemed to steady.

'Skrundigorrrr!' his voice reverberated from the walls and floor in a low growl.

THE DREAM WAS still vivid when Grimli was woken by a chill draught, and he saw that the fire was all but dead embers. He added more sticks from the bundle strapped to his travelling pack and stoked the ashes until the fire caught once again. As it grew it size, its light fell upon the face of Dammaz who was sitting against the far wall, wide awake, his eyes staring intently at Grimli.

'Did you see it, lad?' he asked softly, his low whisper barely carrying across the room.

'I did,' Grimli replied, his voice as muted, his heart in his throat from what he had witnessed.

'So, lad, speak your mind, you look troubled,' Dammaz insisted.

'I saw them slain, and I saw Okrinok fight his way free instead of defending their bodies,' Grimli told the Slayer, turning his gaze from Dammaz to the heart of the fire. The deep red reminded Grimli of the ruby set upon Okrinok's hammer.

'Aye, that was a terrible mistake, you can be sure of that,' Dammaz grimaced as he spoke. The two fell into a sullen silence.

'There is no honour to be found here,' Grimli declared suddenly. 'The curse cannot be lifted from these enduring stones, not while mighty Karaz-a-Karak endures. I shall return there, swear the Slayer oath and come back to Karak Azgal to meet my death fighting in the caverns that witnessed my ancestor's treachery.'

'Is that so?' Dammaz asked quietly, his expression a mixture of surprise and admiration.

'It is so,' Grimli assured the Slayer.

'I told you not to be hasty, beardling,' scowled Dammaz. 'Stay with me one more day before you leave this place. You promised you would come with me, and I haven't shown you everything you need to see yet.'

'One more day then, as I promised,' Grimli agreed, picking up his pack.

THEY ENTERED THE goblin tunnels not far from the chamber where Grimli had slept, following the sloping corridor deeper and deeper beneath the World's Edge Mountains. They had travelled for perhaps half a day when they ran into their first goblins. There were no more than a handful, and the fight was bloody and quick, two of the grobi falling to Grimli's hammer, the other three carved apart by the baleful blade of Dammaz's axe.

'The goblins don't live down here much. They prefer to live in the better-crafted halls of Karak Azgal itself,' Dammaz told Grimli when he mentioned the lack of greenskins. 'But there are still plenty enough to kill,' the Slayer added with a fierce grin.

True enough, they had not travelled more than another half mile before they ran into a small crowd of greenskins moving up the tunnel in the opposite direction. The goblins shrieked their shrill war cries and charged, only to be met head-on by the vengeful dwarfs. In the confines of the goblin-mined cavern, the grobi's weight of numbers counted for little, and one-on-one they were no match for even Grimli. As he smashed apart the skull of the tenth goblin, the others turned and ran, disappearing into the darkness with the patter of bare feet. Grimli was all for going after them, but Dammaz laid a hand on his shoulder.

'Our way lies down a different path, but there will be more to fight soon enough,' he told Grimli. 'They will head up into Karak Azgal and fetch more of their kind, and perhaps lie in wait for us somewhere in one of the wider spaces where they can overwhelm us.'

'That's why we should catch them and stop them,' declared Grimli hotly.

'Even if we could run as fast as them, which we can't lad, the grobi will lead us a merry chase up and down. They know every inch of these tunnels and you do not,' Dammaz countered with a longing look in the direction the goblins had fled. 'Besides, if we go chasing willy-nilly after every grobi we meet, you'll never get to see what I have to show you.'

With that the Slayer turned away and continued down the passage. After a moment, Grimli followed behind, his shield and hammer ready.

GRIMLI WAS SURPRISED a little when the winding path Dammaz followed led them into a great cavern.

'I did not think the grobi could dig anything like this,' he said, perplexed.

'Grobi didn't dig this, you numbskull,' laughed Dammaz, pointing at the ceiling. Grimli followed the gesture and saw that long stalactites hung down from the cave's roof. The cavern had been formed naturally millennia ago when the Ancestor Gods had fashioned the mountains. Something caught the young dwarf's eye, and he looked futher into the hall-like cave. A massive mound, perhaps a great stalagmite as old as the world itself, rose from the centre of the cavern.

Grimli walked closer to the heap, and as he approached his eyes made out the shape of a small arm stuck out. And there was a tiny leg, just below it. Hurrying closer still, he suddenly stopped in his tracks. The mound was not rock at all, but built from the bodies of dozens, even scores of goblins, heaped upon one another a good ten yards above his head. Walking forward again, amazed at the sight, Grimli saw that each goblin bore at least one wound, crushed and mangled by what was obviously a heavy hammer blow. He looked over his shoulder at Dammaz, who was walking towards Grimli, axe carried easily in one hand.

'You recognise the handiwork, lad?' Dammaz asked as he drew level with Grimli and looked up at the monumental pile of greenskin corpses.

'Okrinok did this?' Grimli gaped at the Slayer, wondering that he could be even more astounded than he was before.

'Climb with me,' Dammaz commanded him, stepping up onto the battered skull of a goblin.

Grimli reached for a handhold and as his fingers closed around the shattered arm of a goblin, it felt as hard as rock beneath his touch. There was no give in the dead flesh at all and his skin prickled at the thought of the magic that obviously was the cause. Pulling himself up the macabre monument, Grimli could almost believe it had been fashioned from the stone, so unyielding were the bodies beneath his hands and feet. It was a laborious process, hauling himself up inch by inch, yard by yard for several minutes, following the glow of Dammaz's axe above him. Panting and sweating, he pulled himself to the top and stood there for a moment catching his breath.

As he recovered from his exertions, Grimli saw what was located at the very height of the mound. There stood Okrinok. He was unmistakable; his ruby-encrusted hammer was still in his grasp, lodged into the head of a goblin that was thrusting a spear through the dwarf's chest. The two had killed each other, and now stood together in death's embrace. Grimli approached the ancient dwarf slowly, almost reverentially. When he was stood an arm's length away, he reached out and laid a trembling hand upon his ancestor's shoulder. It was then that Grimli looked at Okrinok's face.

His helmet had been knocked off in the fight, and his long, shaggy hair hung free. His mouth was contorted into a bellow, his scowl more ferocious than any Grimli had seen before. Even in death Okrinok looked awesome. His beard was fully down to his knees, bound by many bronze and gold bands and beads, intricately braided in places. Turning his attention back to his ancestor's face, he noted the familiar ancestral features, some of which he had himself. But there was something else, something more than a vague recognition. Okrinok reminded him of someone in particular. For a moment Grimli thought it must be his own father, but with a shiver along his spine he realised it was someone a lot closer. Turning slowly, he looked at Dammaz, who was stood just to his right, leaning forward with his arms crossed atop his axe haft.

'O-Okrinok?' stuttered Grimli, letting his hammer drop from limp fingers as shock ran through him. He staggered for a moment before falling backwards, sitting down on the goblin mound with a thump.

'Aye, lad, it is,' Dammaz smiled warmly.

'B-but, how?' was all Grimli could ask. Pushing himself to his feet, he tottered over to stand in front of Okrinok. The Slayer proffered a gnarled hand, the short fingers splayed. Grimli hesitated for a moment, but Okrinok nodded reassuringly and he grasped the hand, wrist-to-wrist in warriors' greeting. At the touch of the Slayer, Grimli felt a surge of power flood through him, suffusing him from his toes to the tips of his hair.

GRIMLI FELT LIKE he had just woken up, and his senses were befuddled. As they cleared he realised he was once again in the mine chamber, witnessing the fight with the goblins. But this time it was different – he was somehow *inside* the fight, the goblins were attacking *him*! Panic fluttered in his heart for a moment before he realised that this was just a dream or vision too. He was seeing the battle through Okrinok's eyes. He saw Frammi and Gorgnir once more fall to the blades of the goblins and felt the surge of unparalleled shame and rage explode within his ancestor. He felt the burning strength of hatred fuelling every blow as Okrinok hurled himself at the goblins. There were no thoughts of safety, no desire to escape. All Grimli could feel was an incandescent need to crush the grobi, to slaughter each and every one of them for what they had done that day.

Okrinok bellowed with rage as he swung his hammer, no hint of fatigue in his powerful arms. One goblin was smashed clear from his feet and slammed against the wall. The backswing bludgeoned the head of a second; the third blow snapped the neck of yet another. And so Okrinok's advance continued, his hammer cutting a swathe of pulped and bloodied destruction through the goblins. It was with a shock that

Okrinok realised he had no more foes to fight, and looking about him he found himself in an unfamiliar tunnel, scraped from the rock by goblin hands. He had a choice; he could return up the tunnel to Karak Azgal and face the shame of having failed in his sacred duty. Or he could keep going down, into the lair of the goblins, to slay those who had done this to him. His anger and loathing surged again as he remembered the knives plunging into Gorgnir and he set off down the tunnel, heading deeper into the mountain.

Several times he ran into parties of goblins, and every time he threw himself at them with righteous fury, exacting vengeance with every blow of his hammer. Soon his wanderings took him into a gigantic cavern, the same one where he now stood again. Ahead of him the darkness was filled with glittering red eyes, the goblins mustered in their hundreds. He stood alone, his hammer in his hands, waiting for them. The goblins were bold at first, rushing him with spears and short swords, but when ten of their number lay dead at Okrinok's feet within the space of a dozen heartbeats, they became more cautious. But Okrinok was too clever to allow that and sprang at the grobi, plunging into the thick of his foes, his hammer rising and falling with near perfect strokes, every attack crushing the life from a murderous greenskin.

To Okrinok the battle seemed to rage for an eternity, until it seemed he'd done nothing but slaughter goblins since the day was born. The dead were beyond counting, and he stood upon a mound of his foes, caked head-to-foot in their blood. His helmet had been knocked loose by an arrow, and several others now pierced his stomach and back, but still he fought on. Then, from out of the bodies behind him rose a goblin. He heard a scrape of metal and turned, but too slowly, the goblin's spearshaft punching into him. With blood bubbling into his breath, Okrinok spat his final words of defiance and brought his hammer down onto his killer's head.

'I am a dwarf! My honour is my life! Without it I am nothing!' bellowed Okrinok, before death took him.

TEARS STREAMED DOWN Grimli's face as he looked at Okrinok, his expression grim.

'And so I swore in death, and in death I have fulfilled that oath,' Okrinok told Grimli. 'Many centuries have the Skrundigor been blamed for my act, and I have allowed it to happen. The shame for the deaths of Gorgnir and Frammi was real, and the High King was owed his curse. But no longer shall we be remembered as cowards and oathbreakers. The goblin king was so impressed that he ordered his shamans to draw great magic and create this monument to my last battle. But in trapping my flesh they freed my soul. For many years my spirit wandered these tunnels and halls and brought death to any grobi I met, but I am weary and wish to die finally. Thus, I sought you out, last of the Skrundigor, who must be father to our new line, in honour and in life.'

'But how do I get the High King to lift the curse, to strike our name from the Dammaz Kron?' asked Grimli.

'If you can't bring the king under the mountain, lad, bring the mountain over the king, as we used to say,' Okrinok told him. He pointed to his preserved body. 'Take my hammer, take it to the High King and tell him what you have seen here. He will know, lad, for that hammer is famed and shall become more so when my tale is told.'

'I will do as you say,' swore Grimli solemnly. Turning, he took the haft of the weapon in both hands and pulled. Grimli's tired muscles protested but after heaving with all his strength, the dwarf managed to pull the hammer clear.

He turned to thank Okrinok, but the ghost was gone. Clambering awkwardly down the mound of bodies, Grimli's thoughts were clear. He would return to Karaz-a-Karak and present the hammer and his service to the current High King, to serve him as Okrinok once did. It was then up to the High King whether honour was restored or not. As he planted his feet onto the rock floor once more, with no small amount of relief, Grimli felt a change in the air. Turning, he saw the mound was being enveloped by a shimmering green glow. Before his eyes, the mound began to shudder, and saw flesh stripping from bones and the bones crumble to dust as the centuries finally did their work. Soon there was nothing left except a greenish-tinged haze.

Hefting Okrinok's hammer, Grimli turned to leave. Out in the darkness dozens of red eyes regarded him balefully. Grimli grinned viciously to himself. He strode towards the waiting goblins, his heart hammering in his chest, his advance quickening until he was running at full charge.

'For Frammi and Gorgnir!' he bellowed.

OATHBREAKER

Nick Kyme

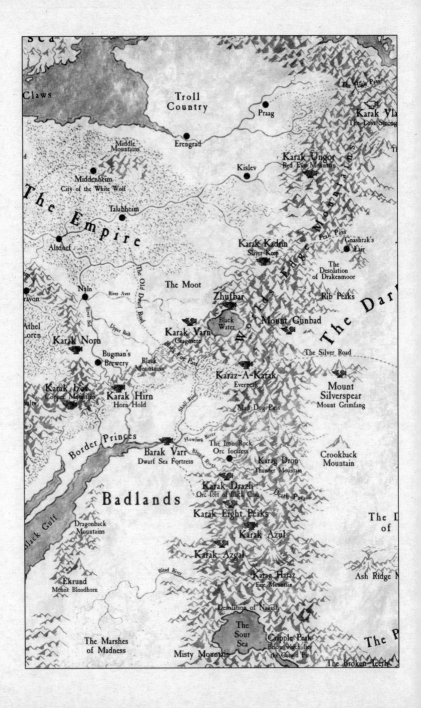

PROLOGUE

RALKAN FLED THROUGH the crumbling ruins of the underdeep, feeling his way frantically along the craggy tunnel. The ancient walls were warm, just like the stagnant air wafting languidly towards him, and dried the dwarf's sodden clothes. The heavy stink of sulphur pricked at his nose, but he ignored it.

Heart pounding, Ralkan risked a quick glance behind him. The tunnel stretched on forever, its vaulted roof creeping higher and higher until it was lost in a firmament of stars. There was nothing else, no monsters following, yet still he fled. Looking ahead again quickly, he didn't see the narrow cleft in the tunnel floor. He stumbled over and fell into it, down deep into the bowels of the earth, all sense of time and space passing away until he was brought thunderously to the ground. A dagger of white heat burned into Ralkan's hand, where the rock had cut a bloody gash into it, and he realised he was back in the very same tunnel.

Struggling to his feet, Ralkan bundled himself around a corner, the nameless fear at his heels driving him. He fell again, tearing his leather jerkin. Muttering an oath to Grungni, he got up. Then, enshrouded by the creeping dark and the waiting silence of the underdeep, he stopped. Breath held painfully in his chest, he felt along the wall again. Not for guidance, for his dwarf eyesight pierced the thick shadow well enough to see, but to try and remember.

As Ralkan's gnarled fingers traced pitted rock and jagged stone they found a runic symbol. It was a massive diagonal cross, with four short lines capping the end of each longer one, so large that it should have been impossible to feel and recognise. But know it, he did.

'Uzkul,' Ralkan muttered. Icy terror gripped his heart as the dwarf discerned its meaning instantly. It was a warning. It also meant something else – he had no memory of this place and with that came a crushing realisation.

He was lost.

Hurrying on further, he saw a wan light up ahead – the flickering flame of some burning brazier or the lambent glow of coals in a hearth hall. He made an oath to Valaya for it to be either. Getting closer to the light, the tunnel opened out and the foul sulphur smell assailing his nostrils grew more pungent. Heat radiated off the walls, without the need for Ralkan to touch them to feel it. By the time he reached the opening from where the light was spreading his clothes were bone dry.

Ralkan stepped tentatively into the corona of light, and gripped the talisman of Valaya around his neck.

'By the everlasting beard of Grungni…' His voice was barely a whisper as he regarded the huge cavern before him and basked in a lustrous aura.

Beyond the threshold of the room there were mountains of gold the likes of which Ralkan had never seen in all his long days. So vast and immeasurable was the hoard that it and the massive cavern appeared to have no end. Before he knew what he was doing, the dwarf had already wandered into the room, stepping into a diffuse shaft of natural light coming from above. Appeasing his desires, Ralkan blundered headlong into the nearest treasure mound, delving gleefully. The heady scent of gold filled his nostrils; the taste of it in the air tingled on his tongue as he immersed himself. Coins and gems spilled freely but as Ralkan dislodged them in his frenzy something else was revealed beneath – a desiccated dwarf head. Ralkan recoiled, and as he did so a different aroma assailed him, overpowering the whiff of gold – the stench of something old, as old as the world, a sentient presence.

Rasping wind emanated from a distant patch of thickening shadow at the back of the grand chamber. No, it wasn't wind… It was something moving slowly, gradually uncoiling, hidden in the dense shadows where the aura of light seemed too afraid to venture.

Running into the chamber was a mistake.

Ralkan's gold lust, which lay in the heart of every dwarf, bled away to nothing. The sound of heavy snorting echoed off the walls. Ralkan would have fled, had his dwarf legs allowed it. Instead he was like a statue, staring at the dark. The sulphur stink came at him again, so strong it made his eyes water, and he was certain he felt warm, wet breath against the back of his head. Whatever lay in those shadows had slipped past the dwarf somehow and was now behind him. The snorting abated, replaced by a deep, resonant sucking.

The eyes to the desiccated head sprang open, defying all laws of nature.

'Flee!' it hissed with decaying breath.

Ralkan turned…

White, blazing heat blinded him. Intense pain surged over the dwarf's body as fire ravaged it, hungrily devouring leather, metal and cloth. It flooded his senses, the nerve endings searing shut until he felt nothing; saw nothing but an empty, beckoning void. Ralkan opened his mouth to scream but fire scorched his throat, sealing it, and stripped the flesh from his bones…

RALKAN AWOKE WITH his gnarled hand covering his mouth to stop from shouting out. He was drenched in sweat despite the cold stone chamber surrounding him. He blinked back tears, a sense memory of the vision, as his eyes adjusted to the dark. He waited a moment, listening intently to the silence… Nothing stirred. Ralkan exhaled his relief but his heart still pounded at the nightmare – no, not a nightmare. It was a portent – a portent of his doom.

ACT ONE
HEARTH AND HOLD

CHAPTER ONE

THE VAST EXPANSE of the Black Water stretched out in the valley below like some infinite obsidian ocean. Dense fog, cooling in the early chill, sat over it like a vaporous white skin. Even at its craggy banks, it did not stir but sat like stygian glass: vast, powerful and forbidding. In truth it was a mighty lake, massively wide and impossibly deep, set in a huge crater that yawned like a giant maw, jutting with rocky teeth. Ribbons of glistening silver fed down through clustered stones and hidden valleys, filling the chasm-like basin of the lake with the melt waters of the surrounding mountains. Its glassy surface belied, in its apparent tranquillity, what dwelled in the Black Water's depths. Rumours persisted of ancient things, alive long before elves and dwarfs came to the Old World, slumbering in the watery dark.

'Varn Drazh,' muttered Halgar Halfhand almost wistfully.

A smile creased the old dwarf's features, near smothered by his immense beard braided into ingots of gold and bronze clasps, as he surveyed the vista laid out before and beyond.

Even standing upon a ridge overlooking the deep basin of the Black Water, rugged plateaus and dense groves of pine scattered amongst the sparse landscape were visible. Wending trails and precarious passes made their way across the rock. Halgar followed one all the way up to the zenith of the mountains. Peaks, jagged spikes of snow-capped rock, weathered by all the ages of the world, raised high like defiant sentinels. This was the spine of the Karaz Ankor, the everlasting realm of the dwarfs, the edge of the world.

Halgar smoothed his thick greying moustache absently, with a hand that had only two fingers and a thumb; the other, replete with all of its digits, rested lightly on the stout axe cinctured at his waist.

'Ever am I impressed by the majesty of the Worlds Edge Mountains,' came the deep voice of Thane Lokki Kraggson beside him, the dwarf's breath misting in the cold morning air.

Halgar frowned. A wisp of brooding cloud scudded across the platinum sky filled with the threat of snow.

'Winter is a time of endings,' he said dourly.

'The cold will be hard pressed to vent its wrath beneath the earth; we have little to fear from its asperity,' Lokki returned.

Halgar grunted in what could have been amusement.

'Perhaps you are right,' he muttered. 'But that's the thing about endings, lad, you never see them coming.'

'We are close, my old friend,' said Lokki, for want of something more reassuring, and rested his hand, encrusted with rings etched with the royal runes of Karak Izor, upon the longbeard's shoulder.

Halgar turned to his lord, released from his reverie, and clapped his hand upon Lokki's in a gesture of brotherhood. 'Aye, lad,' he said, all trace of his earlier melancholy gone.

There was a strength and wisdom in Halgar's eyes. The old dwarf had seen much, fought many foes and endured more hardships than any other Lokki knew. He was the thane's teacher, instructing him in the ways of his clan and of his hold. It was Halgar that first showed him how to wield axe and hammer, how to form a shield wall and become a link in the impregnable mail of a dwarfen throng. Halgar still wore the same armour of those days; a thick mail coat and metal shoulder guard that displayed his clan-rune, together with a bronze helm banded by silver. The ancient armour was an heirloom, fraught with the attentions of battle. Though it was routinely polished and cleaned, it still bore dark stains of blood – ages old – that would not be removed.

'I for one will be glad of the hospitality of Karak Varn's halls,' said Lokki, walking back from the ridge and through the long grasses, pregnant with dew, to the Old Dwarf Road. They had travelled far, a journey of some several months. First, north from Karak Izor in the Vaults – the Copper Mountain – then they'd taken a barge across the River Sol in the shadow of Karak Hirn, the Horn Hold. Crossing the spiny crags of the Black Mountains had been hard but the narrow, seldom trodden roads had led them to Black Fire Pass. They'd ventured through the wide gorge stealthily, keen not to attract its denizens, until at last they'd reached the edge of the mammoth lake. Now, just the undulating, boulder strewn foothills of roiling highland stood between them and the hold of Karak Varn.

'The soles of my boots grow thin, as does my appetite for stone bread and kuri,' Lokki complained.

'Bah! This is nothing,' snapped Halgar, his mood darkening abruptly. 'When I was a beardling and Karak Izor in its youth, I trekked from the Copper Mountain all the way to Karak Ungor, curse the grobi swine that infest its halls.' He spat and winced sharply as he got back onto the road, clutching at his chest.

Lokki moved to the longbeard's aid, but Halgar waved him away, snarling.

'Don't fret, 'tis just an itch,' he grumbled, biting back the pain. 'Wretched damp,' he added, muttering, shading his eyes against the slowly rising morning sun.

'Why have you never removed it?' Lokki asked.

Piercing his armour, and embedded deep into Halgar's barrel-like chest, was the tip of a goblin arrow. Its feathered shaft had long since been snapped off, but a short stub of it still remained.

'As a reminder,' returned the longbeard, eyes filling with remembered enmity, 'of the blight of the grobi filth and of the treachery of elves.' With that the longbeard tramped off down the road, leaving his lord in his wake.

'I meant no disrespect, Halgar,' Lokki assured him as they crested another rise.

'When you are as old as me, lad, you'll understand,' said Halgar, softening again. 'It is my final lesson to you,' he added, holding Lokki's gaze. 'Never forget, never forgive.'

Lokki nodded. He knew the tenets of his race all too well, but Halgar drove them home with the conviction of experience.

'Now, let us–' Halgar stopped and pointed towards a shallow ravine below them, where the road went down into the basin and to the edge of the Black Water. Lokki followed his gaze and saw the wreckage of several ore chests. They were old, the wood warped and overgrown with moss and intertwined by wild gorse, but there could be no mistaking it. It was what lay next to the chests, though, that gave the thane greater pause – skeletons; bones and skulls that could only belong to dwarfs.

Halgar descended down into the ravine, picking his way through rocky outcrops and stout tufts of wild grass, Lokki close behind him. They reached the site of the wreckage in short order.

Grimacing, Halgar crouched down amongst the skeletons. Many still wore their armour, though it was ravaged by time and tarnished beyond repair.

'Picked clean by the creatures of the wild,' said Halgar, inspecting one of the bones. 'They have been gnawed upon,' he added with distaste and sorrow.

'There are more…' Lokki uttered.

Beyond where the two dwarfs were crouched there stretched a windswept highland plain, the fringes edged by shale and shingle from the lake's shore, scattered with more bones.

'Grobi, too,' spat Lokki, throwing down a manky piece of leather as he ranged across the rugged flatland. Skeletons were everywhere, together with more broken ore chests. Preyed on by wild beasts, the battle that had unfolded there ranged far and wide, making it impossible to discern its scale or significance.

'I don't like this,' said Lokki, going to another chest – this one empty, too.

'This was a party headed from Karak Varn,' Halgar muttered, having followed Lokki, running his fingers across old tracks.

'How many?' asked the thane.

'Difficult to say,' murmured Halgar, examining one of the wooden chests more closely. 'Wutroth,' he said to himself, remarking on the rare wood the chest was made from.

Above Lokki, a thick tongue of rock hung over the grassy plain, blotting out the harsh winter sun. A narrow path, little more than a thin scattering of scree, wound up to it from the ancient battlefield.

'I'm going to try and get a better vantage point,' he said, forging up the pathway, beard buffeting as the wind swept across him.

There upon the rise, Lokki saw the full extent of the battle that had taken place. There were at least a hundred dwarf bodies, twice that number in goblins and orcs, though Grungni knew how many others had been dragged away by the beasts of the foothills to be gnawed upon in caves. There was a large concentration of bones at the edge of the Black Water where Lokki saw Halgar crouched – dwarfs and greenskin. The dwarfs seemed to be arranged in a tight circle, as if they had fallen whilst defending fiercely. Orc skeletons spiralled out from this macabre nexus, likely the remains of those repulsed. The shattered remnants of maybe thirty chests were in evidence, too. Old tracks, made with heavy, booted feet moved away from the site, too large and brutish to be dwarfs. It had not ended well for the warriors of Karak Varn and Lokki muttered an oath.

Returning from the overhanging rock spur, Lokki found Halgar tracing a flame seared rune on one of the chests.

'Gromril,' said the longbeard without looking up, indicating the chest's contents. 'Most likely headed for the High King in Karaz-a-Karak,' he surmised, based upon the direction of what tracks still remained.

'What's that?' asked Lokki, his keen eyes picking out something amidst the carnage in the centre of the formation he had espied from above. Around one dwarf skeleton's neck was a talisman. Its chain was tarnished, but the talisman itself remained pristine as the day it was forged. There was a rune marking upon it. Lokki showed it to Halgar. The old dwarf squinted at first then took it from Lokki for a better look.

'It bears the personal rhun of Kadrin Redmane,' he said, looking up at his lord, grim recognition on his face.

'The lord of Karak Varn?' Lokki's tone was similarly dark.

'None other,' said Halgar. 'Doubtless he fell guarding the gromril shipment to Karaz-a-Karak.'

'He must have been dead some time,' said Lokki, 'and yet no word of it has come from Karak Varn.'

Halgar's expression grew very dark.

'Perhaps they were unable to get word to the other holds,' the long-beard suggested. 'I saw no dawi tracks leading from this runk,' he added, indicating the bone-strewn battlefield. 'It is likely the fate of Kadrin Redmane is unknown to his kin.'

Lokki looked down at the dwarf skeleton that had worn the talisman, the remains, it seemed, of Lord Redmane. Its skull had been nearly cleft in twain. A split metal helm lay nearby. He ran his finger, the skin brown and thick like leather, across the wound. 'The blow is jagged and crude,' he said, 'but delivered with force.'

'Urk,' Halgar said, showing his teeth as he ground them.

'I saw their tracks, trailing away from the fight. There was a mighty battle here,' Lokki told him. 'How old do you think these skeletons are?' the thane asked, accepting the talisman of Kadrin Redmane back from Halgar.

The longbeard was about to respond when he sniffed at the air suddenly. 'Do you smell that?' he asked, getting to his feet and unslinging his axe.

A bestial roar echoed from the surrounding rocks. Lokki looked up and felt hot bile rise in his throat. Charging down the east side of the ravine, following the route taken by the two dwarfs, there was a group of five orcs brandishing bloodstained cleavers and crude spears. Seven more emerged from behind a cluster of boulders in the opposite direction, armed with brutish clubs. At least three more came from a second path, across the overhang of the grassy rise, bisecting the route of the other two groups, wielding wooden shields and crude, fat-bladed swords. Decked in filth-stained leather, studded with rusted iron and rings punched through their thick, dark skin, the orcs yelled and bawled as they piled across the flatland.

'They have been watching us,' Lokki realised, on his feet and moving back-to-back with Halgar as he drew his hammer and lifted his shield.

'Aye, lad,' Halgar growled, sniffing contemptuously.

'Never forgive, never forget,' Lokki snarled as the orcs met them.

UTHOR ALGRIMSON FILLED his lungs with a mighty breath of icy air as he regarded the mist wreathed peaks of the distant Worlds Edge Mountains. Standing in a patch of lowland in the foothills of the mighty range, he worked out the cricks in his back and neck. The sun was just breaking the horizon as he appreciated the view, his home of Karak Kadrin to the far north a distant memory now as the shadow of Zhufbar loomed close to the west, and beyond that Karak Varn.

The wings on the helm the dwarf wore fluttered in a highland breeze, his short cloak disturbed into small fits of movement. The errant wind cleansed him of an otherwise dark mood and committed the desperate plight of his liege-lord and father to the back of his mind.

Below him, down a steep escarpment, the wide, dark shadow of Black Water glistened. He had emerged at its western edge, about halfway down.

'A wondrous sight, is it not?' a voice said from above Uthor. The dwarf, momentarily startled, looked up and saw a balding dwarf with a thick, ruddy beard. He was sat upon a rocky outcrop, overlooking the gargantuan lake. Smoke rings spiralled from the cup of a bone pipe pinched between the thumb and forefinger of his right hand and a strange-looking crossbow rested on his lap. Perched in profile, he wore a stout leather apron over a tunic that bore the rune of Zhufbar.

'Legend tells that the crater was formed by the impact of a meteorite in ages past. Nowadays, the rushing lake waters wash the ore extracted from the mines and turn great water wheels that drive the forge hammers of Zhufbar and Karak Varn,' said the dwarf, and looking over to Uthor added, 'Rorek Flinteye of Zhufbar.'

'Uthor Algrimson of Karak Kadrin,' Uthor responded with a nod, noticing as the dwarf faced him that he wore an eye patch.

Rorek got to his feet and came down from the rocky outcrop. The two dwarfs shook hands heartily. Uthor noticed a ring upon his brethren's finger was inscribed with the crest of a dwarfish craft guild.

'An engineer *and* a tour guide,' he said when he recognised the crest.

'Indeed,' Rorek answered, chewing on the end of his pipe throughout the exchange, seemingly unfazed by Uthor's mild derision directed at his encyclopaedic utterance.

Smiling thinly, Uthor released his grip. Judging by his hands, Rorek could only have been a craftsdwarf, for they were coarse, ingrained with oil and metal shavings, and he smelled like iron.

'You are far from home, Uthor Algrimson,' Rorek said.

'I have been summoned to a council of war by a distant member of my clan, Kadrin Redmane of Karak Varn,' Uthor replied, straightening up. 'There are greenskins around Black Water that seek the taste of my axe,' he added, grinning.

'Then we are brothers in this deed,' said Rorek, 'for I too am headed to Karak Varn.'

'Your crossbow is impressive, brother,' said Uthor, who had never seen its like.

Rorek looked down at the weapon, and cradled it in both hands so that Uthor might see it better. 'It is of my own design,' he boasted proudly.

The crossbow was larger than those wielded by the quarrellers of Karak Kadrin. Uthor was well acquainted with the missile weapon, having used one during the many goblin hunting expeditions he had accompanied his father on. A dark memory sprang unbidden into Uthor's mind as he thought of his liege-lord. He crushed it, instead focusing his attention on the engineer's creation.

It was well made, as was to be expected from the dwarfs of Zhufbar. A small metal crank attached to a circular base was bolted to the stock and its large wooden frame accommodated a heavy-looking metal box filled with bolts. Uthor couldn't help but notice a similar looking box attached to the engineer's thick tool belt, but this one contained bound up rope with a stout metal hook at one end.

'It is… *unusual*,' he said.

'I've yet to declare it to the guild,' Rorek admitted.

Uthor was no engineer, but he knew of the traditions established by the Engineers' Guild and of their reluctance to embrace invention. To impress such a device upon the guild could place Rorek's tenure in jeopardy and would likely be met with scorn and disgruntlement.

Before Uthor could say anything of this to the engineer, the sound of clashing steel and the cries of battle carried on the breeze. Words of Khazalid were discernible through the clamour of the distant melee. Rorek's good eye grew wide as he turned towards the source of the commotion. 'Not far,' he said. 'South, just beyond this side of Black Water.'

'Then we had best hurry,' said Uthor, his top lip curling into a feral smile. 'It seems the battle has started without us.'

GROMRUND OF THE Tallhelm clan, hammerer to the great King Kurgaz of Karak Hirn, and so named because of the mighty ancestral warhelm he wore upon his head, stalked down the Ungdrin road, his companion a few short steps behind him. Great was the subterranean underway of the dwarfs, carved into the rocks in ages past in an effort to connect the many holds of the Worlds Edge Mountains. Runic beacons that could be made to glow, and even blaze, with a single word of Khazalid, the language of the dwarfs, provided guidance and illumination through myriad tunnels that ever since the Time of Woes had become, at least in part, the domain of fell creatures: orcs, goblins and even worse denizens all stalked the ruined passages of the Ungdrin road now.

'The gates of Karak Varn are not far,' said Gromrund, raising a lantern as he noted a runic marker inscribed in one of the ornate columns set along the tunnel walls. Statues of the ancestor gods sat in between them, wrought into the very walls themselves. At their feet were thick stone slabs of grey and tan, rendered into knotted mosaic interweaved with the runes of Karak Varn. 'This way,' said the hammerer and forged off into the darkness.

'Have you ever seen the gilded gates of Barak Varr, my friend?' asked Gromrund's companion, a dwarf who had introduced himself as Hakem, son of Honak, of the clan Honak, bearer of the Honakinn Hammer and heir to the merchant houses of Barak Varr, Sea Gate and Jewel of the West. The longwinded title had failed to impress the hammerer.

'No, but I suspect you are about to describe them to me,' Gromrund replied with gruff disdain.

The two dwarfs had met at a confluence of the Ungdrin road by sheer chance at a point where the subterranean tunnels that linked Karak Hirn and Barak Varr met. Three days they had been travelling together. To Gromrund, it felt like months.

'They rival even the great gates to Karaz-a-Karak in their majesty,' boasted Hakem, 'eclipsing even the Vala-Azrilungol with their beauty. Wrought of iron, inlaid with coruscating jewels that shimmer in the refracted sunlight, each gate bears the likeness of Kings Grund Hurzag and Norgrikk Cragbrow forged into the metal, founders of the Sea Gate and my esteemed ancestors. Bands of thick, lustrous gold filigree mark it in the rhuns of the royal clan of Barak Varr.' The merchant thane's eyes grew misty at the mention of the architectural masterpiece.

'A wonder, I am sure,' remarked the taciturn hammerer, wondering if he could silence his travelling companion with a blow from his great hammer, doubtful that the merchant thane would be missed. Yet in truth, even Gromrund was moved, as all dwarfs were when talk was made of the elder days, but he did his best to hide it.

Hakem's merchant garb was almost as grandiose as his tongue: gilded armour, ringed fingers and a purple velvet tunic spoke of wealth, but nothing of heritage, of honour. Gromrund found such ostensible opulence distasteful and decadent. He knew that the War of Vengeance had hurt the purses and the pride of the merchant thanes of Barak Varr. Now, some four hundred or so years later, trade had ceased with the elves. They needed to establish stronger links with their kin, to garner favour and forge new contracts wherever possible. He could think of no other reason for Hakem to have been summoned. To invite such a dwarf to a council of war seemed incongruous at the very least; at most it was an insult.

The Ungdrin narrowed ahead; the roof had become dislodged and sloped downward sharply, doubtless the result of the earthquakes that had ravaged Karak Varn and all of the Karaz Ankor. It forced the hammerer's mind back to the matter at hand. The damage only affected a short section of the underground tunnel, but Gromrund had to stoop to get his helmeted head, replete with two massive curling horns and the effigy of a bronze boar, through it.

'Why don't you just remove your warhelm, brother?' Hakem offered, just behind him, ducking only slightly as he took off his own jewel-encrusted helmet. Gromrund turned to glare at the Barak Varr dwarf, his face hot with indignation. 'It is an heirloom of my clan,' he snapped. 'That is all you need know. Now, keep to your own business and stay out of mine,' he added, and continued through the tunnel without waiting for Hakem's reply.

Once they had traversed the narrow passage, the Ungdrin opened out again into a much larger cavern with three portals leading off from it. A great circular bronze plaque set into the floor at the centre of the room bore further runic symbols. It was a *bazrund*, a way marker that indicated they were close to the hold and showed the roads that led to Zhufbar and Karaz-a-Karak.

'I know of heirlooms, kinsdwarf,' said Hakem, seemingly unfazed by the hammerer's outburst as he stepped onto the plaque. 'What say you of this?'

Out of the corner of his eye, stooping over the plaque as he confirmed they were indeed headed in the right direction, Gromrund saw the dwarf hold a rune hammer aloft. So beauteous was it that even he stopped to look at it.

The rune hammer was clearly crafted by a master. It was plainer than Gromrund might have imagined, a simple stone head – inscribed with three runes that glowed dully in the gloom – topped an unadorned haft carved from stout wutroth, studded with fire-rubies. The grip was made from bound leather and a thick thong attached it to Hakem's bejewelled wrist.

'Have you ever witnessed a thing so truly magnificent?' said Hakem, his eyes alight with pride. His immaculately preened black beard bristled, the gemstones set in braid clasps within it glistening with the reflected rune-glow of the hammer.

'It looks a fair weapon,' Gromrund said, feigning his indifference as he turned away again and started walking.

'Fair?' said Hakem, in disbelief. 'It is worth more than the entire wealth of most clans!' he said, brushing down his tunic when he realised some dirt from the narrow tunnel had marred the velvet.

'Why does a merchant have need of such a weapon anyway?' Gromrund remarked, feigning disinterest.

'*That*,' said Hakem, clearly relishing the moment, 'is *my* business.'

Gromrund snorted, contemptuously.

'Silk-swaddled cur,' the hammerer muttered beneath his breath.

'What did you say?' Hakem asked.

'We're nearly there,' Gromrund lied, a wicked grin ruffling his beard, before Hakem continued to boast of the wealth of the merchant thanes and the house of Honak. They couldn't arrive soon enough.

ROREK WAS GASPING for breath by the time they crested the final rise. Below them, in a narrow ravine, a battle was being fought. Two dwarfs, one clearly a thane and carrying an axe and shield; the other much older, a longbeard, similarly armed. They fought back-to-back. Rorek counted nine orcs surrounding them, another six dead at their feet. He watched as one of the greenskins waded in with a reckless spear thrust. The longbeard hacked the haft down whilst the thane reached over his back and stabbed the spike of his axe into the orc's neck, blood fountaining from the wound.

Uthor had seen enough and a wild grin crept across his face as he bellowed, 'Uzkul urk!' and charged into the melee.

One of the orcs, a thickset beast with broad tusks jutting from its slab-
like jaw and an iron ring through its nose, turned to face this new threat.
There was a flash of silver and the deep, *thwomping* retort of a blade
slicing air. The orc was smashed off its feet and hit the ground before it
could throw its spear, an axe embedded in its cranium.

ON THE RIDGE, Rorek watched as Uthor flung his axe end-over-end into
the nearest orc. He waded in quickly after it, ducking the savage swing
of another greenskin before punching it hard in the face with his
leather-gauntleted fist, shattering its nose. He stooped to retrieve his axe,
wrenching it free with one hand. More blood spurted from the mortal
wound as he did so. Uthor then used the haft to block an overhand
cleaver swing from the orc with the shattered nose.

Further down, the thane and the longbeard were still pressed hard by
the remaining orcs, one of whom looked like some kind of chieftain. His
flesh was much darker than the rest, his body bigger and more muscled,
and he wore an antlered leather helmet. He wielded a heavy-looking
morning star and pummelled the thane's shield with the crude weapon.

Uthor had dispatched a second orc, the top half of its skull cut off by
the keen edge of his axe, the matter within spilling onto the ground. He
was breathing hard and two more orcs came at him wielding wicked
cleavers and crude, curved blades.

Rorek unslung the crossbow from his side, released the safety catch
and turned the crank at the wooden stock. A fusillade of bolts peppered
the ravine. One of the orcs was struck in the jaw, a second bolt pierced
its neck, and a third pinioned its foot to the ground, though at least four
more bolts thundered harmlessly into the ground. The engineer roared
with glee, then exhaled sharply as an errant bolt careened off Uthor's
winged helmet while a second whistled closely by his ear. The dwarf
cursed, scowling at Rorek before dispatching the pin-cushioned orc with
his axe and then turning his attention to its unscathed kin.

Thinking better of it, Rorek shouldered his crossbow and drew his
hand axe. He'd have to do this the traditional way.

'Kruti-eater!' Uthor snarled at Rorek as the engineer reached him from
atop the ridge, disembowelling the second orc, though more were coming
to replace it. 'Though it might suit you, I've no desire to wear an eye patch!'

Rorek nodded apologetically, before hacking off another orc's hand at
the wrist. Uthor finished it, beheading the creature. 'Stay behind me,' he
said, 'and keep that crossbow well harnessed.'

AT THE BASE of the ridge, as he was slowly being crushed beneath his
shield under the continued blows of the orc chieftain, Lokki saw the two
strangers rushing to their aid.

'Halgar!' he grunted.

The longbeard kicked an orc in the shin, shattering the bone, and cut the greenskin down as it crumpled in pain. 'I see them,' he growled, half-turning to regard his liege-lord as another two orcs demanded his full attention.

'No, old one,' said Lokki, pain spiking up his arm as his shield was pounded incessantly. 'I need a little help.'

Halgar swung his axe in a wild arc, forcing the two orcs in front of him to give ground. He then whirled around and rammed his shoulder into the flat of Lokki's shield, the thane doing the same. 'Push!' he roared.

The blow from the orc chieftain came again, but this time it was met with the force of two angry dwarfs and his morning star was parried aside. Lokki and Halgar followed through, smashing the shield straight into the body of the orc chieftain, who staggered backwards, stunned.

Halgar cried out as a spear struck him in the side. It split some of the chain links of his armour and grazed bone, but didn't impale him. Lokki's expression was fraught with concern for the venerable dwarf, but Halgar just bellowed at him.

'Kill the beast!' The longbeard gestured toward the staggering chieftain, before swatting the spear aside and turning back to face his foes.

Lokki did as ordered, swinging his axe around full circle to reaffirm his grip, and lifting his shield to work out some of the pain and stiffness in his shoulder. The orc shook its head, a long drizzle of blood and snot shooting from its ringed nostril as it snorted. It snarled at the advancing dwarf.

'Come on,' Lokki growled, meeting its bestial gaze with his.

UTHOR BATTERED ANOTHER orc with the flat of his axe blade before hacking up into its chin, his face and beard sprayed with greenskin blood as the orc's jaw caved. He shrugged it disdainfully off his blade then hawked and spat on the cooling corpse.

'I count another five since we joined the fight,' he said to Rorek, who was watching his back.

'I saw at least three more come from the rocks cresting the western ridge,' Rorek returned, 'but they are thinning,' he added, breathing hard.

The two dwarfs had left an impressive trail of greenskin dead in their wake. Another group had emerged from the rocks almost as soon as they had arrived, though, placing themselves between them and the other dwarfs. But with the orc reinforcements dispatched, only a handful remained, and Uthor had a clear route through to their two embattled kin.

The longbeard faced three, while the thane made ready to fight the orc chieftain, wielding his axe and shield with practiced ease. Two further greenskins – bigger than the others and more heavily armoured – stood behind the chieftain, presumably at the orc's bidding. Uthor snorted.

'I'll get to you later,' he muttered and fixed his steely gaze on the three fighting against the longbeard.

THE ORC CHIEFTAIN facing Lokki was about to commit to the attack when, as if abruptly aware of its surroundings, it backed off and grunted in its debased language. Two heavily armoured orcs behind it rushed forward suddenly and into the thane's path. Behind them, the chieftain bellowed again, a shrilling cry that ululated in its throat. Lokki flashed a brief glance over his shoulder to see the remnants of the orc horde retreating.

The two left alive against Halgar were already running. Three more fled the other two dwarfs making their way across the flatland, now only a few feet from Lokki and Halgar. One of the fleeing greenskins was pitched off its feet, squealing, as an axe *thunked* into its back. When Lokki looked back, he saw another two, together with their chieftain and his bodyguards, making good their escape. They scattered back up the ravine and into the nearby foothills at the edge of the Old Dwarf Road. The will of the orcs was broken it seemed and, by the time it was over, some sixteen greenskin carcasses littered the ground.

'Filthy urk,' growled Halgar. 'No stomach for a fight, not like in the old days.'

Lokki decided not to give chase. He doubted Halgar could keep the pace, despite the longbeard's undoubted protestations to the contrary, and in truth, he was weary himself. He wiped blood from a cut on his brow, caused by a wound he hadn't realised he'd received, and watched as one of their new found allies, a dwarf wearing a winged helmet and bronze armour etched with the runes of Karak Kadrin, wrenched his axe from a greenskin body.

'You have our gratitude, kinsdwarf,' said Lokki, slinging his shield to his back and hitching his axe back to his weapons belt, before proffering his open hand to the axe-wielding dwarf. 'I am Thane Lokki Kraggson of Karak Izor.'

'Of the Vaults,' the axe-wielder said, trying to keep his tone even and without derision. There was some ill feeling between the dwarfs of the Worlds Edge Mountains and those of the other ranges. Exiles, some called them. Others had less pleasant names.

'Yes, of the Vaults,' Halgar returned proudly, daring the stranger's scorn as he stood beside his lord.

'*Gnollengrom*,' the axe-wielder muttered to Halgar, bowing deeply. Rising again, he clasped Lokki's hand in a firm grip. 'Well met, my brother,' he said. 'I am Uthor Algrimson of Karak Kadrin, and this,' he added, gesturing towards his companion, a dwarf bearing an eye patch and carrying a strange looking crossbow, 'is Rorek Flinteye of Zhufbar.'

'We are in your debt,' Lokki said, nodding his appreciation.

'You are of the royal clan of Karak Izor,' said Uthor, noting the gilded earring that Lokki wore. It was a statement, not a question.

Lokki nodded.

'Then it seems the rumours of the urk gathering in the mountains must be true, if royal clans are taking an interest,' Uthor remarked. 'The greenskins are bold indeed to venture all the way to Black Water.'

'You too have been summoned to Karak Varn?' Lokki asked, inferring it from Uthor's comment.

'Indeed,' he said, 'and we would be honoured to travel at your side, noble thane.'

'Yes, yes. Enough talk,' growled Halgar, wrinkling his nose as he surveyed the carnage. 'These urk are starting to stink.'

HALGAR MUTTERED WORDS of remembrance over the cairn tombs of the skeletal remains of Lord Kadrin of Karak Varn and his followers. The dwarfs had carried the bones reverently from the battlefield of the narrow ravine to the western ridge in the shadow of Karak Varn. They were well equipped, as was prudent for long journeys, carrying short shovels and picks, and buried the remains deep so they would not be disturbed. As the longbeard conducted the brief ceremony, the other three dwarfs stood silently around him with their heads bowed as a mark of deep respect. Below them, and in the distance, the oily smoke rising from a burning pyre, on which the orcs smouldered, stained the air.

'May Gazul guide you to the Halls of the Ancestors,' Halgar whispered, invoking the name of the Lord of Underearth. Making the rune of Valaya – goddess of protection – over his chest, the longbeard got to his feet and the four dwarfs moved away in silence.

After a time, Uthor spoke.

'You are certain it was the body of Kadrin Redmane?' He regarded the talisman of his distant kinsdwarf thoughtfully as he slowly traced the rune markings with his finger. Lokki had given him the heirloom immediately after he had explained how he and Halgar had come across the old battle site, the dead dwarfs with the ore chests and the subsequent ambush by the orcs. As he was a relation of Redmane it was only right that he have it.

'I cannot be certain, but the bones we found bore that talisman and they were old, as if he had been dead for some time.'

'Was there a hammer amongst the remains?' Uthor asked.

'None that we discovered,' Lokki replied.

Uthor sighed lamentably.

'Dreng tromm, then I am doubly saddened. Lord Kadrin's rune hammer was presented to him many years ago, when he was in his youth, by the then High King, Morgrim Blackbeard,' Uthor said. 'If my ancestor is dead then it means the hammer is lost, either to the urk or the Black Water,' he added, tucking the heirloom back under his armour. 'We had best make haste,' he said grimly, 'this does not bode well for Karak Varn.'

CHAPTER TWO

IT WAS WITH some relief that Gromrund and Hakem finally reached the gate to Karak Varn. The hammerer's mood had grown steadily more belligerent the longer they travelled together and the prince of Barak Varr feared the two of them might have come to blows. His tunic was freshly tailored and he would not have it soiled in a brawl, nor would he be received into the hold of Karak Varn in such a state of disrepair.

'Behold,' said Gromrund. It was the first time he had spoken in over an hour. 'The southern gate of Karak Varn.' The hammerer seemed to straighten as he said it, and was made impossibly tall by the mighty warhelm that sat upon his brow, the two great horns spiralling from it almost touching the roof of the tunnel. The helmet incorporated a half mask, too, that concealed much of the hammerer's face, but still his moods were easy to discern.

The gate was impressive. Tall and wide, it was set into a vaulted antechamber that ended the narrow tunnel. Etched with gilded spiral designs and elaborate crosshatching, it was the height of the fully helmeted hammerer five times over. With the intricate gold framing and knot work the past histories of the karak were described in painstaking mosaic. Truly, it was a stunning piece of craft and a testament to the dwarfs' mastery of metal, displayed ever proudly, for what was merely a side entrance into the hold. To Hakem, it was little more than an ornate door, plain and austere – nothing like the bejewelled entryways of Barak Varr.

'There is something wrong here,' Hakem said suddenly, his mood darkening quickly.

'If you remark of the lustre of the gilded gates of Barak Varr, once more...' Gromrund warned, brandishing his great hammer meaningfully.

'No, it's not that.' The seriousness in Hakem's tone demanded attention as he gripped his rune hammer.

'Yes, I see it,' Gromrund said, facing the southern gate, gripping his hammer haft a little tighter.

'Where are the guards?'

GROMRUND LED THE way through the gate. Deciding against hailing for it to be opened or even knocking, the dwarfs had to push hard against it to force an opening. Worryingly, it was neither locked nor barred. Once inside, a long and lofty hall stretched before them. It was lined with stone statues; thanes and kings of Karak Varn and lit by flickering braziers mounted in sconces. One of the statues was toppled over. Its fall had shattered the terracotta slabs beneath and removed its head. Rubble was strewn all about. On the left wall, a huge tapestry depicting a great battle fought against the elves during the War of Vengeance was torn. Shreds of material hung down like strips of flayed skin.

'This was not the welcome I had envisaged,' Hakem said humourlessly, gaze ever watchful in the deepening shadows of the hall. 'Where are our clan brothers?'

'Karak Varn is invaded,' Gromrund hissed, fear edging his voice. 'These halls should be the dominion of Kadrin Redmane, lord of this hold.'

'Yet they seem abandoned.' Hakem finished for him, saying what the hammerer was thinking.

'Indeed,' Gromrund concurred, noting the absence of any dwarfs at the south entrance, even dead ones.

'Is it possible that Redmane and his kin merely moved on, following another seam of ore? It is the way of our people,' Hakem reasoned, stepping carefully, every footfall a clattering din in the abject silence.

The two dwarfs advanced slowly and cautiously, and spoke in low tones. Something was desperately wrong here. Both knew that this was no dwarf migration; no pursuit of a more promising vein of ore. Some terrible fate had befallen the karak. It appeared empty – in a place where guards at least should be present – and utterly bereft of life; even the hammer falls of the forges, usually an ever-present and reassuring clamour, were silent.

The long hall soon gave way to another area of the hold, perhaps a merchant quarter – it was wide and dark, shadows cast from the illuminated entryway suggesting another hall with associated galleries and antechambers. Unlit braziers, growing cold, were set in the walls and the detritus of trade lay all about: ruined casks, broken carts and broad barrels, wrecked wooden stalls and racks.

'I thought the hold had been resettled,' Hakem remarked, biting his tongue about the great merchant halls of Barak Varr. 'If it was recently contested, where are the signs of battle? What in the name of Grungni happened here?'

'I know not,' Gromrund breathed. 'Karak Varn was wrested back from the rat-kin and the grobi years ago. The entire upper deeps were conquered by dawi, though much of the lower levels are ruined and flooded still from the Time of Woes.'

'It is as I read it,' agreed Hakem. 'Though this place looks dead, as if...'

'Hsst!' Gromrund motioned for quiet, raising a clenched fist. With the same hand he pointed towards a runty-looking figure, swathed in shadows and crouched with its back to them, in the middle of the hall.

With unspoken understanding, Hakem ranged wide of the figure, moving silently to catch him at his flank. Gromrund headed straight ahead, low and quiet as he stalked his prey.

As the hammerer drew close, he saw more of his prey's appearance. Its clothes were ragged: coarse and filth-stained garments, the stink of which rankled at his nostrils. Gromrund could not keep the sneer of contempt from his face – if it was a grobi swine his hammer would crack its wretched skull, though as he got closer he realised it was too big for a mere goblin. The creature wore a helmet upon its head, too, dented and tarnished. Doubtless the foul greenskin, whatever its breed, had stolen it from some noble dwarf's corpse.

Anger swelled in Gromrund's breast and a red rage overlaid his vision, before he saw Hakem ready to strike at the creature's flank.

'Turn, filth!' Gromrund bellowed, all thoughts of caution gone. He wanted to see the fear in the greenskin's eyes before he smote it. 'Turn and feel the wrath of Karak Hirn!'

The runt-like shadow figure seemed to leap up in sudden shock and whirled around to face the hammerer.

'Hold!' it cried in Khazalid. Gromrund's hammer stalled a few inches from stoving its skull in. Hakem, frozen momentarily, held his rune hammer aloft and ready to strike. 'Hold!'

It was no goblin. The bedraggled swine before them was a dwarf. Gromrund, now facing him, recognised the dwarf's garb as belonging to that of the Grey Mountains. Known as 'Grey dwarfs', they were the poorer cousins of the Worlds Edge Mountains, the Black Mountains and the Vaults. The hammerer then noticed a large pack behind the dwarf, who held up his hands plaintively. Some of the contents had spilled out: spoons, a silver ancestor idol and even a dented firkin were amongst the booty. It was unlikely that these trinkets were the Grey dwarf's belongings.

Gromrund's lip curled up with distaste as he saw the scattered treasure, but he lowered his hammer.

The Grey dwarf exhaled in relief, shaking slightly at almost being sent to his ancestors prematurely, and nodded his thanks.

'I didn't hear you approach,' he said, voice quivering a little as he extended a grubby hand. 'Drimbold Grum,' he offered, 'of Karak Norn, in the Grey–'

'Doubtless you were too intent on whatever it was you were doing,' Gromrund grumbled, staring from Drimbold's hand to the bulging pack. 'And I already know of your heritage, dawi,' the hammerer growled, keeping his hands firmly at his side, 'and of your name. The Grums are well recorded in the Tallhelm Clan's Book of Grudges. One hundred years ago, you supplied us with a stable of shoddy lode ponies, weak of back and bowel. Recompense for which is yet to be made by the reckoners,' he added through gritted teeth.

'Ah, no, that was the Sournose Grum's,' said the Grey dwarf. '*I* am one of the Sour*tooth* Grums,' he added, smiling.

Gromrund glowered.

Drimbold lowered his hand and his eyes, and quickly set about replacing the items that had spilled from his pack.

'He smells worse than a narwangli,' hissed Hakem behind his hand, not entirely convinced the Grey dwarf hadn't soiled himself when they'd surprised him.

Gromrund ignored him.

'What do you know of the fate of Kadrin Redmane and his kin?' the hammerer demanded, once Drimbold had turned back around to face them and was on his feet. Even the dwarf's mail was rusted and ill kept, and his beard was infested with gibil.

'I do not know, my kinsdwarf. I only just arrived myself. I was *adjusting* the items in my pack when you found me. I noticed one of the straps was loose,' he added by way of explanation.

'Indeed,' muttered Gromrund, not bothering to disguise his suspicion.

'Has Karak Norn made a pledge to Karak Varn, also, in ridding the Black Mountains of the urk tribes gathered there?' Hakem asked, wrinkling his nose at the Grey dwarf's stink.

'Precisely that,' Drimbold confirmed brightly.

'Then, Grum or no, you had best come with us,' Gromrund returned. 'Perhaps the Grey dwarfs have something to contribute if they are willing to send an emissary across the mountains. Besides, I have an ill feeling about this place,' the hammerer added, looking around the large hall of the merchant's quarter again, before returning his gaze to Drimbold. 'It smells foul.'

With that, the hammerer stalked off into the gloom, Hakem following at his side. Whatever differences were felt by the Karak Hirn and Barak Varr dwarf, they were nothing compared to the mutual distaste they held for a resident of the Grey Mountains. They were poor dwarfs, scratching a living off rocks, without the breeding or heritage of the other holds. Still, a dawi he was and if part of the war council they should travel together. In any event, it was far better that a stern eye was kept upon him, lest he get into trouble and bring it down on all their heads.

'Where are we going?' Drimbold asked, adjusting his cumbersome pack, an eye on the way he had come.

'To the audience chamber,' Gromrund replied, 'where the rest of the war council are due to assemble.'

'What if they're gone too?' Drimbold asked again.

'Then we wait,' Gromrund snarled, turning briefly to set his steely countenance upon the Grey dwarf, 'for as long as it takes!'

In truth, Gromrund did not know what else *to* do. His role here was merely to hear of Lord Redmane's grievances and commit what forces to staunching the growing grobi hordes that he was permitted. With Redmane absent, and his hold deserted, he was slightly lost and getting steadily more annoyed.

'An ufdi and a wanaz,' he muttered, bemoaning his travelling companions as he followed the runic markers that would lead them to the audience chamber. 'Why, Valaya, do you test me so?'

THE GREAT GATE of Karak Varn loomed large and imposing – two immense slabs of stone, bound with steel and gold set into the very mountainside.

''Tis quite a sight,' breathed Lokki, arching his head properly to survey the gate's majesty.

'Aye lad, an eye opener you might say,' Halgar agreed.

'Indeed,' said Uthor.

Rorek nodded sagely, supping on his pipe.

The four dwarfs were standing on a short but wide road fashioned from stone tiles of ruddy terracotta and grey granite that led up to the massive gate. The walkway, a preamble to the majesty of the entrance proper, was decorated with square spiral devices and inset by a band of runes on either edge. Shallow stone steps met the short road and ended in a wide plateau of smoothed rock, similarly inscribed with gold intaglio.

The main gate itself was a full two hundred feet at its highest point and framed by a stout arch of fashioned bronze, inlaid with intricate copper filigree. A cross-hammers device encompassed both sides of the gate, the stone haft of each inset with large gemstones. Judging by the crude scratch marks around the jewels, efforts had been made to remove them but to no avail. On either side of the gate was a symbolic rendering of a dwarf face, each wearing helmets, but one with an eye patch, the other bearing horns, and forged from bronze. At the gate's apex was a carved stone anvil.

At each end of the immense structure there stood an eighty-foot statue, set proudly upon a rounded stone dais, banded with runic script. On the left there was Grungni, clad in long mail, a forge hammer in his hand. On the right, the imposing figure of Grimnir, war-like with his noble crest standing sternly from his shaven skull, the mighty axes forged by his brother god gripped in both hands. Other, smaller statues gave way to the ancestor gods – kings and thanes of Karak Varn all – set in mighty alcoves carved into the mountain rock. Harsh weathering had worn the statues down, some were even toppled over.

'Praise Grungni for his skill and wisdom that we humble dawi might fashion such beauty,' Uthor breathed reverently.

'For his hand guides all things, and is felt in the hammer blow of every forge,' Rorek completed the litany.

Uthor clapped the engineer heartily on the shoulder then turned towards Lokki, his expression serious.

'We had best keep word of their liege-lord's death to ourselves until we are admitted,' the dwarf suggested.

Lokki nodded. 'Agreed,' he said and cast his gaze up to an empty parapet carved out of the rock and above the gate itself. It was a watch station, yet strangely there were no quarrellers in evidence to garrison it. Still, Lokki noted the crossbow slits and murder holes warily.

'Ho there!' he bellowed. 'The emissaries of Izor, Kadrin and Zhufbar seek an audience with the lord of Karak Varn.' The last part nearly stuck in the thane's throat, given his foreknowledge of Kadrin Redmane's demise. It was likely, given the condition of the bones they'd found, that the dwarfs of the hold already knew of it, but then a successor would have been chosen, or at the very least a warden appointed to act in Redmane's stead. In either case, it did not explain the fact that there were no guards at the main gate.

'Fellow dawi beseech admittance and the hospitality of Karak Varn,' Lokki cried again. He was met by silence.

Though it was only late afternoon the sun was dipping in the sky, thick black clouds, pregnant with rain, smothering it. From the north, a fierce wind was blowing, its howling chorus tearing through the peaks.

'The weather bodes ill,' grumbled Halgar, casting a look behind him at the deepening shadows.

Uthor stepped forward and hammered on the door with his fist. It only made a dull thud. 'Teeth of Grimnir,' he swore, 'this is hopeless! How are we to attend a council of war if we are unable to enter the very hold at which the council is to take place?'

'I fear we may already be too late, Uthor, son of Algrim,' said Lokki. 'But still we must try to get inside. Perhaps if we were to take the Ungdrin road, there is an entryway a few leagues east, and approach through the southern gate?' he wondered.

'A journey of two weeks at the very least and we have no way of knowing that the entryway is still open to us,' said Halgar, wincing as he sat down upon a rock. The spear wound was still a little raw but the tenacious dwarf had refused any treatment. 'It'll take more than an urk blade to finish me off, lad!' he'd bellowed to Lokki when the thane had expressed his concern. The longbeard mastered the pain quickly and took out a small clay pipe from within his beard. He stuffed it with weed from a pouch on his belt and lit it with a small flint and steel device. Taking a long draw, he blew out a large smoke ring and added, 'The hour grows late and soon grobi will swarm this mountainside. They are curs, and would likely shoot us in the back from behind a rock,' he spat, taking another pull on his pipe.

'Two weeks is too long,' said Uthor with uncharacteristic urgency. 'I would gladly fight an army of grobi should circumstances require it, but we need to get inside now and find out what fate has befallen our kinsdwarfs.'

'There might be another way,' said Rorek from the back of the group, chewing the end of his pipe as he eyed the lofty watch station a further twenty feet above the two hundred foot gate. He paced forward then stopped a short distance from the entranceway. Raising his left hand in front of him – his right still holding the pipe as he supped on it – he stuck up his thumb and pointed his forefinger. Looking down the extended finger, squinting slightly with his good eye, he mumbled something and took three paces backwards. Then he unslung his crossbow from around his side and detached the metal box attachment filled with quarrels. With the others rapt in silent incredulity, he hung the metal box back onto his tool belt and replaced it with another, except this one harboured a coiled up rope with a hook at one end.

Rorek then crouched down on one knee and aimed the crossbow, complete with new attachment, towards the watch station parapet. Squinting slightly, he flipped up a metal catch on the crossbow's stock – it was a small steel ring with a cross in it. Trapping the crossbow in his right armpit and against his shoulder, he tucked the pipe back in his belt, stuck the thumb of his left hand in his mouth and raised it up to catch the wind. Satisfied, he aimed down the steel cross and fired.

There was the sudden *crack* and *twang* of a heavy spring as the hook exploded from the end of the crossbow, followed by the whirring of rope unwinding from a metal pulley as it was carried with the hook, flying upwards and then arcing in the direction of the parapet. Each of the four dwarfs followed it, mesmerised. The hook sailed over the parapet and into the open watch station, followed by the clang of steel against stone. Rorek wound the crank at the end of the stock furiously, steel scraping stone above them until the hook caught and the rope pulled taut.

'Grungni's steel tongs,' said the engineer.

'May they ever bend the elements of the earth to his will,' Uthor finished for him. 'What now?' he asked, slightly dumbfounded.

If any guards were present above the gate, they would have come to investigate by now. It seemed the dwarfs had no choice.

'Now I climb,' Rorek returned, setting the crossbow against a rock as he strapped a set of shallow spikes to his boots. 'Look after these for me,' he added, shrugging off his weapon's belt and pack. He then proceeded to walk forward slowly, all the time steadily winding up the slack from the rope. Once he reached the gate wall, he attached a small clasp on the crossbow's stock to his tool belt, and placed a spiked boot against the mountain rock. He wound a little farther, and when he was certain the rope supported his weight, placed a second boot against the rock. Now suspended above the ground, he wound the crank slowly and carefully, one steady step after another as he climbed up the sheer wall.

'Impetuous youth,' Halgar mumbled from his seat on the rock, puffing smoke rings agitatedly. 'Beardlings,' he muttered, despite Rorek's gnarled leather skin and broad beard making him at least a hundred, 'no respect for tradition.'

It took Rorek almost an hour to climb the two hundred and twenty feet to reach the edge of the parapet. By the time he did, the sun had all but faded in the sky as the engineer scrambled over it. Rorek gave a short wave to indicate his success and then disappeared from view. All the dwarfs could do now was wait for Rorek to try and open the gate.

'I HAVE TRAVELLED far to reach the hold of my kinsdwarf,' Uthor remarked, 'but to venture from the Vaults, across Black Fire Pass no less, that is indeed a perilous journey and Redmane, to my understanding, was not your clan brother.'

The dwarfs had set up camp outside the gate upon the roadway, far enough from the edge of the mountains to ensure they were not surprised by a grobi ambush or unknowingly preyed upon by some other beast. Like the rest of their kin, they had little need for shelter, hardy enough to weather even the harshest conditions, though the lack of a roof, together with several tons of rock, above their heads was a little unsettling.

Uthor sat facing Lokki. Both dwarfs had their weapons laid in front of them, their hands locked around stout tankards, and were seated on their shields. They had made a small fire, surrounded by a thick belt of stones. If they were to attract the attention of grobi, they would do so with or without the flames in their midst. Besides, greenskins hated fire, as did many other denizens of the night – it would be a useful weapon, if it came to it.

The dwarfs were arranged so each could look over the shoulder of the other at the high crags into which the main gate of Karak Varn was wedged, should any threat present itself.

'Halgar and I...' Lokki began, looking towards his venerable mentor. Halgar was nearby, and sat unmoving on the rock, his eyes fixed forward, unblinking. His hands were sat upon his lap, restfully. Uthor followed Lokki's gaze and saw the statuesque longbeard for himself.

'He bears many scars,' he said, noting the lack of fingers on Halgar's right hand.

'He lost them long ago, but won't speak of how. At least he never has to me,' Lokki told him.

'Is he… all right?' said Uthor, a hint of concern in his voice as he continued to regard the still form of Halgar.

'He's sleeping,' Lokki explained with a thin smile.

'With his eyes open?'

'Grobi will as sure as kill you in your bed as on the battlefield, he always taught me,' said Lokki.

'Truly, the wise have much to teach us.' Uthor nodded his deepest respect in the direction of the slumbering longbeard.

'Halgar and I,' Lokki tried again, once he had Uthor's attention, 'are here on a debt of honour,' he explained. 'Almost nine hundred years ago, during the War of Vengeance, Kromkaz Vargasson, my ancestor and grandsire of Halgar, was ambushed on the way to Oeragor by a band of elf rangers.'

At the mention of elves, Uthor hawked a great gobbet of phlegm into the fire where it sizzled briefly.

'The elves were swift and cunning,' Lokki continued, the glow of the fire casting his face in increasing shadows with the gradual onset of night. 'Four of Kromkaz's kin lay dead before a shield was raised, an axe drawn, and yet still more fell,' Lokki went on, repeating by rote the tale that Halgar had taught him. 'Hiding behind their bows, they herded Kromkaz and his warriors into a narrow defile and my ancestor would surely have died – he and his warriors – were it not for miners from Karak Varn. They emerged from a hidden tunnel, part of the Ungdrin road, at the ridge from where the elves had Kromkaz pinned. The miners, dwarfs of the Copperhand clan, fell upon the elves, chasing them from their hiding places. His foes revealed, Kromkaz ordered his warriors to attack and the elves were crushed. Kromkaz reached Oeragor that day. They fought alongside the Copperhand clan and witnessed Morgrim, cousin of Snorri, son of the High King, slay the elf lord Imladrik,' Lokki said, and the reflected glare of the fire made his eyes seem as if they were ablaze. 'We come to honour that debt, to repay the dwarfs of the Copperhand clan and the hold of Karak Varn.'

Uthor nodded solemnly, wiping a tear from his eye as he did so.

'Great deeds,' he said, his voice slightly choked. 'Great and noble deeds.'

'Ho there!' the distant voice of Rorek broke the reverie.

The engineer was nowhere to be seen. Lokki and Uthor got to their feet, and took up their weapons and armour.

Halgar blinked once and was awake, the old dwarf standing up as if he'd never been asleep.

Uthor kicked out the fire and went over to stand expectantly beside Lokki and Halgar, outside the great gates.

'About time,' Uthor muttered. Halgar's low grumblings were indiscernible, though Uthor thought he caught the word 'wazzock'.

'What are you doing stood over there?' came the engineer's voice again, echoing throughout the canyon.

This time all three turned in the direction of the sound. Still there was nothing. With Lokki leading them, the three dwarfs moved cautiously away from the great gate and towards where Rorek's voice was coming from. Negotiating their way around the right-hand side of the gate, to where one of the long galleries of statues was arrayed, they saw Rorek's head about fifty feet up and poking over a shallow lip of stone. Such was the ingenious geology – part natural, part dwarf-made – of the stone overhang that were it not for the fact that his voice had guided them and that his head was sticking out, the engineer would have been invisible.

'Take this,' he hollered from above and shortly afterwards a trail of rope came down to them.

One by one, the trio of dwarfs climbed up a stark, flat face of rock that got them to a short ledge from where Rorek's seemingly disembodied head was watching them keenly.

When they found the engineer, he was sat inside a narrow, dank-looking tunnel. Only a dwarf, and one that was being particularly observant, would have been able to detect the opening. Stretched over the narrow ledge, Rorek was holding up an ironbound grate, thickly latticed and stained in brown and yellowish hues that were visible even in the fading light. A trail of darkly stained water, long since dried up, fed away from the opening into a shallow rut in the ledge and was carried in long streaks down a section of the rock face, away from the statues.

'I have found our entrance,' the engineer said proudly.

'Wazzock!' bawled Halgar, cresting the ledge. 'You have found the tunnel to the latrine.'

Uthor wrinkled his nose when he noticed the concealed pit far beneath the grate.

Unperturbed, Rorek crept back from the ledge, retreating back into the tunnel to allow the others to pass. 'I could not operate the mechanism to open the great gate, try as I might,' he explained, 'and this was the only other way in. I've disarmed any traps but you'll have to duck, though.'

Lokki went in first, pausing for a moment at the mention of traps, but traversing the short ledge quickly. Halgar followed, grunting and muttering all the while. Uthor brought up the rear, gathering the engineer's rope up after him and giving it back to Rorek, along with the rest of the engineer's possessions.

The latrine grate slammed shut in their wake. Rorek bolted it shut from the inside, before ramming down a heavy-looking second gate. Three clockwise turns of a stylised, bronze ancestor face wrought into the wall completed the ritual and was accompanied by the dull retort of more, hidden, locks. 'Just a short crawl to the outer gateway hall,' the engineer said and started off down the narrow tunnel. It was disgusting; a long dark yellow stain ran down the middle of it and the walls of the tight space were encrusted with dried filth. The stink of it was palpable.

'I have smelled urk less foul,' Halgar grumbled again as the dwarfs set off after Rorek.

TRUE TO ROREK'S word, the dwarfs emerged from another iron grate into the outer gateway hall. It was a fairly spartan room, but vast, designed to accommodate huge throngs of dwarfs as they entered from the main gate. Any nobles, craft guild masters or other notable dignitaries could then be received by the lord of the hold in the audience chamber that resided at the bottom of a lengthy stairway connecting it to the outer gateway hall.

'This is how I found it,' said the engineer. The chamber was deserted and barren save for a dwarf helmet resting forlornly on its side in the centre of the room. 'Not mine,' Rorek added.

'Draw your weapons,' Halgar growled, glancing first to the gate on the left and then to the gate on the right – beyond them were the barracks, where a throng's warriors could be housed temporarily. Lastly, his gaze fell to the gate at the far wall, that which led to the stairway.

Axe in hand, shield raised, Lokki said, 'We head for the audience chamber and make oaths to Grungni that we are not too late.'

Beyond the next gate the long stairway wended down into the darkness, great columns of stone carved with clan symbols and runes punctuating it. Though lit by hulking iron braziers set at regular intervals, the shadows cast upon the stairway were long and could hide any number of lurking dangers.

The dwarfs moved swiftly and in single file, two watching the left, and two the right, until they reached the entrance to the audience chamber.

'Someone has been here before us,' Lokki hissed, standing on one side of the double gate that was slightly ajar. Uthor quickly took up a position on the opposite side, axe in hand. Halgar and Rorek waited pensively behind them, ready to charge in.

'Make ready,' said Lokki.

Uthor nodded.

The two dwarfs thrust the door open and charged into the audience chamber, weapons drawn and bellowing war cries. When they saw the dwarf wearing the massive warhelm sitting at a long oval table, the merchant thane bedecked in fine velvet and the dishevelled looking creature huddled in the corner, counting silver spoons into a burgeoning pack, they stopped abruptly and were lost for words.

'HOW LONG HAVE you been waiting here?' Lokki asked.

The dwarfs were seated around the wood table, carved of mountain oak and inlaid with intricate runic designs rendered in gold. Introductions had been made and it had been quickly established that they were all there for the same purpose: to attend a council of war at the behest of Kadrin Redmane, to discuss the best way to rid the nearby mountains of the gathering greenskin tribes.

'Three weeks, is as near as I can reckon,' said Gromrund, his eyes fierce behind the faceplate of his warhelm. He was the only dwarf not to have divested himself of his helmet – a fact Lokki was wise enough not to press.

'And you have seen no one in that time?' Uthor chipped in, leaning back in his stool as he lit up his pipe.

'I ventured a look up the great stair and even explored two of the clan halls, but there was no one. I returned to the audience chamber and waited as I was bidden,' Gromrund explained. 'I had hoped to be received by Lord Redmane,' he added.

Uthor flashed a glance at Lokki, who then turned to the hammerer.

'Kadrin Redmane is dead, slain by urk, may he sit at the table of his ancestors,' he said grimly. 'Halgar and I found his remains on the Old Dwarf Road at the edge of Black Water. The four of us buried him and his companions in the earth, under the shadow of the karak.'

'Remains?' said the hammerer. 'How can you be sure it was Kadrin Redmane?'

'He wore this talisman,' Uthor told him, holding it aloft in the light cast by the torches in the room.

'Dreng tromm,' Gromrund muttered, bowing his head, momentarily lost in his thoughts. 'Then we are too late,' he said, grimly meeting Lokki's gaze.

'Many years too–'

'Quiet!' Halgar cut Lokki off before he could speak.

The sudden outburst spooked Drimbold, who dropped a gilded comb that he was using to preen the gibil from out of his beard.

Hakem's expression showed that he recognised it, but before he could take it up with the Grey dwarf, Halgar was on his feet and stalking to the back of the room. He edged towards a stone statue of Grungni set upon a large octagonal base, axe in hand. Lokki followed him, knowing by now to always trust the longbeard's instincts. Rorek waited just behind him and readied his crossbow. Uthor went the other way around the table, Gromrund right at his back.

'What is that stench?' the hammerer whispered, sniffing at the air.

'It matters not,' Uthor snapped, drawing his axe. 'Make ready.'

Hakem followed them, the Barak Varr dwarf stealing a reproachful glance at Drimbold, who waited pensively at the table, clutching his pack.

Halgar stopped at the statue and listened intently. He motioned to Lokki. The thane came forward and examined the statue. Looking down, he saw something.

'Rorek,' he hissed, beckoning the engineer, who quickly joined him, shouldering his crossbow, as Halgar stepped to the side.

Rorek followed Lokki's gaze to the octagonal base and noticed a strange configuration of carvings, slightly outset from the rest. Crouching down, the engineer carefully ran his fingers over the stone, seeking out any imperfections. He pulled a piece of the design out, a perfectly round dwarf head effigy and rotated it. When he pushed the head back into place, there was a grinding sound and the dull scrap of a sliding bolt of stone, then a small crack appeared at the lip of the octagonal base.

'Help me lift it,' Rorek said, getting his fingers beneath the lip. Lokki did likewise, catching on quickly to what the engineer wanted him to do. Halgar stood poised with Uthor, whilst Gromrund and Hakem had gathered torches and held them at the ready to be thrust at whatever lurked beneath them.

'Heave!' Lokki cried and the two of them lifted off part of the octagonal slab, revealing a small, darkened chamber within, below the statue itself, with several tunnels leading off from it. Inside, blinking back the glare of the torches was a dwarf, a thick, leather-bound book clasped to his chest.

'Ralkan,' he mumbled, half-crazed, trying to ward off the bright light with his hand, 'Ralkan Geltberg,' he repeated, louder and with greater lucidity. The dwarf's eyes were pleading as he added, 'Last survivor of Karak Varn.'

CHAPTER THREE

SKREEKIT WRUNG HIS paws together, and fought the urge to squirt the musk of fear. Beneath filth-caked robes, daubed in the bloody symbols of Clan Skryre, the skaven's fur was moist with sweat. A furtive glance at another agent, a warlock of low breeding, drowning in his own blood from a dagger thrust in his lung, and he found his voice at last.

'Three hundred warp tokens, four cohorts of warriors for protection against Clan Moulder and a hundred slaves is our price, yes. Make deal, quick-quick,' Skreekit blathered.

STANDING BEFORE THE warlock, in a dank chamber edged in filth, dirty straw, and other signs of skaven habitation, was Thratch Sourpaw. He called it his 'scheming room' but in truth it was merely one of the many antechambers appended to the subterranean warren of the skaven. The black-furred warlord of Clan Rictus sneered his dissatisfaction, looking at Skreekit down his long snout and revealing an old, but horrific, wound on his neck. Coarse, brown stitching was still embedded in his flesh, made visible by the pink scar tissue. Thratch's cold reddish eyes picked out something behind the nervous warlock, who had just soiled his robes further.

Thratch watched as something detached itself from the cavern wall at the agent's back, a layer of swiftly moving shadow, silent and at one with the darkness. There was the sound of metal tearing flesh and blood exploded from the warlock's mouth, spraying the dirt-encrusted stones in front of him with crimson, a jagged blade punching through his chest. The knife was withdrawn savagely and Skreekit slumped forward. Sheer terror twisted his face, lying in a puddle of his own filth and viscera, blood bubbles bursting on his froth-drenched muzzle as poison ravaged his innards.

Thratch was one of the many warlords of Clan Rictus as well as dwarf slayer, goblin killer and conqueror of Karak Varn. Clad in thick metal armour, wreathed in a fine patina of rust, stray black tufts of his fur eking out beneath the pauldrons and vambraces, he looked formidable. The warlord knew this and played on it as he approached the last of the three warlocks that had come to make deals with him.

'Now,' the warlord said, signalling for his assassin, Kill-Klaw, to emerge fully from the shadows, certain there would be no attempt on his life. The Clan Eshin adept obeyed dutifully and lingered at the warlock's side, just enough so the skaven was aware of his presence, just enough so the warlock couldn't see him.

'You build device for me, yes-yes.' Thratch pointed a claw towards a crude design he had scratched on the wall with the spike he had instead of a paw – the three warlocks had winced as he had done it. 'Your promise-price,' he demanded.

The last representative of Clan Skryre gulped audibly before he answered – a half glance at the lurking assassin.

'*One* hundred warp tokens, *two* cohorts of warriors and… *fifty* slaves,' he ventured.

Thratch loomed close, hot breath making the agent's eyes water.

'Accepted, yes,' he hissed, a long and terrible grin wrinkling his features.

'WHAT HAPPENED HERE, brother?' Lokki asked, his tone soothing.

Ralkan sat in front of him, still. He was fairly diminutive, even by dwarf standards, and the great tome he clutched to his breast only made him seem smaller still.

'Red eyes,' he murmured. 'Red eyes in the dark… everywhere.'

The crazed dwarf wore the scholarly robes of a lorekeeper, one of the few chosen to chronicle and remember all the great events of a hold – its deeds, its heroes, its grudges. A talisman bearing the rune of Valaya hung around his neck – it seemed the goddess of protection had heeded his pledges. He wore a series of belts and straps over his scribe's attire, Lokki assumed they were designed to secure the book should the lorekeeper require the use of his arms. The dwarf's beard was dishevelled, wretched with dirt and encrusted filth, as were his skin and nails. He looked wasted and thin, like he could do with a good meal inside of him. How long he had been there, hiding within a warren of tunnels, scrabbling in the dark, Lokki could only guess. Rorek was in the secret chamber beneath the statue of Grungni at that very moment, trying to ascertain how far the tunnels went and how many there were. Of the others, Uthor and Halgar were with Lokki, while Gromrund and Hakem stood guard at each of the entranceways. Drimbold sat sullenly in the corner, occasionally glancing at the way out of the audience chamber, before returning to his thoughts.

'Bah,' snarled Halgar, the old dwarf getting to his feet. 'He has said nothing else since we dragged him from his hole.' The longbeard walked away to go glare at Drimbold, the end of his pipe flaring to life as he lit it.

Lokki watched him go, then turned back to Ralkan and reached for the book he had pinioned to his chest. The lorekeeper seemed reluctant to part with it, but, with some gentle urging from Uthor accompanied by several dried strips of meat, released it.

"'Tis the Karak Varn Book of Remembering,' Uthor said solemnly.

Lokki opened it, thumbing carefully through the thick parchment pages. Names in their hundreds of thousands were etched within, names of all the dwarfs of Karak Varn that had lived and died: their clans, their deeds and how they met their end.

Lokki skipped ahead to the last of the entries and read aloud.

'*Marbad Hammerfell, journeyman ironsmith, fell to a skaven blade in his back. Fyngal Fykasson, stonecutter, died by drinking water from a tainted well. Gurthang Copperhand, miner, inhaled deadly skaven gas.*' He lingered on this last one and mouthed a silent oath to Valaya. 'There are hundreds like this,' he said, 'killed by the rat-kin, stabbed in the back with spears and daggers, poisoned in their sleep!'

Uthor clenched his fists until his knuckles cracked. He was breathing loud and heavily, his face flushed a deep red.

Before he could say or do anything, Rorek emerged from the secret chamber beneath the statue of Grungni.

'As far as I can tell, there are several tunnels,' he began, 'extending far into the hold and across many deeps. But they are narrow; I doubt any of us could get through them.'

'Little wonder he is so filthy,' Lokki remarked with a short glance at Ralkan. The lorekeeper, having devoured the meat given to him by Uthor, was staring aimlessly.

'I found markings scratched onto the wall in the chamber immediately below...' said Rorek, arresting Lokki's attention. For the first time the thane noticed that Ralkan had a small rock pick tucked into his belt.

'...made by some tool or other,' Rorek continued. 'If they equate to years, he has been here for a while.' The engineer's expression was grim as he regarded Lokki.

'How did this doom befall Karak Varn?' Lokki asked the lorekeeper again. 'How long have you been in hiding?'

Ralkan's lips moved soundlessly. There was desperation in his eyes as he met the thane's gaze.

'Red eyes...' he sobbed at last, tears flowing down his face, making pale streaks in the grime. 'Red eyes, everywhere.'

* * *

'IT IS SIMPLE,' Uthor said firmly, on his feet and pacing the length of the audience chamber, 'we find the hold's book of grudges – that will tell us all we need to know.'

'And risk alerting whatever sacked this hold to our presence?' Gromrund countered. 'It is reckless folly.'

Uthor rounded on the hammerer, who was sat on one of the stools, an imposing sight in his warhelm and full armour. 'The hammerers of Karak Hirn are obviously of less stern stock than those of Kadrin,' he snarled.

Gromrund shot to his feet, thumping his hand down so hard upon the table that it shook, spilling ale with his vehemence, much to the annoyance of the other dwarfs.

'The brethren of Horn Hold are ever bold, and not lacking in courage,' he bellowed. 'I would not sit here and have their name–'

'Quiet fool,' hissed Halgar, reproachfully, 'lest you have forgotten your own desire for caution at rousing the denizens of this place.'

The entire dwarf throng were once again arrayed around the table – all except Ralkan, who had retreated to a corner and was mumbling quietly. Some smoked pipeweed, others nursed tankards forlornly – ale supplies were running low. This was despite the fact that Rorek had discovered a hidden vault inside the room that contained several reserves of beer, doubtless left there in preparation for the council. The assembled dwarfs were locked in a long and hard debate, not to be rushed into rash action without due and proper consideration, about what they should do. All except Drimbold, who was eyeing the finery of Hakem's merchant attire, before averting his attentions to Halgar as something else caught his interest.

'I say we venture into the deeps,' said Uthor, eyeing Gromrund as the dwarf sat back down, clearly disgruntled and chewing his beard in agitation. He switched his gaze to Lokki, knowing as a thane of a royal clan and with his venerable companion, it was his favour he needed to sway. 'It is our duty to discover the fate of our kinsdwarfs and avenge them! What do we, sons of Grungni all, have to fear from ratmen?' he added, top lip curling in a derisive sneer. 'We can scare those cowards away.'

Lokki remained thoughtful throughout Uthor's impassioned rhetoric.

'How are we to find the kron?' asked Hakem, using a second beard comb to preen himself. 'I for one have no desire to scramble around in the dark, looking for something that might not even be there.'

'Indeed,' Gromrund chipped in, suddenly emboldened again. 'Even the ufdi sees the madness in what you are suggesting.'

If Hakem thought anything about the slight, he did not show it.

'The lorekeeper can guide us,' Uthor said simply, addressing the group again. 'But he is *zaki*,' Rorek whispered, casting a furtive glance at Ralkan before he twirled his finger around his temple.

Uthor turned to the lorekeeper. 'Can you guide us?' he asked. 'Can you take us to the dammaz kron of Karak Varn?'

There was a flash of lucidity in Ralkan's eyes and a moment's silence before he nodded.

Uthor looked again at Lokki. 'There you have it, the lorekeeper is our guide.'

Lokki returned Uthor's gaze, and was careful not to look to Halgar for guidance. This was something he would have to decide for himself. As member of a royal clan, be that of the Vaults or nay, hereditarily he had the highest status, despite the fact that both Halgar and Gromrund had longer beards. He was the leader.

'We head into the lower deeps,' he said, ignoring the grunting protestations of the hammerer, 'and retrieve the dammaz kron. The fate of Karak Varn must be known and these facts presented to the High King.'

'It is settled then,' said Uthor, with no small measure of satisfaction.

'It is settled.' Halgar spoke his approval.

'I have one question,' Drimbold piped up, beer froth coating his beard as he supped from his own weather-beaten tankard. 'Wise grey beard, why do you have an arrow sticking out of your chest?'

Halgar scowled.

THE DWARFS TRAVELLED down a long and narrow tunnel. They had passed numerous hallways, clan chambers, armouries and galleries during that time. So far, no more dwarfs of Karak Varn – not even skeletons – save for Ralkan, were found in the creeping dark of the deep. All that remained, it seemed, were the last vestiges of a toppled kingdom, its reclaimed glory wrecked by calamity, its once proud stature rendered to rubble. Dust lay thick in the air and it was tainted with the bitterness of regret and defeat.

The dwarfs had discovered, during Ralkan's more lucid moments – which were becoming ever more frequent – that the dammaz kron, the book of grudges, was in the King's Chambers located in the second deep. Much of the hold, even the upper levels, was in a state of utter ruination – fallen columns and statues, collapsed ceilings and gaping chasms all in evidence – and the dwarfs had been forced to take a fairly circuitous route. The narrow tunnel, fraught with rubble and jutting rocks where the walls had split, was merely part of that route.

Uthor strode alongside Ralkan, who was at the head of the group, the lorekeeper leading the way. Often he stopped suddenly, causing a clash of armoured bodies and muffled swearing behind him, pausing to regard his surroundings and then set off again without a word.

'Like I said, zaki,' Rorek, immediately behind them, had whispered in Uthor's ear. 'Are you sure he knows where he's going?'

Gromrund walked beside the engineer and wore an expression like brooding thunder. The hammerer had been silent throughout the trek, positively bristling at the will of the 'council' going against him. He gripped his great hammer tightly, glowering behind the mask of his helmet as he focused meaningfully on the back of Uthor's head.

Behind them Hakem and Drimbold, a bizarre pairing of wealth and poverty. Hakem cast frequent, sideways glances at the Grey dwarf, who stooped occasionally to pick something up and add it to his pack. The merchant-thane took great pains to ensure the strings of his purse were tight and his possessions securely fastened. Drimbold paid no heed to his discomfort and smiled back at Hakem broadly, using a silver fork, encrusted with jewels – Grungni only knew where he had appropriated it from – to pick strips of goat meat from his blackened teeth.

Lokki and Halgar brought up the rear, taking care to watch the route the dwarfs had taken, lest anything be following them.

'What do you think of the son of Algrim?' Lokki asked, keeping his voice low.

Halgar thought on it a moment, scrutinizing Uthor carefully and considering his answer before he spoke. 'He is a hazkal, to be sure. But he fights as if the very blood of Grimnir flows in his veins.' The longbeard blinked twice and rubbed his eyes with the back of his hand. 'And he bears a heavy burden, I know not what.'

'Are you all right, old one?' Lokki asked the longbeard. Halgar had been rubbing his eyes intermittently for the last hour, gnarled fingers kneading out whatever fatigue ailed them.

'An itch, is all,' he growled, 'Damn grobi stink is everywhere.' The longbeard stopped rubbing and stalked on a little harder, making it clear the conversation was at an end.

Halgar was old, so old that Lokki's father, the King of Karak Izor, had urged the longbeard not to take the road with Lokki, that one of his hammerers could accompany him instead. Halgar had snarled his derision at the stoutness of hammerers in 'these times' and more placidly had said he wanted to 'stretch his legs.' The king had relented, unwilling to go against the wishes of one of the oldest of the clan. Besides, there was the debt of Halgar's grandsire to consider, and the king would never oppose the pursuit of a pledge of honour. But throughout their journey to Karak Varn, Halgar had been prone to dark and reflective moods. Lokki had often woken in the night, after quaffing too much ale and needing to empty his bladder, to find the longbeard staring off into the dark as if looking at something just beyond his field of vision, just beyond his reach. It was as if he sensed an end was coming and he had no desire to wither and atrophy in the hold, scribing of his last days in some tome or scroll. He wanted to die with an axe in his hand and dwarf armour on his back. Lokki hoped his own end could be so glorious.

After that, Lokki fell into silence, remaining watchful of the dark.

THE LONG STAIRWAY stretched down into the waiting blackness of the second deep. Much like that which led to the audience chamber at the great gate, it was broad and illuminated by gigantic iron braziers wrought into the fearsome image of dragons and other creatures of ancient legend. The flames cast dancing shadows on the walls, throwing ephemeral slashes of light onto finely carved mosaics fashioned into the rocks. Each one was broken up by thick stone pillars, marked by rune bands of the royal clan of Karak Varn.

'Here, does High King Gotrek Starbreaker slay the elf king and take his petty crown,' intoned Halgar, pointing to one of the mosaics. On it, Gotrek Starbreaker was depicted in refulgent, golden armour, his axe drenched with blood. An elf corpse lay at his feet, the Phoenix Crown held aloft in the High King's hand and presented to a mighty throng of dwarfs arrayed about him.

'Lo, does the Bulvar Troll-beater, three-times grandson of Jorvar who did flee at Oeragor, face the grobi hordes, and reap a doom worthy of the sagas of old,' he said wistfully. Bulvar was a slayer, and bore a massive crest of red hair upon an otherwise shaven head. Half his body was painted to resemble a skeleton – an affectation common among the cult and indicative of the slayers' death oath – the other half was scribed with swirling tattoos and runic wards of Grimnir. Bulvar was alone, surrounded by orcs, goblins, trolls and wyverns. His last stand was made upon a great host of greenskin carcasses, the twin axes in his hands slaying goblins for all eternity.

'And there,' added the longbeard, 'King Snaggi Ironhandson, son of Thorgil, who was sired by Hraddi, atop his oathstone at the Bryndal Vale after the sixth siege of Tor Alessi.' The noble figure of the dwarf king stood upon a stout, flat rock with the rune of his clan carved onto it, his warriors with shields locked around him as they faced off against a host of elves with levelled spears. 'Great was Snaggi's sacrifice that day,' said Halgar, his expression faraway as he became lost in remembrance and the expedition moved onward.

At last the dwarfs negotiated the stairway, taking care to avoid numerous pitfalls that bled away into the dark nothing of the underdeep far below.

From there they passed through a great, wooden door that only yielded when Lokki, Uthor, Gromrund and Hakem heaved on the mighty iron ring bolted to it, and into a feast hall – its hearth cold and long extinguished. A guild hall followed, of the Ironfinger miners, if the runic rubrics lining the walls were any proof, and then a long, vaulted gallery, until the dwarfs were before another great gate.

Standing almost fifty feet tall, it was decorated with a final mosaic – rendered in copper, bronze and gold – surrounded by a gilded, jewel-encrusted arch. There were voids in the arch where some of the gemstones had been prised loose and stolen. Such defilement brought about ambivalent feelings of sorrow and rage in the onlooking dwarfs.

'Ulfgan…' Halgar struck a sombre note, barely a choked murmur, as if his voice held the burden of ages. 'The last king of Karak Varn.'

The mosaic was cracked, some of the gemstones set in it missing, each empty socket like a wound in stone.

'It is the King's Chamber,' he breathed.

'IT IS NO use,' stated Gromrund. 'The gate is barred, and no locksmith can grant us entry. We have no choice but to turn back.'

The dwarfs had been outside the gate to the King's Chamber for almost an hour. A thick, steel bar lay across it on both sides that would only be opened by means of a great iron key – that which was carried only by the hold's gatekeeper and chief of the hammerer guards, or by the king himself. Since the dwarfs had neither, their quest to retrieve the Karak Varn Book of Grudges had stalled.

Rorek worked slowly and painstakingly at the lock hole, ignoring Gromrund's naysaying and derogation.

Uthor, stood patiently by the engineer's side, would not be baited into another argument.

'I am in agreement with Gromrund,' said Hakem, deliberately keeping his distance from Drimbold, who was lurking at the edge of the gallery in the shadows, doubtless looking for more trinkets to further burden his weighty pack. 'There is no more we can do here.'

The hammerer looked around the throng for further supporters but found none.

Halgar's eyes were far away as he regarded the King's Gate. Lokki seemed intent on thoughts of his own as he watched intermittently between the engineer cycling through his many tools and the darkness that lay behind them. Uthor was predictably tight-lipped, and maintained a certain grip on his axe haft.

Again, it seems the ufdi is the only one willing to side with me, thought Gromrund, with some annoyance.

'Hakem may be right,' Lokki said at last.

Hakem! Hakem the ufdi! You mean Gromrund Tallhelm, son of Kromrund, who fought at the steppes of Karak Dron is right, thought the hammerer with growing ire.

'Though it galls me, there is no way past the King's Gate without the key and I will not take up arms against it.'

Uthor bristled, looking as if he were about to protest, when he was interrupted by the voice of Drimbold.

'I've found something,' said the Grey dwarf, stepping out of the shadows, 'What's this?' He pointed out a concealed rune marking set in the stone and glowing dully in the gloom.

Halgar snapped out of his thoughts and stalked over to investigate, grumbling beneath his breath.

'Stand aside, wanaz!' he bawled at Drimbold, scowling. The Grey dwarf ducked quickly out of the furious longbeard's path, allowing

Halgar to get up close to the rune, which was set just above head height into the rock itself.

'*Dringorak*,' Halgar said, tracing the rune with his finger, rather than reading it. 'Cunning Road. It is a rhun of disguise.'

'I thought only rhunki could detect such things,' said Gromrund, eyeing the Grey dwarf suspiciously.

'Aye,' Halgar replied, 'but this one has lost much of its potency. Doubtless from the grobi filth and rat-vermin infesting these once great halls,' he snarled, hawking a gobbet of thick phlegm onto the ground. 'Still, 'tis remarkable that you saw it.' Halgar glared at Drimbold.

'Just luck,' said the Grey dwarf diffidently.

The longbeard turned his attention back to the rune and carefully felt the rock beneath, then drew a rune of passage in the dust and grit. He waited a moment and then used his gnarled fingers to find the edges of a door. Halgar opened it carefully.

'A tunnel lies beyond,' he said.

Lokki looked at Ralkan, but the lorekeeper was *elsewhere*.

'Bring him with us,' he said to Hakem. 'We enter the tunnel.'

THE TUNNEL WAS short and narrow, the dwarfs emerging quickly through a great, cold hearth and into the King's Chamber.

'A secret door,' remarked Uthor as he stepped out into a large room.

It might once have been splendid, but decay had visited itself upon it without restraint. It was also painfully clear that the dwarfs were not the first to have walked this chamber since the fall of the karak. Dried grobi dung smeared the walls and the desolation of shattered statues, torn tapestries and even the defilement of a small shrine to Valaya lay all about.

'Where are our enemies?' said Gromrund in low tones, gripping his great hammer.

'The hold is vast, hammerer,' said Lokki. 'If we are fortunate, they will not show themselves at all.'

There were three other ways leading off from the room, besides the barred King's Gate. All were open, their doors shattered or archways collapsed in on themselves. It was here that the current denizens of Karak Varn had gained entry and egress. It was a sorry sight. The king's bed was painstakingly carved from stout wutroth and in a state of disrepair. His brooding-seat had been upended – one of the arms ripped off. But there was no sign of the book of grudges or indeed, a lectern or mantle that might once have held it.

The dwarfs had gathered in the centre of the room, wary of the darkness that persisted beyond the three open doorways, enraged at the despoliation.

Drimbold was the last of them and, as he joined the throng, began surreptitiously poking about the room, aghast at the finery on display. Rummaging around a rack of kingly robes, weighed down by dust,

Drimbold heard a low *thunk*, followed by the scraping retort of a hidden mechanism, beneath the floor. The Grey dwarf lifted his hand from where he'd been supporting himself on the wall and noticed a small stone depressed into the stonework behind the robes. It would have been easy to miss, and avoided altogether, had the dwarf's palm not pressed upon it in such a way and with sufficient force.

Six pairs of accusing dwarf eyes fixed upon Drimbold, but quickly turned towards the back of the room, where the king's bed resided. The once-magnificent artefact swivelled to the side on a concealed stone dais. In its wake another door was revealed. It too slid to one side with the grinding protests of stone against stone. Beyond it lay a vault, the flickering luminescence of glowstones set into the walls striking great mounds of coins and gemstones casting shadowy penumbra.

'Thindrongol,' said Lokki, stepping forward into the threshold of the room. It was one of the many secret vaults of the dwarfs used to hide treasure, ale or important artefacts from invading enemies. Given the fate that had befallen Karak Varn it seemed a prudent measure to take. The rest of the throng quickly gathered by Lokki's side and gaped in wonder.

Uthor had lit a torch and, stepping inside, used it to better light the room. Flickering half-light revealed something else, hidden at first in the wan illumination.

There at the back of the long vault was a gilded throne, and sat upon it a dwarf skeleton. Strands of thick, dust-clogged spider web wreathed it, cloaking the entire room. The gruesome thing wore kingly robes, now moth-eaten and age-worn. On its head rested a crown, its lustre only slightly dulled by time, a few ragged hairs poking beneath from the bleached yellow skull. A few errant tufts of beard remained too, and in the skeleton's bony grasp, fingers still clad in tarnished rings, there was a rune axe – unblunted and its glory undimmed.

'King Ulfgan,' uttered Halgar, standing beside Uthor, and bowed his head.

They all did, even Drimbold, and observed a sombre moment of respectful silence. Ralkan bowed deeply, going down on one knee and weeping.

Lokki gripped the lorekeeper's shoulder and looked back up. 'May he walk with the ancestors, his tankard ever full, his seat at Grungni's table,' he said solemnly.

'For his wisdom is great and his craft everlasting,' Uthor, Gromrund, Hakem and Rorek replied in unison.

Halgar nodded his approval.

Off to the king's right hand, several feet away, there stood an unadorned iron lectern. In its cradle sat a thick book, its parchment pages old and worn, the leather of its binding cracked.

'We have found the dammaz kron,' Lokki intoned softly.

* * *

THE DWARFS HAD brought several more torches into the hidden vault, lit from Uthor's, and set them in wall sconces to augment the light of the glowstones. The illumination had revealed a counting table in one corner, a large pair of iron scales upon it. Oddly, though there wasn't much gold or many precious jewels in the treasure vault; it felt bare, as if some of it was missing. Hakem had reasoned that it could not have been stolen by grobi or skaven – why would they have resealed the room?

It was easy to imagine a lorekeeper scribing dutifully at the lectern as his lord dictated a raft of wrongs perpetrated against their hold and clans, but it was now Uthor who stood before it. As Redmane's descendant, it was deemed he should be the one to read from the kron. With tentative fingers, the other dwarfs standing patiently before him as if he were about to deliver some sermon or lecture, Uthor turned to the first page. The Khazalid script was scribed in dark, brownish blood – the blood of Ulfgan – as were all books of grudges. By the blood of kings were the oaths within them sworn, and the misdeeds of others recorded for all time. Reading quickly to himself, Uthor skipped ahead – with due reverence – until he reached the final few pages.

'*Let it be known that on this day, Ogrik Craghand and Ergan Granitefist of the miner's guild were slain as a pall of poison gas did infest the southern mines. The foul cloud did then boil up the southern shaft and kill many more dawi. Their names will be remembered,*' he read, skipping ahead further.

'*Our lord Kadrin Redmane has not returned. Incensed at a spate of urk attacks on the road, he was to lead a shipment of gromril to High King Skorri Morgrimson personally. No word has reached the karak of his fate, or that of his expedition. As if to compound this dark turn of events, a horde of grobi did attack the first deep and slay many dawi. Skaven gather in the lower deeps and we cannot contain them,*' Uthor continued, looking up briefly to regard the grim faces of his kinsdwarfs.

'It goes on,' he said, reaching the final entries. '*The third deep falls, grobi and skaven attack in vast numbers and we cannot hold them. There are few of us left. Thane Skardrin makes his last stand at the Hall of Redmane… He will be remembered.*

'*A beast is awoke in the underdeep. Rhunki Ranakson, apprentice to Lord Kadrin, does venture into the fifth deep in search of it but does not return. We cannot prevail against it. It is our doom.*'

'That is the end of it,' Uthor breathed, slowly closing the book of grudges.

Silence descended, charged with anger and sorrow, each dwarf lost in his own thoughts at the account of the last days.

A raucous clattering broke the moment abruptly. The throng turned as one to see Drimbold, the rune axe of Ulfgan in his grubby hands, a pile of spilled coins and gemstones sprayed at his feet.

'Must you touch everything?' Gromrund raged, incensed at the Grey dwarf's curiosity.

'This is a weapon of kings,' said Drimbold in response, without hint of trickery or subterfuge this time. 'This axe is your birthright,' he added, turning to Uthor. 'It should not fester in this tomb, for the grobi to defile and plunder.' He pulled the axe carefully from the dead king's skeletal grasp and held it out for Uthor to take.

The scowls of the dwarfs lessened, though Halgar muttered something about 'desecration' and the 'slayer oath'.

Uthor approached Drimbold, the others parting to let him through. His gaze never left the mighty weapon. The runes on the blade still glowed dully; magical marks of cutting and cleaving inscribed long ago. The long haft was wrought in knots of gold and studded with emeralds. A talisman, engraved with the rune of Ulfgan's clan and bearing the face of one of his ancestors, was bound beneath the blade by a thick strap of leather. The axe was the most beautiful thing he had ever seen.

'It is wondrous,' he breathed, reaching out, almost fearful to touch it. As his hands grasped the tightly bound leather grip and he felt the weight of it for the first time, the head of Ulfgan slumped to one side. The dwarfs turned to witness the old king's shoulders slump and cave. The spine split, ribs cracked and the entire skeleton fell in on itself, crumbling into a mass of bone.

'And so passes Ulfgan,' said Halgar, 'last king of Karak Varn.'

A sudden scratching sound filled the air.

'What is tha–' Hakem began.

Halgar hissed for silence, closing his eyes to better hear the noise.

The scratching was getting steadily louder and the sound of squeaking accompanied it; a shrill and discordant chorus of hundreds of voices converging on the dwarfs.

'We are discovered,' said Halgar, unslinging his axe and shield. 'The skaven come!'

The other dwarfs quickly followed suit, steel scraping leather.

'Into the King's Chamber,' bellowed Lokki. 'We must not be trapped in here!'

The throng piled back into the King's Chamber, Ralkan taking up the dammaz kron after strapping the book of remembering to his back by means of his many belts. Rorek was the last out of the vault, shutting the door once the others were clear, the king's bed swivelling back into place to leave the room looking just as it had when they'd first entered.

The dwarfs closed together, shields locked and faced in three directions, towards each of the open doorways.

'Make ready,' Lokki shouted above the now deafening screech of the skaven.

Countless pairs of tiny red eyes glinted menacingly in the dark void beyond all three of the doorways and the skaven surged into the room like a pestilential tide of fur and fangs.

'Grimnir!' Lokki cried, invoking the name of the warrior god as skaven steel clashed with dwarf iron.

The first wave of skaven crashed against the sturdy shield wall and was thrown back, broken. Lokki, Halgar, Uthor and Hakem all dug in their heels, bracing themselves against the swell. Skaven bodies were everywhere, their foul sewer stench assailing the dwarfs' nostrils.

The shield-bearing dwarfs were formed in a locked triangle formation, with Lokki at its apex. Uthor guarded his left; Halgar his right. Hakem stood next to Halgar, while Gromrund, whose great hammer precluded the use of a shield, protected their backs.

Behind the shield wall was Rorek, his crossbow unhitched. Drimbold was next to him, his duty to protect the lorekeeper at his side.

Shrieking war cries and curses, the skaven – foul parodies of giant rats walking on two legs – regrouped and charged again, stabbing with spears and cruel daggers.

Lokki bore the brunt and felt a great dent punched into his shield. His brother dwarfs steadied him, their interlocked shields a nigh on impenetrable wall of metal.

'Heave!' cried Halgar.

Boots scraped against stone, and the dwarfs pushed back together. The skaven were repulsed and the dwarfs broke formation for but a moment to swing axes and hammers. A skaven fell dead for every blow. A flurry of crossbow bolts flew above their heads; even Rorek could not miss at this range with the foe packed so tightly, and more of the rat-kin squealed.

The King's Chamber was filling rapidly with the ratmen, scurrying in a seemingly endless deluge from the open doorways.

At the back of the dwarfs' shield arc, Gromrund roared, splitting skulls with every stroke of his great hammer. Blood flecked onto his armour and the face plate of his warhelm but he gave it no heed. He swung left and right, corded muscles in his arms and neck bulging as he exerted himself.

'We are surrounded!' he cried to the others, smashing a black-furred skaven in the snout with an eruption of blood and yellowed fangs.

Lokki heard the hammerer's warning and knew they could not hold out. His axe was slick with skaven blood, his armour and shield badly dented. 'They are endless,' he breathed to Halgar, thumping a ratman to the ground with the flat of his blade before severing its neck with the edge of his shield.

'They are doomed!' laughed the longbeard, grinning wildly as he hacked a skaven from groin to chest. His axe blade jarred in the ratman's sternum and he had to step from the protection cordon of the shield wall as he used his boot to free it. A spear thrust flew in and took Halgar in the arm; the dwarf bellowed in rage.

Hakem turned, smashing the spear haft in two with his rune hammer before he stove the rat's head in. He closed tighter, until the longbeard regained his position.

Halgar roared, redoubling his efforts.

Uthor rent armour, flesh and bone as if it were nothing. Wherever the axe of Ulfgan fell a skaven died. A hulking brute of a ratman waded in towards him, brandishing a heavy looking halberd. Before the creature could swing, it was cut in twain down the middle, viscera spilling onto the ground in a sanguine soup.

The skaven were thinning, but Lokki knew the dwarfs could not battle forever, despite the protestations of Halgar.

'We cannot win this fight,' he said, and saw the way to the hearth and the dringorak was relatively clear. 'Break and make for the hearth,' he cried.

'Aye,' Gromrund replied, followed by the squealing retort of another felled skaven.

No one countermanded Lokki's order, not Uthor or Halgar. They all saw the wisdom in his actions. He led and they followed.

The dwarfs retreated into their shield wall, crushing closer, until they were almost arranged in a circle. The skaven surged against them, pressing hard and screeching fervently.

When the swell became almost unbearable, Lokki bellowed. 'With all your strength… Now!'

The dwarfs pushed as one, Gromrund, Drimbold and even Ralkan lending their weight, and the skaven were smashed back. Without pausing to take advantage of those skaven prone or stunned, the dwarfs broke, the shield wall dismantling as they ran for the hearth. The few skaven stood in their way were hacked and hewn aside as Uthor took the lead, carving a red ruin in their feeble ranks.

The dwarfs barrelled into the hearth and into the dringorak. They negotiated the tunnel quickly and emerged into the vaulted gallery outside the great gate of the King's Chamber. With no time to seal their route off they ran headlong up the long hall, the enraged squeaking of the skaven close behind them.

Rorek paused a moment part way down the gallery and fired a fusillade of crossbow bolts at the pursuing skaven as they poured from the hidden doorway. Most of his shots missed, but two of the ratmen fell with quarrels in their necks and bodies.

'Come on,' Lokki urged, tugging on the engineer's arm. The thane had been the last to leave the King's Chamber, ensuring everyone had made their escape.

Rorek shouldered his crossbow and gave chase as the others pounded onwards.

Ahead, a horde of skaven spilled out of hidden crevices in the walls, scurrying quickly to form a blockade.

Unrestrained by the formation of a shield wall, the dwarfs struck the skaven picket line in force and the killing began in earnest.

In an orgy of blood and screeching death, the ratmen were scattered with the dwarfs barely stalled in their stride.

Through the long gallery they went, back the way they had come across the guild hall, the feast hall and through the wooden gate, skaven harrying them without respite.

'You expect me to flee the length of the hold!' Halgar bawled to Lokki as they forged up the long stair that led from the second deep.

'I thought you trekked all the way to Karak Ungor,' Lokki gibed, grinning broadly.

'In my youth!' Halgar replied, snarling.

Lokki laughed aloud and the dwarfs drove on: negotiating the dilapidated tunnel and through manifold rooms, passageways and halls until they reached the audience chamber, hands on their knees and breathing hard. The scratching, squeaking retort of the skaven echoed after them.

'They are persistent bastards,' Uthor said, begrudgingly between breaths.

'We must make for the outer gateway hall,' said Lokki, readying himself for flight once more as he regarded the throng. 'Wait–' he added. 'Where is Drimbold?'

Drimbold was nowhere to be seen. In the frantic race through the deep, Lokki had lost sight of many of his companions – the Grey dwarf could easily have fallen without his notice.

'Does anyone know of his fate?' he demanded quickly, acutely aware of the rising din of the skaven as they closed on them.

The shaking of heads met his steely gaze. The thane's expression lapsed briefly into sorrow and then hardened.

'He was a greedy wanaz,' said Gromrund, 'but it is no way for a dawi to die, fleeing through shadow.'

The stink of skaven grew abysmally strong as their screeching became ear-piercingly loud.

'Onward,' said Lokki, 'or we shall all share his fate.'

The dwarfs hurried from the audience chamber and were halfway up the second stairway that led to the outer gateway hall when the skaven reached them. The ratmen flung spears and crude knives, and pelted the dwarfs with stones launched from slings. The throng stopped and raised shields to ward off the missiles as the first of the skaven overtook them.

The dwarfs hacked left and right, fighting a running battle as they pounded up the last half of the stairs. The throng had almost reached the archway to the outer gateway hall. Uthor was carving a path through the skaven who had got in front of them, Gromrund and Hakem defending the lorekeeper, striking down any ratmen who got too close. As Hakem smashed one of the skaven warriors into the floor with the flat of his shield, another got past him and advanced upon Ralkan.

Red, beady eyes gleaming maliciously, the ratman brandished a long knife and made to stab the lorekeeper in the heart. Months of waiting in the darkness, cooped up in the dank tunnels, every noise sending shivers of dread down his spine welled up in Ralkan and he snapped.

Bellowing a battle-cry that resounded around the stairway he smashed the creature aside with the book of grudges itself. The skaven crumpled under the furious blow but was then battered down by the book again as the lorekeeper bludgeoned it, all of his pent-up fury and anguish vented in a few seconds of bloody battery. In the end, Hakem hurried him on, the skaven a smear of red paste on the ground.

'Feel better?' said the Barak Varr dwarf.

'Yes,' Ralkan replied. His face and beard were flecked with blood, the book of grudges drenched in gore.

'Good, because there are more…'

LOKKI BEHEADED A skaven warrior before impaling another on the great spike at the top of his axe blade. Halgar was at his side, battling furiously, the two dwarfs fighting the rearguard as always. Looking down at the massing horde, Lokki thought he saw something nearby – nothing more than a fleeting scrap of shadow – dart into the darkness at the edge of the stair. He wondered on it no further, his attention diverted to a diminutive skaven, wearing robes daubed in wretched symbols and bedecked in foul charms. In its greying paw it clutched a bizarre, arcane-looking device. It was like a staff but almost mechanical in nature. The creature raised the staff high and devoured a chunk of glowing rock, swallowing it labouredly, throat bulging.

A strange charge suddenly filled the air as Lokki's beard spiked.

'Sorcery,' he breathed, making the rune of Valaya in the air.

Greenish lightning arced from the skaven's staff, zigzagging wildly until it struck the stairway roof, earthing into the stone. There was a low rumble and a tremor rippled across the ground, great chunks of masonry plunging downward, shattering as they struck the stair.

Halgar staggered and nearly fell.

Lokki looked up. A great slab of granite dislodged itself from above and was plummeting down, about to crush the longbeard.

Lokki smashed him aside, rolling furiously as the massive rock missed him by inches. It splattered several skaven and began rolling slowly down the stair. It granted the dwarfs a brief reprieve as the skaven wailed, fleeing in all directions.

Wiping a swathe of sweat from his face, Lokki got up and helped Halgar to his feet. The thane didn't see the scrap of shadow creep up behind him. At first he didn't feel the blade sink into his back.

'That was close, lad, Grungni be–' Halgar stopped as he saw Lokki's wide eyes and the blood seeping from his mouth.

The longbeard was paralysed as a skaven thing bound in black cloth – its eyes blindfolded with a filthy, reddish rag – snarled from beneath a long hood revealing a stump of flesh for a tongue. It emerged slowly, tauntingly from behind the thane and ripped out its dark-stained dagger.

Lokki lurched, spitting blood, and fell backwards down the stair, his armour clattering.

Disbelief then rage filled Halgar and he roared.

His anguished cry was crushed by the screeching retort of another bolt of lightning surging from the robed skaven's staff. The eldritch energy exploded against the archway, which shuddered and started to collapse completely. The violent quake that accompanied it threw Halgar down as the skaven assassin bled away into the darkness, Lokki lost from view.

A sound like pealing thunder echoed menacingly above him and Halgar prepared to meet his doom with grief in his heart.

HAKEM CRUSHED A skaven skull, his rune hammer exacting a fearsome tally, and looked back from the threshold of the outer gateway hall to see Lokki fall. He watched as a black scrap of shadow seemed to withdraw from the dwarf and shaded his eyes as harsh, green light flared below in the stairway tunnel. He staggered, but kept his feet as the archway to the outer gateway hall started to crumble, Halgar beneath it.

Hakem raced back through the arch, and hauled the longbeard backwards with all his might.

'Nooo!' Halgar bellowed, as the archway and part of the roof collapsed downward, smashing into the stair and crushing any skaven in its path. The route down to the audience hall was blocked. The dwarfs had become separated from the ratman hordes.

RIVULETS OF DUST and grit flowed readily from the ceiling cracks and the small chunks of dislocated rock that crashed down to the ground added to the imagined peril that the outer gateway hall was about to cave-in.

Eventually though, the tremors subsided and only dust motes remained, clinging to the air like a thick fog.

Uthor coughed in the dust-clogged atmosphere and beheld the huge slabs of granite that effectively sealed off the route to the first deep. He knew that Lokki's body was behind it. In the end, just ahead of Hakem, he had witnessed their leader fall. He watched the other dwarfs stunned by their own grief, silently regarding the mass of fallen stone. Drimbold too was lost it seemed, to Grungni only knew what fate. They had the book of grudges, but at what price?

'Old one,' said Uthor, his voice low and reverent. 'We must not linger here.'

Halgar had his hand on the wall of stone. He bowed his head and listened carefully. Muttering something under his breath – it sounded like a short pledge – he turned and looked Uthor in the eye. His face was like chiselled stone for all the emotion it betrayed.

'Let it be known,' he said aloud for all the throng to hear, 'on this day did Lokki, son of Kragg, thane of the royal clan of Karak Izor fall in battle, stabbed in the back by skaven. May Grungni take him to his breast. He will be remembered.'

'He will be remembered,' the other dwarfs uttered.

'The skaven still gather at the other side of the rock fall,' said Halgar, stalking toward the great gate. 'They will seek a way to get through to us,' he added, turning to Uthor. 'You are right, son of Algrim. We should not linger.'

'I think we might not have to traverse the latrine tunnels to escape the hold,' Rorek said, his back to the others as he examined the great gate, its antediluvian mechanism wreathed in a fine white patina of dust. 'The five of us may be able to open the gate from inside.'

'PUSH!' ROREK CRIED and the dwarfs heaved with all their collective might. The engineer had disengaged the massive locking teeth on the gate by means of six circular cranks. With the aid of Uthor, Hakem and Halgar he then released the three huge, metal braces barring it. It was then just a matter of opening the gate itself. Two large, thick chains hung from the ceiling. As each was dragged downward, by means of an immense circular reel set flat into the stone – ten broad handles on each – a series of interlocking cogs and pulleys would go to work, hitching each gate, inch by laborious inch, along an arc carved into the rock. Slowly but surely the gateway would open. The throng only needed to work one gate – that would be enough to allow them egress – but with only six dwarfs, instead of ten, gathering in one of the chains it was extremely hard going.

'Enough!' shouted Rorek again. The left-hand gate was open a shallow crack – just three feet wide but enough for them all to squeeze through. Hazy light was spilling onto the open courtyard.

'Follow me,' said Uthor, taking the lead.

As he emerged into the harsh, late afternoon sunlight of the outer world, he covered his eyes against the glare. When he saw what lay beyond, he quickly lowered his hand and bellowed, 'Grobi!'

A small horde of orcs and goblins gathered in the crags outside Karak Varn. They appeared to be making camp – seated around crude fires and the debased totems of their heathen gods – eating, squabbling and sleeping.

The first orc died with Uthor's flung axe in its chest. The beast stared down stupidly at the ruin of its torso – at first stupefied – then it let out a low gurgle and slumped dead.

A goblin fell, its skull crushed by Hakem, before it could let out a warning. A third, then a fourth was killed by Halgar, holding his axe two-handed, meting out death with silent determination.

Gromrund killed another, smashing an orc in the back, brutally collapsing its spine and crushing its neck.

Rorek put his crossbow to work and pitched several goblins off their feet, their torsos pinioned by tightly bunched quarrels.

Before the greenskins even realised what was happening, eight of their number were dead. The thirty or so that still lived roared and snorted in anger, frantically taking up weapons. A host of snarling green faces all turned in the direction of the onrushing dwarfs, drawing up into a ramshackle picket line of bristling spears and curved blades.

'Charge through them!' Uthor cried, wrenching his thrown axe free of the orc carcass before sheathing it and drawing the blade of Ulfgan. The dwarf of Kadrin surged into the masses, the undeniable spike of the throng's attack. Gromrund and Halgar were at his heels. Hakem followed with Rorek, the two of them keeping the lorekeeper safe as he was carried along by the charge.

A flurry of arrows came at the dwarfs as they ran, the hooded goblins loosing short bows and screeching madly. Uthor took one in his pauldron, two more struck his shield but he did not slow, ducking an overhead cleaver swipe and, as he rose, hacking off his attacker's arm.

In the end, it was over quickly. The dwarfs smashed through the camp like an irresistible hammer, leaving the greenskins bloodied and bewildered in their wake. They didn't stop running until they could no longer hear the bestial calls and cries of the orcs and goblins. They weren't followed. Foolishly, they had left a way in to the karak and doubtless the greenskins were exploiting that mistake.

THE DWARFS HAD made camp in an enclosed crag, a fitful fire at the centre. There were only two ways in and out. Gromrund stood ready at one, hammer held across his chest; Hakem was at the other, watching the road ahead.

Night was drawing in, the last vestiges of sunlight bleeding blood-red as they slowly vanished into the horizon. Uthor warmed his hands by the fire. None of them had spoken since the battle with the greenskins.

'We make for Karaz-a-Karak,' Uthor muttered darkly across the crackling embers of the fires.

'It is a fair march from here,' said Rorek, smoking his pipe. 'At least two days over rough terrain and our rations are few – the ale has all but run dry.'

'Then we had best tighten our belts,' said Uthor.

'Hsst!' The warning came from Gromrund. 'Someone approaches,' he hissed, just loud enough for the others to hear. The dwarf crouched low, adopting a stalking position. He held his great hammer in one hand, the other raised in a gesture for the rest to wait.

'It is Drimbold,' he said aloud in surprise. 'The Grey dwarf lives!'

Drimbold walked into the camp, his face cut and his already worn attire ripped in several places. Even his pack appeared lighter. The dwarf quickly explained to the others how he had become separated from them, the skaven blocking his path. He had taken another tunnel and wandered in the dark until he'd luckily found another way out – a secret door in the mountain that led to the Old Dwarf Road. He'd watched the dwarfs fight through the orc camp at the gate, but had been too far away to do anything. After that he'd followed their trail, until it led them here.

'I am lucky to be alive,' he confessed, 'by the favour of Grungni.'

He smiled broadly, reunited with his erstwhile companions, and then said, 'Where is Lokki?'

'He is dead,' said Halgar, before any of the others could speak. 'Slain by skaven treachery.' The longbeard's expression was like steel. There was but one thing concerning him now, Uthor could see it in his eyes. Vengeance. And he meant to exact it.

Uthor got to his feet and regarded his kinsdwarfs.

'A great wrong has been done this day,' he uttered, with fire in his eyes. 'But it is one among many. One that began with the death of my kin, Kadrin Redmane and now Lokki, too, rests in a stony tomb. Karak Varn lies in ruins; its once great glory rendered to nought.'

Many of the dwarfs began pulling at their beards and growling in anger.

'It cannot stand!' Uthor bellowed, watching the grim faces of his companions alight with the flame of vengeance, the dwarf's rhetoric emboldening.

'It *will* not stand,' he added solemnly. 'I Uthor, son of Algrim, lord-regent to the clan of Dunnagal do hereby swear an oath to reclaim Karak Varn in the name of Kadrin Redmane, Lokki Kraggson and all of the dwarfs that gave their lives to defend it.'

'Aye!' cried the dwarfs in unison.

Only Halgar kept his silence.

'Until the end,' said the longbeard, holding out his open palm.

Uthor met his stony gaze and laid his hand on top of Halgar's. 'Until the end,' he said.

The others followed. The oath was sworn. They would go to Karaz-a-Karak and return with an army. Karak Varn would be retaken or they would die trying.

FROM ATOP A lonely crag overlooking the camp a dwarf sat in solitude. The faint flare of a pipe briefly lit his battle-scarred face, his nose pierced by a line of three gold rings, a chain attached to the opposite nostril running to his ear. A huge crest surged from his forehead, appearing like a spike as he was silhouetted against the night.

'Until the end,' he muttered, crushing the smouldering pipeweed with his thumb and leaping down off the rocky promontory into the darkness below.

LOKKI AWOKE, NOT in the halls of his ancestors, his place made ready at Grungni's table, but coughing and spluttering amidst the ruination of the long stair. He was alive; a terrible, searing pain in his back where the knife had gone in reminded him of that fact. He'd lost his helmet somewhere – there was a large gash on his forehead, the blood was still slick and filled his nose with a copper-like scent.

Rubble lay all about and the air was thick with dust and grit, his once dark brown beard was wretched with it. A brazier still burned from a sconce attached to a nearby wall. Its flickering aura cast long, sharp shadows. The skaven were gone, as were their dead. They must have thought him slain, else he would be dead too.

Lokki tried to look around and found he couldn't move. A huge slab of granite crushed his legs. With some effort he heaved himself up onto his elbows and pressed both his hands against the rock but it wouldn't yield. He slumped back down again, gasping for breath. He was weak; the blade that had stabbed him must've been coated in poison. Dwarfs were a resilient race though, and could survive all but the most potent venoms – at least for a time.

Mustering his strength Lokki glanced around, hoping to find something he could use to lever the slab off his legs. His axe lay just beyond his reach. He tried desperately, gloved fingers clawing, to touch it but it was too far.

A stench wafted over him on a weak-willed breeze emanating from some unseen source. He knew it well. It was the cloying, rank and musty odour of skaven. The reeking stink was overpowering; Lokki felt bile rising in his throat and his eyes water. Then he heard something, the tiny sound of claws scraping stone.

'Poor little dwarf-thing,' said a horrible, rasping voice.

A skaven, clad in thick rust-ridden armour, with black and matted fur, loomed over Lokki. The creature gave a half snarl, half smile revealing yellowed fangs. Lokki noticed a scar beneath its filthy snout; the stitches were still evident in the pinkish flesh. On the fingers of its right paw the ratman wore a golden ring; a rune marked it out as treasure stolen from the vaults of Karak Varn. The other ended in a vicious-looking spike. A crude helmet sat on its head, two small ears poking through roughly sheared holes. Lokki had fought enough rat-kin to realise this was one of their clan leaders – a warlord.

'This is skaven territory, yes-yes,' hissed the creature.

Lokki fought the urge to retch against its foetid breath as it crouched down close, beady little eyes scrutinising, mocking.

'Neither dwarf-thing nor green-thing rule here now. Here, Thratch is king. Thratch will kill, quick-quick, any who set foot in his kingdom, yes. Dwarf hold is mine!' he snarled, slashing a deep wound in Lokki's cheek with a filthy spike.

Lokki grimaced and spat a thick gobbet of blood into the skaven warlord's face. 'Karak Varn belongs to the dawi,' he growled, defiantly.

Wiping the dwarf's blood away with the back of his remaining paw, Thratch stood up, a feral grin splitting his features. Lokki watched as the creature slowly backed away into the darkness, and at exactly the same time another skaven emerged from it as if the shadow were an extension of his very being.

It was clad in black rags, its eyes blindfolded, its gait slightly stooped as it crept towards Lokki menacingly.

'Tried to cut my throat, Kill-Klaw did, yes…' hissed the warlord, who was lost from view. 'Took his eyes, took his tongue – but Kill-Klaw not need them to stab-stab, quick-quick. Now Thratch is master, and he bids Kill-Klaw… stab… stab… slow… slow.'

The blind skaven assassin loomed over Lokki, dagger in hand. For the first time, the dwarf noticed it wore a necklace of severed ears strung around his neck. Kill-Klaw screeched – a terrible sound emanating from the very gut – and darkness engulfed Lokki utterly. Agonised screams ripped from the dwarf's mouth, echoing through the ancient halls of Karak Varn and into the uncaring blackness, as Kill-Klaw went to work.

CHAPTER FOUR

BLOODY BUT UNBOWED, Fangrak trudged through the winding goblin tunnels of the Black Mountains and thought of how he might avoid a grisly demise. The orc chieftain was accompanied by a band of his warriors; the greenskins – orcs and goblins both – that had survived the attack by the dwarfs at the gate.

Twice now, he had been defeated. After the massacre in the foothills at the edge of Black Water he had gathered more warriors. He knew the dwarfs were headed for the old city, but he hadn't bargained on how long they would be down there. Two days he had waited, his patience thinning with every hour. Even choking the odd goblin hadn't alleviated his boredom. They'd erected totems, made offerings to Gork and Mork out of dung, and lit fungus pyres – the thick fumes cloying and potent. A stupor had descended from the heady fug exuded by the smouldering pyres, and the dwarfs had surprised them as the greenskins had awaited their return outside the gate of the hold. All of this he would have to explain to Skartooth.

The long tunnel opened out into a wide cavern. Daubed upon the walls in dung and fungus paint were the markings of the orc gods. Fires were scattered throughout the vast room beneath the mountain, goblins clad in thick black robes hunkering together and stealing malicious glances at Fangrak as he passed them by. Some hissed and snarled at him as he went, navigating the clutter discarded by the greenskins and the ubiquitous filth that pervaded everything. Fangrak wasn't scared of any of them, orc or goblin. He growled back, brandishing his flail meaningfully. The brutal weapon was slick with greenskin gore – he'd had to take his wrath out on someone before they returned…

At last, Fangrak reached the end of the chamber. Flickering torches clasped in crude iron sconces threw slashes of light on scattered bones that lay in abundance there. Orc, dwarf and skaven were all picked clean, even the marrow sucked dry by Skartooth's 'pet'. The beast was ever hungry and it was unwise to let him starve for too long.

Ungul was the first thing that Fangrak noticed as he approached the seat of his warlord with shoulders slumped, his defeated warriors in tow. The troll languished on a cot of straw and flayed skin – brown and coarse like leather, and curled at the edges. Chewing on a bloodstained, meaty rib bone, the beast grunted at the orc chieftain, the chains that shackled it to the ground rattling agitatedly.

Fangrak kept far enough away from Ungul so that it couldn't reach for him with its long, gangling arms, relieved as the beast went back to chewing at the bone. The orc chieftain bowed down on one knee before his warlord.

Skartooth was seated upon his 'throne', as the goblin warlord liked to call it. Wrought from bone, divested of flesh and meat by Ungul, the 'throne' took on a macabre aspect. A skull rack served as a back rest, crested by the heads of dwarfs and skaven, and any greenskins who displeased the agitated goblin. Rib, thigh and shin bones fashioned the seat, while the arms, legs and feet were made from an assortment of other parts, each surmounted by more skulls. Skartooth liked skulls; he had one on top of his great black hood, a mere rat skull – else the towering peak would collapse into his eyes. Around his neck he wore an iron collar, infested with spikes. It was a grotesque talisman. As Fangrak stooped he imagined tightening it around the goblin warlord's neck until his eyes burst from his tiny head and his thin tongue lolled from his simpering little mouth. The orc chieftain allowed himself a grin at that, careful to conceal it from Skartooth as the warlord spoke.

'So, you is back then,' sneered the goblin, enveloped in his voluminous black robes, stained with the symbol of the blood fist – his tribe. ''Ave you killed them stinking stunties yet?'

'No,' growled Fangrak, keeping his head bowed.

'Useless filth!' Skartooth spat, lobbing a handful of rotten meat he'd been playing with, rather than eating, straight at Fangrak. The wretched meat struck the orc chief in the head, knocking his helmet askew. Fangrak went to right it without thinking.

'Leave it,' Skartooth screeched, getting to his feet and yanking hard on Ungul's chain. The troll, who had been busying himself picking scabs from his stony flesh, grunted in annoyance, but the goblin warlord held the creature's gaze and it became placid.

'You want to feel the insides of Ungul, do ya?' Skartooth snarled.

Fangrak looked up at the goblin warlord, but betrayed no emotion.

Skartooth took a step forward. Fangrak could see the goblin's dung staining the furs laid out on the seat of his throne.

'You want to get in 'is belly where 'is juices will melt ya away to nuthin', eh? You worthless scum, you dung-eating swine.'

Fangrak responded levelly, his voice deep and unmoved.

'We 'ave found a way through the gate.'

Skartooth halted in his menacing tirade to listen intently.

'But there's a rock fall in the way,' Fangrak said calmly. 'I reckon we can get in, but I'll need a few lads to clear it.'

Skartooth looked Fangrak in the eye, scrutinising him carefully to try and detect if he was lying. Satisfied, the goblin warlord sat back down.

'You'll 'ave what you need,' he whined, squeakily. 'But Ungul is still 'ungry.'

Fangrak got back to his feet and pointed to one of his warriors. It was Ograk – he'd been the lookout at the gate, sprawled on a rock, snoring loudly when the dwarfs had attacked.

'Oi!' said Fangrak, gesturing Ograk towards him. 'Come 'ere.'

Ograk pointed dumbly to his chest, to make sure it was him that his chieftain meant. Fangrak nodded once, very slowly. The orc shuffled forward, one eye on Ungul, who was licking his lips.

Fangrak got up close, eye-to-eye with Ograk, then took a knife slowly and quietly from a sheath at his thick waist and slit the backs of Ograk's legs with two fiercely powerful swipes. The orc howled in pain and rage, collapsing to his knees. He ripped his cleaver from its sheath, spitting fury, but Fangrak swatted it from his grasp with a heavy backhand blow.

'You'll not be needin' that,' he said, grabbing Ograk by the scruff of the neck and growling in his ears, 'and you'll not be runnin' away, 'iver.' With a grunt of effort, Fangrak hurled Ograk into the reach of the troll. Ograk screamed as Ungul battered him down with a meaty fist, the splintering retort of bone echoing around the cavern.

'Are we done?' he said to Skartooth, belligerently.

'Go clear that rock fall,' Skartooth said, 'or it'll be you in its belly next time.'

Fangrak turned, snarling harsh, clipped commands at his warriors before going off into the cave to press-gang others for his work crews. In his wake, he heard the wet tearing sound of rending flesh and the dull crunch of slowly mashed bone. He didn't stay long enough to hear the sucking of juices or the swallowing of innards; he was hungry enough as it was.

UTHOR LED THE procession of dwarfs as they approached the Great Hall of Everpeak, Seat of the High Kings, behind Bromgar, one of the High King's hammerers and bearer of the key to the King's Chamber. It was a great honour indeed and Bromgar bore it with stoic fortitude and irresolute dourness.

The gatekeeper had met them at the mighty entrance to the hold – an impregnable bastion of flat stone that defied the ravages of the ages. He'd been waiting there as they'd approached from the Everpeak road – a lone dwarf made seemingly insignificant before the edifice of rock and iron.

The dwarfs of Everpeak had been expecting them.

A series of secret watchtowers set into the highest crags offered a view of many miles and were a ready early warning of approach. Quarrellers had stood at sombre guard from a final pair of watchtowers, flanking the outer gate. They were wrought with massive statues of the ancestors and the High Kings of old, the imposing sentinels glaring down at all-comers. The venerable image of Gotrek Starbreaker was amongst them, holding aloft the Phoenix Crown of the elves, a trophy won at Tor Alessi and which still resided in Everpeak as a reminder of the dwarfen victory.

At the loftiest upper wall the glint of armoured warriors could just be seen, patrolling diligently. The gate itself was a colossal structure. Some four hundred feet tall, its zenith seemingly disappeared into sky and cloud. So solid, so formidable was the great gate to Karaz-a-Karak it was as if it was carved from the very mountainside itself. Valaya's rune was inscribed upon it in massive script, a sure sign of the protection of hearth and hold.

They had been granted entry mainly due to Halgar's presence and the fact that they bore dire news and the Karak Varn Book of Grudges as proof of it. Bromgar had turned then, rapping five times with his ancient runic hammer on the immense barrier of stone and tracing a symbol with a gauntleted hand. Uthor had stared, enrapt, as a thin silver seam appeared and a portal no larger than four feet tall opened and allowed them all admittance.

'Ever since High King Morgrim Blackbeard ordered them shut during the Time of Woes, the great gates to Everpeak have not been opened,' the gatekeeper had said dourly, by way of explanation.

Having been received by an honour guard of Bromgar's hammerers in the audience chamber, the dwarfs now walked down a vast gallery, flanked by the royal warriors in silent vigil, their great hammers held unmoving at their armoured shoulders.

NEVER HAD UTHOR witnessed such beauty and such immensity. The audience hall rose up into a vast and vaulted roof, banded by gold and bronze arcs. Columns of stone, so thick and massive it would take a dwarf several minutes to walk around them, surged into that roof, resplendent with the bejewelled images of kings and ancestors. A mighty bridge, a thousand beard-spans across and covered in a mosaic representing the past deeds of Everpeak, stretched across a gaping chasm that fell away into the heart of the world. It led to a broad gallery lined by a veritable army of gold statues, each one a perfect rendition of the royal ancestors of the hold. So wondrous was Karaz-a-Karak that even Hakem was stunned into abject silence.

Of their company, only six now remained for an audience with the High King himself. Rorek had parted ways with the throng at the edge of Black Water. He would take the long road back to Zhufbar, taking care to avoid the greenskins lurking in the mountains and petition his king to grant troops for the mission into Karak Varn and the reclamation of the hold. Lokki, of course, had fallen. It was a bitter blow, felt by all, but none so keenly as Halgar who had said little since they'd made their oaths.

After a bewildering journey, they stood at last before the doorway to the Great Hall, resplendent with runes, etched in gold and gromril and bedecked with a host of jewels. Uthor quailed within, humbled to be at such a place. It even banished the dark spectre that haunted the edges of his mind – the memories back at Karak Kadrin – if only for a moment.

Horns bellowed throughout Karaz-a-Karak, their notes deep and resonant, heralding the arrival of the visitors to the king's court. The great stone doors opened slowly, grinding with the weight of ages. Another hallway stretched before the dwarfs, so long and wide it could have held several small overground settlements. Its vaulted ceiling seemed to disappear into an endless firmament of stars as an infinite array of sapphires and diamonds sparkled high above. Light cast from huge iron braziers, forged into the dour faces of high kings and ancestors, inlaid with huge fist-sized rubies, created the glittering vista and made it seem as if the hold was open to the very heavens.

The awesome planetarium made Uthor feel insignificant, as did the hundreds of beautifully carved columns stretching away in the shadows, much further than he could see. They were etched with the deeds and histories of the clans of Everpeak. Bare rock was visible on some, where a clan's line had been wiped out. Even now, high up in the lofty space, artisans were at work dutifully engraving with chisel and pick.

Like the thick tongue of some immense beast of myth, a mile-long red carpet swept down the centre of the massive hall. As the dwarfs made their way along it, treading down the mighty crimson causeway in awe-struck silence, Uthor noticed the great deeds of his forebears etched onto the walls. These vistas were much, much larger than those of Karak Varn, over a hundred feet tall: the ancestor gods, Grungni and Valaya, teaching their children the ways of stone and steel; mighty Grimnir slaying the dark denizens of the world and his long trek into the unknown north; the coronation of Gotrek Starbreaker and finally the great deeds of High King Morgrim Blackbeard and his son, the current lord of Everpeak, Skorri Morgrimson. Uthor wiped away a tear at their magnificence.

At the edge of a vast circular dais of stone, Bromgar bade the dwarfs stop. Around the far side, the ancient faces of the Karaz-a-Karak council of elders regarded them. Every one of them sat upon a seat of stone,

the high backs decorated with ancestor badges wrought of bronze,
copper and gold. Each seat bore its own particular device to reflect the
status and position of the incumbent. A gruff-looking dwarf, his long
black beard flecked with metal shavings, bound in plain iron ingots
and with tan skin that shone like oil, could only have been the king's
master engineer; his chair was decorated with tongs crossed with a
hefty wrench. The high priestess of Valaya, a wise old matriarch wearing long purple robes, was seated in a chair that bore the image of a
great dwarfen hearth, the rune of the ancestor goddess above it. There
were others too; the head victualer had a tankard, the longbeards of
the warrior brotherhoods bore axes and hammers, and the chief lorekeeper an open book.

In the centre of this venerable gathering, atop a set of black marble
steps and sat upon a further dais was the High King himself, Skorri
Morgrimson.

He wore a doublet of white and royal blue, edged in silver thread
over a broad, slab-like chest. Thick and rugged, his black beard – the
namesake of his father – was bound up in ingots of gold. Dappled with
grey hair, it hinted at his age and wisdom. Thick, heavily muscled arms,
banded with rings of bronze, copper and gold, and inscribed with swirling tattoos were folded across his chest. On one arm, the various devices
of the ancestors were depicted; on the other, a rampant red dragon, its
coiling serpentine tail made into a runic spiral.

THE SEAT OF the High King broke the semicircle of elders into two
smaller, but equal, arcs and was altogether more grandiose.

Backed with a bronze motif of a hammer striking an anvil, the face
of Grungni wrought above it in a triangular apex of gold, the Throne of
Power was a mighty symbol of Karaz-a-Karak and all the dwarf people.
It bore the Rune of Azamar, forged by Grungni and the only one of its
kind, and was said to be all but indestructible. For if the rune's power
was ever broken, it was believed that it would signal the doom of the
dwarfs and an end to all things.

Stood just behind the king, two at either side, their gromril armour
resplendent in the light from the roaring braziers, were Skorri's throne
bearers. During times of war, and at the king's command, they would
bear the mighty throne of power into battle, with the High King sat
upon it reading from the Great Book of Grudges. They were the finest of all Karaz-a-Karak's warriors. Uthor would have bowed to them
alone and yet here they all were before the High King himself!

'Noble Bromgar, whom do you bring before this council?' asked the
high priestess of Valaya.

'Venerable lady,' said Bromgar, bowing deeply. 'An expedition from
Karak Varn seeks the wisdom and the ear of the council of Everpeak on
a matter of dire import.'

'Then let them step forward,' the priestess replied, observing the custom of the High King's court.

As one, the dwarf throng stepped into the circle as Bromgar stepped back into the shadows, his immediate duty done.

'Lord Redmane is the master of Karak Varn,' said the High King. The dwarfs were almost twenty feet away, such was the size of the circle, and yet the king's voice came across loud and resonant to all. 'A grudge is scribed in his name in the Dammaz Kron,' the king continued, 'for failing to deliver a shipment of gromril as was his oath. What have you to say on this matter? Who speaks for you?' snarled the king, glowering at each of the dwarfs in turn. Only for Halgar did he hold back his ire.

Uthor stepped forward from the throng.

'*Gnollengrom*,' he said, bowing down on one knee and removing his winged helmet, cradling it under his arm, to observe due deference. 'I do, sire – Uthor Algrimson of Karak Kadrin.'

'Then be heard, Uthor, son of Algrim,' boomed the voice of the king, brow beetling beneath the golden dragon crown of karaz sat upon his head.

'I bring dire news,' Uthor began. 'Kadrin Redmane, my ancestor and lord of Karak Varn, is dead.'

A ripple of shock and despair from across the council greeted this stark revelation. Only the High King remained stoic, shifting in his seat and leaning forward to rest his chin on one fist. His eyes regarded Uthor intently and bade him continue.

'Slain by urk at the edge of Black Water; his talisman is proof of this fell deed.' Uthor held it aloft for all to see. Grim faces, etched with grief, looked back at him.

Uthor gestured to the rest of his companions. 'We ventured deep into his hold and found it abandoned, overrun by skaven.'

The High King scowled at that. Uthor went on.

'Through death and blood we recovered the book of grudges,' said Uthor and Ralkan came forward, head bowed low, the Karak Varn Book of Grudges held before him in his outstretched arms. It was still spattered in skaven blood from when he had used it as a bludgeon.

'Ralkan Geltberg, last survivor of Karak Varn.' There were tears in the lorekeeper's eyes as he said it.

'It tells a sorry tale indeed,' Uthor interjected. His face fell as he returned to a dark memory. 'One of our party… Lokki, son of Kragg, royal thane of Karak Izor, died retrieving it.'

Halgar straightened; the mention of his charge's name still felt like a raw wound to the longbeard.

'Venerable Halgar Halfhand of the Copperhand clan was his kinsdwarf,' Uthor explained.

Halgar came forward now, removing his helm and bowing in the time-honoured fashion, but with his fist across his chest as was the custom in years gone by.

High King Skorri nodded his respect to the longbeard.

'Fell deeds to be sure,' he said. 'The great holds fall and our enemies grow ever bold. This slight will not be forgiven and will be forever etched in the great kron.'

'Noble King Morgrimson,' Uthor said boldly, the entire assembly shocked by his impertinence at speaking before being asked to. 'We seek vengeance for our kinsdwarfs and the means to take back the hold of Karak Varn from the wretched rat-kin. Each of us has sworn an oath in blood!'

Incensed at this act of disrespect, Bromgar stepped forward but a glance from the High King stayed the gatekeeper's hand.

Passion blazed in Uthor's eyes so bright and powerful that none could have helped but be moved by it. Skorri Morgrimson was no exception.

'Your cause is noble,' said the High King, levelly, 'and no oath is ever to be taken lightly, but I cannot help you in this deed if it is the might of my warriors you beseech. There are precious few to spare; our kin have been ever dwindling against the attacks of the grobi and their kind. There are other, more pressing matters that demand the strength of Karaz-a-Karak. Alas, the plight of Karak Varn is dire, but one that will have to wait.'

'My king,' said a voice from the council below. It was a female dwarf, one of the attendants of the high priest of Valaya. She had been shrouded in the shadow of the matriarch and Uthor had not noticed her before. Long, golden plaits cascaded from her head and a round stubby nose sat between eyes of azure. She wore a purple sash over simple brown robes, but also bore a talisman bearing the rune of the royal clan.

The High King turned to her, incredulous at the interruption.

Many of the longbeards on the council grumbled loudly about the impetuousness of youth and their lack of respect. Even the matriarch turned to scowl at her attendant.

'My king,' she repeated, determined to be heard, 'with Karak Varn in ruins, surely Everpeak must act.'

The High King fixed the maiden with his gimlet gaze and, noting the courage in her eyes, breathed deeply.

'With war to the north beckoning and the retaking of Karak Ungor, I can spare but a handful of warriors to this cause, my clan daughter,' said the High King, content to relent and indulge her for now, before turning to regard Uthor once more. 'Sixty warriors is my pledge and that is a generous offer.'

'My liege,' the attendant continued, 'I must protest–'

The High King cut her off.

'Sixty warriors and no more,' he roared. 'And I will hear no more of it, Emelda Skorrisdottir. The High King of Everpeak has spoken!' The High King's glowering gaze went to Uthor and the others, ignoring his clan daughter's indignation.

'Take these dwarfs back to the audience chamber,' he growled. 'There they shall await my warriors, but I warn them...' the High King stared at Uthor sternly, '...this is a foolhardy mission and one that I do not condone; they would fail it at their peril. Now...' he said, leaning back in his throne, breathing in deeply as he puffed up his mighty chest, 'Dismissed!'

CHAPTER FIVE

'HE IS RECKLESS,' growled Gromrund. 'A reckless fool,' he said. 'Sixty dwarfs to retake a hold full of skaven… It is madness.'

Three months they'd been at Everpeak as the warriors were gathered and prepared. Careful note had been taken of the cost of weapons and armour afforded to the clans and made in the reckoner's log, so that it might be levelled against the coffers of Karak Kadrin, Norn, Hirn, Izor and Barak Varr. With everything in order, at last they had made for Karak Varn once more. The throng was bolstered by forty warriors of the Firehand, Stonebreaker and Furrowbrow clans, and a coterie of twenty ironbreakers led by the ironbeard Thundin, son of Bardin, and the king's emissary in the mission to reclaim the karak. He walked alongside Uthor, clad in thick gromril, his ironbreakers keeping measured step behind him. Thundin was possessed of a warlike spirit and had been eager to join the throng to recapture Karak Varn. His helmet device, a miniature hammer striking an anvil, rocked up and down vigorously in time with the great wings on Uthor's warhelm as the dwarfs forged on in search of glory.

'Doubtless he will add Gunbad next to his list of conquests,' Gromrund grumbled, as they were led west along the Silver Road.

Mount Gunbad was a pale shadow on the northern horizon and the dwarfs were keen to avoid it on their journey back to Karak Varn. The great and prosperous gold mine there had fallen over three hundred years ago, sacked by grobi, and no attempt had yet been made to retake it – at least none that was in any part successful. The richest mine in all

261

of the Worlds Edge Mountains and the sole repository of *brynduraz*, the rare 'brightstone' sought by miners and kings with equal fervour, and it was lost to the greenskins.

'And what of his plan?' the hammerer continued. 'We know nothing of that.'

'You would not renege on your oath?' said Hakem, who had been travelling with Gromrund since Everpeak. Ill-suited as they were, Gromrund at least felt he had an ally in the ufdi, despite his garish sensibilities and boastfulness. In truth, since Karaz-a-Karak, the dwarf had said little of the 'wealth and glory of Barak Varr,' and it meant the hammerer could stomach his presence.

'I am no unbaraki,' hissed Gromrund, keeping his voice low as he said the word. To be an 'oathbreaker' was the worst insult to any dwarf and to even say it in company was frowned upon. 'But I seek neither personal glory, nor to settle my own account before I stand in front of the gates to the Halls of the Ancestors… It is for Lokki we do this deed,' Gromrund added solemnly with a glance at Halgar.

The longbeard walked alone, a few feet away. No one spoke to him, none dared for he wore a scowl the likes of which might be forever ingrained onto his face and a deep burden that fell like an eclipsing moon across his eyes.

'For Lokki then,' said Hakem – he too was looking at Halgar – full of honourable bluster. 'By the Honnakin Hammer it is sworn.'

'For Lokki,' murmured Gromrund, as the throng left the Silver Road, following a tributary of Black Water and, once they'd reached that great pool of jet, back to the hold once more.

DRIMBOLD WALKED AMONGST the throng of warriors from Everpeak, with Ralkan beside him. The Grey dwarf didn't know what had happened to the lorekeeper. He never fought in the final battle to escape the karak; he had long since taken his leave by then. But though he was no longer the shell he had been, he didn't carry much in the way of gold either, so Drimbold wasn't interested either way.

Reclamation, that's what he was doing and he was determined to return to Karak Varn so he could continue his endeavours, but he'd rather do so with a band of stout warriors than by himself, although alone he could probably enter undetected as he had done previously. For now though, other thoughts occupied his mind.

For several days the Grey dwarf had kept a close watch on two of the travelling throng, intent on their wares. Both were nobles of Everpeak, a beardling and his older cousin if Drimbold's memory served, and possessed of a desire to honour their clan by retaking Karak Varn. *In a way*, he thought, *we are all reclamators really*.

As they trod amongst their kinsdwarfs Drimbold eyed the ringed fingers of the elder dwarf, the bands of polished bronze bent around his warhelm and vambraces. Drimbold's eyes widened as he caught the flash of something bright and shiny around the beardling's waist. It took but a moment for the Grey dwarf to realise what it was.

Gold no less! These Everpeak dwarfs are rich indeed, thought Drimbold. He picked up his pace, just a few steps behind them, and reminded himself of something very important: on the road, there's always a chance that things will get dropped.

UTHOR TURNED AND gave the signal for the throng to leave the Silver Road at last. The tributary that would lead them to Black Water beckoned, and though the terrain would be fraught with crags, clawing bracken and scree underfoot it was the most expedient way to Karak Varn en masse.

A warhorn resonated down the short marching line of the dwarfs, five abreast, and the column wended north-east following Uthor's lead, Thundin and the ironbreakers in tow. It wasn't long before the shadow of Karak Varn loomed large once more, though they faced a different aspect to that which Uthor had confronted on their first foray to the hold. But it was another sight – an altogether more welcome one – that caught his attention this time.

'BEHOLD,' SAID ROREK to the thong of dwarfs gathered around him, 'Alfdreng – Slayer of Elves!'

A stout, wooden stone thrower sat behind the engineer, lashed to a heavy-looking cart hauled by three lode ponies. Thick metal plates were bolted to its carriage and they in turn attached it to an iron-plated circular platform inset into the base of the cart itself. A crank, wide enough for two dwarfs to work it, was driven into a second plate next to the circular platform and a supply of expertly carved rocks sat in a woven basket at the end of the cart. Each stone bore runic slogans and diatribes directed at the race of elves. During the War of Vengeance, the stone throwers the dwarfs had used to bring down the walls of Tor Alessi had been renamed grudge throwers as the practice of inscribing the ammunition they flung came about, reflecting the deep-seated fury the dwarfs felt against their once-allies during those days.

There were mumbles of approval as the engineer paraded the ancient grudge thrower before the warriors of Karaz-a-Karak and his companions. The dwarf had also brought with him no less than two-hundred warriors from Zhufbar, a pledge from the king. The Bronzehammer, Sootbeards, Ironfinger and Flintheart clans all plumped up their chests and twiddled their moustaches and beards as they regarded the appreciative gestures of their Everpeak kinsdwarf.

'Only an engineer would bring a machine to a tunnel fight,' muttered Gromrund to anyone who was listening. 'We dwarfs have been fighting battles without such contrivances for thousands of years; I fail to see how it would advantage us to do so now.

'Elf slayer you say,' Gromrund bellowed.

Rorek nodded proudly, one foot rested on the side of the cart and striking a dynamic pose.

'We go to kill grobi and rat-kin, not elves,' the hammerer grumbled.

'Bah,' said Rorek, taking a long draw on his pipe, 'it will crush grobi and ratman as well enough as elf. So speaks Rorek of Zhufbar,' he added, laughing, backed up by a chorus of cheers from his kinsdwarfs.

THE GREENSKINS ATTACKED quickly and without warning, descending down the steep-sided ravine like a bestial tide. Night goblins, hooded and cloaked, poured from hidden mountain burrows and sent black-fletched arrows into the dwarf throng. Three warriors fell in the first volley, before the dwarfs had shields readied. Hulking orcs, led by their black-skinned brethren, surged forwards cleavers upraised, spears outstretched, and crashed into a hastily prepared shield wall of Karaz-a-Karak clan warriors. A horde of trolls, lashed and goaded into battle by a cruel orc beastmaster, fell among the ironbreakers at the head of the group, stamping and goring. A belt of foul-smelling stomach acid wretched from one, engulfing one of the veteran ironbreakers, his stout armour no proof against the foul stuff.

In a few, brutally short moments the dwarf army was embattled.

'Gather together!' Uthor bellowed, shielded from the trolls for now by Thundin and his ironbreakers. A nearby warrior, his kinsdwarfs fighting hard against the pressing orc horde, heard the order and blew a long, hard note on his warhorn. A second note from farther up the line responded and the throng began to form up in a thick wedge of steel and iron. Beset to the front and on one flank, it was slow going and some dwarfs got left behind as they fought.

Goblin wolfriders, howling and hooting as they scampered into view from behind a dense cluster of crags on their lupine steeds, harried the rear of the dwarf column, shooting short bows and making daring lightning raids on the stragglers.

FROM ATOP A viewing tower fixed to the side of the cart, Rorek bellowed furious orders to his crew below. Two dwarfs pumped the crank frantically and Alfdreng was rotated on the circular platform to face the hordes spilling forth from the ravine sides like malicious ants.

'Brace!' he cried and six metal clamps with broad teeth at the ends swung down from the cart and dug deep into the ground, securing it firmly. The lode ponies snorted and kicked in agitation but Rorek gave them no heed.

'Hoist!' he bellowed and the giant throwing arm of the grudge thrower was wound back on a stout wooden spindle. The wutroth of which the arm was carved bent and creaked under the strain; Rorek felt it tense even in the watchtower.

'Load!'

A heavy boulder was rolled into the throwing basket by two sweating crewmen, its grudge runes angled to face the enemy.

Through his good eye, the engineer fixed his gaze on the rampaging night goblins and a wave of orcs about to hit the dwarf column. The tension of the throwing arm persisted, resonating throughout the wooden structure.

'Wait…' he said.

The hordes were thickening into a densely packed mob, goblins and orcs taking up positions with short bows.

'Wait…'

The greenskins halted at a rocky ridge and began to draw back their bow strings.

'Fire!' yelled Rorek.

A belt of air whipped past him and a dark shadow became a blot in the darkening sky before the boulder crashed into the dead centre of the ridge, crushing orc and goblin alike. With the sound of wrenching stone, the ridge collapsed, and several more of the greenskins were buried.

A terrible aim with a crossbow he might be, but the engineer was a deadeye with any machinery.

A cheer went up from the crewmen and the Zhufbar dwarfs surrounding the war engine protectively, but Rorek had no time to celebrate as he eyed more greenskins.

'Five degrees to the left,' he bellowed. 'Crank!'

SHOULDER TO SHOULDER with warriors from the Firehand clan, Gromrund and Hakem fought a mob of spear-armed urk. A dense forest of sharpened stone tips thrust at them as the orcs pressed. One Firehand dwarf fell, gurgling blood as a spear pierced his mail gorget.

Hakem smashed one haft in two and parried another away with his shield, a third struck his pauldron and he recoiled but quickly righted himself to fend off a death-blow aimed at his neck.

Without the room to swing his great hammer, Gromrund used the weapon like a battering ram, making pummelling drives with the hammer head. Wood splintered and bones cracked before his weighty blows but more orcs came on. Nearby, he could hear the battle-dirge of Halgar above the din of clashing steel.

UTHOR STOOD WITH Thundin, his axe carving through troll hide as if it were nothing. Every wound left a searing mark, hissing as it struck the hideously pale grey flesh. Trolls were known for their miraculous ability to regenerate from even the most heinous of injuries. Even now, one of the gruesome beasts recovered from a host of axe wounds inflicted by three of Thundin's ironbreakers. One was battered into the dirt by the creature; a second swatted into his kinsdwarfs before the veterans came at the troll again and proceeded to dismember it. Wherever the blade of Ulfgan fell skin did not reknit or bones reset; where it fell was death and it was the reason the dwarfs were winning.

'You fight with the fire of Grimnir; may his axe be ever sharp,' Thundin said as he ducked a vicious sweep of a troll club and moved in to open its bloated gut. The beast recoiled in pain, bellowing in fury. The iron-beard rushed passed it, armour clanking, having created the opening he needed.

Between blows, Uthor watched as Thundin came face-to-face with the orc beastmaster. The snarling creature sent out its barbed whip, hoping to tear chunks off the ironbeard, but Thundin caught the lash around his armoured wrist and yanked the orc towards him. The beastmaster was nearly barrelled over. Thundin beheaded it, a gout of crimson gore erupting from its ruined neck as it fell. With the rest of the ironbreakers pressing and Uthor's axe blade carving ruination, the trolls broke, their long, gangly legs taking them back into the hills.

'It seems I am not the only one,' Uthor replied, having fought his way to Thundin's side.

The ironbeard followed his gaze to the two nobles from Everpeak.

They fought like slayers at the head of the Stonebreaker clan, hewing greenskins with controlled fury. Several goblins had already lost heart and were scampering away from their flashing axe blades.

All across the line the dwarfs fought. Some had fallen and their names would not be forgotten, recorded in Ralkan's book of remembering, which the lorekeeper still carried, strapped onto his back. Though they were tightly packed, and the orcs assailed them on two sides, the green-skin dead were tenfold that of the dwarfs. They piled in great stinking heaps, the brethren who still possessed the will to fight clambering over the rotting corpses. With a stout row of mountain crags at their backs, and shields locked to the front and sides, the dwarf formation was virtually impenetrable. The greenskins would not break it.

We will win this fight, Uthor thought.

An ululating war cry broke suddenly above the roaring battle-din, echoing through the narrow pass. Uthor's gaze swept west to the crags at the dwarfs' backs.

'Valaya's golden cups,' he breathed.

'May they be ever bountiful,' Thundin concluded, having followed Uthor's gaze.

A second horde of greenskins, vastly outnumbering the first, barrelled down the opposite slope howling like daemons.

Uthor saw the chieftain Lokki had fought at Black Water riding a snorting, thick-hided boar. He was surrounded by a guard of stoutly armoured orc warriors, also riding boars who were much bigger and darker-skinned than the rest. One carried a ragged banner adorned with skulls and black chains, the symbol of a clenched and bloodied greenskin fist daubed upon it. The glint of massive spear-tips twinkled in the moonlight like ragged stars and Uthor realised the greenskins had brought machineries of their own.

ROREK SAW THE goblin bolt throwers, ramshackle war engines hammered together with crude greenskin craft and carrying a massive spear of thick, black iron. Too late, he bellowed, 'Turn!'

The whipping retort of six bolt throwers loosing in quick succession found Rorek's ears on the fitful breeze. The sound of splintering wood followed quickly and the engineer gaped in horror as he realised he was crashing to the ground, one of the watchtower's supports brutally severed. Another bolt pierced the throwing arm of Alfdreng just as it was being frantically rotated into position and its arm tautened. A crewman was flung into the air screaming as the wutroth snapped and flipped backwards. A second dwarf was killed by the rope wound on the spindle as it lashed out and garrotted him.

Three more bolts buried themselves in the Zhufbar ranks, piercing armour as if it were parchment, pinioning three and four dwarfs at a time.

NIGHT WAS NEAR as the orcs from the western slope fell upon them, the sun dipping beneath the mountain peak, washing the sky with blood. It fell swiftly as the dwarfs fought, the last diffuse vestiges of day giving way to twilight and then dusk. The orcs became primeval in it, the false light casting them in an eldritch aspect.

The orcs and goblins swarmed, Rorek was lost from sight and many of the Zhufbar dwarfs would now be dining in the Halls of the Ancestors – this was not how Uthor had envisaged his glorious return journey to Karak Varn.

With the onset of darkness the greenskins became further emboldened, until a discordant note rang out, resonating around the high peaks.

The greenskins at the back of the western horde were turning, their screams rending the air. An urk in the fighting ranks noticed it too and turned for but a moment. Uthor cut it down contemptuously. He was about to press his attack when the front rankers started to waver and fall back, distracted by the events unfolding behind them. Then Uthor saw them, a band of at least thirty slayers, axes sweeping left and right, their blazing orange crests like a raging firewall even in the darkness. The orcs quailed before them and trapped between two determined foes their will broke. The chieftain's guttural cry split the air again, but this time it was to signal retreat. Dwarfs on both sides redoubled their efforts until both the east and west greenskin hordes were repulsed and the few that remained were cut down.

Uthor wiped a swathe of orc blood from his face and beard, chest heaving painfully so that his voice was barely a whisper. 'Thank Grungni.'

* * *

'Borri, son of Sven,' the beardling replied gruffly and over-deep. Uthor suspected the dwarf was compensating for his youth. The beardling wore a full face helmet, metal eyebrows and a beard fashioned into the design all supplemented by a long studded nose guard. Although the shadows cast by the mighty helm shrouded Borri's eyes they flashed with fire and pride.

Small wonder he fought with such vigour, thought Uthor at the steel in the beardling's expression.

With the battle over, the dwarfs were gathering up the wounded and burying their dead. A careful watch was maintained by the slayers, with whom Halgar had much to say, throughout. An early count by Ralkan estimated that the throng had lost almost sixty, the slain mostly amongst the Zhufbar clans, and around another thirty grievously wounded. They'd found Rorek amidst a pile of wooden wreckage, inconsolable at the destruction of Alfdreng but otherwise alive and not badly injured. Gromrund, Hakem and Drimbold had all survived the battle, too.

While the dwarfs made ready, Uthor felt it was his duty to recognise the efforts of his warriors and speak with the mysterious group of slayers whose timely intervention had turned the tide. He resolved to get to them later.

'Barely fifty winters, eh?' Uthor said, 'and yet you fought like a hammerer.'

Borri nodded deeply.

'As did you,' Uthor added to Borri's older cousin, Dunrik of the Bardrakk clan.

This dwarf had clearly seen much of battle, Uthor realised immediately. A patchwork of scars littered his face and his beard was long and black, banded with grudge badges. He wore a number of small throwing axes around a stout, leather belt and shouldered a huge axe with a deadly looking spike on one end. It was much like Lokki's. Incredibly, given their efforts, both had emerged from the fight almost completely unscathed.

'Son of Algrim,' growled the voice of Halgar.

Uthor turned to face the venerable longbeard and bowed his head as always.

'Meet our ally, Azgar Grobkul.' Halgar stepped to one side, allowing Azgar to come forward.

The slayer's bare chest bore numerous tattoos and wards of Grimnir. A spiked crest of flame-red hair jutted from his skull that was otherwise bald, barring a long mane of hair that extended all the way down his muscled back. Across his broad, slab-like shoulders, Azgar wore a trollskin pelt, stitched together by sinew. A belt around his thick waist was cinctured by goblin bones and adorned with a macabre array of grisly trophies. The call to arms he had issued in the throng's defence was made by a wyvern horn he slung across his body on a strap of leather and he gripped a broad-bladed axe – a chain linking it to his wrist by means of a vambrace – in one meaty fist.

'*Tromm*,' the slayer muttered, his voice like scraping gravel as he met Uthor's gaze steadily.

The slayer's eyes were like dark pits, exacerbated by the tattooed black band across them, but Uthor knew them, and knew them well.

'It is ever the burden of those who take the slayer oath to seek an honourable death in battle, in the hope to atone for their past dishonour,' Uthor replied, his expression tense.

'Perhaps I will meet it in the halls of Karak Varn,' said Azgar dourly. 'It seems a worthy death.'

Uthor's fists were clenched. 'Perhaps,' he muttered, relaxing, 'Grimnir willing.' Uthor nodded once more to Halgar and then stalked away to find Thundin.

'He bears a dark burden, lad,' said Halgar, momentarily lost in his own thoughts. 'Think nothing of it.'

'Indeed,' said Azgar, a noble cadence to his voice despite his wild appearance. 'Indeed he does.'

The slayer watched Uthor walking away. His face betrayed no emotion.

ACT TWO
OATH AND HONOUR

CHAPTER SIX

THE DWARF THRONG reached the outer gate of Karak Varn in confident mood. The greenskins had been put to flight and, though only some two hundred or so strong, the army was now bolstered by a band of ferocious slayers. It also seemed word of the orcs' defeat had spread, for no such creature opposed them as they made camp in the long shadow of the mountain.

The dwarfs gathered in small groups, heavy armour clanking noisily as they came to a halt and took in the impressive sight of the hold. Mutterings of wonderment and dour lamentations could be heard on the silent breeze that such a jewel in the crown of the Karaz Ankor could have fallen into depredation. Others, those older members of the clan who had seen greater glories, merely sighed in relief that the first part of the journey, at least, was over.

Strangely, the orcs had closed and barred the great gates left open in Uthor and his companions' flight several months ago, and so, with a day passed since the battle in the ravine and night approaching once more, the dwarfs pitched tents. They were large, communal structures that were used to house some twenty or so dwarfs at a time. Standards of bronze, copper and steel were staked in the ground at the encampments of each individual clan to indicate who lodged there. Warriors removed weapons and helmets as they huddled together, looking for casks of ale to moisten parched throats, and shake the grit from their boots. It had been a long march through the mountains. Tonight they

273

would rest, before making their initial excursion into the karak come the morning.

'THERE IS BUT one sure way to secure the hold,' stated Gromrund. 'We clear one deep at a time and seal all ways in and out.'

'There is little time for that, hammerer,' Uthor argued.

Several of the dwarfs gathered in the largest of the tents, a broad but squat affair made of toughened leather and supported by stout metal poles. So low was the roof that Gromrund's warhelm would occasionally scrape the ceiling. There were a few muttered comments between dwarfs as to why the hammerer did not remove it, but as of yet no one had asked him. No guide ropes were required to keep the tents up, such was the ingenuity of the design, and each took on the bulky and robust appearance of rock. A shallow flume was cut into the roof and through it the smoky vapours of a modest fire billowed. Red meat on a trio of spits dripped fat and oil into the flames, making them sizzle and hiss sporadically. A large, flat table had been erected and each of the assembled war council sat on small rocks around it, drinking from tankards and firkins, and smoking pipes.

'According to the lorekeeper,' Uthor said, gesturing to Ralkan who sat quietly and supped at his ale, 'there is a great hall in the third deep, big enough to accommodate our forces. It is defensible and a fitting place to stage our reconquest.'

Uthor switched his attention to the rest of the gathered dwarfs. Halgar, Thundin, Rorek and Hakem all sat around the table, watching and listening to the two dwarfs debating.

'We get to it and secure a bridgehead,' Uthor continued. 'From there we can launch further attacks into the hold, striking deep at the skaven warrens, and reclaim Karak Varn for good!' He thumped his fist down on the table – the assembled throng wary, of such outbursts, astutely raised their tankards a moment before – for emphasis.

'Delving so deep without knowing the dangers ahead and behind us is folly.' Gromrund would not be dissuaded. 'Have you forgotten the battle in the King's Chamber and how quickly we were surrounded?'

'We were but a party of eight back then.' Uthor stole a glance at Halgar. Yes, eight, old one, he thought, when Lokki was still alive. 'Now we are many.' A fire glinted in Uthor's eyes at that remark.

'I maintain we will stand a better chance if we take the deeps one at a time. We have Thundin's ironbreakers to consider, far better employed as tunnel fighters than holding a single massive chamber, and let's not forget the Grim Brotherhood–'

'The slayers will do as they will, but they seek to die in this mission,' Uthor snapped, a bellicose demeanour possessing him suddenly. 'I for one do not want to be honoured posthumously, hammerer.'

Gromrund snorted his breath through his nostrils, and the part of his face that was visible behind his warhelm's face plate flushed red.

'A vote then,' the hammerer growled, through clenched teeth, slamming down his ale to the rapid upraising of tankards around the tent. He held up a coin that shimmered in the firelight. On one side was an ancestor head; the other bore a hammer. 'Heads, we clear the deeps one by one–'

'–or hammers, we head for the Great Hall and make our stand there,' Uthor concluded.

Gromrund slammed his coin down first, head facing upward.

'Venerable Halgar,' said Uthor, matching the hammerer but with his coin, hammer upturned, 'yours is the next vote.'

Halgar snorted derisively, grumbling at some unknown slight and set his coin down upon the table, but left his hand over it to conceal his decision.

'The vote is secret, as it was in the old days,' he snarled, 'until all parties have made their choice.'

Hakem nodded, placing his coin down and covering it. In turn the process repeated, until each and every dwarf present had placed his voting coin.

'Let us see, then, who has the support of this council,' Uthor intoned, eyeing the table with the concealed coins upon it eagerly.

As one, the assembled dwarfs revealed their decisions.

GROMRUND LEFT THE tent muttering heatedly under his breath and went off in search of his own lodgings for the night. Drimbold, who was sitting a short distance from the tent, watched him as he ladled a stew over a low fire. Gromrund stalked right through the Grey dwarf's encampment, tripping on the stones surrounding the fire and accidentally kicking over a steaming pot of kuri.

'Be mindful!' Drimbold said as his meal was unceremoniously splattered over the ground.

Gromrund barely broke his stride as he snarled, 'Be mindful yourself, Grey dwarf.'

'Grumbaki,' Drimbold muttered. If the hammerer heard him, he did not show it. Must be that warhelm clogging up his ears, he thought with a wry smile. Looking down at his spoilt food he scowled but then dipped his finger into a portion of the kuri he'd made with troll flesh, before putting it in his mouth. He chewed the cured flesh for a moment, the fire putting paid to any regenerative qualities the meat might have once possessed, then sucked at the juices, grinding the added dirt and grit in his teeth. 'Still good,' he said to himself and dipped his finger in the spilled stew again.

Drimbold ate with a small group of Zhufbar dwarf miners of the Sootbeard clan, sitting around a fitful fire. Not all of the dwarfs were sleeping in tents tonight and, as none had wished to share with him on account of the fact that several personal items from around the camp had already gone missing with a fairly strong suspicion as to who the culprit was, he was amongst those unlucky few. The Grey dwarf didn't mind, and neither, it seemed, did the Sootbeards, one particularly enthusiastic and slightly boss-eyed dwarf by the name of Thalgrim regaling them with tales of how he could 'talk' to rocks and the subtleties of gold. The latter subject interested Drimbold greatly, but Thalgrim was currently entrenched in matters of geology, so the Grey dwarf paid little attention to the conversation and instead contemplated his evening beneath the stars.

In truth, Drimbold was as at home looking up at the sky as he was beneath the earth at Karak Norn. He came from a family of kruti and had worked the overground farms of his hold since birth. His father had taught him much of fending for oneself in the wild and the art of kulgur was one such lesson.

Chewing on a particularly tough piece of troll flesh, Drimbold noticed another fire, higher up, on a flat rock set apart from the closely pitched tents. He could see the slayer, Azgar, up there in the light of a flickering fire sitting with his Grim Brotherhood as they were known. They ate, drank and smoked in silence, their gazes seemingly lost in remembrance at whatever fell deed had meant they'd had to take up the slayer oath.

Bored of watching the slayers, Drimbold decided to observe the Everpeak nobles instead. They were close by, just north of his encampment and farthest from the gate. Typically aloof, they sat in their own company and spoke in low tones so that none could hear them. Both wore short cloaks, etched with gilded trim, and finely wrought armour. Even their cutlery looked like it was made from silver. He had yet to catch a second glimpse of the belt the beardling wore around his waist, but he was certain it was valuable. They even possessed their own tent, which had an ornate lantern hanging from the apex of its entrance. The Grey dwarf watched as the beardling retired for the night and his cousin dragged the rock he was sitting on over by the entrance flap, sat back down and lit up a pipe. Drimbold had seen it earlier, as they were setting up camp. It was made of ivory and banded with copper. The Grey dwarf was wondering what other objects of worth they might own when the conversation with the Zhufbar miners turned to gold again and his attention went back to Thalgrim.

UTHOR SAT ALONE outside one of the dwarfen tents in darkness, deliberately apart from the fires of his kinsdwarfs, and found some solace in it. He stared into the distance, absently polishing his shield. The night formed shapes before his eyes, the long shadows cast by the flickering light of faraway fires resolving themselves into a familiar vista in his mind's eye...

The trading mission at Zhufbar had gone well and Uthor was full of boastful pride as he entered his clan's halls at Karak Kadrin in search of his father to tell him the good news. His hauteur was abruptly quashed, however, when he saw the grave expression of Igrik, his father's longest-serving retainer.

'My noble thane,' uttered Igrik. 'I bear grim tidings.'

As the retainer spoke, Uthor realised that something fell indeed had transpired in his absence.

'This way,' Igrik bade him and the two headed down for his father's chambers.

Uthor could not help notice the dark expressions of his kinsdwarfs as he passed them in the clan hall and by the time he reached the door to Lord Algrim's rooms, the two warriors stood outside wearing grim faces, his heart was thumping so loudly in his chest he thought he might spit it from his mouth.

The doors opened slowly and there was Uthor's father lying on his bed, a deathly pallor infecting his usually ruddy complexion.

Uthor went to him quickly, uncertainty gnawing at him at whatever fell deeds had transpired in his absence. Igrik stepped inside after him and closed the doors quietly.

'My lord, what has happened here?' Uthor asked, placing a hand upon his father's brow that was damp with a feverish sweat.

Algrim did not answer. His eyes were closed and his breathing fitful.

Uthor whirled around to face Igrik. 'Who did this?' he demanded, anger rising.

'He was poisoned by rat-kin,' Igrik explained dourly. 'A small group of their black-clad assassins entered through the Cragbound Gate and attacked your father and his warriors as they toured the lower clan holdings. We killed three of their number once the alarm was raised but not before they slew four of our warriors and got to your father.

'As Algrim's oldest son, you are to act as lord-regent of the clan in his stead.'

Uthor was incensed, his gaze fixed to the floor as he tried to master his rage. His mind reeled at this trespass – there would be a reckoning! Then a thought occurred to him and he looked up.

'The Cragbound Gate,' he said, seeing the wound to Igrik's face for the first time, partially hidden by his thick beard. 'It is guarded at all times. How did the assassins get by the door warden?'

Igrik's face darkened further. 'I'm afraid there is more…'

Uthor's reverie was broken by the hacking cough of Halgar. The long-beard also sat alone on a shallow ridge overlooking the camp, and despite hawking most of his guts up drew deeply of his pipe and rubbed his eyes with his knuckles. The venerable dwarf had insisted he take first watch, and who was there to argue with him.

Uthor's thoughts returned to his past. He gritted his teeth as he recalled his hatred for the one that put his father on his deathbed. 'Never forgive, never forget,' he muttered and went back to staring down the darkness.

FROM A HIGH promontory, away from where dwarfish eyes might find them, Skartooth watched his enemies in the deep valley below, a

malicious sneer crawling across his thin features. Greenskins needed no
fires to see and so the warlord waited in the thickest shadows, weapon
sheathed should an errant shaft of moonlight catch on his blade and
give his position away. A small bodyguard of orcs and goblins was
arrayed around him, including the troll, Ungul, and his chieftain,
Fangrak.

'We could kill 'em in their sleep,' growled the orc chieftain, nursing the
stump of his missing ear as he peered downward at the resting dwarfs.

'No, we wait,' said Skartooth.

'But they is 'elpless,' Fangrak replied.

'The timin' ain't right,' Skartooth countered, backing away from the
ridge, not wanting to be discovered.

'You zoggin' what?' Fangrak's face screwed up into a scowl as he
regarded his warlord.

'You 'urd and if you don't want to lose that other ear you'll shut your
meat-ole,' he screeched.

'Hur, hur, meat-ole,' Ungul parodied, the troll's hulking shoulders
shrugging up and down as he laughed.

'We wait until the stunties get inside…' Skartooth added, striking
Ungul hard on the nose with the flat of his small sword to stop him
laughing. The troll rubbed the sore extremity but fell silent, glowering
for a moment.

'We wait,' Skartooth began again, 'and then we attack from secret tunnels only greenskins know about,' he added, his mouth splitting into a
wicked grin.

'Oi!' squeaked the goblin warlord, remembering something.

Fangrak was already trudging away and turned to face Skartooth.

'Oose clearin' that rubble?'

'Gozrag's doin' it; must be almost finished,' Fangrak replied. Realisation
dawned as he looked back down at the dwarfs encamped below.

'Aw zog…'

THUNDIN STEPPED BEFORE the great gates of Karak Varn, morning sun
cresting the pinnacle of the mountain, and pulled a thick iron key
attached to a chain around his neck from beneath his gromril armour.
The ironbeard, and emissary to the High King himself, was standing at
the head of the assembled dwarfs who had mustered in their clans, fully
armoured and bearing weapons ready.

With the other dwarfs looking on, Thundin placed the key into a
hitherto concealed depression in the stone surface of one of the gates
and it glowed dully. The dwarf muttered his gratitude to Grungni and
with a broad, gauntleted hand turned the rune-key three times counter-
clockwise. Beyond the gate from inside the hold, there came a dull
metallic *thunk* as the locking teeth barring the door were released.
Thundin turned the key again, this time clockwise but only once, and

the scraping, clanking retort of the chains gathering on their reels could be heard faintly. Thundin stepped back and the great gates began to open.

'We could have used one of those earlier,' griped Rorek, standing at Uthor's side a few feet behind Thundin. The other dwarfs from the initial expedition into the hold were nearby. 'My back still aches from the climb.'

'Or from when the war machine collapsed on top of you,' Uthor replied, smirking beneath his beard.

Rorek looked crestfallen as he remembered back to the collection of timber, screws and shredded rope that was Alfdreng. He was still trying to devise a way that he could break the news of its destruction to his engineer guildmasters back at the hold. They would not be pleased.

'I'm sorry my friend,' said Uthor, with a broad smile. ''Tis a key from the High King, forged by his rhunki. Only his gatekeeper or a trusted emissary may bear one. Your efforts were just as effective though, engineer,' he added, 'but far more entertaining.' He laughed, slapping Rorek heartily on the back.

The thane of Karak Kadrin was clearly in ebullient mood after his dark turn towards the end of the war council. Ever since the battle in the ravine, Uthor's demeanour had been changeable. The engineer was baffled by it. With the loss of his war machine, shouldn't he be the one in the doldrums? He had little time to ponder on it as with the way laid open, the dwarf throng started to muster inside. It was a sombre ceremony, punctuated by the din of clanking armour and scraping boots. A grim resolve welled up in the throng as they followed Thundin, a charged silence that was filled with determination and a desire for vengeance against the despoilers of Karak Varn.

'URK!' SHOUTED ONE of the Grim Brotherhood. The slayers were the first to enter the hold and, once through the great gate, barrelled past their comrades to set about a band of around thirty orcs labouring in the outer gateway hall. The greenskins looked dumbfounded as the slayers charged, midway through hauling rocks away to the sides of the chamber in crude-looking wooden carts and bearing picks and shovels.

An orc overseer, uncoiling a barbed whip, could only gurgle a warning as Dunrik's throwing axe thudded into its neck. A second spinning blade struck the greenskin's body as it clutched ineffectually at its violently haemorrhaging jugular vein.

A troll, whom the overseer had been goading to lift a large boulder out of their path when the dwarfs attacked, stared stupidly at its dead keeper then roared at the oncoming slayers. It tried to crush Azgar beneath a chunk of fallen masonry from the cave-in but he dodged the blow and weaved around behind the beast. Looking under the rock, the troll was dismayed to discover no sticky stain where the dwarf had been and was dimly wondering what had become of its next meal when Azgar leapt onto its back, wrapping his axe-chain around the creature's neck. The troll flapped around, trying to dislodge the clinging slayer, crushing several orcs in its anguished throes. Azgar's muscles bunched and thick veins bulged on his neck and forehead as he strained against the creature. Eventually though, as the rest of the Grim Brotherhood butchered what was left of the orcs, the troll sank to its knees and a fat, purpling tongue lolled from its sagging mouth.

'You're mine,' the slayer snarled between clenched teeth.

With a final, violent twist of the chain, the beast fell prostrate into the dirt and was still. Quickly on his feet, Azgar caught a flaming torch thrown to him by Dunrik and set the troll ablaze.

Several dwarfs muttered appreciatively at the display of incredible prowess. Even Halgar nodded his approval of the way Azgar had slain the beast.

By the end, it was a massacre. Dismembered orc corpses lay everywhere, splayed in their own pooling blood.

Dunrik approached the dead overseer and wrenched his axes free in turn, spitting on the carcass as he did it. He gave a last hateful look at the barbed whip half-uncoiled at the orc's waist and turned to find Uthor in front of him.

'Well fought,' he said. The other dwarfs barely had time to draw their axes before it was over. Only Dunrik had shed orc blood with the slayers.

'It was a runk,' he replied bitterly, as if dissatisfied with the carnage and walked away to stand by his younger cousin.

Uthor's gaze met that of Azgar but he said nothing.

One of the Zhufbar miners, a lodefinder by the name of Thalgrim, if Uthor's memory served, broke the charged silence.

'Shoddy work,' he muttered, observing the crude braces the orcs had rammed in place to support the roof, though much of the rubble had been shifted and a gap made that was wide enough for the dwarf throng to traverse, 'shoddy work indeed.' Thalgrim smoothed the walls, feeling for the subtle gradations in the rock face. 'Ah yes,' he muttered again. 'I see.'

A bemused glance passed between Uthor and Rorek before the miner turned.

'We should move swiftly, the walls are bearing much of the weight and in their dilapidated condition are unlikely to hold for long.'

'I agree,' said Rorek, appraising the braces himself. 'Umgak.'

'That,' added Thalgrim, 'and the rocks told me so.'

Rorek flashed a worried glance at Uthor, mouthing the word 'Bozdok' and tapping his temple.

Mercy of Valaya, the dwarf thought to himself, as if one zaki wasn't already enough.

* * *

THRATCH WAS PLEASED. Before him stood his pumping engine, a ramshackle edifice wrought by the science and sorcery of Clan Skryre, that even in its latter stages of construction was easily worth the meagre price he had paid for it.

The vast device was located in one of the lowest deeps of the dwarf hold, where the worst of the flooding was, held together by a raft of crudely welded scaffolding and thick bolts. Three immense wheels, driven by giant rats and skaven slaves, provided energy to the four large pistons that worked the pump itself. Even now, as the Clan Skryre warlocks urged the wheel runners to greater efforts with sparking blasts from their arcane staves, green lightning crackled between two coiled conductor-prongs that spiked from the top of the infernal machine like some twisted tuning fork.

As the warlord watched, standing upon a metal viewing platform, nervously eyeing the vast body of water below him and taking an involuntary step back, a streak of errant lightning wracked one of the wheels, immolating the slaves within and setting the wheel on fire. Clan Skryre acolytes wearing hooded goggles and bizarre, protruding muzzle-bags over their faces, scurried in and pumped a billowing cloud of gas over the fire. A few slaves from the adjacent wheel were caught in the dense yellow fug and fell, choking, to their knees. Syrupy blood bubbled from their mouths as their lifeless bodies smashed around the impetus-driven spinning wheel, but the fire was quickly extinguished.

Thratch scowled, wrinkling his nose against the stink of singed fur.

'Ready-ready very soon,' a representative of Clan Skryre squeaked, cowering before the warlord. 'Humble Flikrit will make fix-fix,' it blathered.

Thratch turned his venomous gaze on him and was about to mete out some form of humiliating punishment when a shudder ran up the viewing platform. The skaven warlord thrashed about as he lost his balance and fell. The skaven's eyes were wide as he landed just a few inches from the platform's edge near what would have been a deep plunge into the water below had he fallen any further. Thratch squealed and hauled himself quickly to his feet, scampering backwards. He almost collided with a skaven warrior, whose bounding approach had very nearly pitched Thratch off the side of the platform. The ratman was lightly armoured and slight – one of Thratch's scurries, a message-bearer.

'Speak. Quick, quick,' the warlord snarled, recovering his composure.

As the scurrier whispered into Thratch's ear, the warlord's scowl grew deeper. 'You have done well, yes-yes,' said Thratch when the skaven was finished. The scurrier nodded vigorously and risked a nervous smile.

Thratch turned to the warlock still cowering behind him. 'Strap him to the wheel, yes…'

The scurrier's face fell and he turned to flee, but two burly stormvermin, Thratch's personal guard when Kill-Klaw was not around, blocked his escape.

'And no more mistakes,' snarled the warlord, 'or Thratch will have you fix-fix.'

'DIBNA THE INSCRUTABLE,' Rorek said to the throng as they paused at the threshold to a mighty guild hall. Like much of the hold, it was illuminated by eternally blazing braziers. They were filled with a special fuel created in collaboration by the Engineers' and Runesmiths' Guilds that could last for centuries. Uthor had heard such things spoken of only in whispers by the guilders of Karak Kadrin, and knew the precise ingredients of the fuel, as well as the rituals that took place to invoke its flame, were closely guarded secrets.

An immense stone statue stood before the dwarfs, venerating one such guildmaster, though Dibna was an engineer of Karak Varn. It was erected, column-like in the centre of the vast chamber, carved to represent Dibna holding up the walls and roof with his back and arms, dour-faced as he bore the tremendous burden stoically.

'This has been added recently,' Thalgrim added, noting the hue and coarseness of the rock from which Dibna was wrought. He approached the statue cautiously, bidding the others to wait. Once he'd reached it, the miner carefully ran his hand across the stone, sniffing it and tasting a patch of dust and grit picked up by his thumb.

'Fifty years, no more,' he said, wandering off into the shadows.

'Where are you going, lodefinder?' Uthor, waiting at the head of the throng behind Rorek, hissed loudly as Thalgrim disappeared briefly behind the statue before reappearing through the gloom several minutes later in the glow of a brazier. He was standing at the back of the room, something else obviously having caught his eye.

'There's a lift shaft here too,' said the lodefinder. He was looking through a small portal made in the rock, delineated by gilt runic carvings that flashed in the brazier flame. 'It goes deep.' His voice carried over to the dwarfs as it echoed.

'Perhaps we could use it to get to the Great Hall,' muttered Uthor.

Halgar stood next to him.

'With no way of knowing where it leads, I wouldn't risk it, lad,' the longbeard replied.

Uthor acceded to Halgar's wisdom with a silent nod.

Rorek was surveying the roof. He eyed it suspiciously, noting the dark streaks running down the walls. 'The statue shores up the chamber,' said the engineer, 'Lord Redmane must have commissioned it as a temporary measure to prevent the Black Water flooding the upper deeps.' He turned to Uthor, several ranks of dwarf warriors standing patiently behind him. 'We can pass through, but must tread with the utmost caution,' he warned them.

* * *

'THIS WAS HERE before even Ulfgan's reign,' Halgar muttered, tracing his gnarled fingers across the mosaic reverently.

The dwarfs had been travelling for over a day, traversing Dibna's guild hall without incident, through long vaulted tunnels and numerous halls and were already at the second deep with still no sign of opposition.

Uthor had planned it that way, instructing Ralkan to take them down seldom trodden paths least likely to be infested by skaven and to the Great Hall in the third deep. On no less than three occasions though, the lorekeeper had led them to dead ends or cave-ins, his recollection of the hold growing increasingly unreliable the farther the dwarfs delved. Often Ralkan would stop completely, and peer around, perplexity etched on his face as if he had never been in the tunnel or chamber in which the throng was standing. Strangely, a word from Drimbold in the lorekeeper's ear and they were on their way again. The Grey dwarf merely said he was 'urging the lorekeeper to concentrate' when asked what he'd said to Ralkan.

Another day from their goal, according to Ralkan, and Uthor had decided to make camp in a huge hall of deeds – the entire throng, almost two hundred dwarfs strong, barely took up a quarter of it such was the immensity of the room. Mosaics, like those upon the long stairway to the King's Chamber, were etched onto the walls and he and Halgar regarded one as most of the other dwarfs were setting up camp.

'From before the War of Vengeance then?' Uthor asked.

The image was that of a huge dragon, a beast of the elder ages. Red scales like incandescent flame covered its massive body and a yellow, barrel-ribbed chest bulged as it spewed a plume of black fire from its flaring nostrils.

'Galdrakk,' Halgar murmured beneath his breath.

Uthor's look was questioning.

'Galdrakk the Red. It was a creature of the ancient world, old beyond reckoning,' the longbeard said, deigning to elucidate no further.

Uthor was reminded of the dire words in the dammaz kron, '*A beast is awoke in the underdeep…*'

A dwarf hero, wearing archaic armour, was depicted warding off the conflagration with an upraised shield. A host of dwarf dead lay around him, rendered as charred skeletons.

'*…it is our doom.*'

A second image showed the hero and a group of his kinsdwarfs sealing the dragon in the bowels of the earth, a great rock fall entrapping it for all time.

'It stirs the blood to think of such deeds,' said Uthor proudly.

'And yet it reminds me of our faded glories,' muttered Halgar with resignation. 'I will take the first watch,' he added after a momentary silence.

'As you wish, old–' Uthor began after a moment, but stopped when he realised the longbeard was already walking slowly away.

* * *

'YOU'D THINK HE would remove that grobi arrow,' said Drimbold to Thalgrim.

The two dwarfs were taking second watch, sat outside one of the two grand doorways into the hall of deeds, and to pass the time were observing their comrades.

'Perhaps he cannot,' Thalgrim replied, 'if the tip is close to his heart.'

Halgar was laid on his back, the snapped black arrow shaft protruding upwards. Apparently the longbeard was asleep, but his eyes were wide open.

'How does he do that?' Drimbold asked.

'My uncle Bolgrim used to walk in his sleep,' offered Thalgrim. 'Once he excavated an entire mine shaft whilst slumbering.'

Drimbold looked back at his companion incredulously. The lodefinder shrugged in response. His face was illuminated in the blue-grey glow of a brightstone; a fabled piece of brynduraz hewn from the mines of Gunbad. Several chunks of it were set throughout the hall; though the dwarfs could see quite well in the dark, a little additional light never hurt.

Uthor had forbidden the lighting of fires, and ordered the few torches set in sconces around the chamber to be doused as they slept. They would impair the dwarfs' otherwise excellent night vision and they needed every advantage they could get against the rat-kin. The stink of smoke or cooking food might also attract the skaven and he wanted to fight them on his terms only, once they had reached the Great Hall. No cooking also meant the dwarfs were reduced to eating only stone bread and dried rations. Thalgrim fed a hunk of the granite-based victual into his mouth and crunched it loudly.

Drimbold had no taste for it – he'd been on stone bread for the last two days having consumed all of his other rations – and made a face. Then he watched as Thalgrim reached underneath his miner's pot helmet, a clump of stubbed out candles affixed to it by their waxy emissions, and produced what looked like a piece of moulding fungus.

'What is *that*?' The pungent aroma made the Grey dwarf's beard bristle, but it wasn't entirely unpleasant.

'Lucky chuf,' Thalgrim explained. The ancient piece of cheese in the lodefinder's hand looked half-eaten.

'I've only needed to use it once,' he said, taking a long, deep whiff. 'I was trapped for three weeks in a shaft made by the Tinderback miners… Weak-willed and thin-boned that lot, much like their tunnels.'

Drimbold licked his lips.

Thalgrim saw the gesture and put the chuf back under his helmet, eyeing the Grey dwarf warily.

'Perhaps you should get some sleep,' he said. 'I can manage here.'

It wasn't a request.

Drimbold was about to protest when he noticed the stout miner's mattock, one end fashioned into a pick, at Thalgrim's side. He nodded instead, and dragging his pack with him – now burgeoning with loot once more – went off to find a suitable alcove out of the lodefinder's eyeshot.

Drimbold sat down against one of the massive columns that lined the edge of the hall of deeds. So massive was it that he was shielded from Thalgrim's view. Satisfied, he went back to surveying the slumbering throng.

Almost everyone was asleep. Dwarfs were lined top to toe, despite the fact they had the room to spread out – gregariousness and brotherhood amongst their own kin was ingrained since the time of the ancestors. One or two were still awake, smoking, supping or talking quietly. The majority of the Grim Brotherhood looked comatose, having swigged enough beer to kill several mountain oxen. It seemed the slayers had a nose for alcohol and had discovered another hidden ale store in the deep. 'Brew stops', as they were sometimes known, were not uncommon – the holds were vast and should a dwarf be forced to undertake a long journey, he would have need of such libations. Of course some were merely secret stores left by forgetful and ageing brewmasters.

Azgar was the only one of the Grim Brotherhood still up. He was sitting at the perimeter of the camp, axe in hand as he stared at the outer darkness. The tattoos on his body seemed to glow in the light cast by the ring of brightstones nearby, giving the slayer an unreal quality. Drimbold recognised some as wards of Grimnir, he'd also heard the slayer mention that he bore one for each and every monster he had ever slain. The Grey dwarf suppressed a shudder – Azgar was nearly covered head to foot. Drimbold looked away, in case the slayer caught his eye.

Reverberant snoring emanated from the prone form of Gromrund through his mighty warhelm that the hammerer – for reasons unknown to the rest of the throng – still wore, his head propped up on a rock. He was divested of his other armour, which sat next to him in careful and meticulous order.

Hakem was close by – it seemed the two had reached some kind of understanding – laid with his hands across his chest, one clamped over his gold purse. The ufdi wore beard-irons clasped over his finely preened braids and softened his sleep with a small velvet pillow. Rather unnervingly, the merchant-thane had one eye open and was looking directly at Drimbold! The Grey dwarf quickly averted his gaze again.

Deciding he was finished observing, he began to settle down for what was left of the night. His eyelids felt heavy and were sloping shut when a shallow cry snapped him awake. He reached for his hand axe instinctively, but relaxed when he realised it was Dunrik, waking from some night terror. Borri was quickly at his cousin's side, a few other dwarfs who had been disturbed by the sudden commotion grumbling as they got back to their own business.

The beardling was whispering something to Dunrik, so low and soothing that Drimbold could barely hear it. His interest was piqued when he caught something about a 'lady' and 'a secret'.

Was Borri marrying into money and he didn't want the others to know? Drimbold then wondered if the dwarf had joined the mission to Karak Varn to secure part of his bride's dowry. The thought made his blood run cold. It meant that Borri was a salvager, just like him!

CHAPTER SEVEN

'THE GREAT HALL should be just ahead,' Ralkan announced.

The two hundred-strong throng had reached as far down as the third deep, eschewing the use of scouts as the lorekeeper was the only one who knew where they were going and he couldn't be risked sent ahead with only a small bodyguard. Should they be slain or the rest of the army cut off from them they would surely meet with calamity. Strength in numbers: that was the dwarf way. The dwarfs need not have worried, for they had got this far without encountering any resistance. That very fact unnerved Halgar, who peered anxiously into every shadow, stopping and raising his axe in readiness at any incongruous sound or tenuous sign of danger.

'Can't you feel it?' he hissed to Uthor, as the throng marched though what must once have been a mighty feast hall, its hospitality long since eroded.

'Feel what, venerable one?' Uthor asked, genuinely curious.

'Eyes watching us…' uttered the longbeard, squinting at the darkness clinging to the edges of the hall, '…in the blackness.'

Uthor followed Halgar's gaze but could feel or see nothing.

'If they are,' he said assuredly, 'then we will put them out, one by one.' Uthor gave a bullish smile at the thought, but the longbeard seemed not to notice and continued his paranoid vigil.

The throng left the feast hall and proceeded down a short but broad passageway. As they rounded a corner, Ralkan leading them, the lore-keeper said, 'Just beyond this bend and across the gallery of kings, there lies the Great Hall…'

Peering through a wide arch as he joined a dumbstruck Ralkan at the threshold to the room, Uthor saw a massive, open plaza stretch away from them. Immense stone statues of the kings of Karak Varn lined both flanking walls, though some were diminished by time and bore evidence of dilapidation. Magnificent though the statues were, it was the gaping chasm rent into the cracked and crumbling flagstones that got his attention. Like a vast and jagged maw torn in the very earth, it filled the entire width of the room, exuding thick trails of smoke, and blocked the dwarfs' progress.

'IT'S DEEP,' MUTTERED Halgar, 'all the way down to the mountain's core. Likely a wound made when Karak Varn was wracked by earthquakes and the Black Water first flooded its halls, so the legends hold to be true.'

Uthor and Rorek stood beside the longbeard and peered over the edge of the chasm. Darkness reigned below; only a hazy, indistinct glowing line in the blackness dispelled the myth that the tear in the earth had no end and yawned into eternity.

Uthor imagined a great reservoir of lava at the nadir of the gaping pit: bubbling and spitting, venting great geysers of steam, chunks of molten rock dissolving in its heat and carried by a thick syrupy current. Briefly his mind wandered to what else might lurk in that abyss, kept warm beside the cauldron of liquid fire. He dismissed the thought quickly, unwilling to countenance such a thing.

'We have to find a way across this,' he said instead. 'Is that strong enough to bear our weight?'

Uthor pointed towards a wide but ramshackle, bridge spanning the mighty gorge. It was crudely made, seemingly bolted together without design or care. Such slipshod construction was anathema to the dwarfs, especially an engineer.

'Umgak,' Rorek muttered. The engineer was crouched down next to the bridge, which was little more than a roped affair with narrow struts of weather-beaten wood. He turned to Uthor. 'Not of dawi manufacture,' he added, much louder. 'Likely it was made by grobi or rat-kin.' The engineer curled his lip in distaste.

'We should find another way,' Gromrund stated grimly, having joined the dwarfs at the precipice of the chasm. 'I do not trust the craft of neither greenskin nor skaven, and I have no wish to fall, honourless, to my doom.'

Uthor chewed it over. Crossing the bridge was not without risk.

'We cannot go back,' he said after a momentary silence. 'And I doubt the lorekeeper could even *recommend* an alternative route, let alone lead us to it.' He gestured to Ralkan, who was stood off to one side of the throng with Borri and Dunrik, muttering incessantly.

'I don't understand...' he garbled. 'I don't remember this being here.' The words spewed from his mouth repeatedly like a mantra, his gaze lost and faraway.

'It's all right,' Borri said, trying to soothe the addled dwarf but without success.

'I will not trust my fate to a grobi bridge,' Gromrund asserted, planting the pommel of his great hammer into the ground as if that was an end to the discussion. 'This is folly,' he added, 'and I am not the only one who thinks it so.'

Uthor moved his glowering gaze from the hammerer and swept it over the throng waiting behind him.

The warriors mustered close together, banners resplendent with their ancestral badges touching. Dour-faced clan leaders stood at the forefront; ironbreakers, their grim faced masks unreadable, were alongside. Slightly removed from them were the slayers – wild-eyed and bellicose of demeanour. There were dissenting voices – Uthor heard them grumbling to each other.

'We have come this far,' he said, addressing the throng, 'and endured much. The names etched in the book of remembering are testament to that,' he added, pointing to Ralkan, who wore the tome on his back. 'I would not be thwarted by a lowly bridge and have those names besmirched; the honour of their deeds – Nay! Their *sacrifice*, be for nought.'

Silence descended at Uthor's impassioned rhetoric. Several shame-faced dwarfs looked back at him; others couldn't meet his fiery gaze and looked down at their boots instead.

Uthor stood there for a moment, basking in this victory and then turned to scowl at Gromrund, the hammerer almost livid.

'We take the bridge,' Uthor stated.

Rorek was getting to his feet, fairly oblivious to the tension and the speech. The engineer took a good, long look at the bridge and sucked his teeth.

'I'll need to test it.'

ROREK YANKED ON one of the guide ropes, attached to a broad metal stake rammed into the rock and earth, and the entire bridge shuddered. But it held.

He was aware of the charged silence around him as he took his first faltering step onto the bridge itself. The engineer felt for the rope around his waist to make sure it was still there. He daren't look back to see if Thundin and Uthor were still holding onto it. The rope was his. At least he knew *that* would hold.

After what seemed like an hour, Rorek had reached the middle of the bridge. It creaked menacingly with every step and swayed slightly with the warm air currents emanating from below. As far down as it was, the dwarf could still feel the heat from the subterranean lava stream; smell its sulphur stink faintly in his nostrils. Some of the wooden struts were placed far apart, or were simply missing, and the engineer needed to concentrate hard on his feet to prevent any mishap. He stared downward and swallowed as the abyss stared back.

Having got this far and with a hand on each guide rope, Rorek was growing more confident and progressed steadily. Relieved, he reached the other side at last and waved the others on.

'No more than four at a time,' he called back to the throng, 'and watch your step, the way is perilous.'

Thundin's expression darkened as he turned to Uthor, who was gathering up the rope.

'This is going to take a while.'

UTHOR HAD POSTED lookouts at the entrance to the gallery of kings, and at the edge of the chasm to watch the exit to the vast plaza. Whilst they crossed the bridge the dwarfs would be vulnerable. He did not want to be caught unawares by skaven saboteurs lying in wait for them on the other side, or ready to spring out and cut the ramshackle structure from under them as they were crossing en masse.

Steadily, in groups of four, the throng made its way across the bridge. The dwarfs crossed without incident and soon there were many more warriors on the far side than the near. Uthor instructed the guards at the edge of the chasm to cross. It left him, Halgar and two miners from the Sootbeard clan, Furgil and Norri, who'd been stationed at the gallery entrance. As he called them over Uthor noticed a straggler, hunting around the statues on their side of the chasm.

'You too, Grey dwarf.'

Drimbold looked up from his rummaging, having detached himself from the main throng long ago to explore the vast room, and started to wander over.

Uthor turned to face Halgar.

'I will guard the way,' he said.

The longbeard grumbled and went to step onto the bridge, but missed the guide rope, clawing air as he fought to snatch it. The bridge swayed violently with his displaced weight.

'Venerable one!' Uthor cried, reaching out for Halgar's arm. The longbeard found the guide rope at last and smacked Uthor's hand away.

'I can cross well enough unaided,' he snarled and started to tramp gingerly away, feeling for the rope with his hands, rather than looking for it with his eyes.

Uthor turned back to Drimbold, who was getting ready to set foot on the bridge, the Sootbeards waiting behind him.

'I will follow the great beard,' he whispered, with a glance at Halgar who had already reached the halfway point. 'Wait until he is safely across before you proceed.'

Uthor hurried on after the longbeard, but in his haste misjudged his footing and trapped his boot between two struts. He swore out loud and by the time he'd freed it, Halgar was on the other side, rudely refusing any offers of help and bustling past the clan dwarfs in his way.

Nearly two-thirds of the way across and with his boot now loose, Uthor made to move on, aware that the rope bridge was creaking ominously. He glanced back. Drimbold was at about the halfway point, his massive pack thumping up and down on his back with every step. Furgil and Norri were a short way behind him.

There came a sudden, tearing sound and Uthor's eyes widened as he saw the rope tied to the nearside stake begin to fray. It coiled apart seemingly in slow motion, the thin strands unravelling inexorably as he watched. Already, the bridge was beginning to sag to one side as the shredding rope yielded to the tension put upon it.

'Move,' he cried, waving the dwarfs on urgently even as a violent shudder passed through the bridge. 'It will not hold!'

Uthor heaved the Grey dwarf past him, nigh-on pushing him. He looked back to the Sootbeards, urging them on. They moved quickly, determination in their eyes.

The rope snapped.

The sudden feeling of the world giving way beneath him filled Uthor's senses. His vision blurred as the crumbling bridge below and the vaulted ceiling of the gallery merged as one. Smoke-drenched darkness came rushing towards him. His breath pounded in his chest and he thought of his hold, the lofty, cloud-wreathed peaks he would never see again; of his quest unfulfilled and the shame it would bring to his clan; of his father lying on his deathbed, as he faded away bereft of glory and unavenged; of Lokki, slain with a skaven knife in his back. Uthor wanted to cry out, to shout his anger at the ancestors, to defy them, but he did not. Instead, he felt the coarse brush of twined hemp against his fingers and grabbed it tightly.

A bizarre sensation of weightlessness passed quickly and Uthor was slammed into the side of the chasm, his shield and weapons – mercifully well-secured – clanking as they struck rock. The dwarf's shoulder blades were nearly yanked from their sockets as the weight of his armour pulled at him. White heat blazed up his arms and a dizzying fog obscured his vision. For but a moment, he lost purchase and the rope burned through his grasp, tendrils of smoke spiralling from his leather gauntlet. Uthor roared, biting back the pain as he gripped the rope hard to arrest his descent, one-handed, the other arm flailing about as he spun and thrashed. At last it was over and a hot line of pain gnawed at his arm, back and head. Through the dense aural fug of resonating metal in his ears from his helmet, the dwarf heard shouting.

'Uthor!' the voices cried.

'Uthor!' they said again.

Uthor looked up through a haze of dark specks, a spike of pain flaring in his neck and saw Rorek. The engineer had a rope around his waist and was peering over the edge of the chasm.

'Here,' Uthor said groggily. He didn't recognise the sound of his own voice.

'He lives!' He heard Rorek say. The dwarf's vision kept coming in and out of focus. When it returned, Uthor noticed Drimbold being hauled up the dangling bridge by Gromrund and Dunrik. The Grey dwarf clung to his pack, trinkets spilling out of it as his rescuers heaved. The lost treasure shimmered in the torch light – Uthor's world was darkening – they looked like falling stars...

'HE IS SLIPPING,' said Rorek urgently, turning to Thundin and Hakem who were holding the rope with feet braced. 'Lower me down...'

Rorek watched as Uthor drifted into unconsciousness... and let go of the rope. Before the engineer could cry out a half-naked dwarf barrelled past him out of the corner of his eye.

AZGAR WAS LEAPING through the air, a pledge to Grimnir on his lips as he swung his axe-chain rapidly in a wide circle. Over the edge of the chasm he went, through a faint wall of heat and plunged into the endless abyss. He turned his body in mid-flight, releasing the axe-chain and flinging it upwards in the direction he had just come. He watched for a moment to see the heavy blade arc over the lip of the gaping gorge and then wrapped both hands firmly around the chain. The links clattered and the chain pulled taut as the axe blade bit home above him.

Azgar felt the tension jar violently through his shoulders and back, but, grunting back the discomfort, he held on. The chasm wall rushed to meet him, promising to shatter his bones in a single crunching impact. Azgar absorbed the slamming force with his feet, bending his knees as solid stone made its presence felt. As he did, the slayer ran sideways like a mountain goat herder: nimble, light and assured. He reached out and caught Uthor's arm in one meaty fist. The slayer roared with the effort, thick cords of muscle standing out in his neck, arms and back. The chain lurched in his grasp for a moment and the two dwarfs fell a few feet. Azgar looked up in alarm as he imagined the axe blade churning a furrow in the flagstones above.

UTHOR OPENED HIS eyes to see a wild-eyed slayer looking at him. Azgar's face was red. Veins stuck out on his forehead that was beaded with sweat.

'Hold on,' he snarled through gritted teeth.

Uthor looked down and saw the gaping blackness, a vague line of distant fire running through it. He gripped the slayer's arm with one hand and held onto the chain with the other, bracing his feet against the chasm wall.

* * *

AT THE CHASM'S edge, Rorek breathed a sigh of relief. He stepped back, untying the rope from around his waist. He checked to make sure Thundin and Hakem still gripped it and then tossed the end of the rope into the gorge.

'Coming down,' he bellowed.

Rorek took hold of the rope, wrapping it loosely around his wrist, just as it went taut. He felt the pull against his arms lessen as several more dwarfs joined him.

'Take the strain...' he cried. 'Now, heave!'

The dwarfs hauled as one, dragging the thick rope through their fingers, hand-over-hand in perfect unison.

'Heave!' Rorek bellowed, and they did again.

The command repeated several more times until two dwarf hands – one wearing a shredded leather gauntlet, the other hairy-knuckled and tanned – reached up over the edge of the precipice clawing rock with their fingers.

With Rorek and the others holding the rope firm, Gromrund and Dunrik reached down and hauled Uthor over the edge and onto solid earth once more. Two of the Grim Brotherhood grasped the thick wrist of Azgar and soon enough the slayer too was no longer imperilled.

Gasping for breath, Uthor regarded him sternly and gave a near-imperceptible nod of gratitude. Azgar reciprocated, dour-faced, and yanked his axe blade from where it had carved its way into the rock. After he'd gathered up the attached chain, ignoring the muttered admiration of a few of the clan dwarfs, he walked away from the chasm edge to be amongst his kin.

'Where are Furgil and Norri?' Uthor asked of Rorek, looking around once Azgar was out of eyeshot.

The engineer's face darkened, as did the faces of those dwarfs stood around him.

Drimbold was amongst them, sat clutching his pack. The Grey dwarf's expression was distraught.

'They fell,' he breathed.

'They fell,' echoed Halgar, stalking through the throng, dwarfs barrelling quickly out of the grizzled longbeard's way. 'They died without honour,' he snarled at Drimbold. Halgar's ire was palpable as he eyed the bulging pack the Grey dwarf clung to.

'The bridge, it was–' Drimbold began.

'Overburdened,' said the longbeard.

'I thought it would–'

'You do not get to speak,' Halgar raged. 'The bodies of our kin were smashed on rock, immolated in the river of fire. Forever they will wander the catacombs of the Halls of the Ancestors, bodiless and with deeds unreckoned. Your greed has condemned them to that fate. You should throw yourself off into the underdeep...' the longbeard growled.

'Half-dwarf, I name thee!' he bellowed for all the throng to hear.

Shocked silence followed the declamation.

Halgar stormed off, grumbling heatedly as he went.

Several amongst the throng muttered in the wake of the insult he had levelled against Drimbold. To be so besmirched... especially by a venerable longbeard, it was a heavy burden indeed. A host of accusatory faces gazed down at the Grey dwarf. Drimbold did not meet their gaze but, instead, held onto his pack tightly like it was a shield.

Uthor watched the Grey dwarf thoughtfully, his head still thundering from his fall. He saw the borrowed helmet, the tarnished armour, the blunted hand axe: these were not the trappings of a warrior.

'You were not summoned to the war council, were you, Drimbold?' said Uthor.

'No.' Drimbold's voice was barely a whisper, shoulders slumped and mournful.

'You know this place too well.' Uthor's eyes narrowed. 'All the times you have guided our guide, you knew which way to go, didn't you? When we thought you lost to the rat-kin as we fled for our lives, you escaped another way.'

Drimbold's face fell further still as the weight of his leader's discovery struck him like a physical blow. The Grey dwarf exhaled deeply, his shame could be no greater, and then spoke.

'When Gromrund and Hakem found me, I had been looting from the hold for months,' he admitted. 'There is a cave – I have hidden it well – not far from the karak, where the treasure lies. I knew there were dangers, of the grobi and the rat-kin, and I took steps to avoid them.' Drimbold's voice grew more impassioned. 'Karak Varn was lost and its treasures laid bare for any greenskin to steal or defile. My clan and hold are poor–' he explained fervently, 'far better that the lost riches be in the hands of the dawi, so I sought to reclaim them.' The look in Drimbold's eyes was one of defiance. It faded quickly, replaced by remorse.

'You knew of Kadrin's death and the fall of the hold, yet you said nothing?' Uthor said, clearly exasperated.

'And likely he is a Sournose Grum and not a Sourtooth as he alleged,' snarled Gromrund, the hammerer having bustled his way forward upon hearing his name mentioned.

Uthor fixed him with a reproachful glance.

Gromrund scowled back and stood his ground.

'My clan knew of the prosperity being enjoyed by Lord Kadrin,' Drimbold continued, 'so I ventured to the hold in the hope of panning some of the ore from the edges of Black Water. I did not think the Karak Varn dwarfs would miss it.'

Uthor's expression darkened at that admission, but Drimbold went on, regardless.

'I discovered the skeletons by the Old Dwarf Road, just as you did,' he said shamefully. 'And yes, I am one of the Sournose Grums.'

He could not meet the thane of Karak Kadrin's gimlet gaze any longer, nor the fierce anger of the hammerer, and lowered his eyes.

With the throng looking on, Uthor regarded the Grey dwarf in stony silence.

'Yours is a heavy burden,' he uttered prophetically. 'Furgil Sootbeard and Norri Sootbeard,' he added, 'may they be remembered…

'We've lingered here long enough,' Uthor said after a moment, addressing the throng. 'Make ready, we muster out for the Great Hall at once.'

The throng was forming up into organised ranks, gathering at the exit and waiting for Uthor as he strode purposefully to the front to meet Ralkan.

Rorek followed in his stead.

'With no bridge to speak of,' said the engineer, 'how are we to go back?'

When Uthor turned to him he was smiling darkly.

'There will be no turning back.'

CHAPTER EIGHT

HOISTED UP ON Ungul's back in a crudely woven basket, Skartooth looked over the goblin runners hurrying ahead of the greenskin horde as they tramped through the narrow tunnel. The roof was low and, on more than one occasion, the warlord had thumped the troll hard with the pommel of his sword after his head had struck a jutting rock.

Fangrak trudged alongside, the chieftain's thick hobnailed boots crunching gravel underfoot. A great mob of orcs followed close behind him, shoulders hunched in the tight confines of the tunnel. Behind that there came yet more goblins. Wreathed in their black, hooded cloaks, they were little more than scurrying shadows in the gloom.

Skartooth had almost gathered the entire tribe for his 'cunnin' plan'.

'You is sure this is the way?' moaned Fangrak, again, snarling at an orc bumping into him.

"Ow many times ave you gotta be told?' whined Skartooth. 'These is gobbo tunnels and I knows 'em like the back of my 'and.' Sneering, the goblin warlord showed Fangrak his puny claw for emphasis. A look of surprise briefly crossed his face as he saw something there as if for the first time, before he continued. 'All that snotling rutting must 'ave addled your brain,' Skartooth said with a malicious grin.

'Hur, hur, ruttin',' droned Ungul.

Skartooth started laughing uncontrollably in the basket, spittle flicking from his tiny, wicked mouth. The hilarity stopped abruptly when he almost fell out, for which he struck Ungul viciously across the back of the neck. The troll turned to snarl at him, but when it met Skartooth's gaze, fell quiet and acquiesced.

'You leave the thinkin' to me,' warned Skartooth, his attention back on Fangrak.

Fangrak clenched his fists. No one spoke to him like that. When Skartooth looked away again, bawling at the goblin runners, he rested one meaty claw on the hilt of a broad dagger at his waist. Ungul glared at him as he did it, regarding the chieftain hungrily. Fangrak let it go – if it weren't for that beast… He was averting his gaze when he saw an ephemeral glow emanating from some symbols etched onto the spiked collar Skartooth wore around his neck. They looked like shamanic glyphs…

AFTER CROSSING THE chasm, the throng had been forced to take yet another detour. The main gate leading into the Great Hall was blocked by rubble; so massive was the ruination that even with the clan of miners they had, it still would have taken several days to get through. Another gallery had brought them to this point, the Wide Western Way. The tunnel was aptly named. Such was its girth that the throng could have marched fifty dwarfs across in four long lines, gazing up at its thick, vaulted arches in the light of the smouldering brazier-pans chained above. They did not. The long tunnel's state of dilapidation prevented it, with its broken pillars and sunken floors. Instead they strode in a column no more than four shields wide and in deep ranks, ever watchful of the pooling shadows that stretched from walls they could not fully see.

Naturally Uthor took the advance party, though even he was forced to concede the head of the column – that went to the Sootbeards. Though expansive, the Wide Western Way was fraught with pit falls and rock-strewn in places. It would be easy to slip in the gloom and never be seen again. The miners were ensuring the passage was clear and safe. There'd already been too many lost needlessly to the creeping dark.

Thalgrim was amongst them, overseeing their endeavours. It was painstaking work. Uthor had instructed that the throng stay together and in formation, lest anything be lurking in the darkened recesses of the tunnel. It meant excavating the scattered rock falls that impeded the dwarfs' path, and quickly. He paused a moment, his miner's mattock over one shoulder and lifted his pot helmet a little to wipe away a swathe of sweat.

'Mercy of Valaya, may her cups be ever lustrous, what is that stench?' said Rorek, wrinkling his nose. He looked back to Uthor for support, but the thane seemed lost in another of his dark moods.

The engineer was in the advance party, too, his structural expertise invaluable as they made progress down the Wide Western Way.

'Nothing,' said Thalgrim, sitting his helmet back down on his head quickly.

The pungent aroma still clung to the air and Rorek gagged.

'A pocket of gas, perhaps – nothing to worry about,' the lodefinder assured him.

Rorek mouthed the word 'gas' to Uthor, who looked askance at the lodefinder with some concern.

'Shouldn't we make certain?' he ventured.

'No, no. It's probably just some cave spores we've disturbed. Foul smelling, perhaps but certainly harmless, my brother.' Thalgrim was about to busy himself with something, thus avoiding further questioning, when he saw that the passageway narrowed ahead. The two walls on either side arced in dramatically in a cordon of around six shield widths. Bereft of brazier-pans, it was also miserably dark.

'Call a halt,' he bellowed, as the Sootbeards started to gather in the sudden bottleneck .

'DO YOU THINK this route will finally lead us to the Great Hall?' Hakem asked.

Dunrik shrugged, seemingly distracted as he kept one eye on his cousin walking just ahead of him.

The Everpeak noble had offered little by way of conversation, despite the hour that they had been traversing the Wide Western Way, which Ralkan claimed would get them to their destination.

The lorekeeper travelled with them for now, in the middle of the column, staying out of the way of the miners' excavations. The last thing the dwarfs needed was their guide crushed beneath a slab of fallen rock or lost to the underdeep, in spite of his occasional befuddlement.

'I have my doubts,' whispered the Barak Varr dwarf conspiratorially, careful not to raise his voice so that Ralkan could hear him.

Still Dunrik gave him nothing.

The column was slowing. The armour of the ironbreakers, who were a few ranks in front, clattered as they started to bunch up. Thundin raised his gauntleted hand in a gesture for the throng to stop.

The message went down the line, a hand raised every ten ranks or so, until it reached Azgar and his slayers who were guarding the rear. Halgar had joined them, the longbeard preferring their silent, fatalistic company to that of the rest of his kin.

Hakem tried to look ahead to see what the delay was, but all he got was a small sea of bobbing dwarf heads.

'Perhaps it is another wrong turn?' the merchant thane offered.

It seemed Dunrik had no opinion on the matter.

Hakem was a gregarious dwarf by his very nature. He liked to talk, to boast and regale people with tales, and was not prone to long bouts of brooding like some of his kin. As a trader, his livelihood and the prosperity of his clan depended on the bonds he could forge, but despite his best efforts Dunrik was proving tight-lipped.

He was not the only one, either. Since the tragedy on the bridge, Drimbold had become like an outcast. He travelled in the column, much like the rest, but he kept his eyes down and his mouth shut. At least it meant Hakem didn't need to keep such a hawk-like watch over his purse and belongings. It was small recompense for the grief he felt in his heart.

The merchant thane brought his attention back to Dunrik. It was clear that he too had his own travails.

'I heard your screams when we last made camp,' said Hakem, his tone abruptly serious. 'Your scars go deeper than the flesh, don't they? I have seen their like before…'

Dunrik didn't bite.

Hakem persisted, anyway.

'…from the barbed whips of a grobi slave master.'

Dunrik twisted sharply to face him, his expression fiery.

Borri overheard and was turning around, about to intervene, when Dunrik's fierce gaze stopped him.

'I mean no disrespect,' Hakem said calmly, noting that Borri had continued on his way, albeit slightly uncomfortably. Gromrund, who walked on the other side of Dunrik, shifted a little in his armour, too.

'My great, great grandfather was captured by grobi for a short time, taken whilst driving a caravan to one of the old elgi settlements before the War of Vengeance,' Hakem went on. 'The greenskins ambushed them and slew many of our warriors. They turned the wagons into cages for our kin and were taking them, my three-times grandsire included, to their lair when a party of rangers found them.

'Three days my kin had been on the road before they were rescued and in that time the grobi had visited much pain and suffering upon them.'

Gromrund, having heard the entire recounted tale, turned to regard Hakem with newfound respect but stayed quiet.

'His face and body were scarred much like yours,' Hakem said to Dunrik, 'he showed me just before he passed on into the Halls of the Ancestors.'

Dunrik's anger drained away and a look of resignation passed across his face.

'I was held at Iron Rock,' he said, voice low and full of bitterness, 'taken whilst patrolling the Varag Kadrin.' Dunrik breathed deep as if recalling a dark memory.

'Of the twenty-three of my kin brought there in chains, only I escaped the urk fortress alive.' Dunrik was silent for a beat as he revisited the stinking dungeon, heard again the tortured screams of his brethren, felt anew the savage beatings of his vindictive captors.

'I did not do so unscathed,' he added, not just referring to his lasting physical injuries.

The Everpeak noble's face was wretched with the greenskin's 'attentions'. A long, jagged line ran from forehead to chin; some of Dunrik's beard was left patchy in its path. Weals of still-reddened flesh pock-marked the right side of his face, burns left by the brander's iron, and he was missing three teeth.

Gromrund, who had respectfully remained silent throughout the exchange, could not help but be moved by such tales of honourable for-bearance and grievous loss, gripped the dwarf's shoulder. As he did, he caught sight of where Dunrik's left ear had been almost chewed off – a wound kept mostly hidden by his helmet.

'Dreng tromm,' the hammerer muttered.

'Dreng tromm,' echoed Hakem.

Dunrik stayed silent.

Hakem, suddenly aware they had fallen into solemn lamentation, and slightly regretful of his questioning, sought to quickly lighten the mood.

'Tell me,' he said to Dunrik, eyes brightening, 'have you ever seen a more magnificent hammer than this?'

'A fine weapon,' Dunrik remarked.

'Indeed, it garners that reaction often,' Hakem replied, a little per-turbed as he noted the smirk on Gromrund's face just visible below his massive warhelm.

'It is the Honakkin Hammer,' he explained, aware of Gromrund's sud-den interest, 'and I bear it proudly as an ancient symbol of my clan. As heir to the fortune of my father, merchant lord of Barak Varr, it is my great honour to carry it into battle. Make no mistake, this is a very seri-ous undertaking,' Hakem told them, indicating the thick leather strap that bound the weapon to his wrist. 'This cord has never been cut, for if it ever was and the hammer was lost, the prosperity of my clan and my line would be lost along with it.'

'A noble undertaking,' said Dunrik solemnly.

'Indeed,' Gromrund muttered reluctantly.

'Certainly, the fall of the Honaks would dull the lustre of the hold,' Hakem went on. 'Tell me, Everpeak dwarf, have you ever seen the won-der that is the Sea Gate?'

Gromrund grumbled loudly. 'Whether you have or have not, you are about to be regaled of its splendour,' he barked. 'I have no stomach for it,' he added gruffly and stormed off, shouldering his way further up the column to find out what was causing the delay.

'PUT YOUR BACKS into it,' Thalgrim chided, standing atop a flat stone so he could see his miners working at the door impeding their path.

The stone barrier sat right at the end of the bottleneck ed section of the tunnel and Thalgrim assumed the Great Hall was beyond it, this lesser door a secondary way into the room. The lodefinder realised now that the Wide Western Way was narrowed by design, to make it easier to defend should it be invaded. A wise strategy and one he applauded, only not right now.

Most of the throng were grouped together in the narrow defile, shoulders touching, with a wall at either flank. The stone door being pushed by the Sootbeards wasn't particularly tall or broad, but it was obviously thick and heavy. Rorek, with Uthor at his shoulder, had already released a series of stone bolts by carefully manipulating the door's ingenious locking mechanism. Much of its resistance came from the fact that it hadn't been opened in many years, but eventually the door yielded to the miners' exertions, and ground open noisily.

'At last,' breathed Uthor, finding the closeness of his kinsdwarfs around him and the enveloping darkness disconcerting. 'This tunnel is the perfect place for an ambush.'

THUNDIN SAW A strange globe-like object fly overhead then heard the gurgled warning of his kinsdwarfs before he saw the billowing cloud of yellowish gas. Bordak, one of his fellow ironbreakers, fell back clutching his throat as bloody foam bubbled down his face and beard.

They were wedged in the bottleneck of the Wide Western Way, many other dwarfs of the throng having already moved through the stone door and into the Great Hall beyond it. Thundin and his ironbreakers were trapped with the rest, shoulder-to-shoulder with their kinsdwarfs and strangely vulnerable.

'Gas!' cried the ironbeard. The acrid taste of the noxious fumes was upon his tongue before he could clamp his mouth shut. He watched as three more filth-stained globes soared out of the darkness and into the packed ranks of the dwarfs. He was powerless to intervene as they shattered on raised shields and unsuspecting helmets, disgorging their foul contents amongst the throng.

The dwarfs retreated instinctively, and those that remained on the near side of the door were herded back into the bottleneck .

Thundin caught a snatched view of the Great Hall through the small portal and massing bodies. He could only guess at its immensity as the others, seemingly so far away and oblivious to the attack, gathered inside.

'Back into the Wide Western Way,' he bellowed, risking another mouthful of the gas, his voice croaking as the virulent poison wracked his throat and insides. Head reeling, he felt the press of warriors at his back moving steadily out of the bottleneck. He vaguely saw the opening through his blurring vision when two concealed alcoves opened up on either side of him. Ratmen wearing strange, sacking hoods tied at the neck with a filtered muzzle and dirt-smeared goggles, poured out brandishing knives.

One came at him with vicious abandon, cackling with malevolent glee as all around Thundin his ironbreakers died, their armour no defence against the invasive poison.

Choking on his own blood, Thundin smashed aside the skaven's dagger thrust with his shield and hacked off its head with his axe. A loud crack echoed inside his helmet as he caught a flash of fire in the darkness and the whiff of burning. Another ironbreaker fell, a smoking wound in his chest plate.

Thundin was slowing now. He couldn't breathe, tasted blood in his mouth and felt it trickle from his nose and ears. He clutched at his throat, dropping his shield to claw at the metal gorget around his neck. An immense flare of green and incandescent flame surged from an alcove further up the bottleneck to his left. Thundin was blinded for a moment. In his disorientation he thought he heard screams, as if he were listening to them from the bottom of a deep, dark well. Through the mucus and blood in his nostrils, he caught the stench of burning flesh. The ironbeard wanted to retch but couldn't. He slumped to his knees, his armour heavy, and removed his helmet. The effort to hold his breath with it on was suffocating. As he gazed bleary-eyed at the carnage of dead dwarfs all around, something large loomed over him. Thundin's nerveless fingers let the axe slip from his grasp.

'Valaya,' he croaked with his final breath as the beast crushed him.

DUNRIK ROLLED; THE lumbering rat beast tore into the ground with its claws in the dwarf's wake as he desperately tried to reach Thundin who lay prone in a rapidly expanding miasma of sulphurous fog. Trapped in the bottleneck , the fighting was fierce and close. All around him his brothers fought hammer and axe against a seemingly endless tide of skaven. The creature before him had come with the rat-kin, lumbering out of the shadows like some cruel experiment. It was huge and grotesquely muscled; a horrific fusion of ogre and skaven. Its body was wrapped in thick, pus-soaked bandages and ravaged by sores and overly distended muscle growth. Dagger-like claws extended from fingers encrusted with dirt and dwarf blood. Blinded, the beast tracked the dwarf by smell alone and with lethal efficiency. The rat ogre sniffed for his prey and came at the Everpeak dwarf again, its savage backswing sending a hooded skaven screaming backwards into the melee.

Dunrik ducked the swiping arm of the rat ogre, its claws digging four deep furrows into the bottleneck wall. The dwarf came forward quickly, beneath the creature's guard and rammed the spike of his axe into its frothing jaw, so hard that it punched straight through and came out of the rat ogre's skull. Dunrik ripped the axe free with a roar of defiance, gore and brain matter showering from the gaping wound. In its death throes the beast came on still. It was about to lunge for Dunrik with the last of its fading strength when Hakem, who was also trapped with the skaven attackers, shattered its wrist with a blow from the Honakinn Hammer. The weapon's runes glowed dully as the merchant thane fought, a second blow crumpling what was left of the rat ogre's skull.

Dunrik nodded a hasty thanks and then pointed to the door to the

Great Hall. Nearly half the throng had already filed through, but the
tail end was being ravaged by poison gas as they struggled to turn and
fight the skaven massing behind them, realising slowly they were under
attack.

Hakem nodded his understanding and the two dwarfs ran to the stone
door, covering the short distance quickly. They held their breath in unison as they plunged into the cloud of poison gas eking through it. A few
dwarfs of the Firehand clan were battling furiously against a horde of
hooded skaven at the threshold to the room. Borri, having been pushed
further down the bottleneck in the press of the fighting, was amongst
them just beyond the door arch and inside the Great Hall itself.

He met the gaze of Dunrik across the open doorway, hacking down
one of the ratmen with his axe. Borri's eyes were pleading when he
realised what Dunrik was about to do.

Anguish crushing him, Dunrik heaved against the stone door with
Hakem at his side and a few of the Firehand dwarfs, the rest of the clan
warriors forming a hastily arranged shield wall to protect them. The
door yielded quickly this time and scraped shut with a thudding echo
of stone on stone, the thick bolts sliding into hidden recesses automati-
cally. Dunrik looked down at the locking mechanism and smashed it.
There would be no opening it.

'MAGNIFICENT...' UTHOR GAZED in wonderment at the Great Hall of Karak
Varn. As leader of the throng, he was the first through and was vaguely
aware of the others amassing in his wake.

By far the biggest chamber they had been in yet, the Great Hall was
supported by a veritable forest of symmetrically arranged columns that
stretched down its full length. At one end of the mighty room there was
an immense hearth fashioned to resemble the ancestor god, Grungni,
his wide open mouth giving life to the flames that must have once
blazed in it. Statues lined the walls, interposed with bronze brazier
pans made into the image of the engineers who had fashioned them,
immortalising the dwarfs for all time, their outstretched hands cup-
ping the dormant coals within. Shadows hugged the walls and pooled
thickly around each of the columns. The Great Hall was gloomy,
despite the firelight. There were stone tables throughout. The king's
resided at the top of a rectangular plateau – broad stairs leading up to
it – and overlooked the rest.

'Here, it begins,' Uthor murmured beneath his breath, privately con-
gratulating himself. 'Here, we take it all back.'

'Dunrik!'

Uthor heard Borri's cry from the front of the throng before the thunderous, booming retort of the stone door to the Great Hall slamming
shut, and was arrested from his brief moment of vainglory.

Skaven infested the doorway behind him, cut off from the rest of the horde, and tendrils of gas evaporated around it. Several dwarfs littered the floor of the Great Hall, spitting blood and snot.

'Turn!' he bellowed. 'Turn, we are under attack!'

AZGAR THROTTLED THE skaven warrior with one hand, right in the thick of the fighting at the edge of the bottleneck and the broader section of the Wide Western Way, trying to battle a way out for his kin. The rat-man's eyes burst with the sheer pressure exerted by the muscle-bound slayer, coating the inside of its goggles in sticky crimson. Discarding the creature like an unwanted rag, Azgar freed up his hand to disembowel a second onrushing skaven with a brutal upswing of his chained axe.

The fighting was close; so close he smelled the sweat of his brothers around him, tasted blood on the air, and heard their deathsongs in his ears. The sound of killing became a macabre chorus to the doleful dirge as ratmen funnelled into the churning blades of the Grim Brotherhood, held in the bottleneck and unable to get out. From the Wide Western Way the skaven came at them in their droves, hemming the dwarfs in.

Azgar cursed loudly as one of his tattooed kinsdwarfs was dragged silently to his doom by a vicious swarm of rats. No way for a slayer to meet his end, he thought bitterly, hoping that his own death would be more glorious.

A muted scream and a wash of hot fluid splashing against the side of Azgar's face got his attention – the stink of copper filled his nostrils and the slayer realised it was blood. He turned and looked up as a gargantuan rat ogre loomed over him, the beast casting aside two wet hunks of armoured flesh that had once been a dwarf warrior.

Metal plates, ravaged by rust, were fused to the monster's body like scales and it wore a cone-like helmet with a perforated grille at the muzzle – but hinged so that it could still bite – and two holes for its malevolent, red eyes. It swung a gore-splattered ball and chain that had been bolted to its wrist; a serrated boar spear was grafted to the other in place of a hand.

Azgar's flesh burned. He noticed the tattoos of Grimnir blazing brightly on his body and then the glowing, black-green rock studding the rat ogre's torso from between the cracks in its scale-armour.

Roaring a challenge, spittle frothing from beneath its helmet, the beast loped forward, with ball and chain swinging.

Azgar smiled, gripping his axe as he fixed the hulking mutant in his sights.

'Come on,' he said. 'Come to me.'

'OPEN THE DOOR,' Uthor demanded. 'I will not leave them to be massacred.'

The half of the throng inside the Great Hall of Karak Varn had slain the meagre few skaven that had got through before Dunrik and Hakem had shut out the rest.

The throng waited in pensive silence behind the thane of Karak Kadrin, listening to the muted sounds of battle, dulled by thick stone, through the closed entry door.

'The locking mechanism is ruined, I cannot release it,' said Rorek, one of those to have made it through, crouching by the doorway and replacing his tools in his belt.

'Can it be broken down?' Uthor asked desperately, switching his attention to the lodefinder, Thalgrim, all of the Sootbeard miners having made it into the Great Hall.

'Given several days...' said Thalgrim, rubbing his chin. 'Perhaps.'

'We must get through,' urged Borri, a slightly high-pitched, hysterical tone to his voice. 'My cousin is on the other side. I saw the rat-kin hordes through the fog, they couldn't possible prevail against such numbers. We must get to them.'

'We cannot!' Uthor snapped, enraged at himself more than the beardling. His face softened abruptly at the pain on Borri's face.

'I'm sorry, lad,' he said, placing his hand upon the young dwarf's shoulder and looking him in the eyes. 'Their names will be remembered.'

It was not supposed to be this way: desperate, divided... defeated. The thane felt his shoulders sagging as the burden of his oath exerted itself upon him. Had he been wrong? Was Gromrund right? Had he led them to folly? Aware of all eyes upon him, Uthor found inner steel and straightened up to address the throng.

'Secure the Great Hall, make barricades and set guards on every exit,' he ordered the clan leaders. 'We are but a hundred dwarfs,' he added, 'let them come in their thousands. They are but the rancid surf that breaks upon our rocks; each of us is a link in a suit of mail. Stay together, remain strong, and their blades will blunt and break against us.'

Chittering, squeaking laughter filled the massive room, coming from everywhere at once.

Uthor had heard it before.

Like miniature balefires, hundreds of eyes flashed in the outer darkness ringing the room – No, not hundreds... *thousands*.

Uthor gaped at the sheer size of the skaven horde closing in on them, rusted blades held ready in a vast sea of wretched, stinking fur. He *had* been wrong; this *was* folly.

'Valaya preserve us,' he breathed.

STONE SPLINTERED AS the ball and chain smashed against the ground. Azgar leapt back to avoid its deadly path and then ducked swiftly as the rat ogre swiped at him, the boar spear spitting sparks as it raked the wall. The beast swung again with the spiked ball. Azgar cut the chain in two with a blow from his axe and, stepping past the fierce swipe, reversed his cut to lop off the rat ogre's arm at the shoulder despite the armour plate. The creature howled in pain, the sound muffled and tinny through his cone-helm, and drove at Azgar with the boar spear, blood fountaining from its ruined stump. The slayer avoided the strike, which embedded deep into the flanking wall and held fast. The monstrosity heaved at the weapon impaled in the stone but couldn't free it.

Azgar regarded the rat ogre darkly as it struggled... and cleaved off the other arm. The beast fell back with the impetus of its own exertions. The slayer went to finish it but the rat ogre lashed out with its tail, taking Azgar's legs from under him. He hit the ground with bone jarring force and the slayer barely had time to get his bearings when a rust-brown blur came at him. Azgar reacted instinctively, holding onto the beast's jaws, one in each hand, a hair's-breadth from biting off his face.

He shook with effort, every muscle straining as he fought to keep the rat ogre back. Saliva flicked his face and neck as the rat ogre's rotten meat breath washed over him. Digging deep, he summoned all the reserves of his strength and roared as he snapped the creature's jaws back, twisting metal and breaking bone. A howl of pain tore from the rat ogre's broken mouth. Azgar crawled out from under it, as the beast thrashed in fits of agony, gathering up the chain that was attached to his wrist and reaching for his axe.

'Chew on this,' he said and buried the blade in its tiny cranium.

MOST OF THE Firehands were dead, either suffocated or impaled by rat-kin spears, though the gas was all but dissipated. Dunrik risked a breath as he briefly surveyed the carnage.

The skaven assault had split the dwarfs still holed up in the bottleneck into two. The ironbreakers were all dead. Of the advanced part of the force on Dunrik's side of the door only him, Hakem and a handful of clan warriors remained. If they could rejoin with the other forces further back down the Wide Western Way, they might be able to fight their way free.

Dunrik, his left eye bloodshot from ingesting some of the skaven gas, took an involuntary step back as two rat ogres lumbered into view, filling up the passageway. They demolished the feeble shield wall easily, one of the beasts biting off the head of a Firehand dwarf as he fled from it. All thoughts of escape disappeared from Dunrik's mind. He felt the stone door at his back, the closeness of the walls at either side, Hakem's tension as he raised his shield. There would be no escape.

HALGAR GASPED FOR breath through clenched teeth, making the most of a brief respite in the furious melee unfolding in the bottleneck around him. He'd watched as the stone door was sealed, effectively trapping them with their enemies and was glad of it. At least he would go down fighting. The longbeard's arms and shoulders burned, the weight of his axe like a fallen tree in his gnarled hands. Blood – both rat-kin and dawi – splattered clothes, armour and skin. Halgar's vision blurred sporadically in time with a persistent throbbing in his skull; he put it down to when a skaven warrior had struck a lucky blow against his helmet – he would have to work out the dent later.

The longbeard tramped slowly through the carnage, past his battling kinsdwarfs as he tried to reach Drimbold. Having been near the back of the group, the Grey dwarf would never have reached the Great Hall, even if he'd tried. Instead, he had fought. Drimbold was a vague outline at times when Halgar's eyesight worsened, but he knew it was him – he could smell him. Ralkan was behind the Grey dwarf, clutching a borrowed hammer like his life depended on it. It did.

Out of the gloom, a hooded skaven came hurtling at the longbeard. Halgar sidestepped its attack, upending it with a smack of his axe haft against its ankles and then hacking the blade into the ratman's back to finish it. He shouldered a second rat-kin in the gut, using his armoured plate-mail like a battering ram and was rewarded with the crunch of bone. An elbow smash broke the skaven's skull wide open, blood and matter spilling freely. He felled a third with a hefty kick to the shins and then decapitated it with the edge of his shield to reach Drimbold's side.

'Stand firm!' he bellowed, cutting a savage diagonal blow against an onrushing skaven. More ratmen were pressing, their numbers seemingly endless. Even Azgar and his slayers were being slowly herded towards them.

'Fight until you've no breath–'

A massive ball of green and incandescent flame lit up the passageway, burning shadows into the walls and illuminating the conflict like some gruesome animation. Dwarfs fell screaming to the terrible conflagration – cloth, metal and hair melting before it.

'There!' cried Drimbold, fending off a rusty dagger with his hand axe. He pointed to a pair of hooded skaven lugging some kind of infernal weapon between them. One carried a bulbous cannon rigged with coiling pipes and a pull chain affixed to the fat copper nozzle. The other bore a large wooden barrel with bolted on plates that fed the cannon, bent-backed against the weight of whatever liquid was stored within.

A small band of dwarfs from the Stonebreaker clan charged toward the deadly arcane device, bellowing war cries.

The skaven gunner squeaked gleefully as he tugged at the pull chain, opening the nozzle. The Stonebreakers were immolated in a blazing inferno, their charred remains still smoking long after the flame had abated.

Halgar blinked back the afterimage of the fiery destruction wrought by the skaven cannon.

'We must destroy it,' he snarled, as the nozzle swung in their direction.

The longbeard flung a throwing axe towards the weapon but missed, the blade *thunking* harmlessly against the wall, before clattering to the ground. He stared down the gaping maw of the cannon, an indistinct circle of fathomless black, and closed his eyes.

The searing heat, the wash of flame didn't come. Skaven screaming filled his ears and Halgar opened his eyes to witness the bent-backed fuel carrier flapping at the barrel he carried. A hand axe was buried in its side and a volatile chemical mixture sprayed out eagerly. Patches of the ratman's fur burned and smoked where the fluid touched it – the stink of cooking skaven flesh was redolent on the breeze.

The gunner seemed oblivious to the screeching protestations of its partner and yanked backed on the firing chain with reckless abandon.

Halgar, Drimbold and all those dwarfs in the vicinity of the cannon were thrown back as an explosion wracked the tunnel, leaving a blackened scar on the ground fraught with tangled skaven corpses.

DUNRIK WAS SMASHED to the ground by a sudden, powerful shock wave. Dazed, he got to his feet, helping up Hakem and the few Firehand dwarfs that still lived.

Body parts littered the tunnel in steaming, fire-scorched chunks. The rat ogres were dead, engulfed in the fearsome explosion. Moreover, the way was clear to Halgar and the others. They'd have to run for it and close the short distance up the tunnel quickly. The skaven were already gathering their wits and regrouping to attack again.

'COME TOGETHER!' UTHOR cried in the Great Hall, his throng forming up in disciplined ranks around him, making a square shape with shields locked.

The skaven masses came from the shadows, spilling from their hiding places and concealed tunnels in a foetid, flea-infested swarm. They were on the dwarfs quickly, several warriors torn down before they had shields readied.

Uthor fended off a hail of missiles before hacking down an emaciated ratman with his rune axe. More came at them in their droves, almost throwing themselves suicidally onto the dwarfs' blades and hammer heads. Blinking back a swath of foul-smelling skaven blood as it splashed against his face and helmet, Uthor saw these diminutive rats were nought but fodder, cast into the melee and urged on by the cruel whips of their masters. The skaven sought to tire them, wear them down until exhaustion took them and then death. Uthor raged against it and redoubled his efforts.

'Give no quarter,' he bellowed, turning left and right to bolster his warriors with his stirring rhetoric. 'Have no fear, for we are the sons of Grungni!' Uthor caught the eye of Borri, who fought furiously beside his kinsdwarfs, anger lending him vigour. Another hail of sharp stones and wicked throwing knives filled the air, flung from behind the skaven slave fodder. Uthor raised his shield to repel the missiles. When he looked back, he couldn't see Borri anymore.

* * *

DUNRIK AND HAKEM stood shoulder-to-shoulder with Halgar and the others in the bottleneck. Azgar and what remained of the Grim Brotherhood backed up to join them, having aborted their attempts to break through the innumerable rat-kin hordes, and the trapped dwarf forces were finally reunited but being pressed into an ever diminishing circle.

Ralkan was at the centre of it, several stoutly armoured dwarf bodies between him and a vicious death at the claws of the skaven. The lorekeeper had abandoned his borrowed hammer – Drimbold wielded it now, in lieu of the weapon he'd thrown to destroy the rat-kin's fire cannon – and was frantically feeling the rock wall at the dwarfs' backs with his hands, muttering feverishly.

Dunrik watched the lorekeeper incredulously and caught Halgar's eye.

'His mind has finally given in to despair and terror,' said the longbeard, hacking down a skaven with his axe, before breaking the nose of another with his fist.

No matter how many the dwarfs killed, the numbers of the rat-kin did not dwindle and their vigour showed no sign of lessening.

'No way out,' growled Azgar cutting a ratman in half, 'and an endless horde to slay,' he added with no small amount of relish. 'It is a worthy death.'

Halgar nodded, battering a hooded skaven with his axe pommel.

'There is my seat made ready,' said the longbeard, his voice rising above the battle din so it might be heard by all of his kinsdwarfs. *'At the table of my ancestors it doth await me. Upon the rock are my deeds arrayed.'*

'Lo do I see the line of kings,' Dunrik said, joining in the sombre deathsong.

'Lo do I see Grungni and Valaya,' added Hakem, the words taught to him when he was but a beardling.

'Tremble o' mountain.' Azgar's distinctive timbre gave weight to the recitation.

'Rage o' heart,' said Drimbold, last of all. At least he would die with his kin, a hammer in his hand.

'For hearth and hold, for oath and honour, for wrath and ruin – give fire to my voice and steel to my arm that I might be remembered!' Halgar's voice was dominant as the entire dwarf throng rejoiced as one.

Only Ralkan did not sing. Instead, his fingers found the subtle permutations in the rock wall he'd been searching for. As he manipulated them carefully, a thin line ran rapidly up the length of the wall, across the roof and back down again spitting out dust as it went. A vein of light eked through it, shining faintly – a secret door, made in the elder ages, and Ralkan had found it.

GROMRUND CRUSHED ANOTHER skaven skull with his great hammer, but he was tiring. A boot to the groin and a pommel smash to its head as it doubled over put paid to another rat-kin, but the furred abominations seethed in the Great Hall. He had been one of the last to get through, not counting those unfortunates that had been poisoned to death by the gas or stabbed in the back by the rat cowards.

Bitterness filled the hammerer's heart as he fought. Uthor's plan had failed, and failed catastrophically. How the skaven had tracked them to this place in a domain as vast as Karak Varn, he didn't know. His only consolation was that he'd at least die with honour.

Through the curtailed view of his warhelm, Gromrund saw a savage blow come at him. Using his weapon defensively, he caught the attack against the haft of his great hammer. A huge skaven warrior confronted him, clad in thick, cured leather, studded with spikes. The creature's fur was the colour of coal. It wielded a brutal looking glaive, the blade dark and wet.

The ratman pressed, scraping the weapon against the wooden haft of Gromrund's hammer as a second blade thrust at him. Locked with the first skaven warrior, the hammerer was unable to defend himself. He did all he could, and twisted sharply, the second blade grazing against his armour, ripping out mail links and scattering them like silver coins. Gromrund staggered; managed to heave the first skaven back. He saw a blur of grey to the corner of his eye and felt an almighty blow against his head, the metal warhelm deafening him as it clanged loudly in his ears. Vision swimming, Gromrund went down on one knee, almost dropping his great hammer. He could smell blood. Through bleary eyes he saw the huge skaven cackle as it raised its glaive for the deathblow.

'I'm sorry, father,' he whispered and put up his hammer feebly.

The skaven fell; several black-shafted arrows pin-cushioned its swarthy body. The other turned, screeching maliciously towards some unseen threat.

Gromrund got to his feet and saw that a great many of the ratmen had whirled around towards the source of the attack. He looked at the skaven corpse again – a momentary lull in the fighting, as the rules of engagement were seemingly re-established – it had been felled by grobi arrows.

Bestial war cries rent the air and Gromrund watched, open mouthed as hordes of greenskins streamed from unseen tunnels and unknown passageways. Black-garbed goblins, hooded and bearing short bows, loosed arrows into the packed rat-kin ranks; massive, brutish orcs smashed a thin line of slave fodder aside beneath hob-nailed boot and cleaver, whilst trolls were unleashed into the furred mass to gorge and crush and maim.

Where the skaven rushed to meet the greenskin horde their numbers thinned, and an avenue of escape presented itself. Across the melee in which dwarf, skaven and greenskin fought, Gromrund caught the attention of Uthor. The thane had seen the route too – it led to an oaken gate, stout enough to hold an army back if properly braced, but not so massive that it could not be opened and defended quickly.

'To the gate!' Gromrund heard Uthor cry, hoping that their embattled enemies would be too distracted to impede them.

'Go, now!' Gromrund added his voice to the thane's order.

Staying together, the dwarfs moved as quickly as they dared to the oaken gate. The way was diminishing all the time, as rat-kin began filling the gaps, struggling to fight them and the greenskins at once.

Building momentum, the throng adopted a spear-tip formation and drove a thick wedge into the skaven ranks, scattering them as they charged headlong through pressing bodies and the intermittent hail of arrows.

'They are the grobi from the ravine,' Gromrund shouted above the din to Uthor – the two dwarfs were shoulder-to-shoulder in the rush.

'I recognise the urk chieftain,' he added, catching glimpses through the frantic fighting.

'Lokki fought him at the edge of the Black Water,' Uthor offered, cutting down a skaven warrior who stood in his path, before battering another away with his shield.

'We were followed here,' the hammerer growled, shattering a ratman's spine and pummelling the hip of another with a wicked side swipe.

Anything further would have to wait. The gateway loomed.

The throng gathered into a semicircle, arrayed around the gate at their back. Though fighting two foes at once, the rat-kin still came at them but the line was holding and the skaven were repelled by shield, hammer and axe.

As the battle became ever more furious, goblins and orcs found their way to the dwarfs' protective cordon. They too were repulsed with equal violent fervour.

ROREK WORKED DESPERATELY at the gate lock, wiping a wash of nervous sweat from his forehead. A shallow sounding click rewarded his efforts and, with help, he pulled the gate open. The depleted throng piled through quickly, barely half of those who'd made it into the Great Hall, but in good order. A thin line of shield bearers fought a desperate rearguard, allowing the majority of the dwarfs to pass through unhindered.

'Down!' Rorek cried and the rearguard squatted to the floor, shields upraised, as a host of quarrellers loosed a storm of crossbow bolts into the skaven harassing their kinsdwarfs. Rorek added his own rapid-firing fusillade and a score of ratmen were cut down. The short respite was enough time for the shield bearers to hurry through the doorway and those warriors positioned either side of it to slam the gate shut.

Thalgrim and two of the Sootbeards dragged a hefty bar across it before the dull hammering from the other side began as the skaven attempted to batter their way through. After that, Thalgrim took several thick, metal door spikes from a pouch on his belt and smacked them against the base of the door to wedge it shut. Rorek did the same and, satisfied the way back was secure, at least for a time, the dwarfs fled.

'HELP ME PUSH!' the lorekeeper said, grunting as he threw himself against the wall. A few of the dwarfs turned and seeing the rectangle of light lent their own weight.

The secret door opened and Ralkan hurried through, eyes wide when he saw the plateau of stone basked in the white radiance coming from above. Through a long, natural funnel in the mountain the light of the upper world shone down, resolving itself in a hazy aura when it struck stone.

'The Diamond Shaft,' the lorekeeper breathed, in awestruck wonderment.

The plateau led to a set of descending steps and beyond that another plateau. From there a massively long stairwell dropped down into darkness and was lost from sight completely. On either side of the magnificent edifice of stone was a sheer drop into the underdeep, so cavernous and black that it might have been bottomless.

Overcoming his awe, Ralkan surged across the first plateau and was heading down the steps and onto the second, much larger, expanse of stone when the skaven came teeming through the secret door.

Most of the dwarf throng had followed the lorekeeper; the slayers and a few of the clan warriors mounting a fierce rearguard. The throbbing wave of rat-kin smashed against the rock of dwarf warriors and several of the foul creatures were pitched over the edge of the short stairway and fell screaming to their doom in the void below. But as the skaven numbers grew, the dwarfs were pushed back and slowly overrun. The fight came to a stalemate at the second plateau; the ratmen, despite their masses, unable to break the sons of Grungni, and the dwarfs refusing to give any more ground. Bodies, both skaven and dwarf, fell like fat rain into the hungry abyss surrounding them, the stone plateau, as mighty as it was, insufficient to hold them all. Rat-kin thronged on the stairs, bunched so close together that those in the middle were crushed and suffocated, while those on the edges were pushed off the edge into oblivion.

Rune-light illuminated Hakem's face as he struck relentlessly with the Honakinn Hammer, the weapon that was his birthright and a formidable relic of the craft of elder days. As he swung, the merchant thane sang the battle-dirge of his ancestors, the *Ever Blazing Beacon*. He smote his foes gloriously, punctuating every stanza with a hammer strike.

A sudden surge of skaven pushed forward into him and his kinsdwarfs. Hakem used his shield to crush a ratman's muzzle and pitched another over the edge with a swift kick to the stomach. A third was smashed by the dwarf's hammer, its neck snapping back with an audible crack of bone. Hakem raised his rune weapon to smite a fourth but found he was pinned. The ratmen came on like a resurgent tide, literally thrown at him. Two dwarf warriors fell to their deaths in the charge. The merchant thane staggered, boots scraping stone underfoot; he felt the drag on his shield arm as it was crushed to his side. In the maelstrom of fur, flesh and steel a ratman bared its filthy fangs to bite at him. Hakem head-butted it and the creature's nose caved, before falling away into the mass. Bellowing, he freed his hammer.

'Feel the wrath of the Honakinn–'

There was the streak of tarnished steel in the gloom.

Pain seared up Hakem's arm, a dense ball of it throbbing at his wrist. He could no longer feel the weight of his rune hammer. Fear, so thick and palpable it made him almost retch, seized the dwarf and he looked over. In that brief moment of uncertainty, he thought of the shame he would bring to his family and his clan if his grip had failed him and the Honakinn Hammer was lost.

When Hakem saw the bloody stump of his wrist from where his hand had been cleaved off, he screamed.

DUNRIK SHOULDERED HIS way through the rat-kin mob, hacking frenziedly as he went. Hakem's agonised scream was still echoing in his ears as he ducked a blow aimed at his neck, the hooded skaven warrior killing one of its brethren behind the dwarf instead. With a grunt, Dunrik drove the spike atop his axe blade into the dumbfounded creature's chin. He kicked away the corpse and sketched a ragged figure eight with the blade, carving up a cluster of skaven who had sprung at him. Another launched itself over the melee, howling insanely, muzzle foaming and with daggers poised. Dunrik took it in flight on his shield – legs braced against the sudden impact – and using its momentum, propelled the snarling creature off the plateau and into the waiting darkness. He reached Hakem, intercepting a halberd blow aimed for the dwarf merchant's head. Dunrik trapped the weapon against the ground with his axe then stamped on the haft, shattering it. An uppercut with the edge of his shield ripped off the skaven's jaw and it fell in a mangled heap.

Hakem was clutching the bleeding stump of his wrist, his shield hanging limply on his arm by the leather straps as he scrabbled across the ground in search of his dismembered hand and hammer.

'Get to your feet, fool!' snarled Dunrik, fending off another hooded skaven – mercifully, it seemed they had exhausted their supply of poisoned globes.

'I must retrieve it,' the merchant thane wailed, crawling on his knees, heedless of the deadly battle around him.

Hakem's eyes widened suddenly. Dunrik followed his gaze and saw a dwarf hand, bedecked with jewelled rings and still gripping a rune hammer.

A tremor rippled through the plateau, felt even above the thudding resonance of shuffling feet. Deep rumbling, like thunder, came next and a cacophony of splitting stone swallowed up the battle din as if it were nothing but a morsel of sound. Terrified screams of dwarf and rat filled the air as the short stair collapsed, overburdened by the weight of armoured bodies and shaken loose by the exertions of combat.

The impromptu temblor shook Hakem's disembodied hand. It and the hammer pitched over the edge and plunged into the void. The merchant thane's anguished cries merged with the fading death screams of those on the short stair, and he raced forward about to go over the side after the ancient weapon.

'No!' Dunrik bellowed, battering a skaven aside as he reached out and grabbed Hakem's belt. 'Stand fast,' he cried, but Hakem was already on his way and the dwarf's momentum pulled Dunrik with him. The Everpeak dwarf slipped and Hakem was half over the lip on the plateau, staring down the throat of the abyss, when at last he arrested the merchant's flight and dragged him back.

'Idiot,' said Dunrik, leaning down to help Hakem up. 'No relic is worth an honourless death–' the dwarf stopped when he felt the first spear-tip pierce his back. Snarling in rage, Dunrik was about to turn when a second split the links of his armour and drove into his side. He twisted to face his attackers; the snapped hafts of the spears still embedded in him were like ice blades of pain. Dunrik raised his axe, too slowly, as a third spear impaled his exposed chest. His shield arm went limp, a blow from a mace shattering his shoulder guard and bruising bone. The snarling visages of four skaven warriors, since divested of their hoods, regarded him.

Dunrik tried to bellow his defiance and ready his axe for one final swing, when one of the vermin lunged forward and sank a rusty dagger into his neck.

'Emelda…' the dwarf gurgled, and breathed his last.

HAKEM WATCHED IN horror as Dunrik died, snapped spear hafts still jutting from his body. The merchant thane was dazed and weak from blood loss. He still clutched his wrist feebly as the fully armoured Everpeak dwarf fell on top of him, smashing him into the ground. Hakem's head struck stone and he blacked out.

'HERE!' A VOICE cried. 'Quickly, he is alive.'

Drimbold heaved at the body of Dunrik crushing the merchant thane. Azgar arrived to help and the two of them lifted the dead Everpeak dwarf off Hakem.

'He's lost a lot of blood,' said Ralkan, waiting close by.

Azgar raised Hakem's arm carefully. 'He's lost a lot more than that,' he said, showing them the stump.

'Take this,' Halgar offered, the dwarfs all clustering around the wounded merchant. The longbeard held a flaming torch.

Azgar took it and smothered the flame into the stone, allowing the embers to burn with radiated heat.

'Brace yourself,' he told a bleary-eyed Hakem, still only partially conscious.

The merchant thane bellowed in agony as the slayer rammed the glowing torch into his wound, searing it shut. He tried to thrash about but Halgar held him down.

'Easy lad, easy,' he said, waiting for the nervous fits of pain to pass before he let Hakem go.

Ralkan came forward with several strips of cloth and started to bind the bloodied stump.

'Can you walk?' Azgar asked when the lorekeeper was finished.

Hakem staggered to his feet and, meeting the slayer's gaze, nodded slowly. He looked around him, his bearings returning, along with his memories. There was a gaping hole, some forty feet across, from the first plateau to the one on which he now stood with the rest of his kinsdwarfs. He could only assume that was why any of the slayers were left at all – unable to pursue their foes across such a chasm.

Bodies littered the broad expanse of stone; there were scarcely fifty dwarfs left from the hundred or so that must have got through the tunnel. Some of those that remained were throwing rat-kin corpses into the gaping drop on either side.

Hakem noticed the ashen-faced corpse of Dunrik last of all. He was laid on his back. An attempt had been made to wipe some of the blood from his armour and face. Someone had arranged his hands over his chest, as if in quiet repose – the spear heads still lodged in his body helped shatter the illusion. The other dwarf dead were laid down too, but with their cloaks covering their faces, hands made to clasp their hammers and axes, shields rested at their sides. There seemed so few, given those that had survived, but Hakem suspected many of the dawi had fallen into the darkness along with the skaven.

'We won,' said Azgar bitterly when the merchant thane met his gimlet gaze.

Hakem thought of Dunrik, growing cold on the slab on stone, of the dawi falling to their deaths and of the Honakinn Hammer that shared their fate in the abyss.

'Did we?' he said.

FAR DOWN INTO the underdeep, beyond the barriers of even dwarfen curiosity, something stirred. Ancient memory, dark and ill-formed at first, flooded its mind as it woke from a long slumber. The scent of blood and steel filled its flaring nostrils, and it felt the subtle shift of stone down the cragged walls of its lofty cavern through its claws. The ground trembled as it shook away the dust of ages from its mighty body.

They had forgotten it. Thought it perished all these long years. But something had changed – it could feel it. The mountain had... *moved*. Through its slowly resolving vision it noticed the tiny bodies of lesser beings, fallen into its domain. It approached the shattered corpses and once it reached them it began to feed.

CHAPTER NINE

'I CAN RUN no further,' said Gromrund, puffing his cheeks and weighed down by his massive warhelm.

For almost an hour, Uthor's throng had fled through darkened tunnels, down stairways and shafts, with no knowledge of their destination, desperately trying to put as much distance between them and their foes. They gathered now in some nondescript gallery, not nearly as grandiose as some of their previous accommodations, or as large. Gromrund, for one, was glad of it – it meant less places for their enemies to hide and ambush them.

Uthor turned to regard the hammerer, noting that several other dwarfs were bent over with hands on knees, breathing hard.

'Very well,' he said at last. 'We rest for a moment, but then we must move on. It's possible that the others survived. If we can find a way through to reach them, we might–'

'We are defeated, Uthor, son of Algrim,' Gromrund snapped. 'Barely fifty remain out of the two hundred with which we entered. The rat-kin number in the thousands – you know this – and there are the grobi to consider as well.'

'They may have worn each other down. If we were to take advantage of that...' Uthor didn't sound convincing.

'Your vainglory will kill us all!' Gromrund raged, squaring up to the thane, making his intentions clear.

'And your courage deserts you, Karak Hirn dwarf. Why is it that you never remove that warhelm of yours? Is it to hide your shame?' Uthor snarled.

A deathly hush filled the small gallery as the other dwarfs waited in the charged atmosphere, as the fight they all knew was coming slowly unfolded.

Gromrund bristled at the remark, Uthor near spitting the words at him. The hammerer clenched his fists.

'Never, in all the generations of Tallhelms has this helmet *ever* been removed,' he began levelly. 'Only upon my death shall it be prised from my cold skull and given to the next in my line,' he hissed through clenched teeth. 'It is tradition, and to go against it would disrespect the memory of my father, Kromrund Tallhelm, and besmirch the honour of my clan,' he concluded, beard bristling.

Uthor fell silent in an impotent rage.

'Our fallen brothers,' Gromrund continued darkly, now he had the thane of Karak Kadrin's attention, 'the needless death in pursuit of false honour… It ends now,' he promised. 'It is over, Uthor. You have brought enough shame to your clan.'

Uthor roared and right hooked the hammerer across the jaw. Gromrund staggered back, but like a prize-fighter, rolled on his booted heels and threw a punishing uppercut into Uthor's chin. The thane was knocked off his feet, but got up quickly and drew his axe.

Gromrund hefted his great hammer, leather gauntlets cracking as he tested his grip.

'I will show you the courage of Karak Hirn,' he promised, with violent intent.

'Come forward then,' Uthor replied, beckoning him. 'And I will knock that warhelm off your foolish head.'

'Enough!' A high-pitched voice rang out, shattering the violent mood. 'Stop this, now.'

Borri, the Everpeak beardling, rushed to stand between the two dwarfs. As he spoke, Gromrund was struck by the authority in the young dwarf's tone and despite his anger, lowered his hammer.

Similarly moved, Uthor did the same, staring nonplussed at a dwarf he thought was slain in the Great Hall.

'There has been enough death… enough.' Borri sagged, full with sorrow as his indignant fury was spent.

Uthor was incredulous.

'I saw you fall,' he ventured, stowing his axe. 'You could not have survived,' he added, appraising the near-pristine condition of the Everpeak noble's armour.

All eyes went to Borri at once.

The beardling opened his mouth to speak but Uthor was relentless.

'You barely have a scratch on you.' The thane regarded Borri suspiciously – his own armour was bent and broken in numerous places; even one of the wings on his helmet had several feathers torn out.

'I…' Borri began, taking a step back, suddenly aware of the attention fixed on him.

'It is not possible,' Uthor breathed and noticed the gilded cincture around the beardling's waist. He recognised one of the runes on it – he had seen it before… 'Let me see that belt,' he demanded, closing in on the young dwarf.

'Please, it is nothing…' Borri blathered, holding up his hands as if to ward off any further inquisition.

'And your voice,' Uthor said, eyes narrowing. 'It sounds different.'

Borri stepped back again, but quickly found he had nowhere to go.

'Show us what's on the belt, lad,' said Gromrund, directly behind Borri as he put his hand on the beardling's shoulder.

Borri sighed in resignation.

'There is something you should know, first,' he said, placing his hands against the sides of his helmet and lifting it slowly off his head.

ROREK CHIPPED AWAY at the chunk of rock with a small pick. The gallery wall at which he crouched, several feet away from where the rest of Uthor's throng congregated, felt cold to the touch and damp, so he worked carefully and with painstaking precision.

The engineer had noticed the runic rubric when the dwarfs had finally stopped, partly in the belief they were not followed by rat-kin or greenskins; partly from sheer exhaustion. Rorek was oblivious to the rest of his kinsdwarfs, and when his curiosity wasn't sated by merely examining the runes, partly obscured by calcified streaks of sediment, he had begun delicately excavating it. There was a message beneath, of that he was certain – perhaps it would provide some clue as to their location, or offer a way out. It was whilst digging out a particularly recalcitrant piece of rock, scrutinizing the markings he could discern beneath with the light of a candle, that the engineer became aware of a shadow looming over him.

'What are you doing, brother?' asked Thalgrim. The lodefinder was clearly as inquisitive as the engineer.

'There are rhuns beneath,' said Rorek gruffly, turning his attention back onto his work. 'They may indicate where we are.'

Thalgrim watched as Rorek chipped in vain at the hunk of rock obscuring the runic script beneath.

'Stand aside,' said the lodefinder, hefting his mattock and twisting it around in his hands to brandish the pick end.

Rorek paused in his endeavours, annoyed at the interruption. Looking back, he flung himself aside just in time as Thalgrim's pick smacked hard into the wall, the calcified rock crumbling under the impact.

Rorek was mortified at first, flat on his arse as he regarded the impetuous lodefinder; when he saw the broken rock and the intact symbol that it once concealed, he grinned.

'Well struck,' the engineer added, getting to his feet and clapping a hand on Thalgrim's back.

'Indeed,' said the lodefinder proudly, 'I mean no disrespect,' he went

on, 'but though the engineers of Zhufbar fashion true marvels of ingenuity, it is the miners of the karak that know the vagaries of rock and
stone best.'

Rorek nodded solemnly at that – there had ever been a strong accord
between the guild of engineers and miners.

Full of pride, Thalgrim went to remove the pick from where it had
embedded in the wall, but it wouldn't budge.

'Seems to be stuck,' he muttered beneath his breath, giving the haft
of the mattock a tug. 'Release it,' said the lodefinder – Rorek couldn't
be sure if he was talking to him or the rock wall – trying again. Still it
didn't yield.

The engineer went to help and after testing their grip, the two of them
heaved. There was the crunch of stone as the pick end of Thalgrim's
weapon came loose, sending the two dwarfs sprawling to the ground.
Another sound came swiftly afterwards, the wrenching retort of splitting
stone as a large crack ran jaggedly up the wall and a thin trickle of murky
water exuded from the hole made by the lodefinder's mattock.

'Grungni's girth…' Rorek muttered as the thin trickle became a steady
stream.

'May it be ever broad and full,' Thalgrim added, watching the pool
growing at their feet.

'Get up,' said Rorek as a thick chunk of stone fell away and water
gushed out in its wake.

LONG, GOLDEN PLAITS cascaded down as Borri removed his helmet and a
pair of piercing azure eyes regarded Uthor, from either side of a round,
stubby nose.

Gasps and rumbles of amazement greeted the dwarf stood before them.
Uthor was aghast.

'Rinn!' hissed one of the Sootbeard dwarfs and promptly passed out.

Gromrund's hand fell from Borri's shoulder to hang limp at his side.

'By the Bearded Lady!' he heard another dwarf gasp.

Some of the dwarfs began smoothing down their blood and dirt-caked
tunics, faces flushed a deep crimson as they went on to quickly preen
their beards.

'I have not been entirely truthful,' said Borri with royal timbre, straightening up defiantly.

'I am Emelda Skorrisdottir…' She parted the chainmail of her armour,
revealing a golden cincture so wondrously crafted and timelessly beautiful that some of the Sootbeard miners wept. Runes of protection were
etched upon the magnificent belt around Emelda's waist, but one in particular caught Uthor's eye – the rune of High King Skorri Morgrimson.
'Clan daughter of the royal house of Karaz-a-Karak.'

'Rinn Tromm,' uttered Gromrund, bowing deeply on one knee. Still
gaping, Uthor followed suit, the others then taking his lead.

'Arise!' Rorek cried, hurrying towards them with Thalgrim close behind him.

Uthor turned sharply towards the engineer, incensed at the interruption. The thane's anger drained away when he realised his knee was wet. When he saw the torrent of water flooding through the wall in the distance, he did as Rorek asked.

The gallery wall broke away as they were getting up.

'Run for it!' Uthor bellowed, herding the dwarfs down the long gallery.

The last of his throng were barrelling through as the foaming wave slammed into them, smashing the lagging dwarfs like dolls against the opposite wall. Those that weren't crushed to death were drowned soon after. Uthor was blasted by a stinging spray, replete with grit and stone shards. He recoiled against the blow and ran, flashing a quick glance behind him as he fled, hell-bent on a large metal door at the end of the gallery.

As the massive wave crashed into the far gallery wall it demolished columns and archways in its fury. For a few seconds it swelled in the tight space, churning like the innards of some primordial beast, until it found a way through and raced after the dwarfs with gathering momentum.

'THE WAY IS long indeed,' said Azgar, stood on a lower plateau, leaning on his axe as he looked down the wending stairway.

'The Endless Road,' offered Ralkan, enjoying one of his more lucid moments, 'with many winding turns that lead into the lower deeps. It was so named by the stonemaster who built it, Thogri Granitefist. May he be remembered.'

Azgar bowed his head in a brief moment of solemn remembrance.

Those who had escaped the tunnel battles with their lives had made an encampment a few plateaux down from the battle site, too tired and grief-stricken to move on immediately. After disposing of the skaven corpses they had left their slain brothers in quiet repose, unable to convey all the bodies. Only Dunrik went with them, carried on a makeshift hammock between Drimbold and Halgar. The longbeard wrinkled his nose constantly, complaining about the stink of the skaven rotting above them beyond the shattered stairway, the only bodies they couldn't reach to toss into the abyss. It seemed he had put his grievances towards the Grey dwarf aside for the time being, and was satisfied to let Drimbold lead them as they bore Dunrik to his final rest. As the Everpeak dwarf was of royal blood, it was only right and proper that he should be afforded a funeral and interred back into the earth so he might sit alongside his kin in the Halls of the Ancestors. For now, Dunrik was set down on the ground, all of his trappings strapped tightly to his body, so that when the funeral rites were enacted he would have them in the afterlife.

A sombre silence descended and Ralkan retreated away from the plateau's edge to sit alone.

Azgar was left in solitary contemplation as he regarded the abyssal gloom before him. Discernible by the ambient light cast from the Diamond Shaft, and filtered through the dust-heavy air, gargantuan dwarf faces glowered at him. They were the lords of the elder days of Karak Varn, hewn into the very rock face and made immortal in stone. As they looked upon the slayer, he found his mind wandering to the past and could no longer meet their stern gaze…

Azgar's head thundered like the great hammers of the lower forges. Each footstep was a physical blow, as if his skull were the metal pounded beneath the anvil.

It had been a mighty feast, though his recollection of it was dim. He recalled besting Hrunkar, the hold's brewmaster, at the ox-lifting and then of a drinking boast that the broad-girthed dwarf had accepted gleefully. To challenge a brewmaster to a quaffing contest, in retrospect, had been foolish.

Azgar had no time to ponder his misplaced confidence any further; the Cragbound Gate lay ahead and its current warden awaited him.

'Tromm,' said Torbad Magrikson, resting his axe over his shoulder and tapping out his pipe.

'Tromm,' Azgar managed, shuffling into position beside the gate as Torbad slowly walked away into the brazier-lit gloom.

An hour passed and Azgar felt the thrumming of hammers as engineers and metalsmiths worked diligently at the forge, the resonance of their labours carrying through the very rock of the mountain. It was a soothing refrain rippling through his body as he leaned at the warden's post. Azgar's eyelids grew heavy and within moments he was asleep…

Desperate cries woke Azgar from slumber, that and the rush of booted feet.

'Thaggi!' shouted a dwarf voice.

Azgar opened his eyes blearily, suddenly aware that he was slumped in a heap against the wall. He was shaken roughly.

'Awake,' said Igrik angrily, standing before him. 'Thaggi, Lord Algrim has been poisoned!' he cried.

Azgar snapped to at that, heart thumping more loudly than any raging hangover ever could.

'Father?' he asked of the ageing attendant, Igrik.

'Yes, your father,' he said, bitterly.

Then Azgar noticed something else: the wet footprints through the Cragbound Gate, its locks and bolts slipped silently. They were not made by dwarfen boots. They were long and thin with extended toes; they were the pawprints of skaven.

'Oh no…' breathed Azgar. 'What have I done?'

The scene shifted then in the slayer's mind's eye, resolving itself into the lustrous glory of the King's Court.

'Remove his armour,' ordered the king, his dour voice carrying despite the immensity of the mighty hall, 'and divest him of all trappings, save his axe.'

A four-strong throng of hammerers, their faces masked, moved in and solemnly took Azgar's armour, belts and clothes until he was stood naked before

King Kazagrad of Karak Kadrin, his son Baragor looking on sternly at the right hand of his enthroned lord.

'Let him be shorn and his shame known,' Kazagrad decreed.

Four priests of Grimnir came forward from the surrounding gloom. They each bore two buckets, carried via a brace of wutroth across their backs, and bore shears. Setting the buckets down they began cutting off Azgar's hair until all that remained was a rough shock of it down the centre and his beard, the only thing preserving his dignity.

'You have undertaken the slayer oath to atone for deeds that are to remain unnamed,' intoned the king.

The priests brought forth broad buckets filled with thick, orange dye and began combing it through Azgar's hair.

'You are to seek your doom that you might die a glorious death…'

From another bucket the priests took handfuls of pig grease and congealed animal fat. With gnarled fingers, they worked it into Azgar's streak of hair until it was hard like a crest.

'Take up your axe and leave this place, and let your disgrace be remembered by all.'

The priests shrank back into the darkness. Without word, Azgar turned and, head bowed, began the long walk out of the hold. He had no desire to stay. His brother had been espied by the watchtowers returning to the karak. It was best that Azgar was not there when he discovered their father's fate.

THE INUNDATION RAMMED dully against the ironclad door with slow and thudding insistence.

Uthor's fleeing throng had made it through the gallery just in time, slamming the door in their wake when the last of them had got through. Those caught up in the waters were left for dead. It left a bitter canker in the survivors.

'It holds, for now,' said Rorek, noting that the door was at least water-tight.

Exhausted, alongside the engineer, Uthor just nodded.

A great foundry stretched out before his sodden throng, who were huddled around the entrance to the chamber, having been battered and blasted throughout their desperate flight to the iron sanctuary.

Down a short set of steps the foundry opened into a vast plaza of stone, engraved with fifty-foot runes of forging and the furnace. Brightly burning braziers adorned the walls, doubtlessly lit by the hold's previous occupants, and punctuated the runic knots carved into them with perfect regularity.

Deep troughs of glowing coals smouldered and the light of the flickering embers illuminated racks of tools. Fuliginous chimneys were built at the ends of the troughs and rose up into the vaulted ceiling. Each of the stout, broad-based funnels was designed to lock the emanating forge heat and channel it into the roof space and the upper levels in order to keep them warm and dry. A raised stone walkway delineated the entire room and led to a wide, flat plinth with an archway wrought into the face of an ancient runelord overshadowing it. Through the venerable ancestor's mouth there was a mighty forgemaster's anvil, bathed in the fire-orange glow of brazier pans.

The foundry was divided into a central chamber and two wings, broken up by broad, square columns. On the left wing there was a vast array of armour suits, weapons and war machines; on the right wing, a long runway extended that ended in an octagonal platform.

A dais in the centre of it supported a statue of monumental proportions carved into the image of Grungni himself. The ancestor god's plaited beard went all the way to the base and in his hands he held forge tongs and a smithy's hammer. Beneath him there sat another brazier, raging with an eldritch blue-red flame that cast pooling shadows into the stone-worked face. Beyond this temple there was a sheer drop into a pit of fire, which burned so fiercely the coals within it were but a vague shadow in the emanating heat haze.

Great heavy pails were set above the vast pit by thick iron chains, ready to plunge into the fires and bring forth the precious rock to feed the forges.

'Magnificent,' said Thalgrim, tears in his eyes. Other than this laudation, the throng was stunned into silence.

They were arrested from their wonderment by the dull retort of *thunking* metal against the iron door as the armoured dwarfs slain in the flood were butted against it by the swell of the water.

'We should move away from the door,' Uthor said darkly.

UTHOR'S THRONG SAT around the burning coal troughs of the foundry plaza, rubbing their hands and wringing out their beards in silent, grim contemplation. The heat warmed clothes, hair and hearts quickly but Uthor found no solace in their fiery depths as he drew deep of his pipe, lost in his thoughts.

'So is this how it is to end, then?'

Gromrund stood before the thane of Kadrin. The hammerer's armour was battered and broken in places. It was the first time Uthor had even noticed it since the fighting and their flight from the inundation.

'I need time to think,' the thane of Kadrin muttered, peering back into the flames.

Gromrund leaned in towards him, forcing the thane to look at him.

'You were so eager for your reckless glory but a few hours ago. Yet now you sit and do nothing,' he hissed, 'while all around your throng stagnates and festers like an old wound.'

Uthor maintained his silence.

'You have much to atone for already, son of Algrim, do not add to the reckoner's tally further.' With that, the hammerer stalked away out of Uthor's sight.

After a moment, the thane of Kadrin looked up from the blazing coals and regarded his warriors as if for the first time since their defeat in the Great Hall. The wounded were many; some had lost limbs and eyes, a burden they would carry into the Halls of the Ancestors. Others wore bandages over deep wounds or displayed broad cuts openly, but not as the heroic ritual scars of combat; they wore them with the deep shame of the broken and beaten. The dwarfs sat together in their clans. Uthor noticed the large gaps in them, brave warriors all who would not know the feeling of their holds beneath their feet and above their heads ever again. He had condemned them to that fate. Unable to look further, Uthor averted his gaze.

'May I sit with you?' a voice asked. Emelda's eyes flashed in the fire-light as she sat down, more perfect and beauteous than any jewel in Uthor's reckoning, her long plaits like streaks of gold.

'I am honoured,' said the thane, with a shallow nod. Her stealth was impressive; Uthor had not heard her coming.

The clan daughter's noble bearing was apparent in the way she held herself, proud and defiant. The other dwarfs would not sit with her, not because of any slight or ill feeling; rather that they were ashamed of their unkempt appearance and bashful in her presence as a lady and a royal consort. Since none would join Uthor either, it meant that they were largely alone.

'You risked much to follow us here,' he said after a moment's silence, grateful of the distraction she provided.

'I believed in your quest,' Emelda replied. 'Too swiftly are the deso-lated holds left uncontested, for all the fell denizens of dark places to inhabit and despoil. There was honour in your plight and talk of such deeds that could not go unreckoned. Besides that, I have my reasons,' she added darkly.

'It was glory,' Uthor admitted after a moment, reminded of Gromrund's words as he stared into the fire.

'I do not understand.'

The thane gazed up into Emelda's eyes, his expression rueful.

'The promise of glory brought me to this place, not vengeance, and this folly has delivered us all to our doom. Cowering in the dark. Hunted like… like rats.' He curled his lip at that last remark and dipped his head again. It was a bitter irony; rats preyed upon by rats.

Emelda stayed silent. She had no words that would make right what had befallen them. The mood was grim; it chilled the bone despite the cloying heat in the air. Failure and dishonour hung like a palpable fug, and was felt by all.

'And what of Dunrik? Is he even your cousin?' Uthor asked.

Emelda felt her chest tighten at the mention of his name. She made a silent oath to Valaya that he had made it out of the tunnel alive, somehow.

'No,' she said, after a few moments. 'He was my guardian, sworn to protect me. Dunrik smuggled us into the escort from Everpeak,' she confessed.

'So you both defied the will of the High King, as I did.'

'Yes,' said Emelda, shamefaced.

Uthor laughed mirthlessly.

'Milady,' uttered Gromrund, clearing his throat as he appeared suddenly beside them, 'I am Gromrund, son of Kromrund, of the Tallhelm clan and hammerer to King Kurgaz of Karak Hirn.' The hammerer bowed deeply, ignoring Uthor. 'It would be my humble honour to serve as your protector and vouch safe passage for you back to Everpeak.'

Emelda smiled benignly, full of royal presence.

Gromrund, meeting her gaze as he genuflected, reddened.

'You are noble, Gromrund, son of Kromrund, but I already have a bodyguard and we will be reunited soon,' she explained, unable to mask an edge of uncertainty in her tone. 'For now, Uthor son of Algrim will see to my safekeeping,' she said, gesturing in the thane of Kadrin's direction, 'but I will make certain to mention of your pledge to the High King.'

'As you wish, milady,' Gromrund said, a side glance at Uthor to make his displeasure known before he backed away in respectful silence.

GROMRUND STOOD ALONE at the anvil stripped of all his armour, barring his warhelm of course. With a forgemaster's hammer in hand, he worked out the dents in his breastplate with careful and meticulous precision. He was glad of the solace that metalsmithing provided, especially after his recent rebuttal from the Lady Emelda. In truth, he was also working out the anger he felt towards Uthor, but was mindful not to let his ire spoil his re-crafting. The Tallhelms were all forgesmiths by trade, a source of much pride amongst the clan, despite their esteemed calling as royal bodyguards.

Gromrund stopped a moment to check his labours, wiping the sweat from his face as he did so. Out of the corner of his eye, he caught sight of Uthor conversing with the Everpeak lady.

As he watched them, he noticed Uthor's face darken. Despite their grievances, and his earlier words, the hammerer took no pleasure in the thane's distress – though he still believed, as a hammerer, it should be he that saw to Emelda's wellbeing – an oath was an oath and each and every one of them had failed in that. As expedition leader though, the son of Algrim bore that shame most heavily.

The lady, Emelda, seemed to try and soothe him but to no avail.

A rinn! Gromrund thought as he looked at her. Posing as a beardling amongst the throng with not a dawi, save for her keeper, any the wiser – a truly shocking admission.

When she caught the hammerer's gaze, he averted his eyes to the anvil, bashful beneath her scrutiny.

Shocking indeed, he thought, toiling at his armour again, but not entirely unwelcome.

THALGRIM'S STOMACH GROWLED loudly. He went for the piece of chuf beneath his helmet, but stopped himself short. Perhaps it was that which attracted the skaven to them; perhaps he was the cause of the ambush in the tunnel, of so many dawi deaths...

'It was the Black Water,' said Rorek, sat across from the lodefinder, eyes ablaze in the light of burning coals.

The two of them were sitting with some of the Sootbeard dwarfs outside the great arch.

Rorek was tinkering with some spherical object he had fashioned from the materials in the forge. It helped keep his mind occupied.

Thalgrim returned a thoughtful expression, grateful of the distraction, as the engineer went on.

'Five hundred years ago, during the Time of Woes, a deluge from the great lake flooded the hold and ruined it,' said Rorek, carefully screwing a plate on the spiked ball of iron in his hands. 'I think, even in the upper deeps, there are pockets of trapped water. We released one when we split the gallery wall. It at least means the grobi and the rat-kin cannot follow this way.'

'It means we cannot escape the way we came, either,' Thalgrim countered, engrossed with the engineer's work. 'This entire hold groans under the weight of the Black Water,' he added. 'I can feel it through the rock; the subtle vibrations caused by its movement are unmistakable.'

'Then we had best not linger,' muttered Rorek, looking up at the age-old cracks in the vaulted ceiling above them.

DRIMBOLD WOKE AWASH with sweat. A chill ran down his spine as the cries of Norri and Furgil, falling into the chasm as the rope bridge failed, echoed in his ears. Their faces were forever etched on his mind, contorted with sheer terror as they met their doom in the gorge, swallowed by fire. The Grey dwarf realised he was gripping his pack. The lustre of the treasure within had somehow dimmed. He released it quickly, as if stung. Some of the loot spilled out, clanking loudly against the stone plateau. The noise disturbed Halgar, who'd been rubbing his eyes. The longbeard scowled at Drimbold before returning to his dark thoughts.

The Grey dwarf cast his eyes around the forlorn throng, led now, it seemed, by Azgar.

Ralkan lay nearby him, twitching spasmodically, wracked by a fever dream about some unknown terror.

Hakem was awake, nursing the stump of his right hand, an ugly dark red stain emerging through the makeshift bandage. He was muttering.

Drimbold heard the Honakinn Hammer mentioned several times. The merchant's boastful bluster was but a fading memory now. He looked pale and drawn, and not just from the amount of blood he had lost.

'It's time we made a move.' It was Azgar, at the top of the next descending stairway, his face an unreadable mask.

Without word, the dwarfs started to gather their belongings. When they finally left the plateau, only Drimbold's treasure-laden pack remained.

'I GROW WEARY of staring into the fathomless dark,' Hakem moaned, peering over the narrow ledge into a faintly rippling void below. It was the first time the dwarf had spoken since he'd lost his hammer and his hand.

The Endless Stair was above them now, its final plateau leading to a vast stone archway. From there, the dwarfs had found the narrow ledge. So narrow was it that Azgar's throng walked slowly in single file. On one side there was a sheer rock face that seemed to go on for miles in both directions; on the other side yet another deep chasm presented itself.

'This is the Ore Way, the threshold of the once great mines of Karak Varn,' Ralkan said wistfully, walking a few places behind Azgar who led the group with what remained of his Grim Brotherhood.

'I see nothing but darkness,' Hakem muttered bitterly, 'shifting below us like serpents.'

'It is not serpents,' Ralkan interjected, close to the merchant's position in the file. 'These are the flooded deeps.'

The shimmering in the darkness was water, so thick and murk-ridden it was like black ichor. Columns, leaning over and split in twain, languished in it, the stagnant dregs of the Black Water pooling where they broke the water's surface. The reek of wet stone clung to the damp air like a shroud.

'Look there,' he added, voice echoing as he pointed far out into the gloom-drenched cavern.

Hakem followed the lorekeeper's gesture to the wreckage of three lofty towers, wrought of wood and metal. Each tower had a massive pulley set at its apex, with the remnants of what once must have been a long chain. The links had been shattered long ago, but stout buckets clung tenaciously to one of the chain lengths. Hakem then realised the broken columns were supports for bridges that connected the towers to tracked lanes of stone that ran all the way across and down the empty gulf to the walkway they now traversed. One such lane still existed in part, its central support standing defiantly like an island in an ocean of tar.

'All dwarf holds began as mines,' Halgar remarked. 'These are from the Golden Age of the Karaz Ankor.' He and Drimbold took careful steps as they bore the body of Dunrik along the shallow pathway. The longbeard felt the wall with one hand as he went, making certain he was close to it at all times. One slip and all three would likely join the rest of their kin claimed by the abyss.

'Rich were the veins of ril, gorl and gromril,' the longbeard said wistfully. 'Such great days…' he added in a choked whisper.

Apparent that Halgar's reminiscences were at an end, some of the other dwarfs began talking amongst themselves as a slightly improved mood started to settle over the throng.

The longbeard paid them no heed as he allowed the surface of the rock face to pass beneath his hand, taking solace in the roughness and solidity of it against his leather-like skin. Then he heard, or rather felt, something that he did not expect.

Halgar stopped dead in his tracks.

'Stop,' he bellowed, though some of the dwarfs in the file had already bunched up and were bumping into each other with the longbeard's abrupt halt. Drimbold very nearly tripped and dropped Dunrik as he was pulled back.

'What is it?' Hakem called from behind Halgar.

'Be silent!' The longbeard said, admonishing him, before catching Drimbold's gaze.

'Set him down,' Halgar bade him, and they did, reverently. The old dwarf then turned back towards the rock face, placing both hands against it and pressing his ear as close as he could. The stone felt damp and chill against his face. A faint *plinking* sound, dull and faraway, emanated through the rock.

'I hear nothing,' moaned Hakem.

'Save for the sound of your own voice, no doubt. Be still!' Halgar raged, ''Tis a pity it was not your tongue taken by the abyss,' he snarled, plunging the merchant thane into mournful quietude before listening intently.

The sound came again, muted but distinctly metallic.

'A hammer,' he snapped at a dwarf behind him, one of the Stonebreaker clan.

The clan dwarf returned a bemused look as he brought out a small mattock.

'Quickly now!' Halgar snatched the weapon and with his attention back on the rock face started to tap back.

GROMRUND KNEW HE must be a strange sight, wearing only his helmet and little else besides. It had grown so hot in the foundry that he had removed his outer garments as well as his armour and stood in nothing but boots and breeches as he toiled away at a vambrace. Slowly beating out a gouge from a skaven dagger, Gromrund paused in his hammering to wring the sweat from his beard.

A dull *thunk* got his attention. At first he looked down to make sure he wasn't still hammering, that the heat hadn't addled his brain and he'd just *thought* he'd ceased.

The noise came again, insistent and repetitive. He was too far away from the ironclad door for it to be anything beyond it in the flooded chamber. Still, he couldn't place it. Gromrund looked around and caught sight of Thalgrim sat by the arch, silently gripping his stomach.

'Lodefinder,' he called out to him.

Thalgrim looked over and the hammerer beckoned him.

The lodefinder was a little weary as he reached the sweating dwarf wearing nought but his boots, smalls and a massive warhelm.

'Listen,' said the hammerer urgently.

CHAPTER TEN

'IT'S COMING FROM the wall,' said the lodefinder, eyes brightening when he heard the sound. He rushed over, smoothing the wall with his hands to detect the subtle movements in the stone. 'There,' he said again, pin-pointing the exact position from which the noise was emanating.

By now Rorek, the Sootbeards and a number of other dwarfs had noticed the sudden commotion and were heading onto the anvil plat-form.

It was a welcome diversion. The throng had been waiting several hours for Uthor's decision on their next course of action. The thane was brood-ing when the flurry of movement began, drawing deep of his pipe and sitting in abject silence.

'*Grundlid,*' said Thalgrim, ear pressed against the wall. 'There's a mes-sage,' he added. 'We are sons of Grungni. It is them! Our brothers live!'

More and more dwarfs were gathering on the anvil platform as word of Thalgrim's discovery spread quickly.

'Where?' asked Uthor urgently, having fought his way through to the front of his throng.

Thalgrim looked back, nearly beside himself. 'I will find out,' he said, tapping back with meticulous precision using Grundlid, or Hammer-Tongue, the secret language of miners and prospectors. A series of careful scrapes and taps, with varying duration and intensity, could convey a message. Most amongst the dwarfs knew its rudiments but only the most vaunted lodefinders were privy to its intricacies.

'The mines,' said Thalgrim, catching snatches of Grundlid as he

responded with a long scrape of stone and three heavy raps, followed
by a long, lighter one.

'We must get to them,' said Uthor.

'They are below us,' Thalgrim offered, between taps.

'The lodefinder and I will follow the message and bring them to the
foundry. The rest of the throng will await our return here.'

Gromrund stepped forward, about to protest, but a look from Uthor
silenced him. The thane of Karak Kadrin wanted to atone for his mistake, even if only in part.

'The less of us that venture from the safety of the foundry the better,
and the less likely it will be that the skaven and whatever lurks in the
dark will be aware of us. If the others still live, we two will find them.'

'We three.'

Emelda emerged through the pressing masses, the dwarfs respectfully
allowing her passage. 'I'm coming with you.'

Now it was Uthor's turn to bite his tongue. The royal clan daughter's
gimlet gaze told him all he needed to know of her reasons. Dunrik might
be amongst them. She had to know.

'MAINTAIN A WATCH on all ways in and out.' Uthor addressed his throng
as he, Thalgrim and Emelda stood before the only exit to the foundry
that wasn't flooded on the other side. 'When we return, Thalgrim will
provide a simple signal in Grundlid.'

Uthor went to walk forward when Gromrund stopped him.

'Grungni go with you,' said the hammerer, back in his armour again
when he gripped the thane's shoulder.

'And you,' Uthor replied, unable to keep the surprise from his face.

The guards at the foundry door hauled away the locking bar and tugged
on thick, iron chains attached to it. Screeching metal filled the air and a
gaping black void of the unknown opened out before the three dwarfs,
so dark and infinite it swallowed the light from the foundry whole.

'THIS WAY,' SAID Thalgrim, moving off quickly through a dilapidated corridor. 'Very close, now,' he added.

Uthor wasn't convinced that the lodefinder was talking to him or
Emelda as the two of them ventured warily after Thalgrim. The path was
treacherous, fraught with pit falls, sharp rocks and heavy debris. Dust
motes fell eagerly from sloping ceilings with every step and Uthor dared
not raise his voice above a whisper, lest the whole lot come crashing
down on their heads.

'Slow down, zaki,' he hissed, struggling to keep pace. The thane cast a
glance behind him and saw that Emelda was on his heels and showing
no evidence of fatigue. When Uthor looked back, there was no sign of
the lodefinder.

Grimnir's tattooed-arse, he thought angrily, the wattock has probably fallen to his death and left us lost in this labyrinth. The thane increased his pace, stumbled and nearly slipped but got his footing at the last moment, in the hope of catching sight of Thalgrim. He took another step and realised there was nothing beneath his foot. Scrambling for purchase, Uthor's hand gripped the wall but slipped on moisture slick stone. Flapping wildly, he was about to plunge headlong into a drop of sharp rocks when he felt his fall abruptly arrested.

Emelda, holding onto the thane's belt, hauled Uthor back onto solid ground.

'I hope this is the right way,' she said as Uthor flushed with embarrassment at being saved by a woman. The thane of Karak Kadrin looked back at the wall and noticed thin rivulets of water trickling down them and seeping into the porous rock at their feet.

'So do I, milady,' he said, striving to regain his composure.

Their eyes met for but a moment, before Uthor looked away abashedly.

'Not far.' The lodefinder's voice drifted on a shallow and foetid breeze to break the sudden silence.

Relief washed over Uthor, and not just because their guide was still alive. He emerged from the debris-strewn corridor to find Thalgrim standing pensively before a triple forked archway. Each of the three roads were carved into the likeness of a dwarf face and led down still further – they had been steadily descending ever since leaving the foundry. The decline was shallow, but Uthor had felt it, even as he clambered over broken columns, stooped beneath fallen ceilings and crawled through shattered doorways.

'Which way?' Uthor asked, a little out of breath.

Thalgrim sniffed at the air, and felt the rock of each fork in turn.

'Down here,' he said, indicating the left passage. 'I can taste the ore seams, feel them in the rock. The mines are this way.'

'You are certain this is the way?' Uthor asked, unconvinced by the lodefinder's tone.

'Fairly,' he replied.

'And the other tunnels?'

Thalgrim looked Uthor in the eye.

'Our enemies.'

THE SHALLOW LEDGE ended in a narrow archway, through which a much wider and flatter platform opened out. It was a lodecarrier's waystation, one of several in Karak Varn, designed to service the many mines and act as barrack houses for the miners and lodewardens. Upturned ore carts and scattered tools littered the ground and smothered torches were cast aside like tinder. Whoever had been here had clearly left in a hurry.

'The Rockcutter Waystation,' said Ralkan as the dwarfs started filing into the room. 'We are in the eastern halls of the karak.'

'We will wait here,' Halgar decided, at the head of the group with Azgar and his slayers – one of the Stonebreaker clan carried Dunrik's body, along with Drimbold, now. The old longbeard eyed the darkness wearily. In one corner of the modest chamber a broad shaft had been carved into the rock. A wrought-iron lift cage nestled within, battered and bent, the iron rusted and split, with a length of piled chain languishing nearby. A second shaft lay on the opposite side, leading down.

Ralkan approached it carefully. The lorekeeper stuck his head into the shaft and looked up and down.

'The rhun-markers are clear,' he said. 'It leads right down to the foundations of the hold.'

'And up?' Hakem remarked.

'Dibna's Drop,' Ralkan answered, looking back at the mauled merchant thane. 'The room we passed in the third deep is above.' Clearly, the long period of calm had improved the dwarf's lucidity.

'And that?' growled Halgar, pointing.

A third exit lay ahead in the form of a broken down doorway. Even in the gloom, it was possible to make out an ascending tunnel leading off from it. Besides Dibna's Drop, it was the only possible ingress to the waystation.

'I don't know,' Ralkan confessed, memory fogging once more.

The longbeard grumbled beneath his breath. The last message in Grundlid had been close. Their kinsdwarfs were on the way to them. He only hoped they would get there before something else did.

'Someone approaches,' Halgar hissed, gesturing toward the broken doorway. Shallow footsteps could be heard from beyond the threshold to the room, growing louder and with each passing moment. The dwarfs gathered together, the dull chorus of axes and hammers scraping free of their sheaths and cinctures filled the air.

'What if it is not dawi?' Hakem asked, shield lashed to his wounded arm, an axe held unfamiliarly in his remaining hand.

Halgar glanced at Azgar, glowering menacingly at the doorway in the gloom, before he replied.

'Then we cut them down.'

WHEN THALGRIM AND Uthor emerged from the tunnel they were met by a host of axe blades and hammer heads.

'Hold, dawi!' said Uthor, showing his palms.

'Son of Algrim.' Halgar stepped forward, stowing his axe and clasping the thane of Kadrin's forearm in what was an old greeting ritual.

'Gnollengrom.' Uthor reciprocated the gesture, and nodded in respect at being so honoured.

'So you're alive, after all,' the longbeard added, very nearly cracking a smile.

'As are you,' Uthor replied, throwing a dark glance towards Azgar as he noticed the slayer's presence for the first time.

'Round rump of Valaya!' Halgar blurted out suddenly when he saw Emelda emerge from behind Thalgrim, who was currently being slapped on the back and hugged by the Stonebreakers.

'There is much to be told,' Uthor said, by way of explanation. More gasps of shock greeted the revelation from the assembled dwarfs.

'Please,' Emelda said, stepping forward, her eyes bright and hopeful as she scanned Azgar's throng. 'Where is Dunrik?'

Halgar's face fell.

'Yes,' he said, with sorrow in his eyes, 'there is much to be told.'

'So FEW OF you,' said Uthor as he sat around one of the coal troughs in the foundry. The way back to the iron sanctuary had been slow and trod with great care, but had passed without further incident. The returning dwarfs were met with heartfelt joy. The buoyant mood was short-lived however, when it was realised just how many had rejoined them. That, together with the maiming of Hakem and Dunrik's death, had conspired to create a grim, desolate atmosphere.

'We are fortunate to be alive at all,' said Halgar, breathing deeply as he savoured the aroma of the foundry, a chamber unsullied by skaven and redolent of ancient days. After that brief indulgence, the longbeard's face turned grim. 'The rat-kin were ready for us. They have been tracking us ever since we entered the hold…' Halgar looked deep into the coal fires, supping on his pipe. 'Such cunning! I have never seen the like in skaven.'

'How did Dunrik die?' Uthor asked, after a few moments of silence.

'Impaled by ratman spears – he died a noble death, protecting his kinsdwarfs.'

'May he be remembered,' Uthor uttered, his guilt like an anvil trussed around his neck.

'Aye, may he be remembered,' Halgar added.

EMELDA WAS DIVESTED of her armour and instead wore the plain purple robes of Valaya she had beneath her chain and platemail. The clan daughter had even removed the runic cincture – it glowed dully, nearby, in the reflected light of the vast forge pit.

She was alone at the forgemaster's platform in the foundry. Dunrik's cold body lay before her on the anvil. The rest of the reunited throng were sat below, most in hunched silence, contemplating their plight.

'Dunrik,' she whispered, placing her hand on the dwarf's clammy brow. His flesh was pale now, much like it had been when he'd escaped from Iron Rock. She had tended his wounds then as part of her training – for the priestesses of Valaya were battle-surgeons in times of war – and the bond between them had been forged. After that, he'd become her bodyguard and confidant – there was nothing Dunrik would not have done for her; he'd even defied the will of his king to get her to Karak Varn. How she wished to take that back: to be at Everpeak, dreaming of glory and restoring the great days of the dawi to the Karaz Ankor, instead of preparing his corpse for interment.

'Are you ready, milady?' said a small voice.

Emelda turned to see Ralkan stood, head bowed, beneath the archway to the platform. She smeared away the tears on her face with the sleeves of her robes.

'Yes,' she said, mustering some resolve.

Silently, Ralkan walked forward. He carried pails of water, one in each hand, gathered from the vast cooling butts stood against the foundry walls. Setting the buckets down, he helped Emelda remove Dunrik's battered armour. The clan daughter wept as she struggled, with Ralkan's assistance, to pull some of the armour away from the embedded spear hafts. Beneath mail and plate, Dunrik's tunic and breeches were so badly sodden with blood that they had to be cut free. Emelda did this, careful so as not to pierce the dwarf's flesh or defile the body in any way. Next came the extraction of the embedded spear hafts. Each was like a wound against the clan daughter as she removed it.

Naked upon the anvil, Dunrik was washed head to foot and his beard combed. Emelda wrung blood soaked bundles of rags regularly and sent Ralkan back for fresh water on several occasions. After these ablutions Emelda stitched the spear wounds closed and redressed Dunrik tenderly with a borrowed tunic and breeches, uttering a pledge to Valaya as she did it. Ralkan had washed the original garments as best he could, but they were still wretched with blood and cut nigh-on to ribbons, so could not be salvaged.

Gromrund – working at one of the forge troughs below with Thalgrim operating the bellows – had repaired Dunrik's armour, and even given the shortness of time and the state of its degradation it still shone as if new. The hammerer brought it up the platform and left it there without a word.

Emelda dismissed Ralkan and clad Dunrik in his armour by herself. After a few moments, it was almost done and as she affixed the final clasps of Dunrik's left vambrace she went to retrieve the dwarf's helmet. Emelda paused before she placed it on him, setting it down on the anvil next to his head, and traced her finger down the scar the orcs of Iron Rock had given him long ago.

'Brave dawi,' she sobbed. 'I am so sorry.'

'WHAT IS THAT beardling doing?' snapped Halgar, suddenly.

Uthor was grateful of the distraction, so grim was his mood, and looked over to where Rorek – who was anything but a beardling – was tinkering with a globe-like object made of iron and copper. To one side of the engineer there sat a doused lantern. While Uthor watched, the

Zhufbar dwarf picked it up and carefully poured the oil into a narrow spout fashioned into the globe. He then set the globe down and started to unravel a section of rope from that which was usually arrayed around his tool belt.

'I know not,' Uthor answered.

'Mark my words, he'll be for the Trouser Legs Ritual before long or maybe a cogging,' the longbeard grumbled.

Uthor was about to reply when Hakem approached them. His wound had been cleaned and redressed by Emelda in abject silence, before she had gone to tend to Dunrik.

'They are ready,' he uttered.

'HERE LIES DUNRIK, may Valaya protect him and Gazul guide his spirit to the Halls of the Ancestors,' Emelda declared, her voice choked.

She stood at the edge of the great fire pit beyond the statue of Grungni. Dunrik was before her, resting upon a cradle of iron. The Everpeak dwarf was fully armoured, the metal gleaming thanks to the efforts of Gromrund and Thalgrim, and wore his helmet. His shield lay by his side. Only his axe was missing. Emelda carried the ancient weapon as she invoked the funerary rites of Gazul, drawing the Lord of the Underearth's symbol – the great cave and entrance to the Halls of the Ancestors – upon the flat blade. Though Emelda was a priestess of Valaya, she was also learned in all the rites of the ancestor gods, even those lesser deities such as Gazul, son of Grungni.

'*Gazul Bar Baraz; Gazul Gand Baraz,*' she intoned, honouring the Lord of the Underearth, beseeching his promise to guide Dunrik to the Chamber of the Gate. The ritual conferred the dwarf's soul into his axe, and when it was buried in the earth Dunrik would pass from the chamber and be allowed to enter the Halls of the Ancestors proper. Only in times of dire need was such a measure undertaken. Since there was no tomb, no sanctuary for Dunrik's body, Emelda would not leave it in the foundry to be defiled. This was the only way he might know peace.

Inwardly, she pitied those others who had fallen, bereft of honour – left to wander the underdeep as shades and apparitions, ever restless. It was no fate for a dwarf to endure.

The rattling of chains attached to the makeshift bier arrested Emelda from her remembrances. It was time.

Sweating from the emanating heat haze, Thalgrim and Rorek pulled a chain, hand over hand, through one of the pulleys suspended above the pit of fire. Hakem and Drimbold pulled another, the merchant thane managing despite only having one hand. Each chain was split at the very end and branched off into two sections attached to the ends of the iron cradle. As the dwarfs heaved, Dunrik was lifted slowly off the ground. Once he had reached the zenith of the chamber, the chains were locked in place and a third chain dragged by Uthor pulled Dunrik high over the pit of fire. Now in place, and through means of ingenious dwarf engineering, he could be lowered slowly into the raging flames.

As Uthor did so, very slowly, Halgar stepped forward and Emelda, head bowed respectfully, retreated back.

The longbeard's expression was one of solemnity as he opened his mouth and sang a dour lamentation in a sombre baritone, all the while Dunrik getting closer to the forge fires.

> *In ancient days when darkness wracked the land,*
> *'twas Grimnir ventured north with axe in hand.*
> *To the blighted wastes he was so fated*
> *to slay daemons, beasts and fell gods much hated.*
> *Thunder spoke and tremors wracked the earth*
> *Grimnir the Fearless fought for all his worth.*
> *With the gods of ruin arisen all around,*
> *with rhun and axe did Grimnir strike them down.*
> *He closed the dreaded gate and sealed the darkness in*
> *lest it curse the Karaz Ankor again.*
> *Go now brave dawi, go if you are able*
> *to Grungni's table – he is waiting.*
> *In the Halls of the Ancestors with honour at your breast,*
> *you will find your final rest.*
> *Lo there is the line of kings arrayed,*
> *your place among them is assured – they await you.*
> *Go now brave dawi, the hammers ring your passing,*
> *the throng amassing in the deep – your soul will Gazul keep.*
> *Go now brave dawi, in glory you are wreathed,*
> *unto the Halls of the Ancestors received.*

As HALGAR FINISHED, Dunrik's body, already wreathed in flame, was plunged deep into the sea of coal and fire. In moments, he was consumed by it.

'So then does Dunrik, son of Frengar, thane of Everpeak and the Bardrakk clan pass into the Chamber of the Gate to await his ancestors,' said the longbeard.

'May he be remembered.'

'May he be remembered,' the throng responded in sombre unison, all except Emelda who kept her head bowed and stayed silent.

Ralkan, standing near to Halgar, inscribed Dunrik's name in the book of remembering, the massive tome held up for him by two dwarfs of the Stonebreaker clan.

As Halgar fell silent, Uthor stepped forward and turned to the gathered assembly. In his left hand he held a dagger. With a single, swift gesture he drew the blade across his palm, making a fist immediately afterwards, and then passed the dagger to Halgar, who wiped it clean. Uthor then waited for Ralkan to come forward. The lorekeeper carried a small receptacle and held it beneath the thane's cut hand. Uthor clenched his fist and allowed the blood to drip into the receptacle. When he was done, Emelda bound the wound as Ralkan went back to the book of remembering. The entire ritual was conducted in total silence.

'Let it be known,' uttered Uthor, Ralkan scribing the words in the thane of Kadrin's own blood into the tome in front of him, 'on this day did Dunrik of the Bardrakk clan fall in battle, slain by skaven treachery. Ten thousand rat-tails will avenge this deed and even then may it never be struck from the records of Karak Varn and Everpeak. So speaks Uthor, son of Algrim.'

Emelda raised her head and peered into the flames of the vast pit, the axe of Dunrik clutched firmly in her hands.

'AN OATH WAS made,' said Uthor, addressing the throng – less than half that which ventured from their holds to reclaim Karak Varn.

It had been several hours since Dunrik's interment and Uthor had spent that time consulting deeply with Thalgrim and Rorek. Halgar and Gromrund had been privy to their discussions too. Uthor had wanted Emelda to be present as well, but the clan daughter had retreated into herself following her kinsdwarf's passage to the Chamber of the Gate and was not to be disturbed. Once they were done, their decision made, Uthor had bade Gromrund to gather the throng together in readiness for his address.

Uthor was standing on the forgemaster's platform, beneath the arch, and all the dwarfs were arrayed below in their clans. The Bronzehammers, Sootbeards, Ironfingers and Flinthearts of Zhufbar, dark of expression, their numbers thinned by attrition. Alongside them were the Furrowbrows and the Stonebreakers of Everpeak, crestfallen and sullen. The latter bore the standard of the slain Firehands in dour remembrance. Gromrund stood amongst them, slightly to the front. The hammerer knew what was coming and was stern of face. At the back of the group was Azgar, surrounded by his fellow slayers. The Grim Brotherhood were as fierce and threatening as ever. Uthor paid them, and Azgar, no heed as he continued.

'An oath to reclaim Karak Varn in the name of Kadrin Redmane, my ancestor, and of Lokki Kraggson…'

The thane of Karak Kadrin looked over at Halgar, stood beside him, leaning on the pommel of his axe and scowling deeply at the warriors below.

'To wrest the hold from the vile filth that had infested it, the same wretches that took dawi territory, took their very lives in spite of our dominion of the mountain.'

There was muttered discord at that, as all around the throng chewed and pulled at their beards, spat in disgust and gnashed their teeth.

'We have failed in that oath.'

Sobbing and vociferous lamentation accompanied Uthor's remark. Some dwarfs began stamping their feet and drumming axe and hammer heads against their shields.

'And Karak Varn is lost to us.'

Shouting echoed from the back ranks, loud grumblings of discontent and dismay filled the chamber, threatening to turn riotous.

Uthor beckoned for silence.

'And yet,' he said, struggling above the residual din. 'And yet,' he said again as the foundry quietened at a glower from Halgar, 'we will have our vengeance.'

A great, warlike cheer erupted from the dwarfs below and the shield thumping began anew, together with the collective stamping of feet. The noise boomed like thunder, the throng abruptly ebullient and heedless of their enemies.

'If dawi cannot have the karak,' Uthor continued, 'then none shall!'

The thunder rose in great pealing waves, ardent voices adding to its power.

'As it was years ago, so it shall be again. The hold of Karak Varn will flood and all within shall perish.' The thane's gaze was as steel as he regarded his kin. 'So speaks Uthor, son of Algrim!'

From fatalism came defiance and the desire for vengeance. It was etched upon the face of every dwarf present as indelibly as if carved in stone.

'Sons of Grungni,' Uthor bellowed. 'Make ready. We go to war again. For wrath and ruin!' he cried, the axe of Ulfgan held aloft like a rallying symbol.

'For wrath and ruin!' the booming thunder responded.

ACT THREE
WRATH AND RUIN

CHAPTER ELEVEN

UTHOR STALKED FROM the forgemaster's platform and down the stairs into the foundry plaza.

'Well spoken,' muttered Gromrund, the hammerer turning on his heel to walk alongside the thane. The still cheering throng parted like an iron sea to let them through.

'Aye, it was,' Uthor replied, without arrogance then turned to look at the hammerer directly. 'Does this mean we see eye-to-eye at last, then?'

'You are not the only one who has much to atone for, son of Algrim,' came the terse response. 'If it is to be wrath and ruin, then so be it.'

Uthor smirked at that.

'Good enough,' he said then added, 'summon the clan leaders and gather the engineers. We know *what* we must do; now we must devise *how* it is to be done.'

'MAKE NO MISTAKE,' Uthor told them, 'most of us are likely to die in the enactment of this plan.'

The thane of Karak Kadrin sat upon a small wooden coal chest within a circle of his kinsdwarfs, next to the statue of Grungni. All of those who had first ventured into the hold were present – all except Lokki, of course. Thalgrim joined them, too, for the Sootbeards. As an expert in geology, his knowledge of the vagaries of rock and stone would be invaluable. Azgar took his place amongst the council as representative of the Grim Brotherhood – much to Uthor's chagrin – though if death was to be their fate then the slayer would have little qualms. The other clan leaders were present also, for the decisions the dwarf assembly was about to make would affect them all. Only Emelda was absent, still seeking solitude for her grief.

Further off into the plaza there was a flurry of activity as dwarfs sharpened axes, beat the dents from armour and made their final oaths to the ancestors. Strangely, the mood was not one of grim melancholy; rather it was jovial and comradely, as if the spectre of some unknown doom had been lifted.

'Better to die with honour than festering in the uncertain dark, awaiting a long and drawn out demise,' growled Henkil of the Furrowbrows, supping on a long-necked pipe.

'Aye, let us meet our doom with axes to the fore,' said Bulrik – who represented the interests of the Ironfingers – brandishing his axe. The other lords and leaders muttered their approval of these remarks and stamped their booted feet in agreement.

'It is as well,' said Uthor as the bravado died down, 'for I do not expect to live out the rest of my days and neither should you.'

Grim resolution settled over the group. Only Halgar was unmoved, the old longbeard having seen and heard it all before.

'All we can hope for is to do our part and die well. Lorekeeper,' added Uthor, 'tell us all how.'

Ralkan, who had been silent up until now, shuffled forward on his own coal chest and, producing a thick wedge of chalk from within his robes, started to draw onto the flagstones.

'Karak Varn has ever stood beside the Black Water,' he explained, his frantic scribing seemingly irrelevant to his rhetoric. 'In the Golden Age it was a great boon to the hold, for the crater in which the lake's depths resided were thick with seams of ore and precious gromril.'

Ralkan looked up at that and observed the awe-struck expressions of his kin with satisfaction, their eyes alight with the lustre of great days past.

'It was during the reign of King Hraddi Ironhand that the Barduraz Varn was fashioned, a great sluice gate that when opened would yoke the strength of the Black Water to drive wheels that powered the forge hammers of the deeps and allow the prospectors of the hold to sift for minerals.

'Hraddi was a wily king and well aware of the dangers that such a gate presented, should it fail or it be opened too far,' the lorekeeper continued, his audience enrapt. 'He instructed his engineers to build a deep reservoir beneath the Barduraz Varn in which the water could flow and at the lip of this magnificent well he bade miners hew tunnels that would carry the water to an overflow in the form of a vast and heavy grate. Such was the ingenuity of Hraddi's engineers that the grate would always open in the exact same increments as the Barduraz Varn, so that no matter how wide the sluice gate opened the hold would never flood.'

Throughout the explanation, Ralkan pointed to his crude rendering – leastways, it was by dwarf standards – of the gate, reservoir, tunnel and overflow grate.

'But was the gate not destroyed during the Time of Woes?' Kaggi of the Flinthearts interrupted.

Ralkan regarded the clan leader in sudden befuddlement.

'I believe the gate is still intact,' Rorek interjected on the lorekeeper's behalf. 'The flooding we have seen has been isolated to certain chambers. Were the gate to be ruined then the extent of the water would be much greater and there are the records of the hold to consider–'

'Yes,' said Ralkan abruptly, remembering his place again. 'My lord Kadrin did lead an expedition to the Barduraz Varn and found it to be in working order, though he did not linger. Much of the chamber was inundated and the lower deeps – although many of the skaven and grobi had been driven out – still held hidden dangers not so easily persuaded to leave.' The lorekeeper suppressed a shudder as if in some fearful remembrance.

'If we are to flood the hold,' Rorek continued, 'then we must destroy the overflow mechanism.'

An uncomfortable undercurrent of shock and disapproval rippled through much of the assembly. To deliberately set out to sabotage dwarfen craft was almost unthinkable and something not to be undertaken lightly.

'*Dreng Tromm*,' said Henkil, 'that it should come to this.'

'That is not all,' said Uthor. 'Once we have ruined the overflow, so that it stays shut, we must open the Barduraz Varn as far as it will go.'

'The rat-kin are not without wit,' said Hakem, sat across from the thane of Kadrin. The Barak Varr dwarf now wore a bronze hook, fashioned by Rorek and strapped onto the stump in place of his severed hand. 'Even if we are able to block the grate and open up the hold to the Black Water, they will flee before it into their tunnels and return once the flood has drained away.'

'Which is why we must start a second inundation, only from above,' Uthor replied, now looking to Thalgrim.

The lodefinder was busy scrutinising a small rock; the thane of Kadrin fancied he was even conversing with it. Thalgrim snapped upright when he realised the eyes of the council were upon him.

'Yes, above,' he said quickly. 'The temporary shoring we found in the third deep as made by Engineer Dibna can be brought down; it ruptures slightly even now. A shaft from that chamber leads all the way to the underdeep and to the overflow tunnel.'

'We must divide our throng into three *skorongs*,' Uthor said, picking up the slack. 'One will head for the Barduraz Varn; a second will go in the opposite direction, first to the overflow and then to Dibna's Chamber, thus starting the flood.'

'And what of our enemies?' asked Bulrik. 'They will not be gathered together. How are we to ensure they are all destroyed when the waters come?'

'If this plan is to succeed,' Uthor said, 'then we must draw the skaven to one place and channel the bulk of the rushing Black Water to it, ensnaring them until the flood can do its work. Like any rat trap,' he added, 'it requires bait. This is where the third skorong comes in, and theirs is a grim task indeed.' Uthor's face darkened. 'They will hold the rat-kin, here, in this very chamber.'

'And be drowned along with the skaven.' Bulrik finished for him.

'It is possible that some might survive, and any of us who do must take word of this to the High King with all haste. But, yes it is likely most will die.' Uthor's tone was sombre but firm.

'It will be a noble sacrifice.'

'How then are we to goad them?' asked Henkil. 'If the slaughter in the Wide Western Way taught us anything, save for the treachery of skaven' – a bout of spitting accompanied that remark – 'it is that their warlord has some intelligence. Likely they will not come of their own accord.'

'Halgar?' Uthor turned to the longbeard.

The venerable dwarf scratched at the grobi arrow stub embedded in his chest, before leaning forward.

'I have fought fiercer and wilier foes – that is for certain, but this vermin chief is not without base cunning,' he said, chewing on the end of his pipe. 'Like most creatures, even those wretches that prey upon us dawi in the dark and usurp our lands, the rat-kin nest. I can smell the stink of their lair even now, rotting below us like a rancid carcass,' Halgar added, sneering with disgust. 'In my younger days, I once came upon such a nest – I feel its canker crawling over my skin as I remember it. Litters of the foul things were all about, spewed from rat-kin birth mothers that were fattened on urk and dawi flesh. My brothers and I brought flame and retribution to the foul dwelling, slaying the birthing rats first of all. It drove the rat-kin into frenzy and they came upon us with such fervour that we fled back whence we came. Grokki, my clan brother, and I, realising we would not outrun the vermin, cut down the braces to the tunnel which we were in and brought the weight of the mountain down upon us and our pursuers. Of my kin, I was the only one to survive. This,' he said, holding up his ruined hand, 'and the deaths of Grokki and the rest of my brothers upon my conscience, was my reward.'

The longbeard allowed for a moment of sombre silence, before he went on.

'Much like then we must find the filthy rat-kin nest and destroy all that lay within. That will bring them to us, mark my words on that.' With that the longbeard leant back, a heavy plume of pipe smoke issuing into the air around him.

'An expedition must venture from the foundry, once the other skorongs are under way,' Uthor said by way of further explanation. 'It will be small, designed to infiltrate past whatever guards the rat-kin will undoubtedly have in place and delve into the very heart of their nest. Rorek,' added Uthor, looking over to the engineer, 'has fashioned something that will get the ratmen's attention.'

The Zhufbar dwarf grinned, revealing white teeth in his ruddy beard.

'A fine plan,' Henkil concurred, 'but who is to do what?'

'Our most experienced warriors will be in the first two skorongs. The way will be perilous and should either fail then all our efforts will be for nought,' Uthor replied, 'Gromrund shall lead those heading for the overflow and Dibna's Chamber,' – the hammerer nodded his assent – 'together with Thalgrim, Hakem, Ralkan and no more than three warriors from the Sootbeard clan,' he said with a glance at Thalgrim to make sure he was paying attention.

'You, Henkil,' the thane continued, regarding the clan leader, 'will accompany Rorek, Bulrik, Halgar and I to the Barduraz Varn, which leaves the rest to hold the skaven at–'

'No lad,' said Halgar, his face illuminated briefly by his pipe embers before it was cast back into shadow. 'I am too old to be running around the underdeep. I will stay here. I like the smell of the soot and metal; it reminds me of the Copper Mountain,' he added. 'Besides, they will need my nose to find the rat-kin nest,' he said, tapping one of his nostrils.

'But venerable one…'

'I have spoken!' Halgar bellowed, but his expression soon softened, 'I have fought in many battles, more than I can recall; let this be my last, eh?'

Uthor's shoulders sagged. To be without Halgar as he ventured to the gate was almost unthinkable. 'Very well,' the thane said softly. 'Drimbold, you will join us to the gate.'

'I wish to stay here, too,' said the Grey dwarf, 'and fight alongside my kin.'

Halgar raised an eyebrow, but gave no other indication as to what he thought of Drimbold's pledge.

'Very well then,' Uthor said with a little consternation. 'Kaggi, you shall accompany us.'

Kaggi was about to nod but was interrupted.

'Kaggi should remain with his kin,' said a voice from outside the circle.

Uthor's temper was rising; it was quashed in an instant when Emelda moved into the light cast by the statue of Grungni, her armour resplendent before it. She had removed the face mask from her helmet and in her hand she held Dunrik's axe. '*We* shall take Halgar's place.'

Uthor did not have the will to protest. In truth, he welcomed Emelda's presence. Whenever she were near he felt the burden of his past, of his duty to his clan that he now knew he would fail, lift slightly. Her prowess, too, was unquestionable.

'Then please sit, milady, for this last part is crucial,' Uthor said and Emelda took her place amongst the circle, those dwarfs sitting next to her reddening about the cheeks and swiftly smoothing their beards.

Once order was restored, Uthor went on.

'None amongst the first two skorongs must release any flood waters until they hear Azgar's warhorn.' Uthor's jaw tightened only slightly at the mention of the name. 'Only then will we know the rat-kin are committed to the attack. After that, and by closing off tunnels, wells and door dams throughout the lower deeps as we go, the Black Water will be unleashed and channelled into the foundry.'

Uthor allowed a silence to descend as he regarded each and every dwarf in the circle in turn.

'Make your oaths,' he said, getting to his feet. 'In an hour we go to meet our destinies.'

THE THRONG MUSTERED together for one last time. Each and every clan dwarf was decked in their armour and brandished hammers and axes proudly.

At the foundry gate, Uthor and Gromrund, with their retinues, made ready to leave. Their paths would converge for a time, until they reached the triple forked road and then one would head eastward to the mines and the shaft that led to the underdeep, whilst the other would go westward, relying on Ralkan's prior instruction, to the Barduraz Varn.

'If memory serves, the route to both the gate and overflow should be fairly clear of obstruction, fifty years of rat-kin occupation not withstanding, of course.' Ralkan had said as the council were breaking up.

'Of course,' Uthor had replied with a wry glance at Gromrund, the thane noticing that other dwarfs in earshot made similar exchanges.

'YOU ARE CERTAIN its note will carry to the lower deeps?' Halgar asked as he watched the dwarfs slowly depart through the gate.

'The wyvern-horn will make itself heard, you can mark that – its note will carry,' Azgar answered deeply, with a furtive glance at Uthor. The thane of Kadrin was having a final private word with Drimbold. When he was done speaking into his ear, the Grey dwarf nodded and headed back to be amongst the other warriors.

'You fight with honour, slayer,' said the longbeard, watching him. 'But we all go to our deaths now. Perhaps there might be some accord between you and your brother in this moment?'

A slight, near-imperceptible, tremor of shock registered in the slayer's eyes as he looked back at Halgar.

'I have known it from the first time I set eyes upon you,' the longbeard said. 'He even fights like you.'

Azgar considered Halgar's words before he spoke.

'I am sorry, venerable one. You are wise, but there can be no accord between us. I have seen to that.'

The slayer bowed deeply and took his leave.

'Aye,' Halgar said regretfully when he was gone, off to rejoin his Grim Brotherhood and make ready for the coming battle. Uthor, too, had now vanished into the dark, the foundry gate thundering shut in his wake. 'You're probably right.'

DRIMBOLD HEARD THE foundry gate slamming to and the thick bolts scraping across its metal surface as he headed for the weapon racks. The mattock he carried was chipped and battered, and he was unaccustomed to its weight. A stout hand axe, that was what he needed; even Halgar would condone him borrowing one.

Reaching the racks, he looked over to the longbeard, who was wheezing badly and rubbing at the old wound in his chest. He only did it when no one else was watching, but Drimbold was skilled at secret observation and had seen him struggle often. The Grey dwarf remembered Uthor's words to him as he had left.

'I won't let you down,' he said to himself. Really, he had no choice. If this was to be the end, then honouring his pledge to Uthor was his last chance at redemption.

THRATCH WIPED THE flat of his blade on a skaven slave. The wretched creature was so emaciated that it nearly bent double with the warlord's heavy paw pressed on its back. Satisfied that his weapon was clean of goblin blood, despite the pathetic tufts of fur poking between the slave's patches of scar tissue, the warlord kicked the whimpering creature to the floor and stalked away to talk to his chieftain returning from the upper deeps.

'Most of the green-things are dead-dead, my lord,' Liskrit said, cowering slightly before his master, despite his well-armoured bulk.

'And the rest?' snarled Thratch, sheathing his sword as he paced over to the nearby door through which the dwarfs had made their escape.

The warlord had returned to the Great Hall with Kill-Klaw and the majority of his warriors once they had defeated the greenskins. Despite the victory, Thratch had lost many clanrats and almost all of his slaves. The few that did survive were shovelling dwarf and goblin corpses into crudely-made barrows to be taken below to the warrens to feed the birthing mothers.

When the nerve of the goblins finally broke – and Thratch knew it would – he'd sent a small cohort of elite stormvermin and slaves to harry them as far as the upper deeps. No creature, be it dwarf-thing or green-thing, would usurp his domain – this was Thratch's territory now.

'They ran, quick-quick, yes.'

'Good,' said the warlord then screamed suddenly, 'No, no,' smacking the back of a warrior's head into the door as he probed at it with his spear.

'We don't go that way,' Thratch roared, noticing the thin trickles of water eking through the cracks with a slight prickling of fear. The skaven warrior's muzzle had been crushed into its brain with the impact and it did not answer. Suddenly aware of the fact, Thratch about turned and stalked back to his chieftain.

'You stay-stay, make sure the green-things do not return,' he commanded. 'I must check on Clan Skryre, yes,' he added, stalking off again. The progress on the pumping engine was going much slower than Thratch liked and he was debating which one of the Skryre acolytes to kill next when his chieftain spoke.

'Noble Lord Thratch,' said Liskrit, obsequiously.

'Yes-yes, what it is now?' Thratch whirled around, deciding whether or not to have Kill-Klaw gut the impudent chieftain now or wait until later while it slept.

'The dwarf-things… should we follow them?'

A vicious snarl crept across the warlord's snout, revealing glistening fangs, still slick with goblin blood.

'Dead-dead they are, yet they do not know it. Any that are left I will kill-kill or chase down into the dark for the fire-worm to eat.' The snarl twisted into a malicious grin and Thratch walked away, the creeping shadow of Kill-Klaw following silently behind him.

CHAPTER TWELVE

SKARTOOTH WAS DISPLEASED. His cunning attack against the skaven had been thwarted – largely by Fangrak's incompetence, he was sure – the dwarfs had escaped his wrath and his army, together with all his grand designs, was in tatters.

'Idiot!' the goblin warlord shrieked, pacing up and down the flat plateau of rock to which the remnants of the greenskins had fled. The path they had taken led them high into the mountains and three sides of the plateau fell away into a craggy gorge.

Several of the surviving orc tribes had already left, retreating silently into the mountains as Skartooth had led the flight to the lofty promontory. Only he, Fangrak and a meagre horde of other orcs and goblins remained. That and Ungul, of course. The pet troll was sat on its bony backside and paid little heed to the argument brewing between his master and Fangrak, too obsessed was it with watching the viscous drool dripping languidly from its maw and pooling on the ground in front of it.

'It was your plan to ambush the ratties and them stunties at the same time,' growled Fangrak, stood stock still as his warlord paced in front of him.

'There was nuthin' wrong with my plan,' squeaked Skartooth. 'You just didn't listen to my ordas, did ya?' he added, pointing his diminutive blade in the orc chieftain's direction.

'What ordas? "Get 'em"?' said Fangrak, building up to a roar. 'Is them your zoggin' ordas, eh?'

'I knew you were useless, you and your ole stinkin' lot,' snarled Skartooth. 'And now you've ruined everything... Everything!' he cried, apoplectic with rage, the veins in his forehead popping to the surface.

'I've 'ad enough of this,' Fangrak grumbled, turning away from the goblin warlord. 'I'm off.'

'Don't turn your back on me!' Skartooth shrieked, so high-pitched that Ungul waggled a finger in his ear to stop it ringing.

'Zog off,' said Fangrak, already walking away.

Skartooth roared, the goblin's anger getting the better of him as he launched himself at Fangrak, ready to plunge his sword beneath the orc's shoulder blades. But before he could strike the blow, Fangrak whirled around and grabbed Skartooth's scrawny arm in one meaty fist then quickly clamped his other hand around the goblin's neck. With a twist he snapped Skartooth's wrist and the sword tumbled from the goblin's nerveless grasp, clanging loudly as it hit the ground.

Fangrak drew Skartooth close as he started to squeeze his hand around the goblin's neck, slowly choking the life out of him.

Skartooth glanced over towards Ungul, fear in his eyes, but the beast was quite far away and digging deep into its nostril at something that didn't want to be dislodged.

When he looked back at Fangrak, he realised that this had been the orc's plan all along. As that knowledge passed over his face, Fangrak smiled.

'What are you gonna do now?' he murmured sadistically, squeezing just a little tighter and taking great amusement in watching the blood vessels pop in Skartooth's ever widening eyes.

The goblin warlord soiled himself, a long streak of foul smelling dung streaming from his robes to spatter on the ground and Fangrak's leg.

'You filthy–' the orc chieftain began, slightly loosening his grip as he stooped to inspect the mess trickling down onto his boot.

It was all the distraction Skartooth needed. The goblin wrenched himself free enough to bite down hard against Fangrak's hand. The orc chieftain howled in pain and threw Skartooth to the ground as if he'd gripped the wrong end of a branding iron. The goblin warlord scuttled backwards on all fours to the safety of Ungul's presence, the troll having suddenly blinked awake, as if for the first time.

'Kill 'im!' Skartooth squealed, his diminutive voice croaky after nearly being strangled by Fangrak.

Ungul didn't respond. It merely looked dully at Skartooth as if trying to remember something.

'What are you waitin' for? Kill 'im!' the goblin squealed again, smacking Ungul on the nose with his good hand.

The troll snarled at Skartooth, and the goblin warlord saw all the years of pain and mistreatment at his hands felt by Ungul anew.

'Oh no,' he breathed, reaching up to his neck.

The collar was gone.

Fangrak had removed it.

'Ee 'ates you almost as much as I do,' said the orc chief, three of his warriors alongside him, awaiting the gruesome show.

Skartooth shuffled backwards as the troll stood up, its immense shadow engulfing him like an eclipse.

Ungul roared, beating its chest.

Skartooth back-pedalled as fast as he could but suddenly there was nothing beneath his feet and he fell off the promontory, screaming into the jagged gorge below.

Ungul bellowed in rage, watching the goblin disappear. The subject of its ire gone, it lumbered around and turned all of its anger on Fangrak.

'Aw zog,' said the orc chieftain, hunting around with his eyes to locate the collar. When Skartooth had bitten him he'd dropped it. His last memory of the artefact was of it rolling away across the plateau but now it was nowhere to be seen.

'Get it,' he snarled at his warriors, switching to his makeshift back-up plan. The orcs looked bemused at first, but when they realised Fangrak was serious they charged, roaring, at the troll.

Ungul roared back and vomited a searing spray of corrosive stomach acid all over the warriors, who screamed as the toxic liquid ate them up greedily.

Fangrak – seeing his minions turned to bubbling pools of greenish flesh and viscera – ran but Ungul reached out with its gangly limbs and seized him. The orc chieftain squealed as the troll pulled off both his arms and then went for the legs. As the troll sat down to feast, its anger sated for now, the rest of what was left of the horde fled, deep into the mountains.

THE FLICKERING TORCH flame illuminated the fearsome, scar-ravaged visage of Azgar as he led the warriors down the cramped passage.

'These are not dwarf-made tunnels,' growled Halgar, two paces behind the slayer.

The longbeard ran his hand lightly along the walls, smearing away a thin veneer of slime and crusted filth. A trail of effluvia trickled languidly down the middle of the tunnel along the ground in a shallow and foul-smelling rut. Elsewhere, the skaven underway was littered with excreta and other detritus, and the dwarfs needed to traverse it with care lest they slip on clustered droppings or the rank remnants of a discarded rat-kin feast.

'How long have we been down here?' Drimbold piped up suddenly, trudging just behind Halgar.

'Too long,' the longbeard muttered. The twisting, turning route had led them deep into the earth. On several occasions the way had split, spiralling off into the silent gloom in myriad directions, some so obtuse that only one of the rat-kin could hope to travel them. Halgar knew that much of the skaven labyrinth intersected the paths of the Ungdrin road and even undermined and subsumed them in places. In his youth, he'd heard tales of huge, hairless mole rats that the skaven used to dig vast tracts into the rock and earth – whether or not such rumours held any truth the longbeard did not know. He had to suppress a shudder, though, when he wondered how long these tunnels had been here, unnoticed by Kadrin, Ulfgan and even their ancestors, balking at the thought of just how many were bored into the earth and exactly how deep they went.

Azgar was paying little heed to the conversation and was intent on the way forward when Halgar bade him pause a moment as he sniffed at the air. Wrinkling his nose he said, 'The wretched stench of the rat-kin is thickening,' he said. 'We are getting close.'

The slayer nodded and the dwarfs continued into the dark.

The dwarfs that remained in the foundry had waited for an hour before heading out. They too were destined for the triple forked road but preparations to meet and resist the skaven horde first had to be made. The delay would also allow Uthor and Gromrund, who had a much longer journey ahead of them, to get well under way. Azgar's expedition did not dawdle too long, however – in luring the skaven to them, it also meant their brothers en route to the Barduraz Varn and the overflow grate would be less likely to encounter much resistance.

The three dwarfs were not alone as they ventured toward the rat-kin warrens, three of the Grim Brotherhood and another dwarf by the name of Thorig, a warrior of Zhufbar who shouldered a heavy-looking satchel across his back, also accompanied them.

Halgar rubbed at his eyes as the dwarfs stopped in a sloped section of the labyrinthine tunnel network, a two-legged fork in front of them. Azgar brandished the torch light in front of it. His lip curled into a feral sneer as he recognised the foul script of the skaven scratched into the wall above each road. He turned to the longbeard and saw him kneading his eye sockets with his knuckles.

'Are you all right, old one?' asked the slayer.

'Yes,' Halgar snapped. 'This infernal flame is ruining my sight,' he complained, scratching at his chest wound again.

'I am not fond of it either,' Azgar agreed, 'but 'tis necessary,' he added, thumbing over his shoulder in the direction of Thorig, 'for what the engineer has planned.'

Halgar grumbled, his words indiscernible. He pointed to the left-hand opening of the fork, tasting the air as he did so. 'The stink is heaviest there,' he said more clearly, blinking several times before trudging onward. 'Are you coming?' he snarled back at the others.

'WE WILL NEED a rope,' cried Uthor above the raging din of the waterfall.

The dwarfs had been going steadily on a western course just as Ralkan

had told them to. Already they had shut several door dams, which Rorek
assured the thane of Kadrin would help channel the lower flood waters
up to the foundry. They had also sealed a number of wellways, heaving
large stones into their necks to act as stoppers. It was tough and time-
consuming work but necessary. The road had led them downwards after
that, the Barduraz Varn getting ever closer, to a sheer rock face and a
sheet of shimmering, cascading water.

'Can we go around?' Emelda shouted, her voice dulled by the incredible noise of the thundering torrents.

'It is the only way into the flooded deeps and the Barduraz Varn,' Uthor
replied, eyeing the rushing waterfall from the ledge where the dwarfs
were standing. The ledge narrowed abruptly after that, where the waterfall began and had worn it down. Over the edge, the thunderous water
fell away into a deep, dark chasm. Uthor imagined the vast expanse of
the Black Water swelling far above them, its power evident even this far
down, and felt humbled.

Rorek unwound a rope from his tool belt, one of several, and brandished it in front of Uthor. 'This will hold. Dawi twine is not so easily
broken,' he said, errant spray spitting at him and moistening his beard
with jewels of water. He threw one end of the rope to Uthor, who caught
it easily.

'Tie it around your waist and make the knot tight,' Rorek told him then
turned to Emelda. 'You should do the same, milady.'

The dwarfs were moved into single file, first Uthor then Emelda followed by Rorek, Henkil and finally Bulrik. Slowly, with Uthor taking the
lead, they worked their way towards the rushing waterfall.

As Uthor touched the narrowed ledge he instantly felt the slickness
beneath his boots. It would be easy to slip and fall into the endless
depths below, with a forest of razor-sharp rocks at journey's end. The
thane of Kadrin resolved not to look down. Instead, he dug around in a
leather pouch Rorek had given to him and pulled out two broad spikes
of iron. He put one in his mouth – the taste of metal was reassuring
– and reached over to drive the other into the sheer rock. At first he faltered – unaccustomed to the battering force of the water, and recoiled
– breathing hard, his beard, face and arm drenched. Then he gathered
himself and tried again, taking an extra step as he did so.

Icy water smashed Uthor, robbing him of breath and setting his teeth
chattering as he fought against the thunderous swell. Taking a small hammer from his belt, the thane drove the spike into the wall, where it held fast.
Using the spike as a handhold, he eased himself further across the ledge
and drove in another. Then came a third and a fourth, and Uthor reached
the centre of the ledge, where a small crevice in the rock wall allowed him a
moment's respite from the onrushing deluge.

Catching his breath, acutely aware that the others were following
slowly in his wake, he was about to continue when he felt a sharp tug

against the rope cinctured at his waist. The thane turned, his boots slipping on the drenched rock, and saw Emelda losing purchase on one of the spikes and falling backward. She was but an arm length away and Uthor quickly reached out to her, grabbing her by the wrist as she flailed, and heaved her towards him. The royal clan daughter thumped into Uthor's body with the momentum of her rescue and the two of them fell back against the narrow crevice in the rock wall, breathing hard.

'My thanks,' said Emelda, her long plaits dripping wet as she blinked away water droplets from her eyes. A smile starting to form in the corners of her mouth changed dramatically to a grimace as Uthor felt her pulled back again. He held her fast, gripping a wall spike with all his strength as he tried to see what was happening. Beyond the foaming, white veil of water blurred shadows presented themselves and dulled cries carried through the raging downpour.

ROREK WATCHED, POWERLESS, as Bulrik fell. The Ironfinger dwarf stumbled against a jutting rock and slipped. His death-scream was swallowed by the roar of the waterfall, his tumbling body lost from view in the churning mists.

Wisely, the dwarfs had left several feet of rope between each fastening around the waist but even so, Henkil only had a few seconds to untether himself or he too would be lost to the darkness. The leader of the Furrowbrows pulled frantically at the knot he had made. His clan were rope makers, he had boasted as much to Rorek before they had descended the stairway, and as such knew much of knot work, so much so that he had congratulated himself when he'd tied this particular binding, unthinking that he might have to untie it in haste.

Henkil's fingers slipped, the slack of the rope pulling taut and he looked up at the engineer when he realised all was lost. The Furrowbrow was yanked violently off the ledge to his doom, Bulrik an unwitting anchor. The rope started gathering again. Rorek was tugged forward at first, some of the slack piled at his boot, but then he stepped free of it. He pressed his back against the rock wall and braced his legs – no way could he bear the weight of two fully-armoured dawi. Like most of the throng, Rorek carried several throwing axes and with the trailing rope tightening before his very eyes, he pulled one free. With an oath to Grungni that his aim might this once be true he cast the blade, which span end over end scything through the water and smacking into the ledge, cutting the rope with no more time to spare. There it remained, firmly embedded, as the severed trail disappeared into the gloom following Bulrik and Henkil.

'IS IT MUCH farther?' groaned Hakem as he climbed down another few feet through the cramped confines of Dibna's Drop.

The dwarfs had entered the shaft via the mines and were descending gradually to the underdeep and from there to the overflow tunnel – thanks to Thalgrim's rope, secured safely above – which resided a long way below. The going had been hard; much of the shaft was collapsed and in places, sharp rocks jutted out where adjoining tunnels had broken through the shaft wall like stone battering rams. Mercifully, the ancestors of Karak Varn had built a series of short ledges at intervals down the long shaft. Gromrund took advantage of this piece of engineering ingenuity gladly, setting his boots onto the stone outcrop for a breather.

'Not sure. I think we are about halfway,' the hammerer reckoned, peering into the gloom below between his legs.

'In the halls of Barak Varr, gilded lifts allow passage up and down the deeps,' Hakem moaned, struggling to untether his hook from the rope as he too found one of the ledges.

'You must be feeling like your old self again,' Gromrund remarked with a wry smile in the merchant thane's direction, 'to boast of your hold's magnificence. Or do you seek to outdo Halgar with your grumbling?' he added.

Hakem gave a half-hearted and ephemeral laugh. The loss of the Honakinn Hammer still dogged his thoughts. The memory of it vanishing into the darkness beyond his grasp and the subsequent death of Dunrik was like a sudden knife-blade in his heart and his expression darkened.

Gromrund saw it and averted his gaze upward to where Ralkan, Thalgrim and the three Sootbeards descended. Each of them found purchase on the ledges in short order; the relief of Ralkan though was almost palpable.

'How long can we rest?' gasped the lorekeeper, unused to such physical exertion, casting his gaze skyward and scarce believing he had come such a distance.

'Not long,' said Gromrund, 'a few minutes, no more.'

Thalgrim was in his element, as were his clan brothers. They chatted freely, taking the opportunity to eat what rations they had in their packs. One of the miners even dangled his feet over the edge, dropping a small piece of rock into the gloom. Thalgrim turned his ear towards it as it struck the bottom with a shallow and faraway *plink*.

'One hundred and thirty-one feet,' said the lodefinder to the rest of the group, 'give or take a few inches.'

'There,' said Gromrund, looking back at Hakem. 'You have your answer.'

Hakem scowled.

'Definitely more like the longbeard,' Gromrund muttered beneath his breath.

THALGRIM LED THE rest of the way down Dibna's Drop. The darkness was particularly thick here it seemed and he and the rest of the Sootbeards lit candles stuck to their mining helmets to help light the way for the other dwarfs. There were no more stops and after what felt like several more hours to some, they reached the end of the shaft and the ancient rock of the underdeep.

The lodefinder landed with a dull splash, water coming up to his ankles and wetting the mail skirt of his armour. The underdeep was partially flooded. Tramping through the water to make way for the others he gazed in wonder at the vast subterranean halls at the lowest habitable levels of Karak Varn. Massive archways ran down the curved ceiling at precise intervals and stout columns, carved with runic script and the images of fabulous beasts, held the roof aloft. A fizzle of flame got his attention as the rest of the group made landfall. He realised it was his candle and craned his neck to regard the ceiling directly above. Liquid dripped intermittently from a shallow crack, an isolated pocket of flood water obviously trapped beyond it and trying to force its way through. Thalgrim was possessed by the sudden urge to hurry.

'Which way, lorekeeper?' he asked, turning back to the group, all of whom had now exited the mineshaft.

They were standing at a confluence of four tunnels, the crossroads stretching off into the distance seemingly without discerning features.

Ralkan regarded each avenue in turn, his brow furrowed as he tried to remember.

'I thought you knew how to get to the overflow,' said Hakem, with a furtive glance at Gromrund.

The lorekeeper scratched his head. Much of the tunnels were damaged: collapsed columns jutted from the water like miniature stone islands and some of the archway decoration had fallen away leaving them jagged as if gnawed upon. It was not how Ralkan remembered it, though he had seen the desolation before.

'We go north,' he said at last, pointing towards one of the tunnels.

'That way lies south,' said Thalgrim, his expression perplexed.

'South then,' replied the lorekeeper, a little uncertainly. 'Come on, the grate is not far,' he added and started tramping down the tunnel, the bottom of his robes waterlogged.

'*South* it is,' muttered Hakem, exchanging a worried look with Gromrund as the dwarfs followed.

THE FOUL STINK of skaven was overpowering as they reached the entrance to the warrens; even Azgar and the others did not need the nose of the longbeard to smell it.

Halgar slowly and quietly pulled his axe from his belt as he approached the ratman chamber. Azgar was beside the longbeard and he turned to the slayer, first putting his finger to his lips and then showing the slayer his palm in a gesture to wait. The longbeard crept forward to the threshold of the room, his stealth incredible for a dwarf of his age and so armoured, and peered into it.

The skaven warren was made in a large, roughly-hewn cavern around three hundred beard lengths in each direction. Structurally, there were a number of raised stone platforms and Halgar also noticed the edge of several deep pits in the centre of the chamber. Rat-kin guards stood around them, wearing cracked, black-leather hauberks and carrying broad-bladed spears – they must be the birthing pens, where the bloated skaven females gorged upon the flesh of the dead and spawned litters of the mutated ratmen. The thought turned the longbeard's stomach and he gripped his axe haft for reassurance. Two more guards sat near the entrance, noses twitching but otherwise oblivious to Halgar's presence.

Slumbering slaves took up most of the rest of the floor space, heaped on top of one another in clots of fur and cloth, partially obscured by a low-lying, sulphurous fug. Halgar noticed it came from the birthing pens.

A languid, almost comatose, atmosphere persisted. Piles of excreta lay everywhere, along with bones and other debris. Urine stained the walls and sweat clung to the air, on top of the nostril-prickling stench of the sulphur fog. Halgar had seen enough and backtracked to his awaiting kinsdwarfs.

The longbeard beckoned Thorig forward and the Zhufbar dwarf did so quickly. Halgar nodded to him and Thorig unclasped the satchel he'd been carrying since they'd left the foundry. Delving deep, he produced a fist-sized ball of copper and iron. A faint seam was visible in the flickering torch light that ran across the ball's circumference, a hinge at one end and what appeared to be a spring-loaded catch at the other. A spout protruded from one hemisphere with a short length of twine sticking out of it.

Halgar took the ball in his hand and tipped it; the tinny sound of liquid sloshing inside could be heard very faintly. The longbeard raised an eyebrow at the Zhufbar dwarf.

'*Zharrum*,' whispered Thorig with a glint in his eyes. 'The mixture of soot and oil is particularly volatile when exposed to a flame,' he added, echoing the words of Rorek.

'Your clansdwarf will be for a quaffing,' Halgar grumbled quietly.

Thorig shrugged and passed a ball to each of the other dwarfs. He then took the flaming brand proffered by Azgar, crushing it into the ground until only glowing embers remained. The slayer then led them back to warren entrance.

A shallow gurgling of blood and the two skaven at the cavern entrance were dead with slit throats. Azgar and Halgar laid their kills down almost in perfect unison and began the stealthy advance into the chamber. The dwarfs trod in single file, Halgar at the front marking a path through the slumbering slaves. Should any of them be disturbed and manage to raise the alarm then the dwarfs would be quickly surrounded and fighting for their very lives.

Azgar followed on after the longbeard, sweeping his gaze left and right for any sign of movement, chained axe held low in his grasp. So intent was he on what was in front of him that he didn't see the rat tail flick beneath his boot. The bulky slayer stepped on it and the slave to whom it belonged would've screamed but for Azgar reaching down like lightning, wrapping his chain around the creature's neck and snapping it with a vicious twist. Like before, he laid the body down carefully and the dwarfs moved on.

As they came close to the birthing pens and the guards that protected them Halgar bade them silently to spread out, using the shadows and the soporific state of the rat-kin to creep up on them. There were six guards in total; a pair for each of the three pits and one each for Halgar, Azgar, Drimbold and the Grim Brotherhood. Thorig stooped out of sight, fearful that the embers of the torch would rouse the skaven.

When they were all in position, Halgar rose up from a crouching stance and cut the first guard down. One of the Grim Brotherhood smothered the second with a meaty palm over the mouth and then broke its neck. Azgar and another of his slayers, looming out of the mist like ancient predators of the deep, dispatched the other two with equal and deadly swiftness. Drimbold and the third slayer finished the remaining guards, one with a well-flighted axe throw; the other with an axe spike to the throat. So silent was Drimbold that the other dwarfs didn't even see or hear him approach. The assassins shared a nod to acknowledge the task was done and crept over to the birthing pens.

Halgar peered into the deep pit and almost gagged.

Sat on its fat rump, its rolls of fat spilling over each other, was a vile skaven birth mother. The bloated female was mewling faintly with its scrawny legs spread wide in preparation for the expulsion of yet more skaven offspring. She was surrounded by bone carcasses: dwarf, goblin and even ratman were all in evidence. A host of diminutive rat-kin spawn suckled hungrily at a raft of small, pink teats sticking out of the birth mother's torso. Several of the spawn were dead and some of the stronger babies were devouring them, noisily.

In one corner of the pen there was a crude iron brazier. Thick, billowing mist exuded from it as some foul-smelling skaven concoction was burned down within – doubtless, it was the source of the sulphur fog. Attached to the lip of the brazier cup was a thick tube. It ran all the way to a metal pipe that was affixed to the birthing mother's spittle-flecked muzzle. Judging by the inert nature of all the skaven in the chamber, Halgar surmised that the gas was used to sedate the disgusting creatures for when they were birthing the rat-kin multitudes.

Skaven slaves were also present in the pits. They carried long wooden poles at the end of which were filthy-looking sponges. As the dwarfs watched, the slaves dolefully patted the birth mothers down with the sodden sponges, presumably in an effort to keep them cool throughout their exertions.

Halgar could barely contain his revulsion and as he sneered contemptuously one of the birth mothers looked up at him with her beady eyes and squeaked a frantic warning. All around the room, the skaven stirred.

Halgar roared and buried a throwing axe in the birth mother's skull, splitting it open like an over-ripened fruit. The skaven slaves screeched first in horror at the blood fountaining from the birth mother's ruined skull and then with rage as they saw her murderers above. They dropped their poles and drew rusty blades, rushing towards an earth ramp that would get them out of the pit.

Thorig had already sped from his hiding place and lit Azgar's zharrum with the torch's embers. The fuse burned down quickly and the slayer tossed the sphere into the pit where it exploded, the catch releasing on impact and spraying flaming liquid all over the slaves and the birth mother's corpse. The stink of burning fur and the wrenching scream of dying rat-kin filled the air as Drimbold threw in his zharrum too and the pit became a bowl of raging fire.

Halgar rushed over to the second pit, two of the Grim Brotherhood in tow. One of the slaves was coming off the end of the earth ramp, a wicked barbed spear in hand. The longbeard booted it in the groin and sent the creature back down again before he threw his zharrum in after it, engulfing the birthing pen in flame. The third and final pit was immolated shortly after, Thorig tossing two of the fire bombs into it before any of the skaven within could react. Through fire, thick with oily black smoke from burning body fat, the writhing shapes of the birth mothers and their slowly cooking offspring could be seen. The rancid stink of roasting rat meat brought tears to Halgar's eyes.

'Come on!' he bellowed. 'Our work is done. Back to the foundry.'

The dwarfs gathered together, cutting down slaves as they went. From the back of the chamber a cohort of previously unseen clanrats wielding spears and halberds had mustered. They squeaked ferociously and came at the dwarfs with muzzles frothing. Thorig threw a fire bomb into them and the sheet of flame reduced the first rank to flailing torches. But a second rank came on. A thrown spear passed Halgar's ear and *thunked* into the wall behind him.

'Out! Out now!' he cried, rallying the charge once the dwarfs were reunited.

Azgar and the other slayers went first, cleaving a path through a welter of slaves that had sprung up in their path. Thorig was behind them and, with Drimbold at his side, the Zhufbar dwarf cast more fire bombs into the chamber at will, determined to raze the wretched nest to the ground. As he ran, he coaxed the embers of the torch into life and soon the brand was aflame. Halgar was the rearguard, backing away quickly as the clanrats closed on them, trampling any slaves in their way such was their fury.

Barrelling through their skaven assailants the dwarfs crossed the threshold of the massive cavern, now wreathed in fire as a mighty conflagration took hold, and out into the tunnel again. The clanrats were almost upon them when Thorig turned and thrust the flaming brand into the satchel. Casting the spent torch aside he whirled the burning satchel around his head like a sling and threw it, fire bombs and all, into the nest entrance. A huge wall of fire sprang up from where the satchel hit the ground, so dense and ferocious that the pursuing skaven came to an abrupt halt and became hazy silhouettes through it.

'Well done, lad,' said Halgar, coughing some of the smoke from his lungs and smacking Thorig on the back.

The Zhufbar dwarf nodded exhaustedly, and lifted his helmet to wipe a swathe of sweat from his forehead.

'But we must not linger,' the longbeard continued, eyeing the inferno that prevented the rat-kins immediate pursuit. Even now, vaguely discernible through the blaze, slaves heaped great clods of dirt into the wall of fire in an effort to extinguish it. 'Destiny awaits us,' he added, grinning.

The dwarfs fled back whence they had came, Azgar to the fore retracing his steps flawlessly. Only the Grim Brotherhood remained. Drimbold noticed the warriors, standing solemnly before the raging fire wall, axes held in readiness.

'Come on,' the Grey dwarf cried at them, slowing his flight, 'the rat-kin will soon give chase!'

Azgar saw Drimbold falter and tracked back to drag him onward.

'But they will surely be slain,' the Grey dwarf said.

'As is their oath,' Azgar told him. 'They knew their part in this. Their sacrifice will stall the rat-kin long enough for us to make ready in the foundry.'

'They are your warriors; you have not even bid them farewell.'

'That is not our way,' Azgar replied. 'They go to meet with an honourable death.' The slayer's tone was almost longing. 'Soon they will be received in Grimnir's hall, to fight the endless battle,' he added, fixing Drimbold with his stony gaze. 'I envy them, Grey dwarf.'

'This is not as the lorekeeper described it,' said Rorek, scratching his head.

'It bears the name of the brewmaster, though,' Uthor replied, pointing out a stone plaque in which the words 'Brondold's Hall – His Brew Will Be Remembered' were carved in Khazalid. 'This must be where Ralkan meant for us to go.'

'It more resembles a lake than any drinking hall I have ever seen,' added Emelda.

The three dwarfs were standing upon a stone-slabbed platform, which fell away at the edge into a vast expanse of turgid, greenish water, many hundred feet long. The murky lagoon of crud was still, like tarnished glass, the upper portions of columns protruding through it all the way to the high ceiling. Foamy deposits lapped around the pillars where they split the surface, and clustered at the edges of the walls. Braziers still flickered, just above the waterline, an incredible feat given that they must have been lit for over fifty years or more. They were a further example of the miracle fuel of the dwarf guildmasters. The light illuminated massive bronze heads, belonging to submerged statues and depicting the ancient brewmasters and lords of the hold, the tips of their beards dipping into the rancid reservoir.

Save for the stone epithet dedicated to the long dead brewmaster, numerous wooden barrels, kegs and steins held fast in the stagnant, reeking water made it clear this was indeed the drinking hall that Ralkan had described.

'You will reach Brondold's Hall, arriving from the northern portal,' the lorekeeper had said. 'Beneath the south wall there is a trapdoor. Though bolted, it will lead into the drainage tunnels below. Traverse this tunnel and you will emerge in the reservoir of the Barduraz Varn.'

Uthor recalled the words dimly – Ralkan had said nothing of a vast, uncrossable lake. Regarding the massive expanse of flood water, he noticed a dwarf skeleton clinging to one piece of floating detritus like some macabre buoy. It was the first time the throng had seen any of their slain brethren in the entirety of the hold, save for the remains of King Ulfgan. Uthor felt a tingle of dread reaching up his spine as he watched the dead dwarf, bobbing lightly in the rank water despite the illusion of stillness, and was reminded of the recent loss of Bulrik and Henkil. He tried to crush the memory quickly, but couldn't prevent his mind wandering back to those frantic moments at the waterfall, the pallid face of Rorek appearing through the spray with news of the clan leaders' deaths.

The rest of the way down the narrow path had been conducted in silent remembrance. So much death, and so needless – I have brought this fate upon them. I have brought it upon us all, Uthor thought darkly, averting his gaze to peer into the impenetrable murk. A raft of unseen terrors that might be harboured in the water's depths sprang unbidden into his mind. All dwarfs knew of the slumbering beasts that lay in the bowels of the Black Water, awaiting prey foolish enough to quest there.

'Let us quit this place with all haste,' said Emelda quietly at Uthor's shoulder. The thane of Kadrin turned to her and saw the concern for him etched upon her face.

'Yes,' Uthor agreed, his grim disposition diminishing before her countenance. 'But how are we to cross,' he added, moving away from the clan daughter to stand at the edge of a grand stairway that had once led down to the revelry of the hall but was now swallowed by a greenish mire. 'I can see no rafts.' Uthor crouched down and dipped one finger into the water, removing a thin piece of clouded film that overlaid the surface of the unnatural lagoon.

'We cannot swim it,' Emelda replied, gazing out across the stagnant plain, 'the distance is too long.'

'We would not get far in our armour, anyway,' Rorek piped up, 'even using the barrels for buoyancy.' The engineer was inspecting a statue that had collapsed on the stone platform, leastways the detached head and part of the torso had. Rapping it lightly with a small hammer from his tool belt, a dull gonging sound resonated around the chamber.

'Hollow,' Rorek muttered, scrutinising the statue head further. The fall had made a clean break at the neck and he was able to peer inside its massive confines. 'Perhaps... Uthor,' he added suddenly, turning to the thane, 'we'll need those barrels after all.' The engineer proffered a length of rope with a small metal grapnel attached. 'Have you ever been fishing?' he asked.

THE THWOMP OF whirling rope cut through the air, followed by a snap as Uthor let fly. His aim was true but the barrel shattered under the impact of the grapnel... again.

'You are a warrior born, son of Algrim,' said Emelda, who'd been watching the thane's efforts for several swings, while Rorek busied himself with the statue head. She had no clue what the mercurial engineer was planning, but she felt certain it would not adhere to the strictures of the Engineers' Guild. 'Even fishing for barrels, you cannot resist the killing stroke.'

Uthor looked askance at Emelda, slightly ruffled and reddening at the cheeks. He was about to swing again when he stopped himself and turned to face the clan daughter.

'You think you can do better?' he asked, offering the rope and grapnel, now lathered in the water's stagnant residue.

Emelda smiled and took the rope and hook. She then walked over to the edge of the platform and tested the weight of them in her hands. Taking a step back, she swung the rope around swiftly in a wide arc with practiced ease, the clinging filth attached to it flicking outwards in a vile spray. Emelda then let fly. She noticed Uthor watch it as it landed just behind a barrel.

'A good effort,' said the thane, puffing up his chest slightly and trying to keep the grin from his face.

Emelda didn't take the bait; she merely gathered the rope slowly, allowing the grapnel to trail through the water and snag on the end of the barrel, after which she drew it in effortlessly. When the barrel bobbed against the edge of the platform she turned to Uthor.

'A defter touch was required,' she explained.

Uthor muttered gruffly to himself as he stooped to pick up the barrel and set it on the platform.

'Where did you learn that?' Uthor asked as Emelda cast out again and snagged another barrel.

'My father taught me,' she replied, dragging her catch through the murky water. 'Fishing in the mountain streams and lakes of Everpeak.'

'You mean the High King?'

'No,' said Emelda, bringing the barrel to the water's edge for Uthor to retrieve. 'The High King is not my father.'

'My apologies, milady, when I saw you in the court of Karaz-a-Karak, I thought–'

'My father is dead.' The rope sagged briefly in Emelda's grip and she looked at Uthor. 'He was the king's cousin. When he was killed, King Skorri took me on as his ward in recognition of an old debt between them.'

'Dreng tromm,' uttered Uthor, head slightly bowed in respect. 'May I ask, milady, how did he die?'

'He was inspecting our family's mine holdings and there was a tunnel collapse. We lost thirteen brave dawi that day. When the prospectors recovered their bodies they found that some of the braces had been gnawed upon and a second section of tunnel undermining the upper shaft.'

'Rat-kin,' Uthor assumed.

'Yes.' Emelda's expression was pained but also flushed with contained rage. 'So you see I not only came here to ensure that the great days of the Karaz Ankor return, but on a matter of personal grudgement also.'

Uthor fell silent and then took his leave when Emelda turned away. He went over to Rorek to find out what he wanted with the barrels. The whip and pull of the rope and grapnel followed in his wake as Emelda worked out her anger.

'Do you have any beer skins?' Rorek asked, intent on an inverted distilling funnel set into a metal frame.

'You seek to drink us a way across the lagoon?' Uthor countered, a bemused look on his face as he reached onto his belt. 'Here,' he added, 'though they dried up long ago.'

'Good,' Rorek replied, taking the skins Uthor offered without looking. 'No use in wasting grog,' he added, working meticulously.

'That is the last of them,' said Emelda, appearing behind Uthor with one more barrel. The thane avoided her gaze for the moment, the weight of her grief adding to his own. She set the barrel down. When she rested her hand upon his shoulder, Uthor felt his mood lighten instantly.

'We are almost ready,' said Rorek, interrupting the silent exchange as he got to his feet and revealed the contraption he'd been labouring over.

The small funnel was set over a tiny fire that burned with a white-hot flame. Vaporous heat was visible emanating from a shallow metal cup in which the fire was contained that fed into one of Uthor's beer skins affixed to the narrow spout of the funnel. Uthor's eyes widened as, in seconds, the leather skin inflated and became fat with heat vapour.

Satisfied, Rorek bent down and plucked the skin from the spout and stoppered it quickly. He then raised the skin to his ear.

Uthor was nonplussed and exchanged a worried glance with Emelda. 'Grungni's rump, tell me you are not trying to converse with that skin. I thought only the lodefinder was prone to such madness.'

'I am listening to hear if any air is escaping,' Rorek explained, then lowered the skin to look at Uthor again. 'It is not,' he added.

'Fascinating, I am certain,' Uthor stated, 'but how is this to get us across the lagoon?'

'Alone, it will not,' Rorek told them. 'We need this.' The engineer pointed to the bronze statue head. The Zhufbar dwarf had lashed all of the barrels, save the last, retrieved by Emelda, to the outside and had bored a hole through the very top of the statue's helmet, wide enough for a rope to pass through.

'Have you been eating frongol, engineer?' Uthor asked, staring at the giant bronze head.

'Stand aside,' Rorek growled, muttering beneath his breath as he tramped past the thane. Once he'd reached the platform's edge, he unslung his crossbow.

'You'd best not be pointing that thing anywhere near me,' Uthor warned him.

Rorek ignored the baiting and hunted around on his voluminous tool belt. Finding what he was looking for he attached it to the crossbow by means of its ingenious racking mechanism. After ratcheting the ammunition back, the engineer braced himself and took careful aim, flicking up the sighting ring with his thumb. He pumped the trigger and the crossbow loosed, sending a large, harpoon-like bolt into the roof with a rippling length of rope chasing after it. The thick, metal quarrel stuck fast with a shudder of stone, and three spiked prongs flicked out of a concealed compartment inside the shaft to latch onto the rock like a pincer. The rope was attached to the other end of the quarrel by means of a small pulley.

'Grapnel bolt,' Rorek explained with no small amount of boastful pride, gathering up the slack in his hands until the rope was taut. 'Here, take this,' he added, passing Uthor a section of rope before rushing over to tether the opposite end to the statue head.

'And what am I to do with this, engineer?'

'Pull,' came the laconic response.

Uthor did as he was told, Emelda joining in when she realised what Rorek intended. The engineer added his own brawn to the task and as they heaved the rope running through the pulley the statue head was slowly lifted upright and then off the ground.

'Keep going,' Rorek snarled through clenched teeth; the bronze head was monstrously heavy. As it rose higher, the weight of the statue swung itself out over the lagoon.

Satisfied with its elevation, Rorek shouted, 'Stop!' adding, 'hold it there,' as he let go of the rope before taking the trailing end piling behind Uthor and Emelda. He then tied it around the upper remains of the statue that still sat on the platform until the rope was taut.

'Now,' Rorek said. 'Release it slowly.'

Uthor and Emelda did as they were asked. With a savage creak of metal as it tightened further at its anchor point, the statue head lurched down a few feet before it came to a halt. Rorek wiped a swathe of sweat from his forehead, and not from his earlier exertions.

'It holds,' he announced.

'I can see that, engineer,' said Uthor. 'What would you have us do now?'

'Now,' Rorek said, turning to face them both, 'we get wet.'

UTHOR TIED OFF a makeshift belt of inflated beer skins around his waist and chest as he prepared to walk down the grand stairway and into the wretched water.

'There is no honour in this garb,' he moaned. 'If I am slain and found like this by my ancestors there will be a reckoning against you and your clan, engineer.'

'Without them you will sink like a stone in your armour,' Rorek replied. 'And then where would your honour be?'

Uthor grumbled beneath his breath and started down the steps. Emelda awaited the outcome pensively behind him.

Ice blades stabbed into his legs as the thane of Kadrin waded into the water. Now up to his waist, the stagnant film sheathing the lagoon parted before him like clinging gossamer. At last he found the courage to plunge out into the open depths. Uthor felt the pull of his armour dragging him downward into the murk and for a moment he panicked, seeking the edge of the platform in an effort to heave himself up and out.

'Don't flap,' Rorek snapped at him. 'You will sink and drown.'

'Easy to say stood on dry land,' said Uthor, spluttering water. 'I have already had my dunkin' – dawi are not meant for water.' Taking a breath, spitting the turgid fluid from his mouth, Uthor managed to calm down and spread his arms wide as Rorek had instructed him. Pushing away slightly from the edge, incredibly he found he was afloat.

'By the beard of Grimnir, I can't believe that worked,' Uthor said, relieved and still spluttering – the beer skins only just putting his head and shoulders above the waterline.

'Neither can I,' Rorek muttered beneath his breath.

'Speak up,' growled Uthor, bobbing up and down slightly like a cork in soup, using his arms like oars to slowly position himself beneath the hollow statue head hanging above.

'I said, now milady can try.'

Uthor grumbled some more and fell silent as he waited for Emelda, similarly laden with inflated beer skins, to join him in the water.

Rorek came last of all, the engineer seeming as if he almost enjoyed the swim. All three positioned themselves beneath the shadow of the hanging statue head, staring up into its vast hollows. The engineer ferreted around in the water, reaching for something on his belt and eventually pulled out a throwing axe.

'Give that to me,' Uthor barked, 'you would as likely hit one of us.'

Flushed with embarrassment, Rorek passed the weapon to Uthor.

'You had best be right about this, engineer,' Uthor warned, holding the axe in one hand. 'Now you will see the killing stroke,' he boasted, winking at Emelda.

With a grunt, Uthor let fly. The throwing axe span through the air and sheared the tethered rope in two, sending the hollow statue head plummeting earthward. In the instant before the massive thing plunged into the water, the three dwarfs huddled together instinctively. Uthor noticed Rorek had his eyes closed and his fingers firmly crossed. 'Grungni's balls...' he muttered as the statue head crashed down.

'WAIT, I HEAR something,' Hakem hissed, edging up to the end of the tunnel before peering surreptitiously around the curved corner.

At the end of a short, wide corridor was the overflow grate. Two mighty hammerers fashioned from the very rock of the mountain stood sentinel before the massive gate that dominated the entire back wall of the tunnel. Their hammers were part of the actual mechanism that allowed the water through. At this moment they were clasped together – the Barduraz Varn was obviously still closed.

Huge cogs of iron with broad, fat teeth were bolted to the left facing wall and a bewildering array of interlinking chains and conjoined pistons fed from them to the inner-workings of the grate itself.

Dwarfed by the immense structure was a small cohort of rat-kin, obviously sent to guard the grate from interference – a dozen clanrats and a pair of Clan Skryre engineers bearing another fire-spewing contrivance, similar to that which had caused such havoc in the Wide Western Way.

Hakem rolled back around the curve to where the others were waiting.

'Twelve guards,' the Barak Varr dwarf reported, his demeanour increasingly taciturn and pugnacious since losing the Honakinn Hammer.

Gromrund cracked his knuckles and readied his great hammer, sloshing determinedly through the floodwater. 'There is little time for it,' he said matter-of-factly, 'but needs must.'

Hakem stopped him.

'They also have sorcerous machinery of some sort.'

'Pah,' snorted Gromrund, marching past the merchant thane. 'Skaven engineering is cheap and unreliable. Doubtless, it will misfire before it can do any damage.'

Hakem blocked him again.

'Step aside, ufdi,' Gromrund snapped irritably. 'You will not soil your beard in this fight,' he added, though after the mining shaft the entire skorong was so lathered in soot it would be hard to notice either way.

'I have seen its effects with my own eyes,' Hakem warned, his gaze unwavering. 'And it is deadly. Armour, for one, is no proof against it. Burned to ash by the sorcerous fire of the skaven is not an honourable death.'

Gromrund backed down, planting his hammer head into the ground so he could lean on the haft.

'So then, ufdi, what are we to do? Wait here until the rat-kin die of boredom?'

'Lure them and thin their numbers.' Thalgrim's voice broke up the building tension.

Hakem and Gromrund turned to look at the lodefinder, who was grinning ferally. He lifted up his helmet and at once the dwarfs were assailed by a pungent, if not entirely unpleasant aroma.

'Lucky chuf,' Thalgrim explained, holding out the piece of moulding cheese in his hand.

Ralkan's eyes widened when he saw it, acutely aware of his groaning stomach.

'The skaven have a taste for it,' Thalgrim added, darkly, deciding not to mention his suspicions about the ambush. Plopping the remains of the chunk into his mouth, Thalgrim chewed for a moment then swallowed, savouring the taste.

Ralkan's shoulders sagged, his loudly rumbling belly seemingly inconsolable.

Gromrund was agog. 'Are you mad, lodefinder, you have just eaten our bait?'

'I did not want to waste it,' Thalgrim replied, licking his gums and teeth for any lingering traces of the ancient cheese. 'Besides, it is not wasted,' he added, breathing hard into the face of the hammerer, who gagged at once.

'Very well,' said Gromrund, putting up his hand to ward off any further emissions. 'Go and do what you must. You stay back, lorekeeper,' he said to Ralkan who was happy to oblige.

Thalgrim nodded, creeping stealthily to the end of the curved tunnel. Once he'd reached the end, he peered around once to see that the skaven guards were still there and then blew a breath, thickly redolent of chuf, towards them, hoping that the shallow breeze would carry it. He watched silently from the shadows, acutely aware of the other dwarfs behind him with weapons readied.

At first there was nothing. The skaven just chittered quietly to each other in their ear-wrenching tongue. But then the snout of one of the clanrats twitched and it sniffed at the air. Then another did the same, and another. There was a bout of frenetic squeaking and several of the rat-kin abandoned their posts to follow the cloying stink wafting towards them.

Thalgrim gave them another blast for good measure and then retreated around the corner.

'They come,' he whispered, unslinging his pick-mattock.

The dwarfs hugged the shadows, keeping to the very edge of the tunnel. The sound of padding, splashing feet carried on the cheese-tainted air towards them, getting closer with every second as their curious enemies approached.

Thalgrim held his breath when he saw the first clanrat emerge from around the corner. Incredibly the creature's beady eyes were closed, using smell alone for guidance as it tracked the chuf's scent. Four of its flea-infested brethren followed, wielding a mixture of spears, blades and heavier-looking glaives.

Once they had all passed the threshold of the tunnel, the dwarfs attacked.

Thalgrim smashed the neck of one of the rats from behind, crushing its spine inward as it collapsed with a mewling cry. A second fell to Hakem's borrowed axe, the blade cutting a deep wound in the clanrat's belly through which its innards spilled. The creature looked dumbfounded at the dwarf as it tried to gather up its organs. One of the Sootbeards buried his pick in its forehead to silence it. Gromrund killed another two; one he choked with the wutroth haft of his great hammer, a second he bludgeoned with the hammer head. The last was cut high and low by the remaining Sootbeard dwarfs, its spear falling from nerveless fingers before it could retaliate.

'Tidy work,' muttered Gromrund, wiping a slick of expelled blood from his breastplate. 'That leaves seven, plus the war engine.'

'Let's take them now,' Thalgrim hissed urgently. 'They will only have time for one shot.'

The rat-kin had caught the scent of blood on the breeze and were squeaking at each other agitatedly, pointing towards the tunnel with clawed fingers.

'For Grimnir!' Gromrund bellowed, overwhelmed by battle-fever, and raced around the corner to meet his foes. The others followed – all except Ralkan, who awaited the outcome of the skirmish pensively – making their oaths as they went.

Screeching skaven levelled spears and blades as the dwarfs charged, before parting to allow the fire cannon through. A mighty whoosh of flame swallowed the cackling retort of the Clan Skryre engineers as they unleashed their war engine gleefully and lit up the tunnel in a blinding flare of angry green light. Thalgrim threw himself aside, flooring

Gromrund in the process, but two of the Sootbeards were engulfed in the deadly conflagration and died screaming.

Rising from the floodwater, the hammerer parried a spear thrust with his hammer haft before stamping down on his assailant's shin, breaking it. He finished the clanrat with an overhead blow to the skull. Red ooze flowed thickly from the rat-kin's ruined head as it languished in the water.

Up close, Hakem launched his shield like a discus at the fire cannon. The spinning weapon severed the first engineer's head and embedded in the chest of the second. So mauled, the pair fell back and splashed into the water in a rapidly spreading pool of their own fluids.

There was a gurgled cry as the last Sootbeard was impaled by a spear to the neck. A burly skaven shrugged the dwarf's corpse off the blade contemptuously before rounding on Thalgrim. The lodefinder ducked a savage swipe and came under the blow to ram the head of his mattock into the creature's chin. Dazed, the rat-kin staggered back but, blowing out a billowing line of blood and snot, recovered its composure and came at Thalgrim again. A blur of steel arrested its charge, as the creature was smashed against the wall, a thrown axe *thunking* into its torso. The lodefinder turned to see Hakem snarl as the rat-kin slumped down and was still, and nodded his thanks. The merchant thane nodded back, grimly.

The skaven were all dead. Gromrund finished the last, crushing its skull with his boot as it tried to crawl away through the floodwater. He spat on the corpse afterward and then turned to the others.

'They were still good deaths,' he remarked, regarding the charred corpses of the two Sootbeards and the floating, impaled body of the other.

'We must find a way to break the mechanism,' said Hakem coldly, straight back to business. 'And I think I know of such a way,' he added.

The other two dwarfs followed his gaze to the still twitching Clan Skryre engineers and the volatile fire cannon still strapped to their bodies.

'STEADY…' WARNED THALGRIM as he carefully lifted the broad barrel of the skaven cannon where its volatile mixture was held. 'Easy does it.'

'Filthy rat-kin, I doubt I will ever get the stink from my beard and clothes,' moaned Hakem, carrying one of the dead Clan Skryre engineers and having subsequently wrenched his shield free of its wretched corpse.

'Consider yourself lucky, merchant,' Gromrund countered, lugging the other corpse as he tried to arch his neck away from the vile burden. 'Mine has no head!'

Between them, the three dwarfs heaved the bulky skaven war engine and its mouldering crew to the network of cogs and pistons that were the mechanism for the overflow. Ralkan – having been summoned once the fight was over – was with them, sat on a chunk of fallen rock as he held a burning brand aloft. The lorekeeper stayed back from the heavy

Dwarfs

lifting work, instead recording the names of the slain Sootbeards in the book of remembering that he rested on his lap.

'You are certain this will work,' grumbled Gromrund, on the verge of wedging the entire foul assembly into the grinding and massive cog teeth.

'Aye, I'm certain,' growled Thalgrim, a little put out by the hammerer's obvious lack of confidence. 'We Sootbeards have a close affinity with rock and stone, that much is true, but I also know something of engineering works, master hammerer,' the lodefinder added indignantly, before lumping the barrel and its various attached pipes and paraphernalia into the mechanism.

'Quickly, now,' Thalgrim said, edging backwards urgently. The cogs stalled for a moment, an ugly screeching noise emanating from the mechanism as it tried to chew flesh, bone and wood. 'It won't hold long,' he added, reaching out for Ralkan's torch as the other two dwarfs disappeared from beyond his eye-line. The lorekeeper had since packed away the book of remembering and he too was backing off.

Thalgrim grasped the brand and flung it, end over end, into the wrecked skaven cannon, which was even now haemorrhaging flammable liquid. As he threw the torch, Thalgrim turned and ran before diving into the shallow water. The others rapidly followed suit. The flame caught, igniting the chemicals in the barrel immediately, devouring the crude artifice and its crew hungrily.

Thunder cracked as the force of the massive explosion tore into the tunnel, amplified as it resonated off the stout walls, so powerful that it vibrated armour and teeth. Chunks of dislocated rock plummeted into the water in the aftermath, fire blossomed briefly and dust motes fell like a veil of shedding skin.

Thalgrim was the first to poke his head above the water and check that it was over.

'Clear,' he said, coughing back a cloud of dust and thick smoke.

'It is fortunate we are not dead!' barked Gromrund, after spitting out several mouthfuls of rank floodwater. 'My ears still ring from the blast,' he added, waggling a finger in one.

'At least it worked,' said Hakem, without joy. The merchant thane was on his feet and surveying the carnage wrought upon the overflow mechanism.

'Dreng tromm,' Gromrund muttered breathlessly as he went to stand beside him.

The stout dwarfen mechanism, that which had been built in the reign of Hraddi Ironhand, that which had withstood the wrath of the ages and even endured the Time of Woes, was ruined. A blackened scar overlaid a twisted mess of metal and broken stone. It was all that remained of the once great artifice of the engineers of Karak Varn.

Ralkan was beside himself and could not speak through tears of profound remorse. All of the dwarfs felt it; another small part of the Karaz Ankor meeting with ruination.

Is this how it is all to end, thought Gromrund? We dawi forced to lay waste to our own domains?

'It is sealed,' stated Hakem flatly, breaking the hammerer's solemn pondering. 'We had best move on,' he added, turning away from the gut-wrenching vista.

'Cold is the wind that blows through your house,' uttered Gromrund as the merchant thane walked away.

Hakem did not respond.

'How will we know when we have reached our destination?' Uthor's voice was tinny and resonant within the close confines of the giant 'diving' helm Rorek had constructed.

'It is simple,' the engineer remarked, even the muscles in his face straining as, together with his companions, he half lugged, half pushed the immense hollow helmet of bronze. 'We either reach the trapdoor at the south wall or we don't. The air will not last in here indefinitely,' he said.

At that Uthor looked down briefly at the water that had now reached his upper torso. It had been rising ever since the helm had crashed on top of them; its descent arrested by the numerous barrels that Rorek had assured them provided flotation. Despite that, though, the three dwarfs still needed to heave and push the helm forward, occasionally grinding its severed base against the flagstones beneath when the massive chunk of statue dipped.

Thanks to the Zhufbar dwarf's ingenuity, the dwarfs were able to traverse the murky depths of the lagoon through Brondold's Hall in what the engineer termed a 'submersible'. The thane of Kadrin had no clue to the word's meaning, nor had he any desire to discover it. All he knew was that a pocket of air was trapped in the upper reaches of the hollowed helm that allowed them to breath, whilst submerged far below the waterline.

'Your assurances provide much comfort, engineer,' Uthor growled.

'Speak less,' Rorek snapped abruptly. 'There is only a finite amount of air and the more we use, the less we will have,' he added, indicating the steadily rising waterline.

'Bah,' Uthor muttered. 'Dawi were not meant to be submerged in a tomb of bronze and iron.'

Emelda kept her mouth clamped shut throughout the exchange. Sweat peeled off her forehead in streaking lines that ran down her face. Not from exertion; she too was a warrior born and the equal of any male. No, it was from wide-eyed fear of being trapped here in the watery gloom, of her last breath being a mouthful of rank and foul-tasting water. There was no honour in it. As she worked, just that little bit harder than Uthor and Rorek, to get them to their destination, she surveyed the inner hollows of the diving helm nervously. Tiny fissures had already begun to appear in the ageing bronze, and tiny rivulets of water ran weakly through the smallest of cracks. One of those cracks grew wider, even as she maintained her fearful vigil, so wide the water was nigh-on gushing. She opened her mouth to shout a warning but no sound came out at first. Desperately, and through a supreme effort of will, she found her voice.

'It is splitting!'

Rorek saw the danger instantly and redoubled his efforts. 'Heave,' he bellowed, the timbre of his voice thunderous and urgent inside the helm. 'The south wall cannot be far.'

Uthor grunted, shouldering as much of the burden as he could. A dull screeching sound, muffled by fathoms of floodwater, came to the surface as the dwarfs leant their weight to one side of the helm and pitched it at an angle against the flagstones underfoot.

They panted and gasped with the intense effort. The water level rose, hitting their shoulders. In a few more seconds of frantic endeavour it had reached their necks.

'For all your worth!' Uthor cried, smashing his body into the side of the giant helm, spluttering as the water came over his mouth and nose.

Muffled silence filled the statue helm as the last of the dwarfs' air was expended. Not only was it their lifeline, but it had also provided additional buoyancy. Without it, the three dwarfs took the full weight of the massive bronze helm.

Uthor felt as if leaden anchors had been attached to his ankles as he dragged one heavy foot in front of the other, his urgency suddenly blighted with agonising slowness. His lungs burned; there was little air left in his body. Then he felt the ground beneath his feet change subtly. Stamping down, something bent and yielded beneath him. He tried to peer through the gloomy water but all he saw was a cloud-filled murk. He raised Ulfgan's axe; it was like lifting a tree. The runes etched on the blade shone diffusely, like a submerged beacon, as he struck down towards his feet.

The ground broke away, broad spikes of it funnelled upward into the water-filled helm, and Uthor fell. Rorek and Emelda were lost to him in the clinging, green-tinged darkness. Something pulled at him, a forceful current propelling the dwarf to Valaya knew where. He barrelled and spun at first, smacking into unseen obstacles. Pain flared in his side as something sharp and jagged bit into him.

Fighting hard, Uthor got his bearings and started to swim, pumping legs and arms determinedly as the last of his air was used up. He was in a tunnel. So narrow and tight it could only be the one that Ralkan had spoken off. The way seemed long, black spots beginning to form in Uthor's hazy vision. Soon he too would be lost. His legs felt heavy, his arms seemed to hang limply at his sides and the sense of falling, falling deep into the abyssal gloom overwhelmed him...

Light flared, dim and washed out. Air rushed, unabated, into his body as Uthor was suddenly lifted free of oblivion, coughing and spluttering into renewed existence.

A figure stood over him, serene and benevolent, her arms outstretched and welcoming. Long, golden hair cascaded down her shoulders and a halo rimmed her head, her countenance refulgent in its reflected glory.

'Valaya…' Uthor breathed, bleary-eyed and slightly incoherent.

'Uthor,' said the figure. Strong arms shook the thane of Kadrin.

'Uthor.' The tone was urgent but low.

Emelda crouched over him, her face creased with concern.

Uthor came to his senses, abruptly aware that Rorek supported his back. He'd lost his helmet somewhere along the way, his shield too – thank Grimnir he still had his axe. Together, his two companions held him up, above the shallow water of a vast and expansive reservoir. Hraddi's reservoir, just as the lorekeeper had described. They had reached the site of the Barduraz Varn.

Uthor got to his feet and found the low-lying water came up to his knees.

'Keep down,' Emelda hissed, Rorek moving silently to her side, so low only the tips of his shoulders pierced the waterline.

Uthor did as he was told and crouched next to the clan daughter on the opposite side.

'We are not alone,' she hissed, pointing across the massive, flat reservoir.

Uthor followed her gesture. There, just beyond the edge of where the water ended in a rat-kin made platform of shovelled rock and earth, slaves toiled and hooded Clan Skryre overseers chattered. Thickly-armoured, black-furred skaven carrying curved swords and a number of their smaller brethren equipped with spears milled around in rough cohorts. Two other Skryre agents stood close by the bulkier skaven guards, drenched in filthy robes and carrying bizarre-looking staffs seemingly fashioned from a riot of crude skaven technology. Crackling energy played across spinning diodes and jutting forks. Uthor was reminded of the skaven sorcerer they had faced during their flight from Karak Varn all those months ago. He bit back the memory of Lokki's death during that dark retreat and refocussed his attention.

Mercifully, the ratmen were intent on their labours and had not seen the dwarfs emerge from the underground river.

Uthor's eyes widened as they tracked further and took in a massive, infernal construction that dominated the back of the immense chamber. Huge wooden wheels bolted together with crude strips of copper and iron were connected to the towering, ramshackle device. They ran rapid and wild with the frantic efforts of the slaves and giant rats imprisoned within. Arcs of eldritch lightning flew across spiked prongs far above as the desperate slaves were urged to greater endeavour with the lash and crackling staves of the Skryre agents. All the while in the background, behind a raft of clumsy observation towers and platforms, great pistons thudded up and down in relentless unison and the water in which the device was sat, where the makeshift skaven embankment fell away, gradually drained.

'Valaya preserve us,' Uthor breathed. It was a huge pump; the rat-kin had devised a way to clear the flood waters from Karak Varn. His heart stammered when he perceived what was stood behind the wretched skaven contraption. It was the great sluice gate itself – the Barduraz Varn.

GROMRUND CURSED LOUDLY, striking his head for the seventh time as he and Thalgrim climbed up the narrow shaft of Dibna's Drop.

'You would find the going easier if you removed that warhelm, hammerer,' the voice of the lodefinder echoed down to Gromrund.

'I shall never remove it,' came the caustic response of the hammerer, the warhelm of his ancestors still ringing loudly in his ears. 'Some oaths were not meant to be broken,' he added in a murmur.

They'd left Hakem and Ralkan behind, waiting at the crossroads beneath the lofty shaft through which the two dwarfs now toiled. Ralkan was in no condition to climb; the book of remembering was a weighty burden to bear and with only one hand a climb upwards was too difficult for Hakem. Besides, as he'd muttered when Thalgrim and Gromrund had departed, someone needed to stay behind and guard the lorekeeper. The first part of the climb had been conducted via the lodefinder's rope, tied off at the mine shaft of the Rockcutter Waystation; the second meant scaling a length of thick chain hanging down from Dibna's Chamber, doubtless a remnant of when there had once been a lift cage.

Thalgrim went hand over hand, his pace quick and assured with the ready practice of repetition. The lodefinder seemed to bend and swing from the path of every jutting crag, every errant spike of rock, though the way upwards was largely clear of obstruction.

Gromrund found it harder going in his much heavier full plate, great hammer smacking against his back as he climbed. More than once he slipped, and each time he found his grip again. Thalgrim made no such mistakes and was soon far ahead of him in the soot-drenched darkness, the flame of his helmet candle flickering faintly above like a firefly.

When Gromrund at last reached the zenith of the shaft and Dibna's Chamber in the third deep, he found the lodefinder waiting with hands in tunic pockets and a smouldering pipe pinched between his lips.

'There,' he said, nodding in the direction of the stone statue of Dibna the Inscrutable, still just as they'd left it, bearing the weight of the room. 'A mattock blow to the left ankle, precisely three and three-eighths inches from the tip of Dibna's boot, will collapse the statue and give us enough time to climb back down.'

'And you know this, just by looking at it?' said Gromrund, a little breathlessly.

'Aye, I do,' Thalgrim replied, supping on his pipe. 'That and the rock–'

'Please, lad,' uttered Gromrund, 'don't say it.'

The lodefinder shrugged and test swung his mattock a few times before advancing forward carefully. 'Precision and a deftness of touch is the key,' he muttered.

Gromrund gripped his shoulder before he got any further.

'Wait,' snapped the hammerer.

'What is it? This deep is likely crawling with grobi and rat-kin by now, we should not linger.'

'I have not yet heard the wyvern-horn. We cannot release the waters until the slayer and the rest are ready.'

'Then I hope it is soon, for if the vermin come – and come they will – then we will have no choice but to act,' said Thalgrim.

'Then we had best hope they do not,' muttered Gromrund.

CHAPTER THIRTEEN

AZGAR EMERGED BACK into the foundry, Thorig at his heels with Drimbold and Halgar bringing up the rear.

'Close and bar the gate,' the longbeard growled, through rasping breaths. He was bent almost double, hands clamped to his knees and wheezing.

Drimbold went to his aid but recoiled before the venerable dwarf's bark.

'Leave me be, half-dwarf,' he snarled. 'I do not need the likes of you to help me stand and fight. I was fighting battles before some of your ancestors were beardlings.'

With a resounding clang, the gates to the foundry were shut and the bar slid across. Enraged skaven chittering emanating from beyond it was cut off abruptly as the way into the further deeps was sealed.

'Make ready,' bellowed Azgar, a half glance at Halgar to make certain he was still fit and able. The gnarled old longbeard was back upright and swinging his axe to work the cramps from his arm and shoulder.

Good enough, thought the slayer and marshalled the meagre dwarf forces that stood before him in four lines of iron and steel, axes and hammers ready, shields held to the fore.

Towards the barred gate the foundry plaza narrowed to such an extent it was possible to cover its breadth with twenty-five shields. Three further lines, similarly-armed, stood stoically behind it. If one dwarf fell, another would take his place. They were to hold the skaven as long as they could, defending solidly as only dwarfs knew how and infuriate the vermin hordes so they committed all their forces to the attack. Should the lines fail – and fail they would, Azgar knew – then the forgemaster's platform would be their egress and the site of their last stand, one worthy of a saga the slayer hoped.

'The rat-kin come,' Azgar said as he appraised the dwarfen ranks, 'and they are angered,' he added with a feral grin. A rousing cheer met his words.

Relentless thudding came from the foundry gate. Metal creaked and moaned against the determined assault and the bar bent outwards slightly with every blow.

'They will soon be upon us,' hissed Halgar to the slayer, who had taken up his position in the middle of the first line.

'Yes,' Azgar replied – a glint in his eye as he stood alongside the longbeard. His steely gaze never left the gate. When it shuddered and the bar began to split he tightened his grip on the haft of his axe. 'Let them come.'

Another crash and the gate shook hard. The dwarfs remained in silence, jaws locked and hearts racing in anticipation of the imminent battle. For most, if not all, it would likely be their last.

The gate was rocked again.

It was met with stony silence. The tension was almost unbearable.

'Shed blood with me,' Halgar cried out suddenly to the throng. 'Shed blood and be my brother. We are the sons of Grungni. Alone we are rocks; together we are as enduring as a mountain!'

'Aye!' came the response as almost a hundred dwarf voices responded in unison.

The gate shuddered for the last time and was ripped outwards, wrenched almost off its hinges. From the black void of the unknown came the skaven, squeaking and snarling in apoplectic rage.

'Quarrellers!' Halgar bellowed, and a host of crossbow-bearing dwarfs of the Flintheart clan came forward from the second rank, their clan leader Kaggi amongst them.

'Loose!' cried Kaggi and the snapping retort of flung quarrels filled the air. So densely packed, a rat-kin fell to every bolt but the skaven did not falter and the dead and dying were crushed. With no time for a second volley, the Flinthearts retreated behind the first rank shield wall to draw axes and hammers.

The furred skaven wave fell upon the throng without pause and engulfed it. Blades clashed, shields clanged and blood slicked the flagstones of the foundry plaza in torrents. The dwarfs reeled before the sudden, furious onslaught. Many warriors fell clutching grievous wounds, only to be stomped to death by the relentless rat-kin masses driving forward. Other dwarfs, the Flinthearts amongst them, fought hard to fill the gaps in their shield wall but the skaven pressed with unremitting wrath, their frenzy evident in their foaming muzzles. Halgar was at the centre of it, separated from Azgar somehow but with Drimbold now at his side.

'Remember, King Snaggi Ironhandson at the Bryndal Vale,' the long-beard bellowed as he fought. 'Remember his oaths, my brothers, as I remember mine. Sing your death songs loud, bellow your defiance to the deep, 'til the sound echoes throughout the Halls of the Ancestors!' he said, hacking left and right, using his shield as a bludgeon, his axe stitching a red haze in the air around him. 'Join me now, brave dawi. Join me in death!'

A rallying cry erupted from the dwarf ranks with all the power and thunder of a landslide. Clan warriors dug their heels in and repulsed the skaven horde with all the steel they could muster. Halgar drove at the vermin with added purpose to let the other dawi see his defiance. The stink of killing got into his nostrils and he felt empowered. Perhaps it was infectious; even the Grey dwarf seemed full with battle lust.

What Drimbold lacked in skill, he made up for with effort. He guarded Halgar's side with such vehemence that even the longbeard couldn't help but notice his fervour.

A surge to the left of the skaven horde got Halgar's attention as he cleaved another clanrat down. He felt it ripple down the front rank. Following the source of the tremor he saw the right dwarfen flank collapsing as the rat-kin scurried their way around the edges of the shield wall.

'Reinforce the flank,' the longbeard bellowed above the roar of combat. 'Don't let them get behind us.'

Kaggi saw the danger and, shouting commands, gathered his warriors to bolster the failing flank. As the brave clan leader led the way a spear flung by some unseen hand skewered him in the neck. Kaggi fell, clutching the wound, his lifeblood spilling eagerly. He was quickly lost to Halgar but the clan leader's warriors, enraged at Kaggi's death, pressed with fury and the line was strengthened again.

Halgar averted his gaze. The sorrow pricking at his heart turned to fury as he cut a black-furred skaven from groin to sternum.

'Uzkul!' cried the longbeard, wrenching his axe free in a swathe of dark blood.

'Uzkul!' echoed Drimbold, mashing a clanrat in the maw with the butt of his axe before finishing it with an overhand swipe to the head.

Still the rat-kin came on and Drimbold slipped and fell on the fluid-slick stone. A host of hate-filled skaven faces bore down on him but then recoiled before a swirling mass of steel.

Azgar wove amongst them, slightly ahead of the first rank and swinging his chained axe in a brutal, repeating arc. Limbs rained down upon the plaza floor as the grim-faced slayer was showered in blood.

Drimbold staggered up, two clan dwarfs helping him.

'Stay on your feet,' Halgar snarled, taking a moment to rub his eyes.

The Grey dwarf nodded dazedly. When he went to rejoin the fight he saw the skaven had gathered together and were backing off. The dwarf line, having weathered the first attack, did not press and a gap soon formed between the bitter foes.

'Nice of them to give us a breather, eh, lad?' remarked the longbeard, wiping the blood slick from his axe and readjusting his shield.

'Why don't they come?' hissed Drimbold through gritted teeth. The tense lull was almost more than the Grey dwarf could take. Only when the lumbering shapes came slowly from the skaven ranks, bustling their smaller kin aside violently to reach the killing, did Drimbold understand why.

Huge rat ogres, ten-strong, bristling with muscle and raw, terrifying brawn bellowed challenges and beat their chests with slab-like claws. Confronted by these horrifying, freakish creations the dwarf line took an involuntary half step back.

Azgar, who had rejoined the line, saw it.

'Khazukan Kazakit-ha!' bellowed the slayer, invoking the ancient war cry of the dawi, and stepped forward a pace.

'Khazuk!' came the unified response from the throng who matched him.

'Khazuk!' they cried again and took a second pace.

'Khazuk!' came the final cry as the dwarfs stepped into the killing zone of the rat-kin ogres.

WITH JUST THEIR noses above the waterline, Uthor, Rorek and Emelda stalked across the shallow reservoir towards the guards lingering at the rock plateau. As they drew closer the three dwarfs fanned out at some unseen command.

Uthor's gaze was fixed upon three clanrats, leant on spears and bickering with one another at the base of one of the ramshackle observation platforms. Only a few feet away, the thane of Kadrin arose slowly and quietly from the water, his beard and tunic drenched. One of the clanrats turned just as Uthor raised his axe and balked when confronted by the thane's cold eyes.

That expression remained on the creature's cooling corpse after Uthor buried his rune axe into its forehead. Ripping the glittering blade free, he beheaded another and downed the third with a savage blow to the back after it turned to flee.

He looked over to his companions. Three more rat-kin corpses lay at Emelda's feet in various states of mutilation. Rorek, too, had dealt with his guards. Two skaven pin-cushioned with quarrels floated in the shallow water, exuding blood. With this outer ring of sentries dispatched, the trio of dwarfs grimly moved on.

Crouched low as they sneaked across the rock plateau, the dwarfs converged and reached the threshold of the skaven engine. Up close, the infernal machine gave off an almighty clamour that masked their booted footfalls and shook their armour. As they approached, one of the hooded Clan Skryre agents turned and squeaked a warning. Rorek stitched a line of crossbow bolts across its neck and torso as it went to raise its staff.

Alerted by the sound the black-furred skaven turned, together with their smaller clanrat brethren, and began herding the slaves towards the dwarfs. The rancid, emaciated creatures dropped barrows and sodden sacking filled with earth, and took up spades and picks, the fear of their masters overwhelming their terror of facing the well-armed dwarfs.

FLIKRIT WATCHED AS Gnawquell twitched and fell, a host of feathered shafts jutting from his body like spines. The Clan Skryre warlock grinned with glee at his fellow acolyte's demise. 'Favour finds the survivor,' that was his motto. You cannot be elevated in the eyes of the Thirteen if you're dead. When he noticed the three battle-hardened dwarf-things stalking towards him, ripping through his slaves like they were nothing, he readily squirted the musk of fear.

Mastering the terror that was threatening to loosen his bowels, Flikrit backed away. Delving into his robes he found a chunk of glowing warpstone and ate it up hungrily. The tainted rock tingled on his tongue: bitter, acrid, empowering. Fear ebbed away to faint, gnawing doubt as visions were visited upon the warlock. He raised his staff, full of warpstone-fuelled confidence and incanted quickly. A nimbus of raw energy played briefly around Flikrit's outstretched paw before he channelled it into his staff and unleashed an arcing bolt of lightning.

Green-black energy arrowed into the air, charging it with power and the redolence of sulphur, and split a slave before it earthed harmlessly away.

Flikrit snarled his displeasure and screeched again, thrusting his staff towards the marauding dwarf-things carving up his slaves; slaves paid for with his tokens! Lightning flashed and one of the dwarf-things was struck as the eldritch bolt exploded into the earth nearby, spewing razor chips of rock.

Flikrit cackled with glee, leaping up and down but scowled when he realised the dwarf-thing was alive and getting to its feet with the help of one of its kin. This new foe broke through the stormvermin ranks that were now bearing the full brunt of the dwarf-thing's fury with the slaves dead or running. It was beardless with long, golden fur hanging from beneath its helmet. Determined anger was etched on the beardless-thing's face and Flikrit squirted the musk of fear again as the effects of the warpstone chunk wore off. The warlock hunted around quickly for another hunk of the tainted substance and plopped it nervously into his mouth with quaking fingers. The dwarf-thing was almost upon him as he unleashed another lightning bolt.

Flikrit squeaked with relief and joy as his assailant was engulfed by a furious storm of warp energy. He closed his eyes against the flare of light, expecting to see a charred ruin when he opened them again.

Armour smoking, the dwarf-thing was alive! A faint glow emanated from a gilded belt around its waist. Having been brought to its knees, it got up in an even fouler rage than before, axe swinging meaningfully. Flikrit backed away, looking right and left for aid. Most of the stormvermin were dead. All of the Clan Rictus warriors were slain. He was alone.

Desperate for survival, the warlock dug his filthy paw deep into his robes and pulled out the last of his warpstone. Three massive chunks went into his mouth. Flikrit swallowed loudly. Dark energy rushed into his body, setting his nerves on edge, like he was on fire. About to unleash a final bolt of terrifying power, Flikrit realised he *was* on fire. He tried to pat out the greenish flames in his smouldering fur but to no avail. Opening his mouth to scream, the warp-blaze ravaged him utterly, stripping fur and flesh, and rendering bones to ash.

EMELDA SHIELDED HER eyes from the skaven torch before her, lightning arcing wildly from its body and striking the roof of the chamber. The wretched sorcerer crumpled into a blackened heap of nothing as the deadly magic it had tried to unleash consumed it. The clan daughter's armour was still hot from the lightning blast and she smelled scorched hair before muttering an oath to Valaya. As the skaven magic dissipated, the runes at her cincture dulled and became dormant once more.

Slightly dazed she looked around at the carnage.

Rorek shot down a group of fleeing clanrats with his rapid-firing cross-bow before rushing forward to finish a rat-kin slave crawling across the ground with the weapon's weighted butt.

Uthor dispatched the last of the burly black skaven, Ulfgan's axe flashing fiercely as it shredded armour and bone with ease.

They were victorious. The skaven were all dead. Only those trapped within the thunderously turning wheels remained, utterly oblivious to the battle and locked in a hellish, spinning nightmare.

But the destruction was not at an end. Even as Emelda stowed Dunrik's axe, slabs of rock broke away from the ceiling where the lightning had damaged it, plummeting into the pool of water surrounding the pumping engine. A massive chunk, one of the dilapidated archways of the vast chamber, crashed down onto one of the wheels that drove the pistons crushing it and the creatures within utterly.

'We must destroy that abomination,' bellowed Uthor as he fought the din of the engine, his steely gaze softening as it went from the skaven construction to Emelda.

'Are you…?'

'Valaya protects me,' she replied.

'We need only to open the Barduraz Varn,' said Rorek, the sporadic lightning generated by the two remaining wheels casting his face in ephemeral flashes. 'The flood waters will bring what is left down.'

'How are we to reach the gate?' asked Emelda.

'That stairway will take us to the opening mechanism,' Rorek answered, pointing to a set of narrow, stone steps – partially obscured by the extremities of the pumping engine – leading to the huge bar of gold, copper and bronze that prevented the Barduraz Varn from opening.

Uthor at the lead, the three dwarfs rushed the steps quickly, taking them two at a time.

'Mind the wheel!' shouted Rorek above the incredible noise of the engine.

Part of the stairway brought the dwarfs perilously close to one of the whirring generator wheels. Uthor had to press his back against the stone to make sure he wasn't dragged off the steps and into it. Edging by slowly, he felt the whip and pull of the air as it was smashed against his face, thick with the stink of burning flesh. Through the blurring effect of the rapidly spinning wheel he caught snatches of the slaves labouring madly within. Their bloodshot eyes bulged with intense effort, panting for breath through froth-covered mouths, fur pressed down under a thick lather of sweat. The thane saw other shapes in the kaleidoscopic vista, too, the remains of the wretched creatures that couldn't maintain the pace or that fell, their broken bodies bouncing up and down with the wheel's momentum and slowly being smashed to pulp.

Traversing the deadly stretch of stairway, Uthor finally reached the locking mechanism of the gate, the way opening out into a simple stone platform with a large wheel crank in the centre, riveted to the floor via a broad, flat iron plate. The others were not far behind when the thane of Kadrin took up a position at the wheel crank. He pushed hard but it wouldn't yield, not even a fraction.

'It's tough,' he yelled. 'Lend your strength to it.'

'It can't be opened that way,' Rorek told him, arriving on the platform just after Emelda. 'We must first release the lock,' he added, pointing at the magnificent gold, copper and bronze bar that spanned the entire width of the gate.

'Here,' cried Emelda, stood before a shallow alcove in the wall.

Upon closer inspection, Uthor noticed there was a round metal recess in it with four square stubs of iron sticking out.

'What now?' asked the thane of Kadrin, turning to his engineer.

'It is rhun-sealed,' Rorek replied, scrutinising the indentation in the rock before he looked directly at Uthor. 'We cannot open it without a key.'

STANDING ATOP THE great anvil, chained axe dripping blood, Azgar surveyed the swell of the battle below. Teeming rat-kin hordes thrashed against the thinning dwarfen shield wall that had been pressed all the way back to the forgemaster's platform. Death frenzy was seemingly upon the foul creatures, muzzles frothing as they squealed madly to get at the dawi through the great arch. An endless, undulating sea of furred bodies stretched beyond it as yet more ratmen piled into the foundry.

Azgar kept his hand on the wyvern-horn hunting through the thronging skaven with narrowed eyes. The dwarfs were but half the number they were at the start of the battle. They would not last much longer. Yet the slayer resisted the urge to blow the note that was to signal all of their deaths. He was waiting; waiting for something to show itself...

HALGAR WAS TIRING. He would not admit it to himself but his aching limbs, the fire in his back and shoulder, the thundering breaths in his chest told him so. He slashed open a rat-kin's throat before breaking the snout of another with a savage punch. Three more of the vermin came on at him – the skaven seemed to surround them now – and he was forced back, defending a flurry of blows. For a moment his vision blurred and he misjudged a parry. The errant blow struck his thigh and the longbeard cried out.

Drimbold stepped in and hacked the cackling ratman down before it could take advantage.

Halgar nodded to the Grey dwarf, heaving more air into his lungs.

'Stay by me,' he barked, mustering what breath he could.

'You do not need to watch me,' Drimbold replied, slicing the ear off a slave fodder. 'I will stay in the fight.'

'No, lad, not because of that,' Halgar replied, his axe held uncertainly in his hand, 'because I'm going blind.'

'I will,' said Drimbold determinedly, taking up a position at the longbeard's back and fending off a reckless rat-kin spear lunge.

Halgar had gone past pain, surpassed exhaustion now. Raw hatred for his foes kept him going, made his axe blade swing and take more lives. The killing became almost ritualistic in the dense fug of battle and everything else; every sense, every feeling was swallowed by it. When the longbeard felt the rock at his back slip away, all of that changed. He looked over his shoulder to see Drimbold slumped on one knee, clutching his chest.

'To your feet!' he cried, cutting through the shoulder of a rat-kin slave. Drimbold wasn't listening or, at least, he couldn't hear the longbeard. The Grey dwarf cried out when a curved blade ran him through, punching out of his back, shearing his light armour easily. Halgar whirled, blinking back his blurring vision, or tears – he couldn't tell which – and cut Drimbold's attacker down.

'To me!' the longbeard cried, gathering the Grey dwarf up in his arms as he fell back, a cohort of clan warriors surrounding them both in a shield wall. Halgar dragged the Grey dwarf back bodily, a geyser of blood spitting from his chest, into the rear ranks and set him down.

'Uthor… told… me…' Drimbold gasped through blood-flecked lips – every word was a struggle. 'He said… I was to protect you…'

Halgar patted the Grey dwarf's shoulder, unable to speak as he regarded the dwarf's wounded body.

'I… failed,' Drimbold uttered with his dying breath, the light in his eyes fading to grey.

'No, lad,' Halgar replied with tears in his eyes. 'No you haven't.'

The longbeard rested his gnarled hand over Drimbold's dead, staring eyes. When he took it away again they were closed. He then leant down. The words were choked as he whispered in Drimbold's ear.

'You are a half dwarf no longer.'

Halgar wiped the back of his hand over his eyes and stood up, brandishing his axe.

'Guard him well,' he ordered three shield-bearing warriors sternly, who nodded sombrely before arraying themselves around the Grey dwarf.

With that the longbeard stalked away, back to the front and back to the killing.

AT LONG LAST, Azgar found what he was looking for. Across the skaven ranks he espied their warlord, squeaking orders and forcing his way to the front.

It was an unusual trait for a rat-kin leader, the slayer thought to himself, to throw itself into the fight. There could be no mistaking it, though. Decked in thick armour of tarnished metal, wielding a weighty-looking glaive and ragged cloak dragging in its wake, this was the opponent Azgar had been waiting for.

Now he knew the skaven were committed to the attack.

Bellicose glee in his heart, the slayer raised the wyvern-horn to his lips and, with his mighty chest bulging, blew out a long and powerful note.

CHAPTER FOURTEEN

THE WYVERN-HORN ECHOED throughout the hold, a reverberant and sonorous blast that carried through earth, stone and flood.

'There!' cried Gromrund, waiting inside Dibna's Chamber.

'I hear it,' Thalgrim replied, poised before the statue of the engineer. As the lodefinder lifted his pick-mattock he looked over his shoulder at the hammerer. 'Once this begins, there will be little time.'

Gromrund nodded his understanding. 'Make your strike well.'

Thalgrim let fly and met the statue with precise force.

'It is done,' he said, turning on his heel as a shallow crack emerged in the rock, running rapidly up Dibna's leg, across his torso, beyond his shoulder and up his outstretched arm until it finally reached the ceiling.

Gromrund watched the fissure's course slightly agog, small chips of rocks falling from its terminus at the ceiling.

'Flee, now!' Thalgrim urged, leaping into the shaft and disappearing from view.

Gromrund followed quickly, a final nervous glance behind him before he descended. Water was trickling through the ever-widening cracks and one of Dibna's fingers fell away, shattering as it struck the floor. Darkness beckoned the hammerer as he approached the shaft and raced into it.

GROMRUND HALF CLIMBED, half slid down the shaft. Wisps of smoke spiralled from his armoured gauntlets with the intense friction of his descent. There was a nervous moment when he switched from the thick chain dangling from Dibna's Drop to the lodefinder's rope but he made

it without falling to his doom. A growing sense of urgency had started
to overwhelm him, exacerbated by the speck of flame from Thalgrim's
candles diminishing rapidly beneath him as the lodefinder made expedient progress.

'You'll get yourself killed at that pace,' Gromrund called down to him.

'As might you if you don't pick up yours,' came the distant, echoing
response.

Gromrund intensified his efforts as much as he dared and, looking
down again, swore he could make out a faint corona of washed-out light.

We will make it, thought the hammerer, as an almighty crash resonated above them, followed by a thunderous roar. Time was up.

Water fell like rain at first, droplets splashing harmlessly off
Gromrund's armour. Then it became a torrent, growing more violent
with each passing second. The hammerer slid now, almost free falling,
determined to arrest his descent when he neared the bottom of the shaft.
That plan was reduced to tatters when the full fury of the deluge above
smashed into him, and he was forced to grip the rope tightly to avoid
being ripped away from it and cast like tinder into the darkness.

Gromrund roared his defiance and tried to edge down an inch. He
did but had to grip hard again as the icy cascade battered the hammerer remorselessly. Gromrund had his head down and the pounding
water thumped against his neck, so hard he thought it might snap.
Thalgrim was below him, he was sure of it. He could just make out
the hazy figure of the lodefinder through the downpour. The shaft
shuddered against the elemental onslaught, chunks of loose rock
sent spiralling earthward. One smacked against Gromrund's warhelm, setting it askew. Another *thunked* his pauldron armour and the
hammerer nearly lost his grip, crying out in anguish.

Chilling heat blazed up his arm and back. Gromrund shut his eyes
against the pain, it taking all of the hammerer's effort just to hold
on. When he opened them again, he tried to gauge the distance to
the ground – thirty, fifty feet, perhaps. If he dropped now he could
survive. The decision was made for the hammerer when a great slab
of stone sheared away from the shaft wall. Its jagged edge rammed
the rope into the opposite side, cutting it loose. Gromrund fell and
the hunk of rock fell after him.

PAIN SEARED UP his right leg and something cracked as Gromrund struck
the ground, spluttering as the gushing Black Water engulfed him.
Underwater, his heavy armour anchoring him, the hammerer's world
grew dim and quiet. Sound, light and feeling seemed to lose all meaning as the icy deluge robbed him of his sense and bearings. Memory
reached out to Gromrund from the past, the day when he had taken the
warhelm of his clan to continue the Tallhelm legacy.

Father…

Kromrund Tallhelm lay before him in a gilded sarcophagus carved from stone by the master masons of Karak Hirn. Ashen-faced and in repose, his lord and father was no more. Upon his breast there sat the mighty horned warhelm of the clan, a prestigious symbol of their lineage and the oaths they had made to serve King Kurgaz, founder of the Hornhold, as his bodyguards.

As Gromrund reached out for the warhelm he felt himself being pulled away and the sound of distant voices rushing closer.

Spitting and cursing, Gromrund emerged above the floodwater, cascading readily into the underdeep.

'Pull him clear!' he heard Thalgrim bellow and his body was heaved away again.

Blinking back rivulets of water eking into his warhelm and down his face, he recoiled, landing hard on his rump, as a massive chunk of rock and debris crashed down onto the confluence of the crossroads. A few moments ago, he had been floundering in that very spot. Looking around, Gromrund noticed his companions were with him. Thalgrim and Hakem helped the armoured hammerer to his feet. Getting up, he saw that the flood water reached his lower torso.

'We cannot stay here,' Thalgrim cried above the crashing din of the waterfall, wading frantically in the only direction left to them, the rock fall having demolished and blocked off the other three.

Breathing heavily Ralkan slogged after the lodefinder, struggling in his drenched robes and dragging the book of remembering after him as if leading a lode pony. 'Farther ahead,' he gasped, 'I am sure there is a way upward.'

With no time to question or verify it, the dwarfs drove on.

Hakem and Gromrund laboured at the back – the two warriors wore the heaviest armour and were finding it hard going.

'Can you walk?' Hakem asked of the hammerer, supporting him beneath the shoulder.

'Aye,' Gromrund replied, but didn't refuse the merchant thane's help.

'You are limping badly,' Hakem told him, feeling the hammerer's laboured gait as the merchant thane bore his weight.

'Aye,' was Gromrund's reply.

'If we survive, you may need a stick.'

'There'll be no stick. The hammerers of the Tallhelm clan walk on two legs, not three!' Gromrund raged as the pair struggled on.

WADING THROUGH THE rapidly rising swell, the dwarfs made pitiful progress. Barely fifty feet from the crossroads and the water was already up to their shoulders.

Thalgrim gazed up at the lofty arches of the vaulted tunnel ceiling and realised they wouldn't make it like this.

'Remove your armour,' he cried to the others as a column behind them cracked and fell into the flood water, scattering debris. 'We will have to swim for it.' The lodefinder unbuckled his mail vest and let it plummet into the river surrounding them.

The other dwarfs followed suit, shrugging off chainmail, unclasping breastplates and greaves, divesting themselves of leather hauberks and vambraces. They shed the armour clumsily but quickly. Each piece was an heirloom, the loss of which was felt profoundly, and discarded with an oath to one of the Ancestor Gods that reparations would be made.

By the time it was done, the water had reached their chins.

'Your warhelm,' said Thalgrim. 'You must leave it behind – it will weigh you down.'

Gromrund folded his arms.

'The Tallhelm has never been removed in five generations of my clan, since before the Horn hold was founded. I will not break that tradition now.'

'You will drown,' Hakem reasoned, now wearing only his tunic and breeches. 'Leave it and come back to reclaim your honour.'

'Upon my death you may prise it from my head,' the hammerer snarled, still fully armoured.

The water rose again, up to the dwarfs' shoulders and getting deeper with each moment.

'Help me,' Hakem burbled, spitting mouthfuls of the Black Water as he tried to lift Gromrund. Thalgrim and Ralkan swam over to him, and hoisted the hammerer up from beneath his armpits.

'Leave me,' he roared, his head popping above the turbulent waterline with their combined efforts.

'Remove the warhelm!' Hakem begged him, staring the hammerer in the face as he said it.

'Never!' Gromrund raged back before his snarling visage softened. 'Go. Find your dooms and, if you're able, tell my king that I fought and died with honour.'

They could hold him no longer. The hammerer was like an anchor and dragged them all down with him.

Hakem felt his fingers slipping and watched as Gromrund – the hammerer had his arms folded still – fell away into the gloomy water, bubbles trailing from beneath his warhelm. The merchant thane, swimming hard, broke the surface of the now swelling river and drew great gulps of air into his lungs.

The current that surged through the underdeep was strong and carried the three dwarfs along by its will alone, smashing them into columns, plunging them beneath the water only for them to resurface desperately a moment later. Hakem was lost in it, lost in a maelstrom of spitting foam and churning water.

'Here!' he heard Thalgrim cry. Seeing something in the water, he reached out and grabbed it.

The lodefinder hauled him around the corner of a massive column, he and Ralkan crushed against it by the pressure of the flood. In his other hand he had his pick-mattock, lodged in the wall for grip. A brutal-looking gash was etched upon his forehead where it had been struck by a jutting stone.

'The rock is weak here,' Thalgrim shouted over the thrashing surf. 'I can break through it.'

'Where will it lead us?' Hakem replied, looking to Ralkan.

The lorekeeper shook his head, just trying to hold on.

Though they had only been carried by the water for a few minutes, they could have travelled a great distance. There was no way of knowing where they were now.

'Does it matter?' cried the lodefinder. 'This path will end in our deaths.'

The water was getting steadily higher. There was only a few feet left before it engulfed the tunnel completely.

Hakem nodded.

'Hold on,' Thalgrim said and ripped his pick free. Using the column for support, he smashed the weapon, two-handed, into the bare rock. The wall crumbled and an opening was made wide enough for the dwarfs to pass through. Thalgrim went first, diving into the unknown, then Ralkan and finally Hakem.

First there was darkness then the sense of falling as the merchant thane struck the ground hard. He was rolling and skidding on his backside down a long and narrow tunnel, an undercurrent of rapidly rushing water beneath carrying him. So black were Hakem's surroundings and so disorientated was he, that all he could discern was that he was going down; down into the darkest depths of the hold.

'IS THERE NO other way,' Uthor cried over the din of the thunderous skaven pumping engine.

'Rhun-seals are wrought by rhunki using rhun magic, as are the keys that unlock them. It is far beyond my skill. Without such a key we cannot release the bar and as long as the bar is engaged the Barduraz Varn will not open.'

As if to mock them, the echoing report of the wyvern-horn rang loudly through the chamber.

'We must release the Black Water now,' Uthor raged. 'In this deed at least, I *will* succeed.'

'We cannot,' Rorek told him. 'Besides the rhun-key, there is no other way.'

'Grimnir's hairy arse!' Uthor slumped down on his backside, Ulfgan's axe in his lap. 'The lorekeeper mentioned nothing of this. If we survive, I will personally see to it that his beard is shorn.' He gripped the haft of his axe as he thought about the retribution he would visit upon Ralkan. Regarding the glinting blade, the runes glowing faintly as he held the weapon in his grasp, something dawned on him.

'These rhun-keys,' said Uthor suddenly, getting to his feet. 'Who would bear such a thing?'

Rorek stared back at him, slightly dumbfounded. 'What does it matter?'

'Who would bear it? Answer me!'

'The rhunki that made it, of course,' Rorek blathered, unsure as to the reason for Uthor's sudden, urgent behaviour.

'Who else?' The thane of Kadrin was delving beneath his chainmail shirt.

'The king,' Rorek finished. 'The king of the hold.'

'Do you remember the King's Chamber?' Uthor asked the engineer.

'Of course, you bear noble Lord Ulfgan's axe to this day.'

'Yes, I do. But the axe was not all we salvaged from his private rooms.' Realisation dawned on Rorek's face.

Emelda stood watching the entire display nonplussed.

'The talisman,' said the engineer.

Uthor found it beneath his armour, where he'd put it for safe keeping after fleeing the hold, and held it aloft.

Ulfgan's talisman – it bore the rune marking of the royal clan etched around the edge and in the centre was the badge of his ancestor, Hraddi. Flickering brazier light shone through two square holes in the eyes and a third in the mouth. Without looking, Uthor knew they would fit the mechanism perfectly. They had their key.

Uthor placed the arcane device into the recess in the wall, fixing the three holes in position over the iron studs. It clamped into place with a dull, metallic *thunk*.

'Turn it,' said Rorek, standing just behind him and looking over the thane of Kadrin's shoulder. Emelda waited next to the engineer, silently apprehensive.

Uthor did as Rorek told him and turned the rune key once. Beyond the wall, he heard the sonorous retort of a hidden mechanism at work. Screeching metal filled the chamber, smothering even the sound of the chugging engine, as the mighty locking bar disengaged spitting out dust and stone chips. Hinged at one end, the huge bar split into two from a previously imperceptible join and fell away to clang thunderously into a thick bronze clamp on either side of the Barduraz Varn.

Moving away from the alcove, Uthor took his place at the huge wheel crank in the centre of the stone platform. His companions followed him, and together they turned the massive device that set yet more hidden feats of engineering in motion.

From below, a sudden onrush of water could be heard as the Barduraz Varn rose magnificently. Hauled up by a raft of iron chains, the great gate ascended vertically in slow and juddering increments, feeding gradually into a long and deep recess set into the chamber roof way above where the dwarfs stood on the stairway. Pushed past the point of no return, the gate would keep opening, its momentum as inexorable as the flood waters crashing through it, until it was fully released.

From their vantage point on the stone platform, Uthor gazed across the gradually deepening reservoir to another set of stone steps on the opposite side of the vast chamber. They led up to a thick, wooden door. With the destruction of Rorek's diving helm the way back was shut; this might be their only possible escape route.

'Head for that portal,' he cried, starting down the stone steps. 'Make haste,' he called back, 'the chamber will soon be flooded.'

The dwarfs negotiated the stairs quickly, slowing only slightly when they edged past the still whirring wheel. When they reached the bottom, the crude struts of the pumping engine were beginning to buckle under the sustained battering of the emerging Black Water. Several of the observation platforms had already been felled and swirled in the growing reservoir amongst the rotting debris of rat-kin corpses.

Slogging back across the carcass-ridden lagoon, making the most of the few islands of rock that had yet to be submerged, the dwarfs finally reached the second stairway, plunging waist deep into the water to get to it. Tramping up the stone steps was a great relief and once they had gained the upper platform and the threshold to the portal, they looked back.

The Barduraz Varn was a third of the way open and with smashing force the inundation unleashed by it crushed the pumping engine utterly. Rat-kin slaves mouthed silent screams as they were pummelled into the thrashing depths, together with their wheeled prisons that collapsed and split against the swelling water. Like a fallen standard conceding defeat, the metal prongs at the zenith of the engine were the last to crumble. Arcs of lightning flared defiantly as a massive wave engulfed the tower and it was dragged into the depths. Flashes, stark and diffuse, raged for a moment and were still as if the infernal engine had never existed.

Having seen enough, Uthor turned away and made for the wooden door.

HAKEM WAS FLAT on his back, his clothes sodden and torn. Dazed, he got to his feet absently feeling a fat bruise bulging on his head. Darkness surrounded the merchant thane and an old, stagnant stench wafted over to him on a warm and shallow breeze.

'Thalgrim,' he hissed, crouching down and scrambling around for his borrowed axe. It was nowhere to be found. Patting down his body, he realised he still had his beard-irons. Hakem looked at them for a long moment then unhitched the irons from his belt and dropped them to the ground.

'Here,' came the whispered reply of the lodefinder, close by.

'Lorekeeper,' Hakem called quietly again, detecting Thalgrim's vague outline just ahead.

'Am I dead yet?' Ralkan answered.

Eyes adjusting to the gloom, Hakem made out the prone form of the lorekeeper, flat on his back and languishing beneath a faintly trickling waterfall that fed into a thin, downward wending stream. It seemed the rushing waters had been diverted at some point during their descent. Hakem wasn't about to question it.

'You're not dead,' he said, standing next to the exhausted lorekeeper. 'Now, get up,' he added, helping Ralkan to his feet.

Thalgrim joined them. Incredibly he still carried his pick though, try as he might, he couldn't light the clutch of candles gripped in his meaty fist.

'Waterlogged,' the lodefinder explained unnecessarily.

Hakem ignored him. These were the lowest deeps, that much he was certain, and as a thane and bearer of the longest beard it was his duty to get them through it and somehow out of Karak Varn.

'What is this place?' he asked Ralkan.

The lorekeeper rubbed the water from his eyes and wrung out his beard, before peering intently at the surrounding gloom.

'We are at the lowest part of the underdeep,' he murmured, picking out age-worn runes and sigils carved into keystones.

The tunnel was wide but low. The three dwarfs were gathered where it flattened out to a level plain. Just beyond it the tunnel fell downward in a gradual slope. Other than that, the only other way was back up, over the lip of stone from which the dwarfs had been disgorged and a long, hard climb through the rapids.

'Is there a way out from here?'

Ralkan scratched his head and fell silent. It wasn't a good sign.

'I don't remember this place,' he admitted. 'I do not think I have ever been here… Yet…'

'Yet?'

'There is something familiar,' he said. 'This way,' the lorekeeper decided finally as he headed down the slope.

IT FELT LIKE they'd been wandering the tunnels for an hour, though Ralkan could not be sure – his judgement of the passage of time had been irrevocably damaged during his period of hidden isolation in the hold.

With each step that carried him further into the lower reaches of the underdeep a strange disquiet gnawed at him. Smothering it to the back of his mind for now, the lorekeeper led them on until they reached another crossroads.

The Barak Varr dwarf said something – Hakem, that was his name – Ralkan didn't hear what it was. His head was hurting. Nothing looked right.

East, he thought suddenly. East – that feels right, and took the left fork.

About halfway down the tunnel, the lorekeeper thought he heard something – faint, but it was definitely there. Vile squeaking drifted over to Ralkan on the weak breeze. Fifty years in the dark. Squeaking and scratching. Squeaking and scratching.

No – it wasn't right. Something boiled up inside the lorekeeper, something he'd buried. It slid, leaden in his gut, and icily up his spine until it dried his tongue to sand. Ralkan turned on his heel and fled.

'SKAVEN,' RALKAN HISSED as he rushed passed Hakem.

The Barak Varr dwarf looked ahead down the tunnel. His heart caught in his mouth when he saw the skulking shadows against the wall, stretching towards him. Then came the squeaking, chittering sound of the rat-kin as the horde grew ever closer. Judging by the terrible cacophony, there must have been hundreds. Hakem's first thought was the flood waters might not reach them here; his second was he couldn't fight them and live. He gave chase after the lorekeeper with all haste, urging Thalgrim, who was dawdling in the tunnel, to follow him. The lodefinder was not far behind as Hakem fled by the crossroads and went after Ralkan, straight down the western fork.

'Lorekeeper,' bawled the merchant thane. 'Lorekeeper, slow down.'

In his frantic flight after Ralkan, Hakem raced through a myriad of tunnels. After a while, it became clear they had lost the skaven or that they had deliberately given up the pursuit. As he slowed, and a sense of creeping, ancient dread came over him, Hakem could understand why.

Ahead of him Ralkan was still running, though the lorekeeper was obviously exhausted now and had slowed down considerably. Hakem picked up his pace, trying to close the gap. He saw Ralkan look behind him, though the lorekeeper gave no indication he had seen the merchant thane. Then he slipped and fell to his knees. Ralkan was up swiftly and bundling himself around a corner was lost from sight.

Hakem hurried on. Sweat dappled his forehead and he noticed the air was getting warmer – his sodden clothes were gradually drying in it.

This tunnel is ancient, thought the merchant thane as he reached the corner, a sulphurous stench pricking at his nostrils, mixed with old fear. Hakem caught up to Ralkan at last. The lorekeeper's leather jerkin, the one he wore beneath his robes, was torn and he was feeling his way slowly along the wall.

'What is it?' Hakem asked, aware that Thalgrim had just reached them both.

Ralkan traced his fingers over a dust-shrouded symbol.

'Uzkul,' he muttered. He turned to the merchant thane, his face an ashen mask.

'Uzkul?' Thalgrim asked.

Ralkan nodded slowly.

Something was wrong; the lorekeeper was behaving more strangely than usual. Slightly on edge, Hakem looked past him and further down the tunnel. He saw a faint glow ahead.

'Perhaps it is an ancient hearth hall,' Ralkan offered, following the merchant thane's gaze. The lorekeeper's voice seemed far away as he said it, padding calmly down the tunnel and towards the light.

'You are sure this is the way?' Hakem asked as he followed, sharing a worried glance with Thalgrim alongside him. The sulphur stink was getting stronger with every step.

Ralkan didn't answer.

'Heed me, lorekeep–' the merchant thane began as he reached Ralkan, standing at the mouth of a huge cavern. The words stuck in Hakem's throat, gaping in awe as he was bathed in a golden aura.

'WE MUST TURN back,' said Rorek.

'There is no *back*,' Uthor replied, angrily.

Before them was a narrow stone bridge, spanning a deep gorge. A rushing spout of water surged violently across it, falling away into the dark recesses of the crevice beyond and below.

After they'd left the chamber of the Barduraz Varn, the dwarfs had sealed the door shut behind them. Making haste, for they knew the floodwater would reach them soon enough, they had reached the bridge. Uthor had tried to cross, tied to Rorek and Emelda, but the force of the spouting deluge had crushed him flat and nearly pitched the thane right over the edge. He'd crawled back, drenched and defeated with the rushing water battering him at every clawed inch.

'Then this is the end,' Emelda uttered with resignation. 'We cannot cross and we cannot retreat. I envy Azgar and the others,' she said, noting the tightening of Uthor's jaw at the mention of the slayer, 'at least they will die fighting.'

'I see something,' said Rorek, suddenly, squinting past the pounding water. The engineer pointed to the other side of the bridge and the mouth of another, small, portal. 'It's not possible,' he gasped.

From beyond the bridge, shrouded in darkness, a vaguely outlined figure hailed them. Any words were lost, swallowed by the roar of the thrashing water as the figure waved to them with an outstretched arm. Though mostly sketched in silhouette, the shape and size of the figure's warhelm was unmistakable.

'Gromrund?' breathed Uthor and suppressed a shudder, uncertain as to what he was actually seeing.

Gromrund's silhouette waved again and pointed down to the bridge.

Uthor followed the gesture but couldn't see anything past the rush of the water.

'I thought he was at the overflow grate in the opposite end of the hold,' Emelda whispered, clutching the talisman of Valaya around her neck for reassurance.

'He was,' Uthor replied darkly, searching through the pounding river for some sign of what Gromrund wanted them to find.

Then he saw the frayed edges of a rope. It was only a few feet away; Uthor could reach it at a stretch.

'Hold onto my ankles,' said the thane of Kadrin as he got down onto his stomach.

'What?' Rorek asked, still staring at the shadow beyond the bridge.

'Just do as I ask!' Uthor barked.

Rorek crouched down with Emelda beside him, and the two of them gripped Uthor's ankles as he crawled back across the bridge, the river battering him relentlessly.

Fingers numbing from the cold, Uthor reached out and gripped the rope.

'Pull me back,' he cried.

Dragged from out of the swell, Uthor clutched one end of the rope in his hand. On the other side of the bridge, Gromrund showed them the opposite end and beckoned for them to cross.

'Are you sure about this?' Rorek muttered, his voice a little tremulous as he eyed the dark portal and the shadow inside it.

'It is our only chance.' Uthor pulled the rope until it was taut. He saw Gromrund take the strain on the other end. With an oath to Valaya, he stepped bravely onto the bridge. At first he was battered to his knees but using the rope for support he got back to his feet and crossed, hand over hand, inch by painful inch. Rorek and Emelda followed.

It felt like hours but they reached the other side, collapsing into an exhausted heap on a small stone platform.

'My thanks, hammerer–' Uthor began but as he looked over to where Gromrund had been standing the rope fell slack. The Karak Hirn dwarf was gone.

AZGAR LEAPT FROM the forgemaster's anvil, clearing the last lines of dwarf defenders and landing amidst a clutch of rat-kin warriors who scattered before him. Before the vile creatures could close in again, the slayer swung his chained axe in a punishing circle, slicing meat and bone. Churning deeper into the fray, amidst a storm of severed limbs and shredded torsos, Azgar found his prey.

Shrieking a challenge, the rat-kin warlord came on fearlessly, ducking the first swing of the chain as it stepped inside the killing arc and swatted away the second revolution of the deadly blade with the flat of its glaive. Pulling the weapon down, it made a powerful lunge that Azgar was hard pressed to dodge. The slayer twisted from the glaive's path, though it nicked the skin of his left side and drew blood.

Snarling exultantly, the warlord then licked the crimson droplets bejewelling its blade and surged at Azgar again. The slayer rolled beneath a wild, overhead swipe, gathering up his chain axe as he did so and gripping the haft to wield it conventionally. A vertical strike from the glaive followed, and the slayer dived forward to avoid it, gutting a black-furred skaven that got too close before whirling on his heel and side swiping the overstretched warlord. The blow carved into the rat-kin's back, ripping off plates of armour. The warlord cried in pain, blocking a second blow with the haft of its glaive. Roaring back, Azgar struck again and again, until he sheared the glaive haft in half.

Staggering backward, the rat-kin warlord tossed the bladed end at the slayer, who smashed it aside with the flat of his axe. It slowed Azgar enough for the rat lord to draw its sword.

Slowly, the duelling warriors were afforded room to fight, neither skaven nor dwarf willing to step into the path of their whirling blades.

Azgar swung again, releasing a little chain for additional reach and surprise. The rat-kin warlord saw it coming and weaved out of the weapon's death arc. Rushing forward, the blurring steel flicking past its ear, the creature cut the slayer across the torso, using the momentum of the blow to carry it beyond the dwarf's reach.

Azgar felt wet blood between his fingers, clutching at the wound as he nearly fell to one knee. Screeching, high-pitched and sporadic, emanated from the rat-kin warlord's mouth in what the slayer could only assume was laughter. The dwarf stood and turned, the blood from his torso was already clotting, grinning contemptuously.

'Come on,' he growled, beckoning the skaven on. 'We're not done yet.'

HALGAR SAW THE slayer dive from the anvil but quickly lost him in the melee. There were no tactics, no scheme to the battle now. It was about dying and surviving, pure and simple. The remaining dwarfs, although few and surrounded by foes, fought as if the very spirit of Grimnir were with them. Halgar's heart swelled, belting out his deathsong with every blow and thrust of his axe. During the carnage he had lost his shield and wielded the weapon in two hands.

Cutting down a rat-kin slave, the longbeard screwed up his eyes again – the blurring was getting worse and dark patches lingered menacingly at the periphery of his vision. When Halgar opened them he saw something advancing toward him. Whether it was his failing eyesight or some brand of foul sorcery, he could not tell but it seemed as though it were a ragged blanket of drifting blackness. Shadows, as if drawn like moths to a lantern, mustered to it until the thing resolved itself in front of the longbeard. Out of the gathered darkness came a flash of metal. Halgar, acting on instinct, parried the dagger blow and took a step back as a second blindingly fast swipe cut through the air in front of him.

The longbeard bellowed defiantly, stomping towards his assailant and swinging his axe. Eyesight blurring badly now, Halgar missed by a foot.

The assassin recoiled, the old dwarf knew now it could only be such a creature, dodging the blade with effortless grace. Regrouping quickly it struck out again, severing the tendons in the longbeard's wrist. The axe clanged to the ground from Halgar's nerveless fingers. The second dagger punched into his chest and the longbeard suddenly found he could barely breathe.

Halgar fell onto his knees, trying in vain to staunch the blood flowing eagerly from his chest.

Drawing near, certain of its kill, the skaven assassin hissed with gleeful, undisguised malice. Ironically, it was blind and upon opening its mouth to gloat revealed it had no tongue, either. But something else caught the longbeard's attention, so close that even he could see it – the last thing he would ever see as his vision darkened completely. It was an ear, cut from the head of some unfortunate victim. Embedded in the lobe was a gilded earring that bore the rune of the royal clan of Karak Izor. It had once belonged to Lokki.

Halgar roared, reaching out blindly to strangle the creature that had killed his lord. He grasped air and felt two dagger thrusts in his torso. Doubling over, one hand supporting his weight lest he collapse, the longbeard tasted copper in his mouth as he spat out blood. His nose twitched. He could smell Lokki's killer close by. Halgar dropped his head submissively, knowing that the creature would draw in to finish him. The stench of it grew so pungent it must be upon him. Halgar reached across his body with his half hand, the other no more use than a prop with the tendons slashed, and gripped the grobi arrow embedded in his chest. The air and scent shifted around him. This was it.

Halgar tore the arrow free, blocking the overhead strike of the skaven assassin with his other arm, and rammed it into the rat-kin's throat. He felt it flail; slash weakly at his back and side. Strength failing, Halgar held it there, pushing the arrow tip even deeper. The thrashing stopped and the skaven assassin slumped. Halgar fell onto his back, lifeblood eking across the foundry floor. Though he couldn't see, as the longbeard heard the onrush of flood water smashing into the chamber and the shrieking terror of the drowning rat-kin, he smiled.

'GRUNGNI'S HOARD,' HAKEM gasped. 'May its glittering peaks reach the summit of the world.'

Gold: a shimmering, gilded sea of it stretched out in front of the dwarfs who stood agog at the threshold to the immense chamber. Illuminated by the natural light of a narrow and lofty shaft far above, piles of the lustrous metal soared into its vaulted ceiling like mountains, touching the ends of dripping stalactites. Gems and jewels glittered like stars in the shining morass, together with copper-banded chests that jutted like wooden islands between refulgent straits. Ornate weapons: swords, axes, hammers and others of more elaborate artifice protruded from vast treasure mounds. So immense was the hoard that it was impossible to take it all in with a single look. The chamber itself was cavernous and appeared to tail off into an anteroom at the back that was lost from view.

Hakem could taste the gold on his tongue; its strong, metallic scent filled his nostrils. He had to fight the urge to run wildly into the room and immerse himself in it. But then he noticed something else amidst the hoard's lustrous mirage, skeletons picked clean, and fire-blackened armour and snapped blades. Great pools of heat-emanating sulphur confirmed Hakem's sudden suspicions and the creeping dread he had felt earlier returned. The chamber was inhabited.

Thalgrim mumbled something next to him. Hakem turned to find the lodefinder glassy-eyed and slack-jawed. A thin trail of drool came off his bottom lip and stretched all the way down to the floor.

'Gorl,' he garbled drunkenly.

'No,' the merchant thane cried, reaching out to grab him. But he was too late. Thalgrim stumbled madly into the chamber, burbling 'Gorl, gorl, gorl!' as he went.

Hakem went after him, despite every fibre of his being willing him not to. Ralkan followed in an entirely different delirium.

'Thalgrim,' Hakem hissed, stalling a few feet from the cavern mouth, not daring to raise his voice much above a whisper. 'Wait!'

The lodefinder was oblivious and, after diving amidst a mountainous pile of gold, went barrelling onward.

An inferno of roaring, black-red flame engulfed Thalgrim from an unseen source. The wave of heat emanating from it was incredible and felled Hakem to his knees. Ralkan collapsed into a heap before it, screwing his body up into a ball and whimpering. Hakem lost sight of Thalgrim in the fearsome blaze, shielding his eyes against its terrible glare. When he looked back, there was nothing left of the lodefinder except ash – he didn't even scream.

Survival instinct got Hakem to his feet. He rushed over to Ralkan and dragged him up by the scruff of his neck.

'On your feet,' the merchant thane snarled beneath his breath.

Ralkan obeyed as whatever fear seizing him drained his will.

Tremors shook the ground, sending coins and gems cascading from their lofty summits, so violent that Hakem struggled to stay standing.

From around the collapsing mounds of gold there emerged a beast so ancient and evil that many who lived had never seen its like.

'Drakk,' Hakem whispered, Ralkan murmuring next to him and gripping the merchant thane's tunic for dear life. Hakem felt his courage, his resolve and his reason stripping away as he beheld the snorting behemoth.

So massive was the dragon that its bulk pushed the mountainous treasure peaks aside, nearly filling the width of the immense chamber. Red scales that glistened like blood covered a brawny body fraught with scars. Its barrel-ribbed chest was broad and sickly yellow. Deep, black pools of hate served for eyes and regarded the dwarfs hungrily. Claws the length of swords three times over and half again as thick, scraped the ground as the creature sharpened them raucously. Raising its long, almost elegant, neck the dragon stretched its mighty, tattered wings and roared.

Mind-numbing terror gripped the dwarfs as they fought the backwash of dragon breath, rancid with the stink of sulphur and rotting meat. The beast made no attempt to advance. It merely snorted and hissed, tongue lathing the air as it tried to taste the fear of its prey.

Hakem gritted his teeth and forced his arm to move, prising Ralkan's fingers off his tunic one-by-one. Released from the lorekeeper's grasp the merchant thane felt a sudden epiphany come over him, a surety of knowledge that let him bury his fear beneath something raw and primal.

'Go,' Hakem said calmly.

Rigid with fear, Ralkan responded with a murmur.

'Go,' he said again, more fiercely this time.

Eyes locked on the beast, the lorekeeper took a half step back.

'I have lost my honour,' Hakem uttered with absolutely certainty and took off his tunic. 'There is nothing left,' he continued, throwing down his belt. 'Perhaps if I die here, there will be some honour in that.' He tore off the hook that was strapped to his arm and unravelled the bandage – the wound was still bloody and seeped through it.

'Go, lorekeeper,' Hakem said, reaching down and taking up a hammer from amongst the scattered treasure. 'Recount my deeds that my name at least might live on.'

Ralkan took another fearful step.

'Flee you fool – now!' Hakem raged, shouting in the lorekeeper's face.

Ralkan found his will at last and fled.

'Now we are alone, you and I,' said the thane of Barak Varr, the frantic footfalls of the lorekeeper diminishing behind him as he allowed his bloodsoaked bandage to fall to the ground. He bit into the stump of his wrist, reopening the wound and bringing fresh blood to the surface. Daubing it ritualistically over his bare chest in the arcane sigils of old, he muttered an oath to Grimnir.

The dragon sloped forward, baring its long and deadly fangs – its gaping maw could snap an ogre in two.

Hakem gripped the hammer.

'Come,' he said with grim finality. 'Face me and forge my legend.'

Rearing up on its haunches, the dragon snarled. There was the faintest trace of amusement in its eyes as it dove towards Hakem with bone-crushing force.

CHAPTER FIFTEEN

UTHOR HAD DESCENDED into a ravine of fire. Here in the very bowels of the underdeep the blood of the mountain itself ran in thick channels of lava. Blistering heat haze emanated from the syrupy magma rivers, gouts of liquid flame spitting sporadically to the surface. Igneous rock clusters swam the lava tributaries, shifting like miniature archipelagos, and ran as far as the eye could pierce dust and flame down a long and craggy catacomb.

Columns, carved from the rock in the earliest days of the world, supported a ridged and spiked roof that rose high into a billowing pall of grey-black smoke.

'I do not like the look of this path,' said Rorek, sweating profusely.

Stretching out in front of them was a long and wide road, wretched with cracks venting intermittent plumes of steam and sharp, jutting rocks.

'It is the only road we have left,' Uthor told him, exhaustedly. The thane of Kadrin was finding it hard to speak. Vapours of thick, repressive heat made legs and arms leaden and lungs burn. Carried on an arid, air-choked breeze that robbed breath and will, the effect was stifling.

'Then it is the way we must go.' Emelda mustered her resolve, swallowing back the taste of soot and ash on her tongue.

After the Barduraz Varn and the shallow bridge, the trio had rested for but a moment on the stone plateau, none of them wanting, or willing, to talk about the sudden appearance of Gromrund or what it meant for the hammerer. Gathering up their strength, they'd pressed on down shallow corridors bereft of light, going deeper and deeper into the hold aware that the flood waters might be just behind them.

At one point, Rorek had noticed a marker stone etched in runic script. 'The Lonely Road' it read – it was aptly named. They'd ploughed on in silence, finding no further signs, no indication of where they might be headed. Thunder roared above them constantly and small rock chips fell from the ceiling and scattered down the walls as the Black Water did its work. Then, at last, it caught them, a crushing wave of such fury that they'd fled before it. An ancient door of the underdeep had impeded their escape but together they'd released the elder portal and sealed it shut behind them with the last of Rorek's door spikes, descending into the magma caves at the very nadir of the karak.

Emelda took the first steps across the plateau, treading the most solid route through a cracking path rimmed with piles of hot, burning ash and cooling cinder. Uthor and Rorek followed tentatively behind her.

'Stay away from the edges,' she called from the front.

Uthor peered over the crumbling plateau periphery into deep pits of boiling lava, bubbling with submerged eruptions and gaseous emissions. When a section of rock broke off and fell away into it, only to be devoured instantly, he shrank back and stepped a little faster. All the while, the earth shook and the ceiling rattled, the sound of muted thunder emanating loudly through it.

'Watch out!' Uthor cried.

Emelda looked up and leapt aside as a dislodged spike of rock came crashing down and impaled into the hot earth where she had been standing. The clan daughter got to her feet, just as Uthor arrived, quickly dusting off a thin patina of scorching ash.

'Tromm,' she breathed, her face red and sweaty.

'Tromm,' Uthor returned.

'We had best not linger,' Emelda added, noting more errant chunks of stone impacting against the ground and shattering.

Uthor nodded and the three of them moved on hurriedly.

HAKEM WAS DEAD. Ralkan knew it in his heart, even if he didn't see him fall. Galdrakk the Red was a legend, a dark tale to scare beardlings to sleep or taunt a wazzock. The lorekeeper did not think for a moment that such a beast still existed. Yet he had seen it with his own eyes, even envisioned his own doom at its claws. Hakem had changed that doom and made it his own.

Ralkan cursed aloud, tripping and smashing his knee as he scrabbled in the darkened corridors, stumbling blindly, not knowing where he was but desperate for a way out. Honour was of little consequence to the lorekeeper now. He had to try and live or Hakem's noble sacrifice, his great deed would be for nought. That thought drove him and the certainty that once it was finished with Hakem, Galdrakk's appetite would not be sated and the beast would be coming for more…

THRATCH'S HEAD WAS spinning. He smelled damp fur and realised he was wet. Cold stone was hard and sharp against his back. Blurring memories filled his mind as he struggled to wake fully, of the battle with the dwarf-things, of the terrible thunder…

The painted dwarf-thing was fast, maybe faster than Thratch. No – that wasn't possible. No warrior, dwarf-thing, green-thing or skaven had ever bested him – even the assassins of Clan Eshin had failed in all their clumsy attempts to slay him. No, Thratch was king of his domain and no half-naked, furless dwarf-thing was going to change that.

Ducking instinctively, Thratch was forced to the task at hand and the raging dwarf-thing with his chain-cutter. More out of defensive self-preservation than any measure of sword skill the warlord swatted the shiny blade away, though he took pains to snarl his indifference at his enemy.

Thratch lunged, trying to gut the fat dwarf-thing like a stuck pig. The painted creature was fast but not fast enough and the warlord squealed inwardly with delight as he cut it, licking the shed dwarf blood from his blade. Frenzy filled his mind at the taste of it, the imminence of the kill intoxicating. Thratch would wear the dwarf-thing's head like a hat when he slew it.

The warlord drew down a wicked swipe to finish it but the painted dwarf-thing disappeared at the moment of victory. Searing pain flared in Thratch's back, dispelling his blood frenzy. Keen, skaven ears heard the split sections of plate hitting the ground as they were torn free. Silver flashed as the painted dwarf-thing came on.

Thratch blocked madly as the blows rained down – such fury! The glaive haft snapped under the barrage. Thratch threw the bladed end at his assailant desperately, fighting the urge to squirt the musk of fear and flee blindly. The skaven took a step back and came close to flight. No – he was master of this realm. Thratch had never fled; his strength was what marked him for greatness, it was the very thing that would get him noticed by the Council of Thirteen and cement a vaunted position in the highest echelons of Skavenblight.

Thratch drew his sword. Rushing forward, he cut the dwarf-thing across the stomach. The skaven licked his muzzle – how succulent its entrails must taste. Another swipe, savage and unrelenting now – the dwarf-thing was tiring and Thratch could feel it. He shaped for another pass, the final blow, when the ground started shaking. Using his tail as a third leg, Thratch kept his feet.

Something didn't smell right. Thunder was rising; he could hear it distinctly getting closer. Thunder? Beneath the earth? Thratch turned. A mighty wave rose up before him, edged with white, frothing foam, thick with skaven and dwarf-thing bodies swept up in its watery maw. Thratch's fur stood on end, eyes widening in abject terror as he faced the pounding inundation. He pumped the musk of fear into the air around him as the remorseless wave crashed down…

Pain flared in Thratch's back from where the painted dwarf-thing had struck him. The skaven warlord winced as he got shakily to his feet and wiped the blood from his muzzle, trying to remember what had happened after the wave hit. Memory was sparse, like scratchings of meaning at the back of his mind. Darkness came first and then sound had fallen away as he was carried off into the gloom.

Trying to piece together the time between then and now, Thratch wandered wildly through the dwarfen deeps, too dazed and incoherent to do anything else. Scent, faint but distinct wafted over him on a hot breeze. Thratch's nose twitched; the stinking aroma of soot and iron was familiar. It was like acrid bile in his throat – the hated stink of dwarf-things.

Thratch was angry as he followed the stench. His lair was flooded, his engine was likely destroyed and his army decimated. He still had his sword, though it was chipped and a little bent, that was good. He'd need it to exact his vengeance.

'THIS WAY,' UTHOR bellowed, treading carefully across a rock path that fell away at one edge into a deep, undulating pool of liquid fire.

Emelda followed wearily. She had dispensed of her armour – too heavy and hot to bear any longer. Shimmering around her waist in the reflected glow of the lava was the cincture, her only remaining protection. Rorek followed the clan daughter, some distance behind as the trio passed the narrowing path and came upon a wide tunnel that wended upward but was fraught with shadowed alcoves and pits of flame.

'Do you smell that?' asked the thane of Kadrin, letting Emelda catch him up.

'I smell only ash and fire,' she replied, her expression haggard.

'Breathe deeply,' he told her.

Emelda closed her eyes and took a long and lingering breath. Beyond the scent of ash-laden, fire-scorched air was another smell – something much clearer and colder.

'The upper world,' she said, opening her eyes as tears were forming.

'And there,' added Uthor, pointing in the distance to a faint corona of light. 'The way out.'

'We have escaped...' said Emelda, her face alight with joy then twisting horribly in pain. The end of a rusted blade punched savagely through her chest as she spat a thick gobbet of blood into Uthor's soot-stained beard. Emelda sagged forward as the lustre of the runic cincture dimmed ever so slightly and the blade was wrenched free. The thane of Kadrin rushed to catch the clan daughter and saw past her falling form the visage of a burly skaven, wielding a bent and broken sword. The creature grinned maliciously and snarled at the dwarf.

Holding Emelda in his arms, Uthor was defenceless. He saw the blood-slicked blade poised for a second strike, one that would finish them both. Uthor let Emelda go and tried to unhitch his axe, knowing already it would be too late that, even so close to freedom, his death was assured.

Rorek bellowed a war cry, launching himself at the rat-kin with axe in hand. The creature turned, well aware of the engineer's presence, scraping its blade along the ground and flicking a cloud of burning ash and cinder into Rorek's good eye. Clutching his face and screaming, the dwarf's charge failed and he stumbled to the ground in a dishevelled heap.

Uthor was up, though his arms were leaden, and ready to fight. He stood protectively in front of Emelda who lay prone in the dirt. Rorek was off to his left, wailing in agony and rolling back and forth. Before him was the rat-kin lord, bloodied and breathing hard, its tiny eyes full with vengeful desire.

The skaven must have followed them, somehow got ahead and waited in one of the darkened alcoves to strike. There were so many hiding places, so many ways for unseen lurkers to attack and here, in the flattened plateau of the tunnel the creature had chosen to make its move.

Rocks were falling swiftly now and teeming lances of water came down from the ceiling in several places where the flood had found its way through. Steam hissed where they struck the ground and vaporised.

Uthor squared off against the rat-kin lord, side-stepping slowly, not daring to wipe the trail of sweat eking into his eyes.

'Come on then,' he gasped, the challenge unconvincing as he brandished Ulfgan's axe.

Chittering with glee, the skaven warlord was about to rush the dwarf when another figure stepped from the shadows and into his path.

'Go,' said Azgar, the slayer's muscle-bound back a cross-hatch of cuts as he came between Uthor and the skaven. 'Get the other two out,' he added. He too must have survived the flood waters and followed the rat-kin lord to them. 'This one and I have unfinished business.' With that Azgar charged at the rat-kin and battered it back with a rain of savage blows.

Steel crashed in Uthor's ears, the rock fall a deep and resonant chorus to the cacophony as he went to Emelda.

She was pale as he cradled her in his arms, the light dying in her eyes.

'Leave me,' she begged through blood-spattered lips, her voice little better than a shallow rasp.

'We are close,' Uthor whispered, shielding her instinctively as a chunk of rock fell and shattered close by, showering him with cutting shards. 'Lean on me,' he pleaded, trying to get beneath her and use his shoulder as a crutch.

Emelda coughed as she exerted herself, spitting blood from her mouth.

'No,' she managed. 'No, I can't.'

Uthor set her down carefully.

'I go to my father now,' she rasped, clutching Uthor's hand. 'Tell the

High King that I died with honour and take Dunrik to his rest.'

'Emelda...'

The clan daughter's hand fell away. Uthor clenched his eyes tightly shut, his grief overwhelming. Rage forced it down into the pit of his stomach and opened his eyes. He took the cincture from around Emelda's waist reverently and secured it around his own. He took the axe of Dunrik and strapped it to his back. Muttering an oath to Valaya and to Gazul, Uthor got to his feet and was about to go after the rat-kin when he heard Rorek, sobbing not far away.

Anger wilted as the thane of Kadrin's gaze fell upon the stricken engineer. For a moment he flitted from it to the duelling form of Azgar, his brother, as he battled the skaven warlord fiercely. The slayer's chain axe was shattered and he wielded the broken end like a lash to hold the darting rat-kin at bay. As Uthor watched, a fiery column burst through the ground, flinging rock and magma into the air. Another jet broke the surface, then another and another. Azgar was all but lost beyond the barrier of flame.

'I TOLD YOU we were not done yet.' Azgar snarled at the skaven warlord and charged.

Reeling against the barrage of blows, the rat-kin parried and countered furiously. At last, Azgar's frenetic onslaught wavered and as the slayer unleashed a scything swing with his chain axe, the warlord weaved aside and stamped its foot down upon the chain as it flew past harmlessly. Having trapped the weapon, and without stalling, it brought its sword down two-handed, shearing the chain in half.

Bladeless, Azgar fell back as it was the skaven's turn to attack, using the length of chain that remained like a whip to keep the creature at bay. Thick beads of sweat trailed eagerly down the slayer's body, working their way into the pronounced musculature as the two fought on a narrow precipice. Lava bubbled below the duelling warriors, exuding gaseous smoke and radiating intense heat.

Behind him, Azgar heard the raging eruption of flame and magma as the chamber slowly started to disintegrate. If forced to back off much further, the slayer would be consumed by it. Instead, he lashed out with his chain one last time, smacking the skaven's blade aside for but a moment and barged into the rat-kin warlord. The rat-kin bit and clawed viciously, stabbing with the spike of its left hand when it dropped its sword as the slayer slowly crushed the creature's body. The blade fell into the lava pool and melted away. Heedless of the grievous wounds inflicted upon him, Azgar drove forward, lifting the skaven warlord up in a fierce bear hug. Claws digging into the ground, the rat-kin tried to arrest the slayer's determined drive but Azgar was not to be denied. He reached around to the creature's neck and, with his bare hands, tore out a raft of crude stitches. It squealed as he did it, the old wound opening readily as Azgar lifted his prey higher and up off the ground.

The edge of the precipice beckoned.

Azgar roared and flung himself and the rat-kin warlord over the edge…

A STRUGGLE, so indistinct that the details were lost, ensued through the shimmering heat haze as skaven and dwarf grappled. Then they fell, off the edge of the precipice to be swallowed by the lava pool.

'Brother…' Uthor muttered, and felt his grief two-fold.

With no time to mourn, the thane went to Rorek quickly, picking him up and hoisting the engineer onto his back with a grunt.

'I cannot see,' Rorek sobbed, rubbing at his freshly ruined eye.

'You will, my friend,' said Uthor, putting one foot in front of the other, just trying not to fall.

'Are we leaving now?' Rorek asked as he passed out.

'Yes,' Uthor replied. 'Yes, we're leaving.'

The chamber shook with all the natural fury of an earthquake as a beast, so old and terrible that Uthor felt the strength in his legs abandoning him, emerged into the wide tunnel behind the fire columns. Even through the flame Uthor recognised this creature as a dragon, the creature called Galdrakk the Red and enemy of his ancestors. With a powerful flap of its wings that staggered Uthor backwards, Galdrakk battered the fire down and launched through it. Lava hissed at its scaly hide but did nought but scorch it as the beast landed heavily on the other side.

Uthor found the strength to back away as the dragon regarded him hungrily. The foul creature's snout was broken and its right eye was crushed as if it had fought recently. The wounds served only to make its appearance all the more terrifying as it came on, one thought filling Uthor's mind as it did so.

We cannot make it…

An almighty wrenching of stone filled the air as a veritable avalanche of rock crashed down upon Galdrakk. The beast was so massive; it couldn't help but be struck. A spiked rock sheared into the soft membrane of its wing, and it roared in pain, followed by a heavy boulder that bashed its snout as others rebounded from its back, neck and forelimbs.

Uthor ran, head low as the ceiling crashed down, the thunderous cry of Galdrakk resonating in his wake. He kept running, not daring to look back, fearing that the beast might still be alive, that it might have gotten free and be on their heels. Uthor fled until, blinking, he emerged into the blazing day, a clear sky supporting an orb-like sun above him. Even then, he still ran, picking his way through mountainous crags, hastening past caves and negotiating patches of scrub and scattered scree until, gasping so hard for breath he thought his lungs might burst, he collapsed in a clearing encircled by rune-etched menhirs. Vision blur-ring, he recognised the sigil of Grungni and fell unconscious.

IT WAS A shrine to the ancestor gods. Runes for Grungni, Valaya, Grimnir and their lesser children were in evidence upon the foreboding menhirs that felt like the walls of some impenetrable citadel.

Uthor sat in front of a small fire as he read each and every one. He didn't know how long he had been out, but he and Rorek had not been bothered by beasts as they'd lain comatose on the bare earth.

As far as Uthor could gather, they'd emerged far south of Karak Varn at a tributary of Skull River, which flowed quietly below them in a narrow, sloping defile. The deaths of his comrades weighed heavily upon him, but none more so than that of Emelda. For that and the failure of his oath, there would be a reckoning.

Rorek was stirring, and it arrested the thane of Kadrin from his mel-ancholy thoughts.

'Where am I?' the engineer asked, blinking his fire-scarred eye, red-raw and blackened from the burning ash. 'I... I'm blind,' he said, trying to get to his feet as he started to panic.

Uthor laid a hand upon his shoulder.

'Rest easy, you are among friends.'

'Uthor...?'

'Yes, it's me.'

'Uthor, I cannot see.' The engineer's voice was edged with mild hysteria but he lay back down again.

'I know,' the thane of Kadrin replied, sorrowful as he regarded the milky white orb of Rorek's once good eye. The thane of Kadrin had hoped that the loss of sight might not be permanent but in the harsh daylight the wound looked grievous. He had brought this fate upon Rorek.

'I smell open air, grass and fresh water, and feel wind against my face. Where are we?' the engineer asked.

'Near Skull River, south-east of Karak Varn and, by my reckoning, a day's trek across the mountains to Everpeak,' Uthor told him.

'Are we escorting the Lady Emelda back to Karaz-a-Karak?' the engineer asked.

'No, Rorek. She fell.' Uthor couldn't keep the dark edge from his tone.

'Then are we the only survivors?'

'Yes, we are.'

A sound beyond the shrine circle broke the solemn silence. Uthor stood up, axe in hand.

'What is it?' Rorek was panicking again.

'Stay here,' Uthor hissed and stalked out of the circle, crouched low against the ground, using the long grasses and scattered rocks to cover his advance.

Something moved towards him in the shelter of an earthen overhang.

Uthor stooped to grasp a handful of gravel and cast it quickly ahead of him. Then he gripped his weapon in readiness and, ducking into the shadows, waited for his quarry to approach.

'By Grimnir,' he whispered through clenched teeth, 'I'll split your sides.'

Stone crunched as whatever had wandered across their camp tramped over the gravel noisily.

Roaring, Uthor sprang from his hiding place with his axe raised, ready to mete out death.

Ralkan recoiled from the sudden attack and fell back, the blade cutting air in his wake as Uthor swiped furiously.

'Lorekeeper!' said Uthor, lowering his blade and rushing to Ralkan's aid as he sat, dumped on his arse.

'Am I free?' Ralkan asked, fearfully. 'Am I alive?'

'Yes. Yes, you are free and alive.' Uthor extended his hand to help Ralkan to his feet.

'Uthor!' It was Rorek.

The thane of Kadrin turned, as he got Ralkan up, to see the engineer staggering toward him, axe in hand as he supported himself on a menhir. 'Is it grobi, rat-kin? Point me to them,' he growled. 'I can still shed greenskin blood.'

'Hold,' said Uthor, his voice jubilant. 'It is Ralkan. The lorekeeper lives! 'Tell me, Ralkan, do you have word of any of our other brothers?'

The lorekeeper's face darkened.

'Yes,' he said, simply.

THE WAY BACK to Everpeak was slow and laborious, Rorek's blindness making climbing of any significance impossible, and conducted in silent remembrance. In any case, Uthor wanted to avoid much of the mountain crags. They were fell places, rife with monsters and the three dwarfs were in no condition for a fight. Instead, they went southward, following the languid flow of Skull River, keeping to the shallows, and descended into a thick forest. Wolves hunted them under the false darkness of the tree canopy and more than once Uthor had been forced to take them off the trail and hide in the wide bole of some immense oak as he heard the chatter of goblins. It stuck in his craw to skulk in the shadows, but peril stalked their every step and if they were brought to the attention of even the most innocuous predator, their doom would be assured.

Karaz-a-Karak was a mighty and imposing shadow on a sun-bleached horizon when they finally reached it, the fiery orb red and bloody in a darkening sky that threatened the onset of night, when the true dangers of the wild were made manifest.

Heavy of heart and of booted foot, the trio of dwarfs trudged down the gilded terracotta and grey stone runway that led to the formidable gate of the dwarfen capital. It had been many months since they'd left Everpeak. It would not be a happy reunion.

* * *

UTHOR HELD HIS head low. He was alone in the High King's Court; both Rorek and Ralkan were being tended by the priestesses of Valaya in a set of antechambers close by.

'Uthor, son of Algrim,' boomed the voice of Skorri Morgrimson, High King of Karaz-a-Karak. 'You have returned to us.'

'Yes, my king,' Uthor uttered with proper deference. The thane of Kadrin went down on one knee. Keeping his eyes on the ground, he dared not meet the High King's gaze.

'And the fate of Karak Varn?' the High King asked.

Uthor mustered his courage as he tried to find the words to relate his failure.

'Speak quickly,' the High King chafed. 'We march to Ungor this very night!'

Uthor looked up.

The High King was sitting upon the great Throne of Power and dressed in his full panoply of war. Clad in shimmering rune armour as forged by the venerable Skaldour in ages past, the dragon crown sat proudly on his beetling brow and with the axe of Grimnir clutched in one hand, Skorri Morgrimson was a truly fearsome sight. In the other hand, he held a quill, the end of which was dark with what appeared to be crimson ink. In front of the High King, upon a gilt and ornate cradle, was the Dammaz Kron. The Great Book of Grudges was open at a blank page.

The king's son, Furgil, stood behind him, also ready for war. The Council of Elders had been dismissed, only the High King's loremaster, his hammerer bodyguard, and Bromgar, the gatekeeper Uthor had met many months ago, were present.

'Karak Varn has fallen. Our expedition failed.' The words were like hot blades in Uthor's heart as he remained genuflect before his king.

'Survivors?' asked the High King, noting the presence of only the thane of Kadrin in his hold.

'Only the three of us that reached Everpeak.'

Skorri Morgrimson's face darkened at that admission.

'My lord,' said Uthor, his voice beginning to choke as he held out the runic cincture. 'There is something you do not know.'

The High King's eyes widened when he saw and recognised the cincture.

'No…' he breathed, tears welling in his eyes.

'My lord,' Uthor repeated, gathering his resolve. 'Emelda Skorrisdottir, clan daughter of the royal house of Karaz-a-Karak joined us in our quest but fell to the rat-kin hordes. She died with honour.'

'Dreng tromm,' the king muttered, pulling at his beard, tears streaming down his face. 'Dreng tromm.'

Bromgar approached Uthor and took the cincture from him to present solemnly to his king. Skorri Morgrimson traced the blood-flecked runes upon its surface as if touching the face of Emelda herself.

'Take it away,' he whispered, averting his gaze from the bloodied artefact. Staring back down at Uthor, all semblances of grief and anguish
drained away from the High King's face as it became as hard as stone.

'At least you can look me in the eye and say it,' the High King stated
coldly. 'You are exiled,' he added simply, getting louder and more vengeful, 'cast out of the Karaz Ankor. You and the names of your companions
will be etched in the Dammaz Kron in blood, never to be struck out –
Never!' he raged, getting up out of his throne and snapping the quill in
half in his clenched fist.

Uthor quailed before the High King's wrath but stayed his ground.

'Now leave this place, unbaraki. You are hereby expelled!'

Hammerers came from the wings and escorted Uthor away, who had
to be helped to his feet, so great was the shame upon his shoulders.

THE NEXT MORNING as the great gates to Everpeak boomed shut in their
wake, Uthor cast his gaze skyward. Flurries of snow were building
amidst darkening cloud and a tinge of chilling frost pricked at the wild
grasses. Autumn was ending and, in a few more weeks, winter would be
setting in. Uthor thought of Skorri Morgrimson as the High King led
his army to Karak Ungor, great marching columns of dawi intent on
vengeance and retribution, standards reflecting the glimmer of the low
lying sun, drums beating and horns blaring. There was a time when the
thane of Kadrin would have relished being part of such a muster; now
he could not wait to be as far away from it as possible.

'What do we do now?' said Rorek, guided by the vacant-looking
Ralkan. The engineer had a blindfold over his eyes foregoing his patch,
which now seemed surplus to his needs.

Ralkan no longer bore the book of remembering. It had been taken by
the loremasters of Everpeak as a record of what had happened. Ralkan
had done much to fill it with all the dwarfs' deeds in the time it had
taken to the reach Karaz-a-Karak in the hope that the names of the slain
would be remembered, if nothing else.

The three of them had been returned their weapons and other
belongings, and even given provisions and fresh clothes before being
summarily ejected from the hold. Only Dunrik's axe remained behind
for the priests of Gazul to inter and set at least his spirit to rest in the
Halls of the Ancestors.

Uthor kept an eye on the horizon as he replied.

'We go northward, to Karak Kadrin and the Shrine of Grimnir. There is
but one more vow we must make, and I would make it there before my
father if he still lives.'

With that the dwarfs trudged away from Everpeak lost in their thoughts.
The wind was gathering in the north. A storm was coming.

EPILOGUE

SKARTOOTH AWOKE IN a deep gorge. His hood was torn, the rat skull ripped free and lost in his plummet over the edge of the plateau. Noises, like crunching bones and sucking meat, emanated from above. Dazed and bruised, sporting numerous small cuts and grazes, the goblin warlord struggled to his feet. Something dug into his bare foot that was swaddled with dirty, black bandages. Skartooth grimaced in pain when he saw it had drawn blood. He looked down, ready to vent his diminutive wrath upon whatever rock or sharp stone had cut him. His mouth gaped open. Beneath his foot was the iron collar, the one that Fangrak had stolen!

Gathering the artefact quickly to his breast, Skartooth hurried away. The goblin was acutely aware of the deepening shadows in the nearby caves and though he disliked the blazing sun overhead he was nervous of what things might dwell in those places. There was also the possibility of disaffected orcs and goblins to consider. Likely, they would not take kindly to Skartooth after their abject defeat, despite any protestations that the failure was all Fangrak's doing.

Skartooth took a wending trail down the gorge, picking through overhanging crags and avoiding the worst of the sun's glare. It didn't last long; something lurking in the gloom set his heart racing and his teeth on edge. He took his chances within a deep cave, its entrance so narrow that no beast of any great size could possibly reside there.

Leaving a cooling trail of piss in his wake as he failed to master his fear, Skartooth wandered into a large cavern. Shafts of hazy sunlight drifted down from a natural amphitheatre and illuminated a large patch of ground. Skartooth's heart was in his mouth again when he saw the bleached bones collected there.

Something stirred behind the goblin, something unseen as he'd wandered aimlessly into its lair. Hot breath lapped at the back of his neck. Skartooth turned slowly and came face to face with a massive, lizard-like creature with a thick, scaled head like a battering ram and broad, flat wings. Skartooth knew the creature's like: it was a wyvern. The shaman he'd stolen the iron collar from rode such a beast.

The wyvern hissed, baring its fangs. Skartooth soiled himself and backed away into the light, clambering over the bone nest, kicking skulls and rib bones loose as he fled. The wyvern followed. Skartooth noticed it only had one horn; the other had been shorn off at the nub. The beast snarled and flicked a rasping tail that ended in a savage-looking, poisonous barb. As it opened its mouth, preparing to devour the meagre morsel that was Skartooth, the goblin warlord held up his arms in a vain attempt to fend it off, eyes closed as he waited for the end.

At once the wyvern backed down and hissed its obeisance.

Skartooth opened his eyes, realising he wasn't languishing in the wyvern's gullet. He saw that the creature had retreated. The collar glowed warmly in his outstretched hand. Skartooth brandished it experimentally in front of him.

'Bow to me,' he murmured tentatively.

The wyvern went down onto its knuckles and lowered its head submissively.

An evil grin spread across the goblin's face.

'Skartooth got a wyvern.'

HONOURKEEPER

Nick Kyme

ACT ONE
WROUGHT IN IRON

CHAPTER ONE

Beginnings and Endings

BEYOND ARCHER RANGE, King Bagrik surveyed the carnage of the battlefield from atop a ridge of stone. Across a muddy valley riddled with trenches, earthworks and abatis his army gave their blood, sweat and steel. Sat astride his ancestral war shield, carried by two of his stoutest hearth guard warriors, the king of Karak Ungor had an unparalleled view.

The silver moat the elves had fashioned shimmered like an iridescent ribbon, reflecting the flames of burning towers. Bagrik watched keenly as gromril-plated bridges were dropped over it, landing like felled trees for the siege towers and warriors with scaling ladders to cross. On the opposite side of the ridge where it fell away into a shallow ravine, Bagrik could hear the heartening din of smiths at their forge fires, toiling in the dwarf encampment making more bridges, bolts for the ballista, quarrels and pavises. The smell of soot and iron drifting on the breeze was like a taste of home.

Bagrik's expression hardened as a siege tower lurched and slipped on one of the bridges, falling into the molten moat and taking most of its crew with it. Others had better fortune, and battles erupted across the length of the elven wall with spear, hammer and axe.

He swelled with pride at the sight of it, all of his hearth brothers locked in furious battle with a powerful foe. Sorrow tempered that pride, and wrath crushed both emotions as Bagrik glowered at the city.

Tor Eorfith the elves called it. Eyrie Rock. It was well named, for the towers at the zenith of the city had soared far into the sky, piercing cloud and seemingly touching the stars. They were the dominion of mages, great observatories where the elven sorcerers could contemplate the constellations and allegedly portend future events.

Bagrik wagered they had not seen this coming.

He had no love for sky, cloud and stars; his domain was the earth and its solidity beneath and about him gave him comfort. The earth contained the essence of the ancestor gods, for it was to the heart of the world that they had returned once their task was done. They had taught the dwarfs how to work ore to forge structures, armour and weapons.

Grungni together with his sons, Smednir and Thungni had shown them the true nature of magic, how to capture it within the rune and etch it indelibly upon blades, talismans and armour in order to fashion artefacts of power. Bagrik had no love for the ephemeral sorcery of elves. Manipulating the true elements of the world in such a way was disharmonious. At best attempting to control them smacked of hubris, at worst it was disrespectful. No, Bagrik held no truck with such transient things. It angered him. The mage towers had been the first to go.

Crushed by hefty chunks of rock flung by dwarf stone throwers, the towers had exploded in a conflagration of myriad colours as they were destroyed, the arcane secrets and the alchemy of their denizens turned against them, and only serving to affirm Bagrik's vehement beliefs. They were just blackened spikes of stone now, broken fingers thrust into an uncaring sky, their communion with the stars at an end.

It was a fitting epitaph.

For the briefest of moments the air was on fire as elven sorcery met dwarf runecraft, forcing Bagrik back to the present. Further down the ridge, their litanies to the ancestors solemn and resonant, the runesmiths worked at their anvils. Not mere forgesmiths' anvils, no. These were runic artefacts – the Anvils of Doom. Agrin Oakenheart, venerable rune lord of Karak Ungor led his two apprentices, esteemed master runesmiths in their own right, in the rites of power as they dissipated hostile elven magicks and unleashed chained lightning upon the foe. With each arcing bolt, Bagrik felt his beard bristle as the charge ran through his ancestral armour.

Death wreathed the battlefield like a sombre shroud, but it was at the gatehouse where its greatest harvest would be reaped.

Break the gate, break the elves. Bagrik clenched his fist as his gaze fell upon the battle being fought there. He would settle for nothing less…

'Heave!' Morek bellowed above the thunder. The dwarf's voice resonated through the bronze mask of his helmet as he urged his warriors again.

'Heave with all your strength. Grungni is watching you!'

And all thirty of his hearth guard warriors did.

Beneath the gromril-plated roof of a battering ram, the armoured dwarfs pulled the ram back for another charge. Runes etched down its iron shaft blazed as the gromril ram-head, forged into the bearded visage of the ancestor god Grungni, smashed into the gate. It was a barrier the likes of which Morek had never known, adorned with gemstones and carved from seemingly unbreakable wood. The eagle device upon the gate barely showed a scratch. The elves, despite his initial beliefs, knew their craft. Morek was determined that it would not avail them. Sweating beneath his armour, his orders were relentless.

'Again! There will be no rest until this gate is down!'

Shock waves ran down the iron with the impact as dwarf tenacity met elven resistance and found each other at an impasse.

Breathing hard as he wiped his beard with the back of his glove, Morek paused a moment and detected the groan of metal high above. It was the third day of the siege; he'd had plenty of time to survey the city's defences. The elves had cauldrons above the gatehouse.

'Shields!' he roared, long and loud.

The hearth guard reacted as one, creating a near-impenetrable shield wall to protect the vulnerable flanks of the battering ram.

Near-impenetrable but not invincible.

There was a whoosh of flame and an actinic stink permeated Morek's nose guard as the elves released their alchemical fire.

Screaming drowned out the roar of the conflagration as hearth guard warriors burned down like candles with shortened wicks. Reflected on the underside of his shield Morek saw a blurred shape fall from the narrow bridge where they made their assault and land in the moat beneath. A pillar of blue-white fire spiralled skyward as the burning dwarf struck the moat, so high it touched cloud. The elves, employing more of their thrice-cursed sorcery, had filled a deep trench around their city with molten silver and the alchemical fire's reaction with the shimmering liquid was spectacular yet terrifying.

A second deluge of the deadly liquid smashed against the battering ram, as the elves vented their stocks in desperation. Heat came through Morek's shield in a wave, pricking his skin despite his armour. He grit his teeth against the onslaught, watching iridescent sparks crackle and die upon the stone at his feet as the elven siege deterrent spilled away.

No screams this time. The attack abated. Two cauldrons had been expended. The elves had no more. It would take time for them to replenish the deadly liquid fire. In the brief respite, Morek took stock and smiled grimly. Only three hearth guard dead: his warriors had closed ranks quickly. But the elves had more. As the battering of the gate resumed, a flurry of white-fletched arrows whickered down at the dwarfs from above, thudding into shields and plate. Despite the armoured canopy of the ram, Morek took one in the pauldron. The dwarf at his flank, Hagri, was struck incredibly between gorget and face-guard, and died gurgling blood. Morek chewed his beard in anger. Hagri had fought at Morek's side for over seventy years. It was no way for such a noble warrior to die.

The arrow storm was relentless, the dwarfs effectively pinned as they raised shields again, unable to work the ram and protect themselves at the same time. Peering upwards through a crack between shield tip and the ram canopy, Morek saw white-robed elves – stern of face with silver swan helmets gleaming – loose steel-fanged death with ruthless purpose. Archers lined the battlements and as Morek scanned across he saw one of the elven mages incanting soundlessly as the battle din eclipsed his eldritch tongue. In a thunderclap of power, the mage was illuminated by a crackling cerulean aura. Forked lightning arced from his luminous form and the mage's silver hair stood on end as the energy was expulsed, straight towards Morek and his warriors. But before the bolts could strike they hit an invisible barrier and were deflected away. Blinking back the savage after flare, and muttering thanks to Agrin Oakenheart's runesmiths, Morek tracked the bolt's erratic deviation.

One of the distant dwarf siege towers assaulting the eastern wall exploded as the lightning found a new target and vented its wrath. Dwarfs plunged earthward from the high parapet of the tower, mouthing silent screams. The assault ramp and the upper tower hoarding were utterly destroyed. Fire ravaged it within and without, and the siege tower came to a grinding halt. In its place though, three more towers moved into position, dragged and pushed by hordes of dwarf warriors, those at the front protected by large moveable pavises of iron and wood. As one, the heavy armoured ramps crashed down upon the elven parapets, crushing them before disgorging throngs of clansdwarfs.

All across the churned earth, as far as the deepening black of oncoming night in the distant east and west, the dwarfs marched in droves. Teams of sappers flung grapnels, heaving as they found purchase to tear down ruined sections of tower and wall. Quarrellers, crouching behind barricades or within shallow trench lines, kept up a steady barrage of bolts in an effort to stymie the heavy death toll being reaped by the elven archers and ballista. On the bloody ramps of the siege towers, and battling hard upon scaling ladders, dwarf warriors fought and died. But it was at the great gate, the principal entrance to the elven city, that the fighting was fiercest. Knowing this would be so, Morek had taken his finest hearth guard warriors and told his king he would break it. He had no intention of failing in that oath.

'We are like stuck grobi sat out here,' said Fundin Ironfinger, a hearth guard warrior crouched behind Morek, his shield locked with that of his thane.

Morek had to shout to be heard above the insistent thud of raining arrows.

'Bah, this is nothing, lad – a light shower, no more than that. They can't shoot at us forever, and once the elgi run out of arrows we'll have this gate down. Then they'll taste dawi steel–' Morek was forced to duck down as the storm intensified.

'Eh, lad?' he said during a short lull in the arrow fire, looking back at Fundin.

The hearth guard didn't answer. He was dead; shot through the eye.

Dutifully, another hearth guard moved up the line to take his place and Fundin's body was edged beyond the relative protection of the canopy to be punctured with further arrows.

No, Morek thought grimly, he had no intention of failing in his oath but if the arrow storm didn't end soon, he'd have no warriors left to break down the gate and fulfil it. Touching the runic amulet around his neck, he made a pledge to Grungni that this would not be so.

THE AIR WAS thick with arrows, bolts, fire, lightning and stone. Bagrik watched as a battery of mangonels flung massive chunks of rock that had been hewn from the hillside and smashed them into Tor Eorfith, shattering walls and pulverising flesh and bone. With grim satisfaction, he saw one missile strike the central arch of the elven gatehouse where his hearth guard stood beleaguered beneath their battering ram.

Elven bodies fell like white rain.

CHEERS GREETED THE destruction of the gatehouse, the arrow storm brought to an abrupt and bloody halt. Debris fell along with the elven dead, fat pieces of rock and limp bodies bouncing off the gromril roof of the battering ram.

Morek urged the hearth guard on to even greater efforts. They swung and pushed, swung and pushed with the thunderous insistence of an angry giant. At last, the runes upon the ram-head were doing their work, forcing cracks into the sorcerous wards that galvanised the gate. Magic permeated all that the elves did; it was even seeped into the very rock and wood of their settlements. Tor Eorfith was no different. It had been enchantment that had repulsed the dwarfs for this long. That protection had ended with the life of the silver-haired mage, now nothing more than a shattered footnote in history, dead and broken at the foot of the outer gatehouse wall.

Thickening cracks appeared in the eagle gate as it finally yielded to the punishing efforts of the hearth guard.

Morek could sense they were close.

'One last pull!'

With an almighty splintering of wood, the elven gate was split in two. Through the rough-hewn gap, Morek glimpsed azure robes and shining elven mail. A cohort of spearmen faced them; tips angled outward like a forest of razor spikes. Then as one the elves parted like a crystal sea to reveal a pair of bolt throwers of ivory-stained wood, and both fashioned into an effigy of a hawk.

The dwarfs raised shields as the javelin-like projectiles flew at them. Three more of the hearth guard were killed, impaled on the sharp missiles. Morek swung his axe once the barrage was over, working out the stiffness from his shoulder. The spearmen had closed ranks again, ready to skewer the foe. Morek raised his axe, runes upon the blade shimmering, and signalled the charge.

BAGRIK WATCHED THE gatehouse fall and the hearth guard rush forward to meet the elven spearmen within. The high ridge was an excellent vantage point to view the battle from and the king took in the full spectacle. Even as the elves fought, as they spat arrows from their tower walls, unleashed arcane fire and lightning and thrust with gleaming spears and swords, Bagrik could tell that this was the final push. The dwarf army was on the brink of breaking through.

Three long days, and the cusp of victory was within his grasp. It did nothing to satisfy him, it did not slake his thirst for vengeance, nor did it quieten his anger. No protracted siege this; no picket lines had been erected, no wells blocked or provisions destroyed or tainted. Full assault. That was all. Come his reckoning at Gazul's Gate, the final portal before admittance into the Halls of Ancestors and the dwarf afterlife, Bagrik would be held to account for the blood expended.

He cared not.

'My king,' the voice of Grikk Ironbeard, captain of the ironbreakers, interrupted Bagrik's thoughts. Grikk bowed low before his king as he announced himself. Not one inch of the ironbreaker's body could be seen beneath the all-encompassing suit of gromril. Even his face was concealed behind a stylised dwarf mask. Only Grikk's wiry black beard was visible. It was a necessary precaution. As an ironbreaker, Grikk was responsible for guarding the dwarf underway, a dangerous underground road between the holds that was fraught with many monsters. Today, Grikk had a different task. But it was one for which his ironbreaker armour and his skills as a tunnel fighter were ideally suited.

'Rugnir and the sappers are ready. The final assault can commence.'

Bagrik nodded, his gaze drifting over to the south wall of the city where Rugnir and the hold's engineers were tunnelling in preparation to undermine it. Bagrik had five throngs of clan warriors held in reserve, together with the hold's longbeards to exploit the breach when it came.

Bagrik's gaze remained fixed as he replied gruffly.

'Secure the tunnel, kill any opposition.'

'Yes, my king.'

Grikk departed swiftly, the sound of clanking armour left in his wake.

Bagrik watched a moment longer before he gave the order to advance. An entire phalanx stood upon the flat ridge, clan warriors and hearth guard all. Ten thousand more dwarfs. The hammer with which to crush the elves beneath the anvil of warriors already breaking through the elven defences below. War horns blared down the line one after the other, raising a thunderous clamour. The dwarfs' march towards the elven city was resolute and relentless. Bagrik went with them, brought to the forefront of the attack and into the cauldron of battle by his shield bearers.

Regarding the bloody fire-wreathed vista, the swathes of dead, the wanton destruction levelled at two great civilisations, Bagrik couldn't help wonder.

How did it all come to this?

CHAPTER TWO

Fateful Meetings

KARAK UNGOR WAS the northern-most fastness of all the mountain holds of the Karaz Ankor, the everlasting realm of the dwarfs. The rocky edifice of stone and bronze was a monument of dwarf tenacity and their expertise in the building of impregnable fortresses. For over two thousand years, Karak Ungor had stood stalwart against ice storms, cataclysm and the predations of greenskins. In the eyes of the dwarfs, this was but an eye blink in the grand chronology of history, for the mountain dwellers made things to last and endure the capricious ravages of time and conquest.

In the vastness of the hold's outer gateway hall, a small welcoming committee awaited their guests from across the Great Ocean. These dwarfs were little more than specks in a huge expanse of stone, standing before the immense gate that led out of the hold and into the northern Worlds Edge Mountains.

Gigantic figureheads of the ancestor gods that were carved into the rock of the mountain loomed over them. Grungni, Valaya and Grimnir, the greatest of all the ancient deities of the dwarfs, each dominated one of the three open walls of the chamber. Craggy-featured, the ancestors were stern and imposing as they regarded their descendants as if in silent appraisal. No dwarf would ever wish to be found wanting under their gaze.

The fourth wall was taken up almost entirely by the great gate. It was encompassed by a sweeping arch of bronze, and inlaid with runes of gold and myriad gemstones dug from the mountain. The gate itself was

431

a huge slab of smoothed stone with copper filigree describing an effigy of two dwarf kings upon their thrones. It was a magnificent sight and the main entrance into and out of the hold. Either side of it were a pair of statuesque hearth guard, their faces hardly visible beneath their stout, half-face helmets and braided beards. Each carried a broad-bladed axe, resting against the pauldron of their ancient armour, their stillness belying their readiness. One bore a large bronze-rimmed warhorn at rest next to his chest. He was the gate warden and the hold's chief herald.

Above the quartet of warriors, patrolling a stone platform that rose over the great gate arch, were ten quarrellers with crossbows slung across their backs. These dwarfs were the interior gate guard, the first line of defence of the hold and from whom the call to arms would be raised should it come under attack.

Morek, at the edge of the welcoming party, fidgeted restlessly in his armour. He had wanted to double the troops on the gate and supplement it with a cohort of thirty more hearth guard by way of a show of strength and intent, but the queen would not have it – they were negotiating trade with the elves, not war.

Queen Brunvilda, wife of the great king Bagrik, was at Morek's right, occupying the centre of the delegation. She was royally attired with deep blue robes, fringed with gold and threaded with runes of copper and bronze. Upon her brow she wore a simple mitre with a single ruby in the middle. Her long hair was the colour of tanned leather, bound up in concentric knots and pinned in place invisibly. Around her waist was a bodice of leather that squeezed her matronly figure and accentuated her ample bosom. It was augmented by a gilded and bejewelled cincture. Her eyes were grey like slate but held warmth akin to the forge fires of the lower deeps. All told, Morek thought she was a remarkable woman.

The dwarf thane had his own claim to royalty, albeit a weak one. His clan was a distant cousin to that of High King Gotrek Starbreaker. There was noble blood in his veins, though he had never sought a regal claim, always content to serve the kings and queens of Ungor.

To the queen's right was Kandor Silverbeard, a merchant, diplomat and the royal treasurer. Kandor wore expensive garments of emerald and tan, a testament to the profit of his gold gathering and silver-laced tongue. He was festooned with gilded accoutrements, including a lacquered wood cane encrusted with gemstones. Though Morek had no clue why Kandor needed it; the merchant could walk perfectly well without a stick. Kandor's reddish beard was well groomed and immaculately braided, his hair combed and pristine. Despite himself, Morek brushed down his armour surreptitiously with a gloved hand in an effort to make its gleam more lustrous. He saw the merchant look askance at him, halting Morek's pre-emptive preening in its tracks. The captain of the hearth guard's response was gruff and inaudible.

The rest of the party was made up of ten more hearth guard, the only additional warriors the queen had conceded to, imposing in their ranks behind them. None of the dwarfs had spoken for some time since their arrival in the outer gateway hall, though a dulcet chorus of hammers striking anvils carried from the lower deeps on air heavy with the smell of soot and thick with forge-warmth.

Morek broke the silence.

'Your elgi guests are late.'

Kandor Silverbeard didn't look over as he answered.

'They will arrive soon enough, Morek. Don't you have any patience?'

'Aye, I've plenty. I could stand here until Grimnir returned from the Northern Wastes and still wait another fifty years if needs be,' barked Morek, feeling challenged as he levelled his steely gaze at the imperious merchant.

'They are guests of our hold, Thane Stonehammer, not merely that of Kandor Silverbeard's,' said Queen Brunvilda, her tone soft yet powerful.

'Of course, my queen.' Chastened, Morek averted his gaze from her, feeling a sudden burning at his cheeks, and was glad his armour largely hid his face. 'But we dwarfs have strict habits and routines. All I'm saying is lateness is no way to gain our favour.'

'Their ways are not our ways,' the queen counselled, though she didn't need to remind Morek of the fact. To his mind, elves were utterly unlike the dwarfs in both appearance and demeanour. These stargazing explorers were not content in their own lands it seemed, and deliberately sought out others to satisfy some innate wanderlust. Morek thought them effete and brittle; he fancied they would be ill-suited to life within the hold. He smirked beneath his faceplate at the thought of their discomfort and hoped they would soon leave as a result of it.

'It begs the question then, my lady, how we ever think an agreement can be reached between our peoples?' Morek returned, choosing his words carefully so as not to offend his queen.

Kandor answered for her.

'You are a warrior, Morek, so I shall leave the defence of the realm to you,' he said, turning to look at the captain of the hearth guard. 'But I am a merchant and ambassador, so I ask you to leave matters of trade and diplomacy to me. This pact will succeed. What's more, it will strengthen our realm and ensure its continued prosperity.'

'You'd do well to remember that all dwarfs are charged with the protection of the hold,' Morek replied. 'And do not think me so foolish as to be unaware of your eye for profit in this.'

'As royal treasurer, it is for the wealth of the clans of Ungor that I–'

'Enough!' said Queen Brunvilda, halting Kandor's retort before it could continue, 'Our guests are here.'

Slowly, a portal within the great gate was opening. Much smaller than the gate itself, the portal was the true entryway into the hold. The grand doorway of Karak Ungor had not been opened in over two thousand years, not since it had first been founded and the entirety of the hold's armies had marched forth to join the forces of the then High King, the venerable Snorri Whitebeard. Dwarfs and elves had come together then, too, but despite the intractable nature of the dwarfs, things had changed during that time and alliances were now being forged anew.

A clarion call resonated throughout the large chamber as the gate warden blew hard on his warhorn, announcing the arrival of the elves. At his signal, his fellow warriors stood to attention, the stamp of their booted feet in perfect unison, and the quarrellers stopped patrolling as they observed an honourable stillness before their new allies from across the sea.

The elves were fey creatures, tall and proud, whose pale skin shimmered with an otherworldly lustre. They glided across the dwarf flagstones as light as air, their white and azure robes fluttering on some unseen breeze. There was a stark and wondrous beauty about them, powerful and frightening at the same time. Yet to Morek's eyes, they seemed delicate and thin. Despite their unearthly aura, what could these lofty creatures possess that the dwarfs had any need of?

The party of elves was led by what Morek assumed was an ambassador amongst their people. He was dressed in white robes. Golden vambraces, worn for decoration, gleamed beneath wide sleeves trimmed with tiny sapphires. The ambassador's hair was the colour of silver and rested upon either shoulder evenly, and though his smile was benign, sadness lingered behind his eyes that he could not hide.

A warrior wearing ceremonial half-armour of fluted plate and overlapping scale of glimmering silver followed closely behind. His eyes, almond-shaped like the rest of his kin, seemed perpetually narrowed, and a long angular nose spoke of royal bearing. A slender sword, its hilt encrusted with rubies, was scabbarded at a plaited belt at the elf's waist. Golden hair cascaded from his stern countenance, and a gilded crown set with gemstones framed the elf's brow as he regarded the hall with haughty indifference. This then was their leader, Morek decided, the elf prince.

Two others came in the prince's wake, also nobles. One was a male with long, black hair, also enrobed, though his garb was ostensibly more opulent than that of the ambassador. This one had an ill-favoured look about him, and Morek saw the implied threat in the way the elf toyed idly with the hilt of the sword that he wore at his waist.

His companion was a female, similarly attired, though she wore a small circlet of silver around her head. The pair were muttering quietly, in such close consort that Morek found it uncomfortable to watch them. Certainly, the female possessed a… *presence* that the hearth guard was at once attracted to and repelled by. He had to fight to stop himself from lowering his gaze. The male alongside her, walking with a disdainful swagger, seemed to notice the dwarf's discomfort and whispered something into the female's ear to which she laughed quietly. Morek felt his cheeks redden and his annoyance grow.

One other elf stood out from the rest of the entourage that trailed in after the nobles in pairs, an entourage that consisted of musicians, gift bearers, pennant carriers, servants and some fifty elven spearmen. He was bigger than the rest, not just taller, but broader too, and seemed the most ill at ease with their newfound surroundings. His straw-coloured hair was wild and bound into a series of plaited tails. A thick pelt of white fur was draped over his muscled shoulders and he wore scale armour over which was a gilt breastplate. A long dagger was sheathed at his hip and a doubled-bladed axe slung across his back.

The bodyguard, Morek thought, noting the way that this elf surveyed the chamber, searching every darkened alcove for threats and enemies. Perhaps, Morek wondered, not all elves were so weak and fanciful. Was it possible he had misjudged them?

PRINCE ITHALRED WRINKLED his nose at the foul stench of the dwarfs' domain. A 'magnificent hold' he had been told. It looked like little more than a tomb buried into the earth, gladly forgotten but now exhumed for some unconscionable reason. This 'great gate' Malbeth had spoken of was little more than roughly hewn stone peppered with gemstones. It had none of the flowing lines, the smoothness and artful consideration of elvish architecture. Worse still, the air was stiflingly hot and thick with acrid fumes. Ithalred smelled oil, tasted soot in his mouth and at once longed for the high silver towers of his realm at Tor Eorfith.

What is this place you have brought us to, Malbeth? he thought, his eyes upon the ambassador's back as he led them to the awaiting dwarfs.

'They call this hole in the ground a *kingdom*?' Lethralmir whispered to Arthelas, echoing his prince's thoughts as he strode behind him. The seeress laughed quietly, her musical voice arousing more than just the simple pleasure of companionship in the blade-master.

'They build such grand chambers, though, Lethralmir,' she whispered back.

'Mighty indeed,' the elf replied sarcastically, casting his gaze about in the gloom. 'Yet *they* are so diminutive. Do you think, perhaps, that they are compensating for something?' he added, smirking.

Arthelas laughed out loud, unable to control herself. A scathing glance from Prince Ithalred silenced them both.

'Your brother is ever the serious diplomat, is he not, dear Arthelas?' scoffed Lethralmir in an undertone.

The seeress smiled demurely, and the elven blade-master felt his ardour deepen.

'WELCOME DEAR FRIENDS, to Karak Ungor,' said Kandor, bowing before the elf ambassador. The dwarf merchant's gaze extended the greeting to all, in particular the prince, who seemed unmoved by the gesture.

'*Tromm*, Kandor Silverbeard,' said the ambassador warmly, in rudimentary Khazalid, and clasped Kandor's hand firmly.

'Tromm, Malbeth. You honour us with these words,' Kandor returned, glowing outwardly at the elf's use of the dwarfs' native tongue – 'tromm' was used by way of greeting and a mark of respect amongst dwarfs at the length and quality of their beards. The incongruousness of an elf saying it was not lost on Morek, however.

Honour us? Kandor, you are a grobi-fondling wazzock, the elgi has no beard! If anything, he besmirches us with his hairless chin, thought Morek, gritting his teeth at the merchant's obsequiousness, and wondering if Kandor's ancestral line was tainted with elf blood.

This was not Malbeth's first visit to the hold. The elf was a ranger, as well as an ambassador, and had travelled from Yvresse on the east coast of Ulthuan, across the Great Ocean and to the Old World. There he had met Kandor Silverbeard, who was delivering shipments of ore southwards to the other holds of the Worlds Edge Mountains. The two had struck up a firm friendship, echoing that of the elf lord, Malekith, and the first High King of the dwarfs, Snorri Whitebeard. It was but an echo of that halcyon time. That former alliance was now cast in an inauspicious light, the traitorous son of Aenarion the Defender having fled Ulthuan before the might of Caledor the First, and now seeking succour in the lands of Naggaroth.

Such things were not of consequence, however, and talk between dwarf and elf had soon turned to trade, and after accompanying Kandor as far south as Mount Gunbad, they had returned north to Karak Ungor. The elf's stay had been brief, and Morek had never met the ambassador during that time, though he looked as effeminate as he had imagined.

'We too are honoured, by your generous hospitality,' the elf, Malbeth, replied before turning to the dwarf queen.

'Noble Queen Brunvilda,' he said, bowing. 'It seems like only yesterday when I was last a guest in these halls.'

'Aye, Malbeth,' began the queen, 'It has only been twenty-three years, little more than a shift in the wind,' she said, smiling broadly.

Malbeth returned the gesture, before announcing the rest of his kin. 'May I present Arthelas, seeress of Tor Eorfith and the prince's sister.' The demure elf came forward and gave a shallow bow to the queen, before Malbeth continued, 'Lethralmir, of the prince's court.' The ambassador's gaze seemed to harden as it fell upon the lean-faced blade-master, who gave an overly extravagant bow towards their dwarf hosts. 'This is Korhvale of Chrace, the prince's champion,' Malbeth added. The muscular elf preferred to stand as he was, with his prince in eyeshot, and only nodded sternly.

'Finally,' said Malbeth, stepping back, 'Prince Ithalred of Tor Eorfith.'

The prince came forward of his own accord, eyeing each of the dwarfs in turn, his gaze lingering on the warriors especially.

'I do not see your king,' said Ithalred abruptly, dispensing with all bonhomie as if it were an enemy run through on his sword.

Morek bristled at the elf's impertinence, about to speak, before a glance from Queen Brunvilda stopped him.

'I am Queen Brunvilda of Karak Ungor,' she said to the prince, stepping forward and inclining her head in greeting. 'The king will meet us in the Great Hall once you are settled. Alas, an old wound makes walking for my liege lord difficult and I was sent to greet you in his place.'

Prince Ithalred glanced around, not deigning to look the queen in the eye as he replied. 'I look forward to our first meeting,' he said, his own mastery of the dwarf language, unlike Malbeth's, was crude as if the words were uneasy on his tongue.

'He dishonours our queen!' Morek hissed to Kandor who had retreated to stand alongside the hearth guard captain.

'They do not know our customs, that is all,' Kandor snapped back in a harsh whisper, his withering gaze demanding silence.

Ithalred seemed not to hear and turned and spoke in elvish to his attendants. Upon his beckoning, the servants and gift bearers came forward.

'We bring riches from our island realm as a token of our friendship.' The prince's words were neither warm nor obviously sincere, though the array of gifts was fine indeed with belts of silks, beauteous elf potteries, opulent furs and spices.

'We are honoured by these tokens,' said the queen, still observing due deference to the prince.

'Yes,' Prince Ithalred answered, 'and yet I see your hospitality extends to meeting us with armed guards.'

A slight ripple of indignation crossed the queen's face but she did not act on it.

'They are the ceremonial honour guard of Karak Ungor,' she explained carefully, her tone calm but taut. 'In our traditions, these warriors greet kings and nobles of other holds. So it is the same with you, good prince.'

'Are we to be "guarded" then, whilst we visit this... *hold*?' the elf continued. 'Under house arrest until we are due to return? This does not smack of alliance, being met by warriors at your kingdom's gate like an enemy laying siege to its walls.'

'It is a great honour to be received by the royal hearth guard!' bellowed Morek suddenly, unable to keep his patience any longer.

'Captain Morek,' snapped Queen Brunvilda, before the elves could reply. 'Hold your tongue!'

Ithalred was fashioning a retort when Malbeth intervened. 'Please, there is no need. My prince is tired from our journey and acknowledges this gracious welcome,' he said with a glance at Ithalred, who, to the ambassador's apparent relief, seemed suddenly disinterested in the exchange. Though Malbeth also caught a look from the black-haired elf, the one called Lethralmir, who smiled mirthlessly at him. The ambassador averted his gaze, focussing his attention back to the dwarf queen.

'Perhaps we can be shown to our quarters?' Malbeth suggested. 'A rest will clear all our heads of fatigue.'

'Of course,' Queen Brunvilda said politely, turning to Kandor.

'We have prepared extensive chambers for you and your party,' the merchant said quickly, his relief at the crisis having been averted obvious on his face.

'They expect us to dwell in caves like them, no doubt,' hissed the black-haired elf.

Morek found his distaste towards Lethralmir deepening by the moment as he spoke to the eldritch female, Arthelas. She seemed to wane as the talk went on, her beauty slowly fracturing as if the travails of the elves' journey were taking a heavy toll.

Kandor seemed not to hear the black-haired elf's remark, or at least he chose to ignore it, determined as he was to win over the delegation.

'If you would follow me,' he said courteously.

Cringing wattock, thought Morek then said, 'Wait,' and showed his palm. 'No weapons may be carried by an outsider beyond the outer gateway hall,' he told the elves, 'You must relinquish them here.'

At a signal from their captain, the hearth guard came forward to collect the elves' spears, bows and blades. At the same time, the one wearing the furs, Korhvale, stepped between his prince and the advancing dwarfs. Though he didn't speak, his intentions were clear. No elf would be handing over their arms.

The prince muttered something in elvish to the warrior who stepped back, though his eyes never left the hearth guard.

'Is this how you establish a bond of trust, by surrounding your allies with troops and then demanding they submit their weapons?' the prince asked with growing agitation.

'We request it only,' said Kandor, still trying to recover the situation. 'Your weapons would be stored in a private armoury.'

'Private?' queried the prince, waving away his ambassador's nascent protests, 'I see little privacy or consideration here, *dwarf*.'

'Even still,' Morek asserted, stepping forward in spite of the six elf spearmen that had come swiftly, almost unnoticeably, to their prince's side and were brandishing their arms with meaning. 'You *will* be disarmed before you enter the hold proper.'

Though Morek was over three feet shorter than the elves, he stood before them unshakeable like a mountain and would not be disobeyed.

The elven bodyguard, Korhvale, interceded again, knuckles clenched and aggression written across his face.

'Then you shall have to *take* them from us,' he muttered, his elven accent thick as he struggled to pronounce the words. This time Ithalred was content to let it play out, his face a mask of stone. Behind him, the black-haired elf watched with profound amusement, an ugly smile upon his lips, whilst the female seemed suddenly fearful and unsure of where the confrontation was heading.

Morek had no such concerns.

'By Grungni, I *will* do it,' he snarled belligerently, reaching for his axe. His hearth guard moved up behind him, enclosing the other dwarf nobles and preparing to brandish their own weapons.

'Thane Stonehammer!' bellowed Queen Brunvilda, who had kept her silence throughout the heated exchange until now. 'Do not dare draw your weapon in anger before me,' she ordered. 'Return your hearth guard to the west hall barracks at once.'

Morek turned and made a face behind his armoured mask, the substance of his mood obvious in his eyes.

'I would not leave you... *unattended* my queen,' he protested with a fierce glance at the glowering elves. 'No hearth guard in the history of the hold has ever–'

'I am well aware of our hold's history, my thane, and have lived many long years within its halls. What need have I of warriors at my side with you as my honour guard,' she added with a thin smile, by way of maintaining Morek's reputation and standing. 'Your concern is unnecessary. Now, please dismiss the hearth guard.'

Morek opened his mouth again, made clear by the movement of his beard, but clamped it shut when the queen's own expression made it apparent that she would brook no further argument.

The captain of the hearth guard's shoulders sagged slightly, though he took care to fire a warning glare at Korhvale before he retreated.

You were close to tasting my axe, it said. Morek meant every word.

Morek bowed once in front of the queen, who nodded in turn, before ordering his warriors from the outer gateway hall. Dutifully the dwarfs departed, the sound of clanking armour echoing in their wake, and Morek went to stand back alongside his queen having to content himself with glowering at the elves.

'Now, dear *friends*,' Queen Brunvilda began anew, 'as queen of Karak Ungor, I humbly ask you to leave your blades and bows here. No armed force has ever entered Karak Ungor, save those of us dawi. I will not break with that tradition now,' she said, her voice soft but commanding. 'I, nor any of my warriors, shall take them from you. Rather you will be *asked* to relinquish them. There is an antechamber to this very hall where you may take your weapons until you are ready to leave us. Noble Prince Ithalred,' she added, facing the prince, 'your fine sword is clearly an heirloom and we dwarfs know the value and importance of such bonds. I would not ask you to part with it and, as such, I give you my personal sanction to carry it in this hold. A dwarf's oath is his bond,' she said, 'and it is stronger than stone.'

The prince was about to respond when a meaningful glare from his ambassador, Malbeth, made him hesitate. Understanding passed between them and when Ithalred spoke again, his truculent demeanour had abated.

'That is acceptable,' he said, this time looking her in the eye.

'Very well then,' replied the queen. 'You are invited to the Great Hall once you are settled in your quarters. The hold of Karak Ungor has prepared a feast and entertainments in your honour.'

'You are most gracious, noble queen,' Malbeth interjected.

With that Queen Brunvilda bowed again as did the elves in turn, passing slowly from the outer gateway hall to stow their weapons in the antechamber. After that was done, closely watched by Morek, they were then led by Kandor to their quarters.

Once she was alone with the hearth guard captain, Queen Brunvilda sighed deeply. The elves had barely got through their doors and already hostility was rife.

'That could have been worse,' said Morek honestly, aware that his own enmity towards the elves had only fuelled the fires of discord.

The queen offered only stern-faced silence by way of response.

'The elgi are rude and without honour,' Morek said to fill the uncomfortable silence.

'Yet, we managed to match them,' Queen Brunvilda replied, her gaze upon the disappearing train of elves as they walked down the long corridor to their quarters.

'But, my queen, they disrespect us… and in our own domain!' Morek cried, and regretted raising his voice at once.

Queen Brunvilda's glare was now fixed upon him, and laden with steel.

'They disrespected *you*, my queen,' the captain of the hearth guard said, his voice tender as he looked into the matriarch's eyes.

For a moment, Queen Brunvilda's expression softened, then, as if catching herself, her stone-like disposition returned together with her anger at Morek.

'Let us hope that their mood improves,' she said quietly, and headed off to the Great Hall where her king was waiting for her.

'This dank, this dark, I feel it seeping into my very marrow,' said Prince Ithalred, a scowl creasing his face as he watched the elven artisans erect his grand marquee.

Kandor, the dwarf merchant, had brought the elves to what he described as the 'Hall of Belgrad' in the eastern wing of the hold. These 'quarters' consisted of an expansive central chamber, where it was presumed the elf prince and his entourage would stay, flanked by two wide galleries where his warriors could be barracked, and four antechambers, two each feeding off the barrack rooms, for servants and storage.

Though long abandoned by the dwarfs when the seams of ore nearby were exhausted, the rooms were still magnificent and lavishly decorated. Flagstones of ochre and tan decked the floors and were polished to a lustrous sheen. Gilt archways, glittering with jewels, soared overhead into vaulted ceilings supported by thick, stone columns inlaid with silver and bronze. Flickering torches, ensconced along the walls, cast a warm glow that shimmered like burnished gold. This 'opulence' had failed to move or impress the elves, and once the dwarf had taken his leave, the prince was quick to set his servants to work.

According to Kandor, the Hall of Belgrad was formerly the dwelling of a long-dead dwarf noble. At least that was as much as Ithalred could discern with the few words of Khazalid he knew.

'It is every inch the crypt that the dwarf described,' he said, as the cohorts of servants laboured hard to fashion something more to his liking.

Belts of flowing white silk were unfurled across the flagstone floor then taken up and affixed to wooden stanchions to make large tents. Elven designs had been stitched into the luxurious cloth: runes of Lileath, Isha and Kurnous, preying hawks and soaring eagles, the rising phoenix and rampant dragon. They represented Ulthuan, their gods and the symbols of their power.

Once the tents were up they were filled with thick rugs and furs, hanging tapestries and carved wood furnishings such as beds, stools and chests decorated with elven imagery and fine jewels. Ithalred had brought several draught horses and elven carts with him from Eataine. This baggage train had entered the hold with the servants, and its horses were housed within the overground stables of the dwarfs – elvish steeds ill-suited to life under the earth.

Each of the marquees the elves had brought with them that were reserved for the nobles had several rooms. They were sumptuously decorated according to their specific tastes with pillows and pennants. Long velvet curtains contained the aroma from silver dishes of slowly burning spices intended to ward off the stench of soot and oil from the underground hold.

As ambassador to the prince, Malbeth, too, was afforded a separate abode. The remainder of the elven cohort had less grandiose accommodations, their tents smaller and bereft of the outrageous finery and luxury prevalent in the grand marquees, but not without comforts of their own.

'It is not what we're... *used to*, my prince but this hall obviously has some significance to the dwarfs. By granting us such accommodations they are bestowing great honour,' counselled Malbeth, the inauspicious start to their visit at the forefront of his mind.

'Malbeth, are you so beguiled by this soot-stained race that you cannot see the cave we are meant to dwell in, or has Loec tricked you with some glamour that hides the truth of the matter?' Lethralmir asked, arriving at the prince's side with Arthelas in tow.

The ambassador stiffened at the noble's presence but bit his tongue when he felt his heart quicken with anger. Lethralmir was Ithalred's closest companion, his best friend. They had shared swords on the field of battle many times over and a bond forged in blood was unwise to challenge. Malbeth would only lose Ithalred's favour if he spoke out against the blade-master, and he would need the prince on side if they were to come to any agreement with the dwarfs.

'An honour you say?' Lethralmir continued. 'I do not see it as such. These earth-dwellers may be content to roll around in muck, even consign their royal households to such ignominy, but the purebloods of Ulthuan will not bow down to such debased levels.'

Arthelas giggled quietly. Even Ithalred suppressed a smile at the blade-master's remark.

A servant approached before Lethralmir could speak further, though he did manage to flash a furtive grin at Arthelas. It was not so secretive that it escaped Ithalred's notice, however, or that of his towering bodyguard, Korhvale, who had appeared silently behind them.

'My lord,' said the servant, bowing as he addressed the prince, 'where should I put this?' The plain-robed elf carried a small chest of dwarf design, one that was obviously intended for the prince. From the clinking sound emanating within, it seemed that there were bottles of some description inside.

Ithalred stared at the item as if it were something unpleasant he had stepped in.

'Put it with the rest,' he said, and looked away. The servant took it as a gesture to leave.

Malbeth watched him take the dwarf chest into one of the antechambers where he saw the shadowy outline of other furnishings and victuals from their hosts. The dwarfs had laid on a small banquet of food and drink, together with stools and tables that their guests could use. The elves had swept it all away swiftly, stashing the items unceremoniously where they'd be out of the way and out of sight. It pained Malbeth to see it. He had hoped Ithalred would have tried to embrace the dwarfs' culture. It seemed, though, that he had no desire to.

Even the dwarf torches had been doused, the prince complaining of the smell and the smoke they exuded. In their place the servants had hung elven lanterns from gossamer-thin cords of silver. Immaculately carved wooden stanchions supported the loping lengths of silver that carried the lanterns and these in turn were decorated with some of the native flora of Ulthuan. The scent of the flowers did, in part, mask the heady stench of soot, oil and damp stone that permeated the air, and were supplemented by incense burners, great golden cauldrons set around the main hall, that cast an eldritch glow.

Once they were finished, it was as if the elves had created a small corner of Tor Eorfith within the subterranean halls of Karak Ungor.

'It will have to do,' said Prince Ithalred, striding towards his marquee. 'Lethralmir,' he added. The other noble stopped in his tracks as he sidled up to the prince's sister.

Korhvale's face darkened abruptly when the blade-master approached Arthelas.

'Yes, Ithalred?' said Lethralmir.

'Have my servants pour me a bath, and send a maiden to bathe me. I have need for this stink to be washed from my body.'

'Of course, my prince,' Lethralmir replied, masking his annoyance well as he stalked off to gather the servants.

'What of the trade pact, Ithalred?' Malbeth interjected, just as the prince was about to disappear through the door flap of his tent. 'We have much to discuss.'

'I will attend to it later... over wine,' he replied, and entered his dwelling without looking back.

Korhvale was quick to follow, though he stopped short of going inside, contenting himself to standing at the door. He was a White Lion, the traditional bodyguard of the nobles of Ulthuan, and a native of the mountainous region of Chrace. Malbeth liked Korhvale. Though sullen and taciturn, he spoke plainly and honestly, and without the venom-tongued bile that Lethralmir favoured. The ambassador noticed the White Lion linger a little too long on Arthelas as she departed to her tent, averting his gaze when she made eye contact.

It seems you have many would-be suitors, thought Malbeth as he retired to his own dwelling, a fact that will displease your brother, seeress.

THE TENT FLAP closed behind him and Malbeth sighed deeply, before dismissing his servants so that he could be alone. He had worked hard to forge this meeting with the dwarfs, in spite of Ithalred's resistance. He knew it would not be easy, that his greatest obstacle would be the prince's attitude, his arrogance. As a child of Eataine, his blood carried within it the royalty of Ulthuan and Ithalred was as noble and proud as any of his forebears. His grandfather had even fought alongside Aenarion himself, aiding the greatest and arguably most tragic of all the elf heroes to cast the daemon hordes back into the abyss that had spawned them.

History was not the only thing working in Ithalred's favour. The estates of his father and uncle were extensive, his family amongst the most afflu-ent of all the Inner Kingdoms. Ithalred, though, had no desire to cement his fortune in lands and title, he was an explorer, and in that he and Malbeth were kindred souls. Small wonder having seen the Glittering Tower – that glorious spike of purest silver, blazing like an eternal bea-con before the Emerald Gate of Lothern – that Ithalred had turned to the life of the wayfarer and desired to set sail for lands across the Great

Ocean. He could no more deny its call than a dwarf could suppress his urge to dig into the earth and explore the mountains. It was in his blood.

Malbeth knew it had been personally hard for the prince to come to the dwarfs, even under the mask of a trade agreement, but come he had and now they needed to make the best of things, to ingratiate their hosts if they could. Ithalred's narrow-mindedness, his imperious superiority was always going to make things difficult, but Malbeth had fostered hopes that the first meeting with the dwarfs would have gone better in spite of all that.

Their need was a dire one, if only the prince would acknowledge it. Establishing a trade pact with the dwarfs was a small but necessary thing; without it the elves would never get what they truly wanted from them.

CHAPTER THREE

Goblin Hunting

SIX DWARFS STALKED down a narrow, rocky gorge. Despite a distance of some several miles, the towering peaks of Karak Ungor still loomed in the background like rocky sentinels watching the party's progress. The dwarfs moved in single file, against the wind, their cloaks fluttering in a chill breeze. Wearing tunics over shirts of mail, each with a low slung crossbow over his back, the dwarfs were hunting, and their prey was not far.

'We are close, Prince Nagrim,' said Brondrik at the head of the group. He was crouched by a cluster of rocks jutting out on the snow-dappled trail. He eyed the edge of the gorge ahead, the scree path rising to a natural plateau.

Nagrim nodded at the old pathfinder, watching him sniff the cold mountain air, his nose wrinkling as he detected the scent of greenskins.

'Their foul stink is heaviest here,' added Brondrik, spitting onto the ground as if the stench had left a bitter taste in his mouth.

'How many?' asked Nagrim, peering through the fitful drifts of snow funnelled down the ravine by the wind.

'Nineteen, I think,' Brondrik replied, before moving on. 'Very near, now.'

Brondrik wore his ranger's garb, a green-grey tunic with a small cloak of *hruk* wool. The hruk were a hardy breed of mountain goat that the dwarfs reared on overground farms and mining settlements. The beasts produced hard-wearing wool, perfect for ranging over the crags of the mountains. Brondrik wore scars too, across his cheek and right ear. His beard was tan with flecks of grey, left to grow as it will. When the venerable pathfinder had smelled the goblin musk, he'd snarled, showing three missing teeth.

Nagrim grinned broadly as he thought of the quarry just ahead.

He would beat his father's tally this day.

The dwarf prince, in contrast to the pathfinder, was dressed in a deep blue tunic. Its hue indicated his heritage and the legacy he carried as a member of the royal household of Karak Ungor. Thick bronze vambraces were clapped around Nagrim's wrists, whilst copper torques banded his muscled arms, and gold ingot pins secured his plaited dark brown beard. Over his shoulders sat bronze pauldrons, the mantle of his ranger's cloak clasped to them. He was armed for the hunt, his crossbow slung over his broad back, and a hand axe cinctured at his waist by a strip of leather.

The hunting party reached the end of the rocky gorge, filing out onto a barren plateau of rock. Out of the narrow defile they could see the mountains again. There in the open, the wind whipping about them, it was as if the dwarfs stood at the zenith of the world.

'Magnificent…' breathed Brondrik, misting the air as a tear ran down his face.

The lofty crags of the Worlds Edge Mountains were wreathed in white, and encroached upon the horizon like broad, rocky fingers. Snow peeled off the distant peaks like a phantom veil, shawling the thick clusters of lowland pine below. Melt waters shimmered like frozen glass as they fed into valleys and basin lakes; thin trails of silver-grey veining the mountainside. Clouds gathered overhead in a steel sky pregnant with the threat of a heavy snowfall. The trail behind the dwarfs was dusted with the drifts, several booted footprints disappearing slowly as the errant snow filled them.

A slighter-built dwarf, armed only with a small hand axe and dressed in a silken coat and velveteen breeches, tramped after the prince.

Nagrim had approached the edge of the plateau, and gazed down the long, winding road that led into a forested valley scattered with rocks.

'Our quarry is close, eh, Tringrom?' said the prince as the smaller dwarf reached him. Wisps of snow caught on Nagrim's beard as he smiled warmly at his kinsdwarf.

'We'd best hope so, Prince Nagrim. We cannot be late for the feast. Your father would shear a foot from my beard if I allowed that,' Tringrom replied. The royal aide wore a permanent scowl, ill-suited to ranging outside the hold. He'd been ungainly as he'd trekked through the chasm, his once fine clothes ripped and scuffed by the rocks and brush. Even now, standing beside the prince, he worried at the gold trim of his coat that had snagged on a clawed branch, the stitching partly torn.

'Finding it hard going?' said Nagrim, watching the royal aide with amusement as he huffed and puffed at the ragged trim of his coat.

'How much longer are we staying out here?' he grumbled. 'King Bagrik expects us back before nightfall to meet the elves. It would not–'

'Aye, and we'll bring back a host of grobi trophies to impress the pointy ears, eh, ufdi?' bellowed a red-faced dwarf appearing beside Tringrom. From the slur in his voice he was obviously drunk and stomped about the trail with all the subtlety of an ogre. He was clad in worn clothes, and his fingers were covered in tarnished rings that might once have been beautiful. His tattered attire and drunken disposition conspired to give the dwarf a decidedly unkempt appearance.

'My *name* is Tringrom,' said the royal aide through gritted teeth, 'of the Copperback Clan, and my family have been attendants to the royal line of Ungor for over a thousand years, Rugnir *Goldfallow*.'

The red-faced dwarf, Rugnir, stiffened with anger at the insult, but the reaction was fleeting. His ire seemed to vanish with the breeze and he was quickly his bawdy self again.

'Calm down, lad,' said Rugnir. 'You'll always be an ufdi to me.' The dwarf gave a wide grin that showed off his teeth. 'Pretty as a winter's bloom with your pressed silks and perfumed beard, a preening red-feathered crag sparrow,' he said. 'If I didn't know better…' he added, closing one eye as he appraised the dwarf mockingly, '…I'd say you were a rinn!' Rugnir laughed uproariously, clapping Tringrom hard on the back. The royal aide was inspecting the damage done to his coat and ripped off the gold trim completely when his drunken kinsdwarf smacked him.

'Quiet down!' snarled Brondrik from part way down the valley path, whirling around to fix them both with a fierce stare. 'The wind is shifting, and our voices will soon carry into the lowlands,' he warned, adding, 'And the grobkul will last until we find the grobi and burn their nest.' The pathfinder patted a bulging leather satchel, slung over his shoulder, at this last remark, before moving on.

Tringrom's straw-coloured beard bristled as he flushed with embarrassment at Brondrik's admonishment. Rugnir on the other hand, his own beard rust-red like his drunk-blushed cheeks and ringed eyes, merely chuckled and held up a hand to show his compliance with the pathfinder's wishes. For his part, Nagrim grinned over at the ebullient Rugnir. The two were constant companions and drinking fellows.

There was none better than Rugnir during a feast or celebration. The prince liked his boisterous demeanour and easy company. It was welcome relief from the intensity of his father, the king, and the royal flunkies he insisted on having accompany Nagrim whenever he left the hold. It was only by the prince's request that Rugnir had joined the hunting party. Many in the hold who knew him did not like him, claiming he was destitute and a *wazlik*, an honourless dwarf that borrowed gold from another and did not pay it back.

Wealth, for a dwarf, was a measure of success and therefore prestige.

With that came respect. Rugnir's clan, once Goldmaster, but now referred to in whispers as Gold*fallow*, were once vaunted members of the Miners' Guild and renowned as the greatest lore finders and tunnel-hewers in all of the northern holds. Their fame had even stretched as far as Karak Eight Peaks, the Vala-Azrilungol, one of the southernmost kingdoms of the Worlds Edge Mountains. Fate, though, had been cruel to the Goldmaster clan, and the great fortune amassed by Kraggin and Buldrin Goldmaster, Rugnir's father and grandfather, was eroded over the years. Tunnel collapses, flooding and a series of bad investments had all but left them destitute, and their holdings worthless. Rugnir, the last of the Goldmasters of Karak Ungor, after his father was slain by trolls, had frittered what funds remained on beer and gambling. The Goldmaster coffers had dried up.

Now Rugnir satisfied himself with Nagrim's patronage, which paid for his debts and wagers and kept him fed, much to the distaste of the other dwarfs of the hold. The shadow of his ignominy was long indeed, and some feared it would touch the prince before long. Nagrim would not hear of it, however, and so Rugnir had accompanied the hunters into the mountains.

'Tringrom,' said Nagrim, venturing after Brondrik once he'd seen that the rest of their party, two of the pathfinder's rangers, Harig and Thom, had caught up. They followed in Rugnir's wake, taking great pains to cover the rowdy dwarf's tracks, lest they attract attention. There were deadlier things than goblins lurking in the mountains and it was wise to be cautious, or sooner or later the hunter would become the hunted. Though the dwarfs held sway beneath the earth, they did not have such dominance over the mountain crags that they could tread with impunity.

The royal aide had tucked the gold trim of his silken coat in his pocket and was somewhat disconsolate as he followed the prince.

'What is my father's tally?' Nagrim asked.

Tringrom took a heavy-looking, leather-bound book from a satchel slung over his shoulder. Using his body and cloak to shield it from the worst of the wind and snow, he started to leaf through its pages. Finding what he was looking for, he stopped and read aloud.

'Lo did Bagrik Boarbrow, of only seventy winters, reach a tally of five hundreds and three score plus one grobi.'

'And what is my tally?'

'Your tally, Prince Nagrim, is only five short of that,' said Tringrom.

'Six grobi,' Nagrim thought aloud, grinning broadly. 'Do you think I can beat my father's count, Brondrik? Is there enough quarry for that?' the prince called out to the pathfinder who was crouched by a fork in the valley road, inspecting tracks invisible to the others.

'Aye, my prince, they'll be enough grobi for that,' he answered gruffly, and stood up. 'This way,' he said. 'And no more talk. The grobi stink is very strong, my eyes water with it.'

'Are you sure your nose isn't too close to your arse, pathfinder?' Rugnir asked, and roared with laughter.

Brondrik turned on his heel and unslung his crossbow. His eyes were like granite, his mouth a thin, hard line of anger.

'Have your travelling companion be quiet or I will shoot him myself,' he said to Nagrim.

'Easy, Brondrik,' said the prince, showing his palms, a look over his shoulder at Rugnir warning the ex-miner to keep his mouth shut from here on in. The colour drained from the drunken dwarf's face when he saw the loaded crossbow pointed at him and the apoplexy on Brondrik's face.

'Can we move on?' asked Nagrim. 'There are grobi to kill and precious little light left to do it in.'

The low winter sun was setting behind him, filling the valley path with shadows. They had but an hour, maybe less.

Brondrik saw it, too, and nodded, stowing his crossbow and leading the dwarfs onward to their prey.

'BRONDRIK,' NAGRIM WHISPERED, settling down into a comfortable position amongst the rocks. His kinsdwarfs were close by, hidden well in the crags.

The fork at the long valley path had led them to a high, boulder-strewn ridge. Snow fell readily from the sky now and draped the craggy rise. The goblin camp was below them, down a shallow slope, at the base of a wide canyon. The vermin had made their nest in a small cave, their crude daubings marking it from the outside. There were no guards. Only dung and the gnawed bones of lesser creatures – rats, birds and elk calves – lay outside the greenskins' lair.

Closing one eye, Nagrim sighted down the shaft of his crossbow and took aim on the cave mouth. 'Hurl the *zharrum*, now,' he said.

The venerable pathfinder did as asked, reaching into the satchel he carried and taking out a small round keg with a length of fuse poking through the lid. Lighting the fuse quickly with flint and steel, Brondrik launched the fire bomb into the air. The lit fuse fizzled dangerously as the bomb's parabola took it just outside the cave, only for it to clank against the ground and then roll in.

Nagrim and his fellow hunters winced as the fire bomb exploded. Jagged silhouettes were revealed in the ephemeral blast of light that followed. A chorus of high-pitched screams came from inside the cave, together with a plume of issuing smoke. Moments later, the first goblin came scurrying out, patting his head frantically to try and put out the flames in his topknot.

Nagrim put the creature down with a bolt through its neck.

'Tally-marker,' he shouted to Tringrom, who cradled the leather-bound tome in his arm, a quill at the ready, 'scratch one up for Nagrim Boarbrowson!'

Three more goblins emerged from the cave with scorched faces, coughing up phlegm.

'He's mine!' roared Rugnir, nearly slipping over in his enthusiasm to
peg a greenskin drooling black snot from its bulbous nose. The dwarf
had been going for the head but his aim was off and he only succeeded
in pitching the creature's furred helmet off. Confused, the goblin first
patted its skull to find out why it felt suddenly cold then, realising he'd
lost something, turned in a circle to try and find it.

Nagrim stood, eschewing the cover of the rocks for a better target, and
put a bolt through the hapless creature's eye. The impact spun it around
and it fell face-forward into the dirt.

'Ha!' he cheered loudly. 'Are we shooting grobi or just playing with
them, Rugnir?'

The ex-miner muttered drunkenly beneath his breath.

As the flames within took hold in earnest, burning straw, leather and
whatever else the greenskins kept in their foul abodes, a stream of goblins came staggering from the cave. Some, the paltry few with their wits
about them, loosed arrows from crude short bows at the dwarfs, but
most fell pitifully short of the target or broke against the rocks.

With the fleeing goblins in disarray, Nagrim and the rangers came
out of their hiding places, loosing quarrels with deadly accuracy at the
yelping greenskins. The dwarfs made their way steadily down the ridge,
disturbed scree tumbling ahead of them as they closed on the nadir of
the canyon, and the goblins' lair. Only Rugnir slipped, and tumbled
headfirst down the slope. He laughed as he landed on his rump in front
of the others. He quickly flung a throwing axe at a screeching goblin that
had tried to skewer the dwarf on its spear. The greenskin took the axe
blade in the face, blood spurting from the wound, and lay still.

'That one counts,' Rugnir hollered, as he struggled to his feet and set
off after the other goblins.

After Rugnir's unceremonious arrival at the base of the canyon,
Nagrim was next to level ground. Blinded by the flames, a burnt
greenskin blundered past him, heedless of its surroundings. Nagrim
unslung his axe and buried it in the creature's skull, tearing the
weapon out with a wet crunch of bone. Another was running back
into the cave, despite the raging conflagration within, and Nagrim
changed weapons again, lifting his crossbow and puncturing the creature's back with his shot. It fell dead just before the cave mouth.

Breathing heavily, the prince was aware of the other rangers alongside him, making their kills and calling them out to their tally-marker,
Tringrom. The ufdi's fine silken tunic and velvet breeches, already ruined
from the trek through the gorge, were covered in dirt and grobi blood.
A bulging knapsack at his waist held goblin ears, noses and teeth, and
when the hunters threw their trophies to him he'd not been fast enough
to stop the blood from marring his clothes.

'Maiming doesn't count,' shouted Nagrim, beheading one of Rugnir's 'kills' that still had some life in it.

The drunken dwarf muttered something in reply that was lost in the scream of another goblin cut down by his axe.

The slaughter lasted only minutes, just as well given the sun had all but faded in the sky. Goblin corpses lay everywhere, the dwarfs moving amongst them removing further trophies.

'Eighteen, all told,' announced Brondrik, sucking his teeth before he muttered, 'Could've sworn by Grimnir there were more…'

'How did we fare, Tringrom?' Nagrim asked, wiping the blade of his axe on one of the steaming greenskin corpses.

The royal aide paused in his shovelling of the trophies into his knapsack to refer to his leather tome.

'A score of six for you, Prince Nagrim,' he told him.

Nagrim glowed inwardly. He had beaten his father's tally.

'Four for Brondrik,' the royal aide continued, 'and three each for Harig and Thom.'

'And what of Rugnir,' said the drunken ex-miner, 'what of his tally, eh?' he asked eagerly.

'Two,' Tringrom replied, stony-faced.

'Eh? Two? Two? I slew more than that!' he raged, stomping towards Tringrom for a better look at his tally-marking.

'Two!' the royal aide confirmed, slamming the tome shut and locking the clasp.

Rugnir was incensed, balled fists on his hips as he glowered at Tringrom.

'There is falsehood here,' he growled, before turning away in disgust.

'What was it?' said Nagrim, 'Fifty pieces of copper that you'd outshoot me?'

Rugnir grumbled again, looking into the distance.

'Wait, I see one!' he declared suddenly, fumbling to get his crossbow to a shooting position. Brondrik had been right – there was a survivor. The last remaining goblin had somehow evaded the dwarfs and was scampering madly back up the valley road. When a furtive glance behind it revealed that the dwarfs had seen it, the goblin redoubled its efforts.

'Double or nothing that I can peg this grobi swine,' said Rugnir, boastfully.

'Be my guest,' Nagrim replied, gesturing for him to proceed.

'One hundred copper pieces you'll owe me, lad,' he grinned, sighting down the crossbow.

Rugnir missed by a yard.

'A good effort,' said Nagrim with false sincerity. He took up his own crossbow, the goblin a diminishing green smudge in his eye-line by now, and fired.

'Yes!' he cried, making a fist in triumph as the goblin was pitched off its feet by the shot and lay dead on the trail.

'Mark that as seven kills, tally-marker,' said Nagrim, before he turned to look at Rugnir.

'Impossible...' breathed the dwarf, the drunken ruddiness of his face paling suddenly.

'A hundred copper, then...' Nagrim goaded him.

'Er... perhaps you'll let me owe you it, prince?' Rugnir asked, hopefully.

Nagrim looked serious at first but then laughed out loud, slapping Rugnir hard on the back.

'Don't worry old friend, your copper is no good to me.'

'What copper?' Tringrom mumbled to himself, still scowling.

'Which, er... reminds me,' said the ex-miner, ignoring the remark. 'I have certain outstanding... financial obligations to Godri Stonefinger and Ungrin Ungrinson...'

'How much?' sighed the prince.

'Twenty silver pieces each,' Rugnir replied.

'Tringrom,' Nagrim said to the royal aide. 'Have the amount taken from my coffers and settle the debts upon our return.'

'Yes, Prince Nagrim,' said Tringrom, his eyes like daggers as they fell upon Rugnir, who was careful to avert his gaze.

'Lead us back to the hold, Brondrik,' said Nagrim. 'I must tell my father his grobi tally has been beaten! There is celebrating to be done, and I must drink quickly if I'm to catch my friend here,' he added, throwing his arm around Rugnir's back in comradely fashion and laughing loudly.

'Indeed you must, my prince,' muttered the pathfinder, who fired a withering glance at Rugnir before heading back up the trail. The ex-miner didn't notice and laughed along with Nagrim. His smile faded when he saw the disapproving glances of the other dwarfs.

CHAPTER FOUR

Pacts

KING BAGRIK SAT in his counting house, surrounded by the month's revenue from the clans of the hold. Smoke drifted from a pipe pinched between his teeth, filling the room with the heady scent of tobacco. The king was dressed in a simple brown tunic, his bald pate reflecting the glow from the ensconced torches set around the room. He pored over the stone tablets and curling parchments strewn across the table in front of him, sat bent-backed in a broad throne, which, like the table, was fashioned from lacquered wutroth, a rare and incredibly strong dwarf wood. The bare stone walls of the small austere chamber were carved with the klinkarhun, the numerical dwarf alphabet.

Pieces of gold, silver and copper – some made into coins stamped with the royal rune of Ungor, others nuggets of purest ore gathered in bags – were stacked around the king, their order fathomable to Bagrik alone. With careful deliberation, the king checked off the tributes and taxes of the clans, the leaseholds on mines and overground farms, statutory beard tax and ale tithes. As liege lord of the realm, a percentage of all the hold's remunerations went to the king and Bagrik was meticulous about its acquisition.

'How do we fare so far with the taxes, Kandor?' asked the king, his voice deep and gruff as he sifted through the requisitions.

'The Firehand and Flinteye clans still owe thirty pieces of gold each for anvils and picks,' the merchant replied, sat behind a smaller desk next to the king's, checking parchment and tablets of his own. As royal treasurer it was part of Kandor's duty that he attend the monthly gold gathering, to log in taxes and dispatch reckoners, the king's bailiffs, to reclaim late payments or act on the behalf of other clans who had cause for grudgement against their fellow dwarfs.

'Mark that!' bellowed the king. Bagrik's edict was followed by the measured scratching of a quill from one corner of the room where Grumkaz Grimbrow, his chief grudgemaster, was sitting shrouded in shadow. The longbeard recorded each and every late or missing payment in the form of grudges, writ in the king's blood and set down in the massive tome resting on a stone lectern next to the venerable dwarf.

'I have here a claim from the Ironfingers, who say they were sold knackered ore ponies by the Leatherbeards and lost a day's tunnelling on account,' said Kandor, leafing through the pile of papers.

'Denied!' said Bagrik. 'The Ironfingers should learn to better examine their stock before buying.'

'Another from Grubbi Threefinger, a reckoner, requests remuneration for worn boot leather in prosecution of the king's duties.'

'Granted–' the king began, but then turned swiftly to the shadowy form of Grumkaz, who was halfway through noting the king's order.

'How much in taxes has Grubbi recovered this past month?' he asked.

The grudgemaster leafed back through the hold's records.

'One hundred and fifty-three gold pieces, fifteen short of his required tally,' the grudgemaster announced.

'Denied!' the king bellowed again, and went back to the parchments on his desk as the sound of frantic scratching came from the grudgemaster as he made an abrupt adjustment.

'Tell me, Kandor,' Bagrik said after a moment, his head still in the parchments on his desk, 'what do you think of these elgi? Is there trade to be had between us?'

The merchant set down a stone tablet, surprised at the sudden question.

'They have travelled far, my king and the elgi, Malbeth, has much honour. I do not think they would have done so if they meant to waste our time,' he said.

'I care not for their ambassador,' the king responded curtly. 'What about their prince, this... Ithalred? It is he that holds power amongst the elgi. Morek tells me he is an arrogant bastard.'

'Morek knows nothing of diplomacy–' Kandor began, before the king interrupted.

'Neither do I, Thane Silverbeard. That's why I'm asking you.'

Kandor's reply was frank.

'The elves are utterly unlike us in every way, my liege, and... *difficulties* between our cultures are inevitable, but open trade between us could be very profitable for Karak Ungor. We would be foolish not to at least listen to what they propose.'

'You do not think me a fool then, Kandor?' Bagrik asked, looking up from his tallying.

'Of course not, my liege,' Kandor blathered, face reddening with sudden concern.

'Then you'll know that I'm aware of the disrespect they've shown towards my queen, that they have turned the Hall of Belgrad into an elgi dwelling, yes?'

'My liege, I–'

Bagrik scowled, and waved his hand for silence.

'I trust your judgement, Kandor. Aye, I do, as sure as stone,' Bagrik told him. 'And a king's trust is no small thing. I know you won't have brought these elgi to my halls without good reason. And I know your talent for gold making. But know this, too,' he added with a steel-edged glare, 'If I receive word of our guests dishonouring my queen again, or besmirching her in any way, I will have them thrown out. And your beard will be shorn, Kandor of the Silverbeard clan, for bringing them to my gates in the first place!'

'Please accept my apologies, liege. I've spoken to Malbeth and made it clear to him that such behaviour will not be tolerated again,' said Kandor, trying to sooth the king's sudden ire.

'You are right. It will not,' Bagrik added simply, staring at Kandor a moment longer to make his point, before turning his attention back to the taxes piled on his desk.

'All seems in order here,' he said. 'Dispatch reckoners to the Firehands and Flinteyes to settle their accounts, and add on ten pieces of copper each for late payment.'

'At once, King Bagrik,' Kandor replied, quietly relieved that he'd escaped with only a mild tongue-lashing.

'Go then to your duties!' bawled the king. 'And make your oaths to Grungni that these elgi put me in a better mood.'

Kandor bowed and left the parchments where they were on the ground.

'It shall be done, my king,' he said, and as he was leaving met Queen Brunvilda with Tringrom in tow coming the other way. He bowed to them both before walking on and out of the counting house.

'My queen,' Bagrik said warmly to his wife as she approached. Brunvilda bowed once she'd reached her husband. The king then dismissed Grumkaz who shuffled quietly out of the room, his work done for now.

'And Tringrom,' added the king, 'you look like a wanaz.'

'My lord, Tringrom has been on a grobkul with your son,' said the queen before the royal aide could reply. 'Late, again,' she added, stern of face. 'He is being readied for the feast, as should you be.'

'Bah! I'll be ready soon enough,' Bagrik snapped. 'But tell me, Tringrom,' he added, conspiratorially, 'how did my son fare?'

'He has beaten your tally, my liege,' the royal aide replied.

'Ha!' cried the king, slapping his hands down upon the desk and sending parchments spilling onto the ground. 'Barely sixty-nine winters, and he beats his father's tally,' Bagrik said proudly. 'Go… mark it in the Book of Deeds, so all shall know of my son's achievement!'

'At once, my king,' Tringrom replied and left his king and queen alone, gazing longingly at one another.

'Our son, he will make a fine king,' said Bagrik, once the royal aide was gone.

'Indeed he will,' Brunvilda replied, resting a hand upon her husband's shoulder. 'But he is reckless, and I do not like his friendship with Rugnir, either. Brondrik has made a damning report to Morek that you should hear.'

'He is young,' counselled Bagrik, 'it is to be expected. And as for Rugnir,' said the king, seizing his queen around the waist, who yelped mildly in surprise and delight, and pulling her close, 'let the captain of the hearth guard deal with it.'

'Bagrik Boarbrow, unhand me at once!' cried Brunvilda, though her demand was distinctly half-hearted as she looked lovingly into the eyes of her husband.

'Is that really what you want me to do, lass?' he asked.

'No…' she answered demurely, smoothing down his beard with the palms of her hands.

'You smell like hops and honey,' he said, breathing in her scent like it was nectar.

'And you reek of gold, my king…' she replied, smiling. 'Bagrik?' she asked after a moment.

'Yes, my queen,' he replied, voice husky with the ardour of their embrace.

'I would like to see our son.'

'You will see him,' Bagrik replied, nonplussed. 'He will be at the feast, Grungni willing he is ready in time.'

'No, not Nagrim…' Brunvilda said quietly, shaking her head.

Bagrik's face darkened as soon as he realised what she meant. Silently, he released his grip and gently let her go.

'That… *thing* is no son of mine,' he said, his voice now hard like stone.

'He *is* your son, whether you care to admit it or not,' insisted Brunvilda, stepping back into Bagrik's eye-line when the king averted his gaze to stare at parchments he had already read. 'I will not abandon him, even if you have disowned him,' she continued.

'Abandoned?' said the king, facing her again. 'Yes, he should have been abandoned. Cast out at birth and left in the mountains for wild beasts to devour!'

Brunvilda's face was pinched with anger, and tears were welling in her eyes at the king's harsh words. Bagrik regretted them at once and tried in vain to make amends.

'I'm sorry, but the answer is no. I have agreed to stay my hand, and I've honoured that pact. But that is all I will do.'

'He is your son,' the queen repeated, imploringly.

Bagrik hobbled from his throne, wincing in pain at an old leg wound, and turned his back on her.

'I will speak on it no further,' he whispered.

Queen Brunvilda said nothing more. Bagrik heard her footsteps clacking on the stone, fading as she left, and felt his heart ache once she was gone.

CHAPTER FIVE

The Serpent Host

ULFJARL OF THE Skaeling tribe stood upon the skull-headed prow of his Wolfship and bellowed defiantly at the gods.

Crimson lightning answered, flashing across the storm-wracked horizon and turning the sky the colour of blood. Massive waves, churned up by the wind, rolled over the surface of the thrashing Sea of Claws and sent stinging spray into Ulfjarl's face and body. The Norscan warlord ignored it, exultant as the power of the terrible storm filled him.

Nothing would stop him reaching the mainland. There lay the Old World and the silver tower of the elves that haunted his dreams. Upon those white shores, Ulfjarl would find his destiny.

Bondsmen fought the rumble of thunder with their dour baritones, pulling at the oars with determined fury and bringing the Norscan warlord back from his reverie. Stoic, fur-clad huscarls sat beside them, clutching axes and spears, their round wooden shields strapped to their arms. Norsca, their frozen homeland, and the rest of the Skaeling tribe, was a distant memory now as they drove across the ocean with a ragged fleet of thirty other Wolfships. Their black sails, daubed with the symbol of a coiled crimson snake with three heads, bulged with the hellish gales, the mast pennants snapping like dragon tongues.

Ulfjarl had the same snake symbol seared into the skin of his bare and muscled chest. It was the icon of his army, the Serpent Host. He wore a mantle of furs thrown over his massive shoulders. Skins covered his wrists and ankles, leaving his legs and arms, fraught with battle scars, naked to the elements. Furred boots covered Ulfjarl's feet and were bound with chains. A war helm, festooned with spikes and wrought of dark metal, sat upon his head crested by two curling horns. Only the warlord's eyes were visible through a narrow cross-shaped slit, hard like rock beneath a jutting brow.

The beat of drums kept the oarsmen in time. It echoed the pounding of Ulfjarl's feral heart. Every pull brought them closer to the mainland, and through the boiling clouds he could just see it as a thickening black line, lit sporadically by the storm. Neither man nor elf nor daemon could keep him from it. The fire-blackened wrecks of the elven catamarans, left burning in their wake, were testament to that. Ulfjarl had lost no less than five ships to the immortals, who'd fought with skill and desperation. It was a small price. Ulfjarl had cut their warchief's head from his shoulders with his axe, shearing the elf's silver mail as if it were bare flesh.

Like his war helm, Ulfjarl's blade was forged from the ore of a black meteorite that had destroyed his village in fire and fury. Its coming was heralded in the stars, the impetus for his conquest, and he had gathered warriors at once. The Norscan had never seen the metal's like before, his crude mouth could not even form the words to describe it.

Obsid…

Ulfjarl cared not. It slew his enemies well. The elf had learned that lesson to his cost; his flayed skull was now tied to the Norscan's belt as a trophy. Destiny, Ulfjarl's glorious fate, lay at journey's end. Veorik had promised it, seen in a vision, and the shaman was never wrong.

Ulfjarl gazed up to the crow's nest. Eldritch green light crackled and spat like a miniature thunderhead as Veorik used his sorcery to guide them through the storm, just as he had through the ice flows, maelstroms and razor-sharp bergs of the Norscan coast.

Screams pierced the rising tumult of the storm as another ship was lost, swallowed whole beneath a mammoth wave. Ulfjarl watched the mast splinter and crack, watched the tearing sails and scattered rigging, as the vessel was pulled asunder with its crew. Some cast themselves into the sea, flailing as they struggled for life, but endless wet oblivion claimed them all.

Ulfjarl knew each and every one who drowned beneath the waves. He gave their names as sacrifices to Shornaal, one of the Dark Gods, that he would reach land unscathed. The muttered pledges had barely passed his lips when a huge curtain of water, crested by frothing surf, loomed up before the ship.

It seemed the gods had answered.

He saw faces in the watery blackness; a host of daemon visages with needle-pointed teeth and hollow eyes hungering for his soul and the souls of his men. Ulfjarl roared in defiance of it, as if it were an enemy that could be cowed by his fury. He heard the oarsmaster urge his charges to row harder, and they pulled with all their might. Some sang lamentations, others screamed in maddened terror as they faced their doom. Ulfjarl merely laughed, long and loud into the wind, his cry echoing across the sky where it could be heard by heathen gods. He felt the prow rising as the Wolfship surged up the monstrous wave and roared again at the stygian sea, bellowing his name.

Hard and fast they raced up the thrashing waters, nearly pitching prow over stern so severe was the angle of their approach. Ulfjarl ran forward to the very tip of the prow as they rode higher and higher. Misshapen hands with taloned nails seemed to reach out for him as the waters closed. Sibilant threats, half-heard in a tongue he did not understand, filled his ears. Ulfjarl ignored them, his cry of triumph eclipsing the daemon voices as they crested the apex of the wave before it broke.

Smashing down on the other side, foaming water engulfed the Wolfship and for a moment the vessel was swallowed beneath the sea before it emerged again like a cork in a barrel, water cascading from its sails and rigging.

Drenched from head to foot, Ulfjarl beat his chest with a mighty fist and bellowed at Tchar, god of storms and the bringer of change, daring his wrath. His warriors cheered with him, the relief at their survival violent and palpable. Raging winds ripped at the sails, driving them harder, and rain lashed down against the Norscans like knives of ice. Ulfjarl saw another Wolfship draw up alongside them. The warriors onboard yelled and cried in reckless victory. Expressions of triumph turned to horror as the wooden hull of their ship tore open and a huge, serpentine creature surged from the ocean through the debris.

The beast, its silver-blue scales shimmering as the water peeled away from it, towered above the Norscan ships, its broad snout flaring with rage and hunger. Flanged fins, edged in poisonous spikes and attached to a long saurian head, flared as the monstrous serpent regarded its prey. The warriors of the stricken Wolfship mewled in abject terror, their pathetic vessel cleft in two, its jagged halves sinking into the murky waters. The beast roared. Its keening cry smothered the thunder and shook the very ocean, before it dove down onto the hapless Norscans and cast their broken bodies aside like tinder.

Ulfjarl saw a barbed tail disappear beneath the waves, before a curious silence reigned in the creature's wake. He knew this monster. He had heard tales of its terror. It was an ancient denizen of the deep – an ice drake. Stirred from a long slumber beneath the Sea of Claws, it was angry.

Clambering to the edge of the skull-headed prow Ulfjarl leaned over, searching the water for some sign of the creature; a plume of foam, a shadow, anything. But there was nothing. Nothing until the monster erupted from the thrashing sea near the prow on Ulfjarl's blindside, its razor-snout shearing through the surface like a spear. The Norscan warlord staggered back, craning his neck to see the towering ice drake. Black eyes, like pools of endless hate, regarded him as he retreated slowly to get a more secure footing on the deck. It was an epic sight. Man facing monster as the maelstrom of the storm whirled around them.

Ulfjarl took a throwing axe from his belt, bracing his legs for balance as he tested the weapon's weight. Just as he was about to fling the blade, the ice drake dove into the depths again. Ulfjarl spun around, running further onto the deck and screaming for his warriors.

The beast emerged on the Wolfship's starboard side, bellowing its fury. Those bondsmen not unmanned by the terrible creature loosed arrows, and hurled spears and axes, only for the weapons to shatter and rebound from the monster's thick, armoured hide. Thordrak, a jarl chieftain, shouted orders above the tumult of the storm and a group of his bondsmen grabbed rope and barbed bone hooks. Roaring oaths to the gods, Jarl Thordrak and his bondsmen loosed their hooks, desperate to snag the monster's scales or bite into flesh that they might bring it down to the deck to let the huscarls do their grisly work.

A cheer went up as several of the barbed hooks took hold. Thordrak roared for his men to heave. The thick ropes attached to the weapons went taut as the warriors pulled, the ice drake screeching as it resisted them. For a moment the beast appeared cowed as its head dipped, but this false hope was fleeting as it surged upright again with a bellow of power. The ropes snapped, and warriors were yanked off their feet and cast overboard with the force of the monster's escape. Thordrak groaned in anguish as the drake twisted free of the biting snares. Like quicksilver, the beast's head flew deck-ward, smashing into the jarl and what remained of his warriors. He and a clutch of bondsmen were crushed in the ice drake's jaws as its neck snapped straight again. Throwing back its head, the hapless Norscans were tipped down into the beast's gullet and devoured whole. The rest were scattered across the deck, bloodied and with bones broken.

A band of huscarls hefting spears and bearded axes, charged at the creature, shouting war cries. The ice drake came level with the deck and roared back, exhaling a blast of deathly frost from its gaping maw. The huscarls were engulfed in a cloud of frost. As it dissipated the Norscan warriors were left frozen solid, belated screams forever etched on their faces. The deck became a sheet of ice in the wake of the attack, and bondsmen slipped and fell as they fled and fought.

Grabbing a baleen spear, and a length of rope that he slung over his shoulder, Ulfjarl fought his way through the carnage, beheading a screaming bondsman who had lost his mind to terror, and heaving him over the side of the ship. He smashed the corpse of a frozen huscarl to ice shards with his axe as he strove to reach the Wolfship's mast through the chaos. As he slid to the mast and launched himself at the rigging, Ulfjarl heard the oarsmaster extol his charges with threats and curses. Even if they slew the beast, the Sea of Claws might yet drag them all to its watery hells. Ulfjarl would yield to neither, and climbed the bone-hard rigging that was chilled with frost, hand over hand, muscles bunching with effort. Above, he saw the crackling magicks of Veorik in the crow's nest, the shaman lost in a magical trance as he guided the ship despite the deadly battle. A sideways glance revealed the creature was close. Its dank breath reeked of cold and dead blood as it exhaled over the deck, and tore bondsmen apart with its jaws.

Reaching the top of the sail, Ulfjarl heaved himself up and stood on the vertical spar of the mast, ramming the baleen spear into the wood and then lashing himself to it. The ice drake was ravaging the Wolfship, tearing chunks from the hull and butchering Ulfjarl's warriors. The deck was slick with ice and blood. Men slipped and were flung over the side into the raging waters as the Wolfship pitched and yawed.

Hefting a hurling axe, Ulfjarl waited until the ice drake turned its ugly head towards him then threw it with all his strength. The monster screeched in agony as the blade pierced one of its eyes, purple-black blood gushing from the wound. Overcoming its pain, the beast found its attacker and roared at Ulfjarl who was battered back by the fury of its cry. As the ice drake came at him, the Norscan tore the baleen spear free and lunged. The monster recoiled then came at Ulfjarl again, who fought hard to keep it at bay. A fierce jab opened up a gash in the creature's flanged fin and it twisted forward in pain. Seeing his chance, Ulfjarl rammed the spearhead through its other eye, burying the weapon halfway up the haft.

Blinded, the creature thrashed about in a rage, ripping apart the rigging and smashing the mast. Ulfjarl cut himself loose before the spar collapsed, snapped in two by the ice drake, and leapt onto the creature's back. Its long neck was thick like a tree trunk, but ridged and not so wide that Ulfjarl couldn't grasp it. He found purchase beneath its scales as the creature bucked and thrashed to try and shake him loose.

With his free hand Ulfjarl drew his axe and hacked into the beast's hide. Chunks of scale sheared away and soon he was cutting into meat. Below, the huscarls and bondsmen continued to throw spears and loose arrows. Some found chinks in the creature's armoured hide. Ulfjarl felt it weakening as he clove into it, and rode the beast as it sagged downward.

Crashing against the deck, Ulfjarl was thrown off the ice drake. Taking up a fallen spear as he got to his feet, left by a slain huscarl, Ulfjarl impaled the monster through the neck. He rammed another through its upper jaw, a third through its snout, pinning it to the deck. Swinging his axe in a wide arc, he brought it down against the ice drake's neck, again and again, until it was severed. Burying the axe into the deck, Ulfjarl gripped the ice drake's jaw and tore its head away from its neck, thick threads of skin, scale and flesh splitting with his grunting efforts. Raising the head aloft, he roared in triumph, the beast's shedding arteries bathing him in blood. The creature's decapitated body slid off the deck and was swallowed by the sea.

Through the clamour of warriors surrounding him, baying in adulation, Ulfjarl saw the twisted form of Veorik. The shaman hobbled over slowly, parting the throng with his mere presence, and stood before his king in supplication. He took a cup, made from a child's skull, from beneath the ragged skins of his robes. Plunging it into the pooling blood and gore beneath Ulfjarl, the shaman drank deep. Veorik's eyes flashed with power within the shadows of his hood, and he smiled.

Now the Serpent Host had dominion over the ice drakes of the deep…

CHAPTER SIX

An Uneasy Alliance

THE GREAT HALL of Karak Ungor thronged with dwarfs. Clans from throughout the hold had been summoned by their king for an audience with their eldritch guests from across the Great Ocean. Soot-faced miners of the Rockcutter, Stonehand and Goldgather clans sat alongside the blacksmiths of the Ironbrows, Anvilbacks and Copperfists. Fletchers, brewmasters, gold and silver smiths talked loud and readily with venerable runelords, engineer guildmasters, merchants and ironbreakers.

Truly the gathering of dwarfs that night was one of the largest ever in the long and prestigious history of Ungor.

The room was filled with many broad tables, low wooden benches set alongside them and occupied by the dwarfs. Brewmasters surveyed the Great Hall with beady eyes, watching their apprentices dispense immense barrels of ale. Never was a tankard to run dry, a stein to be empty. Flickering torches cast shadowy light onto a bawdy scene as dwarfs spoke and drank, wrestled and boasted. A thick syrup of smoke lay heavy just above the heads of the merry makers, a greyish fug exuding from numerous pipes that flared in the half-light.

In the middle of the vast and impressive chamber was a massive firepit, the coals within glowing warmly, filling the place with the heady aroma of rock and ash. Wrought from bronze and inlaid with strips of silver and copper, the ornate basin was sunk partly into the ground and set inside a ring of flat stones inscribed with runes of fire and burning.

The edge of the chamber had a series of stone ledges, fringed with shadow, where the musicians, victualers and other servants were sitting.

The Great Hall had three doorways: two led to the east and west halls, the oaken portals banded with iron and protected by a pair of hearth guard each; the third entrance was the grand gate of the hall itself. This massive, wooden door was inlaid with gemstones, its magnificent, sweeping arch rendered in gold and chased with silver filigree. It, too, was stout and defensible, for the dwarfs were concerned with the practical as much as they were the grandiose. The splendour of that fine ingress into the king's vaulted chamber said much of dwarf ambition and pragmatism.

A stone platform, reachable only by a central stairway of red carpeted rock, rose at the back of the hall and it was here that the king and his charges were seated. The King's Table, as it was known, was broad and long. It stretched almost the length of the stone platform and was fashioned from dark wutroth with gilt tracery, its stout feet made into effigies of dragons, griffons and eagles. Banners and standards capped with ancestor badges hung behind it on bronze chains. Together they described a tapestry of battles, heroic deeds and the hold's founding, taken directly from the ancient chronicles of the dwarfs.

The great Bagrik was in attendance, surveying all that fell beneath his beetling brow. A tunic of red and gold swathed his kingly form, with a coat of shining silver mail beneath. Vambraces of polished bronze, inlaid with ruby studs, clasped his forearms. Rings with emeralds, malachite and agate festooned his broad fingers and a great talisman, wrought from gold with a single giant ruby at its heart, hung around his neck. Across his shoulders and head sat a dried boar pelt, of which Bagrik took his honorific, Boarbrow. Beneath the dead beast's skin, under the sweeping tusks capped with silver tips, was the crown of Ungor and symbol of Bagrik's lordship over his realm.

Beside him was his queen, bedecked in her own royal finery, the same attire she had worn to greet the elves at the outer gateway hall. Nagrim, his son, was also at Bagrik's table sitting to his father's right as was the custom for heirs apparent. Lamentably, Rugnir was with him, bawdier and more raucous than the entire host of dwarfs put together. Bagrik noted with distaste, as the penniless miner taunted Tringrom who stood biting his tongue in the background, that Rugnir had quaffed more ale than anyone else in the room. He suspected, with reluctant praise, that the wanaz could probably drink Heganbour, the king's chief brewmaster, under the table.

Next to the King's Table was the Seat of the Wise, as occupied by the venerable longbeards of the hold, and then came the lords and thanes, then the priests of the Ancestors, Grungni, Valaya and Grimnir. The last table upon the stone platform was that of the Masters, the vaunted leaders of the dwarf craftguilds. Here sat the runelords, the engineer guildmasters, chief lodewardens and the captains of the hold's warrior brotherhoods, the hearth guard and the ironbreakers. In the Great Hall proximity to the king was an indication of wealth, prestige and respect.

The closer a dwarf was to the table of his liege, the more power he possessed. These then were the greatest of the dwarfs. It was no small matter that Bagrik had allowed the elves to sit at his table. It was the greatest gesture of honour he could afford them. He hoped, sourly, that they would live up to it.

The sounding of horns reverberated around the chamber, announcing the arrival of the elves. Under Bagrik's withering appraisal, the assembled clans ceased their merrymaking at once, observing dutiful silence as all eyes turned to the gate of the Great Hall.

With the scrape of stone and the groaning of ancient wood, the doors eased open and the elven delegation from Tor Eorfith came through. A small cohort of dwarfs led them in with Kandor striding at their head, followed closely by Morek and the king's banner bearer, Haggar Anvilfist. The dwarfs were dressed in shining gromril mail with open-faced helms and glimmering beard locks. Crimson cloaks, trimmed with silver, sat upon their shoulders. Haggar bore the king's banner, held in both hands, one flesh and blood, the other forged from bronze and bearing runes of power.

The great standard of Karak Ungor was fashioned into an effigy of Grungni, the ancestor god depicted in his form as the miner, wielding hammer and chisel. Below this gilded icon was the stylised image of a red dragon, coiled in on itself and stitched into the cloth banner. It was surrounded by a knotted band of gold, with the royal runes of Bagrik's household woven into it. The banner was a relic, as ancient as any in the king's possession, and it was a great honour to bear it.

Their booted feet clanked loudly against the stone, as the dwarfs tramped into the chamber. The elves were close behind them, dressed in white robes with silver adornments. Though he had not met them face-to-face, Bagrik had listened intently to his queen's descriptions of them, her mood still icy following their argument in the counting house. Bagrik resolved to try and make it up to her later. For now, he was intent on his guests.

Prince Ithalred strode imperiously into the chamber, as was the wont of the elves. He carried a sword at his hip and wore a crown upon his forehead. An azure cloak that seemed to shimmer with an enchanted lustre was draped over his shoulders. He kept his gaze ahead, his cold face unreadable. His sister, the one Brunvilda had said was called Arthelas, and the raven-haired Lethralmir stood either side, seemingly serene. Malbeth the ambassador, who was just behind the dwarfs, smiled warmly at his hosts, exchanging the occasional nod with clansmen who seemed to remember him from his previous visit to the hold. The muscular brute, bulky for an elf and who eyed the room with suspicion, was obviously Korhvale. He seemed ill at ease to Bagrik and kept his fists clenched, regarding the dwarfs like a threat.

The elves seemed to move slowly and regally, yet crossed the vast carpeted aisle that led to the King's Table with the utmost swiftness. They were strange creatures, like drifting white veils or half-glimpsed shadows. It was like they were made of air and light, their voices musical and yet ancient all at once. Bagrik had only had a few dealings with elves, but each was chiselled onto his mind, a memory carved in stone.

Together with the royal household of Tor Eorfith, were a host of servants, gift bearers and the prince's warriors. As Ithalred gained the steps to the stone platform, the servants stopped, arranging themselves upon the carpeted concourse in two lines. The warriors peeled away from the royal entourage, too, taking up their positions next to tables below. It had been the suggestion of Kandor and Malbeth to split the elves thusly, to allow the warriors of the two races to mix with one another and feel able to speak freely outside of the presence of their liege lords.

Kandor, Morek and Haggar halted before their king, and bowed deeply. Bagrik nodded back, grumbling for them to take up their positions. The dwarfs obeyed dutifully, Kandor and Morek assuming their places at the King's Table, while Haggar stood behind the throne with Tringrom and Bagrik's hearth guard shieldbearers.

'Noble King Bagrik,' said Kandor, who had remained standing. 'May I present Prince Ithalred of Tor Eorfith.'

'You may,' Bagrik said impatiently, 'now be seated. I am sure the prince and his charges did not come to my hold to stand on ceremony before a foreign lord, am I right, Prince Ithalred?'

The corner of Ithalred's mouth twitched in what could have been a smile, before the elf nodded slightly and took his place at the King's Table. The rest of the royal household followed, though they were careful not to sit before their prince had taken his own seat.

'I am King Bagrik Boarbrow,' Bagrik declared proudly, 'and you and your kin are welcome here, elgi.' He noticed Ithalred's lip curl in distaste as he regarded him, but he chose to ignore it for now.

Following the king's declaration, Kandor and Malbeth made the rest of the introductions respectively. With these formal observances out of the way, the rest of the elves, the warriors in the lower section of the Great Hall, were seated. An awkward silence descended, the total opposite of the bawdy bonhomie that had been prevalent before the elves' arrival, and Bagrik clapped his hands loudly to break it.

'Behold, Prince Ithalred,' he said, gesturing a servant carrying an ornate iron chest over to him, 'a token of our forthcoming alliance.' Bagrik took the chest, dismissing the servant with a scowl, and opened it to reveal a gold drinking horn. The wondrous artefact was festooned with gemstones and fashioned into the likeness of a rampant dragon with emeralds for eyes.

'May you drink to many victories from it,' added Bagrik as Ithalred received it. The elf clearly found the item unwieldy, and was quick to pass it to Malbeth for safekeeping.

'The chest comes with it,' explained the king, somewhat curiously.

Ithalred nodded, as if he had known this all along, and took the chest, passing that to Malbeth also.

'And here,' the king continued, as another dwarf servant came forward, 'is a mantle of finest gromril scale.' Bagrik held the garment before him, which shimmered goldenly in the torchlight. A looping chain of silver was held in place against the cloak with burnished bronze clasps wrought into the faces of dwarf ancestors.

This, too, the prince took gingerly as if uncertain what he was supposed to do with it and promptly dumped the cloak on Malbeth, who had since got the attention of two elven servants to take the gifts and look after them until his prince was ready to inspect them further.

'You honour me, King Bagrik,' said Ithalred by way of reply, his sincerity unconvincing. 'With these fine... offerings,' he struggled. 'Allow me to return the favour.' He turned and gestured to the gaggle of gift-bearing servants below him.

'This bow,' the elven prince began as the gift bearers hurried up the steps to his side, 'was carved with wood taken from the forests of Eataine, its string woven from the hair of elven maidens.'

Bagrik took the weapon as it was proffered. It was smaller than a conventional elven longbow and obviously finely wrought, but Bagrik held it like it was a fragile thing in his thick fingers, his expression wary as if he expected it to break at any second. After a moment he twanged the string, much to Ithalred's horror, and smiled.

'It makes a curious sound this instrument,' Bagrik told him. 'A weapon, you say?' he asked.

'One of the finest ever crafted in all of the Outer Kingdoms of Ulthuan,' the prince replied, paling with disbelief.

Bagrik shrugged, passing the gift to one of his servants.

'Spices,' said the prince hurriedly, indicating a trio of large, silver urns brought forth by more servants, 'from beyond these shores.'

Bagrik eyed the urns suspiciously in turn, before licking his finger and plunging it inside one.

Ithalred went from pale white to incensed crimson as he watched Bagrik root around the spice urn with his saliva-coated finger.

Malbeth, noticing his prince's building apoplexy, interceded quickly on Ithalred's behalf.

'The spices, noble king,' he began, 'are particularly aromatic. Perhaps,' he ventured, 'you might like to sample their scents first?'

Bagrik looked up at the ambassador, and gave an almost inaudible grunt as he pulled his fist from the urn he'd chosen, fragments of spice clinging to his skin, and sniffed deeply. Bagrik's expression went from disinterest to distaste in a moment, his nose and brow wrinkling with the heady scents of the spices.

'Pungent,' he remarked with a scowl. 'Intended for cooking, yes,' he

added, plunging the spice-laden finger into his mouth and sucking off
the contents. Bagrik smacked his lips and flicked his tongue, a scowl
upon his face as he experienced the taste. Then his face reddened and
a sudden hacking cough wracked his body. Bagrik slammed his fist
onto the table, upending tankards and goblets, as he tried to master his
coughing fit.

'The king is poisoned!' cried Morek, leaping from his seat with his axe
drawn. The hearth guard throne bearers were beside him in an instant,
Haggar too. A commotion erupted from the Great Hall below at the
hearth guard captain's pronouncement. Angry voices were taken up as
elf and dwarf shouted at each other in their native tongues.

Prince Ithalred was stunned into enraged silence, while Malbeth and
Kandor tried desperately to calm the situation, though their assurances
only seemed to enflame the opposite race. Korhvale was on his feet
immediately, stepping between his prince and the axe-wielding Morek.
Lethralmir and Arthelas merely laughed at the absurdity of it all, the
elves and dwarfs in the grand chamber at sudden unexpected logger-
heads.

'Morek!' a stern voice rose above the clamour. 'Put your weapon away
and get back to your post beside your king.' Brunvilda was up, and glowered at the captain of the hearth guard, stopped in his tracks by the
queen's anger. 'Do it at once!' she ordered.

Morek obeyed, stowing his axe, and retreating to the throne. The others dwarfs went with him, red-faced before the fury of their queen. The
impassioned bickering stopped, and all eyes were on the dwarf king as
he slowly recovered from his coughing fit.

Queen Brunvilda was quickly at her husband's side.

'I'm fine, my queen,' he said as she rubbed his back.

She was concerned, but still carried the ire of their earlier words spoken before the feast.

Bagrik averted his gaze as she went back to her place. Looking at
Ithalred, the king smiled. 'Your spices have a mighty kick, elgi…'

A moment of charged silence descended, before the king's smile
broadened and he roared with laughter. At first, the elves seemed
shocked by his reaction but as the other dwarfs joined in the icy mood
thawed and all could relax again. Malbeth laughed heartily, encouraging his kin to do the same, though it was mirth tinged with relief
that another potential disaster had been averted. Only Ithalred was
not amused, though his agitation seemed to have drained away for the
time being.

'Perhaps, it would be wise,' the king announced to all, 'if we were to
leave gift giving until later. For I suspect the hall is hungry,' he added,
struggling to his feet. 'Am I right?'

A cheer erupted from the dwarf throng, much to the elves' alarm.
Korhvale, having previously retaken his seat was almost on his feet

again as if he feared another attack. Malbeth had a swift but harsh word in his ear before the White Lion relaxed, but even then he was still wary.

'Then bring the feast!' the king bellowed in response to the roar of his kin.

The two side portals to the hold were thrown open and dwarf victualers filed in bearing metal platters of rare beef on the bone, hunks of seared goat flesh, shanks of lamb and thick ham hocks dripping with juice. Heat shimmered off the succulent meats as they were paraded around the chamber, the victualers converging first on the King's Table, followed by those nearest to it, until they came to the tables in the lower part of the Great Hall. A pair of dwarfs followed the initial entourage of chefs, a spitted boar carried between them over their shoulders. It was a massive beast, though paled in comparison to the skin hung about Bagrik's shoulders, and was brought to the central fire-pit where it would cook slowly as it was flensed by the victualers. Dwarfs carrying baskets of earth and stonebread followed the boar carriers, together with another four servants who laboured with a stout iron cauldron, a meaty mould broth slopping within. This, too, was placed over the fire-pit on a metal frame, the vast basin more than capable of accommodating both dishes.

Apprentice brewmasters worked alongside the victualers, refilling tankards and flagons, and bringing out fresh casks from the hold's ale stores. Though the elves had brought wine from the vineyards of Ellyrion, Eataine and Yvresse, they were encouraged to try some of the milder brews offered by the dwarfs.

'Here...' said the king, taking a keg from one of the passing brewmasters and filling a goblet for Ithalred, 'Gilded Tongue. It is light and flavoured with honey, delicate enough for even your fair palate I'd warrant, dear prince.'

Ithalred set down a goblet of wine, already poured by one of his servants, reluctantly and took the vessel offered by Bagrik.

'Malbeth,' he said curtly, passing the goblet to his ambassador and ignoring the affronted expression wrinkling the dwarf king's face as he did it.

Malbeth bowed to his host and then to the prince before sipping.

'Bah! That is no way to quaff ale,' a voice slurred from the far end of the table. It was Rugnir, the dwarf's cheeks already ruddy with the consumption of alcohol. 'Tip it down, lad!' he bellowed.

Bagrik was inclined to agree and only watched.

The elf nodded, smiling nervously as he drank. Swilling the ale down, Malbeth's eyes widened before watering profusely.

'Potent...' he rasped.

'That's it, elgi,' said the king, a fierce look out of the corner of his eye reserved for Ithalred. 'That is how we dwarfs drink our ale.'

The elf prince seemed unmoved and nonchalant as he sipped at his wine.

This will be a long evening, thought Bagrik ruefully.

WITH THE INTRODUCTION of the meat, a heady flavoursome aroma had soon filled the Great Hall. Though the elves found the notion of eating with their hands distasteful, whilst the dwarfs gleefully licked grease off their fingers and supped spilled broth from their beards, the food itself was well received. Copious amounts of ale and wine warmed the stilted atmosphere and it was not long before all were talking readily, both races curious as to the habits and mores of the other.

Discrete pockets of conversation sprang up throughout the Great Hall, as the elves and dwarfs began to debate in small groups. The King's Table was no exception.

'Yes, we are troubled by the greenskin around these parts. There is no hold of the Karaz Ankor that is not,' explained Bagrik, his mood dark. 'They are vermin and grow in number each year–'

'More for us to hunt, eh, father?' Nagrim chipped in.

As they ate and drank, Bagrik had begun to talk at length to Ithalred about the history of the hold and the long, proud legacy of Ungor. For his part, the elf prince had said little, though listened intently, only mentioning once the greenskins that a party of his warriors had slaughtered in the mountains during their journey to the hold. Bagrik had greeted this news warmly, but then his demeanour had turned bitter as he recalled the encroachments of orcs and goblins upon the dwarf realm.

'That's right, lad,' said Bagrik, his mood lightening at once, throwing his arm around his son's shoulder and seizing him in a fierce grip.

Ithalred looked nonplussed, as if he didn't understand the tactile gesture.

'You kill the beasts for sport, then?' the elf prince ventured.

'Aye, he does,' Bagrik said for his son. 'In fact, earlier this evening, the lad beat his father's tally and before his seventieth winter! A fine deed, eh?' the king exclaimed, turning about to regard those dwarfs in earshot.

Queen Brunvilda nodded politely, a beaming smile reserved for her son, though her eyes carried a small measure of sadness. She had been attending to her husband's words dutifully, but had seldom spoken. Her mind was on other things. She loved Nagrim, and he was worthy of their praise, but whenever Bagrik extolled the virtues of his son, she could not help but think of the other, the one bereft of his father's love and devotion.

Dissatisfied with his queen's muted response, Bagrik looked to his hearth guard captain, whose stern gaze was fixed upon the ebullient Rugnir, further down the King's Table, the ex-miner showing the elves how easy it was to quaff two tankards at once without spilling a drop. To his credit, the wanaz achieved the feat with aplomb.

'Eh, Morek?' the king prompted.

'Yes, my king. None in the history of Karak Ungor have killed so many.

I doubt it will ever be bested, though I'd be happier if we had another one hundred score to that amount. The greenskin overrun the mountains like ants,' he said.

'Indeed,' Bagrik agreed, a little crestfallen as he released Nagrim from his grasp. Morek's dour response wasn't exactly the affirmation he had been looking for.

'And I plan to add to that tally,' Nagrim told the prince, puffing his chest proudly beneath the red and gold tunic that echoed that worn by his father. 'Good Brondrik, the hold's finest and most venerable ranger has offered to take another party into the mountains after the winter. The mines north of the hold are ever plagued. I'll mount a fair few more grobi heads upon my mantle that day, I promise you,' said the dwarf prince, his eyes alight with the prospect of further glory.

'You take trophies off the creatures?' asked Ithalred with slight distaste.

'Teeth, noses, ears,' replied Nagrim. 'Heads, too, if you can carry them all,' he added with relish.

'If the greenskin are so numerous, do you not worry that they will overwhelm you?'

'Bah,' interjected Bagrik. 'They are base and dim-witted beasts. What has the heir of Ungor to fear from them?' he said, clapping Nagrim on the back and smiling broadly.

'And what of you, Prince Ithalred,' said Bagrik. 'Do you hunt in your native lands?'

'Yes,' the elf muttered darkly, 'I hunt. Though of late, the quarry has not been to my taste.' Ithalred stared into space, lost in some dark memory.

'You speak of the troubles in your land, the kinslaying?' asked Bagrik, his tone low.

Word had reached the dwarfs, some months prior to the elves' landfall, and the colonisation of Tor Eorfith, of the civil war in Ulthuan and the treachery of the one they knew as Malekith. It was he that had first brokered peace between elves and dwarfs. It was Malekith that had befriended Snorri Whitebeard, the first of the High Kings of Karaz-a-Karak, capital of the Karaz Ankor. Yes, the dwarfs knew of Malekith. The elves had a different name for him now.

'In my youth, I hunted stag, deer and even pheasant in the forests of Eataine,' Ithalred explained in a rare moment of candour. 'Those days are done.'

An ugly silence came over them, as if a small storm cloud shrouded that part of the King's Table, the rest of the elves and dwarfs seated there conversing easily.

'You are among allies here, Prince Ithalred,' Bagrik told him, saddened by the elf's melancholy but also glad at the bitterness they both understood and shared, albeit for different foes.

'Of course,' replied the prince, his taciturn mask slipping back onto his face again.

The sudden awkwardness was broken by the king's chief victualer and food taster, Magrinson, approaching the table. He had two apprentices in tow carrying the head of the giant boar between them on a silver platter, swimming in dark blood and fatty juices.

'My lord,' Magrinson began, his voice dry and gruff like grit, 'the boar's head.'

The chief victualer ushered his apprentices forward, who then placed the platter before their king. It was the custom of Karak Ungor for the hold's liege lord to eat the flesh of the great boar's head, the meat having cooked in its own juices until it was at its most succulent and flavoursome.

'A fine beast,' said Bagrik, nodding his thanks to Magrinson who bowed curtly and left the King's Table with his apprentices. 'What do you say, Prince Ithalred, are there creatures as fine as this in your forests?'

The elf looked aghast at the steaming boar head, the brute's beady eyes staring at him expectantly. He looked away but found only the skins that Bagrik wore over his shoulders.

'Yes, I ate this one too,' the dwarf king told him, noticing that Ithalred regarded the dried boar carcass that he wore. 'I was not much beyond a beardling when I encountered the beast in the lowland caves to the east of Black Water,' Bagrik explained. 'It was winter then, too, and the snow was foul that year. I was trapped, unable to find my way back to the hold in the growing drifts. So I sought refuge in a cave. Only it was already occupied. It was *his*, you see.' Bagrik tapped the head of the boar skin with something approaching reverence. 'He was a fierce beast, and did not take kindly to me trespassing in his lair. We fought, and he gored me with his tusks. But I slew him. The meat of his body sustained me and his skin warmed me, until I could be found by my father's rangers. Though I did not emerge from the battle unscathed. The wound it dealt me I still carry and I have not walked without pain since that day because of it.'

'Yes,' said Ithalred, seemingly unmoved by the story. 'Your queen explained it was the reason for your absence at our arrival.' There was a barb in the elf's words, and Bagrik felt it keenly.

'Perhaps,' ventured the king, 'you would be more understanding if you, too, bore such an injury, elf.'

'I'm not sure I follow your meaning, dwarf,' Ithalred countered.

Kandor, who had paused in his own conversations to hear of what his king and the elf prince were talking about, chipped in quickly to dispel the sudden belligerent mood.

'You admire the line of kings?' he asked a little too loudly.

Malbeth, who had been doing no such thing, but caught onto his fellow diplomat's ploy immediately, looked around the room with feigned interest.

Arrayed around the Great Hall, cast in stark relief with the jagged fingers of firelight from the wall sconces, were statues of the royal clans of Karak Ungor.

'Yes, they are wondrous,' the elf replied with genuine humility, when he actually regarded the statues. 'Are they carved into the rock of the mountain?'

'That they are,' said the king. 'There for eternity, so that all would know of our proud lineage.'

Glad to have averted yet another disaster, Kandor pointed to one statue sat in a large dusty alcove. 'That is King Norkragg Fireheart,' he said, with a quick glance at his king to ensure that he was happy for him to go on. 'Norkragg was a king of the elder age, one of the first of Ungor,' he continued. 'So the Book of Remembering held, Norkragg was a miner at heart, even eschewing his royal duties to pursue his passion, a fact that left him without queen and heir. In his tenure, Norkragg hauled more coal from the rock face and to the under-forge than any since.'

'A great and noble lord was Norkragg. He had much respect for the traditions of us dawi,' added Bagrik, a meaningful glance at Ithalred to ram his point home.

'And this one,' said Malbeth quickly before the elf prince could reply, gesturing to the next statue in line. 'What is his tale?'

'Ah,' said Kandor, as he regarded the stooped shoulders, were it possible for a statue to stoop, of the liege lord alongside Norkragg. 'King Ranulf Shallowbrow. And to his right, Queen Helgi.'

Malbeth beheld a large and fearsome dwarf woman when he looked upon the effigy of Ranulf's queen.

'She is… *formidable,*' he said, choosing his words carefully.

Kandor went on.

'It was rumoured at the girthing ceremony that Ranulf had to wait another fifty years after his initial proposal of marriage before they could be wed. You see, according to dwarf law a suitor is required to wrap his beard around a rinn's waist twice over before the marriage can be made legal, and Helgi was a mighty woman.'

'It was also said,' Rugnir chipped in, 'that she was of such fine stock that she near bankrupted poor old Ranulf when she sat upon the nuptial scales!'

The ex-miner laughed raucously, Nagrim alongside joining him.

Even King Bagrik raised a smile.

'Aye, Rugnir,' said the stern voice of Morek, who had been listening in to all the conversations around the King's Table, 'that it did, but what a queen Ranulf had. Any wife that you might make for yourself would be as waif thin as these elgi, such is your squandered fortune,' he added caustically.

Kandor balked at the hearth guard captain's remark, hoping that the elves did not take any offence. If they had, they didn't get the chance to voice it as Morek went on unabated.

'Kraggin will be wandering in limbo before Gazul's Gate because of your profligacy. It is no fate for one such as he; no fate at all.'

The entire table fell abruptly quiet at Morek's outburst. Even Rugnir's drunken humour seemed beaten out of him at the mention of his father's name.

'How is this so?' said Lethralmir, who had been apathetically swilling his wine around in his goblet before noticing the apparent discord and seizing upon an opportunity to exploit it. 'Surely, this fine… *individual* cannot be held responsible for the fate of his father. Did he not make his own destiny?'

Morek's face flushed and he clenched his teeth.

Malbeth interceded quickly when he realised what the raven-haired elf was trying to do.

'I think what my kinsmen means,' began the ambassador, 'is we are unfamiliar with dwarf belief. For instance, what is this gate you speak of? It is not a literal gate, like the entrance to this grand chamber, I assume?'

'No,' said Morek, looking daggers at Lethralmir, before switching his attention to Malbeth. 'Gazul's Gate bars the way to the dwarf afterlife and the Halls of the Ancestors,' he explained. 'Every dwarf must face those gates and balance his deeds before Gazul himself. Even if they are found worthy, and pass into the Halls, there is no guarantee they will remain so. The deeds of descendents can throw their place at the table of Grungni into jeopardy. So it is with some,' Morek said, looking askance and angry at Rugnir, 'where their ancestors will wander lost until amends have been made for dishonourable behaviour.'

'Surely, though, this dwarf, if he is indeed enduring purgatory, must have brought it upon himself?' Lethralmir pressed with a sly wink at Arthelas, who was enjoying the show sat alongside him.

'Kraggin was honourable and good,' Morek asserted passionately, 'How dare you besmirch his name!'

'Please, please,' said Malbeth. 'Lethralmir meant no offence, I'm sure. Did you?' he added, looking meaningfully at the dark-haired elf who returned his stern gaze with a look of indifference.

'No, of course not. I would never *besmirch* a dwarf,' he replied at length.

Morek's face darkened and he stood and turned to Bagrik, who was similarly unimpressed.

'My lord, I regret I must leave the King's Table to attend to my many duties,' said the hearth guard captain.

Bagrik was grave as he regarded the elves. It seemed the hope that his guests would live up to the honour of being at his table had been dashed. He sighed deeply, mastering his annoyance. Bagrik knew his hearth guard captain's views – they were not so dissimilar to his own – but he also had no desire to fuel the fire of Morek's anti-elf sentiment. He had promised Brunvilda he would try, and made a similar pledge to Kandor. As king of the hold, he would keep to his word. Yet with Morek in such a foul mood, he had little recourse but to give him leave.

'Granted,' Bagrik said at last.

Morek bowed swiftly, firing a dark glare in Lethralmir's direction before he left the Great Hall.

KORHVALE HAD NOT spoken a word since the elves had entered the Great Hall. He had watched all within the chamber diligently, though, his gaze lingering on Arthelas more than most. Only when she had noticed him looking did he turn away, abashed. He took greater care when watching her after that. It only served to exacerbate the discomfort he already felt. The White Lion did not like the dank halls of earth, the sense of the mountain on top of him. It felt like a threat waiting to make good on itself. Instead, he longed for the wide open spaces of Chrace, his homeland: to feel the breeze upon his face, the warmth of the sun against his skin, and to drink in the scents of the wild.

Korhvale, at his heart, was the beast he wore as a pelt across his shoulders. Wild and untamed, he desired to roam the forests and mountains of Ulthuan. This which he now endured, fettered within a cage of stone, was anathema to him.

'He was always highly strung, that one,' remarked a dwarf sitting alongside him. Korhvale saw he had a thick black beard and dark circles ringed his eyes. He had rough-looking hands, scarred and calloused. Clearly, he was a warrior. He wore a dark grey tunic and pinched a pipe between his lips as he offered a hand to the White Lion.

'Grikk Ironspike, Captain of the King's Ironbreakers.'

Korhvale shook hands with the dwarf, though the tactile gesture felt strange to him.

'Korhvale,' he muttered, uncertain in his use of Khazalid to say much more.

'I get the feeling that grand feasts are not for you, elgi,' said Grikk, struggling for conversation himself.

'No,' Korhvale replied.

'Me neither,' Grikk agreed. 'I would rather be alone in the Ungrin Ankor, the tunnels beneath the hold,' he explained. 'There are many beasts that inhabit them – that is true – but I know what is to be done about beasts,' he added with a glint in his eye.

Korhvale shrugged, unsure how to respond.

'It is at grand gatherings that I am at a loss,' the dwarf said.

'Yes,' the elf replied.

'Seems you and me both,' the ironbreaker muttered, after an uneasy silence, and folded his arms as he supped on his pipe.

A GREAT GONG echoed metallically throughout the Great Hall, struck by Haggar. It heralded the end of the feast and the onset of the

entertainments provided by the dwarfs. The reverberant sound came
as a welcome relief to both races – certainly Bagrik was glad of it. This
Ithalred had proven himself every inch the arrogant warrior-prince
that Bagrik supposed he would be. He wondered, as a veritable throng
of servants issued into the grand chamber to clear plates and platters,
whether or not it had been a wise move to listen to Kandor's counsel
regarding the elves. The merchant guildmaster had insisted that a trade
alliance between their peoples would bring about much prosperity, that
the elves would be all too willing dwarf-friends in light of the troubles
that beset their own shores. So far, though, Bagrik had seen little to
encourage him and would only bite his tongue so long.

The dwarf servants worked quickly, taking the remnants of the feast
back to the hold's kitchens and lesser clan halls. As he watched them
troop out with the giant broth cauldron and the fire-pit, Bagrik felt himself being raised aloft on his throne by his hearth guard. The King's Table
was moved from his path by a group of clansdwarfs, and he, together
with Brunvilda and Nagrim, was carried to the edge of the stone platform overlooking the sunken floor of the vast hall. The other tables, the
Seat of the Wise and that of the Masters and other dwarf nobility, had
already been taken away to be stored. Below, a similar arrangement was
taking place as a large open plaza started to appear where before there
had been many tables.

The ledges that delineated the room were soon occupied, more dwarf
servants providing plump velvet cushions with wooden backboards for
the venerable or important. In short order, the Great Hall took on the
aspect of a roofed amphitheatre, the stone plaza a natural focal point for
the attention of the surrounding elves and dwarfs.

Once the transformation was complete, Bagrik turned again to Haggar
who stood at the ready by the great gong in one corner of the hall. At the
king's command, Haggar sounded the gong again and the hall, which
up until then had been filled with a hubbub of low voices, fell silent.
Bagrik then signalled to his banner bearer to begin the entertainments.

'Grikk Ironspike, Captain of the King's Ironbreakers!' Haggar declared,
his voice resonating around the room like a clarion call.

The black-bearded dwarf came forward from the shadows at the edge
of the Great Hall, approached his king and bowed on one knee, his
clenched fists at either side of his body and touching the floor in the
regal fashion of the dwarfs. He was no longer wearing his dark grey
tunic, instead stripped to the waist and wearing leather breeches with a
skirt of mail, bronze vambraces clapped around his wrists.

'Tromm, Grikk of the Ironspike clan,' said Bagrik to his captain. 'What
feats have you for us?'

'AxE HURLING, MY liege,' Malbeth heard the ironbreaker reply, 'and anvil
lifting.'

Sat next to Kandor, the elf ambassador watched as clansdwarfs marched onto the plaza of stone in the middle of the Great Hall carrying, first, a weapons rack of dwarf hand axes and then a series of wooden stakes on top of which had been rammed the heads of greenskins. Malbeth swallowed back his disgust at the grisly targets, with their lolling tongues and glassy-eyed stares. Ragged skin hung from their necks, together with strips of desiccated flesh caked with dried blood.

They were repellent things, the elf decided, worrying what Ithalred was thinking, who wore a perpetual grimace as he regarded the decapitated heads. As he fretted over his prince, Malbeth also caught the venomous gaze of Lethralmir, who was clearly enjoying the spectacle for all the wrong reasons. Holding the elf ambassador's gaze, the raven-haired blade-master whispered something into Arthelas's ear, who laughed quietly. Malbeth noticed Korhvale, too, his attention rapt, but not on Grikk who was approaching the weapon's rack for his first axe, but rather on Arthelas.

That will not end well, Malbeth thought, and resolved to speak with the White Lion later.

Fraught with concern and misgivings, he gave a false smile to Kandor who gestured for him to watch, as the display was about to begin in earnest.

GRIKK WAS LATHERED in sweat, a line of split greenskin skulls and upturned anvils testament to his endeavours. The dwarfs had cheered as one with each lifted weight, with every orc or goblin head struck and maimed. Grikk never missed, not once, and no anvil, however large, could defeat him. Conversely, the elves seemed not to know what to do and were largely silent throughout, only clapping politely at the end as the ironbreaker captain bowed before his king and then his audience.

Haggar found the elgi to be strange creatures, who lacked the ready camaraderie of his kin. How could they fail to appreciate the skills of the ironbreaker captain? Grikk was one of the finest warriors in the hold, next only to Morek. Would that he, Haggar, be so great... For a moment, the dwarf's mind drifted to a time before, to a shame he must atone for. He eyed the banner of Ungor, resting in its place behind the throne of King Bagrik and felt the dishonour of that day anew.

Thagri, he said to himself, will your dishonour ever linger over me?

So deep was Haggar's remembrance that he very nearly missed the order of his king to announce the next entertainment.

Hurriedly, Haggar thrashed the gong and cried, 'The Miners' Guild Choir, led by Jodri Broadbellow!'

MALBETH WATCHED AS in filed the dwarf choristers, decked in their finest attire, the bronze buttons on their brown tunics gleaming, black metal mining caps polished to a dull lustre. Some wore tiny bells around their fingers, or had cloth tassels bound to their ankles and wrists. There were musicians, too, carrying instruments: large, brass horns curved to resemble coiling serpentine monsters; fat animal bladders, fitted with an array of copper pipes that sprang out at awkward-looking angles; orc-skin drums, rolled out onto the stone plaza; and a strange-looking barrel organ with yellowed-bone keys at one end and a metal turning crank at the other.

It was as bizarre an assemblage as Malbeth had ever seen, and he had been to the dwarf kingdoms before. However odd this array of dwarfs, though, the sight could not have prepared him for what happened next. A dour bass note began the proceedings, the head chorister singing *a cappella* at first, before his fellows joined him in complimentary baritone and tenor. As they sang, some ditty about firkins and a goblin's rump, as far as Malbeth could discern, the musicians struck up their instruments.

A horrific din assailed his senses, and the elf ambassador shut his eyes at first in the hope that the dwarfs had merely mistuned. After a few more seconds of the auditory torture, it became clear that they had not and, grimacing, Malbeth opened his eyes. Puffing cheeks red with effort, the dwarfs pumped out a sound akin to a throttled horse or bone scraped down metal. The elf ambassador noticed King Bagrik seemed to be enjoying himself, as did the rest of the dwarfs watching, slapping his thigh as the miners danced with strange, squatting motions, bells and tassels shaking with every syncopated movement.

Malbeth gritted his teeth, trying desperately at the same time to smile, and prayed to Isha, the elven god of mercy, that it would be over soon.

BAGRIK STOPPED DRUMMING the beat of the choristers' drums when he saw the expression on Ithalred's face. The elf prince looked as if he was in profound agony, his features screwed up so tight they might never revert back to their usual state of indifference.

Hurriedly, the dwarf king got the attention of his banner bearer and urged him vigorously to strike the gong.

After a moment's indecision, Haggar did as he was bidden, the reverberating sound of the gong cutting the performance of the Miners' Guild Choir abruptly short.

'Enough!' Bagrik snarled.

Confused, the miners stopped part way through the first verse of their ditty with a belated toot and crump of a pipe and accordion. Bagrik waved away the looks of the nonplussed miners agitatedly, and they tramped off in disconsolate fashion with a discordant clamour of instruments and much grumbling.

The king then turned swiftly to Haggar, his gaze questioning as to what was next. The dwarf merely shrugged, looking slightly panicked at the sudden interruption in the schedule.

Malbeth came to his rescue.

'PERHAPS, YOU WOULD allow us to grace you with a taste of our native culture,' said the elf ambassador, to Haggar's profound relief.

Bagrik muttered something in response, but then Kandor nodded, similarly relieved.

'Arthelas,' said the elf, turning to the pale maiden at Prince Ithalred's side, 'would you grace our generous hosts with a song of Eataine?'

Haggar saw the elf maiden nod demurely as she rose from her seat, and felt his face flush at her elegance and ethereal beauty. Never had he seen such a creature in all his days. So thin, so brittle, she was like the wind, the reflected light of sun against water, the glitter of gold. She glided down to the plaza, two elf harpists drifting silently to her side as she took her position in the middle of the plaza. The magnificence of the Great Hall seemed dulled in her radiant presence and all within fell silent as she began.

A lilting melody filled the air as Arthelas sang, a haunting, ephemeral sound that seemed to drift in and out of being, as the harpists plucked their instruments in accompaniment. Though he did not understand the words, Haggar felt warmth and a curious sense of lightness spread over his body as he heard them. The effect was bewitching. Time slowed and ceased to have meaning. It was like there was only her in the grand chamber, alone and singing just for Haggar. Her gaze connected with the dwarf's and the burden of his past faded away. Not even a lingering memory remained, there was only Arthelas.

When the song ended and she bowed her head in supplication before the crowd, stunned silence reigned. Haggar wiped tears from his eyes and breathed again. When he saw Arthelas collapse, his heart nearly stopped in his armoured chest.

KORHVALE WAS THE first to come to Arthelas's aid, vaulting down from his perch on the stone ledge, landing deftly, and at her side in a moment. Ithalred was close behind the White Lion, waving the harpists and other elves aside as he took her from his bodyguard and cradled her in his arms, before whispering softly in his sister's ear. She roused, opening her eyes slowly.

'What is wrong with her?' asked Malbeth, the elf ambassador having followed after his prince. A small cluster of other concerned onlookers had gathered, elves and dwarfs both.

'Is everything well, shall I summon the priests of Valaya?' asked Kandor, a little breathless.

'What goes on down there?' called Bagrik from his seat, the dwarf king unwilling to hobble down to see for himself.

'*We have no need of your priests!*' snapped Ithalred beneath his breath, as he flashed a scowl at the dwarf merchant.

'All is well, my friend,' said Malbeth, stepping between the prince and Kandor, and placing his hand on the dwarf's shoulder. 'Arthelas is merely tired from our journey. She feels it more than the rest of us,' he explained.

Kandor nodded slowly, catching a glimpse of Ithalred past Malbeth as he angrily summoned his servants, but did not appear reassured.

'All is well,' Malbeth said again much louder for the benefit of the entire assembly. 'The Lady Arthelas is only tired.'

'We are all tired,' came the voice of Lethralmir, his tone dark, as he emerged through the crowd like a viper. 'These… *games*,' he added, 'have gone on long enough.'

Malbeth was about to say something when Ithalred got up, carrying Arthelas in his arms.

'Lethralmir is right,' said the prince in elvish. 'This ridiculous display is over. I have endured enough of it.'

'But my lord, I'm sure if Arthelas returns to her–' Malbeth began.

'It is over, Malbeth,' Ithalred snapped, his tone brooking no argument.

The elf ambassador, halted in mid-flow, closed his mouth and nodded his assent. Out of the corner of his eye, he noticed Lethralmir quietly smirking to himself.

'Malbeth,' Ithalred said curtly, 'tell our hosts we are retiring for the evening.' At that he stalked out of the Great Hall, Korhvale, his face awash with concern, with him. A clutch of servants came after them, the muttered grumblings of the dwarfs left in their wake.

Lethralmir gave a series of sharp commands in elvish at which the warriors got to their feet and followed the prince with the rest of the servants. The raven-haired blade-master was about to move into step behind them when Malbeth grasped his arm.

'What do you think you're doing?' he hissed, angrily.

The raven-haired elf smiled darkly, 'Keeping my dignity and the dignity of our race,' he said.

'Khaine damn you, Lethralmir.'

The elf sniffed, as if he found Malbeth's remark amusing. 'You first,' he countered, looking down meaningfully at his arm where the ambassador still gripped it.

'Do you really want to make a scene before our generous hosts?' Lethralmir goaded him after a few seconds, and looked back down at his arm again. 'Remember that temper of yours…'

Malbeth let him go.

'What is going on?' asked Kandor, as the elves were trooping out of the Great Hall.

Malbeth turned, having recovered his composure.

'Tiredness has got the better of us all, it seems,' he replied weakly, then raised his voice to address the king.

'Regrettably, your majesty, we must retire for the evening. Prince Ithalred is exhausted, and must rest from his journey. He asked me to convey his appreciation at the fine feast and entertainments you so graciously provided, however.'

King Bagrik said something beneath his breath, clearly unconvinced, and Malbeth took that as his cue to leave.

BAGRIK SURVEYED THE pandemonium of his Great Hall left in the elves' wake: the dwarfs milling around the stone plaza scratching their heads and muttering amongst one another; the disgusted tones of the glowering longbeards, their pipes smoking furiously; the dark glances passing between the guildmasters, and the other clan lords and thanes, that he, Bagrik, had given sanction for this debacle.

He felt the presence of Brunvilda nearby, about to reassure him, and clenched his fists.

'Say nothing!' he snarled between his teeth, turning his furious gaze onto Kandor, who seemed somehow lost standing below him.

Rugnir's voice broke the tomb-like atmosphere.

'Who died?' he asked, jovially. 'Let the elgi get their beauty sleep, there is still more drinking to be done.'

A few of the younger clansdwarfs seemed to warm to the idea at once, Nagrim included.

Bagrik shattered the levity in an instant.

'No!' he raged, struggling to his feet and casting his steely gaze about the room. He had bent over backwards for these elves, allowed them into his home, turned a blind eye to their affronts, their arrogance and rudeness. They had thrown his hospitality in his face like grobi dung. Bagrik was incensed, and in no mood to make merry. 'Back to your clan halls, all of you, the party is over!'

CHAPTER SEVEN

Dark Secrets

IT WAS SEVERAL hours before Malbeth returned to the Hall of Belgrad, now turned into an elven enclave. After leaving the Great Hall, he had waited for Kandor. The dwarf merchant had emerged soon enough, having exchanged curt words with his king, or rather had words foisted upon him, which he had attended to in silence. Ashen-faced from his berating, the merchant had then taken the elf to his private halls and the two had discussed the evening at length, Kandor expressing the king's concerns over the elves' behaviour and Malbeth giving the dwarf his assurances that they were merely teething troubles and an accord could be reached over the trade agreement. The long debate had left the elf weary, but he had managed to convince Kandor that there was still an alliance to be salvaged from the carnage of the feast.

Even so, it was with some trepidation that Malbeth approached the tent of the prince. Korhvale was outside, the White Lion and a handful of other guards and servants the only ones yet to retire to their makeshift abodes. Malbeth knew Korhvale would stay at his post all night, eschewing sleep or even meditation, to watch over his master.

Arms folded like bands of iron, the muscular bodyguard grunted as Malbeth came near, stepping aside so that he could enter.

Low lamps burned within the tent, creating a warm, cloying atmosphere in the opulent surroundings. Ithalred was laid out on a pile of plump cushions and divested of his princely robes, bare-chested and wearing loose-fitting cotton breeches. A soft melody pervaded the room, the two harpists from earlier playing quietly nearby. Two further maidens, wearing precious little, but enough to preserve their dignity, were decanting wine into the prince's goblet and massaging his neck and shoulders. At Malbeth's appearance in the room they looked up and smiled lasciviously before continuing with their duties.

A blue-green smoke drenched the atmosphere, lingering about Malbeth's feet like autumnal glade mist. The elf ambassador saw Lethralmir sitting cross-legged as he supped from a long-handled marble pipe, a fifth maiden combing his long black hair.

The two nobles had been laughing as Malbeth had entered, enjoying the tail end of some jest he was not privy to. Still smiling, Lethralmir blew a large ring of smoke into the air. It held its form for a short while before it dispersed into lingering aroma.

'Prince Ithalred,' said Malbeth, his tone serious, 'we must talk about what happened at the feast. The dwarfs are unhappy.'

Ithalred closed his eyes and leaned further back, wallowing in the decadence of his private pavilion. He beckoned with his ringed fingers and one of the scantily-clad maidens came over with a platter of fruit, which the prince accepted with hedonistic torpor.

'The dwarfs are unhappy, *I* am unhappy,' he replied, nonchalant. 'Let us just be done with these trade talks so that we can return to Tor Eorfith and some semblance of civilisation. I swear by Asuryan, if I spend much longer in the burrows of these hirsute dwarfs, I shall be sprouting hair from my own chin.'

Lethralmir smirked.

Ithalred wasn't jesting.

'With respect,' said Malbeth, ignoring the blade-master, 'amends must be made if the trade talks are to go ahead.'

Ithalred sighed in agitation, waving away the servant girls as he levered himself up onto his elbows.

'What would you have me do, Malbeth? Our cultures are utterly opposite to one another. A clash was inevitable.'

'It is more than a clash,' said Malbeth with growing exasperation. 'We have offended our hosts in their very home! I, too, long for the lofty towers of Eorfith, for the sky and the wind and all that I hold dear about Ulthuan and Eataine, but there is too much at stake here to jeopardise in the name of selfish desire and petulance.'

He'd gone too far. The sneering smile spreading across Lethralmir's face, just visible in the corner of his eye, told Malbeth as much.

'You forget yourself, ambassador,' snapped Ithalred, sitting up and nearly tipping over his wine.

'I apologise, my prince,' Malbeth replied humbly, 'but the fact remains that Tor Eorfith will not survive without the dwarfs' aid.'

'We do not know that for certain,' said Lethralmir, even now stirring the pot.

Malbeth whirled around to face him, though he kept his anger at bay. But only just.

'We know it all too well, Lethralmir,' he said fiercely. 'Do not allow your arrogance to obscure your already clouded mind.

'Prince Ithalred,' Malbeth continued, turning back to his lord without waiting for a response from Lethralmir. 'I am *urging* you – apologise to the dwarfs, make amends for all that has transpired. You know as well as I what this trade pact truly represents, what we hope to gain from it. Please… *please*, do not lose sight of that.'

Ithalred's expression promised another angry retort, but he stopped short as if realising the truth in Malbeth's words and at last capitulated.

'Very well. I'll do as you ask, Malbeth. I will regain the respect of the dwarfs. It is my duty to safeguard the future of Tor Eorfith, so there is little else I can do, is there,' he added, clearly unhappy with the position he was in, with the position that they were all in. 'Now, go…' he said after a moment, his face suddenly darkening. 'It is late, and I tire of politics.'

One of the maidens, seeing her lord's distemper, slid over to resume massaging his neck.

'Leave it!' he snarled, and she shrank back as if scalded by his words. 'All of you,' he added, glaring around the room, 'get out!'

Hurriedly gathering their things, and some of their clothes, the quintet of maidens made a hasty exit, eyes down as they left the prince's private abode for fear of further reproach.

Lethralmir seemed bemused at Ithalred's reaction, particularly his dismissal of the wenches, whose company he had been enjoying profusely.

'Was that strictly necessary, Ithalred?' he asked, taking a long draw on his pipe and reaching for his wine.

'You too, Lethralmir,' the prince said quietly.

The raven-haired elf opened his mouth to protest but thought better of it.

'As you wish, my lord,' he said with forced deference, clearly incensed at being expelled from his prince's presence like a common slave.

Malbeth watched the entire display and felt no satisfaction. He saw only Ithalred at last coming to terms with the gravity of their situation and the stark reality that theirs was a precarious position indeed.

Bowing slightly, he departed immediately after Lethralmir had stormed out, his mood no better than when he had first entered the pavilion.

'WAIT…' CALLED MALBETH, once they were a few feet from the prince's tent and the imposing figure of Korhvale, '…I would speak with you, Lethralmir.'

The raven-haired elf turned. He was on the way to his own tent, determined to summon a pair of the wenches that Ithalred had just dismissed. He let Malbeth come to him before he gave his reply.

'I have nothing to say,' he told the ambassador, still smarting over the prince's rebuttal.

'Then merely listen,' Malbeth countered, guiding the blade-master by the shoulder around the side of one of the tents. Once out of Korhvale's eye-line, he seized Lethralmir by the arm and drew him close.

'Do not think your blatant attempts at sabotage have gone unnoticed,' said Malbeth, his eyes hard. 'I don't know what your reasons are, but it will stop… now. And you would do well to stay away from Arthelas,' he warned.

Lethralmir went rigid at her name. His cerulean eyes were like diamonds as they regarded the ambassador, his dark smile etched as if in ice.

'Your behaviour towards her is unseemly,' Malbeth continued. 'I have turned a blind eye to it for long enough. Do not think that Ithalred will continue to do so, either. The prince has no desire to see his sister sullied by one such as you. Her gifts, her sight – they are precious… I am telling you, Lethralmir–'

'No,' the raven-haired elf hissed, grabbing Malbeth's robes, all trace of his sarcastic vainglory evaporated, and in its place… malicious, undiluted bile. '*I* am the only one doing the *telling* here. Or do you want me to reveal your true nature to the prince, to your precious bearded swine?' He sneered hatefully, though his expression betrayed his fear.

Malbeth's loosened his grip, the sudden creeping dread of discovery shaking his resolve.

It was no idle threat. Lethralmir meant every word. There was anger in his eyes now, the same impotent fury that there had been all those years ago…

Malbeth still held him in his grasp, remembering the day they had first crossed swords, in the sheltered arboretum of his uncle's villa in Eataine, the pale sandstone walls flecked with darkness, Elethya dying in his arms. Her hot blood was a baptism for the rage and anguish that would manifest in Malbeth. And just like that, the feelings that he had fought so hard to repress, the fury that lay in his cursed soul, came boiling to the surface in a tempest.

Lethralmir saw it in the ambassador's eyes, saw him glance to the jewelled dagger the blade-master wore at his belt.

'Go on…' said the raven-haired elf, his lip curling in a sneer '…Do it.' Lethralmir released Malbeth's robe, let his arm drop in submission. 'Give in.'

It would be easy…

Elethya… dying in his arms…

Malbeth let him go, then turned away, heading towards his tent without saying another word.

* * *

LETHRALMIR SMOOTHED DOWN his robes, releasing a long breath as he tried to stop shaking. He told himself it was anger, but in truth he was afraid; afraid of what Malbeth might have done if pushed.

That could be useful, he thought, if properly channelled.

Recovering his composure, he managed to swagger off, imperiously staring down any servants that had seen or overheard his altercation with the ambassador and dared to meet his gaze. He was intent on finding the masseurs – their *attentions* would be a welcome distraction right now – when he changed his mind. He bypassed his own tent, and went straight for Arthelas's instead.

Bastard, Malbeth, threaten me will you?

Lethralmir's route took him back towards Ithalred's domicile and the stern-faced Korhvale, who glared at the raven-haired elf as he approached.

'The prince asked me to see how his sister was feeling,' he lied, flashing a broad smile in Korhvale's direction. The White Lion stiffened in response, his leather gauntlets cracking as he made fists.

Lethralmir gave him no further thought, passing by and continuing on to where Arthelas was waiting.

'I AM BORED,' Lethralmir declared, as he entered the tent, 'and I have charged you with entertaining me,' he added, sweeping into the room and down to Arthelas's side, where she reclined on a chaise-long of white wood, upholstered with sumptuous red velvet and fashioned into the image of a swan in repose. Lethralmir noticed several servants hovering at the periphery, their faces veiled by the thin cotton shrouds that hung throughout the room, and carrying silver carafes and broad, paper fans. There was no food in sight – the seeress seldom ate. Lethralmir dismissed the servants with a few curt commands.

'Finally alone…' he purred, once they were gone, letting the insinuation linger. He drew close to her, the scent of her in his nostrils more potent than any perfume as it enflamed his ardour.

Arthelas pushed him away, but her protest lacked conviction.

'My brother would have you killed if he knew what you were intending,' she said, sighing as she rested the back of her hand across her forehead in an overtly dramatic gesture. 'I am tired Lethralmir, and in no mood for your advances tonight.'

Lethralmir sniffed contemptuously, and recoiled.

'You are in a fouler mood than your brother, the prince,' he replied.

'He is a fool,' said Arthelas, looking at Lethralmir for the first time. There was darkness in her eyes, bitterness in her voice. 'I am a seeress first and a sister second to him. Ithalred's mood is foul because he does not like it when he doesn't get his way. He is annoyed because he must listen to Malbeth's counsel, because he must make parlay with these dwarfs.'

She almost spat the words through clenched teeth as the demure and elegant façade slipped completely.

Lethralmir gazed back at Arthelas, her words meaningless as he drank deep of her azure eyes, and became lost in their fathomless beauty. Determined to lighten the mood, he moved over to the tent flap by which he had entered.

'I have something that will cheer you,' he said, smiling conspiratorially and beckoning her over.

Arthelas exhaled loudly, sitting up, ostensibly annoyed as she padded over.

Lethralmir ignored the histrionics, opened the tent flap and gestured outside.

'Look…'

Arthelas sighed again, signalling her impatience, but did as she was asked. Peering through the flap, she saw Korhvale, brooding outside her brother's tent.

'No more than a crack,' Lethralmir warned, as the White Lion stared in her direction but then swiftly averted his gaze as if suddenly ashamed.

'Look how forlorn he is,' the raven-haired elf said sarcastically.

'I don't like the way he watches me.'

'The dumb and dutiful lion,' Lethralmir sneered, revealing his true feelings. 'His mawkish attempts to gain your favour are only marginally less laughable than the antics of the earth-dwellers,' he added, growing more serious. 'What need do the asur have for these diminutive swine? If Ithalred possessed any backbone at all he would raise the army at Tor Eorfith and turn back the northern hordes closing on our borders. Yet instead, at Malbeth's insistence,' he spat, 'he seeks to yoke the strength of these rough creatures and their crude ways. What will they do, bite the ankles of the northern savages? No,' he scoffed, 'there is nothing to fear from *men*.'

'I am not so certain…' said Arthelas, finding no more amusement in watching Korhvale, and closed the tent flap.

'Why?' Lethralmir asked. His eyes narrowed as he regarded her, suddenly understanding. 'What have you *seen*?'

In that moment, all expression seemed to vanish from Arthelas's face and her eyes glazed over like pale moons. The heady scent of her perfumed boudoir was gone, the smell of the sea, of cold, glacial air, and the tang of salt came in its place.

'Our ships,' said Arthelas, her voice far away, 'ablaze on the ocean…'

'Hasseled's Hawkships,' Lethralmir whispered, realising at once what she meant. Just before they had set off for the dwarf hold, Ithalred had ordered a defensive blockade to be erected far out at sea against northmen vessels the elves had seen from their watchtowers, sailing the Sea of Claws. Commander Hasseled was to lead them, assess the enemy's strength and destroy them if he could. It seemed the good commander had failed.

'Their crude vessels riding through a storm…' Arthelas continued.

'They make landfall… the sentinels are just the beginning…'

'The watchtowers are lost?' hissed Lethralmir.

Arthelas turned to him, vehement, fear in her eyes – the sense of it exaggerated by her dream-trance.

'They already burn… All are dead, all of them.'

She wept, the tears rushing down her face in a flood, and Lethralmir held her.

'Let it go,' he said softly, stroking her hair. 'Let it all go.'

Arthelas looked into his eyes, coming out of it at last.

'All dead…' she whimpered, softly.

Lethralmir took her chin gently, tilting Arthelas's head so she had to look into his eyes. He caressed her neck and drew in close.

'What are you doing?' she hissed, fear and excitement warring in her voice.

'Your brother has no need of a seer, anymore.'

'I can't,' she said in a cracked whisper.

'You must…' Lethralmir replied huskily, parting his lips and pressing them to hers.

BLOOD. ENDLESS BLOOD. The battlefield was soaked in it, a crimson-tinged isle of pounded dirt. Ragged banners fluttered on a fitful breeze that reeked of copper, and smoke from burning cities rendered into ruined shells by the carnage. Hollow, pleading cries and the clash-scrape of metal filled the rancid air, borne upon a hot wind that swirled about in tired eddies and whispered… death…

Malbeth awoke, lathered in sweat. He sat up sharply as if the pallet where he lay were a bed of spikes, and he'd just felt the first prick. His head was swimming, visions slipping in and out of focus – a war against creatures not of this world, screaming terror and a bloody-handed god exulting in the slaughter. A sense memory spoke of metal and fire, the stench of smoke lingering impossibly in Malbeth's nostrils.

The coldness of the dwarf stone, penetrating even the cushioned floor of his tent, brought him around. Sodden sheets clung to his body, and Malbeth cast them off like they were shackles that incarcerated him in the dream. Dull and resonant hammering, the ever-present din of the dwarf forges working day and night, reminded him again of the battle-field as Malbeth lost himself once more to memories that weren't his to recall.

A smoking sword of ruin thrust in a black anvil.

Daemons, their maws hungering, crouched before a dreaded altar.

The world ended in bloodshed and darkness.

Malbeth shook his head to banish the fever-dream images, snapping at the edge of his sight like lashing vipers. It was not his memory. It was the Blighted Isle and the final resting place of the Sword of Khaine, that most cursed of all artefacts, driven into the black anvil by Aenarion the

Defender, the first Phoenix King, and arguably the greatest and most tragic of them all. By first drawing the sword, he had embraced Khaine utterly. In becoming a near god, he had saved the high elf race, and yet, at the same time, his actions had doomed them.

Malbeth got to his feet, revelling in the coolness of his naked form as his evaporating sweat chilled him, and padded over to a shrine devoted to the goddess Lileath. It was a simple thing, a statue upon a raised dais, set aside innocuously in one of the tent's antechambers. His heart was thudding loudly as he regarded her silver effigy, arms wide with her palms upward in acceptance. Malbeth lifted Lileath carefully from her silver, gem-stoned dais and placed her reverently by its side. With two hands, he then lifted off the disc of the dais itself, revealing a small compartment within that housed a wooden chest. Taking out the chest, he set it down on the ground and then sat crossed-legged with it in front of him. It was locked, but Malbeth had the key around his neck – a small golden rune, *elthrai*, attached to a gilt chain. It meant 'hope', but like much of elven symbolism it had a counter meaning, one that could also be interpreted as 'doom'.

Unlocking and opening the chest, Malbeth still felt the pull of anger, the arousal of killing, albeit experienced cathartically, from his dream. The verisimilitude of the battlefield was still strong. There were sixteen vials within, no larger than a finger joint, each containing a pale green milky liquid. With a trembling hand, Malbeth took one of them, ripping off the cork stopper and drinking it swiftly. Rivulets of the thick fluid ran down the curves in his mouth, and Malbeth wiped them away with the back of his hand. Slowing his breath, the thrashing in his heart, the violent desire, subsided and Malbeth began to feel better.

Something had broken in him the day that Elethya died. He'd found solace in rage and death, embracing the will of Khaine. All of the asur held the capacity for those traits embodied by the Bloody Handed God. Murder, hatred, war and destruction: they were part of the elven psyche, as insoluble as stubbornness and gold-hunger was to dwarfs. But it was tempered by peace and love and order – the elven philosophy that one element cannot exist without its counterpart. Malbeth did not possess the same balance that most other elves of Ulthuan did. To his mind, he was cursed, the bloodletting and reaving of his youth, barely justifiable, and an eternal stain upon his soul.

Malbeth returned the chest to its hiding place and remade the shrine. Sinking to his knees, he prayed fervently to Lileath for forgiveness. There were tears in his eyes when he'd finished. He stood wearily, reaching for a robe and soft boots, before drifting out of his tent without a sound.

Outside, Korhvale was the only one left awake. He was scribing something furtively by the dimmed glow of the eldritch lanterns and didn't notice Malbeth as he slipped by him silently.

I'll find no further sleep this night, thought Malbeth, heading out of the Hall of Belgrad and into the hold.

THE SWEEPS AND twists of the elven script were applied with the utmost care and attention. Korhvale took great pains to be exacting and neat in every detail. The wet ink glistened in the low lamp light, the pigments reacting with the oily luminescence that filled the former Hall of Belgrad. The shining runes reminded him of the light in her eyes and that then led to a remembrance of the shape of her lips, the glittering cascade of her golden hair.

He had loved Arthelas for as long as he had known her. A chance encounter with the Prince Ithalred, whilst he was out hunting sparhawks in the Annuli Mountains of northern Chrace, had led Korhvale to his service as a guide and, eventually, bodyguard. It was then that he had met Arthelas, and then that his heart had been lost.

Korhvale did not have the ready wit or charm of Lethralmir, nor the erudite intelligence of Malbeth; he was an intense and brooding soul, but beneath all that there was an artist that desired to be set free. As he sat upon a short, white, wooden stool, he scratched with a sparhawk quill upon a leaf of parchment, just one of many he had already filled as his ode to Arthelas grew. It was a work in progress, having undergone many revisions. He dared not speak his feelings out loud; to do so would reveal the inadequacy of his tongue, the shortfall in his eloquence and charm. Only in these words did Korhvale feel that the depth of his emotion could be expressed. Once finished, he then only needed the courage to show them to her...

The faintest scrape of leather against stone commanded the White Lion's attention and he stopped writing at once, immediately thrusting the leaves of parchment into a nearby knapsack. He stood, surveying the dark for any presence.

A dwarf, their captain of the hearth guard if Korhvale's memory served, appeared in the Hall of Belgrad, holding a lantern.

'Keeping the late watch, eh?' said Morek, moving into the light.

Korhvale noticed the axe, cinctured at his hip, immediately.

'I don't sleep,' he responded in Khazalid, forming the words crudely.

'Must be tiring,' Morek replied, idly casting his gaze about the chamber. The dwarf's expression hardened as his took in all the tents, the elven furnishing and subsequent obliteration of anything resembling dwarf culture.

'I need only to meditate,' said Korhvale.

Morek grumbled beneath his breath, before saying, 'All is well then.'

'All is well.'

'All is well,' the dwarf repeated, but it was as if he'd said the words to himself and with an air of speculation.

Silence fell, elf and dwarf staring at each other uncomfortably.

After a moment, Morek about-faced and tromped from the hall, lantern swinging lightly as he went.

AFTER WALKING THROUGH tunnels, passing galleries, kitchens and stores, Malbeth's wanderings had brought him to a massive, vaulted chamber. The room glowed with starlight, reflected from the upper world. The disparate shafts were diverted through a series of mirrored chambers and funnels until they converged on this place, bathing it in silver. The effect was wondrous, diamonds set around the room's six walls glittering like the celestial bodies whose light they refracted; lines of beaten gold shimmered like liquid and runes carved into the walls glowed with power.

Most impressive of all, though, was the monolithic statue that dominated the centre of the hexagonal chamber. It was a female dwarf, rendered in stone. She was dressed in simple robes; her hands rested across her body serenely, her countenance benevolent and wise, yet also possessing a sense of ageless fortitude.

From his studies, Malbeth knew this to be Valaya, one of the dwarf ancestor gods, in her aspect as teacher and mother. The gravitas invested in this temple, in the statue itself was humbling. There was peace here, Malbeth felt it at once, and whispered a blessing to the effigy of his benefactor.

'You elgi are light sleepers,' complained a voice from behind him, arresting his thoughts.

Malbeth turned to see Morek, one of King Bagrik's captains, regarding him sternly.

'Or do you merely "meditate", as well?' said the dwarf, approaching the statue himself.

Malbeth looked nonplussed, and decided to ignore the remark. 'Elgi,' he said instead, 'I've heard that word several times. What does it mean?' he asked in good Khazalid.

If Morek appreciated the gesture he did not show it.

'It has two meanings; "elf" is one of them,' he replied.

Malbeth followed the dwarf's gaze to the statue.

'Valaya,' he said, changing the subject but confirming Malbeth's initial belief. 'She is the wife of Grungni, goddess of Hearth and Hold, one of our greatest ancestors.' The mood softened a little, as if the power of the goddess was affecting the pugnacious dwarf even through his mere presence in her temple.

'Grungni taught the dawi how to fashion metal into weapons, how to fight when the lands were shrouded in darkness, before the coming of *elves*.' Morek almost spat the last word, Valaya's influence upon him clearly fleeting. 'It is a sacred place,' he added, the implication in his words strong so as to leave no doubt at Malbeth's trespass.

'I meant no offence,' offered Malbeth.

Morek grumbled again, and turned away.

'Elgi; you said it had two meanings,' said the ambassador, 'elf and what else?'

Morek looked back briefly, a scowl on his face.

'Weak.'

The dwarf walked off, expecting Malbeth to follow.

THE ELF WAS not the only one abroad in secret that night, others more familiar with the myriad passageways and ancient, dust-drenched halls of Karak Ungor were also moving clandestinely amongst the shadows.

'I beg you, Queen Brunvilda, reconsider,' Grikk pleaded, a fettered lantern held in front of him in one hand, his ironbreaker's axe in the other.

'If the king finds out about this, I shall tell him I made my own way here,' replied Brunvilda, her gaze upon the armoured dwarf's back as he led them through the catacombs of the hold.

'Aye, my queen, and he'll then shear my beard for letting you walk the Grey Road alone.'

There was no pleasing some dwarfs, thought Brunvilda, and carried on her way.

These vaults, as they were known, were seldom trodden paths. It was as if eons of dust collected on every surface in an all-pervading patina, hence the name given to it by the ironbreakers, 'The Grey Road'. Every alcove, every statue fallen into ruin, every shattered tomb and reliquary was overlaid by a shroud of grey.

Known also as Delving Hold, Karak Ungor was the deepest of all the realms of the Karaz Ankor. Here, in the lowest habitable level it was as if time itself was held fast, like a body in tar. This far down, only ghosts and their whispers frequented the lonely corridors.

Though they were far below the clan halls and the royal quarters of the king, Brunvilda winced with every other thudding report of Grikk's armoured boots. The sound echoed rudely, as if the silence took umbrage at the disturbance. The darkness, too, seemed to shrink reluctantly from the lantern light, as if affronted by its presence. There was sentience in these walls. Dwarfs had lived here once, thousands of years ago. They had mined the rock, and built their lofty chambers until the ore had run dry, and they'd moved on. Only memory lingered. It was an ill-feeling; Bagrik knew it too. It was part of the reason the king had imprisoned *him* here, but it was also something that Brunvilda was prepared to endure.

A sudden draft wafted down the long, pitch-black tunnel. It smelled musty and bitter, the stench of it prickling Brunvilda's nose.

'Stay close to me, my queen,' said Grikk, his voice low as he turned his head slowly, surveying the route ahead. 'One of the fallen gates into the ungdrin ankor is nearby,' he told her in a whisper.

The underway, the subterranean road that linked all of the dwarf holds of the Worlds Edge Mountains, was divided by a series of gates, portals that were guarded and patrolled by the ironbreakers. Though generally considered safe, some of the gates had fallen, the dark creatures that lived beneath the mountain and who vied with the dwarfs for dominance of the underearth having destroyed them. Such gates were sometimes left alone, rather than retaken, clan miners despatched to close them off with controlled cave-ins. Not all of the gates stayed closed, and Grikk was ever mindful of the ones that weren't.

Brunvilda quickened her pace, looking left and right as dilapidated columns were revealed by the wan lantern light, along with the skeletal remains of disused torch sconces. She was so close to Grikk, and so preoccupied with her surroundings that when the ironbreaker finally stopped she barrelled right into him.

Grikk apologised profusely, his eyes wide with shame and embarrassment behind the full face plate of his gromril armour. Brunvilda waved it away with good humour, confessing it was her fault, brushing down her robes and doing her best to placate the mortified dwarf captain.

'We are here, my queen,' Grikk said at last, once he'd finished saying he was sorry.

Brunvilda looked past him to a short length of corridor, at the end of which was the faintest glow of another lantern.

'Thank you, Grikk. I can go the rest of the way by myself,' she said.

'But my queen–' he started to protest.

'Captain – that was not a request. I'll be just fine on my own from here. You need to get back to your duties. If the king finds you absent, he'll know that something is wrong. I have risked his anger once today, already; I will not do so a second time.' Brunvilda placed her hand against his pauldron. 'Your concern is touching – really,' she told him, genuinely, 'but leave me now, Grikk.'

The captain of the ironbreakers obeyed reluctantly, turning back the way they'd come. Brunvilda watched him all the way, until he'd disappeared around a corner. Satisfied he'd done as asked, she checked the satchel she had slung over her shoulder then took a deep breath and headed in a hurry towards the distant lantern and her destination.

Another ironbreaker greeted Brunvilda as she reached the lambent glow cast by his lantern. He was stood stock still in front of an oaken, ironbound door, the hinges embossed with the snarling visage of Grimnir. The dwarf looked shocked when he saw the queen approach from the gloom.

'Queen Brunvilda!' he said quickly, almost dropping the lantern. 'You're not supposed to be here.'

'I know that, ironbreaker,' she answered. 'Now let me pass.'

'I… can't, my queen. The king has forbidden it,' the dwarf answered, clearly flustered.

'Bagrik is not here, but I am, and as your queen I demand that you let me pass,' she pressed. Eyeing him sternly, she detected a chink in his resolve and took a step towards him.

'I cannot, milady. My duty is to guard the gate. None may enter without the king's sanction, I have sworn it.' Despite his protests, the ironbreaker took a half step back as Brunvilda advanced.

'Even still, let me through,' Brunvilda reasserted calmly. 'I have food here going to waste.'

The ironbreaker paused, the dilemma he faced rendering him momentarily mute.

'Let me through, and the king will not hear of it. You have my word,' she said, taking another step forward. 'I am queen of Karak Ungor,' she told him when the ironbreaker maintained his silence, 'and I will not be denied in my own hold.'

The ironbreaker faltered as he fought between the orders of his king and the wishes of his queen.

'It has already been fed,' he said in the end.

It was a poor choice of words that the ironbreaker regretted instantly.

'That is my son you speak of,' Brunvilda snapped.

'Of course, my queen, I didn't mean… it's just. I cannot let you pass,' he urged, his tone pleading. Yet still he did not yield.

'Do you think me weak, ironbreaker?' Brunvilda said after a moment.

'My queen, I only–'

'I ask again,' she said, cutting him off, 'do you think me a weak queen?'

'No,' the ironbreaker said humbly, 'of course not.'

'Then you'll know I will not leave here until I've seen my son.'

Queen Brunvilda came right up to the armoured warrior, her chin almost touching his breastplate. Though he stood a good half-foot taller and was bristling with weapons, the ironbreaker seemed instantly diminished by her formidable presence.

'Let me pass. Now,' she said firmly.

The ironbreaker could only hold her gaze for a moment, then he nodded swiftly and turned towards the portal behind him. With a stout bronze key, held around his neck on a thick chain, he unlocked the door with a loud, metallic clunk and opened it.

At once, the reek of sweat and old meat assailed Brunvilda. It warred with the stagnant aroma of standing water and badly brewed ale. With a last scathing glance at the ironbreaker, she went inside, the door closing firmly behind her.

A small, roughly-hewn chamber lay beyond, guttering torches set at intervals upon the walls offering little light to alleviate the gloom. No statues here, no remnants of former days or remembrances of heroes. It was dank and barren. A hole in the middle of the room, like a crude well, was the only feature. Its purpose was obvious, despite what Bagrik and his ironbreakers might have said – it was a gaol.

Brunvilda steadied herself, trying to master her emotions and the stench wafting from the hole, as she stepped towards it. She got down to her knees in order to peer into the deeper gloom of the well. A faint shaft of light, issuing from some point high above, and reflected into the hole, illuminated a cell. A darkened figure, wearing scuffed dwarf boots and clad in ragged clothes shuffled out of the patch of light and lingered at the shadow's edge.

'Lothvar,' Brunvilda coaxed gently. 'Lothvar, I've brought you food.'

The shadow moved slightly, as if it recognised her voice and after a moment, came forward. It was a dwarf, or at least, some twisted parody of one. Patches of beard clung to his face in sporadic clumps and his eyes were albino pink. A deformed mouth made a jagged line across his features. A flattened nose, one of the nostrils wide and grotesque, sniffed at the air then detected the food in the satchel. As Lothvar shuffled towards the light, enticed by the aroma, Brunvilda saw the withered and twisted hand he held close to his body. His skin was pale, like alabaster, and though the light was weak, it clearly caused him discomfort to endure it.

'Mother...'

The sound of Lothvar's voice nearly broke her heart, and Brunvilda had to turn away.

The queen found her resolve quickly, crushing the sudden rush of guilt she felt at Lothvar's mistreatment, even his existence. She longed to free him of this place, but she had sworn to her king that she would not, and that word was a bond forged in iron.

There was a basket sitting next to the cell entrance. Brunvilda took it and attached it to a pulley system suspended above the well, putting the satchel in the basket before she lowered it. There were leftovers from the feast inside, just scraps, but Lothvar devoured them hungrily, and Brunvilda felt a fresh pang of anguish as she watched him.

'My father, is he with you?' asked Lothvar, his voice hopeful. The creature's intonation, for no other appellation was more suitable for it, was crude and ponderous. He formed his words slowly, as if struggling to grasp them, the droning quality hinting strongly at the malady that debilitated his mind as well as his body.

Lothvar was Brunvilda's first son and his arrival as Bagrik's heir and the future king of Karak Ungor was meant to be a joyous occasion. But Lothvar had developed poorly, his disfigurements obvious at birth and only worsening as he grew older. In spite of it, though, Brunvilda loved him and had pleaded with Bagrik not to cast him out, not to condemn him to death left alone in the mountains. Only a handful of dwarfs knew of Lothvar's existence – the king's captains, Morek and Grikk, and a select group of ironbreakers who would guard Lothvar's cell from interference. The rest of the hold, those that remembered, thought Lothvar dead, lost in childbirth. Great shame would be heaped upon Bagrik should the truth of his first son's survival be discovered. Mercy had stayed the king's hand that day, but the resentment of that decision festered still.

'No, my son, your father meets with the elgi. But he told me to say he loves you,' Brunvilda lied.

'The elgi are here?' Lothvar asked, working his mouth but making no sound as he fought to understand. 'I shall fight them alongside my father,' he said eventually, standing and thumping his chest.

Brunvilda smiled through her tears, glad of the darkness around her.

'No, Lothvar,' she said, 'the elgi are our friends. We will learn much from each other.'

Lothvar gazed up at her blankly.

'I will make him proud,' he said.

'Yes,' Brunvilda whispered, her voice cracking, 'he would be *so* proud.' Her face fell and for a moment she couldn't look at him for fear that her resolve would fail her completely.

'Mother?' Lothvar asked. 'Mother, are you crying?'

'No, Lothvar,' she managed after a long pause. 'I'm fine.' She turned and looked over her shoulder, calling out, 'Ironbreaker.'

'Ironbreaker!' she repeated more urgently, when a response wasn't forthcoming.

There was the clunk of the lock being set loose and then the door opened on creaking hinges to reveal the guard.

'Is everything all right, my queen?' he asked, brandishing his axe and surging into the room as if he expected Brunvilda to be in mortal danger.

'Put that weapon away!' she snarled.

The ironbreaker cinctured the axe quickly as if stung.

'I wish to go down and see my son,' she told him.

The ironbreaker's posture changed, becoming straight and intractable but it was the voice of another that spoke from beyond the doorway.

'I can't allow that.'

'I am your queen!' she insisted, tears in her eyes. 'Who is that? I demand to know who dares disobey me!'

'I think I had best get you back to your quarters, milady.' Morek stepped into the torch light. 'Wait for us outside,' the hearth guard captain said in an undertone to the ironbreaker.

Once they were alone, Morek walked to Brunvilda, risking a furtive glance into the gaol pit before quickly averting his gaze.

'Is he so repellent, Morek?' she said quietly, so that Lothvar could not hear her.

'He is your son, that is all,' the hearth guard captain replied plainly.

'I thought diplomacy was Kandor's arena,' Brunvilda said with a sad smile.

Morek crouched down on one knee and offered her his hand. 'Come now, my queen,' he said softly, 'you have lingered here long enough.'

Brunvilda's defiance evaporated. Taking Morek's hand gratefully, the hearth guard captain helped her to her feet.

'Are you leaving, mother?' asked Lothvar, disappointment in his voice, the sense of abandonment evident in his wretched and pitiable expression.

'I'll return soon, my love,' Brunvilda replied, 'I won't stay away so long, next time,' she said, forcing herself to turn away. Morek ushered her gently out of the room, the ironbreaker who awaited them outside closing the door and locking it behind them.

Brunvilda held her head high as she entered the darkness of the corridor again, the steel in her remade as she strode off towards the royal quarters, Morek in tow. Only when the captain had gone, when she was alone and divested of her royal trappings, when she became just a mother and a wife, and not a queen, only in the dark would she weep. For the dark hid many secrets.

CHAPTER EIGHT

Inexorable Destiny

A JAGGED SPUR of rock crumbled and fell away under Ulfjarl's grasp, and the Norscan was left hanging, one-handed, from the cliff face.

Below, a white-shrouded doom beckoned, the many hundreds of feet engulfed by the mist that had wreathed his ascent, swirling like marsh phantoms in an icy fog. More than once during his climb, Ulfjarl had seen faces in that mist; snarling, monstrous visages that bayed for his blood, and craved the heat of his soul-fire. The Norscan warlord had laughed out loud at every one and drove on through swathes of sleet, icy rain and buffeting winds that howled at his impudence.

With a bellow that matched the thunder ripping through the heavens, Ulfjarl swung his massive frame across the face of the storm-wracked bluffs and found another hand hold. From there he drove on, fork lightning filling every crevice, every cleft and gorge, with shadow as it set the sky alight. Ulfjarl was inured to the elements; they were merely obstacles to his inexorable destiny.

Finally, after three hours of climbing the savage face of the mountain, he reached over and found a stony plateau. Ulfjarl heaved his hulking body over the lip and drew himself to his full height. Veorik was waiting for him several feet from the edge. The mysterious shaman was sitting cross-legged, the cowl of his ragged flesh cloak pulled over his head. Thin slivers of jade, the faint glow of his eyes, were barely visible from beneath his hood. The Norscan couldn't fathom how Veorik had reached the summit – the shaman certainly hadn't climbed as he had, nor could he. The shaman's body was thin and wasted compared to the gargantuan

Ulfjarl. Yet it possessed a wiry sort of brawn with coarse and scaly skin. His veins stood out like cords of rope, the sinews taut and unyielding.

Veorik had appeared mysteriously in Ulfjarl's village the day that fire had rained from the sky. Returning from a raid against the Bjornlings, the Norscan warlord had witnessed the arcing trail of flame cutting across the darkening sky like a portent. He'd killed the three others in the hunting party, a primal instinct driving his hand, and arrived at his village alone. Devastation greeted him. Ulfjarl's village was no more. Crude wooden huts burned like lonely signal fires, the stink of charred flesh redolent on the oily smoke. Blackened bodies lay twisted and broken in a morass of carnage; leather, metal and hair fused to skin. Ulfjarl stepped impassively across the scorched earth, incapable of remorse as he sought to comprehend what could have wrought such utter destruction. His furred boots disturbed wisps of smoke as they scraped at the dust and ash. The Norscan had soon found a long furrow that he followed to an immense smoking crater, a large meteorite burning within its blistered confines. This was the harbinger that had doomed his village. The heat of it had seared him, but he was drawn to the meteorite, to the night-black ore that shimmered like oily veins in the rock. It was then, his skin reddening, and lathered with sweat, that Ulfjarl had seen Veorik.

The shaman was like an ice wraith, detaching himself from the shadows surrounding the otherworldly meteorite as if he had once been a part of it. At first Ulfjarl had thought him a foe, gripping his stone axe and readying to kill the wizened spectre before he entranced him. But then Veorik had spoken. Though he did not know the shaman's tongue, the language sibilant and snake-like, a malicious susurration of old, dead sounds, Ulfjarl had understood its meaning and knew it was his destiny to follow this stranger. Ulfjarl had looked deep into his emerald eyes and felt impelled to thrust his palm against the rock. Pain, agony that tore into every fibre, coursed through the Norscan but when he finally withdrew his hand, a mark had been seared into his flesh. It was the symbol of his destiny – a three-headed serpent.

As the memories faded, Veorik beckoned Ulfjarl with a crooked talon. The Norscan warlord stepped purposely across the stone plateau until he reached the shaman and crouched down by his side. Veorik clutched three vipers that hissed and snapped in his skeletal fist. The shaman ignored their protests, intent on his ritual. Taking a curved dagger from within the folds of his robes, he sliced off the vipers' heads with a single, savage cut, spilling their blood onto the frost-bitten ground. Crimson smoke issued from the vital fluids and, casting the decapitated bodies aside, Veorik thrust his face over the visceral fumes and inhaled deeply. He then scraped his talon through the congealing blood, stone screeching under his scratched attentions, his finger moving as if of its own volition. When he was finished, Veorik looked up and exhaled, a jagged smile splitting his serpentine mouth. Ulfjarl was sure he'd seen a forked tongue, too, slipping out from between the shaman's thin lips and lathing the air. Whatever Ulfjarl had seen, it was clear from the shaman's expression that the auguries were good.

Veorik beckoned again, and this time Ulfjarl helped the shaman to his feet. His grip was as strong as stone, the wretch's apparent frailty belying his true strength. Veorik extended a bone-thin arm to the distant horizon. Ulfjarl followed his gaze and saw a glittering silver spire, fashioned like the watchtowers of the immortals that he had sacked when they'd made landfall, only this was larger, more grandiose. There was power in the bastion of the fey creatures, Ulfjarl could taste it, and the Norscan warlord meant to make it his own.

Impassive, Ulfjarl turned away and walked back to the edge of the plateau. Miraculously, though the Norscan warlord had not even heard him move, Veorik was already at Ulfjarl's side as he peered into the void, the mists receding as if on command. There below, he saw his army.

The Serpent Host had swelled since they'd reached the shore. Lines of warriors bearing the three-headed snake motif still tramped through the passes of the snow-kissed mountains, joining the hordes already taking up assembly at the foot of the cliff. Ragged fires burned like red wounds in the snow-shrouded plain directly below where the army gathered. Great beasts, their shaggy hides matted with frost, bayed and trumpeted as cruel wardens goaded them; whelp masters wrestled with savage hounds that frothed and strained at the leash. Brutish huscarls, bondsmen and the subjugated barbarian tribes held their banners aloft, and brandished spears and axes in honour of their lord.

It was a host of thousands, of hundreds of thousands. The watchtowers upon the shore, where they'd ran their ships aground with wild abandon as a bloodletting frenzy took them, were swept away like chaff. Ulfjarl had beheaded every enemy, had ordered every structure burned as a warning. Fear would range ahead of his host, weakening, sapping, draining. The barbarian tribes of this land had been quick to recognise his strength, quick to appreciate that fear. Every village passed had swelled the ravening horde further. The time for army building was at an end.

Ulfjarl raised his arms aloft and bellowed his name. A guttural chorus, thousands strong, answered, reverberating through the mountain. It was so terrible that the wind cowered, and the lightning fled, and the thunder balked.

War had come and it would engulf the elves completely.

THE ELGI ARE tenacious, I'll give them that, thought Morek, begrudgingly.

It was the fifth day of the trade talks, and the fifth day that the hearth guard captain had waited silently outside the huge gilded doors to the Elders Chamber as Bagrik made his deliberations with the elves.

The Elders Chamber was where all the kings of Karak Ungor, Bagrik included, held council. It was a place of deliberation and of majesty, the atmosphere within heavy with the weight of history and the expectation of legacy. Compared to many of the other halls and rooms of the holds, it was stark with simple square columns, rune-etched without gold or silver or gemstones. Austerity reminded all those within of their duty, and the severity which the dwarfs attributed to the weighty decisions of the king and his council. Morek had seen it many times, but only when considering matters of war or defence. There was an esteemed assembly of dwarfs in attendance today. Morek had watched them pile into the room one after the other, their demeanours a mix of gruff indifference and flint-eyed suspicion.

This was as fine and noble a group that had ever been gathered, with vaunted guildmasters like Chief Brewmaster Heganbour, his many belts and plaited locks festooned with firkins, steins and tankards; Agrin Oakenheart, runelord of Karak Ungor, his bare arms like tanned leather, tattooed with bands of runescript and sigils of power; and Kozdokk, lodemaster and head of the Miners' Guild, ever-present soot-rings beneath his eyes, an array of candles and lanterns affixed to his black pot helmet. In addition to the masters were the venerable longbeards of Bagrik's Council of Elders, whose wisdom was more valuable than gold.

The king had also included his son, Nagrim, in the proceedings. Morek thought this a prudent gesture, for it would be Nagrim that would govern the hold when his father had passed into the Halls of the Ancestors. Rugnir, the hearth guard captain noted, had not been invited, which was just as well. Like Bagrik, he too frowned upon the young prince's association with that wanaz. Kandor, of course, was the first to the table after his king, dressed in his finest tunic, beard preened like the prancing ufdi he was. Alongside him was his mentor, Thegg the Miser, who was as shrewd and cantankerous as any dwarf.

The elves came last of all, late as ever. Morek had scowled behind his beard as the elven prince had stalked into the Elders Chamber, ignorant of the import of that great room and all that had transpired there. The elf's ambassador and the other, raven-haired, lackey were in tow. They were followed by a gaggle of enrobed flunkies – treasurers, smiths and merchants by the look of them.

Servant hosts, dismissed before the council held session, brought silks and spices, silver metals forged into arrowheads and blunted blades, fettered falcons and hawks, and even songbirds – just some of the enticements through which the elves hoped to beguile and impress. What dwarfs needed with such items, Morek was at a loss to explain. Perhaps there were a more sizeable proportion of ufdis in Karak Ungor than he had first suspected. Such things, however, were not the captain's concern. Morek merely performed his duty as the king expected of him. Once the great and the good had been convened, the hearth guard captain sealed the golden doors, and was to allow none to enter until a bargain had been struck.

It rankled that he had been demoted to gate guardian and that Kandor, the feathered peahen, was admitted to the talks. Though begrudgingly, Morek did concede that the merchant thane knew his way around business negotiations. For all of his camaraderie and good nature with the elves, Kandor had deliberately drawn the trade talks out. It was a well-used dwarf tactic, designed to wear down the opposite party in order to get the best deal for the king and his hold. The elves, to their credit, had showed some resilience and had yet to capitulate – if the fact that talks were still ongoing was any barometer.

It was then, as Morek was yet again debating the merits of a union with the elves, albeit only for trade, that Haggar appeared at the end of the wide corridor that led to the Elders Chamber. The young thane was full of purpose as he marched towards the hearth guard captain, his helmet clasped under his arm, the runic hand gifted to him by Agrin Oakenheart gripping the pommel of his belt-slung hammer.

'Gnollengrom, Thane Stonehammer,' Haggar intoned, bowing as low as he could before he would lose his balance and fall.

Morek noticed he used the formal greeting, usually expressed only for elders.

'I am not so old that "tromm", will not suffice,' growled the hearth guard captain.

Morek's gaze lingered for a moment on the runic hand, a simulacrum of one of flesh and blood that had been forged for the young thane by old Agrin himself. Haggar came from the long and noble line of clan Skengdrang, his current appellation referring to the artefact he wore in place of a hand. It was due to his vaunted standing that Haggar had been gifted with it. Though, lamentably, there was a stain upon that once proud lineage. Morek saw it occasionally when the young dwarf thought he was not looking, a fleeting shadow behind his eyes, a severe cast to his face. It saddened the hearth guard captain to see it, and he hoped that one day Haggar would atone for the dishonour of his forebear.

'And call me "Morek", young Haggar,' he said, wrenching himself from remembrance. 'It is my name, after all, and it will do just fine.'

The other thane reddened against the older dwarf's mild admonishment and an embarrassed silence followed.

'I thought you were a statue, at first,' offered Haggar, by way of conversation. 'Three days I have passed the end of this corridor, and for three days I saw you move not an inch,' he added, clearly in awe of the captain.

'It was five days,' Morek corrected him, 'five days and counting,' he said.

Morek sniffed his nonchalance then cleared his throat, as he warmed to a theme.

'And a dwarf must know when to be still, lad,' he told him. 'Once, when I was hunting in the southern forests, three leagues north of Black Water, back when Brondrik was a beardling, I stumbled across a herd of wild hruk. The beasts were in season, rampant and amorous as only hruk can be.' Morek's eyes grew wide. 'They had my scent, and I knew I was in great peril. I could not slay the beasts; the goatherders would have sent the reckoners for me had I done that. Nor could I escape them. So, for seven days and seven nights, I stood stock still in that field, until the hruk moved on and I could return to the hold. I learnt the value of stillness that day,' Morek concluded.

Haggar nodded his appreciation at the imparted wisdom.

'Now, you tell me something,' Morek said.

'Anything, Thane Stonehammer,' said Haggar, his face screwed up in concentration as he devoted all of his attention to the hearth guard captain's query.

Morek sighed before asking, 'What are you doing here?'

'Ah, that is easy,' he said, his face brightening as soon as he realised he knew the answer. 'King Bagrik summoned me to wait for him here before the trade talks had ended. I am to accompany Kandor to the elgi settlement, take possession of any promised goods and return them to the hold.'

Morek couldn't hide the fact that this perturbed him. Why had the king entrusted such a deed to Haggar, and not him? Was he not chief of the king's warriors, aside perhaps from Grikk with whom he had equal standing – but his domain was the ungrin ankor. What if Bagrik had somehow gotten wind of his meeting with Brunvilda in the catacombs? The king would be greatly displeased that Morek had kept it from him. Still, Bagrik was not one to let his annoyances go unspoken...

'It's a pity you left the grand feast so early,' Haggar said, arresting Morek from his thoughts as he noticed the dwarf captain's furrowed brow and attempted to change the subject. 'You missed some fine entertainments. Grikk put on a great display and the elgi maiden, she was...' Haggar was lost for a moment in wistful remembrance.

'Grikk was there, eh?' Morek asked with mild interest, ignoring the elf comment.

'His axe hurling was worthy of the sagas of old,' Haggar adulated.

'I see,' Morek mumbled under his breath, adding, 'Well he'll never beat my hammer throw, no dwarf will...'

Before Haggar could ask him to repeat himself, the dwarfs were interrupted by a clamour of armour emanating from the end of the corridor.

Six fully-armoured hearth guard emerged into the dwarfs' eye line, trooping towards them. A seventh figure, an elf, and not one of Ithalred's party, walked amongst them.

'Hearth guard, explain yourself!' bawled Morek to the first of the warriors that approached him, a veteran of the gate guard.

'Captain,' said the lead dwarf, thumping his chest in salute, 'this one claims he must speak to the elgi prince at once. I thought it best to bring him from the outer gateway hall directly.' At the hearth guard's remark, the elf, who wore silver mail and a cloak of fern and olive, came forward. Throwing back his hood, the elf's eyes sparkled with vehemence.

'My name is Ethandril, I am a ranger of Tor Eorfith and I must see Prince Ithalred on a matter of dire importance.'

Morek raised an eyebrow, noting that the elf was still armed. He cast a reproachful glance at the veteran hearth guard, who showed his palms in a gesture of contrition.

'There was no time to summon you,' pleaded the veteran.

Morek ignored him – he'd deal with him later – and focused his attention instead on the elf.

'Relinquish your arms, first – then you may see the prince,' he told him.

The elf seemed reluctant but he was obviously exhausted and in no mood to haggle, so handed over his bow, a quiver only half full of arrows and a long curved dagger.

'Please,' he implored, once it was done. 'Let me see the prince.'

Morek made a show of inspecting the elf for weapons one last time, a side glance at the lax veteran, who avoided his captain's gaze, before Morek muttered under his breath and turned to face the golden doors.

Haggar stood to one side. This was the hearth guard captain's 'honour' alone.

'He's not going to like this,' Morek muttered, before taking a deep breath and pushing against the doors.

The gilded doors to the Elders' Chamber clanged and boomed as Morek heaved them open. All eyes turned to the hearth guard captain who beheld the king's chisellers going to work on a granite plaque. This, he knew, was the deed of agreement. An accord must have been reached with the elves and now those terms were being ratified and sealed in stone.

Kandor and Thegg the Miser were stooped over the chiseller's work, inspecting every blow, every cut, intent on the deed. The masters were in various states of attentiveness. Kozdokk held up a cage, a song bird twittering within. Whatever he had just said to the elf avian keeper had set an ashen cast to his already pale face. The venerable miner eyed the bird with interest, as he held it up to the light. Morek would learn later that the head of the Miners' Guild had proposed to use the birds to warn lodefinders of gaseous effusions in the mines. Given the mortality rate of this occupation, Kozdokk had suggested to King Bagrik that several hundred birds be traded. Evidently, this had offended the more artful and less pragmatic sentiments of the elf.

Several of the longbeards, slumped in plush chairs, had fallen asleep. One of the venerable elders appeared almost comatose and for the briefest moment, Morek feared he was dead. A nervous eyebrow twitch gave him away, though. Agrin Oakenheart was amongst the somnambulant dwarfs, snoring loudly in one corner. The pipe cinched in the runelord's mouth blew perfect smoke rings as he exhaled. Nagrim seemed interminably bored, chewing his beard, and picking at his teeth with a chisel. The elves looked worn from the deliberations, adding further credence to Kandor's strategy of negotiation by attrition. Malbeth, the elf ambassador, had his sleeves rolled up and a ragged look about him.

All were crowded around a large, slab-like table, its stone surface inscribed with effigies of Grungni and Valaya extolling the virtues of wisdom and temperance. Upon the table sat a huge pair of bronze scales, their use and meaning esoteric to the elves. This archaic device had existed since the early days of Karak Ungor. It was fashioned into the squatting figure of a dwarf goldmaster, his palms open and flat, his arms outstretched. Only the accepted members of the elder council were privy to its significance.

All of this Morek took in after he opened the gilded doors and surveyed the scene. His gaze, unsurprisingly, settled upon Bagrik last of all.

'What is the meaning of this?' bellowed the king from atop his throne on a stone plinth overlooking the Elders Chamber. He leaned forward as he barked at Morek, spittle flying from his lips. It was not wise to interrupt the king during his deliberations but the hearth guard captain had a sneaking suspicion that the elf ranger of Tor Eorfith brought bad news, and that meant the elves' departure from Karak Ungor. For Morek that couldn't happen soon enough. In his opinion, it was worth risking Bagrik's ire.

'Forgive the intrusion, my king,' Morek declared, bowing curtly with all due deference. 'It could not wait.'

Bagrik's stern expression suggested he doubted it.

'An elf, travelled from Tor Eorfith, seeks audience with Prince Ithalred.' Morek couldn't keep the scowl from his face when he mentioned the elf noble by name. He stepped aside, allowing the ranger to enter. The elf bowed stiffly.

'Bring ale,' Bagrik ordered. 'Our visitor has had an arduous journey by the look of him, and is in need of fortification.' One of the hearth guard, who was hovering outside the chamber next to Haggar, hurried off to find a servant.

'You are welcome here, elgi,' Bagrik told the ranger.

Morek chafed at his king's magnanimity, but his mood soured further at what the king said next.

'You, Morek, are not. Grumkaz, mark the hearth guard captain's name and enter a grudge in the kron.'

The king's grudgemaster, his ever present shadow, stirred from the corner of the chamber, so still and grey it was as if he were part of the rock, made animate by Bagrik's bidding. The scratching of his quill against the parchment ran down Morek's spine, making him wince.

'Ethandril.' It was Lethralmir who spoke next. The raven-haired elf came forward, heedless of any royal etiquette he might be besmirching, and beckoned the ranger to approach.

Ethandril did so, swiftly, speaking in hushed tones in their native language.

Morek's face reddened at what was deliberate subterfuge in his eyes, desperate to speak out against it and demand that the elves be open in the presence of the king. But he had affronted Bagrik once already, and even though the king's expression told him he was not impressed, Morek held his tongue.

Lethralmir then went to Prince Ithalred, relating the news in a similar manner to before. All the while, the dwarfs watched in stony silence, Agrin's snoring the only contribution to the susurrus of conversation between the elves.

Ithalred's face had darkened by the time Lethralmir had finished. He turned abruptly to the king, and said, 'With regret, your majesty, we must leave. At once.'

Bagrik's brow wrinkled.

'All is well, I hope?' he asked, his tone probing.

'Yes,' Ithalred replied. 'An urgent matter has arisen at Tor Eorfith that requires my personal attention. I'm sure you understand.'

'Of course,' said the king, though the look in his eyes said anything but. He glanced over at Kandor who was observing the chiseller, as he finished up.

'The deed is set. All is in order,' the merchant thane told Bagrik, as he looked up.

The king nodded, satisfied with the business done, despite the unconventional close to the deal and the subsequent upheaval.

'I give you leave to go back to your settlement, Prince Ithalred,' said Bagrik, once his attention was back on the elf, though Ithalred gave the impression he neither needed nor appreciated the dwarf king's sanction. 'As per our agreement,' Bagrik continued, 'Kandor Silverbeard and Haggar Anvilfist will accompany you as my representatives.' Haggar had entered the room by this time, and bowed at the mention of his name. 'They will bring the promised goods from my vaults and take charge of those offered by you upon your return.'

'As agreed,' snapped Ithalred, obviously distracted as he turned on his heel and stalked out of the Elders Chamber. Lethralmir followed him, deep in clandestine conversation with Ethandril.

Morek watched them go. He could not understand their words, but he was wily enough to discern the note of tension in them. The expression of the ranger, when he had been brought before the hearth guard captain, spoke volumes too. The elves were hiding something. Morek just didn't know what it was.

As they left, a panting dwarf servant rushed into the chamber, a foaming flagon balanced on a wooden dish.

'Ale, my lords,' he said humbly, casting his gaze about frantically for those in need.

'Give it here, lad,' said Bagrik, who quaffed the beer prodigiously, his steely glare fixed on the departing elves as he wiped his mouth with disdain.

'Haggar,' the king snarled, though his wrath was reserved for his former guests. The banner bearer thumped the cuirass of his armour in salute. 'Have a cohort of hearth guard make ready, you are leaving with the elves. You, too, Kandor, and be quick about it!'

The merchant nodded, gathering his things before muttering his respects to the masters and hurrying out of the chamber after the elves. Haggar turned and was about to troop off with him when Morek caught his arm.

'Eyes open, lad,' he said with a wink. 'Eyes open.'

Haggar nodded solemnly, catching on immediately. Whatever was bothering the elves, much like Morek, he had seen it too.

BAGRIK WATCHED FROM the craggy slit of the Dragon's Tooth, the highest watchtower of Karak Ungor, the rocky spire by which all of the ancient skybridges were connected. His expression was stern as he regarded the trail of dwarf carts and mules, diminishing into the mountain passes. He saw the long lines of the elf expedition that had come to his hold, too, and the cohort of twenty hearth guard warriors led by Haggar and accompanied by Kandor. The dwarfs led the group as they made their wending way northward to Tor Eorfith, their knowledge of the secret routes across the Worlds Edge making for a safer and more expedient journey.

A sharp wind was blowing from the north, unsettling the snow-shawled peaks and sending thick drifts across the trees and lowland roads. It blustered through the viewing port of the watchtower, insinuating its way through Bagrik's furs and tunic, chilling him. He suppressed a shiver and his gaze hardened. There was the scent of metal and smoke on the breeze. It did not bode well.

'There is no better vantage point over the northern reaches of the Worlds Edge than the Tooth, my liege.'

Bagrik did not turn to face the speaker. He merely sighed, his earlier anger long since fled to be replaced by concern and doubt.

'Aye, Morek, and it is also a place where a king might find some solitude.' Bagrik had long since dismissed the quarrellers patrolling the Dragon's Tooth and his personal hearth guard who had carried him up the many steps to the lofty watchtower.

'Forgive me, my king, but Queen Brunvilda was looking for you,' said Morek, moving to stand alongside Bagrik, he too now staring at the view beyond the hold.

'All the more reason for me to be up here,' Bagrik muttered, a note of tension creeping into his voice.

'The wind coming from the north is a harsh one,' the king said after a moment of silence, filled only with the howl of the breeze. 'I feel the coming of winter, Morek,' he confessed, no longer talking about the weather. 'I cannot even reach my towers without aid, and all my great deeds are eclipsed in memory, smothered by the dust of ages, soon to be forgotten.'

Morek maintained his silence for a spell, allowing the maudlin atmosphere to thin a little before he spoke.

'You have left a proud legacy, my king. All of us, our time is finite. Grungni calls us to his table in the Hall of Ancestors. Your place is waiting,' he said.

'Is it, Morek?' Bagrik asked, turning to the hearth guard captain for the first time.

Both dwarfs knew of what Bagrik spoke.

'Nagrim's time is dawning,' Morek replied, returning his king's gaze. '*He* is your legacy, my liege. In him the future of Karak Ungor is set in stone.'

Bagrik smiled, though his eyes were still sad. He felt somehow older in that moment.

'Yes, you are right,' he said, turning back to the view port. 'Nagrim is the future.'

'One thing I am less certain about,' Morek grumbled, as he too returned to looking out of the watchtower, the mule train finally disappearing from view, 'is these elgi. For a race that is longer lived than us dwarfs, they have little concept of patience.'

'Indeed,' Bagrik replied, his eyes narrowing. The old leg wound from the great boar gave a twinge. It was a sure sign of troubling times to come. 'They do not,' he concluded.

ACT TWO
BLOOD IN THE NORTH

CHAPTER NINE

Legacy

THE IRON DEEP was akin to an armoury in that within its heavily-guarded confines there resided all the many martial heirlooms and artefacts of Bagrik's royal lineage. Each of the noble clans of Karak Ungor had such a rune vault, but none were as vast and grandiose as that of the Boarbrow's and the line of kings. The mighty room was staggering in its size and ambition. Cavernous in stature, five thousand dwarfs could have marched in and still had room enough to become lost in its numerous galleries and antechambers.

Stone columns, hewn into the image of kings and chased in bronze, shouldered an arched ceiling studded with diamonds. Mosaics were rendered into the walls, depicting ancient heroes and older deeds. The vault had several levels, and an expansive rectangular chasm fell away in the middle of each one, barring the deepest. These upper floors were spanned by bridges carved from the granite of the mountain. Dominating the lowest level of the Iron Deep was the Zharrazak, the Enduring Flame. Reputedly, or at least as far back as records went, it had burned since Karak Ungor was founded and had not once gone out. It was widely postulated that should the Zharrazak ever fail it would be a grave omen, foretelling the doom of the hold. It was set in a simple copper basin and was so large that, despite its depth, the fierce flame cast long, flickering shadows around the entire vault's many nooks and crannies.

Few had seen the Iron Deep, save for the kings of Ungor and their runelords. Agrin Oakenheart was the current custodian, and in addition to all the clan treasures, he kept three of the Anvils of Doom safe within the vault. These artefacts had been forged five hundred years earlier by the master runesmith, Kurgaz, at the heart of Karag Dron. Only the volcanic fire of a mountain could have tempered such potent magical foci. The runes inscribed upon the metal surface of the anvils had only to be struck by a hammer, and for the runesmith to intone the correct forging rite, for their power to be unleashed. Such devices were venerated, and had to be kept under runic seal, so it was with Agrin's Anvils of Doom.

Save for the runelord himself, only King Bagrik had the authority to order the Iron Deep unsealed. With Nagrim in tow, he had done so with a specific purpose in mind. For over an hour father and son had toured the mighty vault, its many floors plunging down into the mountain's core, the effect upon entering through the iron-banded, ward-inscribed, gromril gate not unlike a roofed amphitheatre. Gemstones punctuated the foot and apex of each level in long lines and through them, via some cunning device of the Engineers' Guild, natural light was reflected and refracted creating an aura of myriad hues. Runes of power were described by the cornucopia of light emitted from the stones, wards of spell-baffling and sorcerous annulment that prevented harmful or insidious magic making a mockery of the otherwise stout safeguards.

As they walked, Bagrik showed Nagrim some of the treasures of the hold's long history, the gilded weapon racks, cradles for armour, iron-banded chests and bejewelled plinths stretching far in the glittering gloom.

'It is past time that we walked the Iron Deep together,' said Bagrik as he and Nagrim traversed a concourse of flagstones. Like much of the ancient chamber, it was rendered into a concentric knot pattern, the uniformity occasionally giving way to the artistic flourish of the original masons.

The king wore a simple blue tunic with silver trim and a short woollen cloak. It had been almost two months since Haggar and Kandor had set off with the elves. Winter still clung on tenaciously, reluctant to release its icy grip. Though the first thaws of the nascent spring were now emerging, evident in the subterranean reservoirs filling from the slowly melting mountain peaks, Bagrik still felt the cold and clasped his cloak tightly.

'See here,' said the king, ignoring the ache in his bones as he pointed out a weapons rack, 'the ancient spear wielded by Drekk that slew Kharanak, the great dragon ogre.'

'That must have been some throw to kill such a beast, and with a weapon such as this,' Nagrim remarked, taking in the sight of the simple flint-pointed wooden spear.

'Aye, lad,' Bagrik agreed. 'They did things differently in the elder days when the Karaz Ankor was newly forged, and dwarfs took their first faltering steps into the world.'

'Tromm,' Nagrim intoned respectfully, much to his father's pleasure.

'This Drekk must have been a great hunter. I would have liked to meet him at the grobkul.'

'Ha!' said Bagrik, slapping his son on the back, 'Ever eager to kill the grobi, eh my son?'

'I vow to rid the mountains of the green vermin, father,' Nagrim replied in all seriousness and stopped walking. 'And speaking of it, Brondrik is readying for another hunt. I wish to go with him. Rugnir, too.'

'Is it not enough that you've beaten me, must you crush your father's tally, also?' Bagrik joked, but then regarded his son with thoughtful eyes. He clapped his hands upon Nagrim's shoulders and, with a broad smile, the king nodded at some private affirmation.

'You will make me proud, Nagrim,' he said. 'You will make all of Karak Ungor proud, and your rule shall be the envy of the Karaz Ankor,' Bagrik declared boldly.

'You honour me, father–' Nagrim began.

'But…' said the king, 'I cannot condone of your friendship with Rugnir.'

Nagrim's expression soured and he stepped back from his father's embrace.

'He is a wazlik, son, and his presence by your side is a stain against the good name of this clan, even this hold,' Bagrik told him, wounded at Nagrim's rebuff.

'Have I not always been the son you wanted me to be, father,' said the prince. 'At sixty-nine winters, am I not the finest warrior and hunter this hold has ever known? Matters of clan and council, I will leave to others – Kandor is a more than capable mentor. You have said yourself that I possess the strength and wisdom to rule Karak Ungor, so trust my wisdom in this. Rugnir is my friend, his loyalty is beyond question. I will not forsake him because it raises the eyebrows of the masters and the longbeards.'

Bagrik was about to chastise Nagrim for his wilfulness and lack of proper veneration towards the clan elders, but stopped himself.

'I did not bring you here for us to fight, son,' he told him. 'Please,' he added, 'indulge me. Let us forget about Rugnir for now and walk on.'

Nagrim agreed and together they went further into the Iron Deep, where Bagrik regaled his son with further marvels like Garekk Dragonbane's shield – that which had repelled the flame of the wyrm, Skorbadd – resting on a golden plinth, its edges still scorched black; and the fabled Hammer of Logran, known also as Daemon-killer, glowing with a dull red light, the power of its runes still potent, if diminished. As great and fabulous as these heirlooms were, to Bagrik they paled in significance when compared to the artefact he had brought Nagrim to the Iron Deep to see.

'Your legacy lies ahead,' Bagrik said when they had reached the lowest level of the vault, so close to the Zharrazak they could feel the intensity of its flame, prickling their faces. The king stopped and pointed to another short pathway that led to a shadowed alcove.

Nagrim looked to his father with an expression of uncertainty, as if awaiting his permission.

'Take the road, Nagrim. Your destiny waits at the end of it.'

The dwarf prince obeyed and walked towards the alcove slowly, Bagrik following a few steps behind.

As Nagrim got close, a spit of flame surged from the Zharrazak, its flare so bright that it briefly lit the lower level with a fiery luminance. The light flooded the alcove, just as Nagrim reached it, peeling back the shadows like strips of black parchment. A wave of heat came with it that warmed the skin and set nerve endings tingling with vigour. Revealed in the glow was a suit of armour.

Gilded gromril plate, polished to a fine sheen, caught the light; the reflected flames of the Zharrazak making the surface seem as if it were ablaze. Even when the surge of fire died, the captured lustre in the armour did not. The golden pauldrons, vambraces and cuirass were burning brilliantly. In the glow of its self-made aura details of the armour's exquisite artifice were revealed.

Overlapping gromril plates were secured by ancestor studs, the visages of Grimnir and Grungni promising both strength and fortitude to the wearer. A crimson cloak of velvet hooked onto the breastplate and trailed down the back of the suit, trimmed in silver with runic talismans stitched into the lining. Plates covered the abdomen, and a skirt of gromril hung down like an impenetrable veil to sit just above the wearer's boots.

The ancestral armour was finished off by a full-face helmet, rendered into the stern countenance of a dwarf king of old and fastened to the cuirass by a ruby-studded gorget. Splayed eagle wings, hardened by wax before being gilded, spread from either temple of the war helm, the effect both regal and terrifying.

'This armour was meant for you,' Bagrik said softly, now standing alongside his humbled son. 'It is magnificent, isn't it?'

'I have never witnessed beauty such as this…' Nagrim had tears in his eyes. He reached a trembling hand towards the suit, hardly daring to touch it should he be found unworthy and coruscated in a sudden conflagration.

'It is yours, Nagrim,' Bagrik told him, 'Yours upon the advent of your seventieth winter, but a few short weeks from this day. It's the right of every heir apparent of Karak Ungor to wear it.'

Nagrim turned to his father, his outstretched hand still wavering. The prince's eyes held a question.

'Yes, my son. I wore it too, as did my father, and my father's father and so on to the very beginning of our line. Now it passes to you,' he added simply, gesturing towards the armour.

Nagrim looked back and this time he touched it with the strength of conviction that could only be born of a belief in legacy and destiny. The prince seemed at once uplifted, even empowered, as the physical connection to his ancestors coursed through his body.

'I have been no prouder of you than I am in this moment, Nagrim,' Bagrik told his son when he had turned back from the armour. Its lustre seemed to dim, the gleam only short lived, as if it 'knew' somehow that this was not its time, not yet.

'Thank you, my lord,' rasped Nagrim and went down on one knee to salute his father and his king.

'Rise,' said Bagrik, 'and help your old man back to the gate,' he added with a wry grin. 'We have lingered here long enough, I think. It is time to return to the upper deeps.'

Nagrim smiled, and together father and son made their way back up to the entrance of the Iron Deep, the solid gate slamming shut with thunderous resonance after they left, the dour and silent hearth guard retaining their eternal vigil over it.

Once they were out, Nagrim took his leave, eager to meet with Brondrik and the rangers at the outer gateway hall for the grobkul. Bagrik had his own duties to attend to. He was due in council to meet with the elders over the monthly matters of the hold. Even so, he tarried deliberately in the galleries above the Iron Deep, slowly hobbling the stairways and corridors, regarding the statues of his forebears. Soon his effigy would join them.

'I thought I might find you here,' said a soft voice from the shadows.

Bagrik turned to see his queen stepping into the brazier light.

'Trawling the corridors of the past?' asked the queen, as she approached her king.

'Aye, something like that,' Bagrik replied, stopping before the statue of his father, Thargrik. 'I am old, Brunvilda. I feel the bite of winter, the growing chill in my veins as if for the first time,' he said. 'Vigour abandons me. Age and atrophy creep into my bones and muscles like unseen assassins, making them feel like stone.' Bagrik clenched his fist, watching his fingers wrap themselves slowly together. 'Soon *I* will become stone,' he added, looking back at the granite statue of his father. 'A remembrance only, my body withering and decaying into dust in my tomb.'

Brunvilda laid her hand upon his hand, and the warmth of her touch spread like a rejuvenating salve.

'You are a great king,' she told him, 'who has done great deeds. I do not think your reign is over yet.'

Bagrik looked up at her. There were tears in Brunvilda's eyes.

'Your legacy is strong,' she said. '*That* is how you will be remembered.'

Bagrik smiled back at her.

'He is a worthy heir, is he not?'

'Yes, my king. Nagrim's deeds will also be great.'

For a short time, king and queen enjoyed the moment, allowing a comfortable silence to descend. Both knew it was not to last.

'It feels like you have been avoiding me,' said Brunvilda, her tone soft but candid.

'I have had much on my mind,' Bagrik replied, slipping from her grasp and turning to regard the statue of Thargrik again.

'You only ever seem happy when you are in the company of Nagrim,' she said, stepping forward but just falling short of touching her husband on the shoulder.

Bagrik maintained his silence. He knew what was coming.

'You lavish such love and attention on him, your favoured son,' she pressed.

Bagrik whirled around to challenge her.

'*Favoured* son?' he said, angrily. '*Only* son, you mean.'

Brunvilda's expression hardened. 'I have been to see Lothvar, as you should have done,' she told him. 'He dwells in a prison, surrounded by squalor. It is no way to treat a prince.'

'He is no prince!' Bagrik countered, becoming even more animated. 'He is a *nubunki*, and I should have had him exiled at birth, not compromised my rule with lies and dishonour.'

'He is your son,' Brunvilda maintained, determined to stand her ground in the face of Bagrik's growing fury. 'And the only reason you bestow such affection on Nagrim is your guilt over the treatment of Lothvar.' Brunvilda's mood softened then, as her defiance waned. 'All I ask is that you see him.'

'Never!' snarled Bagrik. 'That thing is no son of mine. He is barely a dawi at all.' The king hissed the words through clenched teeth, suddenly aware that others may be listening or might overhear their argument. Breathing heavily, he drew in close to Brunvilda, his face red with rage.

'Do not mention him in my presence ever again. Lothvar died when he was born, that is all.' Bagrik stared at her for a moment, making sure his words had sunk in. Then he turned and hobbled away, bellowing for his throne bearers.

'Incursions by the grobi into the mines and overground farms have increased this last month,' Morek declared before the council of elders, speaking in his capacity as the king's general. 'The changing season has roused them from slumber, it would seem.'

The assembled longbeards of the council nodded sagely. They were arrayed around the stone table of the Elders Chamber, together with Heganbour and Kozdokk, the two guildmasters summoned to the monthly council meeting to discuss a land leasing dispute between the brewers and the miners. Tringrom, Bagrik's royal aide, was also present. Standing beside the glowering form of his king, who crouched upon his throne like a belligerent gargoyle, Tringrom had already announced the agenda. Beard taxes, ale tithes and the reckoners' ledger were all common fare at such gatherings. But it was the growing numbers of greenskins that demanded the council's attention now, an ever-present thorn in the collective side of all the holds of the Karaz Ankor.

Bagrik muttered beneath his breath at Morek's remarks, his mood more irascible than usual.

'What of the underway?' he growled. 'Do we need to purge the tunnels again?'

'The ungrin ankor is not so overrun with vermin, my king,' Grikk replied. It was a rarity for the captain of the ironbreakers to sit in on the council, but the orc and goblin infestation concerned him most of all. Should the greenskins attack the hold, it was through the underway that they would make their assault. 'All of the gates are holding and the ironbreakers report no incursions through the fallen portals,' added Grikk.

'And the *Grey Road*, is that also clear of intrusion?' asked Bagrik, his lip upcurled. The true meaning of his question was thinly veiled.

Grikk swallowed loudly, before answering.

'Quiet, my liege. Very quiet.'

Bagrik turned to Morek, who shifted uncomfortably beneath his king's gaze.

'We must trust in Brondrik and his rangers to thin the horde,' the king told him. 'Nagrim, my son, and soon to be heir of Ungor, hunts with him even now. He has vowed to rid the mountains of the greenskin, and I have no reason to doubt it.'

'Perhaps we need to take even more punitive measures in the extermination of the grobi,' suggested Morek. 'I could marshal the clan warriors and the rest of the rangers, have them scour the crags. One hunting party, however well led, cannot be expected to cleanse the mountainside single-handed.'

'And I suppose the king's treasury will pay for this campaign, will it, Morek?' growled Bagrik. 'You think my son will fail in his oath to me, is that it?'

'Nagrim is no umbaraki, my liege,' the hearth guard captain, said quickly. 'I only meant that–'

Morek's words would remain unspoken as a thunderous din coming from the golden doors of the Elders' Chamber swallowed them.

'Are my private meetings to be constantly interrupted?' barked the king, glaring at the entrance to the room. 'Is this what the rule of Karak Ungor has come to?'

'Enter then,' he snarled after a moment of silence.

With a sound like churning iron, the great doors opened but a crack and the same hearth guard veteran that Morek had remonstrated during the trade talks with the elves stepped into the Elders Chamber, bowing profusely.

'Lords…' he said, catching his breath, having obviously run all the way from the outer gateway hall, 'forgive my trespass, but the elves and our kinsdwarfs… they have returned.'

BAGRIK AGREED TO meet with Prince Ithalred and his charges in his throne room. There, sat upon his throne, longbeards either side of him, he brooded silently. Surrounded by tapestries and mosaics of the grand deeds of Karak Ungor, Bagrik wondered what ill-news would undoubtedly follow the elves' sudden and unannounced arrival.

The Ithalred that marched into his kingly chamber had lost none of the imperious posturing that had so irked Bagrik in their initial meeting, but the haughty, arrogant noble in him had diminished. The elf prince and several of his kin had been brought directly from the outer gateway hall with all haste, so much so that they still had their weapons. Haggar and Kandor, together with the hearth guard, accompanied them by way of security. They had not – it had come to the king's attention – returned with either the promised goods of the elves or those originally sent by the dwarfs.

'Where is the promised trade, as given in the deed of agreement?' Bagrik's voice boomed like thunder in the vast throne room, the fire in the brazier fans flickering redly in concert with the king's wrath. 'You will answer!'

Kandor stepped forward. His face was ashen, eyes hooded with fatigue. The merchant's usually fastidious appearance was a shambles. Facing the accusatory glances of the longbeards, as well as the stern countenance of Morek, arms folded in disapproval, Kandor had to dig deep to find his voice and his courage.

'We did not bring them, sire,' he confessed.

'I can see that!' bawled the king, 'The empty carts clutter my outer gateway hall, even now. I am asking why that is, Thane Silverbeard.'

Haggar stepped forward before Kandor could answer. In the brazier light, Bagrik saw his banner bearer's armour was dented, some of the mail split. Dried blood spattered his face and tunic, creating a grisly visceral patchwork. There was weariness in his posture that came only from hard battle.

'We arrived at the elgi settlement to find it under attack,' said Haggar, his tone sombre, his face darkening with remembrance. 'A vast horde of heathen men, sailed from across the Sea of Claws, had gathered northwards of the city. By the time we knew what was going on, the elgi had already arrayed for battle. I led the hearth guard to join them, to see what manner of beasts these northmen were.'

'And you met them on the field of war, Haggar?' asked Morek. As general of the king's armies, the hearth guard were his responsibility.

'I did, my captain,' Haggar confessed, looking down at his boots.

'Do not lower your eyes from the king!' snapped Morek. 'Face the shame of your deeds with honour.'

Haggar looked up at once.

Morek scowled back at him.

'Tell me,' said King Bagrik, satisfied until now to let his hearth guard captain take the lead, 'what do the elgi have to say?'

Ithalred, silent until that point, came forth. The elf's eyes were haunted by death. Deep shadows pooled in the sockets and he too was battered and bloodied.

'My army was defeated,' he said simply. 'And it is only a matter of time before the northmen drive on further into the mainland and sack Tor Eorfith, too. I have risked much even coming back here, leaving the city in the hands of my captain, Valorian.'

'Risked?' Bagrik enquired. 'What is it that you think you have come here for, elgi?'

Ithalred unsheathed his sword. There was a clamour of weapons from the hearth guard, and Morek stepped in front of his king, axe at the ready. But the elf prince merely placed the ancient weapon on the ground, and knelt down with it in front of him. The mood relaxed. The hearth guard sheathed their weapons. Morek returned to his position beside the throne.

'King Bagrik Boarbrow, I, Ithalred of Tor Eorfith, Prince of Eataine, humbly beseech your aid,' said the elf. 'I lay down my arms in a gesture of supplication. I cannot defeat the northmen on my own. Join me with your armies so that together we might rid this blight from our lands.'

The room fell into abject silence.

Bagrik smiled cruelly. Leaning forward on his throne, he said, 'That could not have been easy.'

The hard line of Ithalred's mouth, the nerve twitching in his cheek, gave the dwarf king the answer he sought.

'And without the honeyed words of your ambassador or the thinly-veiled slights of the black-haired noble to hide behind,' Bagrik added, a dark glance at Malbeth, who waited in the shadows behind the prince. Lethralmir was not present. It seemed he had not accompanied his lord.

A wise move, thought the king.

'Yes, I believe that was very hard for you to do.' Bagrik stared at Ithalred who, to the elf's credit, returned his gaze without faltering. 'No sovereign would wish to beg at the feet of another.' Ithalred grit his teeth at the remark. 'For make no mistake, that is where you find yourself.'

Bagrik stood up, shooing Morek and his throne bearers away as he hobbled down the three broad steps that led to the throne room's flag-stoned aisle, until he was face-to-face with the elf.

'You came into my hold, my kingdom, and offered only scorn and derision. You mocked our customs and besmirched our culture. For these deeds alone you are already entered into the book of grudges, and this, dear elgi, is severe indeed.' The dwarf king paused, allowing the import of his words to sink in, before he went on.

'Now, you are before me pleading for aid, to fight a foe that harries not my borders, but yours. And in so doing I have learned of a further misdeed. That your trade alliance was nothing but pretence for what you truly wanted, but did not care to admit even to yourself…' Bagrik let the words hang for a moment, the calmness in his voice more unsettling than any rage he could have mustered, '…the might of Karak Ungor.'

Ithalred's expression turned to defiance, and anger. The elf had his answer. The dwarf king was merely making a point.

'Through deception you have tried to garner my favour,' Bagrik continued. 'These northmen will not bother us. We dawi are shielded in our bastions of stone. Let them come – the mountain is our protector. They will shatter against it like twigs against the bulwark of a cliff. No, Prince Ithalred,' Bagrik said at length, turning and hobbling back up to his throne, 'I will not wage war for you,' the dwarf king added once he was seated again. 'We will honour the trade pact, should you survive this trial. Return to me with talk of that, not of war.'

Bagrik sighed deeply, the king grown suddenly weary of talk.

'Now, go,' he said. 'Back to your city, if it still stands.'

Ithalred rose to his feet, still elegant and defiant in spite of it all, picking up his sword and sheathing it. Though his face was contorted with suppressed fury, he managed to bow to the dwarf king before he turned and took his leave. The rest of the elves followed in his wake, escorted by the hearth guard.

'Not you, Haggar,' intoned the king, as the elves departed.

The banner bearer remained where he was, Kandor too.

Only once the elves were gone did Bagrik speak again.

'You saw the forces of this enemy, these *north-men*?' asked the king.

Haggar nodded sternly.

'Tell us of them, now. Spare no detail. I would know what manner of foe we face should their reaving bring them to our walls. And Morek,' added the king, turning to his hearth guard captain. 'Send out rangers to find my son. I will not have him caught up in this war by mistake.'

CHAPTER TEN

Casualties of War

FAR FROM THE throne room of Karak Ungor, high in the fastness of the northern Worlds Edge Mountains, Nagrim hunted greenskins. He was not aware that the dwarfs had returned to the hold and he did not know about the pleas of the elf prince. Nagrim was oblivious to the politics of Karak Ungor. It did not interest him. Let Kandor and Tringrom deal with such matters. Thinking of them now, he was glad that the royal aide had been unable to accompany them. The ufdi only slowed them down. The loremaster would have to record his tally in the book of deeds upon their return. Though, if the current count was any measure, he would have precious little to attribute to any of the hunters on the grobkul.

'Slim pickings,' grumbled Brondrik, cutting the nose off the solitary grobi he'd caught defecating in some brush. The steam of the greenskins' dung was still rising from where it'd squatted before being stuck by the pathfinder's crossbow bolt.

'Aye,' agreed Rugnir, his own axe as of yet unbloodied. 'You've killed too many grobi, Nagrim. Perhaps we should have brought that ufdi with us, his perfumed beard locks seemed to enflame their ardour and brought them running.' The dwarf's roaring laughter echoed across the peaks, carried on the warming winter breeze.

Nagrim didn't join in the banter. He had journeyed from his hold to slay goblins, not trek through the mountain passes.

'We head north-east,' he said without humour. 'There are caves there that may yet harbour greenskin.'

The prince noticed the other rangers in their hunting party, Thom and

Harig, exchange wary glances. Even, Brondrik raised an eyebrow. Rugnir said aloud what they were all thinking.

'North-east, eh lad? That is far from the hold. Are you trying to narrow my girth, Nagrim? The rinns like a dwarf with a bit of meat on him, if you get my meaning,' he laughed thunderously.

Nagrim cut the merriment short, the half-hearted chuckles dying in Rugnir's throat.

'North-east,' he said, ignoring Rugnir's disappointment as the words of his father came back to him. He had been in a strange mood ever since he'd left the Iron Deep and set out into the mountains. When he had touched the ancestral armour of his forebears, the weight of legacy had fallen upon his shoulders like an anvil. His father's time was ending. Soon he would be king of Karak Ungor. The thought, he confessed to himself, filled Nagrim with dread.

'Brondrik, mark our trail,' ordered the prince, checking the load in his crossbow, before slinging the weapon back over his shoulder.

The venerable pathfinder nodded, before something on the ground caught his attention.

'There are other tracks besides grobi here,' he told Nagrim, who came over and crouched beside him. 'See…' said Brondrik, using a gnarled finger, the nail chipped and encrusted with dirt, to describe the irregular pattern in the earth and snow, '…booted feet and larger than grobi.'

'Urk?' the prince suggested, thinking of the goblins' larger and more brutish cousins.

'No,' Brondrik replied, shaking his head. 'No, I don't think it's urk.'

'Which way were they headed?' Nagrim asked. 'They may have driven the grobi in the same direction.'

The pathfinder sighed before he looked up at the prince again. His eyes held a warning that would not be heeded.

'North-east.'

THE DWARFS TRAVELLED for an hour before they caught sight of any green-skins again. Further northward than they had ever ventured, even the wildlife in the barren crags that surrounded them seemed sparse. There were no rivers, the melt waters of the mountain having bled south; just dry, dusty basins. Any trees were reduced to isolated copses of brittle pine with dead brown leaves.

'This is a hollow place, my lord,' said Brondrik from the front of the group, his crossbow low slung and at the ready, 'We should turn back.' The pathfinder seemed wary of his own shadow, his instincts and confidence deserting him. The mood spread to the other rangers, too. Even Rugnir was not his usual ebullient self, and had fallen into a drunken melancholy.

'Come on, Nagrim,' he said, mustering some joviality. 'Let's return to the hold, I'll buy you a drink,' he added with a weak smile.

The prince exhaled his disappointment, and was about to admit defeat when he saw the grobi, scampering through the rocks, some rangy animal carcass gripped fast in its overbite.

'There!' he cried, barrelling off down the trail after the greenskin. 'With me!'

The other dwarfs gave chase reluctantly, especially Rugnir who muttered beneath his breath, something concerning hruk fondling.

For such a gangling wretch the goblin was nimble, picking its way through the crags with apparent ease. Nagrim was hard pressed to keep sight of it, let alone get close enough to catch the creature.

He plunged after it, down a steep-sided valley and into a deep gorge. Nagrim was so intent on slaying the goblin that he slipped, and nearly fell. When he got his footing again, there was no sign of his quarry. He slowed, looking left and right in the wide, flat basin of the gorge. It was scattered with displaced rocks and fallen rubble from the steep sides.

Brondrik was the first to catch up to him, a few moments later.

'I've lost it,' Nagrim hissed to the pathfinder, training his crossbow over the craggy rocks where the shadows were thickest.

'The wretched beast could have slipped out of the gorge unnoticed,' Brondrik suggested, surveying the uppermost ridges of the chasm as an ill-feeling spread over the entire party. 'Do you hear that?' he added.

'I hear nothing,' whispered Nagrim.

Eerie silence persisted in the nadir of the gorge. There were no bird cries; even the wind had died abruptly.

'Exactly,' Brondrik replied.

Rugnir swallowed. The loud noise made the hunters start suddenly. Four stern-faced dwarfs regarded him as one.

Rugnir smiled apologetically, before one of the rangers pointed towards a cluster of rocks at the foot of one of the steep sides of the ravine.

They had found their goblin. He was slumped against one of the rocks, a thick dark arrow with bloodied feathers protruding from his chest.

Out of the corner of his eye, Nagrim noticed Brondrik look up, smelling something on the breeze as the wind changed suddenly. He followed his gaze…

Shadows gathered at the ridge of the gorge on either side, too large to be goblins.

'Defend yourselves, we are under–' the warning died on Brondrik's lips, the arrow in his neck severing his vocal cords and killing the old dwarf a few blood-gurgling seconds later.

'Take cover in the rocks,' cried Nagrim as an arrow thunked in his chest and spun him off his feet.

'Nagrim!' shouted Rugnir, as the other rangers sighted down their crossbows to retaliate. Thom was struck through the eye, then in the arm and neck as he loosed harmlessly into the side of the gorge. Harig made it to the rocks before three arrows thudded into his back, and he slumped forward.

Nagrim was on his feet again. He tasted blood in his mouth, and was finding it hard to breathe. The barbed arrow head had nicked his lung. He fired his crossbow at one of the ambushers and a cry echoed in the mountains as he found a killing shot. Rugnir, having lost his crossbow in the confusion, flung a hand axe, slaying a second. It was never going to be enough. Three arrows put him down: two in the body, one in the leg. Another struck Nagrim in the arm, and he dropped his weapon.

Unable to shoot back and down to one, the dwarf was easy prey. The ambushers knew this and were emboldened, emerging from their hiding places in the crags at the top of the gorge. Moving down the steep slope, spilling scree and with arrows knocked, Nagrim saw the ambushers clearly for the first and last time. The dwarf's vision was fading. His tunic and chainmail was slick with his own blood.

'Grungni...' he breathed, eyes widening.

The creak of bow strings split the air and then the arrow storm began.

CHAPTER ELEVEN

The Death of Legacy

BY THE TIME Morek and the Clan Cragfoot rangers had arrived at the gorge, the ambushers were gone. Blood was splattered everywhere in the dry canyon, thick and black. Arrow shafts stuck out of the ground where they had missed their targets, like feathered grave markers. Dwarf weapons lay strewn about, dropped or abandoned in the chaos.

'This was a massacre,' Morek muttered under his breath as he crouched by the body of a dead ranger. He didn't know the dwarf, but closed his eyes for him as they stared glassily at the clouds scudding across the sky above.

Back at the hold, as he gathered the rangers, the hearth guard captain had been approached by Queen Brunvilda. She had asked him to lead the search party for her son, knowing this is what the king would want. Secretly she feared for Nagrim, but Bagrik would never allow his pride to admit that. Morek had gladly obeyed, amassing the dwarfs with haste and leaving Karak Ungor as soon as they were ready.

Though not as accomplished as Brondrik, the hearth guard captain had spent many summers with the clan rangers and was an excellent tracker. He had found the hunting party's trail quickly. Though, it seemed, it had not been nearly quick enough.

'Another dead, here,' one of the Cragfoots, a dwarf by the name of Lodri, called out. He was standing by the twisted body of a ranger with an arrow embedded through his eye. 'Grungni's oath...' he breathed, when he saw the barbed tip sticking out of the back of the dead dwarf's helmet.

'A grobi, too,' said another, having found a goblin slumped against a rock.

Morek's face only darkened further. He got to his feet and tried to survey the scene. His gaze rose to the ridge line, where another group of rangers patrolled.

'They were lured here, their murderers lying in wait at the ridgeline. They had high ground, surprise and likely outnumbered them,' the captain said, more to himself than any of the other dwarfs present. 'Nagrim,' he hissed, 'how could you have let yourself be goaded?'

Morek had been one of Nagrim's mentors, teaching him the ways of axe-craft and battle tactics when he was but a beardling. The prince was a gifted student, and had excelled in his studies. To see him outwitted and drawn into a death trap like the gorge was galling in the extreme.

'I can find no sign of the prince,' said Lodri as he approached the hearth guard captain. 'He could still be alive.'

Morek surveyed the grim vista again, took in the spilt blood and the disturbed rock and brush as the beleaguered dwarfs had fought desperately but to no avail.

'No,' he uttered sadly. It was one of the hardest things he'd ever had to admit to himself. 'See, there are no tracks leading from the battle, just some rough furrows. Likely the ambushers fled when they were finished, filthy *thagi*, covering up their tracks as they went. This trail here,' he said, indicating the furrows, 'looks like drag marks, possibly from some wild beast...' He stopped, seeing the logical conclusion to his words realised in the ranger's eyes, and decided not to articulate it. Morek did not wish to imagine the prince of Karak Ungor being gnawed upon by some cave-dwelling creature of the mountain. He made an oath to Grungni that none were alive if that was their fate.

'Could he have been captured, then?' Lodri offered. 'For ransom, perhaps?'

'Hmm, it's possible,' Morek's tone gave away that he thought this was a slim hope at best. 'I have heard that northmen covet gold and relish plunder, but taking hostages seems out of character for these beasts.'

As they continued to survey the scene and rationalise the possibility of Nagrim's survival, however remote, another ranger cried out.

Morek's heart caught in his mouth.

It was another body.

The hearth guard captain hurried over, though his haste was utterly unnecessary – all the dwarfs in the gorge were beyond help now. Not even Valaya could save them. The third corpse was face down, and peppered with arrows. Judging by the trail he had left and the position of the body so far from the main battlesite, the dead dwarf had obviously crawled along the ground in spite of heinous injuries. Morek noted with a deepening sense of sadness and outrage that the dwarf's hand, his fingers outstretched and reaching, was just inches from his bloodied crossbow. The hearth guard captain nodded to two rangers standing by the body to turn it over. Morek's heart sank and he felt something die within him in that moment. Perhaps it was hope. The dead dwarf was Nagrim.

Despite what he'd said to Lodri, Morek had still held on to the slight chance that the prince was still alive, that he'd fallen down a chasm and broken his leg, or become lost on an unfamiliar trail – anything but this. Now the irrefutable evidence of Nagrim's demise was before him, it struck like a hammer blow.

'Get them up,' he breathed, finding his voice choked with emotion. Lodri reached out and Morek grasped his arm just before he was about to touch the prince. 'Like the most venerated and fragile heirloom of your clan,' he said, 'Carry him like that.'

Nagrim was raised aloft on the shoulders of four rangers, another four, together with Morek, providing an honour guard as they carried him back up the trail and out of the defile to where a mule-drawn cart was waiting.

Reaching the ridgeline, the path widened out and there was the cart with a cohort of dauntless hearth guard stood at the ready to receive him. Morek had taken no chances with the search party, especially given the possibility of foreign invaders in the mountains, and had brought over thirty dwarfs with him.

As Nagrim was lowered gently onto the cart, the two other slain rangers set down after him, Morek wiped a tangle of dark brown hair that was matted with blood from the prince's face.

'I'm sorry, lad,' he whispered. 'Rest now, soon be home.'

'Dreng tromm, this is a dark day,' said Lodri, as they were leading off the mule.

'Yes,' answered Morek. 'I must find a way to tell the king that his son is dead.'

A SOLEMN PROCESSION of hearth guard carried Nagrim up the central aisle of the throne room upon a bier of shields. They bore him at shoulder height, the prince's hands clasped across his chest as he lay in quiet repose. The ashen complexion, his bloodied face, gave away the illusion that he was merely sleeping. Arrows were embedded in his body, the fatal one piercing his heart through his battered armour.

There were no sounds as Nagrim made his last journey, only the harsh *clack* of metal on stone from the hearth guards' boots. Even the forge hammers had stopped, the ever-present clang of the anvils held fast in respectful remembrance. Morek led the warriors down the central concourse of gilded flagstones, along the heavy path that would bring Nagrim to his disconsolate father.

Word had reached King Bagrik not long after Morek had entered the outer gateway hall, though none had yet related the precise details

of what had happened or said explicitly that Nagrim was dead. It was
unnecessary, the very manner of the prince's return made that fact abun-
dantly clear.

When Morek finally reached the king, at the end of the long, wide
aisle, his face was grave. The hearth guard captain was the only one not
wearing his full-face helmet. He did so out of respect for Nagrim and to
his king on account of the news he was about to give.

'We found him in a gorge, far to the north-east, beyond the grobi
hunting trails,' said Morek in a subdued tone.

Bagrik stared down at the body of his son with ice-cold eyes, his
expression neutral and unreadable. He reached out and was about to
touch Nagrim's face, when he stopped and snatched his hand away as
if scalded. To feel that gelid flesh, the chill of death beneath the skin…
He would not be able to deny the truth before him. Bagrik felt a sudden
tightness in his throat and rubbed it absent-mindedly.

Queen Brunvilda, alongside him, lightly squeezed her husband's
hand. Bagrik reciprocated the gesture and held on as if for dear life,
imagining all the strength dripping out of his fingers as mortality came
to claim him, just as it had claimed his legacy. Kandor was the only
other dwarf present. He was standing below the dais where Bagrik clung
to his throne with claw-like fingers, knuckles white from the constant
effort of gripping. The merchant thane had his head bowed, unable to
bring himself to look upon the slain prince.

'Who was responsible for this?' the king demanded, his voice steady
but carrying an undercurrent of threat. 'Who killed my son!' he cried out
in anguish, coming down from his throne and slipping from Brunvilda's
reassuring grasp to cradle Nagrim's head. 'My boy…' Gently, so gently,
he stroked back Nagrim's hair, the tips of his fingers scarcely brushing
the prince's cold skin. When Bagrik looked up at his hearth guard captain, there were tears in his eyes.

'It was not grobi,' Morek told him, taken aback at first by the reaction
of his king. His expression darkened when he added, 'The arrows are
that of the northmen, the ones plaguing the lands of the elgi.'

Bagrik's jaw line hardened as if carved of granite. A mask of calm fury
came across his face, smothering his grief like a hand upon a candle
flame. There was the briefest glimmer of rogue emotion in his eyes as he
regarded Morek. Regret.

'Retribution,' rasped the king, 'I will have vengeance for this,' he promised, getting louder. 'Send word to the elgi. We'll fight their war for them
and crush these heathen bastards, who think they can attack the royal
clan of Ungor without fear of retaliation.

'Muster the armies. Every axe, every hammer…' Bagrik said. 'We are
now at war.'

* * *

AN AURA OF serenity existed in the Temple of Valaya. In the starlit gloom, a figure hunched over a stone slab below the mighty statue of the beneficent goddess. He was wrapped in a fur cloak, and his shoulders were slumped as if in defeat. Bagrik had ordered that his son be taken immediately from the throne room to the ancestor temple to await internment.

Following his declaration of war, the king had resumed his throne and gave curt orders for his bearers to take him to the temple after his son. To Morek he left the marshalling of the armies. Though grief and hurt unimaginable made him want to strike out, to bring swift retribution to Nagrim's slayers, he knew the mustering would take time. Armouries would have to be stocked, warriors summoned, war machines made ready.

Word had spread throughout the hold with all the force and purpose of an earthquake, the ripples of the king's anguish felt by all. From the hollow tunnels of the vaults to the busy workshops, guild chambers and clan halls, beards were tugged in despair and axes sharpened as all of Karak Ungor mourned and the thoughts of dwarfs turned to revenge.

Anger, hate – that would come. For now, Bagrik dwelt in a well of his own grief. Nagrim was laid before him, pale in death. The blood had been cleaned from his face by the priestesses, his hair was combed, his beard re-braided. The arrows that defiled the prince's body had been removed, the wounds sewn shut, and he wore a robe of deepest purple in place of his battered plate and mail. Alongside him, upon a stone plinth, was the ancestral armour from the Iron Deep. Bagrik hardly dared to look upon it such was the pain of loss he felt. It seemed like so long ago now that he had shown it to Nagrim. All that it once stood for, hope, pride and legacy, was gone like ash before the wind.

Bagrik bent forward, stooping to kiss his son tenderly on the forehead.

'Nagrim…' he whispered, voice choking, and wept. It was a horrible sound, empty and raw, as Bagrik vented his emotions, hollowing himself out until all that was left was granite.

When the king had finally stopped sobbing he looked up, realising that he was not alone.

'I have never seen you cry before,' said the voice of Brunvilda.

Bagrik turned to his queen. Morek had escorted her and was waiting patiently at the threshold of the temple. Brunvilda's eyes were full of pity and sorrow. All Bagrik could return was cold, hard stone.

'It will be the first and last time,' he replied sternly and started to walk past her, out of the temple.

'Your legacy need not end with Nagrim,' Brunvilda said. Her eyes conveyed her meaning.

Emotion returned like black clouds over a bright day, dark and full of promised thunder.

'I have no son,' snarled Bagrik, stopped next to Brunvilda, only a few inches from her face. He fashioned his vitriol into a bladed retort, 'My only son is dead.'

Bagrik stalked away, bellowing to Morek for his armour once he had left the sanctity of the temple.

Brunvilda shared a worried glance with the hearth guard captain, who knew his duty and followed the king.

CHAPTER TWELVE

Those Left Behind

RUGNIR WAS ALIVE. Though when he awoke and opened his eyes he wished he wasn't. Pain seized his body before his blurring vision succumbed to clouds of black fog. It was like an anvil was resting on his chest, and he had to fight to breathe. Rugnir's skull pounded like iron worked beneath a hammer, an almighty hangover vying with his physical wounds for the prize of causing the dwarf the most hurt.

'Nagrim...' Rugnir's first intelligible words since his revival were rasped. He tried to get up but lances of agony brought him down again like a felled oak.

'Be still,' a voice told him, old, like grit worked over sandpaper. It had a cantankerous, chiding edge to it. Rugnir realised it was another dwarf.

His chest hard, like it was filled with too much bone, made his lungs tight, and his leg was stiff like petrified wood. Out of instinct, Rugnir reached down to the source of his pain. He got as far as the rough scrape of bandages before his wrist was seized by a hand that felt like gnarled wood and coarse leather.

'Be still, I said,' the gruff voice repeated.

Rugnir tried to see his saviour, but all he got for his efforts was spikes of hot pain and a vague silhouette. Abandoning that course of action, he closed his eyes and dimly recalled being struck by arrows, though the details were indistinct. He'd hit the ground hard, the stink of blood and metal filling his nose and mouth. That's when the darkness claimed him. Rugnir had expected to awake before Gazul's Gate, and for the ancestor of the dwarf afterlife to bar his passage into the Halls, and consign him to limbo for his contemptible deeds. This was not the Gate, nor was the hazy figure sat beside him Gazul, the son of Grungni and Valaya. This tenebrous chamber smelled of earth and stone and damp.

Howling wind told him he was still in the mountains, the noise oddly hollow and far away. Rugnir suspected his injuries, self-inflicted and otherwise, were to blame for that. Dripping water echoed dully, like he was lying at the bottom of a deep well or inside a cave, but boomed with a thunderous clamour. Rugnir grimaced at every drop, and that too caused him pain. Slowly, as his senses returned through the screaming wall of hurt, he realised he was not wearing his tunic and the softness beneath his recumbent body was from furs and skins.

A sudden panic gripped him as he remembered the gorge. The faces of the ambushers glared at him like ghosts. Rugnir tried to speak but found he lacked the strength. Desperately, he fought to get up again but couldn't move.

'You're still weak,' the voice told him. The distinctive aroma of pipe smoke filled the air. 'Rest.'

Rugnir shaped a reply with his mouth, opening his eyes. Darkness swept over him, clawing its way into his vision and stilling his lips as he blacked out…

WHEN HE AWOKE again, Rugnir had no idea how much time had passed. It could not have been long; the other dwarf was still sitting beside him and smoking his pipe.

'I warned you,' he growled, getting to his feet and stomping over to what Rugnir's gradually returning eyesight discerned was a stove. The old dwarf picked up a steaming cup that had been resting on it and brought it over.

'Up,' he barked, crouching down and lifting Rugnir's head towards the proffered cup, so he could tip the contents into his mouth. 'Drink,' said the old dwarf.

It was some kind of broth, though the likes of which Rugnir had never tasted. Sweet, but with little flavour, it warmed his body and left an acrid aftertaste. Coughing and spluttering, Rugnir shied away from the cup but the old dwarf was insistent.

'All of it,' he growled, and held Rugnir's head fast. It would not have been difficult; he was so weak even the smallest beardling could have forced him. Only when he finished did the old dwarf let Rugnir go.

'What… what was that stuff?' he asked of the old dwarf, able to croak the words.

'Herbs, bark, hruk urine, all the good things a growing dwarf needs,' he replied. 'What does it matter what's in it? You'll drink it, that's all you need know.'

Rugnir's initial, half-comatose impression was right – he was an old, cantankerous bastard.

'You saved my life,' Rugnir continued, and with the affirmation came an overwhelming sense of grief. There was no one else in the cave with them. The others must have perished.

The old dwarf regarded him for a moment. His grey, unkempt, beard ruffled as he chewed on a piece of leather. He wore a dark green tunic with a cloak of furs, and a mail skirt hung down to his iron-shod boots. A mountaineer's cap perched on his head, stuck with sparhawk feathers, and a worn hand axe hung from a thick, brown belt around his waist.

'Keeps my pegs strong,' he said, grinding the leather and showing a perfect set of square teeth, albeit tarnished with age. 'Craggen,' the old dwarf added, tapping his chest with his pipe, before pointing the supping end at Rugnir.

'Rugnir,' the dwarf replied.

Craggen gave a shrug of his mouth, as if the name meant little, then clamped the pipe between his lips and said, 'I live alone in these mountains, hunting grobi, keeping out of the way. What's your excuse for being out here?'

Rugnir told him about the grobkul, about Nagrim and the other rangers. Then he described the ambush, though he left out the attackers. That was only for him to know.

'I must get back,' he said, struggling to rise before the old hermit pushed him down again.

'And waste all the time I've spent bringing you back from Gazul's door? Are you a wattock? You were half-dead when I found you beside the river. You'll last the time it takes for a grobi to stab you in your sleep!'

'River?' asked Rugnir, bleary-eyed. 'What river?'

'The river where I found you, that's what,' Craggen growled. 'Alone, I'm sorry to say,' he said sombrely, blowing out a thick plume of smoke as he considered the stricken dwarf. 'You can barely stand, let alone walk or trek the mountains. No, you'll remain here. The draught will heal you quickly. A few weeks and you'll be back on your feet; a few more and you'll be ready to leave.'

'A few weeks!' cried Rugnir, 'I must return to the karak, immediately,' he said, trying to get up again. His vision swam suddenly and Rugnir slumped back. The effort of even trying to get his shoulders off the ground was exhausting.

'I must get back…' he said, words slurring, his fading strength all but spent. Blackness enveloped Rugnir once more and he slipped into a fitful dream of blood and arrows and death.

BAGRIK'S ARMY MUSTERED at dawn. For the first time in over two thousand years, the great gates to Karak Ungor yawned open and lines of dwarfs emerged like armoured ants.

Word had already gone ahead to the elves, brought by the king's fastest runners, and was returned swiftly by carrier-hawk. One of the hold's mountain rangers had taken the message to the king. They would meet at Broken Anvil Hill, fifty miles south of Tor Eorfith.

With standards aloft, the gold, copper and bronze catching on the rising sun, the dwarfs trooped out with regimented discipline. Six columns deep, they marched in perfect time with pipe, drum and horn. No rousing chorus of voices, no stirring refrain accompanied the instruments – the choristers, heralds and minstrels kept a sombre silence out of respect for the dead. Rangers were dispatched ahead of the main force, swathed in their cloaks and armed with crossbows and throwing axes. They would pave the way for the army, rooting out any threats and securing the path ahead.

It was the hearth guard, though, that led the line, the stern countenances of their bronze masks gleaming dully. Morek marched in the middle of their ranks, first out of the great gate, the horns on his helmet marking him out as captain. Haggar was directly to his right, holding the grand banner of Karak Ungor high, the red dragon snapping in the breeze.

Next came the longbeards, clad in their ancestral armour, which, even though it bore the scars of a hundred or more battles, still shone with polished brilliance. Bagrik travelled with them, carried upon his war shield by the royal hearth guard bearers. The king's face was more severe than that of his bronze-masked bodyguards, as he rocked gently back and forth with the movement of the armoured warriors.

The longbeards were followed by the many clans, led in turn by their thanes and clan leaders. Warriors all, the hues and runes of the clans' fluttering banners described their heritage and craft – rockcutters, lantern-makers, metalsmiths all come together in a mutual cause. Amongst their number were the hold's quarrellers, crossbows shouldered as they marched beside their kin.

Between the massive phalanxes of warriors and longbeards was Hegbrak Thunderhand, master runesmith and former apprentice of Agrin Oakenheart. Though he was not part of the war host, the venerable runelord Agrin and his fellow runesmiths had toiled night and day in the build up to the mustering, fashioning rune weapons upon their anvils of power in the fuliginous depths of sweltering forges.

Hegbrak rode atop one of the anvils as it was heaved along by the Anvil Guard. Clad in rune-encrusted gromril, helmets wrought in the shape of their honorific, the Anvil Guard were warrior elites, devoted solely to the Runesmiths' Guild, who wielded their great hammers with deadly efficiency. A youth compared to the venerable Agrin Oakenheart, Hegbrak was still a mighty runemaster, his rich tan hair fluttering in the breeze as he eyed the horizon.

Mule-trains brought up the rear of the vast column, hauling small carts heavy with baskets of crossbow bolts, axes, hammers and shields. There was ale, too, sloshing in broad casks, and chests of stonebread, oatmeal and other provisions.

War engines drawn by stout lode-ponies followed in the train – wooden stone throwers chased in bronze and brass, and hefty ballista with iron-headed bolts. They were accompanied by engineers, journeymen and warriors. Assorted victualers and brewers walked alongside the baggage train. Priestesses of Valaya, known as the Valakryn, were brought along too as battlefield surgeons. These ladies of the temple were warriors as well as healers, and carried axes and wore mail beneath their purple robes.

Last of all were the slayers, half-naked warrior fanatics that had sworn a death oath to seek their doom against the mightiest foe they could find or by performing the most insane feats of battle. The tattooed berserkers had attached themselves to the war host a few miles after it had left the hold, and acted as its unofficial rearguard.

The slayers were the only dwarfs to break the silence, bellowing oaths and war cries as they trooped along with their brothers. Some wore the skins of beasts like trophies: the shaggy furs of beastmen, hardened troll flesh, even dragon hide. Others painted their bodies to resemble bones and skulls. All wore their hair shaven into a blood-red crest, hardened with lime and grease, and gripped deathly sharp axes. Within their ranks moved the warrior-priests of Grimnir, the robed acolytes of the dwarfs' fiercest ancestor god, ready to swear in others to the cult during the heat of battle.

When the hundred thousand-strong army left Karak Ungor, the great gate had thundered shut in its wake. At the king's order Brunvilda had stayed behind, the queen watching from the Dragon's Tooth as her husband and his throng departed for war. Grikk remained too, together with his ironbreakers, there to protect the hold in the absence of most of its warriors.

Unsurprisingly, the dwarfs had met no resistance on the road and arrived at Broken Anvil Hill in less than three days.

THE MUSTER POINT of the two armies was well named. A huge, rectangular plain scattered with crags and grassy hollows stretched for over a mile. A rocky promontory jutted out at opposite ends, forming thirty foot bluffs that fell away into lowland valleys scattered with trees. It was these vantage points that gave the hill its shape and its name, together with a ten foot deep cleft that ranged partway down the middle.

Ithalred was waiting on one side of the cleft with his glittering host when the dwarfs had arrived, an army of silver knights on horse, light cavalry, chariots and vast ranks of spears and archers. His captains were alongside him, the raven-haired Lethralmir now wearing full armour forged from the elven star metal, ithilmar, a long bejewelled sword sheathed on his back; Korhvale, the White Lion, dressed in his hunter's garb and familiar scale with its golden cuirass. Malbeth, too, was with them, amongst a few other hitherto un-introduced elf warriors, the ambassador unarmed and wearing only robes.

At seeing this meeting of the two races across the cleft in Broken Anvil Hill, the casual onlooker might have supposed it to be a parlay before the onset of hostilities, rather than a greeting between allies. The mood had been tense, the diplomats of both races failing to thaw the ice. Bagrik and Ithalred had exchanged brief pleasantries of sorts, before retiring to their respective sides of the great hill and setting up separate camps.

IT WAS NEARING nightfall on the fourth day since the dwarfs had left Karak Ungor by the time the encampment was finished. The elves held the north side of the hill, their white silken pavilions and grand marquees in sharp contrast to the squat, angular dwellings of the dwarfs on the southern side of the cleft. Trails of smoke issued from the dwarf tents through carefully engineered vents in the roofs. They were made from coarse weave and dried animal hide, and lit by the glow of flaming coals heaped in iron braziers and cauldrons. The elves used their arcane lanterns to light the area around their own domiciles, strung between their campaign tents on silver thread.

Such was the lingering enmity between the two races that they seldom mixed. A few of the more curious occasionally ventured to the other side of the cleft but, when met with hard stares or muttered derision, were quick to return. Dwarfs kept to dwarfs and elves to elves, talking in huddled groups around fires, sharpening blades, stringing bows or simply lost in deep thought. Some, the balladeers, sang solemn tunes or dour lamentations; others prayed at small shrines. The lucky few, the oldest and wisest, slept. Tomorrow would be a hard day – there would be little, if any, time for rest once metal resounded against metal and the blood began to flow.

'Barely more than beasts,' growled Morek, the voice of the hearth guard captain coming from behind Haggar.

The banner bearer was sitting on a stool in front of a wooden bench, a series of tools unravelled from a leather belt on top of it. He had been alone prior to Morek's arrival, isolated upon the rocky promontory of Broken Anvil Hill that faced east.

'You mean the northmen,' Haggar replied, as he gripped his rune hand and twisted. Creaking metal split the air with his efforts, making him wince, before he managed to unscrew the gromril hand and laid it next to the tool belt.

'Aye, lad,' breathed Morek, the scent of pipe smoke in the air as he spoke. 'You fought these dogs with the elgi, what were they like?' he asked.

Haggar's gaze shifted from his works, sweeping across the sloping plain, through swaying grasses and clusters of tightly bunched rock, until after a mile or so it settled upon the distant horizon and the waiting Norscans.

'Like you said, captain, they are beasts. They throw themselves into battle for the sake of bloodletting... 'tis a sobering sight.'

Something had changed in Haggar the day that he'd returned from Tor Eorfith. He'd only spoken once of the Norscan hordes he fought there alongside the elves, and only when the king had asked him expressly. After that, he'd kept his own counsel. This taciturn dwarf, so troubled and moribund, was as different again to the hopeful youth that had spoken to Morek outside the Elders Chamber several months ago.

Slipping into remembrance, Haggar watched the violet campfires of the Norscans burning into azure as they billowed high into the night, issuing spark-filled smoke. Shadows, mere silhouettes of imagined monsters and evil men who made their pacts with heathen gods, cavorted in the flickering light. Emerald lightning crackled sporadically as the sound of depraved pleasures and infernal tortures drifted on the breeze, redolent with the stench of cooking flesh.

'Even the wind is against us,' Morek grumbled, wrinkling his nose against the wretched smell as he came to stand alongside Haggar.

'It will be a hard fight tomorrow,' said the banner bearer, oiling the metal fingers of his rune hand fastidiously. 'I wish Nagrim were with us.'

'Aye, it will,' Morek offered with casual pragmatism. 'And so do I, lad,' he added wistfully. A moment of mournful silence persisted before Morek spoke again to dispel it. 'I'd sooner have the walls of the hold at my back than fight in that cauldron,' he said, indicating the open battlefield, fringed by the mountains on either side.

The Norscans had already set about clearing it, hewing trees in order to erect crude gibbets for their blood sacrifices. Bodies – goblins, beasts and other barbarian men – were splayed in cruciform, and could just be made out hanging limply from the grim scaffolds.

'They defile the very earth,' said Haggar, watching them darkly. 'What manner of beast are we facing, Morek?' he asked, though he already knew the answer.

'A hellish one it would seem, make no mistake of that,' replied the hearth guard captain.

'To bear the banner of Ungor is a great honour, Morek, but to me it feels like a tremendous burden,' Haggar confessed. 'What if I am found lacking?'

'Our great and noble banner is a symbol, Haggar. It is a symbol of our honour, of our resolve and our brotherhood. A symbol is a powerful thing. It can turn the tide when the odds seem impossible, turn defeat into victory...' Morek told him, pausing to put his hand on the banner bearer's shoulder. 'Don't fear failure, Haggar,' he said. 'I know your thoughts are of Thagri. Your destiny is not his; *you* are not him. You'll reclaim your honour come the morrow, lad. Grungni wills it.' Morek gripped the banner bearer's shoulder hard and then let him go.

Haggar turned, about to respond, but the hearth guard captain was already walking away to the camp and his tent. Instead Haggar returned

to his labours, gratefully lost in the ritual taught to him by Agrin when
he had first gifted him the hand. So consumed was he by his work, the
meticulous cleaning and polishing, that Haggar failed to hear another
figure approach until it was almost upon him. At first he thought it was
Morek, come back because he'd forgotten something, but when he turned
around Haggar saw that it was the elf seeress, Arthelas. He fumbled with
his tools in sudden shock and made to stand before she raised her hand,
stopping him.

'Please,' she said musically, sending the dwarf's heart thumping in his
chest. Haggar was about to grip his chest, for fear that Arthelas would
hear, when he stopped himself.

'Don't let me interrupt…' she said, pausing to regard the disembodied
rune hand and the scattered tools, '…whatever it is you are doing.'

'It's nothing,' Haggar replied with gruff embarrassment, covering up
the rune hand with the leather belt and shoving the stump of his wrist
in his tunic.

'You've no need to hide,' Arthelas told him gently, seeming to glide
alongside him. 'Let me see it.'

Haggar felt his face redden; he hadn't been this hot since he'd worked
in Agrin's forge by way of gratitude for the runelord making his hand.
Abashedly, he pulled his arm out from his tunic and showed Arthelas
the wrist stump where a metal cap had been fused, a threaded hole
bored into it in the centre.

The seeress took it gently in her hands – her lightest touch sent tiny
tremors running through Haggar's body. Her face saddened as she
looked back at the dwarf, eyes sparkling like captured stars.

'I…' Haggar began, feeling a strange compulsion to tell Arthelas its
tale, but at a sudden loss for words. 'It was lost long ago,' he managed
after gathering himself together, 'fighting grobi in the tunnels beneath
my hold. King Bagrik appointed me his banner bearer that day when
venerable Skardrin fell, and had Agrin, our venerable runelord, forge a
new hand for me.'

'It is a grievous wound,' she said, letting Haggar go. 'And old…' Her
eyes narrowed, as if she was seeing into his very soul, '…like another scar
you bear, but one that runs much deeper and is still very raw.'

Haggar had kept the shame of his past to himself for nigh on a hundred
years. But he could not resist. He was enraptured by this fey creature, and
spoke in spite of his shame.

'My four-times grandsire, Thagri Skengdrang, once served Norkragg,
one of the first kings of Karak Ungor. He was Norkragg's banner bearer,
an esteemed and privileged position. When Karak Ungor went to
war, Thagri went too, his task to protect the banner and keep it aloft.'
Haggar's face darkened and he looked at his feet. 'Thagri failed in his
oath,' he said. When he managed to raise his head again, his gaze was
far away, lost to memory. 'During a battle against the greenskin tribes

of the east, he allowed the grand banner to slip from his grasp and be sullied on the field. Desperate, he tried to retrieve it, but the enemy, foul urk swine,' he said, scowling, 'swarmed over it. With the banner lost, panic shuddered down the dawi ranks and many were slain. An entire chapter is devoted to them in the dammaz kron, our book of grudges. Thagri was amongst them, beheaded by an urk cleaver as he stooped for the banner. The day was won in the end. King Norkragg rallied the throng, whipping them up into a hateful fervour, but the stain of Thagri's shameful death could not be so easily undone,' said Haggar, blinking as he returned to the present. 'He wanders even now, headless, an unquiet spirit cursed to dwell forever in limbo. This shame has followed the Skengdrangs for over a thousand years. When Thagri failed in his oath, the honour of banner bearer passed to another clan. I am the first of my clan in four generations to reclaim it, and it falls to me to atone for Thagri's mistake by never allowing the banner to fall while I still live.'

Silence fell between them when Haggar had finished.

Arthelas, her expression shadowed with sadness, smiled, and the warmth of her countenance spread to the dwarf, nurturing the coldness within him back to life.

'I cannot pretend to understand your ways and customs, but I sense bravery in you, dwarf. I do not think you will fail in your promise,' Arthelas told him, then bent down and kissed the banner bearer on the cheek.

Haggar was emboldened at once, and seemed to stand straighter.

'There is a word, in my language...' he said, 'dawongi. It means 'dwarf-friend.'

Haggar went down on one knee. 'Tromm, dawongi,' he breathed, nodding slowly with the deepest of respect.

Arthelas smiled.

'Thank you,' she replied, returning the gesture as she took her leave.

Haggar watched her go, determined more than ever not to be found wanting, especially beneath her gaze. Come the morning, the banner of Karak Ungor would soar aloft and never fall until the battle was won or the blood in Haggar's veins had run cold.

ARTHELAS WAS TIRED as she walked back to her pavilion. She moved swiftly through the camp, passing the tents of warriors and knights engrossed in their pre-battle rituals. Those that did see her lowered their eyes respectfully and bowed until she had passed. Approaching her pavilion, Arthelas met the gaze of Korhvale, who was lingering nearby.

All too eager to follow my brother's every whim, she thought spitefully, but smiling benignly at the White Lion.

Korhvale frowned at Arthelas's appearance, her drawn features and weary posture suggesting fatigue. She didn't give him a chance to voice his concern, assuming he would have the confidence to speak it, moving on quickly and reaching her tent.

Upon entering through the narrow flap, Arthelas dismissed her servants and slumped down onto her bed. Stretching over to a small wooden chest, she took out a glass bottle filled with a silvery potion and drank the contents. It was a revitalising tonic, designed to take the edge off her recent exertions.

'You should have let me tour the encampment with you,' said a silky voice from the shadows. 'It isn't safe with all these… *lesser creatures* about.'

'I wanted to be alone,' Arthelas responded curtly.

'Yes, with the bearded swine. I saw that.'

'Are you following me?' The seeress's tone was accusing.

'Yes,' Lethralmir replied brazenly, a look of amusement on his face as he emerged into the lantern light.

Arthelas's annoyance was only feigned and she returned Lethralmir's smile with one of her own.

'You look powerful in your armour,' she said as he approached. When he was standing in front of her, she traced her fingers delicately over his breastplate and arm greaves.

'I am more powerful without it,' Lethralmir breathed lasciviously, leaning in to the seeress.

Arthelas pushed him back and stood up, the effects of the potion invigorating her. 'I cannot believe you were jealous of the dwarf,' she laughed.

Lethralmir sniffed his indifference and went to pour himself a goblet of wine from a silver carafe at Arthelas's bedside.

'I do believe that stunted brute has taken a shine to you,' he said, filling the goblet to the rim.

'He is repellent,' she declared, a wicked smile spreading across her lips. 'Perhaps, a change of *attire* would make us better suited though…'

A sudden flash of light filled the pavilion, not bright enough to attract attention but enough to make Lethralmir avert his gaze. When the raven-haired blade-master looked back Arthelas was gone, an actinic stench drenching the air. Before him stood a comely female dwarf, long plaited hair trailing over her ample bosom.

'Your brother would not approve of you using your magic so flippantly,' said Lethralmir, setting himself down on a plush velvet couch opposite the bed.

'Ithalred has no concept of my true power,' the dwarf replied, caustically. The tone was at odds with the appearance, though the timbre and language were authentic. Its body shimmered with an inner glow that exuded through the flesh, growing steadily brighter with each passing moment until it was utterly consumed by light. When the sorcerous aura died, Arthelas had returned to her true form.

'Let these hairy backed creatures rut with their own kind,' she said, eschewing the bed to recline on a chaise-long next to the velvet couch. 'I can scarcely imagine how such a race would procreate,' she added, taking Lethralmir's wine and drinking it as if to wash the foul taste from her mouth.

'You have beguiled him, though,' said Lethralmir, getting up and pouring himself another drink. 'And he is not the only one.'

'Korhvale,' said Arthelas with a sneer. 'He watches me like a hawk. I think my brother suspects something.'

That piqued Lethralmir's interest. 'Really?'

'Don't come here, for a while,' she told him.

Lethralmir drew close to her, his voice husky. 'But you have beguiled me, as well...'

'I know,' Arthelas replied teasingly, 'but now is not the time,' she hissed, pushing him hard back onto the couch.

Lethralmir frowned, wounded by the abrupt rejection.

'You are about to be summoned,' she said, by way of explanation.

He didn't catch on immediately and stared nonplussed.

'Get out,' Arthelas snapped, her ire lending Lethralmir purpose.

The blade-master got to his feet, swilling down the last of his wine and left with a lustful smile. Lethralmir was met outside by one of Ithalred's aides. The council of war with the dwarfs was in session and his presence was required.

Arthelas smiled to herself when they were gone.

'No,' she hissed, 'now is not the time.'

BAGRIK'S WAR TENT was the largest of all the dwarfs'. It had several chambers, in which the king could sleep, count his gold or eat. The greatest was given over to the war council, a sizeable wooden table dominating the centre and strewn with ragged parchment maps scribed by Bagrik's cartographers.

Flickering firelight from standing iron braziers revealed a crowded scene; dwarfs surrounded the war table, poring over the details of the coming battle, elves stooped next to them, bent-backed with the low ceiling. The aroma of roast pig filled the air, which was thick with pipe smoke, emanating from a spit in the corner of the room set over hot coals. Dripping fat hissed as it caught in the flame.

Bagrik crouched over the table, sat upon his throne in robes and furs. The boar pelt was slung over the back of it, dead eyes scrutinizing all. Morek, Haggar and a few other dwarf captains were standing nearby, smoking, chewing their beards or staring, furrow-browed and with fists on hips, at the maps. Of the elves, Ithalred and Lethralmir had a place beside the table. The other captains stood behind the dwarfs, peering easily over their shoulders.

'The northmen are here, to the east of our camp,' Morek addressed the allied captains, pointing to a place on the map that showed widely spread contours and downward sloping, flat plains almost bereft of any geographical features. The tacticians of the elves, given their recent sorties, had postulated that the Norscan's main camp was to the east, between Karak Ungor and Tor Eorfith. The movements of the Norscan army, and its appearance to the east of Broken Anvil Hill seemed to bear this out.

'Our rangers report a horde of some two-hundred thousand men, together with beasts and… other *creatures*.' Morek didn't elaborate. It wasn't needed. All gathered in Bagrik's tent knew what he meant. There were *daemons*, fell beings summoned from the Realm of Chaos, in the Norscan ranks.

'I suggest a strategy based on us holding this high ground,' Morek continued, setting a small gold marker stamped with a dwarf face on a raised slope indicated by the map. He added several more gold and bronze markers, shaped like coins, to the one he'd just positioned, that represented the other units in the dwarf army. 'We lure the Norscans with ranged attacks and wait for them to come to us. As they draw close, we pound them with our artillery,' he added, pushing forward a line of gold markers. 'When… If,' he corrected, 'they come through the barrage they'll hit a shield wall of hearth guard and elgi spear,' he said, placing a silver coin with an eagle wing on it in the line. 'The hammer and the anvil,' he announced proudly, leaning back and taking a long pull on his pipe, eminently satisfied. 'We won't even need our reserves.'

'Our force is mainly cavalry, what do you propose we do with them?' asked Lethralmir.

'They won't be needed,' Morek replied boldly, and folded his arms as if that was an end to it.

'You would have us linger by the sidelines as whatever ranged weapons the northmen can bring to bear kill us in our saddles? We are asur, dwarf,' he snarled, 'we too have our honour! And what about our spears, you are committing them to a battle of attrition. That way may suit dwarf ways of war, but it does not suit ours.'

'It's true,' countered Morek, rising to Lethralmir's bait, 'that you elgi are not so hardy. Would you like to hide behind our shields, instead?'

Lethralmir smiled mirthlessly, as he fashioned a rejoinder.

'I doubt they would provide much protection. What's to stop the northmen merely jumping over your heads? That's assuming they even see you.'

'Kruti-eating ufdi…' snarled Morek, shoving his way past the other dwarfs to reach Lethralmir, who merely recoiled with distaste.

'Morek,' snapped the king. It was the first time he had spoken during the council, but it was enough to send the hearth guard captain back to his place still fuming from the elf's insult.

Bagrik turned on his throne to address Ithalred. 'Perhaps there is a way to yoke the strength of both our armies,' he said. 'Are you familiar, prince, with the oblique line?'

Ithalred nodded. 'I am, yes.'

'Morek,' added the king, glaring at the dwarf, 'set the markers.'

The hearth guard captain obeyed, setting out a formation of gold and bronze markers upon the raised slope, several ranks deep. To them he added smaller cohorts of silver. Then he spread a long line of silver coins, bunched on one flank and hinged at the middle of the battle-line. When he was done, he stepped away from the table.

'Our south flank,' Bagrik said, 'will consist of our forces, artillery, infantry and quarrellers. Added to it are your archers and spears. On the north, your cavalry.' All eyes were upon the map and the tactical formation arranged by Morek as the king spoke. 'The plan is a simple one,' Bagrik continued. 'The south moves slowly, whilst its bows and machineries hold fast to maintain a barrage. The north will charge at full pace, and engage the enemy first. The attack will split their forces. One flank crushed by the cavalry, their opposite flank will move in support, but it will already have been decimated by our holding troops. Caught in a killing ground, they will falter. Attack the cavalry or march on the distant slope? Either choice is a fatal one, for by that time our slow moving flank will have reached them and they will be destroyed utterly,' Bagrik concluded. There was no relish in his tone, not even the satisfaction in the knowledge of a battle about to be won. There was only stone. 'We dawi call it the bear trap, and employed properly it is deadly.'

Lethralmir sniffed derisively and turned to his prince.

'This assumes, of course, that the northmen will simply attack as a horde. It seems to me our cavalry is greatly exposed by this plan.'

'No plan is without risk!' retorted Morek.

Ithalred ignored the bickering and held the gaze of the dwarf king.

'Very well,' he said. 'We will meet you on the field tomorrow at dawn.' With that he turned and walked out of the tent, his captains following suit.

LETHRALMIR STARED DARKLY at Morek as he left the king's war tent.

The dwarf's face was so red, his teeth gritted, that the elf thought he might immolate himself in a conflagration of his own anger. Lethralmir decided, once he was back out in the open, that he would have liked to have seen that.

'Lethralmir,' the tone in Ithalred's voice punctured the blade-master's good humour.

'Yes, Ithalred,' he replied with a disarming smile.

The prince was on the elven side of the cleft, and clearly did not share Lethralmir's mood as he beckoned the blade-master over.

'Is something wrong?' he asked, feigning concern.

'You were seen,' the prince told him, 'coming out of my sister's tent.'

Ithalred's aide. Lethralmir resolved to discover his name and punish him accordingly.

'Yes… I was merely–'

The elf prince didn't let him finish.

'Stay away from her,' he said meaningfully. 'She is a seer and must remain pure or she'll lose her gift,' he added, telling Lethralmir things that he already knew. 'Now, more than ever, I need her foresight.'

'You cannot shackle her forever, Ithalred,' Lethralmir replied.

The prince came forward, his face a mask of anger. 'Don't challenge me, or your *use* to this court will be at an end,' he promised, eyes wide.

Lethralmir backed off a little, false offence etched on his features.

'I thought we were friends, Ithalred. I would never do anything–'

'We are,' the prince replied, 'but that friendship does not extend to Arthelas. Are we clear about that?'

Lethralmir's expression was contrite, as if the notion of disobeying his prince was utterly beyond comprehension.

'Of course.'

In truth, the blade-master masked his furious chagrin, even keeping it from his eyes.

Ithalred was about to speak again, when he noticed a dwarf, one of the captains from the war council, watching them.

HAGGAR DIDN'T SPEAK the elf tongue, so he couldn't understand what the two nobles were saying. He had heard the name 'Arthelas' though, and it was apparent from their body language and tone that the elves were arguing. Upon seeing him they quickly became silent and went their separate ways. Haggar watched them go. Something wasn't right, and dissension on the eve of battle was a bad omen.

CHAPTER THIRTEEN

A Field of Blood

THE DWARF HORNS pierced the air in a dour baritone. The pounding of drums joined them, signalling the call to arms. Elven horns resounded, too. Combined with those of the dwarfs, it was a discordant cacophony.

Upon the southern edge of an immense sloping plain, vast regiments of dwarfs assembled. Their iron-shod boots churned the earth, and their armour clanked loudly as they tramped into position. A battery of stone throwers and ballista were hauled onto the shallow ridge by mules, the beasts of burden quickly led away once the machineries were in place. From their vantage point, engineers and their journeymen assessed distance and trajectory, making calculations on stone tablets with nubs of chalk.

Hegbrak was set upon an isolated hillock nearby, the stout wheels of his Anvil of Doom sinking a few inches into the soft earth, the Anvil Guard stood silently in front of him. The master runesmith swung his hammer to work the kinks from his shoulder, before tracing his fingers across the runes on the anvil to sense its power.

Just below the lip of the shallow ridge were a throng of quarrellers, smoking pipes and loading their crossbows. Some looked askance at the elf archers waiting nearby, standing in immaculately straight lines, every warrior a mirror image of the elf next to him, their longbows resting against their shoulders with an easy grace.

A sea of armour spread out in front of the bows, an impenetrable shield wall of hearth guard and dwarf clan warriors with standards held high. Rising above them all was the grand banner of Karak Ungor, and

Haggar gripped it tightly as he muttered oaths to Grungni and Valaya.

Morek, fifty or more warriors down from the banner bearer, made his pledges too, for a good battle and a solid victory. His mind was conflicted though as he regarded the elf spears amongst their ranks. Led by the hunter, Korhvale, he hoped they would be able to hold the line.

A greater worry was the cavalry, far off to the northern flank, obscured by the glamour of the rising sun reflecting off their armour. Morek couldn't see their commander, the raven-haired Lethralmir, but knew he was there and felt his wrath deepen. He would use it, the dwarf decided, use it against the enemy. The hearth guard captain hefted his axe and awaited the call to advance.

BAGRIK SAT UPON his throne, several hundred feet from the battle-line on the highest point of the slope. Together with Ithalred, he watched the mustering with cold eyes. Dwarf king and elf prince were joined by their aides, diplomats and other observers, and shared an uneasy silence alongside one another. Each was protected by his own bodyguards and wearing their full panoply of war. Bagrik had a small cohort of hearth guard; Ithalred, despite being mounted, was surrounded by an array of heavily-armoured spearmen. Neither of them was to be involved in the battle. It was deemed too dangerous to risk them in an initial sortie when the enemy's strength was not yet gauged.

Ravens gathered in the sky over the battlefield.

Prince Ithalred scowled at them, muttering in elvish as he limned a ward in the air with his lithe fingers.

Bagrik sniffed at the ritual, dour-faced as the allied army moved into position, just as he had described in the war tent. If only all battles played out like those on the strategy table.

A GREAT CLAMOUR arose from the east as a vast and terrible horde came into view, observed at distance through Morek's telescope. Warriors decorated in blood, and clad in only furs and skins, hollered and raved. Men armed with blades fused into their bones, their faces bound in leather masks, and their skin studded with spikes, cavorted ahead of the main force. In their frenzy, the berserkers tugged at the chains that held them back, blood-flecked foam dripping off their chins from behind the masks they wore.

Snarling packs of feral dogs, their muscular flanks drenched in feverish sweat, strained at the leashes of their whelp masters on either side of the berserkers. One of the frenzied warriors strayed too close and was dragged down by a pack of hounds. His perverted screams were short-lived as the dogs rent him limb from limb in a grisly dark spray.

Hammered shields thrashed out a belligerent chorus as bondsmen and armoured huscarls tramped into view, laughing and roaring like madmen. The fierce din was eclipsed though by thunder as beasts swathed in thick, woollen fur and goaded by Norscans wielding long, barbed spears lumbered into view.

Morek had heard of the war mammoths of the icy north, but had never seen one, let alone fought it. He heard the slayers, given free rein to roam, roar with excitement at the sight of them. A death at the tusks or hooves of one of those beasts would be a worthy doom.

They are certainly ugly, Morek thought to himself as he regarded the mammoths taking up position opposite his flank through the dwarf's far-reaching lens, with their broad shaggy ears, long trailing snouts and beady eyes.

As he watched, Morek's attention was averted to the middle of the ragged Norscan battle-line, where a massive warlord astride another monster pushed his way forwards. He was a huge brute of a man, all brawn with sinew like rope. A black helmet almost encased his head, festooned with spikes, two curling horns surging from its temples. The beast he rode was a sabre-tusk, a muscular predator of the mountains. Morek had seen such a beast before. Feline, their bodies were an undulating mass of hard, slab-like muscles and their short coarse hair was grey-white to better blend in with the snowy peaks where they made their hunting ground.

Never had the dwarf seen somebody ride one.

Unlike the ravenous dogs, the sabre-tusk only eyed the nearby warriors that stood aside eagerly to let it pass. More remarkable still was its master had no lash around the creature's neck, no goad to cow it; the iron of his will alone ensured his dominance. Reaching the front of the horde he raised a mighty double-bladed axe, the haft of the weapon seemingly melded to his flesh, and roared a challenge. His army and the trumpeting of the mammoths echoed his cry. With the terrible sound reverberating around the mountains and across the plain the northmen came, and in their droves.

Horns blared down the dwarf and elf line as Bagrik, from his lofty vantage point, gave the order to advance.

The drums of the hearth guard beat loud and steady in response, a slow rhythm to guide the pace of the refused flank. The sound echoed inside Morek's helmet as the dwarfs began to move.

'Stay together, forward in good order,' Morek bellowed down the line, and heard the other captains echo him. 'We'll drive these dogs back to sea,' he promised, to a resounding cheer, his gaze on the closing Norscan hordes. Baying and howling, these depraved men were indeed the hellish beasts he had supposed them to be, and for a moment Morek's bravado held in his throat.

'Cold beer and soft rinns to any dwarf that stands with me,' he cried, finding his voice at last. More cheers erupted from the ranks. Only the longbeards grumbled, bemoaning falling standards and the bullishness of youth.

Still wet from the last vestiges of thawing winter, the wide plain shimmered in the morning sunlight as the elven cavalry began to canter, their shrilling war horns signalling the attack.

As the hearth guard and clan warrior cohorts made their slow trudge across the battlefield, Morek made out the dispersed groups of lightly-armoured horsemen ranging ahead of the deep wedges of elven knights and chariot squadrons. He was told that these were the horsemasters of Ellyrion, and there were no finer warriors in the saddle in the entire known world. To Morek, horses were for eating, or to draw heavy loads, not for riding. These elven ways of war were foreign to him. But he could not deny their efficacy as the Ellyrians loosed swathes of deadly arrows and launched darting feint attacks across the entire left flank of the Norscan horde, slowly drawing them out to break up their formation.

The heathens responded in kind, frustrated at their impotency to pin the skirmishers at close quarters, with slingers and javelin hurlers, but only a few of the elves were unhorsed. Behind them, Lethralmir and his knights were closing, with the chariots in support.

'Too fast, too fast,' Morek muttered beneath his breath as he recognised the eagerness of the elven knights to whet their blades with blood. The northmen still retained their coherency and the ranged barrage had yet to begin in earnest.

At that thought the skies suddenly darkened and the air was filled with the shriek of thousands of arrows and quarrels soaring overhead. The heavy *twang* and *thunk* of the dwarf war machines added a deeper, more resonant, chorus to the cacophony of death and for a few moments the sun was eclipsed by a storm of wood, iron and stone.

'Ha!' Morek punched the air in triumph as the deadly rain withered the distant Norscan ranks. Tightly packed groups of bondsmen were skewered where they stood, feathered shafts protruding from their bodies like spines. Armoured huscarls writhed in agony as they were pinioned in twos and threes by the immense iron-tipped bolts of ballista, or screamed in despair as the rocks of the stone throwers crushed them. The carnage was relentless, but in truth it was barely a scratch. The Norscans continued to advance, in spite of the certain death that faced them, closing ranks and stepping over the dead and dying as their mighty warlord bellowed his rage.

Morek heard the familiar clarion of elven horns and his gaze moved northward again, to the elven knights riding up the flank.

The Ellyrian horse had withdrawn to allow the elven lancehead to attack. Dragon armour blazed red and hot as the knights charged, war horns screaming, and smashed into a thick square of bondsmen with all the force of a thunderclap. Northmen were crushed beneath flailing hooves, spitted on lances or cut down by swords as the elven mounted elite pressed their irresistible assault. None could get close, the elves' sheer speed and their shining ithilmar plate making them all but invincible.

Desperate to stem the slaughter, the cowardly already fleeing in their droves from the elves' fury, the Norscans unleashed their chained berserkers. Heedless of danger, seemingly impervious to pain, the masked warriors barrelled into the knights, blades hewing. Many were trampled, others cleaved amidst fountaining arcs of blood, but the sheer abandon with which the berserkers threw themselves upon their foes gouged a gory cleft of dead and wounded in the elven ranks, as knights were dragged off their horses, or had their steeds cut from under them by Norscan blades.

Morek observed the deadly skirmish with a small measure of grim satisfaction now that the elves weren't getting it all their own way.

Serves 'em right for going off half-cocked, he thought but was then forced to marvel as the knights marshalled their forces, one wedge breaking off from another to form a second wave with the newly arrived chariots. Together, they smashed into the rampant berserkers who were mown down by the chariots or scythed in two by their bladed wheels. Morek nodded his grudging respect at their prowess as the elves slaughtered the Norscans and reformed their lancehead to converge upon the remnants of the bondsmen.

With the dragon knights' small victory, Morek felt impatient for battle, swinging his axe as the Norscans closed.

'Come on,' he roared, the dwarf warriors echoing his belligerence.

All the way up the line the dwarfs marched, their elf allies small islands of silver in a sea of unyielding bronze and iron, whilst overhead the sky darkened again...

FROM ATOP THE slope, Bagrik watched the second ranged volley fill the air like a massive swarm of hard-nosed insects as it bore down on the advancing Norscan flank. Mere feet from reaping another deadly toll of skewered men, the missile storm struck an immense wave of green iridescent fire that surged violently from the very earth. Arrows burned to cinders and quarrels melted and died in the intense conflagration. Stones flung from the mangonels soared like scorched green meteorites through the wall of flame, cracking and shattering to dust as they hit raised Norscan shields.

'Sorcery,' spat Bagrik, as if the word left a bitter taste in his mouth.

The dwarf king saw Hegbrak come forward off the hillock, the runesmith's power grinding the wheels around and taking him down the slope. He heard the uttered rune rites captured upon Hegbrak's tongue as the runesmith's body was enveloped with the magic bound to the anvil. His hair and beard stood on end, as trickles of lightning coursed through it. A nimbus of raw energy, burning with azure brilliance, built around Hegbrak's sturdy frame. The runesmith, chanting all the while, focussed the power, channelling it into his hammer and holding it there for a moment before he cried out and struck the anvil.

Hegbrak's voice boomed like thunder, echoing across the battlefield as an arcing bolt of lightning was unleashed. It surged from the Anvil of Doom, crackling ferociously before it smashed into the oncoming horde that had been spared the arrow storm. Norscan bodies were flung into the air by the sheer destructive force of the blast, and a great smear of scorched earth and broken men was left in the wake of the terrible lightning.

Blinking back the afterflare, Bagrik searched the rampaging throng of warriors for the Norscan shaman. But before he could find him, a bestial cry rang out from the northern flank where the elven knights were fighting.

The bondsmen had crumbled against their attack, and fled all too easily before the rampant elves. The scattering Norscans revealed a bulky mass shawled with a crude tarp of stitched leather that had been previously obscured by the now fleeing warriors. Ropes tethering the mass were released and a gargantuan war mammoth reared up in front of the elves, trumpeting its fury.

Locked onto their inexorable course, the elven knights had no room to turn. Some tried to arrest their charge but were pushed forward by the warriors behind them or unhorsed in the carnage and trampled. Others rode harder with fatalistic abandon, their lances goring the flanks and chest of the mammoth. Colliding with its unyielding forelegs was like hitting rock, and the elves unable to twist aside crumpled against it, their dragon armour useless against such an immoveable force.

The mammoth howled in pain, swinging its tusks in a rage, stomping madly with its hooves. Further screams rent the air as chariots smashed like kindling against the beast or were upturned by its flailing tusks and snout. Knights, unhorsed in the suicidal charge, were crushed to paste, the gore of their bodies dripping from the mammoth's bloodied feet as they rose and fell.

Belatedly, a horn bearer tried to restore some order but the beast was running amok, the stabbing knights failing to even slow it, the denseness of the mammoth's furry hide repelling all but the most ardent of blows.

As they swarmed like confused insects around the creature, smashing into one another or being carried off by their terrified steeds, the bondsmen returned. The Norscans had regrouped and thundered into those knights and chariots that still retained some sense of coherency in the gruesome melee.

'GRUNGNI'S OATH…' MOREK breathed as he watched the slaughter from afar with detached horror. The anguished cries of the elves further down the line arrested his attention, tormented by the sight of their kinsmen being slain. Morek was more concerned with the fact that their northern flank was collapsing. Only the Ellyrian horsemen were kept in reserve, and their feeble efforts would not break the deadly grind in which the knights were mired. Even as they rallied to loose another flight of arrows, the Norscans unleashed more berserkers, who chased the Ellyrians down even as they were pummelled by slings and javelins.

Morek felt a tremor jolt him as it rippled down the line.

The elves were moving. Fast.

'Hold!' cried the hearth guard captain, 'Hold!' he implored them, but the dwarf's voice was lost in the madness.

Black, like sackcloth, volley after volley from the archers, quarrellers and machineries blanketed the sky. The Norscans were almost upon them now. Soon they would be too close to the allied battle-lines to risk a further barrage. Green fire flared intermittently, as the unseen shaman wrought his magicks, searing arrows to dust and fracturing stone. Hegbrak advanced in the face of it, keeping pace with Morek's slowly marching hearth guard. Lightning arcs crackled from the anvil with every strike of the runemaster's hammer. His face was set in a grimace of concentration, sweat lathering his beard as he shouted the rune rites with fury.

Still the elves moved forward, faster and faster, the spearmen eager to close on the foe so they could vanquish it and go to the aid of the beleaguered knights. Still Morek held the line, bellowing at his charges to keep pace and stay together. Haggar's voice added to that of the hearth guard captain, and the other dwarf leaders followed their example.

'Keep formation,' Morek cried, again and again, watching the approaching Norscan hordes, knowing that the time was nearing when they'd clash. He ducked, as the stone throwers flung a low barrage. Their deadly shadow had made them seem closer than they actually were and he reddened at his foolishness. Arrows and bolts followed swiftly and the eldritch flames of the Norscan shaman rose again to immolate them. Only this time a tapering smoke exuded in their wake, growing and coiling into a thick roiling mist. Clinging to the ground, the mist surged across the plain at a frightening pace, easily faster than the Norscans, and engulfed the foremost elves.

Strange shapes coalesced in that mist as it billowed into a rising fog. Morek's dwarf eyes discerned the lithe bodies of elf females, writhing within the bilious soup. The elf spearmen, ensnared by the tendrils of smoke, were seemingly beguiled. They cried out names in elvish – Morek could only assume they wailed for their loved ones – and more came forward, all of them dropping their weapons to the ground.

As the mist slowly dispersed, the dwarf saw the spearmen held in the embrace of the ethereal maidens of the mist, their expressions soporific as they became utterly enamoured.

'Valaya preserve us,' he gasped in awe and terror.

* * *

THE LINE WAS breaking. Bagrik could see it as plain as the bulbous nose on his face. Impassioned by the plight of their kin, the elf spear regiments in the refused flank had increased their pace; some were even running in order to close with the foe more quickly. Elven captains, the hunter in particular, shouted orders of restraint – Bagrik saw his dwarfs do the same – but it was as if a sudden urge had possessed the elves and forced them into desperate action.

'Is this discipline?' the king barked to Ithalred, who stood stony silent, a nerve tremor in his jaw suggesting his anger.

Slowly, but inevitably like a fraying rope whose threads could no longer bear a weight, the formation fragmented. Closely banded regiments drifted apart almost unconsciously, like floating islands in the grip of a turbulent sea. Where before there was harmony and cohesion, now there was disparateness and disorder working its way insidiously into the refused flank. A staggered formation of elven spear regiments jutted from the wavering line of iron and bronze like silvered teeth slowly being extracted from a giant maw. As they were drawn into the sorcerous mist, the elves became further stretched until even the individual units devolved into a ragged and incoherent mass.

The dwarf line tried to hold, but that only exacerbated the problem, as the elves pulled away and holes started appearing in the allies' wall of armour.

'Follow them, Morek,' Bagrik urged beneath his breath, seeing the danger for what it was. 'Damn the elgi!' snarled the king, heedless of Ithalred's presence and thumping his fist on the side of the throne. 'Damn them!' he cried.

MOREK GRIMACED AS he felt the taint of dark magic gnawing at his resolve. One of the hearth guard alongside him drifted forward out of his rank as the dwarfs' slow march brought them closer to the fading mist and the elven sirens dwelling within. Morek cuffed the warrior across the side of the helmet to bring the hearth guard to his senses.

'Back in line,' snarled the captain. Then Morek held his eyes shut for a moment as he tried to banish whatever sorcery was trying to affect him. When he opened them again, the glamour had lifted and he saw the maidens for what they truly were – foul daemons; female, but with their bodies perverted.

Wrists ended in claws. Pallid, scaled flesh, supple, but gelid and moist, shimmered with aberrant lustre. Their heads had crests or long tendril-like hair that thrashed and coiled in a serpentine fashion. Bent-backed legs ended in talons and the daemonettes' mouths were black like tar pits, filled with tiny spine-like teeth.

The acquiescent elves saw them too, but their horrified realisation was much too late as the daemons tore them apart with tooth and claw, gorging on their necks or eviscerating their bodies with perverted glee.

Those elves following in the wake of their slain kinsmen at first recoiled, but at Korhvale's urging found their courage and fell in to the attack.

Morek could hold his forces no longer. The Norscans were almost upon them and the daemonettes were slashing the elves to ribbons. A second wall of spears charged in, the hunter at their head. Through the spraying blood and the frantic flash of blades and battered shields, Morek could just make out Korhvale as he strode into the daemon ranks, his double-bladed axe swinging like a pendulum.

The hearth guard captain growled in anger. Their carefully laid plans were tearing apart like parchment in the wind. But just as he was about to give the order to attack, the reverberating hoot of warhorns erupted to the south coming from the direction of the extreme flank of the army.

From amongst a clutter of scattered rocks, those eroded by time and weather from the mountain, there came a ragged band of Norscan horsemen. Draped in furs, their sloped brows and muscled bodies daubed in tattoos and festooned with bronze rings and spikes, the warriors hollered and cried out as they rode their brutish, snorting steeds bareback. Wielding hooked chains, long-handled bronze axes and flint-tipped spears, the Norscan cavalry were heading straight for the raised slope and the allied missile battery with deadly intent.

Morek was caught in no-man's-land – halfway between reaching the elves and halfway from the beleaguered missile troops on the top of the slope. Even as he watched the elf archers, those troops at the outermost edge, trying to reform and face their attackers, he knew with stomach-churning certainty that they would not be able to redress their ranks in time. Without the bulwark of the refused flank to protect them, the archers were easy meat. A lightly armoured formation like that, caught to its flank and unable to bring its bows to bear would crumple against a determined cavalry charge, even one as ragged and undisciplined as the Norscans.

Morek had thought the mountains impenetrable. Yet somehow the northmen had found a passage through it and used that knowledge to outflank them. It was galling to think that these debased heathens had outmanoeuvred them. The allies would pay for their hubris with blood.

Yelling their feral war cries, the Norscans crashed into the unprepared elven archers. A paltry few were struck from their beasts by a futile scattering of arrows before the slaughter began. Irresistible, the Norscans ground through the elves like a plough through wheat, cutting off heads and flinging spears and axes with abandon. Bloodthirsty hounds, running with the Norscan horses and snapping at their hooves, fell upon the wounded eagerly, their wild eyes flashing as their maws became stained with gore.

Unable to weather the terrible attack, their ranks in disarray, the elves fled for their lives and the slow erosion of the missile battery began.

In that fleeting moment that heralded the arrival of the Norscan cavalry and the subsequent butchery of the elf archers, Morek imagined the entire back line crumbling like paper before a flame: quarrellers slain, war machines destroyed, the rear echelons of the entire allied army suddenly imperilled. The dwarf looked to Haggar but even in the brief lull of raging battle, he was too far away to be called. Morek turned to his sergeant.

'Narvag, take half the hearth guard and march them back to our lines,' he growled, even as the dwarfs were starting their advance towards the stricken elves battling the daemon horde.

'Captain?' Sergeant Narvag asked in obvious bemusement.

'Look to the rear!' Morek snapped, turning Narvag's head forcefully so he could see the Norscan horse and their continuing rampage, the dwarf quarrellers now bearing the brunt of their murderous attention.

'At once, my lord,' he responded quickly, ordering the horn blower to indicate the break in formation whilst shouting further instruction to the regiments now suddenly under his command.

Two cohorts, fifty strong each, separated from the dwarf throng and started their resolute march back to their lines and the now bloodied rise.

Morek's unyielding line of bronze and iron was weakened but there was nothing he could do. Drums pounding, horns blaring battle orders, the dwarf formation thinned to fill the gaps left by their departed brethren and Morek, with fire in his heart, pressed onward.

So close to the foe now, the black, soulless eyes of the daemonettes glistening wetly, the lesser northmen bearing down in their wake like wild dogs, there was but one thing for the hearth guard captain left to do.

'Khazuk!' Morek bellowed, ordering his warriors to charge.

The dwarfs tromped rather than ran, their heavy suits of iron and gromril armour clanking noisily. With the gathered momentum of the rear ranks, Morek's hearth guard fell upon the daemonettes with all the fury of Grimnir, even as the other dwarfs arrived in line alongside them, preparing to meet the onrushing Norscans.

Grunting, Morek took a blow on his shield, the claw of the daemonette nearly slicing right through it.

Valaya, they are fast... he thought as he was battered back. But the dwarf was not to be denied and clove the daemon in two, the runes on his axe flaring bright as they tasted its unnatural flesh. Black ichor drizzled from the wound like rotting syrup before the creature sloughed away and dissipated into the ether. A second daemon came at the hearth guard captain and he was nearly undone but for an armoured dwarf getting in its way. The daemonette eluded the warrior's clumsy strikes, its body undulating like a snake, before beheading the dwarf with a savage snip of its claws.

The dwarf's sacrifice was all that Morek needed. Still revelling in the kill, licking the blood lasciviously from its claws, Morek cut the creature in two, its waist spilling away from its lower body as it collapsed into a pool of ichorous sludge. With each daemonette slain, a puff of soporific musk exploded into the air, dulling the senses and slowing the body. The dwarfs held their breath against it and pressed on. The elves, too, had now reformed their ranks and were thrusting with their spears to deadly effect, impaling the screeching daemonettes before cutting off their heads.

The elves were swift and skilled, though the daemonettes matched them for pace and dexterity. Where the dwarfs relied on their resilience to bring them through the battle, the spearmen attacked in a silver blur, darting left and right, parrying thrusting, fighting together as one perfect engine of war. The daemons, though deadly, were few in number. Together the elves and dwarfs slew every wretched one of them in a few frantic minutes, but the cost was high. Dwarf and elf dead littered the ground. Sweating, some warriors still shaken from their efforts, the allies closed ranks. They barely had enough time to catch a breath before the Norscans charged them, axes flailing.

'Lock shields!' Morek cried, above the rumble of the battle.

A thousand dwarfs ramming their shields together rose in a metallic clatter. A similar cry echoed from the elven quarter, and they lowered their spears, forming a deadly forest of sharpened silver death.

Like a foul wave of sweat, brawn and brute savagery, the northmen smashed against the dwarf shield wall or rushed the elven spears. At first it was a massacre as the northmen broke against a well-drilled line of bronze and iron or became impaled on silver spear tips, but their sheer masses quickly told as the front ranks of the allies were torn into, screaming elves and dwarfs brought down by crude axes or dragged out of their protective formations and butchered.

A burst of arterial spray resonated in Morek's ears as it struck his helmet, painting the faceplate red. He finished the bearded Norscan with a blow to the chest, ripping out his axe afterwards in a shower of bloody flesh chunks. A second came at him; a powerful hammer blow to the dwarf's pauldron sending spikes of hot pain all the way up his arm. Morek grit his teeth and smothered it, punching the northman in the mouth with an armoured gauntlet, shattering his jaw. Jabbing his axe blade in the warrior's stomach Morek despatched him, before cutting the arm off a third and burying his weapon in the fallen Norscan's head. The agonised scream was loud but brief. The battle whirled around him, a blur of red-ruin and metal-edged death. A dwarf to Morek's left fell, a spear lodged through the eyehole of his helmet. Another hearth guard from the rank behind filled in the gap. Another dwarf nearby was slain, his fate unknown to Morek. The rear rankers came forward again. And slowly, so slowly, the line narrowed.

'Uzkul a umgal!' cried Morek, rending and slaying as his muscles burned with effort.

Death to men! The words echoed in his mind. Another foe looking jealously upon the riches of the Karaz Ankor, another enemy to wear away at his race, another that possessed all the savage barbarity of the greenskins, but who seemed united in their purpose of calculated destruction.

The stink of blood was filling Morek's nostrils. Hot fluid sloshed in his heavy boots. The dwarf was not certain if it were his or that of the foe. The clamour of battle had become an ever-present din, gnawing at his resolve all the while it persisted. Warriors fell. Swords and axes flashed. Carnage churned the once fertile fields of the plains, weighing down the flowing grasses and staining them crimson.

For all the careful planning, for the subtle tactics argued and refined, it had become little more than a melee. Survival was all that drove Morek now, that and the desire to reap as many dead as his axe could take. Ahead, in the growing darkness of a building storm, he thought he saw the flash of lightning from Hegbrak's anvil. It was followed by the roar of some beast that haunted the suddenly benighted field – the sabre-tusk baying in fury at the will of its terrible master.

In the madness as he carved and cut and hewed, Morek thought he discerned the aged standard of the longbeards thrust alongside the banners of the runesmith, together the venerable dwarfs having forged their bloody way through the Norscan ranks in order to bring the chieftain and his elite warriors into battle.

The runesmith's silhouette appeared in the flare of light, tearing back the layers of darkness that now suffocated the field only briefly. Another figure was outlined in the azure flash, one far larger than Hegbrak and astride a beast that seemed dredged from the depths of the world. Two great warriors, dwarf runesmith and Norscan warlord clashed and the ground shook with the fury of their thunder. As soon as it had come, the lightning flare died away and Morek could no longer see the epic confrontation.

Closer at hand was the fluttering standard of Karak Ungor, the dragon rampant still upraised proudly and defiantly by Haggar as he fought with fury alongside his warriors further down the steadily thinning line.

Keep it aloft, lad, thought Morek during a brief lull in the fighting. Keep it where we can see it.

As THE RELENTLESS minutes ground on, even the stoic endurance of the dwarfs was being sorely tested.

Bagrik watched impotently from the ridge as his warriors, both kith and kin, were slain. As he surveyed the faltering battle-line and the swirling melee into which the fight had devolved, his gaze went immediately to the raised slope and the plight of the war machines and quarrellers deployed there. But a few hundred feet away from his position, there was a deadly struggle being fought to reclaim it from the Norscan riders butchering there at will. The toll exacted in blood on that small hill had been heavy indeed.

By the time the cohorts of hearth guard had arrived, most of the elf archers were dead or had fled the field. Even now, they were being marshalled back by reserve forces and rallied for a second push. Ithalred's face had been grave as he'd seen them run. Of the two hundred elves, shimmering brilliant in silver and white at the outset of battle, a mere handful of bloodied souls, with robes dirt-encrusted and armour tarnished, remained.

Several of the war engines were damaged, though mercifully the Norscans lacked the skill or ingenuity to destroy them. But many crews were slain, journeymen and engineers that could not be easily replaced. A regiment of clan quarrellers lay cold on the field, having fought to the last, their defiance a bitter prelude to their inevitable demise.

With a roar of anger, Bagrik had ordered his bodyguard to enter the fray with the diverted hearth guard. Thus combined, the dwarfs had now almost cleared the ridge, saving what quarrellers and machinery crews still lived. Those few Norscan horsemen not dead or having fled into the rocks, were slowly being corralled and put to the axe.

Bagrik maintained his angry demeanour.

It was but a pyrrhic victory on what was fast becoming a field of withering defeat.

In the centre of the plains, now blotted from view by the blood and bodies, the boiling mass of the battle was reaching its height. Lines of bronze and iron were dwindling as the ranks thinned rapidly. Dwarfs and elves lay head to foot in thickening pools of their own blood, face down in dirt: dead, dying and dismembered in the swelling quagmire of viscera.

For a fleeting moment, Bagrik felt his heart emboldened to see such defiance in the face of an implacable foe. Even the elves, he conceded, were unflinching in the face of death.

Even the bastard Lethralmir had distinguished himself, slaying the mammoth with his arcane elven blade and sending the ragged beast thundering to the ground. Its death throes had shaken the horde, but such numbers could not be denied and even now they pressed the elven knights hard, trying to surround them as they fell back. The chariots were utterly destroyed, now so much broken white timber, shattered wheels and twisted elven bodies. Norscan hounds, let slip by their whelpmasters, gorged themselves on the flesh of their slain and stricken steeds greedily.

Though their torn and bloodied banner was still aloft, the pride of Ulthuan was slowly dying in the desperate and protracted battle.

'We cannot win this fight,' said Ithalred through clenched teeth, as if the admission pained him greatly. 'There is no honour to be gained on these killing fields.'

Another agonising minute was allowed to lapse before Bagrik spoke again. His eyes were hard and cold as he observed the battle. For a fleeting second he thought of Nagrim and his stone heart softened.

'I know…' he whispered.

With clenched fists, the dwarf king turned to one of his military aides alongside him. Even as he had the other dwarf under his inscrutable gaze, he still hesitated.

'Sound the retreat,' he snarled at last. 'Withdraw all troops!'

CHAPTER FOURTEEN

Bloodied and Bowed

RUGNIR STIRRED OUT of unconsciousness. The pounding in his head had lessened to a dull throb and the hurt in his chest was easing. As he woke, reality washed over him like ice water. He tried to rise but found he was still too weak. After several painful efforts, Rugnir relented and stayed down. He was still in the cave. It was dark inside, perhaps it was night. The smell of Craggen's broth was heavy on the dank breeze. The old dwarf hermit was nowhere to be seen, though. Rugnir assumed he must be hunting. Rumbling stomach complaining loudly, he hoped that Craggen would bring back something tasty to fill it.

Grungni, I need a drink, Rugnir thought at the aching in his back, the dwarf taking little comfort from the worn furs beneath him. Drifting back into a fitful sleep, he was haunted by the dead faces of old friends.

'MAY VALAYA GUIDE you to the Gate,' Morek uttered softly. Closing the dying hearth guard's eyes, he snapped the dwarf's neck.

Mercy was all he could offer the warrior. His wounds were mortal. Though hardy enough to recover from most injuries, there were some that even dwarfs could not live through.

The withdrawal from the field had been a bitter blow. The armoured line had retreated by degrees, those warriors in more advanced positions helping isolated units like the elven knights break free of the enemy. It had been ordered but messy. At first the Norscans had pressed the advantage but with the upper slope cleared of the foe and the quarrellers and war machines rescued, the deadly missile volleys began again in earnest. Withering fire dampened much of the northmen's bloodthirsty ambition. Bands of slayers, still eager to find an honourable doom amidst the carnage, swept forward in a red-orange wave, axes flashing. Two more mammoths fell to their sharpened blades, now gore-slicked and notched.

In the end, the Norscans too had been dealt a blow of sorts, their dead and dying numbering in the thousands. Though Morek had not seen the warlord again, he'd heard the roar of his commands then echoed by crude Norscan warhorns. Both armies, bloodied and bowed, had quit the field leaving it to the carrion, the mewling wounded and the ghosts of the slain.

The decisive blow that had meant to crush the spine of the northmen and avenge the slaying of Nagrim had finished a bitter and blood-soaked draw. In truth, it was no better than a defeat.

Morek tried not to dwell on it and give in to his anger. He wasn't wearing his helmet, and he wiped a lather of sweat off his brow with the back of his hand. Thunder rumbled overhead in the aftermath of the battle, but it was a dry storm that heated the air and made it thick and stifling. Certainly it did nothing to assist him in the grave task ahead.

Across the bloodied field of churned earth and broken blades Morek and a small group of rangers, together with the Valakryn, moved swiftly and quietly in the doom-drenched night. Dispersed widely, but always in eyeshot of each other, they silenced the enemy wounded or dispensed mercy to those dwarfs and elves that would not recover from their injuries. The few that might survive were taken away by stretcher bearers to the gore-splattered and bone-weary chirurgeons that awaited them in the makeshift infirmary tents.

Besides the throaty thunder, the night was quiet but punctuated horribly by the screams of the injured and the fatalistic moans of the dying. Trekking through the mud and destruction, Morek saw the hafts of weapons jutting from the ground like broken teeth. He heard the guttural curse of a stricken northman silenced by the wet thud of an axe. Morek turned to regard the severe countenance of one of the Valakryn. The robes of the warrior priestess were flecked with blood as she went about her business stoically. Elsewhere, crews of stretcher bearers were ferrying the wounded away. They trailed solemnly from the field, the devotees of Valaya holding onto the grasping hands of the injured reassuringly or whispering benedictions in the name of the goddess.

Mercifully, the northmen had not returned. Though the rangers ensured that if any did they would be heralded and then dealt with swiftly. The barbarian hordes had no time or compassion for the dying. To Morek it seemed a brutal culture. The dwarfs dragged the Norscan corpses together, piling them up so that they could be burned and some of their taint scoured from the earth. In part it was to ward off disease, but it was also because they'd retake the plains come the morrow and no one amongst the allies desired to march across the foetid carcasses of the slain.

As his gaze lingered briefly on one of the smouldering pyres, it struck the hearth guard captain that this army was a mere taste of their numbers. The dwarf shuddered to imagine the actual scale of the foe that they were facing.

The 'mercy parties' were well advanced into the battlefield now, the fires of the Norscan encampment not so distant or abstract anymore.

Tromping through the carnage, Morek saw a ranger approach him swiftly with his crossbow low-slung and ready.

'Ragenfel,' said Morek as the ranger reached him.

'Captain,' the ranger's face was ashen, his reply breathless. 'We've found him.'

Morek shared a glance with one of the nearby Valakryn, Hetga their matriarch. Her face was as grave as he imagined his own to be.

'Take me there, lad,' he rasped, gripping the haft of his rune axe for support.

Hegbrak lay across his Anvil of Doom, his back clearly broken. Shards of gromril plates lay scattered around him, stained dark with the runesmith's blood. His once proud beard was matted with gore and a deep and bloody gouge ran all the way up his open chest and scarred his noble face. Hegbrak's eyes were wide, his expression frozen in a rictus of agonised defiance. The bodies of his Anvil Guard and several of the longbeards lay strewn around him in various states of dismemberment.

'*Dreng tromm...*' the Valakryn whispered, and went immediately to her knees and wept for Hegbrak's passing, and the senseless deaths surrounding him.

Morek could see the horror in the ranger's eyes too. His wide-eyed expression suggested disbelief and the ending of something deep in his heart.

To many in the hold, much like Agrin his former master, Hegbrak had seemed immortal. Not so anymore.

'Ragenfel,' said Morek softly.

The ranger just kept staring.

'Ragenfel,' Morek repeated more forcefully, and the dwarf snapped out of it and turned to face his captain. 'Get the stretcher bearers, lad,' he added quietly. Ragenfel nodded curtly and went off to do as bidden.

When Morek turned back to the runesmith, lying broken at his feet, a tear ran down his dirty face. He wiped it away with his gauntlet. Already tired from the battle, the hearth guard captain felt his weariness deepen. Though this was not bodily, no; this was a weakening of the soul.

The Anvil of Doom was still hot. Morek could feel it as he extended a hand in the runic artefact's direction. The heat did not sear Hegbrak. It had actually kept the other Norscans at bay who might have attempted to mutilate him further. A veritable pyre of the heathens lay stacked around the runesmith and his slain guardians. It gave Morek scant comfort to learn that they had gone down fighting and exacted a heavy toll upon the enemy. The warlord, though, was not amongst them. Morek imagined the brute crowing at his victory, and felt a sudden rush for vengeance seize him. He and Hegbrak had grown up together as beardlings. Together with Kraggin Goldmaster, the three dwarfs had been firm friends since they'd each first held an axe. Now all of that was gone, condemned to bitter remembrance.

The arrival of the stretcher bearers interrupted Morek's reverie.

'Be careful, the anvil is still hot,' Morek warned the trio of Valakryn that came forward to lift Hegbrak onto the stretcher and carry him from the field.

'It burns with the anger of its master's passing,' said one of the priestesses as she stooped down, together with her sisters, to raise Hegbrak up. They bore him reverently. With a pang of painful remembrance, Morek suddenly thought of Nagrim and the slain heir of Ungor's arrival in the hall of his father.

So many dead... all in the name of retribution.

Morek pledged a thousand more until the debt of blood was fulfilled and the grudge against the northmen satisfied. He knew it would never be so, and that fact gave the dwarf captain grim comfort.

'Ragenfel,' Morek intoned. The ranger had returned with the Valakryn stretcher bearers. 'Round up six stout mules and bind the anvil with rope. I want it recovered from the field,' Morek ordered, waiting for the ranger to nod before following the departing Valakryn, Hegbrak carried between them.

MOREK BARGED INTO the command tent unannounced, stalking past the line of captains awaiting an audience with the king and then standing before Bagrik, his face set like stone.

'Hegbrak Thunderhand is dead,' he said, 'slain by the Norscan chief. His Anvil Guard, too.'

Bagrik paused in the scratching of his quill, the assembled thanes and clan leaders naming the dead so that their fates could be recorded in the book of grudges, and one day avenged. The list before Bagrik went to several pages, each name almost carved into the parchment with the vehemence of a vengeful king writing in his own blood.

Stern of face, the iron he placed there masking his deep lament, Bagrik added Hegbrak's name to the hundreds of others. A great many of the dead could not be accounted for. The slayers, cut down to a dwarf, were left unnamed. None in the war party knew them. Like so many of their ill-fated kind, the slayers were loners and had simply arrived unbidden as if Grimnir himself had growled in their ear that war was afoot. Their demise mattered not, it was a form of victory to the dwarfs' minds and in any case there were already more joining the cult, those who had fled the field to return in ignominy or had failed in their battle oaths. Beyond the king's tent, small groups of dwarfs were shaving their heads and dying their beards red. Stripping out of their armour and daubing their bodies with tattoos, they took up axes and swore their death oaths before the surviving priests of Grimnir.

Others, those besides the dead and the dying, licked their wounds and took stock of their losses. By all accounts it was a large tally, and a fell mood had descended upon Broken Anvil Hill as a result.

The elves, too, had lost a great many warriors. An entire cohort of chariots was no more. Morek had later learned that they had hailed from a realm known as Tiranoc, one of those that had suffered grievously during the elven war of strife. The land had been lost, engulfed by a great sundering. It struck the dwarf that these ill-fated chariot riders had been put asunder in much the same way. It was a harsh echo of a painful reality.

Lethralmir, much to Morek's bitter chagrin, had survived. Precious few of his silver knights and dragon armoured nobles joined him though, along with countless archers and spearmen. The elves had their own warriors prowling the battlefield, searching for the wounded, too. Their faces were cold and haunted, their dark hair fluttering in the languid breeze as they'd moved soundless and deadly amongst the fallen. The lines of their stretcher bearers had been just as long as those of the dwarfs, maybe even longer.

'Let it be known,' thundered King Bagrik once he'd finished scribing Hegbrak's name, 'that on this day was Hegbrak Thunderhand, Runemaster of Karak Ungor, slain by north-men. Ten thousand of their dead and the head of their chieftain shall atone for his passing,' he said, scowling, adding solemnly, 'Hegbrak will be remembered.'

The dwarf captains repeated their king's words with heads bowed, Morek amongst them. Every slain dwarf, regardless of his station was afforded the same reverence. All were to be honoured by their kin.

It would be a long night. Long and dark.

THERE WAS A palpable air of tension and barely suppressed anger about Bagrik's command tent early the next morning.

The king had wasted no time, once the Giving of Names was done and all the dead had been accounted for, in gathering together his finest captains and also summoning those of the elves.

It was to be a much smaller assembly than that which had met previously. For the dwarfs, only Morek and Haggar were present. As for the elves, Ithalred had preferred just Korhvale and Lethralmir, the latter captain present in spite of his injuries – the gash upon his forehead spoiling his aesthetically good looks.

'Abject failure,' growled the king to the warriors of both races. 'It is the only way I can think of to describe our ignominious defeat.' The words came through clenched teeth. There were no maps, no coins and no councils this time; just warriors, elves and dwarfs both.

'Had the elgi restrained themselves and not gone off like grobi chasing swine, the outcome may have been different,' said Morek, levelling his gaze at Lethralmir in particular. 'We had a plan, my king–'

'Yes, Morek,' snapped the king, before the hearth guard captain could finish, 'and it was found wanting in the face of the enemy. No single warrior can be made to shoulder the blame here,' he added, now regarding Prince Ithalred closely as he spoke. 'We were all culpable... All of us!' Bagrik breathed deep, the sound wheezing through his nostrils as he fought to stay calm. He then shifted in his seat at the discomfort in his leg.

'The bickering must end,' he told them, as his gaze drifted away to a different place, one where he'd rather not be. 'Nagrim's revenge demands it,' he rasped darkly.

'This horde is bent towards one aim, and one aim alone.' It was Ithalred who spoke, his deep and sonorous voice commanding attention. 'To destroy us,' he added simply. 'I saw it outside the borders of Tor Eorfith when we first fought these curs and I see it again now. There is a malign will guiding these beasts, and I do not speak of the heathen warlord, either.'

'The shaman...' said Bagrik. 'It is him of whom you speak.'

Ithalred met his gaze and perhaps for the first time since they'd met in the Great Hall of Karak Ungor, there was mutual understanding.

'Yes, but I do not think that the shaman is a "he",' said Ithalred, his face as stern as iron. 'I do not think *he* is mortal at all.'

'A *daemon*?' hissed Morek, scowling at the use of the word.

Ithalred looked at the hearth guard captain.

'Exactly that,' said the elf. 'Allied to Slaanesh, the lord of pleasures. My kin are familiar with its caress. The goddess Atharti bears much in common with it. We can all sense it. Those *creatures* that came from the mist are its hand maidens,' he added darkly, before returning to the king.

'I have been a fool, King Bagrik,' Ithalred admitted, 'encouraging the wilfulness of my commanders, even resenting your aid in the face of a common foe. It ends now,' Ithalred promised, a side glance at Lethralmir making it clear that this message was for him, too. 'The heathen northmen worship the Dark Gods of Chaos, but here one of their heralds walks abroad with them in human form. What's more he has chosen a champion, a vessel for their power. Make no mistake, we face annihilation. It was the same in the elder days when mighty Aenarion the Defender fought the daemon hosts of ruin and cast them back into the Realm of Chaos. You dwarfs, shut up in your mountain fastness, did not see it as we elves did.'

There was a ripple of annoyance in Bagrik and his captain's at Ithalred's last remark, but the elf prince ignored it and went on.

'It was only through *our* sacrifice that the world was kept safe. Is *still* kept safe,' he said, his voice impassioned. 'We can ill afford another defeat. I fear if we do, it will be our last.'

A snarl of displeasure had crept upon Bagrik's face after Ithalred had finished, and he spoke with his lip upcurled.

'Then we'll fight together this time. All of us!' His gaze surveyed the room. 'Daemon or no, we will crush these Norscans, we will crush them! So says Bagrik, King of Ungor! In Nagrim's name I make this pledge.'

'Then we will need a plan, my king,' said Haggar suddenly, the young thane clearly fired by Bagrik's rhetoric.

Ithalred smiled.

'Leave that to me,' he said.

'THEY ARE MOVING!'

The cry came from the dwarf rangers who had sat in silent vigil throughout the night and most of the early morning, watching the Norscan camp. The sounding of horns and rap of drums followed the announcement as all upon Broken Anvil Hill were made aware of it.

'Are you sure this is wise, my king?' Morek asked as he tightened the leather wrist strap of Bagrik's vambrace.

'Am I so old and infirm that I need the captain of my hearth guard to fight all of my battles for me?' the king replied.

Morek could find no response.

'Aye, it is wise,' said Bagrik, for him. 'Not so tight!' he added, wincing as Morek pulled hard on the king's gromril cuirass. 'Too much roast boar, eh lad?' he said with a half-hearted chuckle.

'Aye,' Morek agreed. Bagrik hadn't called him 'lad' since he was a beardling. The gesture was not lost on the hearth guard captain, who could not keep the sadness from his eyes, so he lowered them instead, pretending to check the king's weapons belt.

Bagrik had deliberately dismissed his armourers prior to battle, insisting that Morek be the one to help him don his ancestral plate and mail. It seemed fitting somehow, and Morek was only too glad to do his duty to the king.

'Then I will be by your side, my liege,' said the hearth guard captain, gruffly.

'You will not,' was Bagrik's curt reply. 'I need you out in the battlefield, driving our flank, not beardling-sitting an old longbeard like me.'

'But–'

'It is decided, Morek,' Bagrik told him, cutting the other dwarf off. The king clenched and unclenched his fists, rolled his shoulders as he got used to the weight and heft of his armour. Lastly, once his crown and helm were in place, Morek draped the boar pelt across Bagrik's shoulders, completing his panoply of war. The king clapped him on the arm when Morek was done, gripping it in his age-old fingers.

Dwarfs

'You are my best warrior, Morek. You have served me well all these years, but I crave one last duty of you.'

'Please, my king, don't speak like this–' Morek began.

'One last duty,' Bagrik repeated, loud and insistent before his voice softened and the stone in his eyes that had been there since Nagrim's death lifted for a moment. 'Just one. Look after Brunvilda.'

Morek felt like his heart was clutched in an iron fist, so hard that he was unable to speak. Instead he nodded. The movement was barely discernable.

'Good,' said Bagrik. 'Now go and marshal my army and let us write this last bloody saga together.'

THE NORSCAN HORDE took to the field amidst jeering and yelled obscenities. The few prisoners they had captured, dead and alive, were paraded on their banners naked, their skins a patchwork of welts, cuts and bruises. The dwarfs had their beards shorn, the elves their hair shaven as all symbols of respect and nobility were cut away like chaff. The thump of the massive Norscan war drums beat like a raging heart as they strode across the plain in a mob.

Morek's suspicions as to their numbers had been proved correct, as the horde seemed even larger than it was before.

The warlord, on the back of his feral steed, rode between two enormous flanks of bearded and slope-browed warriors from a dozen or more tribes. Surrounded by his armoured huscarl retinue, the warlord paraded like a barbarian king amongst the brutish subjects of his court. Guttural warhorns heralded him as the sabre-tusk pawed hungrily across the plain. The surviving mammoths trumpeted in unison, stomping wildly with their massive hooves before they were goaded into obedience.

Despite its size, it was much the same host as they had faced before, though the riders who had outflanked them yesterday were moving with the main army now. Morek had sent parties of rangers out into the scattered rock debris on the extreme edges of the plain to lay traps and erect barricades. It seemed to have persuaded the flankers into joining their debased brethren, the Norscan warlord favouring a full frontal assault.

The allies had changed tactics too, though, and it was a different battle-line that greeted the Norscans this time. The dwarfs and elves had drawn their forces back, all the way to Broken Anvil Hill, a good two miles from where they had deployed previously. Here, the valley widened, and the mountains fell away as the lowland became hilly and scattered with gorse and pine.

During the night, the mercy parties had buried broken blades in the half mile of earth leading up to Broken Anvil Hill and dug shallow pits festooned with spikes to hinder the northmen's approach. Morek saw one of the mammoths founder as its heavy footfall broke through one of the pit tarps, concealed with a light covering of earth, and fell, crushing several screaming warriors beneath its shaggy bulk. In the end, despite their efforts to raise it, they had killed the beast and left its cooling carcass behind.

Morek smiled.

Already, the fragile order of the heathen army was wearing down.

On the crest of Broken Anvil Hill, at the eastern-most promontory, the archers, quarrellers and war machines were arrayed. Just below, a ring of silver and bronze surrounded them as elf spearmen and dwarf clan warriors and hearth guard stood shoulder-to-shoulder. There were no cavalry this time, and none of the vainglorious eagerness to close with the foe. The face the mustering of dwarfs and elves presented now, was one of stoic resilience.

BAGRIK HELD THE apex of the half-ring of armour, together with most of the hearth guard and the longbeards. Seated upon his throne, he was afforded an excellent view of the battlefield. Haggar stood alongside the king, next to the throne bearers, with the banner of Ungor unfurled proudly, the fabric still stained black with the previous day's warring.

Elf spearmen regiments were interspaced evenly with those of the dwarfs, the proud warriors of Ulthuan facing the coming horde with unshakeable resolve. They towered above their dwarf allies but together presented a unified wall of shields and blades.

Casting his eye across the battle-line, Bagrik saw Ithalred looking back at him far away on the left flank. The dwarf king thought he saw the elf prince nod, so he returned the gesture. He was on foot, the hunter, Korhvale, at his lord's side amongst a thicket of upraised spears held by the elf warriors around them.

To the right flank there was Morek, the dwarf's armoured faceplate masking his expression. Bagrik knew it would be one of determination. Morek had never failed him. He led two hundred clan warriors, the hearth guard captain's presence amongst them designed to embolden them.

There atop their grassy hill, the crest of war machines and archers their tower, the locked shields below their walls and Bagrik himself the mighty gate, the allies stood in fortified unity.

'You will find the way is shut,' Bagrik muttered under his breath, as he willed the northmen to come. He would not have long to wait.

AS IF POSSESSED, the Norscan horde charged across the last few hundred feet of open ground separating them from their foes with alarming speed. As the barbarians closed, a dwarf warhorn echoed across the field. It was quickly taken up by the clarion of further horns, and as one the dwarf regiments in the half-ring marched forward. Twenty feet ahead of the elves, the dwarfs jutted out like an armoured reef before a sheer metal-faced cliff.

Volleys from the war machines, quarrellers and archer remnants punished the edges of the loose Norscan formations, corralling them into long deep ranks. No shimmering fire burned down the arrows and bolts this time, the heathen forces were too close.

With shouted curses on their lips, the Norscans crashed against the dwarf bulwarks like pounding surf striking the rocks.

'Hold them!' cried Morek, ramming his shoulder behind his shield as the heathen men pushed. Somewhere above, resonating through his helmet, he heard a clamour of angry voices as the Norscans found themselves locked in a meatgrinder, and there were no better exponents of a battle of attrition than the sons of Grungni.

The Norscans hammered against them, but the dwarfs weathered the storm, paying for the held ground in blood and sweat. But hold them they did. Even with their rampaging mammoths and suicidal berserkers, the Norscans were pinned. Such an irresistible weight of pressing bodies could not be withstood for long, though, and soon a second cry split the air, this time from the shrilling horns of the elves.

With the enemy engaged to the front, the warriors of Ulthuan swept forward in a silver wave, filling the gaps left deliberately in the dwarf breakers, before crashing into the exposed flanks of the northmen.

Morek felt the weight lifted almost at once and was quick to lower his shield so he could cut down his foes with his rune axe. The hot, copper tang of blood filled his nostrils and he revelled in it. Severing heads, ignoring the battering against his armour as the northmen landed desperate blows, the captain of the hearth guard was like a whirlwind of death.

'Uzkul!' he roared furiously. 'Uzkul a umgal!'

THE BATTLE HAD slumped once more into a bitter grind, but now it was one of the allies' devising, fought on their terms. But despite the battering the Norscans were taking they showed no sign of breaking.

Bagrik winced as a green flash of sorcery erupted in the darkening sky, filling the air with a sulphurous stench. A counter spell seemed to ignite the breeze as Ithalred's mages on the crest of Broken Anvil Hill cast their own magicks. Scouring the battlefield, the king could see no sign of the shaman's whereabouts. Instead, his gaze rested upon another foe.

The Norscan warlord was carving his way through the dwarf and elf ranks with reckless ease, cleaved limbs flung from every swipe of his fell axe. While this chosen one of whatever daemon that favoured the horde lived, Bagrik knew the northmen would not falter. The warlord was only a few feet away and as their eyes locked across the sprawling carnage, Bagrik knew what he must now do.

Tightening the grip on his axe, he roared to his throne bearers.

'Forward! Bring my axe within reach of the heathen's neck!'

The hearth guard shield wall in front of the king broke up instantly, the dwarf warriors laying into the bondsmen and huscarls with brutal determination as they forged a bloody path for their king. Any that broke through were cut down by the throne bearers or crushed by the following longbeards.

'Stay with me, Haggar Anvilfist,' roared Bagrik to his banner bearer who stomped alongside him, cutting left and right through the swell of barbarians with his axe, the noble standard of Karak Ungor clutched firmly in his rune hand.

'Nagrim!' cried Haggar. 'Nagrim!' And the dwarfs around him shouted the dead prince's name.

Bagrik used it, allowed his memory to focus his anger in a burning sharp point at the end of his rune-encrusted axe.

'You and me, north-man!' the king snarled aloud, lowering the face-plate of his helmet and pointing his weapon at the onrushing warlord slaying a path towards him.

Seconds dragged into minutes but at last the two titans clashed, dwarf king versus heathen warlord, the sea of bodies parting around them as if at some unseen command.

One of Bagrik's throne bearers was torn down before it had really begun, the sabre-tusk biting off his startled head after smashing the dwarf down with its brawny body. Bagrik felt the throne wobble as one corner was suddenly left without support. A black blur raced across the eye-slits of his helmet and he parried the warlord's blow just in time.

Grungni's teeth, he is strong, thought Bagrik as the force of it rippled down his forearm, jarring his shoulder. A second blow *pranged* against his pauldron and he felt the blade bite his flesh. Blood started welling in Bagrik's armpit. Never had the king's armour of Karak Ungor been breached so easily. This blade the warlord wielded was like none Bagrik had ever seen. Black, but shiny like polished glass, its curvature seemed to follow his forearm, veins of darkness visible like adders writhing beneath his skin, the weapon nigh-on melded into his very flesh. It rose to a wicked curve, flawless and terrible as if death at that stygian blade would go on for eternity.

A violent shudder ran down the throne again as Bagrik fought the black spots at the edge of his vision. Another of his bearers was ripped apart by a claw-thrust of the Norscan's monster. Unable to bear the king's weight, the remaining warriors collapsed, and Bagrik was dumped unceremoniously to the ground. The Norscan warlord sought to pounce on the stricken dwarf king, have his beast rip out his leathery throat and end the fight, but Bagrik's throne bearers were on their feet swiftly and rushed forward to intercede. They were cut down in moments, their blood-gurgled screams short-lived and lost in the battle din.

Their sacrifice had not been in vain. Bagrik was back on his feet, though he favoured his good leg and used it to support his armoured weight.

'Not done yet, you ugly bastard,' he snarled, beckoning the warlord on with his outstretched finger. 'Come then, let us finish this…'

Roaring as its master urged it, the sabre-tusk lunged for Bagrik's throat, ragged meat strips hanging off its fangs from its kills. The dwarf king ducked and shifted his body at the last possible moment as he went down on his good knee. He carved his rune axe up the beast's stomach, opening it and spilling hot entrails as it leapt over him. Though buffeted to the ground, his head ringing inside his helmet, Bagrik had killed the sabre-tusk. The Norscan warlord was wallowing in its pooling viscera. Shrugging free of the beast's corpse, the northman emerged swathed in gore. If he had a face beneath that helmet of black iron, Bagrik fancied it might look displeased.

'Like I said,' the dwarf taunted, 'just you and me.'

The warlord roared in anger, the sound erupting from his skull-encasing warhelm tinny and strange.

Bagrik matched it with a challenge of his own, struggling to his feet just as the Norscan began to charge. The warlord's muscled gait spanned the distance between them quickly and he leapt into the air as he brought his black blade crashing against the dwarf king's upraised shield. Bagrik reeled from the sheer ferocity of the attack, staggered back as the Norscan followed through and used his shoulder like a battering ram.

Bagrik felt every ounce of the brute's bulk as he was spun like a weather vane struck by a fearsome gale. The dwarf almost fell, crying out in pain as he shifted too much weight onto his wounded leg. The white hot lance of agony brought him to his senses and he realised, readying himself to receive another charge, that his shield was broken. He shrugged the shattered pieces of wood and iron from his arm, and took his rune axe in a two-handed grip.

Bagrik felt his heart thundering in his head, resounding like a rock fall, and his breathing came in laboured gasps.

'For Nagrim…' he rasped, as he marshalled his failing strength.

The warlord came again, but this time Bagrik stepped aside, or rather almost fell, and hammered the spiked pommel of his rune axe into the meat of the Norscan's exposed leg. Without waiting, the dwarf wrenched the weapon free in a bloody spray and hammered a blow against the warlord's head that should have decapitated him. Instead, there was a cascade of sparks as dwarf-forged rune metal met Chaos black iron and the two combatants were flung apart in a backwash of power.

Smoke rose from Bagrik's body in tiny grey tendrils and his armour felt warm to the touch. But it was the dwarf king that was triumphant as he got to his feet and saw he'd chipped away a piece of the Norscan's helmet.

An eye, shot through with ugly pink and violet veins, the flesh around it white and smooth, stared malignly through the jagged hole in the warlord's helmet. At first Bagrik saw incomprehension there, even fear, but it was soon crushed by rage.

'Now we're even,' muttered Bagrik and spat a gobbet of blood against the inside of his faceplate, afraid that if he let down his weapon to lift it he might not be strong enough to wield his rune blade again. Even as the black spots tried to engulf his vision, he held his axe as steady as he could. He bit his lip hard, tasting blood, and the pain kept him going.

The Norscan made to rush at Bagrik, swinging the dark blade melded to his flesh around his head in a wicked arc, when the clarion of war-horns sounded. The duelling warriors faltered at the unexpected noise. The ground was shaking. Cries of panic came from the Norscan ranks, growing steadily louder and more urgent every second. A ripple of discord passed through the horde, palpable to all. The northmen had begun to flee. Fear rushed through the army like a cold wave. As they ran in their droves, like ants deserting a burning nest, the vengeful dwarfs and elves cut them down without mercy.

Before he could try and rally the army, the warlord's huscarl retinue surged forward, presenting shields and stern-faced aggression to the dwarf king, before hauling their chieftain away. At first the warlord resisted, roaring in defiant rage, but as he caught sight of something in the distance behind him he relented.

Bagrik followed the Norscan's eye and saw the shaman for the first time. Shawled in ragged robes, his thin fingers wrapped around a staff of gnarled bone, the lone shaman cut a wretched figure. As he moved, slipping from the dwarf king's sight, he seemed almost serpentine, and Bagrik swore the shaman's eyes flared like the green flash across the horizon line, before he slithered from view. It was but a fleeting glance, a sense of agelessness and malevolence lingering in the dwarf's mind once the shaman had gone. The skies then darkened for Bagrik, and the blackness he had held at bay finally claimed him.

CHAPTER FIFTEEN

No Mercy

THE FIELD BEYOND Broken Anvil Hill was like a charnel ground.

Norscan bodies littered the blood-slick earth, cleaved by axes or pierced by spears. Mammoth carcasses slumped alongside them, being feasted on by the carrion that had descended in the battle's aftermath.

Held in reserve at the western approach to Broken Anvil Hill, and concealed from the Norscans' view, the elf cavalry had ridden slowly through the sparse copses of pine. Once the enemy had committed to the attack, their flanks fully engaged by the elven spears, Lethralmir and his knights had sounded their advance. Exploding from the treeline the charge of the knights was irresistible. The warning cries of the Norscan outriders had been much too late, the feral horseman and their brutish steeds swept away in a red haze. The relentless vigour of Lethralmir driving them, the elf nobles had smashed into the rear of the northmen horde and shut the trap with a line of elven steel. Beset on all sides, the courage of the heathens had cracked like thawing ice pounded by a thousand hammers.

Lances spitted with quivering northmen bodies, their long swords slicked with blood, the elf knights had cleaved through the fleeing horde rending and killing at will. Panic had turned to fear and in moments the Norscans were fleeing with abandon, trampling their own warriors in their urgency to escape certain death.

The will of the enemy broken, the dwarfs and elves had surged forward, intent on dealing them a brutal parting blow, before the order to hold the line was sounded and the allies cheered victory and shouted curses at the disappearing Norscan horde.

Drenched in blood and the bodies of the fallen, the field was theirs.

BAGRIK OPENED HIS eyes and found that he was in the bed chamber of his war tent. Iron braziers burned quietly at the edges of the room. The dwarf king sat up and saw Morek at the foot of his bed, swathed in flickering shadow.

As Bagrik awoke, two priestesses of Valaya emerged from the penumbra at the recesses of the bed chamber. They carried salves and poultices, smiling benevolently as they approached the king.

'You're alive then,' said Morek, a flare of light illuminating his face as he ignited his pipe.

'You look as old as I feel,' Bagrik replied, scowling at one of the Valakryn as she dabbed the purple-black bruise on his shoulder where the Norscan warlord had struck him. The other uncorked the bottled salve and began tending the cuts and gashes on the dwarf king's body.

Morek grunted in half-hearted amusement.

'The elgi's plan worked,' he said, somewhat begrudgingly. 'The cavalry broke the northmen horde in the end.'

'Aye,' agreed Bagrik, 'after we had worn them down. Let them have their glory. We know the truth of it–' he began, but was interrupted with the Valakryn's ministrations.

'Enough fussing,' he snapped furiously, making the priestesses recoil. 'Can a king get no peace?' A confused look suddenly crept onto Bagrik's face and he looked beneath the hruk wool blanket covering his body. 'I am naked under here!' he cried, face reddening. 'Get these rinns out of here, Morek!'

The Valakryn retreated, backing out of the bed chamber quickly with their heads bowed.

'Worse than Brunvilda,' Bagrik muttered shame-facedly once they were gone.

Morek chuckled, smoke escaping from the upcurled corners of his mouth.

'*I* removed your armour and trappings, my king,' he said with a wry smile. 'Your dignity is safe.'

Bagrik groused under his breath and threw off the blanket. Grimacing, the naked dwarf king struggled from his bed.

'You need rest,' said Morek, his tone expressing the futility of his words.

His advice went unheeded as Bagrik hobbled over to his war attire where it lay draped on a plain stone statue. He took his helmet, encircled by his glittering crown, and set it upon his head.

'Gather my army,' said Bagrik, his back to his captain. It was a bizarre image, the dwarf king standing naked in the firelight, just wearing his warhelm. 'Tell the elves we are mustering.'

Morek stepped forward without need for request, and pressed the king's tankard into his hand. Bagrik quaffed the ale in one thirsty gulp, belching loudly as he wiped the foam from his beard.

'Now we chase these dogs down,' he growled.

VICTORY AT BROKEN Anvil Hill gave the dwarfs and elves the impetus they sorely needed. Forged on the altar of battle that day was an alliance of silver and bronze that would not easily be undone. Suspicion and mistrust were washed away by shed blood and sweat experienced mutually on the field, the emergent camaraderie between the two races galvanised through shared triumph.

Winter still refused to relinquish its iron grip on the land as the dwarfs and elves doggedly pursued the fleeing Norscan horde through the snow-capped mountains, through drifts and icy winds. The spring thaw had begun slowly, the white shrouded peaks filling the lowland rivers with their melt waters. At Lake Kagrad, known also as Blood Water, due to its rusted sheen and tang caused by the copper ore embedded in its basin, the allies caught the northmen rearguard. Unprepared, and with the fight beaten out of them, a rout quickly became a slaughter and Lake Kagrad became the Blood Water in more than just name alone.

As the dwarfs and elves pressed on with their campaign, moving ever northward, skirmishes between scouts became common. After several weeks of this guerrilla fighting along the cragged spine of the Worlds Edge, the allies brought the Norscan horde to battle again, upon an immense and lofty plateau surrounded by the soaring peaks of High Pass.

Thunder echoed around the mountains like the angry cries of gods, and lightning tore the sky apart in brilliant forked flashes. Clouds gathered and the rain swept down in a relentless barrage, rattling against armour plates and helmets in a frenetic din as the two armies fought.

Ten thousand northmen plummeted over the edge of High Pass that storm-wracked day, unable to resist the sheer fury of their determined enemy.

The dwarfs formed an impenetrable wall of shields and marched forward resolutely. At the flanks, elf knights and horsemasters killed any Norscans who tried to flee whilst archers and quarrellers thinned the host that was being slowly corralled before the advancing dwarfs. The back ranks fell first, screaming as they were pushed into mist-filled oblivion by their fellow northmen. Death was as inexorable as the passing of the seasons. Those that did escape survived only by virtue of an inexplicable mist that roiled over the edges of the plateau and filled the stony battlefield utterly. Though they were still many, the Norscans had been cut down brutally from an all-conquering horde to a band of raiders. Yet, the Norscan warlord and his shaman had eluded them again, and whilst they lived the dwarfs' and elves' task was not done.

* * *

BAGRIK BROODED IN his war tent, a pipe cinched between his lips, still wearing his armour.

'This is not battle,' he muttered, undoing the straps of his gilded vambrace and letting it fall to the ground. 'It is massacre.'

The victory at High Pass was three weeks behind them and they were now travelling across country, having harried the Norscan horde across the lands of barbarian men and finally to within sight of the Sea of Claws.

'They are running out of earth to flee to,' said Morek, sat opposite his king in the close confines of the tent.

The dwelling was little more than a square-edged pavilion, much smaller and less ostentatious than Bagrik's tent at Broken Anvil Hill. With camp broken every few hours, there was not enough time to erect the larger dwellings. Most of the troops, in fact, shared makeshift bivouacs and were huddled together against the growing cold of the north and the icy rain that had persisted for six straight days.

'Aye, then I'll finish what we started at Broken Anvil Hill,' the dwarf king promised darkly. Since that day when he had fallen at the end of the allies' first triumph, Bagrik had sought his nemesis, the Norscan warlord, in every conflict. Thus far, he had been thwarted. His shaman, the supposed daemon that wore a man's flesh as the dwarf king would wear a cloak or pelt, was also proving elusive. It mattered not – he could wait. Patience was an easy thing for a dwarf. Bagrik knew the enemy he wanted was not so far ahead.

'Something troubles me,' Morek began, easing back on a stool as he regarded his king. 'Why leave the bodies behind, at the gorge I mean. Why leave Nagrim and those with him for the carrion?'

Bagrik's face darkened further.

'Who can say what drives these honourless dogs. I have more regard for beasts than these *north-men.*'

Before Morek could reply the flap to the small tent opened and a wet, bedraggled Haggar entered. He bowed once to his king and then thumped his chest in salute to Morek before he spoke.

'News from the rangers,' he said, breathlessly.

Bagrik imagined that the young banner bearer had run all the way across camp.

'The northmen are holed up in a vast cave that looks out upon the Sea of Claws,' he said. 'They are making their final stand there.'

Morek raised an eyebrow, quizzically.

'I honestly thought they would get in their ships and flee across the ocean,' he said.

'Be thankful they did not,' growled Bagrik. 'Both of you,' he barked, 'prepare your warriors. We march within the hour.'

* * *

ULFJARL SLUMPED UPON his throne, defeated. The noise from the Sea of Claws carried from the mouth of the cave as it boomed and thundered, funnelled through a wide cleft cut into the rock of the cliff. Salt-tainted air tasted bitter and cold in his mouth and every wave smashing against the deadly hidden reef near the shore sounded like mocking laughter.

The seat on which the Norscan now brooded was carved from the bones of his enemies. It was meant to be a trophy of his victory. Instead, it had become a painful reminder of his bitter defeat. Casting his gaze about the hollow cave, Ulfjarl saw his scattered huscarl retinue in the thrall of manifested daemonettes. Daemon and man in varying stages of licentious consort cavorted languidly around him, mewling, moaning, and crying out in pleasurable agony. His warriors were ensnared by the creatures' deadly charms as they flickered in and out of existence in the jade-coloured smoke hugging the ground beneath his feet. Ulfjarl refused their lascivious advances, only the force of his iron will keeping them at bay.

His army was beaten. Many had already fled. Those he had caught deserting he had killed – their flayed flesh was displayed on crude standards rammed into the soft earth around the cave mouth as a warning to the others camped outside, crouched silently around dying fires. Only Ulfjarl's loyal Norscans remained; the subjugated tribes were all gone. The mammoths were nearly all dead. Destiny was slipping through his grasp – the destiny that Veorik had promised him.

The shaman waited patiently in the shadows behind him, almost part of the thickening darkness of the cave. Though he had his back to him, Ulfjarl knew he was there. He felt Veorik's emerald eyes boring into him. The shaman's quiet displeasure was like insidious poison seeping into his body. Ulfjarl felt his glory fading, together with the favour he had garnered through the barter of his undying soul.

What had gone wrong? Had he not sworn his loyalty to the Dark Gods? Had he not shown his might when he had crushed the immortals and their craven watch towers? Had he not demonstrated his will during the slaughter of the elf army in the plains beyond their glittering city? He had offered up their souls as a gift to Shornaal, and the Prince of Raptures had repaid him with boons. Even now Ulfjarl touched the wound in his helmet with tentative and fearful fingers. Through the gaping crevice that the bearded king of the mountain had gouged in him, Ulfjarl could see the world again and the bright vista hurt his eyes. He had thought the meteoric iron was indestructible. He had thought *he* was indestructible. It was not so.

Only the bearded king of the mountain had ever hurt Ulfjarl. At first he had felt anger, a wrathful desire to rend and tear the diminutive warrior apart in the name of the Dark Gods, but then anger had fled, eroded by doubt and the threat of his own mortality. Ulfjarl was in disarray, and Veorik was no longer any comfort or guide. The Norscan warlord's strength, the strength of his rule, was slipping like the dread blade fused into his flesh. He felt it, the black glaive that had become one with his will, reject him. It was a constant struggle now, the black veins in his arm ever restless and eager for egress, to maintain his grip upon it.

The torches at either side of Ulfjarl's throne flickered wildly, their flames bent as if like fiery water rolling down a slope. Except... they were flowing the wrong way, against the wind. Ulfjarl looked up suddenly, his warrior senses prickling with alarm, and saw a sliver of shadow seemingly detach itself from the wall. At first it was like black smoke, an amorphous thing fashioned from the dark that crept slowly towards the Norscan chief like a wraith. Robes emerged from the dissipating smoke, curves and flowing lines that shaped a lithe body clad in iridescent violet. Only the suggestion of a face was visible beneath a voluminous cowl; the edge of a nose, the ridge of a cheekbone, picked out in the wan light.

Rothfeg, a huscarl still with some of his wits about him, noticed the apparition gliding towards his chieftain and hastily grabbing his warhammer charged the clandestine figure. Arms folded benignly across its chest, the enrobed one calmly took its hand out from where it was concealed in its opposite sleeve and Rothfeg was immolated by a flare of violet flame. The huscarl died swiftly, in agony and raptures, the fat of his flesh dripping onto the floor like wax where it first boiled and then cooled. Charred bone ash remained as the enrobed one passed the warrior and came before Ulfjarl himself.

Veorik had not moved. Leastways, Ulfjarl had not heard him move. The warlord raised a hand to stave off his other huscarls who had realised belatedly that their chieftain might be in danger.

'Ulfjarl, Chosen of Shornaal, you languish in defeat,' said the enrobed one, its voice androgynous, ageless and coming from everywhere and nowhere at the same time.

The sense of it was disconcerting and though Ulfjarl did not speak the language that issued from its mouth, he understood every word.

'Do you still desire victory and endless power?' it asked sibilantly.

Ulfjarl rose to his feet and nodded slowly, transfixed by the robed spectre in front of him.

'Slay the bearded king,' it told him. 'Slay him and claim your victory.' The enrobed one slipped its hand back into the folds of its sleeve and when it came out again held a long, serrated dagger. Carrying the cruel-looking weapon in two hands, the enrobed one proffered it to Ulfjarl as if in supplication.

Slowly, Ulfjarl reached for the weapon. He was about to touch the blade to gauge its sharpness, when he saw the leprous-yellow shimmer upon it and stopped short. Instead, reacting to his instincts, the Norscan took the hilt and handle in a firm grip. Removing the long knife from the sheath on his belt, he replaced it with the serrated dagger.

Seemingly satisfied, the enrobed one bowed once and backed away, melting slowly into dark ether as it became one with the shadow once more.

The ash that remained of Rothfeg stirred. Peering deeply, Ulfjarl saw the semblance of a creature within the huscarl's remains. Sobbing, chirruping in what sounded like debased laughter and writhing in agony, something manifested in that purple ash. Wretched and beautiful at the same time, the nascent thing grew at an exponential rate. Scartissue blubber, shot through with bruise-black veins, throbbed into a fat mass of flesh. Muscled haunches pressed outward from it, stretching glabrous skin and extending into saurian legs. Lastly, there came a head, emerging perversely from a crevice hollowed out in the blubber. Its eyes glinted wetly, either side of an equine skull and a thin, spine-like tongue whipped back and forth from its snout as it tasted the air. The flesh-thing reminded Ulfjarl of a giant flightless bird though there was the sense of something disturbingly human about it.

The enrobed one had left a second gift.

Ulfjarl got to his feet and clenched his fist. He felt strength there again. The black veins were no longer restive. Looking to Veorik, he found renewed purpose and knew what he must do.

Ulfjarl gazed down at his throne, raised the obsidian blade aloft and smashed the bone seat into fragments. In the flickering torchlight, he saw that his shaman was smiling.

CHAPTER SIXTEEN

A Final Reckoning

A BITTER WIND was blowing off the Sea of Claws.

King Bagrik was standing upon the war shield of Karak Ungor. Inscribed with ancient runes, the shield's gromril surface blazed with a polished sheen. Runic manacles clasped Bagrik's booted feet, steadying him so he could stand with his wounded leg. He wore a suit of gromril scale, and a mail coif beneath his crowned battle helm, the faceplate having been removed so he could better see the foe. Bagrik's rune axe was cleaned of blood and shone dully in the early dawn light. Its gilded glory did not echo the dwarf king's mood.

Over three months since he had left Karak Ungor. Countless weeks forced to endure bitter cold and spirit-sapping downpours. Seemingly endless nights camped in the wildernesses of the Worlds Edge Mountains, with sky and stars above his head instead of good, solid stone. Bagrik longed for the hearth of his Great Hall and closeness of his queen. All the battles against the northmen, the shed blood, the struggle to bring vengeance for Nagrim's death had brought him to this point.

This then would be the final reckoning, and Bagrik had chosen his shieldbearers with this very fact in mind. Morek and Haggar stood beneath him, shouldering the weight of their king as if he were naught but a feather-filled sack.

As he stared out to the sea, the rising wind disturbing the banner of Karak Ungor mounted on the back of the war shield, the dwarf king fancied he could see the shadow of monsters writhing in its stygian depths. Perhaps they had heard the call to battle; perhaps they too hungered for blood.

585

'This is where we'll end it,' he said dourly to Prince Ithalred.

'I will be glad of it,' the elf answered. 'The constant killing is not to my taste. Let us drive these beasts into the sea at last.'

The two generals waited in the no-man's-land, a few hundred feet from the deployment of their allied army. It was a bleak day, the platinum sky filled with the threat of more rain.

Ithalred was mounted on a white Ellyrian stallion, the steed encased in ithilmar barding much like the armour of its master. A dark mood was upon the prince, the grave look on his face made more severe by the dragonèsque battlehelm he wore, two great wings sweeping out at either temple. A long nose guard, fashioned into the dragon's snout, went all the way down to the prince's snarling lip.

Bagrik sensed that something else was on his mind, besides the impending battle, but chose not to voice it.

'Aye, we'll drown them all right enough,' the dwarf growled instead. 'This day the beaches will be stained in north-men blood. What are you seeking, Ithalred?' he asked, watching the elf as he surveyed the sky overhead.

'Ravens,' Ithalred replied.

'Ravens?'

'They bear ill-omen from the Crone, Morai-Heg,' the elf explained, though Bagrik was none the wiser.

'The skies are clear, elgi,' the dwarf king replied. 'Is that good?'

'Without my sister to interpret their signs, yes, it is good.'

The elf seeress had returned to Tor Eorfith after the allies had won their first victory at Broken Anvil Hill, citing illness and fatigue as the reason for her departure.

'Trust in this,' said Bagrik, patting his arm with an armoured hand, 'not in signs and portents. Are your forces ready, Ithalred?' asked the dwarf, his gaze returning to the horizon and the arc of coastline where the mouth of the Norscan cave was cut into the cliffs. Tendrils of smoke from doused fires drifted forlornly on the salt-tanged breeze over a broad expanse of frozen ground in front of it. Bagrik assumed the north-men were cowering inside.

'I yearn for battle, if only for an ending to all this, as do you, Bagrik,' the elf replied, facing the king. The many weeks campaigning had eclipsed their uneasy accord with solidarity, even something approaching friendship. But it had left the elf weary and with only bitter humour, as if a great burden weighed upon his mind and pulled at his soul.

The dwarf smiled grimly.

An ending to all of this…

'And yes, my warriors are ready,' the elf answered.

Bagrik's reply was gruff and curt.

'Then you had best join them now,' he said, 'for our enemy comes…'

From out of the mouth of the cave marched the remnants of the

Norscan horde. Their warlord led them, riding in a bone chariot that was drawn by some fell creature of the ether that looked like a fleshless bird, only more grotesque and horrifically malformed. In the warlord's wake came a pair of shaggy mammoths, the last of their breed in the war host, followed by a ragged trail of bondsmen and huscarl warriors. Slithering amongst the heavily outnumbered northmen was their enigmatic shaman, though Bagrik kept losing him from sight even when he was staring directly at him.

'To victory, Bagrik,' said the elf prince, holding up his silver long sword.

'To annihilation,' growled Bagrik, and clanged his axe against the elf's blade in salute.

Ithalred gave a snapped command, turning his horse away and galloping to where his kinsmen waited for him. There he would join Lethralmir at the head of the dragon knights, Ellyrian reavers and silver helms alongside them in three deep lines of elven steel. Serried ranks of spearmen and archers, stretching half the length of the ice plain, stood silently in support of the nobles, clutching spears and bows with determination.

'For Nagrim...' Bagrik muttered, once the elf was gone.

Tramping across the frozen shore, its fringes still rimed with ice, the Norscan chief called a halt and the horde stopped.

'They're using the sea to protect their flank,' Morek observed from beneath the war shield, once they too had returned to their lines.

'Why don't they come at us?' asked Haggar alongside him, a hint of wariness in his voice.

'Because they are outnumbered and realise that their doom is upon them,' snarled Bagrik, answering for the hearth guard captain.

'It is madness,' said Morek, taking in the paltry army that opposed them, a mere fraction of its previous size.

By contrast, the dwarf regiments were immense and stretched back into many ranks and across numerous files. There was to be no subtlety, no grand tactics to this battle. The dwarfs would march until they reached the enemy, moving as an implacable wall of bronze and not stopping until the northmen were dead or had been driven into the water and drowned. 'No survivors' Morek had promised his king; it was an oath he fully intended keeping.

'Theirs is a lost hope,' he added. 'They would be better off casting themselves into the sea right now and save us the bother of slaying them.'

'Enough talk. We march,' Bagrik snapped. 'Khazuk!'

'Khazuk!' cried Morek and Haggar.

The war cry was taken up by the dwarf throng and echoed across the ice-bound shore like thunder.

The dwarfs and elves moved slowly at first as they advanced to within a few hundred feet of the Norscans and came to a halt. Still the enemy did not move. By now the chariot riding warlord was lost from view. His huscarl retinue, mounted on their brutish steeds, concealed him behind their shields. Banners were raised aloft throughout the allied army and the armoured front ranks of dwarf warriors and elf spearmen parted to allow a long line of archers and quarrellers through.

'At your order, my king,' said Morek, from beneath the war shield.

Bagrik's gaze was unwavering as he regarded the enemy. No battle cries, no curses or threats. It was as if the northmen knew they were finished and had merely come to play out the final act of this bloody saga.

'Make them run the gauntlet,' the king replied.

Morek took a breath and yelled, 'Loose!'

A flurry of red-fletched quarrels filled the air, pitching up and then down in a razor-sharp arc. The elf archers let fly too, in perfect harmony with the dwarfs.

Faced with the oncoming arrow storm, the Norscans raised shields as one in an act of uncharacteristic discipline. Bondsmen came forward to protect the horses from harm. Such was the sheer number of missiles permeating the air that casualties were inevitable, but the northmen weathered the attack well and once it was over lowered their pin-cushioned shields and roared in defiance.

Bagrik knew then that this was a different breed to that which he had already fought. These were the last of them, the warlord's warrior-brothers. He smiled to himself at a sudden thought – they would be much harder to break.

'Another volley,' said the king.

Morek responded with the order and the sky darkened again.

And again the northmen raised shields and did not falter in the face of whickering death from above. Instead, once the deadly rain was done, they charged, parting like a ragged wave as they ran and allowing the mammoths through their ranks. The earth shook as the beasts of the northern wastes tromped forward. Snapping hounds, let loose by their whelp masters, bounded in front of them. Swarms of hirsute and tattooed bondsmen marauders followed in their wake whirling axes and hammers, the masked berserkers amongst them. After that there came the armoured huscarls on foot, skull-faced death masks grinning madly as they ran in perfect formation. The mounted warriors were content to canter slowly behind the horde alongside their chieftain, and allow the foot-sloggers to bear the brunt of their enemy's initial wrath.

The allies responded with steel-fanged death, the elves loosing with such swiftness that the dwarfs could scarcely see, let alone try to match.

Peppered by a swathe of bolts and arrows, one of the mammoths rocked unsteadily. Its fore-feet collapsed in front of it and it fell hard onto the frozen ground, driving a furrow into the earth with its bloodied snout until at last the beast came to a dead stop and expired.

Within bow range themselves, the Norscans retaliated, small groups of bondsmen archers checking their runs and loosing off arrows into the dwarf and elf ranks. A scattering of warriors fell to their attacks, their death screams raking the air, but it was as nothing. Sling stones and javelins followed, and the unprotected allied missile troops took further casualties.

Bagrik was about to order the quarrellers back when an ululating cry ripped from the northmen ranks, and there was his nemesis – the Norscan warlord atop his chariot of bone, armoured riders trailing behind their chieftain towards the dwarf left flank.

'Take him down!' Bagrik cried, suddenly impotent in the thickly serried dwarf centre. Somehow, the Norscan warlord had manoeuvred behind his horde's advance and slipped from sight to strike at a weaker point in the dwarf king's wall of bronze.

The quarrellers aimed and shot but the few bolts that struck spun away from the hardened frame of the macabre war machine. The daemon beast driving it, charging like a flightless bird, carried the Norscan with unearthly swiftness.

Fast, thought Bagrik with sudden concern as he watched the chariot eat up the ground between him and the dwarf line like it was nothing; too fast!

'Quarrellers, fall back!' thundered the king, 'Armour… For-ward!'

Too late, the dwarf crossbows started their retreat. The chariot struck, scythed wheels churning a bloody path into the quarrellers and punching right through to the slow-moving hearth guard and clan warriors behind. The sudden assault shook the front ranks of the dwarf flank as they were spun and cleaved and crushed.

Laying about him, the warlord severed heads and limbs with enraged abandon. There was no time for the dwarfs to regroup as the mounted huscarls charged in after their warlord, exploiting the sudden gap in the shield wall, slaying the battered and exposed warriors in a blur of bloodshed and pitted metal blades.

From the far opposite flank, an elven battle cry tore into the building maelstrom. Ithalred and his knights were on the move. Bagrik saw them canter at first, then peel away and charge towards the approaching mass of northmen foot-sloggers, pennants snapping gloriously in the rising wind from their raised lances.

It was a call to arms, and slowly at first, but with gathering momentum, the allies not already engaged advanced forward. Though laboured, the dwarf warriors kept a steady pace, their armour clanking loudly as they picked up speed.

Closer and closer they came to the jeering northmen who barrelled at them from the opposite direction, war cries building to a crescendo.

The dwarfs roared in anger, while the elves gave voice to their own fury.

The din of clashing metal rose up like a thunderhead of sound as the armies met in a cauldron of blood and death.

* * *

BLADES FLASHED BY in a frenzy of motion. Screams filled the air that was redolent with sweat and breathless anger. Rage came like a wave, tempered by fear. The noise of war and the cries of furious desperation fuelled by a desire to kill, to live, gathered to a tumult. Death, endless death, reigned on the blood-soaked ice.

'Onward!' raged Bagrik, hacking down either side of his war shield as he and his hearth guard carved up a horde of bondsmen. Beneath the king, Morek and Haggar slew with all the fury of Grimnir reborn.

'None survive!' snarled the king as he buried his axe in the skull of a passing northman.

'Slay them all!' A second blow sent a severed bondsman head spinning off into the throbbing mass, a gory fountain erupting from his cleaved neck. Hate took Bagrik over as he spat diatribes against the Norscans and butchered the host.

From the corner of his eye, an arterial spray impeding his vision for a moment, Bagrik saw the chariot-riding warlord shredding the left flank. Such was the speed and ferocity of his daemon-driven war machine, the dwarfs arrayed against him could scarcely land a blow. They were dwindling slowly, yet the warlord's murderous vigour showed no sign of ebbing.

'Take me there,' said Bagrik, pointing his axe at the chariot as it scythed through the thinning throng of dwarfs. 'Morek, Haggar… for Grungni!' he thundered.

The dwarf thanes turned in their advance, the small cohort of hearth guard turning with them, and headed for the distant flank cutting a gore-soaked swathe through the horde. Bondsmen and huscarls were everywhere. Morek and Haggar parried, and hewed, and roared, driving through the Norscan mass like a battering ram. None that came before their blades, or the blade of their king, lived.

Morek sang, loud and strong, the sagas of the old heroes: of Skanir Helgenfell as he fought the Bloodtooth Tribe on the slopes of Ungor; of Duganar Umbrikson, slayer of the Green Wyrm; and of Thengaz Stonespike, saviour of the underway, who fought a horde of rampaging trolls single-handed. Haggar joined him, and the mournful dirge punctuated every blow, every axe fall.

Though impossible in the clamour, it was as if the Norscan warlord heard the war song, turning as he did in his bloody rampage. His swollen eye, staring wildly through the gap in his black iron helmet, found Bagrik and his thanes. Now he came for them.

The Norscan warlord drove headlong at the dwarf king, even cutting through his own warriors to reach him. His first charge rushed by like caged lightning, scythed wheels *pranging* violently against the axes of Bagrik and his thanes. Several of the hearth guard were crushed or eviscerated by the whirling blades. A severed dwarf head bounced off the bloody war shield.

Unwilling to be mown down by the irresistible chariot, the bondsmen and huscarls clamouring around Bagrik and his hearth guard withdrew. In their zeal to close with the Norscan warlord, the dwarfs had ventured deep into the enemy ranks and the small knot of warriors, shields facing in every direction, was like a bronze island surrounded by foes.

Reaching the end of the open ground that had suddenly appeared around him, the Norscan warlord turned his chariot and charged again. The attack came swiftly, and more dwarf warriors fell to the chariot blades without even striking back. Bagrik and his thanes were staggered by the brutal assault and the dwarf king nearly fell.

'While he rides that machine, we cannot touch the heathen,' said Morek, breathing hard from below the war shield. 'We need to upend him.'

Bagrik scowled as the foe rode out his momentum, gathering speed for another deadly pass. He quickly regarded the handful of hearth guard warriors that remained. From the edge of his vision, he saw the distant lancehead of elven knights falter, Prince Ithalred clutching his throat suddenly as if being strangled. The elf fell from his steed and was lost from view. He was in peril and the elf lay prone. This final reckoning was not unfolding as Bagrik had envisioned.

'Set me down,' he snarled at his thanes, returning to his own battle.

'My king, you can barely walk,' said Morek.

'Do it!' snapped Bagrik, ignoring the hearth guard captain's protests.

The thanes obeyed and put the war shield on the ground, the hearth guard that were left locking their shields together in a feeble wall of bronze and iron in front of them. Quickly, they unclasped the manacles around Bagrik's boots and the king hobbled off the shield to stand with his thanes. Looking over the shield wall, Bagrik saw that the Norscan warlord had whirled around and was coming again.

'Crouch down,' he said, stowing his axe and gripping the lip of the massive war shield with both hands. 'Here and here,' he added, nodding to either side for the thanes to follow his lead.

Stowing their blades, Haggar first yanking the banner of Ungor free and ramming it hard into the earth beside him, both dwarfs gripped the war shield like their king.

'When he tears through the hearth guard, lift the war shield up and get behind it,' Bagrik told them. 'Stay strong and don't give any ground, not even an inch!'

'We are unyielding...' said Morek.

'...strong as stone and steel,' Haggar concluded.

As Bagrik had predicted, the Norscan warlord smashed through the hearth guard wall, killing those unlucky enough to be in his path in a chorus of screams and showered blood. Beyond the slain warriors, he found a stern-faced dwarf king and his thanes waiting.

'Heave!' Bagrik yelled.

The three dwarfs lifted the war shield as one, thrusting it up at a high angle.

Carried by the momentum of his charge, the Norscan warlord didn't have time to slow and the chariot crashed against the gromril bulwark. Bagrik and his thanes roared together, ramming their shoulders against the underside of the shield, boots gouging into the frozen ground as they were pushed back. The crack of wrenching bone echoed dully through the metal, as the war machine lurched madly to its side, frame splintering when it struck the ground.

Gasping for breath, Bagrik staggered backwards and together with Morek and Haggar, let the war shield drop. It fell with a clatter of resounding gromril and was still. The three dwarfs turned on their heels.

The chariot was a broken mess of shattered bone. A spear of it impaled the daemon beast through its grotesque body. Ichorous fluid leaked from the wound.

Bagrik hobbled the few feet to the bone wreckage, unslinging his axe as he followed the long furrow gouged in the earth left by the chariot. He severed the mewling creature's head with a grunt.

Morek and Haggar were behind the king when the Norscan warlord emerged out of the carnage, skin cut in a dozen places but very much alive.

'Find the shaman,' Bagrik snarled over his shoulder at them, gaze fixed on his foe.

The clank of armour told the dwarf king that his thanes had no intention of leaving him.

'Find him now!' he snapped. 'Save Ithalred.'

MOREK'S FACE WAS set like stone. Haggar turned to him, unsure what he should do. In that brief moment, Morek saw that victory was close. A cohort of longbeards had broken through to them past the clot of bondsmen and huscarls. In the distance, he saw a band of triumphant slayers take down the last of the mammoths, its shaggy hide set ablaze by torches before they butchered it.

'Take the banner,' the hearth guard captain told Haggar. 'Lead them,' he said, pointing to the beleaguered warriors that had just broken through.

Haggar nodded, tramping back to the banner and wrenching it from the earth. Bellowing belligerently, he joined the embattled longbeards and waded into the fight.

'You,' said Morek, turning to the startled handful of hearth guard from the king's bodyguard that still lived, 'with me.'

Though he knew little of sorcerers and their distrustful ways, Morek was experienced enough to realise that their ilk often cowered in the rear ranks of an army where they could practise their magic unopposed. This, he felt in his gut, was where he'd find the shaman. Only a thin line of bondsmen stood between Morek and the rear echelons of the dwindling horde. Beyond that was only the sea. There was nowhere else left to hide. Gripping the haft of his rune axe tightly, he made for the foe he had in his sights, the name of Grimnir on his lips.

EMBOLDENED BY THE presence of the banner of Karak Ungor in their midst, the longbeards redoubled their efforts. As they fought the Norscans back, Haggar at their fore, a throng of clan warriors waded in on the flank, having slain a pack of vicious war hounds and their whelp masters. Together the dwarfs drove the northmen back, foot by bloody foot, to the crags at the bottom of the cliffs.

'Victory is near!' Haggar cried, determined to keep the banner aloft, the grip of his rune hand like iron. Blood spurting across his eyes, he saw one of the Norscan leaders raise a warhorn to his lips. A keening cry ripped out of the curled instrument, echoing discordantly across the craggy shore.

It was answered by a bestial call, throaty and reverberant. The sound of it hurt Haggar's ears and he winced in pain. From amongst the crags, from out of the shallow caves and dark hollows, monsters emerged.

Dank-looking skin, gnarled by warts, red scar-tissue weals and patches of discolouration swathed the tall and sinewy bodies of the creatures. Bent-backed with spiked protuberances erupting out of their spines, they loped forward in a gangling fashion. Long talons scraped against the ground at the end of rangy arms, covered in tufts of coarse hair. Flat ears, scarred and chewed, flared from ugly heads that snarled in anger.

'Trolls,' Haggar muttered with distaste, and knew that the fight was far from over.

BAGRIK SPAT ON the purple ash remains of the daemon steed.

'You need to find a stronger beast, north-man,' he told the Norscan.

Through the gouge in his black iron war helm, the warlord's eye narrowed in anger. He leapt over the wreckage of the chariot and threw a thunderous blow at the dwarf king.

Bagrik was taken off guard by the sudden attack and only just parried it. A punch swept in to his left temple and the dwarf blocked with his vambrace. Ignoring the pain seizing his forearm, he smashed his axe haft into the Norscan's stomach. It was like striking iron. The black blade flashed in a blur of movement as the Norscan rained frenzied blows against Bagrik's hard-pressed defence.

Waiting for an opening, after a second flurry of attacks, Bagrik smashed the top of his axe into the Norscan's armoured chin. The blow rocked him, and the heathen chieftain staggered only for the dwarf to shoulder barge him in the chest. Bagrik was about to end the move with an overhead strike when one of the warlord's huscarls from those gathered around them threw himself forward. Bagrik reversed his blow, stepping aside with his good leg, and cutting the huscarl in half as he charged past

screaming. His legs ran on for a few seconds, before slumping over next
to his steaming torso.

'Like I said at Broken Anvil Hill,' snarled Bagrik to the Norscan warlord, who had since recovered. 'Just you and me.'

KNOTS OF STRUGGLING warriors littered the field now, order and discipline
breaking down into individual combats. Morek dodged his way through
the scattered melee of isolated groups of fighters. Hacking foes as he
went, the hearth guard in tow, the dwarf captain reached the thin line
of bondsmen. Cutting through them quickly, the small throng found
themselves at the rear of the Norscan horde. Morek saw they were close
to the right flank, where the elven cavalry had split. One force, mainly
made up of the dragon knights, encircled the prone form of Ithalred.
Morek caught glimpses of the stricken prince through the legs of the
elven steeds. The second, led by Lethralmir, continued the charge, cutting through the northmen ranks with horns blaring.

Morek reasoned that if Ithalred was indeed ensnared by the shaman
then the wretch must be close by. He headed for the dragon knights. It
wasn't long before the dwarf got his reward.

Seemingly alone, scattered elf corpses littering the ground around him,
Morek saw the shaman. Like summer haze, the Norscan shifted in the
dwarf's eye-line. Morek blinked, twice, three times before he appeared
to solidify. With his back to the Sea of Claws, the shaman gestured with
needle-like fingers as he worked his sorcery.

He was only fifty feet away.

'Uzkul!' yelled the dwarf, axe upraised.

The shaman twisted to face the dwarf. His movements were clipped
and rapid like a snake as he outstretched a hand with his palm facing
out.

Morek and the hearth guard had run half the distance when the shaman closed his palm into a fist and the Sea of Claws exploded.

Erupting from the freezing depths was a fell creature of the deeps.
A watery torrent announced the monster's sudden emergence, raining
down in sheets from its long serpentine body somehow held erect in
the thrashing waves of the sea. Its keening cry chilled the air around it
and turned the blood in Morek's veins to ice water. Silver-blue scales
shimmering wetly, the ice drake glared down at the pathetic dwarfs,
its black orbs full of malign intelligence. Lowering its saurian snout,
the monster opened its mouth, baring fangs. Its breath smelled like
cold copper and rotting fish.

'Valaya's mercy,' breathed Morek, rigid with terror, as he realised he
was already dead.

ANOTHER LONGBEARD LOST his head as a troll bit it off. Most of the clan
warriors were already dead, so too were the Norscan bondsmen, as

many eaten by the monsters as were slain by the dwarfs. Slowly, Haggar and the remaining longbeards were being forced back. One of the trolls reached for him, acidic drool dripping from its bottom lip that hissed as it struck the ground. Haggar hacked off its claw at the wrist. The creature squealed in agony, before the dwarf thane lunged forward and put his axe blade into its misshapen skull. The monster fell back, and was trampled by its ravenous kin.

To his right, Haggar saw a wretched plume of bile and fluids erupt from a troll's extended maw. Awash with the foul acid, a longbeard went down screaming. Another lost an arm as one of the monsters, its flesh already knitting together from the stomach wound the longbeard had delivered, ripped through his upraised shield and staved in his head.

'For Ungor!' Haggar cried, determined not to let his clan's honour slip again. But it was an impossible task. For every troll they slew, another with its wounds regenerated, came back at them.

'Hold the line in the name of the king!' he yelled, hoping that Morek was faring better.

MOREK WAS DEAD. Bones smashed against the ice-hard earth, blood oozing from his armour where the monster of the deep had mauled him.

Or so the dwarf had imagined his fate until he was thrown aside, the ice drake diving downwards like a spear. Chunks of rock and frozen debris erupted from the impact as the dwarf felt himself skidding on his armoured stomach across the ice-slick ground.

Slightly dazed, Morek came to his senses and found he was staring into the stern face of the elf bodyguard Korhvale. The dwarf captain nodded reluctant thanks, inwardly chagrined at being saved by an elf. The king may have found some peace with the fey creatures from across the sea; Morek had not.

Struggling to his feet, he saw that the hearth guard were up too, and charged the ice drake as it lurched upwards for another strike. Morek was running towards them, Korhvale in tow, when a blast of freezing air roared from the monster's gaping maw. Three of the charging hearth guard were frozen solid, weapons raised in attack. Surging forward like silver lightning, the last of the dwarfs was snapped up in the creature's jaws and devoured before he even had time to scream.

Morek ground to a halt, watching the beast warily as it rose up like a scaled column and chugged the hearth guard's body down its gullet.

'We must kill that thing,' he said to Korhvale, standing alongside him. From the corner of his eye, Morek saw that the shaman's attention was back on the elven prince.

'And that bastard is next,' he added, pointing him out.

The White Lion nodded, eyes flicking quickly from the shaman and back to the ice drake.

'One of us must try to distract it–' Morek began, but Korhvale was already running towards the beast. Upon seeing fresh prey the ice drake darted towards the elf, opening its hungry mouth for another morsel.

The creature was inhumanly fast.

Korhvale was faster. He sprang forward as the ice drake came for him, rolling beneath its jaws as they clamped thin air. Korhvale came out of the roll and onto his feet in a single fluid motion, unhitching his axe as he braced himself. The White Lion was mere feet from the creature, elf runes on his axe blade blazing white as he held it aloft.

'*Charoi!*' The dwarf heard him cry, as Korhvale brought his weapon down against the ice drake's neck in two hands. Scales sheared away like parchment as the blow went through skin, flesh and bone to emerge on the other side embedded in the rock.

The ice drake let out a surprised shriek before its severed head lolled over on its side, and the blood and viscera in its neck gushed out in a grisly flood.

'Or you could just lop its head off,' Morek muttered to himself, suddenly aware of a group of elves approaching.

'The beast is dead,' uttered Korhvale upon his return. 'Thelion of Saphery and his sword masters,' he added, gesturing to the new arrivals.

The elf called Thelion bowed curtly, his robes and trappings indicating that he was a mage. His warriors were a different breed however, clad in long coats of silver mail, wearing pointed helms and carrying great swords that were nearly half as tall again as Morek. Each one hefted the huge blade as if it were a feather.

'Sword masters indeed,' Morek said to himself. Muttering an oath to Grimnir for the fallen hearth guard, frozen and devoured by the slain ice drake, the dwarf turned his steel-hard gaze upon the shaman. He'd be damned if the elf was going to kill him, too.

A small band of huscarls, evidently seeing the shaman's approaching assassins, and having just despatched a vanguard of spearmen, charged Morek and the elves. The sword masters swept forward unbidden and carved the northmen up in a web of flashing steel. It lasted only seconds, dismembered limbs and impaled bodies already growing cold against the earth.

A cry ripped from Thelion's mouth and they surged towards the unprotected shaman, who now gave them his undivided attention. Korhvale fell in behind his kinsmen, a few feet back, whilst Morek brought up the rear unable to keep pace with the long strides of the elves.

Thin mouth curled into a snarl of displeasure, the shaman splayed his talon-like fingers towards the charging sword masters and a host of serpentine heads spat out on arcs of emerald fire. There was a gurgled cry as one of the sword masters was impaled, his impressive blade clattering to the ground beside his lifeless body. A second died with a flaming emerald band wrapped around his throat, armoured fingers clutching ineffectually at the sorcerous bindings. The last two sword masters were burned down like candles, their bodies engulfed in a green conflagration.

'It has power,' Thelion said to Korhvale and Morek, using Khazalid so the dwarf would understand him. 'Stay behind me.'

'A dwarf cowers behind no one, especially an elgi!' Morek raged, ignoring the mage as he strode forward.

An explosion of green fire knocked Morek from his feet, gromril armour smoking. Patting out the eldritch flames, the dwarf said, 'What are you waiting for, mageling, work your magic.'

At the shaman's bidding the flaming serpents snapped at the survivors, but they recoiled upon striking a shimmering azure shield.

Back on his feet, Morek saw that Thelion had stepped forward. Beads of sweat were dappling his forehead already as he forced the probing serpents back and flung a bolt of incandescent silver at his sorcerous opponent. The shaman caught and crushed it, the dying light of the spell exploding through the gaps in his fingers. He fashioned the writhing serpent forms into an emerald lash. Thelion cried out in agony as it wrapped around his outstretched wrist, bilious green smoke issuing from his seared flesh. Making a cutting motion with his free hand, an azure blade appeared and sliced through the binding lace, dissipating it.

'Go now,' the elf snarled, through gritted teeth. 'I can't hold it for long.'

Morek and Korhvale went around the mage, the dwarf flinging a throwing axe at the shaman's skull only to see it deflected by a glowing green palm. He saw Korhvale dodge an incandescent dagger, before sweeping his axe at the foe. Slithering away with preternatural speed, the shaman avoided the blow. Morek waded in moments later, a downward strike from his axe hitting dirt as the shaman's whickering body made a mockery of his skill.

Elf and dwarf threw attack after attack at the snake-like shaman, who twisted and weaved and undulated away from every one. Slowly though, he backed away, Thelion taking a painful step forward with every foot the heroes bought him. Thrusting his gem-encrusted staff into the air, the elf mage called down thunder bolts from the heavens to smite his foe, but to no avail. Using his body like a lightning rod, the shaman captured the ferocious energy and instead of being destroyed by it, released it back at Thelion. Struck by the cerulean barrage, the mage was brought to his knees. The last thing the elf saw was the shaman's eyes aflame with emerald fire… then there was only agony and darkness.

Morek saw Thelion immolated in a blaze of green fire. Finishing the mage seemed to take something out of the shaman, though, as Korhvale at last landed a blow, cutting a deep gash in his arm. The shaman staggered, dark green blood flowing from the wound, and Morek stepped forward. Sweeping his axe in a punishing arc, he cut the shaman in half, all the way across his waist. The two disparate parts flopped to the ground, spilling bloody intestine.

'Wasn't so hard,' said Morek once he'd got his breath back. The dwarf was about to congratulate himself when he realised that the shaman wasn't dead. The Norscan's hood had slipped off when the upper half of his body was severed. Beneath it was a serpent-like visage, utterly bald with scaled flesh, snake-slit eyes and fangs. The shaman laughed, forked tongue flicking back and forth from his lipless mouth, as his body shuddered. Morek and Korhvale backed away as the shaman convulsed and spasmed. Their eyes widened as something moved beneath his bloody robes. The thin, barbed tip of a tail emerged, growing steadily with each horrific moment. By the time they reacted, it was too late. The shaman lashed out with his new appendage, upending elf and dwarf.

Struggling to his feet, Morek saw the shaman had righted himself also and balanced on the thickening snake tail replacing his severed legs. As the dwarf watched, the shaman's robes fell away revealing a scaled body not unlike the Chaos gorgons of legend.

'*Mother Isha*,' whispered Korhvale as the snake-shaman loomed over them, its tongue lathing the air through its fangs.

Flicking out a talon, the creature sheared through the White Lion's gilded vambrace, severing the tendons in his wrist. Korhvale screamed, his axe slipping from his nerveless fingers. Blood began oozing through the shredded armour plate and he clutched it with his other hand to staunch its flow. Sweeping its serpentine body around in a swift arc, the snake-shaman took the elf's feet from under him again and put him on his back. Korhvale gasped as the air was punched from his lungs, and he writhed on the ground winded.

Roaring, Morek came at the snake-daemon with his rune axe. It dodged the first swipe, chittering in what sounded like profound amusement then raked a talon across the dwarf's face, putting four red gouges in his cheek and ripping off his battle helm. Morek shook his head, blinking back stars, and was about to attack again when the snake-shaman slithered towards him with blinding speed, sweeping his sinuous body around the dwarf and constricting in an eye blink. Morek grunted, dropping his rune axe as the snake-shaman crushed him in its serpentine coils.

The sudden wrench of metal filled his ears, and the dwarf felt his armour being slowly dented inwards. Despite himself, he cried out and smashed his balled fists against the scaled hide but the shaman would not release his deadly embrace. Instead, his glabrous head hove into view, a wicked smile curving his lipless mouth, sadistic malice in his slitted eyes.

Morek felt himself suddenly drawn to the shaman's penetrating glare, relenting in his struggles as sibilant whispers probed at his mind's defences, visions manifesting slowly in his consciousness...

An island wracked by terrible storms, its earth scorched by fire and drenched with blood...

An army of elves, hatred in their hearts led by a cursed and vengeful king…

A warrior of the line of Ithalred, fighting in the glittering host, a war cry on his lips…

A daemon, like a serpent fused with a man, run through by Ithalred's ancestor and cast screaming into the waiting void…

The image changed, bleeding away like streaks of paint across a slickened canvas, resolving itself into a new vista…

King Bagrik, lord of the under-mountain, stabbed by a poison blade…

A red-eyed goblin squatting on the throne of Karak Ungor wearing a pelt of beards, its kin capering around it…

Morek crowned king, Brunvilda in his arms cradling a beardling child, his heir…

Only Morek's innate dwarf resolve saved him from madness. Remembered pain came back and he growled in anger as the battlefield returned to him.

'*Give in,*' hissed the snake-shaman. '*Give in to the Prince of Rapturessss…*' it goaded sibilantly.

'Bugger off,' Morek snarled through gritted teeth and headbutted the snake-shaman hard in the mouth. Shrieking painfully the daemon recoiled, spitting out a broken tooth as it relinquished its death grip on the dwarf. Morek was dumped onto the ground and, despite the pins and needles forcing white hot pain into his body, took up his fallen axe and cleaved the snake-shaman's head in two. Without waiting, he ripped his blade from the cloven skull and hacked again and again, chopping the daemon into pieces.

When he was done, Morek bent over with his hands on his knees, a warm sensation spreading across his forehead, chest heaving as the snake-shaman dissolved into ichorous sludge in front of him. When he'd caught his breath, the dwarf walked over to Korhvale. Extending a hand, he helped the elf to his feet. He winced as he did it, realising that at least one of his ribs was broken.

The dwarf smiled despite the pain, the rune of Grungni that was inscribed just above his brow and usually concealed by his battle helm cooling.

'Now, he's dead,' said the dwarf, hoisting Korhvale to his feet.

Once he was up, the elf tore a strip from his robes and used it to bind his wound.

Morek stared around the battlefield.

'This way,' he said, already off and running.

Bagrik was alone. His king needed him.

BELLOWING THE NAME of Grimnir, the slayers fell upon the trolls with axes cleaving. Their death songs were like sweet music to Haggar's ears, and the thane made an oath to the ancestor god, himself. As they cleaved, the rampant slayers threw flaming torches, those left after the destruction of the mammoths.

Fire was anathema to trolls, their rugged flesh unable to regenerate if it was burned. The wretched creatures screeched and groaned in terror at the mere sight of it. Haggar marshalled what longbeards were left and set about surrounding the few remaining trolls, deliberately picking on the injured. Though formidable foes, once their will was broken, trolls were easy meat. The attack of the slayers with their fiery brands was enough to make the trolls panic and they fled, hooting and shrieking back into the caves. Not to be deprived of their worthy doom, the slayers gave chase.

'Hold here,' said Haggar, gasping for breath. He looked around and behind him, trying to gauge the stage the battle was at. To the distant right, the elf knights were carving through scores of fleeing northmen being crushed under hoof or spitted on lances. Lethralmir seemed to revel in the slaying. Nearby, the dwarf could see Ithalred being helped back onto his horse. Everywhere the final few Norscans were being cut down or driven to an icy doom, just as Morek had promised the king. In the middle of the carnage though, a last bastion of enemy resistance remained. Here were the majority of the warlord's best and most loyal warriors. Shields out and tightly packed, they were proving difficult to crack. Haggar knew that amongst the sea of foes Bagrik was fighting for his life. He knew also that they needed to hold this flank, ensure that nothing else emerged from the caves. Even so, the young thane was not about to leave his king to his fate.

'With me,' Haggar ordered, 'King Bagrik needs us.' With that he hared off, the longbeards muttering disparagingly as they followed, the banner of Karak Ungor swaying back and forth as Haggar ran to the throng of Norscans and to the king.

'HEH, HEH, IS that all you've got north-man?' Bagrik laughed, spitting a gobbet of blood onto the frozen ground. His chest felt heavy inside his armour, every breath an effort, and his old wound was now so stiff that he could barely move. Lamentably, Bagrik glanced at the dents and tears in his gromril scale from where he'd been a little too slow to parry the Norscan's blade.

Fifty years ago this cur would not have even touched me, thought Bagrik, using the brief lull to gather his strength. Only it wasn't fifty years ago, and the Norscan had cut him; he'd cut him deep.

In contrast the warlord was barely scratched. Every blow Bagrik landed was shrugged off or what should've been a killing strike manifested as a graze or nick. With every swipe, the king felt his strength fading, the power behind the blow lessening as if his muscles were atrophying aggressively all the while they fought.

One good hit, Bagrik thought, that's all I need.

In a blackened blur, the Norscan's blade fell upon Bagrik again, the brief amnesty in the battle having ended. The dwarf king struggled desperately to fend him off, knowing in his heart that he was losing. Blows rained in and Bagrik was battered to his knees. Gasping for breath as the Norscan sought to crush him, the dwarf king searched deep within himself for the last vestiges of his strength. There at the core of his being, he tapped into the one thing he had left that could save him. Anger.

Swiping madly, the dwarf caught the Norscan a glancing blow against his war helm, his enemy having opened up his defences when he'd believed that Bagrik was all but defeated. He spun on his heel a little, staggered by the dwarf's sudden lucky strike. Bagrik used it to his advantage. He managed to heave his good leg to a standing position, though the pain was crippling him, and with a roar of fury severed the Norscan's forearm in two. The obsidian blade clattered to the ground and shattered into glassy fragments, its power suddenly broken. Protruding from the lopped off stump of the Norscan's arm, his writhing black veins searched desperately for the weapon. Like a floundering fish gaping for air on the shore, the tentacled veins slowly ceased, flaking away into nothing.

Bagrik didn't stop. To stop now would mean death. He rammed the spiked pommel of his rune axe into the Norscan's thigh, tearing it open and felling the warlord to his knees. They were face to face. Bagrik snarled as their eyes met.

'Now you die,' he promised, aiming for the Norscan's neck. As he lifted the blade, he exposed his side. The warlord ripped another weapon from its sheath and stabbed the king. Bagrik felt nothing more than a pinprick, glancing quickly to see a serrated dagger in the Norscan's meaty fist. It was nothing. Even driven by the warlord's formidable strength, it had only grazed the dwarf king's flesh, slowed by his rune armour.

With a roar, Bagrik decapitated the Norscan. His armoured head *thunked* onto the icy ground and rolled, his body slumped over next to it pooling blood.

Then the poison hit. Coldness seized Bagrik's bones. Paralysis in his fingers saw the rune axe fall from his desperate grasp. The dwarf king reached down to the wound, though he could no longer feel it. The blood on his gauntlets, his blood, was tainted yellow. He gritted his teeth against sudden agony. Gripped by palsy, he fell. Barely able to keep his eyes open, Bagrik stared into the cold lifeless orbs of the Norscan's severed head. Huscarls still surrounded him. He could hear them closing.

ONE OF ULFJARL'S ambitious hurscarls, Heimdarr, had raised his axe and was about to claim the life of the bearded king, and with it lordship over the tribes, when he heard a heavy object spinning through the air towards him. Too late, he turned. Blurring silver was the last thing he ever saw.

* * *

'TO THE KING! To the king!' Morek cried, whipping his last thrown axe into the bestial brow of another Norscan. Korhvale was alongside him, severing heads and limbs one-handed with his hand axe, his wounded arm bound to his side, even as the dwarf barrelled into the huscarls hacking, punching and butting.

In seconds they had forged a way through to Bagrik. The hearth guard captain's heart held in his throat when he saw the ashen-faced king on his side, fearing his liege lord was dead. With relief, he noticed that Bagrik was still breathing, though it was with shallow, laboured gasps.

'Uzkul umgi,' he shouted, cutting down a northman as he dared to take a step toward the stricken dwarf king.

Together, elf and dwarf circled Bagrik keeping the foe back.

War horns rent the air as the back of the Norscan mob suddenly crumpled. From the north, Haggar emerged through a swathe of carnage with a band of dour longbeards. To the east came Ithalred at the head of his dragon knights, crushing Norscan skulls and cutting them down where they stood. In a few bloody moments, the battlefield was clear and the last of the northmen were being destroyed. Some were rounded up and slaughtered, others were harried into the sea. Desperately, these last remnants dove into the icy water. They only reached a few hundred feet from the shoreline before they were dragged asunder by the denizens of the deep, their screams eclipsed by the crashing waves. The Norscan beasts were burned, greasy smoke already staining the air black.

Satisfied the foe was vanquished, Morek went to his king.

'Victory my liege,' he said, thinking at first that Bagrik was only winded.

Far from it. The king was alabaster white. His fingers were shaking, eyes wide, as he hissed through gritted teeth, fighting to speak.

'Back to the camp,' rasped Morek, fear gripping his chest as he looked at Haggar. 'Back to the camp!' he cried.

ACT THREE
ELF BANE

CHAPTER SEVENTEEN

Broken Bread, Shattered Alliance

'HOW IS HE?' Morek asked. He kept his voice low; the king was only in the next room.

The allies had returned slowly and wearily to their encampment, twenty miles from the battle site upon a flat ridge overlooking the distant sea. A thin, lonely trail had led them down to the ice plain, now slicked with blood, and it was by this path that the victorious allies returned in dark mood. The camp was little more than scattered pavilions and sparsely dotted stone-ringed fires. Most of the troops had been committed to the final battle, only disparate knots of wounded and a paltry group of guards awaited the allies upon their return. Morek had sent rangers ahead of the war host to ensure that Bagrik's grand tent was put up, determined his king would have every comfort as he was tended to. The squat structure, smoke issuing through the chimney vent from an already stoked fire, dominated the flat ridge. Drifting in and out of consciousness, Bagrik had been taken there immediately and the Valakryn summoned in force.

'He'll live... for now,' replied Hetga, matriarch of the priestesses. She was a grizzled matronly woman, her robes and trappings cinched tightly around her impressive girth and bosom. Her long hair, bound into a tight bun, was once golden but had since faded to an elegant silver-grey. She carried several scars and much like her uncompromising appearance, didn't sweeten her words. 'The poison still runs through him. He's weak, but some of his strength may return given time. The cantankerous old bastard is awake though, refusing help

605

and banishing my priestesses from his bed chambers, the prude. Truth be told,' said Hetga, lighting up a pipe and supping deep, 'there's nothing more we can do anyway. Whatever venom was upon that blade is beyond our arts to heal completely. Only Valaya, bless her name, can decide his fate now.'

Morek's face hardened. He'd hoped for better news.

'Tromm,' he intoned, bowing his head slightly.

'Tromm, Thane Stonehammer,' Hetga replied, bowing too, and took her leave.

The hearth guard captain took a deep breath before he passed through the flapped entrance to Bagrik's bed chamber.

'This is becoming an all-too familiar occurrence, my king,' he said with forced good humour.

Bagrik muttered a reply that Morek didn't quite catch. He gestured weakly for the dwarf to come to his bedside. Morek obeyed the pale-faced king, seemingly more old and frail that he'd ever known him. Bagrik looked even worse up close. Dark blue veins were visible beneath skin that was white and thin like parchment. Liver spots flared angrily as did the harsh purple bruises where his dented armour had nicked him. The king's eyes, though, were the worst. Rheumy and old, sunken into gaunt cheekbones, they lacked purpose and vigour. It was if the angry fire behind them had died in the hearth.

Bagrik reached out and grasped Morek's tunic, dragging him close. It seemed the old king had strength in his body yet.

'Get me... out of this... damned bed,' he snarled. Every word was an effort, but Morek was still taken aback by the king's vehemence.

'You have to rest,' he told him, shaking his head.

Bagrik tightened his grip. Morek felt his collar pinch his neck and his breathing get a little more difficult.

'If I... am to die,' said Bagrik, gritting his teeth against the pain, 'then... I'll do so with the rock... of the mountain above me, not on this Grungni-forsaken plain... Now, help me up!'

Morek swallowed with effort, managing a nod as he hooked his arms beneath the king's and lifted him out of the bed.

'Enough...' Bagrik said breathlessly, content to sit on the edge of the bed for a moment to gather his strength. 'I need a moment...'

'My king, are you sure–'

'A moment!' snapped the king, cutting Morek off as he glared at him.

When he was ready, Bagrik nodded and Morek heaved him off the bed and helped him into his boots and robes. As he did so, the hearth guard captain saw the ugly yellow wound that had been caused by the poison dagger. It was only small, little more than a graze, but the flesh around it festered and stank.

It reminded Morek of what he'd been shown when in the shaman's thrall. He thought about confiding in his king but in the end decided against it. Bagrik had enough to worry about. Knowledge of the future foretold would avail him nothing.

'Throne bearers!' cried Morek, once the king was back on his feet and the crown of Karak Ungor upon his head.

Four hearth guard marched into the room, the king's seat carried aloft between them. When they reached their captain and the king, they set the throne down and kneeled, heads bowed. Morek assisted Bagrik as the king mounted his throne, then draped heavy furs, together with the boar pelt over his back and shoulders.

'This'll keep out the cold,' he whispered, pressing a tankard of ale into the king's wasted fist. Bagrik had to clasp it with both hands, but as he drank he straightened, eventually holding the tankard in one hand, as if some of his strength was returning.

'A good drop,' remarked the king, some of the colour coming back to his cheeks as he wiped the foam from his mouth. 'I'll need more if we're to travel,' he added, forcing a determined smile.

Morek filled the tankard. The king raised it to his lips.

RUGNIR DRANK THE last of the broth, upending the warm cauldron into his mouth, allowing rivulets of the thick soup to run down his face only to be sopped up by his beard.

Whilst in the cave with Craggen, time had lost all sense of meaning. Drifting in and out of consciousness, it could have been days, weeks or months. Rugnir simply did not know. He knew only that he had to return, and with all haste, to Karak Ungor.

When he was finished, the dwarf set the cauldron down and belched.

'You're a fine cook, Craggen,' he noted.

The old hermit was watching him from the shadows of the cave, smoking his pipe as ever.

'Perhaps I can recommend you to King Bagrik, upon my return, and once all of this sorry business is behind us,' Rugnir added, getting up from where he'd been sitting. At last his strength had almost returned, his wounds had nearly healed and he could even walk without aid. Probably believed dead, Rugnir was finally ready to leave. He only hoped it wouldn't be too late.

'There's a pack for you,' said the gruff voice of Craggen.

Rugnir turned towards where the old hermit was pointing and found a leather knapsack resting against the cave wall.

'Provisions,' he explained, 'ale, stonebread and the like. You'll find rope too, as well as a little pipeweed for the journey.'

Rugnir turned back towards the old dwarf and bowed deeply.

'*Gnollengrom*,' he intoned. 'I am forever in your debt, Craggen.'

'Bah!' scowled the dwarf. 'I'll be glad to be rid of you. Least now I can get back to the grobkul,' he said, shuffling off his rocky perch and tromping over to where the other dwarf was standing.

'Here,' said the hermit. 'It's no heirloom, but it'll kill urk and grobi right enough.' The old dwarf pressed the haft of a hunting axe into Rugnir's hands.

The younger dwarf's face conveyed his deep honour at the gift.

'Nah, don't worry on it,' snapped Craggen, tramping away again. 'Plenty more where that came from,' he said, his voice slowly fading as he was engulfed by the darkness of the cave until he'd disappeared from view.

'I won't forget you,' Rugnir promised, stowing the axe and then hoisting the knapsack onto his back before he left the cave, blinking into the harsh morning light.

RUGNIR FOUND HIS bearings quickly. Only just over an hour on the trail that led off from the cave and he saw a cluster of crags he recognised. Incredibly, it seemed, he was not that far from his hold. A few days solid march across the mountains and he would be able to see the gates of Karak Ungor again. Rugnir's jubilation at his imminent homecoming was tempered, however, by the thought of what he might find there and what he must do as soon as he was back.

Walking with a heavy heart, Rugnir crested a rocky rise and saw corpses strewn upon a battlefield below him. Most were picked clean, bones bleached by the sun. Huge pyres littered the darkened plain, their fires long since gone out. Scattered weapons lay strewn about, along with fallen banners.

Rugnir knew this place. He had been here before, long ago. It was called Broken Anvil Hill.

A HUGE CHEER erupted from the gathered warriors as King Bagrik and Prince Ithalred entered the Great Hall of Karak Ungor. Together, their crowns glittered like halos in the flickering torchlight of the hall. Both lords wore robes and ceremonial armour plate with runes of dwarfish or elvish design as appropriate. Ithalred came on foot, whilst Bagrik was carried upon his throne. Where Ithalred wore a cape of star-blue silk, Bagrik shouldered the boar mantle of his namesake.

The king's health had improved slightly each day since leaving the encampment near the edge of the Sea of Claws. Dwarfs were fast healers. There was little that didn't kill them that left them debilitated for long. Even still, Bagrik was a shadow of the dwarf he once was, a constant grimace cast upon his face like a mask as his every moment was pained by the poison inside him. The onlookers surrounding him, except the few that knew the truth, would assume it was his natural wrathful demeanour that forged the king's expression.

The hall was teeming with dwarfs and elves, mingling with one another as a mood of solidarity pervaded. By joining blades with the dwarfs, through the blood they'd shed on the field, the elves had atoned for their previous dishonour. And while it would never be forgotten, at least the relationship between the two races could move forward. They exchanged words, patted one another on the back and shoulder, even laughed together. Some, mainly the dwarfs, were sombre and reflective, seeking isolated corners to raise their tankards or goblets in remembrance of the deeds done and fallen friends. Others, predominantly elves, were ebullient and self-aggrandising, enjoying the moment for what it was – a celebration of victory.

Captains followed in the wake of their conquering lords. First Morek, clad in his finest gromril armour and best tunic, then Haggar similarly attired, the banner of Karak Ungor held up proudly. Other thanes and clan leaders followed behind him in a dazzling array of battle helms, ancient mantles and ornate regalia. For the elves there was Korhvale, the hunter wearing a magnificent lion pelt across his bare shoulders and a silver ithil-mar cuirass over vermillion robes. Lethralmir followed him, the other elf nobles stepping into line after him. The raven-haired elf wore a perturbed expression in addition to his silver-trimmed azure robes and gilded head-band, at being only second in the processional column behind his prince.

Of the original elven delegation that had come to the hold several months before, the ones who had not fallen in battle, only Arthelas was not present, deciding to stay in solitude at Tor Eorfith until her brother had returned for good. This fact had only further soured Lethralmir's already caustic demeanour.

Morek noted the look in the raven-haired elf's face, following his venomous gaze as it came to rest on the ambassador, Malbeth. The hearth guard captain reserved his own ire for the dwarf alongside him.

Kandor, you ufdi, he thought. Where were you when the call to war was sounded? Preening your beard, no doubt!

He scowled as the ambassadors were the first to receive the triumphant heroes, offering their weak congratulations and honeyed platitudes. Kandor brought a tankard of ale for the dwarf king, and Malbeth a goblet of wine for his prince.

'From the vineyards of Eataine, Prince Ithalred,' said the elf, his tone respectful and not obsequious.

The prince nodded his thanks.

'From Brewmaster Heganbour's finest stocks,' chipped in Kandor, proffering the tankard to his king, who took it with difficulty. 'You gift me with ale from my own stores and expect me to be grateful?' Bagrik growled.

Morek smiled to himself, and then followed the gaze of the king as it pierced the throng and came to Brunvilda waiting patiently upon her throne. She was a sight for sore eyes, right enough. Though outwardly composed, Morek saw the relief at the return of her husband fracture her guarded expression, the suggestion of tears glistening in the corners of her eyes.

The hubbub fell to a dull murmur in the Great Hall, as the doors were shut and Bagrik addressed his hold.

'Long have we fought,' he said, 'far from our home, far from our hearths.' The king lingered on Brunvilda. 'The north-men are dead!' Bagrik stated flatly. 'And Nagrim…' Bagrik's voice was nearly cracking, 'and Nagrim,' he repeated after he'd regained his composure, 'is avenged.'

Solemn muttering from the dwarfs greeted the pronouncement, amidst much head nodding and beard biting.

Prince Ithalred spoke up, breaking the melancholy mood with his musical voice.

'Alliance,' he said, 'is an easy word to use. It is much harder to *mean*. This day, we asur have forged that alliance. It is a bond of hot iron, cooled and hardened by blood,' he continued, the analogy not lost on the attentive dwarfs. 'But it is more than that.' Ithalred turned to face the dwarf king, and offered his hand. 'It is friendship.'

Bagrik nodded, and clasped the elf prince's hand in his own and then embraced him.

Malbeth was still translating Ithalred's words into Khazalid when the roar from the crowd drowned him out. The gesture between king and prince said far more than words ever could. The dwarfs and elves in the Great Hall followed the example of their lords and a warm air of camaraderie slowly filled the massive chamber.

'Drink for all!' bellowed the king. 'We drink to battles won, and to the passing of kith and kin. Remember them, one and all.' Bagrik nodded once to Ithalred and the lords made their way together to the King's Table where Brunvilda waited for them.

'I am glad you are safe,' she whispered into Bagrik's ear once the throne bearers had set him down.

'Aye lass, as am I,' the king replied, grimacing as he went to pat Brunvilda's hand.

She didn't know about the battle on the ice plain.

'You're hurt,' said the dwarf queen, her face awash with concern as she leaned over.

'It's nothing.'

'No, you're wounded–'

'Please Brunvilda,' Bagrik snapped, then lowered his voice. 'It is over now,' he said, looking out to the celebrating throng. 'Let them have their moment.'

Brunvilda bit her tongue, leaning back and facing the crowd with a stony expression.

MOREK WATCHED BRUNVILDA'S face darken and knew that she had discovered the truth about the king's injury. As she surveyed the crowd, her eyes met with the hearth guard captain's and she smiled weakly. Morek chastened himself. Averting his gaze, he found himself locking eyes with Grikk Ironspike. The captain of the ironbreakers, his face smeared with a thin patina of soot, folded his arms in reproach. This was not the triumphant return that Morek had hoped for.

THE FEAST WAS over an hour old before Brunvilda slipped away from the Great Hall. She padded quickly on soft sandals, weaving through the darkened corridors of the hold in silence. Hearth guard warriors gave her murmured greeting as she passed them, but none dared impede the Queen of Karak Ungor. Soon, she had reached the lower halls and the entrance to the vaults. Pausing at the iron-bound door, she reached for a hanging lantern. Her heart was pounding. The Grey Road lay beyond, and the ironbreakers who Bagrik had stationed there to guard it. But neither them, nor the fear of that lonely place would stop her from seeing her son.

Braving the shadowy catacombs of the vaults as she trod the Grey Road unaccompanied, Brunvilda brow-beat every ironbreaker patrol that sought to challenge her. Even the guard at the gate, the one who bore the key to Lothvar's dungeon, fell victim to her withering iron-hard stare.

With the door yawning open, its guardian unable to meet her gaze, Brunvilda covered her mouth against the stink from within and went inside. The place was much as she had left it, dank and smeared with filth. She'd seen pigs in the sties of the overground farms at Zhufvorn and Undvarn in less squalor. Ignoring the rank surroundings, Brunvilda stepped quickly to the opening in the floor that led down to Lothvar's cell. When she looked inside, she found the pitiable dwarf with one mis-shapen ear pressed hard against the cave wall.

'I hear noises from above,' he said, in halting speech. 'Are we under attack? Does my father need me? I am ready.'

Despite his obvious afflictions, Lothvar possessed far superior hearing and olfaction than other dwarfs. Evidently he had heard the merrymaking far above, even through the many thick layers of stone between the Great Hall and his wretched pit. As if to prove his other 'natural' aptitude, Lothvar sniffed suddenly at the rancid air of his cave.

'I can smell elgi. Are we at war, mother? Lend me an axe and I'll drive them from the hold. Nagrim and I will do it. No enemy of Ungor can stand against us brothers!' he declared proudly standing tall, at least as tall as he was able to given his misshapen spine.

'Nagrim is dead,' Brunvilda told him softly, leaning down over the hole and bringing the lantern close, so that Lothvar could see her. It was dark in the cave, night having fallen over the mountains, but Brunvilda could still make out her son. Unlike Lothvar, her nocturnal vision was excellent. 'To a northmen ambush,' she said. 'I told you this long ago.'

'Dead?' Lothvar gasped, halted in his belligerent posturing. The dwarf's face twisted as he struggled to comprehend at first. 'Yes, I remember...'

612

Dwarfs

he said at last, falling into a sudden melancholy.' Gazul, guide him to the Gate.'

'Lothvar,' said Brunvilda, patiently, 'I came to tell you that your father has returned, that he is safe.'

'Did he slay the elgi?' the dwarf asked, sorrow turning to aggression in an eye blink.

'No. The elves are our allies, our friends.' It was like coaxing a frightened mule though it was a timid naïve dwarf Brunvilda goaded, and towards understanding and the truth rather than the edge of a lode tunnel.

'I wish I could have fought beside him,' Lothvar bemoaned wistfully, his earlier melancholy returning.

It was worse than usual. Lothvar was barely lucid for a moment, before he drifted back into the imagined history of his inner world. His speech devolved into muttered ravings, and he shrank back into the darker shadows.

Brunvilda could endure no more of it.

'Give him this,' she told the guard, who lingered at the portal behind her.

She left a bundle of food wrapped lovingly in cloth, and returned to the Grey Road in silence.

BRUNVILDA'S MIND WAS tormented. Seeing Lothvar so debilitated, sinking ever deeper into a mire of madness, was an agony she felt scarcely fit to bear anymore. And what had it driven her to? Defiance of her king, skulking in the shadows like a thief? Perhaps Bagrik had been right... perhaps it would have been better if Lothvar had been exiled and left to the beasts of the mountain. No, he was her son, she could not countenance that, even if it meant going against tradition and ritual, even if it meant lying to Bagrik. Her husband or her son, it was no choice for anyone to make. Brunvilda was so preoccupied agonising over her thoughts that she failed to see Morek standing in the passageway in front of her.

'If the king finds you here, he'll know you have been to see Lothvar,' he said sternly, standing outside the antechamber that led back to the Great Hall.

Brunvilda was startled by Morek's voice, but calmed down as soon as she realised it was him.

'Have you been taking him morsels from the feast, again?' he asked.

Brunvilda nodded, 'And to tell him that his father has returned, and remind him that his brother is dead...'

A fissure was cracking through the queen's resolve that she could not prevent. She sobbed and broke down.

Morek couldn't watch Brunvilda suffer. He came forward and held her in his arms.

'I fear for him, Morek,' she confessed. 'I fear for Bagrik.'

The hearth guard captain paused, unwilling at first to voice his concerns should speaking them suddenly make them real.

'I cannot lie, Brunvilda,' he replied. 'The king's wound is grave. Whatever poison was on that blade–'

'Poison!' She recoiled, though Morek still held her, albeit at arm's length. 'I knew nothing of this–'

The creak of an opening door echoed dully behind them.

'Do you covet my queen, Morek Stonehammer?' asked a dour and sonorous voice.

Morek and Brunvilda stepped away from one another as if scalded, and turned to face the speaker.

Bagrik emerged from the shadows, the door to the antechamber closing quietly behind him.

'You should not be without your throne bearers,' Brunvilda told him, walking towards him. The queen was stopped in her paces by Bagrik's wrathful glare.

'I've strength enough to stand, rinn!' he snapped. 'Though, you obviously think me weak in mind as well as body if you believed that this... *deceit,*' he snarled waving his hand over them both, 'would go unheeded.'

'You misunderstand, my liege,' Morek told the king firmly, putting himself deliberately in Bagrik's eye-line. 'I love my queen,' he said, 'as I love my king. I would gladly give my life for either. It would be the greatest honour you could bestow upon my shoulders,' he said vehemently. 'I have served you for over one hundred years. I cannot believe you could think this.'

Bagrik's face was hard as stone at first but then his resolve cracked, and his weary shoulders sagged.

'My line is dead, Morek,' he said, close enough to rest his hand upon the hearth guard captain's pauldron for support. 'And I am so very tired...'

Catching sight of his queen again, Bagrik's demeanour changed.

'Your continued defiance of my will is not excused!' he raged, before she approached any further. 'Where else could you have been but visiting that *thing*. I was wrong to spare its life. It should have been cast out long ago.'

'If only you would speak to him,' Brunvilda pleaded. Morek stepped out of the way. It was unwise to get between a dwarf king and his queen.

'And say what?' asked Bagrik. 'What sense would it make to a *zaki*?'

'Don't call him that,' she warned.

'You'd prefer nubungki? For that is what *he* is.'

Brunvilda was furious. Morek feared the heat from her face and her fiery glare would melt the iron in Bagrik's ceremonial armour.

'He is *our* son,' she said calmly, through clenched teeth.

There was no time for a bellicose rejoinder. The door to the passageway was thrown open and Kandor barrelled through with several other dwarfs behind him. Amongst them were the king's throne bearers. Mercifully, Kandor's sudden arrival had dispersed the pressure cooker of building tension.

'King Bagrik,' he said breathlessly. 'You must come quickly.'

'What is it?' growled the king, annoyed by the interruption.

'Rugnir,' Kandor replied. 'He's alive.'

ABJECT SILENCE FILLED the Great Hall as all within awaited the return of Rugnir Goldmaster. Against all odds it seemed, he had survived the northmen ambush and found his way back to Karak Ungor after almost four months in the wild mountains.

Runners had been sent ahead to the outer gateway hall – Rugnir was to be brought before Bagrik at once. The king would know of the final moments of his son Nagrim. All would hear of it. Apparently, the dwarf had said little upon his arrival back at the hold. Only that he must see the king with all haste on a matter of the direst importance.

Bagrik steepled his fingers, bent low over the arms of his throne so that his broad back was arched and his chin nearly touched his knees. Gargoyle-like, he stared at the double doors to his hall without moving. After what felt like an age, remarkable given the patience and tenacity of dwarfs, the sound of booted feet could be heard echoing down the long corridor beyond. A few minutes later and the massive gates to the Great Hall were thrust open, a group of six hearth guard trooped in beside the lone ambush survivor.

Rugnir kept his gaze level and straight ahead. He met the eyes of his king and did not falter as he strode down the narrow aisle and past the tables thronging with dwarfs, some confounded, their mouths agape or scratching their heads; others thoughtful as they supped on pipes, longbeards muttering disapprovingly. The elves alongside them looked disconcerted.

Morek noticed two in particular, Ithalred and Lethralmir, sharing a dark glance between themselves furtively.

There was no announcement, no herald to usher him, just Rugnir, alone, with the hearth guard left behind him.

The dwarf, still laden with Craggen's pack, his hunting axe in a loop on his belt, bowed before his king at the edge of the stone dais beneath his throne.

'Approach,' Bagrik growled, taking the utmost care not to look at Brunvilda sitting beside him.

Rugnir rose quickly and moved forward to kneel at the foot of his liege lord, placing the knuckles of both fists on the ground as he did so.

'*Tromm*, King Bagrik,' he uttered, head bowed, his voice harsh and rasping like grit.

The dwarf king squinted at him with one eye, before he leaned forward and prodded Rugnir hard on the shoulder. It made the dwarf look up. Satisfied that Rugnir was indeed corporeal, Bagrik leaned back again, and began stroking his beard.

'You are no apparition then, Rugnir Goldmaster,' declared the king. 'Welcome back,' he added, somewhat belatedly.

Morek was watching the entire display intently, between glances at the elf nobles, who seemed so stiff as to be easily mistaken for petrified wutroth. Rugnir, though, seemed different. No raucous pronouncements, no drunken swagger. Even the alcoholic cherrying of his cheeks was gone, replaced by a rawness, a hollowing out of something inside. Something had happened to him, and it was more than just merely surviving the ambush.

'I bring news,' said Rugnir, when it was clear he was expected to speak. 'Of Nagrim's death and the ambush in the gorge,' he added, much louder than before.

'Tell me, Rugnir,' urged Bagrik in little more than a harsh whisper as tears gathered at the corners of his rheumy eyes. 'Tell me what happened to my son.'

'My king,' Rugnir began, standing to his feet as his voice cracked with emotion, 'it was not northmen that attacked us in the gorge, though that is what you were meant to think no doubt.' He turned to face the elves and levelled an accusing finger at Lethralmir. 'It was them.'

Shocked silence descended like an anvil.

'Ridiculous,' Kandor piped up. 'He is raving,' he said, getting to his feet as other dwarfs also started to voice their dissent. 'Most likely drunk, as well.'

'He's sober, right enough,' said Morek, his words carrying over the growing hubbub. He shook his head, saying, 'And I've never seen him like this before.'

'The elgi are our allies,' Kandor protested, clearly unable to believe what he was hearing. 'They fought with us against the northmen hordes.'

Morek sniffed derisively at the remark.

'You feast with vipers,' Rugnir roared, taking a step towards the King's Table before a pair of hearth guard interceded. 'Dawi slayers and murderers sit at your table... Thagi!' he cried, glowering at the elves with fists clenched. 'Thagi!'

'No,' said Kandor with half an eye on Malbeth, who seemed stunned into silence. 'Impossible. Nagrim was stuck with northmen arrows,' he petitioned the king, 'We all saw it.'

'Arrows, nothing more,' said Rugnir. 'Shot by the elgi,' he scowled. 'I saw it with my very eyes,' he added, pointing at them with two fingers.

'The dwarf lies,' snapped Lethralmir, getting up from the table.

'Sit down, Lethralmir,' Ithalred ordered in an undertone.

'Whilst we are accused of murder and treachery?' replied the raven-haired elf. 'I will not, my lord.'

'Do as your prince commands,' Malbeth told him, the ambassador rising too so that he was level with Lethralmir.

A clamour of disgruntled voices – both dwarf and elf – was gathering momentum throughout the hall. The mood, so genial at first, had soured swiftly and was becoming more riotous by the minute.

'Watch your temper, Malbeth,' Lethralmir warned, sneering, before he turned his attention back to Ithalred. 'We are insulted,' he said, continuing the earlier theme, 'and I demand to know what is to be done.'

'Nothing,' said Morek simply. 'Nothing will be done, until we get to the truth of this.'

The hearth guard captain was already standing. He had moved to within a few feet of Rugnir – the dwarf looked ready to snap at any moment.

'For isn't the truth that the northmen came here for vengeance and not conquest at all,' said Morek, remembering the visions bestowed upon him by the Norscan shaman. 'That we dawi were never a part of whatever fell purpose drove them. You,' – Morek pointed at Ithalred – 'you were the one the daemon sought. There was a debt against your blood, ages old.'

'I can't believe this,' said Kandor. 'How is it possible you know this, Morek?'

The hearth guard captain turned on the dwarf merchant. His eyes were like blazing coals of vehemence.

'I know it, because I saw it when the daemon tried to addle my mind!' he hissed through his teeth.

Kandor could only gape.

Bagrik turned his gaze on Ithalred. The king was stony faced, bereft of all emotion. Morek had never seen him look more dangerous.

'Did you murder my son?' he said with a level voice, looking the elf prince in the eye. 'Do not lie to me, elgi,' he warned, shaking his head then nodding as he narrowed his eyes, 'for I will know.'

Ithalred mustered as much presence as he could, matching the dwarf king's steely glare as one lord to another.

'It was not supposed to be this way,' he admitted with profound sorrow.

The Great Hall exploded in uproar. Like a rampant summer flame over dry fields of wheat and corn, the furore swept across the entire chamber. It infected everyone like a virulent contagion, with anger, belligerence and hate. Everything that had been built over the many months, all the painstaking endeavour to bring the two races together, the warrior bond forged on the fields of blood against the Norscans came tumbling down like a fortress with its foundations cruelly ripped away.

Quickly, the elves found their fellow kinsmen and banded together in protective circles, surrounded by mobs of wrathful dwarfs. The longbeards demanded action and swift vengeance.

Korhvale, seeing the imminent danger, cried out in elvish and he together with a handful of the prince's bodyguard gathered to Ithalred.

But because the two lords were still sat next to each other, the elves fought for position with the hearth guard. Both sets of warriors were only inches away from one another, bristling with anger, one wrong step, one slight away, from going over the edge to bloodshed.

'In Lileath's name, Ithalred I beg you, say this is not true,' pleaded Malbeth from within the circle, anguish etched upon his face.

The prince's eyes were hollow.

'I cannot.'

Frantically, desperate to salvage something, anything from this abject disaster, Malbeth turned to Kandor.

'This was not known to us,' said the elf, looking down at the dwarf beside him. 'We came here out of a desire for lasting peace.'

'You knew of it,' spat Lethralmir, the vitriol was palpable. 'You were as complicit in this as any of us.'

Malbeth's face went as white as chalk, as the life seemed to drain away to be replaced by something colder and harder. To look at him, you would think he had died suddenly. In many ways, he had. The elf's eyes grew wide. All the pent up rage, the dark desires of his past he'd kept at bay for so many years were finally unleashed in a flood of red-hazed catharsis.

'Lying scum!' Malbeth flew at Lethralmir, flinging one of Ithalred's guards aside who had been unfortunate enough to get in his way, and smashed a heavy blow against the blade-master's exposed cheek.

Lethralmir was thrown to the floor under the savage impact. Sprawled on his back the raven-haired elf, supported by his elbows, craned his neck to regard his attacker. A thin drool of blood hung from the corner of his mouth. Lethralmir touched it with his naked fingers, before licking off the hot metallic fluid with his tongue.

'See the killer,' he said, eyes on Malbeth the whole time. 'He even slew his own wife, *murdered* her in cold blood. He is the worst of us all.'

'*Elethya…*' Malbeth scarcely uttered the word. He was breathing raggedly, as he searched in his robes for something. When he couldn't find it, he locked his gaze with Lethralmir. The raven-haired elf smiled, oh so slightly.

The entire hall was enrapt for the moment as Malbeth and Lethralmir played out the tragedy. The elf ambassador was about to reach for a blade to finish his raven-haired aggressor, when he felt a presence on the arm of his robe. Without thinking, Malbeth lashed out. Blinking back the crimson rage that blanketed his vision, he was horrified when he realised he had struck Kandor. The dwarf shrank away from him, rubbing his jaw. Malbeth watched as something died, there and then, in Kandor's eyes.

With the performance over, Morek decided to take matters into his own hands.

'Dreng elgi,' he snarled, unslinging his axe, 'Dreng thagi!' Scraping metal resounded in the hall as the hearth guard drew blades; Rugnir, too, and any other dwarf that carried a weapon. Those who were unarmed balled their fists and chewed their beards in fury. Some of the elves unsheathed daggers, Korhvale amongst them. Lethralmir slipped a hidden blade from his vambrace. Ithalred didn't move as his kin made to defend themselves.

'Cease!' The gravel voice of King Bagrik stopped the fight before it could begin. 'Stow your blades,' he growled at length, glowering around the room at every dwarf in his eye-line. 'Do it now or be entered into the dammaz kron for defying your king,' he promised. A side glance at Grumkaz Grimbrow, the leathery chief grudgemaster, confirmed to Bagrik that the old granite-faced dwarf had his quill readied.

No other dwarf in the Great Hall of Karak Ungor had greater claim to blood for the elves' heinous deeds than Bagrik. His bellow for cessation of hostility was not about to be challenged and, for now, the dwarfs lowered their axes.

'You saved my life, Ithalred,' the king told the elf prince, speaking to him as if they were the only ones in the mighty room, 'and for that I grant you one concession,' he added, raising a gnarled finger for emphasis. The king abided for silence, waiting until even the recalcitrant longbeards had stopped their pugnacious grumbling.

'Get out,' he said simply. 'Take your kin and go. But mark this: do it quickly. I am a hair's breadth from killing you all in this very chamber,' Bagrik promised. The king's eye was twitching as he said it, drawing on all of his will not to just cut the elves down where they stood and let that be an end to it. 'But I will not stain its legacy with blood, especially that of thagging traitors. There has been enough shed in my hold to last me five lifetimes,' he added with the faintest trace of lamented remembrance.

'Go, now. Seven days hence, I will meet you on the field of battle on the lowland outside your city. Then…' he muttered, nodding darkly to the prince, 'then you can atone in full for this treachery.'

Wood scraping on stone announced Ithalred as he rose from his seat in silence. His gaze lingered on Bagrik for a moment longer, before he turned, waiting for the surrounding dwarfs to back away – who did so eventually, but only at Bagrik's snarled urging – and walked down the aisle, up to the gate and through it to the halls beyond.

A hearth guard escort accompanied the elves. Morek was ordered to go with them should any get the idea to take matters into their own hands. Once at the outer gateway hall, the elves were stripped of any armour or weapons, aside from Ithalred's ancestral blade, which Bagrik had allowed him to keep out of respect for him saving his life, and cast out. The elven trappings were then piled up on a mule cart and taken to the lower deeps where they would be melted down in the forges and remade into bolt tips and arrow heads.

The accord between the dwarfs and elves was at an end, their victory

over the Norscan hordes a pyrrhic one. In seven days' time, Karak Ungor
and Tor Eorfith would meet again, and there would be blood.

'CURSE THE WILES of Loec and his perfidy,' muttered Ithalred as the elves
tramped listlessly from the dwarf hold. 'How did this happen? There
was to be no survivors, no chance of the truth of what we did coming
out.'

All told, almost three thousand elves were banished from Karak
Ungor and its slopes. Many of the warriors, mainly rangers, spearmen
militia and archers, were encamped in the crags around the hold. The
reaction to the treatment of their lords when they'd emerged from the
postern gate bereft of their belongings was one of dismay and anger.
The elves' belligerence had cooled somewhat though when the ranks
of quarrellers had appeared in the watch station overlooking the great
gate and the towers and skybridges either side of it. Once the ballista
and stone throwers had been wheeled into position, the elves packed
up their fluted pavilions and elegant tents and marched away.

It was a few miles down the road before Ithalred gave voice to his frus-
tration. By now he, and the other exiles from the Great Hall, had been
given travelling cloaks, weapons and armour.

'It was inevitable,' said Lethralmir.

'How so?' Ithalred stopped walking and rounded on the raven-haired
elf. 'Did you let one escape?'

'I meant, my prince,' he said, subtly clearing his throat, 'that war with
the mountain-dwellers was inevitable.'

Ithalred backed down, seemingly satisfied. About to continue on his
way, he noticed Malbeth trudging down the road towards them. He
appeared catatonic, staring straight ahead at some unseen horizon, one
foot in front of the other like an automaton. After the elves had been
expelled from the dwarf hold, the ambassador had immediately started
scrabbling around in his baggage. Ithalred had paid him little mind, he
had his own crisis to contend with. Whatever Malbeth had been looking
for, the prince assumed he had not found it.

When he approached the two nobles, Ithalred saw a flicker of recognition in the ambassador's eyes and the blank slate expression fell away,
consumed by rage. A roar of anguish ripped from Malbeth's lips as he
tore a sword from the sheath of one of Ithalred's guards and lunged at
Lethralmir. The raven-haired elf saw the attack late, but was swift enough
to weave his body from the killing stroke. Instead, the blade grazed his
ribs and he cried out in pain.

Like lightning, Korhvale, the prince's shadow, seized Malbeth's wrist
before he could strike again.

'Drop it,' he growled. The White Lion had seen the attack a fraction
before it took place. Only he knew that he had delayed for a second to
see if Lethralmir got what he deserved, before he'd intervened. When

Malbeth didn't relinquish the blade immediately, Korhvale twisted the ambassador's wrist and the weapon fell from his agonised grasp with a yell. The White Lion was about to let him go when he saw Malbeth's expression twisted with fury, his eyes full of hate and loathing. He tried to break free and Korhvale, fearing that he would, called for help. Two more guards came to his aid, holding onto one arm whilst Korhvale grabbed the other.

'Khaine has him,' snarled Lethralmir, staunching the blood from his wounded side as he watched Malbeth struggle. 'What's the matter,' he said quietly, drawing close to the pinioned elf. 'Have you lost your medicine?' he asked, smiling.

Malbeth thrashed against his captors, screaming curses at Lethralmir as his rage swallowed him utterly.

'Hold him down,' Ithalred said calmly. 'You,' he added, nodding towards a gaping onlooker, 'bring rope to bind his legs and arms.' The prince looked back at Malbeth with pitying eyes. '*By Isha's grace...*' he whispered, realising that he regarded that which dwelt in all the asur, their raw warrior spirit and violent potential. Here was the Bloody Handed God made manifest. It had destroyed Malbeth, engulfed him with rage and a desire to kill.

Ithalred averted his gaze and found Lethralmir looking back at him, still clutching his bloodied side.

'And get a surgeon for this one,' added the prince, lip curling in distaste. 'You'll get your war with the dwarfs, Lethralmir,' he promised fatalistically. 'I'm going to need every sword.'

Ithalred stalked away. The skies overhead were darkening. Ravens circled.

CHAPTER EIGHTEEN

Fallen Lion

ITHALRED STARED OUT across the plain from the tallest tower of Tor Eorfith. He was naked barring the thick velvet cloak that trailed all the way to the marbled floor. It chilled his bare feet, but the elf hardly noticed. Ithalred felt numb, and not from the cold stone. Below he heard the sounds of battle preparation, of spears and longbows being racked, the dry-loosing of bolt throwers and the clank of hammers as forgesmiths fashioned suits of armour. Saddles were made ready, horse barding polished, lances and arrows stacked. The entire population of Tor Eorfith, man and woman, bustled in quiet urgency. For come the morrow, they would be at war with the dwarfs.

Eyrie Rock was the other, perhaps more prosaic, name for Tor Eorfith. It was a fitting appellation. The beauteous bastion was set upon a vast rugged spur of basalt and granite. Seven silver spires pierced cloud and soared into the stratosphere as if reaching for the very stars. The wondrous towers punctuated a stout outer wall of smoothed alabaster and grey-veined marble. Minarets branched out from the main towers that also supported many balconies. Those edifices that stood behind the outer wall were joined by narrow arching bridges, dripping with ornamentation and bejewelled downward-thrusting spikes. Gem-encrusted obelisks lay sunken in the verdant earth beyond the elven city. They were waymarkers and potent magical foci through which Tor Eorfith's mages could practise their arcane arts.

When he left Ulthuan, Ithalred had brought some of the finest mason-artisans of Lothern and Eataine with him. The glorious citadel where he now stood, this city of silver and jewels, was the glittering fruit of their labours, a masterpiece of the aesthetic, protected by enchanted wards and bound with spells of resistance. As the elf prince stared into the wind at the distant fires of the dwarfs, as they made their encampment a few miles from his gilded gates, he wondered if those magicks would be enough to stop them.

'Ravens flock to the towers, my prince,' said the grim voice of Korhvale from behind him. The two warriors were alone on the balcony. Ithalred chose to no longer keep company with Lethralmir, preferring solitude.

'They foretell our destruction,' intoned the elf prince, his golden hair disturbed by the growing breeze. 'Do you think we are doomed, Korhvale?' he asked, facing the White Lion.

'We reap what we have sown,' he answered tacitly.

'We faced annihilation at the hands of the northmen, what else was I supposed to do?' asked the prince.

'We acted with dishonour.'

'It is not so black and white, Korhvale,' Ithalred pressed, becoming more animated. 'You saw the aftermath of their attack on the watch towers. And what of Hasseled's hawk ships? Fifteen vessels led by our finest naval captain, gone, destroyed. Our army was not strong enough to defeat them.'

'Had I known of your plan to kill the dwarf prince, and trick his kin into a war that was not theirs to fight, I would have stopped it,' Korhvale told him.

'It is much too late for that,' Ithalred scoffed, laughing despite himself.

After a brief silence, Korhvale said, 'We should leave. Take what ships we have left and return to Ulthuan. Your sister ails more by the day, she is constantly fatigued. She has not been seen out of her chamber for weeks. Isha knows it is her home that she craves.'

'*This* is her home, Korhvale,' Ithalred snapped, pointing to the marble at his feet. 'As it is yours and mine, and all of the other damned souls within these cold walls.'

He showed his back to the White Lion.

'Begone,' the prince said brusquely. 'I tire of you, Korhvale.'

The White Lion's lightened step made little sound as he walked away.

For over an hour after Korhvale had left, Ithalred looked down on the dwarfs below. They milled around like ants, tramping back and forth in their armour, raising their tents and unshackling cavalcades of ballista and mangonels from a string of draught mules. Ithalred's keen eyes discerned it all. The armoured dwarfs were like a blanket of bronze and iron blighting the verdant green of the land for miles. Hawk-eyed as he was, though, the elf failed to notice a figure moving through the rocks, several miles away from where the dwarfs were camped, but getting steadily closer.

* * *

KORHVALE HEARD THE soft tread of his own boots echo down the lonely corridor from the spire where Prince Ithalred had made his eyrie. It was a doleful refrain to the beating of his heavy heart. The White Lion was in disarray. His conscience warred with his sense of duty. No warrior wearing the pelt could ever be accused of disloyalty. For was it not the woodsmen of Chrace who went to the aid of Caledor the First, saving him from death at the knives of druchii assassins? But slaying in cold blood... the very act stuck in Korhvale's craw and no matter how he rationalised it, the White Lion could not dislodge the feeling that such a deed made them no better than druchii themselves.

To face the dwarfs meant certain death. A pang of fear seized Korhvale at the sudden thought. Not for him; the prospect of mortality held no terror for a White Lion of Chrace. No, it was Arthelas whom Korhvale feared for. He could not leave her to be slain along with the rest. A desperate plan began to form in his mind. If he could get her onto a boat, there were Lothern sailors eager enough to leave the Old World to ferry her. He could smuggle her away in secret, ensure that she was safe. It was dark enough now for that.

As he plotted, the simple act of it leaving an uncomfortable sheen over his skin, Korhvale remembered the scroll he had hidden beneath his cuirass. Stopping in the darkness he reached for it tentatively. The parchment pages seemed so innocuous rolled up in his hand. Yet they held his desires, his yearnings; the profession of his true feelings for Arthelas.

Her quarters were not far. It might be the last chance he would ever get. Full of purpose, Korhvale returned the scroll delicately to its hiding place and went off swiftly down the shadowed hall. He had only passed a single sentry on his way to Arthelas's chambers in the next tower. Most of the warriors were below, watching from the battlements or making their final preparations for the fight to come. Korhvale had said nothing to him, he'd not even made eye contact so obsessed was he with his mission. First he would tell her of his feelings and then he would get her away from this place.

Korhvale was so anxious by the time he arrived at Arthelas's door that he felt sick. He was about to knock, when he thought better of it. It was deathly silent in the corridor, though the White Lion heard some muffled noises from within the room – perhaps she was singing – any commotion, however insignificant, might rouse unwanted attention. So instead, he eased his weight against the door. To the elf's relief, it was unlocked and opened quietly.

Stepping inside Korhvale closed the door behind him, making only a dull thud as the wood came flush against the alabaster arch. It was gloomy inside and a pungent aroma permeated the air in a thick violet fug. Thin veils were suspended from the ceiling made from gossamer and silk that obscured Korhvale's view into the room.

'*Arthelas*,' he whispered, searching for her in the pastel-hued darkness.

Korhvale thought he saw the hazy glow of fettered lanterns or perhaps candles with their wicks shortened to dull the flame. Passing through the first wall of veils, he noticed carafes of wine, platters of half-eaten fruit. A lyre lay discarded on a wooden bench carved into the effigy of a swan. Through a second layer of overlapping veils, and the muffled sound he heard outside the door became louder and more discernible. It was not singing. Rather, it was more breathless, repetitive but without harmony.

Beyond a narrow arch, through a circular anteroom festooned with plump cushions, was Arthelas's bedchamber.

A final azure veil impeded him. There was the shape of two figures moving softly beyond it. Pulling back the drape, Korhvale whispered again.

'*Arthelas…*'

The words died on his lips. He'd found his true love, the woman he had watched from a distance for all the years he'd been in Ithalred's service. She was in the bed… with Lethralmir. The two of them writhed like adders beneath the orchid, silken sheets.

'Korhvale,' said Arthelas, noticing the White Lion first. The perverted serenity on the seeress's face brought a fresh rush of nausea. Then Lethralmir, with his back to him, looked over his shoulder at the Chracian and smiled in malicious pleasure. With her fingernail Arthelas had carved a symbol in Lethralmir's back in blood.

Korhvale recoiled in horror.

It was the mark of Atharti, the underworld goddess of pleasure.

The White Lion felt the scroll of parchment fall from his nerveless fingers, those words and feelings made cheap and worthless in the face of his horrified revelation. He couldn't breath and clutched at his chest in sudden panic. It was as if a dagger had been thrust into him. Korhvale wished he could take that dagger and use it to cut out his eyes.

'No…' The sound that issued from his mouth was a gasp, but it was raw and primal. Tears fled from Korhvale's eyes, the corners of his mouth curling in disgust.

'Noooo!' he roared with such anguish that it rent his heart and left it forever ruined. Mortified, the White Lion fled. Lethralmir's mocking laughter echoed after him, like wraiths tugging at the Chracian's resolve. Korhvale was a veteran warrior. He had fought countless battles, alone in the mountains of his homeland and the forests of Cothique, on the shores of Nagarythe against the druchii and now for his lord versus the northmen hordes, but Korhvale had never before been wounded like this.

ARTHELAS'S SMILE SOURED into a scowl as she lay beneath the sweating body of Lethralmir and watched Korhvale claw through the veils.

'Don't let him escape,' she hissed urgently. 'Ithalred must never know…'

The smirk on Lethralmir's face vanished. The raven-haired elf grabbed his sword from where he'd left it alongside his discarded armour next to the bed, and leapt naked from the sheets after the White Lion.

Lethralmir knew his way around the chambers. He was also well-accustomed to the soporific fumes that laded the air. Weaving through the veil is like a serpent, his narrowed eyes like slits upon the White Lion as he blundered in blind grief, Lethralmir caught his prey.

THE SILVER FLASH of a sword blade reflecting off the lanterns caught Korhvale's attention. Instinct took over, burning through his tortured misery like a beacon. A hot line of pain seared his side and the White Lion realised he had been cut. Grabbing a fistful of veils, he tore them down and threw them into Lethralmir's face. The raven-haired elf sliced through them with ease, his diamond-sharp blade paring the fabric like he was slicing through air. It slowed him long enough though for the White Lion to unsling his axe.

Chest heaving with the effort of his grief, Korhvale regarded his enemy a few feet across the pastel chamber. Despair boiled away, turning into something more substantial; something the White Lion could use – hate.

'I'll tear you limb from li–'

A FLASH OF light blossomed swiftly, lighting up the chamber, and then died. An actinic aroma, merged with the stench of burnt flesh, overwhelmed the soporific musk.

Lethralmir, blade poised at the ready, looked down at Korhvale's chest and saw why the White Lion had ceased his threats so abruptly. A gaping crater of cauterised flesh and blood existed where his torso should have been. Metal from his ithilmar cuirass fused with bone and boiled viscera. Smoke eking from the terrible wound, Korhvale slumped first to his knees and then fell face forward onto the ground. Arthelas was revealed behind him, draped in a violet gown, crackling tendrils of black energy fading slowly across her outstretched fingertips.

The surprised expression on Lethralmir's face turned amorous.

'Murder is such an aphrodisiac,' he purred.

'Get him up,' Arthelas snapped, in no mood for copulation. 'We must dispose of his body before he's missed.' She swept quickly to her bedside, let the gown slip from her shoulders and put on her robes and trappings.

Despondent and frustrated, Lethralmir set down his blade and threw the White Lion over his shoulder.

'He is heavy,' he complained through clenched teeth.

'Quiet!' Arthelas hissed, adding, 'In here,' as she opened the lid to a large ottoman.

Lethralmir dumped Korhvale's corpse inside unceremoniously and shut the lid.

Arthelas had moved back over to the scene of the fight. She scowled at the blood-stained floor.

'Clean it,' she snapped, looking around her chambers for further evidence of Korhvale's presence there.

'What about this?' Lethralmir asked as he crouched over the bloody smear left by the White Lion. He held a scroll of parchment between his fingers and showed it to Arthelas.

'Burn it,' she told him coldly.

'GONE, MY LORD,' said Commander Valorian.

'"Gone", what do you mean "gone"?' asked Ithalred, strapping on his final leg greave.

The elves were mustering. The arched gates of Tor Eorfith were open and its drawbridge lowered to enable snaking columns of dragon knights, silver helms and reavers to sally. Squadrons of chariots from the partly sundered realm of Tiranoc followed; phalanxes of spearmen and archers in their wake. Bolt throwers, aptly named 'reapers' were wheeled out along the bridge and bedded in quickly upon the high ground. After the war machines marched the sword masters, their massive blades held in salute as they encircled Tor Eorfith's mages who trod solemnly within the web of steel carrying their orbs, staffs and other magical arcana. Though there were just a handful of the warrior-scholars, their deadly great swords could shear through even the thickest dwarf armour.

Tor Eorfith's spellweavers were led by the silver-haired archmage, Rhathilan. He was Arthelas's teacher and mentor though unknown to Rhathilan she had since surpassed him, yoking her power from darker sources. Having seemingly overcome her fatigue, the seeress had insisted she be allowed to fight in the battle. Ithalred had wanted to keep her safe behind the gates of the city, but even they would not persevere forever. In the end he had relented, and so she too joined her fellow mages behind the sword masters' steel circle.

As the elves filed out of the city gates they arrayed themselves upon the plain in disciplined ranks and formed their regiments, banners snapping in the wind. Several miles to the south were the army of the dwarfs, waiting patiently for the elves to finish mustering.

'Precisely that, my prince,' Valorian replied. The warden of Tor Eorfith would be taking command of the interior troops during the first sortie. 'Korhvale is no longer in Tor Eorfith,' he concluded.

'Fled?' Ithalred's voice was tinged with disbelief as he donned his golden hawk-helm. 'He expressed his reservations about this conflict with the dwarfs... that was the last time I ever saw him. But to run?' the elf prince shook his head. 'It is not his way. Something is amiss,' he muttered.

'Would you like me to investigate the matter?' Valorian asked.

'No,' Ithalred decided, looping his foot in the stirrup of his mighty great eagle. The magnificent beast was called Awari, and he was one of three rookery brothers. To forge a bond with such a creature was not easy and no one other than Ithalred ever rode these eagles. Awari was his favourite – intelligence and nobility shone behind his avian eyes. 'There is no time. Marshal the defences,' he said, swinging into the saddle, 'when the dwarfs beat us outside the city you'll need to be ready to interrupt any pursuit so that as many of us as possible can get back behind the walls.'

It sounded fatalistic, but Ithalred was not so vainglorious as to be unrealistic. The dwarfs drew upon all the armies of their entire hold. The elves, though their colony was large, had no such force at their disposal and no time to request reinforcements. Such negative strategy was prerequisite when so badly outnumbered.

With nothing further to say to Valorian, Ithalred arched his head back and uttered an ululating command that shrilled like a bird cry. His great eagle spread its mighty wings, its armoured head and beak glittering in the morning light. With a piercing shriek the ancient creature rose magnificently into the sky to join its unmounted rookery brothers, Skarhir and Urouke, amidst the darkening cloud.

IT WAS FIVE days since the elves had been expelled from Karak Ungor in ignominy. Brunvilda thought it a rare miracle that none had lost their lives in the Great Hall, that scarcely no blood had been shed.

In a few hours Bagrik's armies would leave Karak Ungor for the long, slow march to the elven city. The road to the north would take around two days to travel, two short days before the grand dwarf army would assemble on the lowlands before Tor Eorfith. Using his influence and power as king, Bagrik had assembled such a force as to leave the hold almost empty, barring a skeleton company of thinly spread miners, clan warriors and ironbreakers. There were some, amongst the most venerable ancestors and longbeards, that would also remain but few in the Delving Hold had seen or heard of them in many years.

The scarcity of troops patrolling the corridors was to Brunvilda's advantage as she hurried towards her destination. The queen was shrouded in a thick cloak of hruk wool, voluminous enough to hide what she needed it to. Cowl drawn over her head she moved anonymously, down into the farthest deeps. Brunvilda suppressed a pang of regret and sorrow. It would probably be the last time she ever did this.

Dimly, she recalled her last conversation with Bagrik, what had passed between them now fully occupying her thoughts. After the elven treachery had been revealed, Bagrik had slipped into a bitter melancholy. Brunvilda, once she had him alone in their royal quarters, had tried desperately to bring him out of it, but to no avail. Instead, she had only worsened the king's buried choler.

'Please, I beg of you, don't go into battle,' she had urged him. 'Let Morek reckon this misdeed of the elgi. You are not fit enough–'

'I am fit enough!' Bagrik had raged. 'You'll never meet the dawi king that is not fit enough to reckon his own deeds. I'd have to be dead before I allowed another to settle this grudge,' he vowed. 'My son... Nagrim was slain by these pointy-eared, pale-arsed bastards. His kinsdwarf left for dead, too. And that,' he had told her, his eyes widening with vehemence as he wagged his finger, 'was their biggest mistake. They reckoned on a dwarf being as soft and effeminate as their own silk-swaddled race. What folly!' Bagrik laughed, but it had been a bitter, mirthless expression. The coldness of it had struck to Brunvilda's core.

'I feel for Nagrim, too,' the queen had assured him. 'I loved him dearly, and I would see these elgi pay with their lives for what they did, but I would not see you give up yours so wastefully.'

'It is not profligate to avenge one's kin, Brunvilda,' Bagrik had barked. 'My only son is dead. My *only* son,' he repeated, with a warning in his tone as he had turned away from her to face his armour. 'Upon my return, the other will be exiled,' Bagrik had said without emotion, 'left to die in the mountains, as it should have been years ago.'

Despite her impassioned protests, Bagrik had not listened. Reason had fled in his mind. Whether caused by the poison running in his veins that would surely kill him, or the fact that his heart and soul were hollow lifeless husks, Brunvilda did not know. All she was certain of was that she could not allow Lothvar to be so callously discarded. If he was to die then at least it would be upon the field of battle, fighting for the honour of his father and his clan.

The door to the Grey Road had come upon Brunvilda swiftly. She took no lantern this time; she would need the darkness and the shadows to conceal her. Silently, with only her nocturnal vision to guide her, Brunvilda moved down the long subterranean passageway that led to Lothvar's cell. Approaching the corona of light cast by the hanging lantern at the door, she noted with some dismay that the guard was still present.

Swathed in her dark woollen cloak, the ironbreaker did not see her until she was almost upon him.

'Hold–' he began, starting to show Brunvilda his armoured palm in a gesture for her to stop.

Brunvilda swung the hammer she carried out from beneath the cloak and smashed it, two-handed, against the ironbreaker's helmet. When he didn't go down from the first blow, she struck him again. This time, he went to his knees and his arms dropped to his side. Whilst he was still dazed, Brunvilda pulled off his helmet and then smacked him again over his bare, bald pate. That did it. The ironbreaker fell onto his back unconscious.

Satisfied he was still breathing, and would only be nursing an unearthly headache when he eventually awoke, Brunvilda, leaving the hammer behind, stepped over the prone dwarf and into Lothvar's cell using the key stolen from the guard.

Using the wooden bucket and some patient cajoling, Brunvilda got Lothvar out of his pit. She brought a bundle of tightly wrapped clothes: a coarse jerkin, some woollen leggings and boots. Flicking anxious glances back in the direction of the supine guard, she dressed her son. Though it was a struggle, she managed it quickly and with a few quiet words of encouragement took Lothvar out of the dungeon for the first time in over eighty years. Brunvilda forgot to douse the lantern outside as they fled and Lothvar cowered against the light. She had been tempted to extinguish it, but her son would need to get used to it if he were to achieve the destiny she had in mind for him.

'Where are you taking us, mother?' asked Lothvar, holding Brunvilda's hand as she led them through the Grey Road as fast as she dared.

'To see your brother,' she promised. 'Move swiftly, Lothvar. No one must know you have gone… not yet, at least.'

'Does our father need us?' he asked. 'Together, we will drive the grobi from our gates… No, wait…' said Lothvar, his sudden bravura overcome by solemnity, 'Nagrim is dead…'

'Quietly now, Lothvar,' Brunvilda told him, gripping his malformed hand just a little tighter, 'we are leaving the Grey Road.'

Lothvar did as his mother asked and together they used all the seldom trodden paths, the forgotten corridors and dust-clogged passageways of Karak Ungor, moving in secret until they had reached their destination.

When a noble of a dwarf hold was slain, tradition demanded that a long period of mourning be observed before the dead were allowed to pass into the Halls of the Ancestors. Like with everything, dwarfs took their time over this ritual. Nagrim's internment had been interrupted by the sudden need for war, the abrupt desire to mete out vengeance in his name. So it was then that he had remained in the Temple of Valaya, beneath the goddess's watchful gaze.

Between the magic embedded in the runes of that sacred place and the unguents and oils lathering his body, the dwarf prince was kept preserved and had not decayed even slightly when Brunvilda and Lothvar finally reached him.

'Nagrim,' breathed Lothvar, setting eyes on his younger brother for the very first time. He staggered forward, limping free of his mother's grasp to stand before the cold body of his sibling laid in quiet repose.

'He looks like he's sleeping,' said Lothvar, reaching out with trembling fingers.

'Don't touch him, my son,' warned Brunvilda. 'He is awaiting his ancestors' call. Gazul will guide him when the time comes.'

Lothvar wept, though it was a brief mourning. As he wiped away the last errant tear from his ravaged face, he turned to Brunvilda.

'Why have you brought me here?'

Brunvilda smiled warmly. Out of the corner of her eye she could see the ancestral armour of Karak Ungor, that which by right and tradition would go to the heir of Delving Hold, he who was eldest of the king's offspring upon reaching his eightieth winter.

Lothvar was over eighty winters old.

'I've brought you here for your destiny,' Brunvilda told him. 'Now listen to me Lothvar, listen carefully to what you must do.'

CHAPTER NINETEEN

For Vengeance

AT LAST THE elves were ready. Regal dragon knights glared imperiously astride shuddering steeds, vermillion armour gleaming as if aflame. Silver helm knights, with lances upraised and banners dipped, shimmered in their ithilmar mail. The spear tips of the elf infantry shone in forests of silver spikes. Archers stood motionless, a long unbroken line of sapphire and white. This was an army of the elder race, the immortal sons and daughters of Aenarion from across the Great Ocean. Truly, it was a wondrous sight.

'The glittering host,' Morek growled from atop the ridge, voice thick with contempt. He was standing alongside King Bagrik in his full hearth guard regalia, battle mask drawn over his face. The dwarf stroked the runic talisman around his neck with absent-minded affection. Below him were the batteries of war machines arranged in half-rings. The quarrellers were beneath them strung out in ragged lines to compensate for the uneven terrain. Below that was the sheer wall of iron and bronze that Morek would use as a hammer to crush the elven host and send them fleeing back behind their walls.

'T'would be a pity to bloody them,' remarked the hearth guard captain after he'd received his final orders from the king.

Bagrik grunted beneath his own battle mask.

'But bloody them we will,' he promised darkly, 'and more besides.'

The horn call rang out like clear thunder on a summer's day. It split the air and signalled the first advance. Dwarf trumpets bayed in response, and the staccato beat of drums was struck up in earnest. The sons of Grungni were moving.

The battlefield was dominated by a broad expanse of flat lowland consisting of coarse grass, isolated copses of pine and scattered rocks. Hillocks formed a shaggy undulating spine across the far left flank, developing into much heavier-contoured ground that culminated in the ridge of sparsely grassed rock where Bagrik watched and waited. To the right was the rocky debris of the mountains, eroded by weather and age to encroach a fair distance onto the killing field.

Alongside King Bagrik there stood his runelord, Agrin Oakenheart. The venerable dwarf had said nothing during the long trudge from Karak Ungor. He and his apprentices had kept their own counsel, maintaining a watchful eye on the Anvils of Doom as they were hauled by mules to the battlesite. Skengi and Hurbad were below, amongst the main dwarf throng. The two master runesmiths would be needed to counter whatever sorcery the elves might throw at them.

'There's a change in the earth,' growled Agrin, his voice like metal scraping rock. 'I fear this will be the end of it.'

'The end of what, old one?' Bagrik asked.

'The end of all we know,' replied the runelord, 'and the beginning of change.'

Blinking, Agrin gazed up into the sky, where a pale yellow sun struggled to shine through the gathering clouds, and scowled.

'S'been a long few years since I've seen the sky, felt the wind on my face,' he remarked. 'Now I know why.' Expression souring, he returned to his silence.

STONE FELL IN a relentless hail from the dwarf mangonels arrayed on the hill. It blotted the limpid sun before crashing down like rock-hard thunder against the elven reapers. The bolt throwers were smashed into elegant kindling, their crewman maimed or pulped in the sudden avalanche of granite. Isolated elven mages endeavoured to protect the war engines with shimmering magical shields but their attention was divided between attack and defence. Occasionally thwarted by the efforts of the dwarf runesmiths, the elves could only do so much.

Punitive strikes against the elven machineries had been one of Bagrik's priorities. It had proven a wise stratagem, for even depleted as they were they spat a deadly fusillade that tore up dwarf armour like parchment. Even the stoutest shields were rent apart. Reapers – they were well named, for theirs was a bitter harvest.

'DO YOU REMEMBER what that is for?' Morek shouted above the clang of chafing armour and rattled shields, as the hearth guard marched up the left flank.

'Aye, I've not forgotten my axe-craft, Thane Stonehammer,' Kandor growled back at him. The dwarf merchant wore an open-faced helmet with a long noseguard that showed off his reddening cheeks as they puffed and blowed.

'A little thick around the waist, too, I see,' observed the hearth guard captain. 'More fat than muscle, I'd warrant.'

Kandor looked down at the suit of lamellar armour bulging at his girth and frowned.

'I don't see why we must go to the elgi. Why don't we let them come to us?' he grumbled.

Kandor had joined the army at his own request. His dealings with the elves had left his honour in tatters. Already, his name had been entered into the book of grudges for his singular lack of wisdom in entreating the foreigners. Kandor himself felt partly to blame for what had transpired. Short of taking the slayer oath, he would exact his toll of revenge against those who had tricked him with honeyed words and gilded promises in blood. It would not erase the stain of his ignominy, but it would at least settle some of his account when he met with Gazul at the Gate.

'Ah,' replied Morek conspiratorially, tapping the noseguard of his battle mask with a gauntleted finger, 'that's because our king has a surprise in mind for the pointy-eared bastards,' he explained. 'Don't worry, ufdi, I'll make sure you live long enough to reap a tally that'll see you into the Halls.' Morek laughed loudly, the sound oddly metallic through his helmet.

This will be a grand battle. Nagrim would have wanted to fight in it, thought Morek sadly, as the mangonels continued their barrage.

HAGGAR ANVILFIST HELD the dwarf centre. The banner of Karak Ungor was clenched firmly in the thane's iron grip, and swayed as he moved. The clan warriors arrayed around him followed it like a beacon. This was a day of destiny; Haggar felt it as sure as the rune axe in his hand and the armour on his back. Facing the northmen had been a time of trial, which he had passed. Already, he felt the mark that Thagri had made against his clan's honour lifting. Here upon the fields outside Eyrie Rock that legacy would be forever expunged and a new saga of honour forged in its place.

A violent fulguration erupted before the thane, arresting his thoughts. Haggar watched arcs of lightning dissipating into sparks on the ground as they earthed into Skengi's outstretched runestaff. The thane nodded his thanks to the runesmith whose beard was spiked from the sudden bolt charge. Further down the dwarf battle-line, Haggar saw a distant regiment of clan warriors succumb to the fury of an elven firestorm. The entire front rank died in the conflagration, the dwarfs' magical defences breached at last. Dourly, the clan warriors behind stepped over the scorched remains of the dead and raised their blackened banner in defiance.

'Keep with me!' Haggar shouted to his own warriors, looking to see that they were holding firm. Musicians beat their drums, dictating the pace of the march and clan leaders reaffirmed the thane's orders further down the file. Arrows loosed by the elven archers whickered into their ranks, the occasional gurgled cry indicating that some found their mark, but the dwarfs were unperturbed. Haggar kept them moving until they reached the standing point, the one that Bagrik had shown to all of his captains when they had convened in his tent for the war council.

The thane called a halt, signalling with the banner. Horns blared, carrying the order, and the drummers beat a frantic staccato until they too ceased. Three hundred dwarfs, twenty ranks deep, spanned across the ironclad centre of King Bagrik Boarbrow's army in their regiments of fifty. And this was just Haggar's throng. Two more, equally massive, infantry cohorts bolstered the armoured lynchpin either side, with three further throngs behind them as reserves.

'Here we stand, rocks of the mountain,' Haggar cried to his warriors, 'unshakeable, resilient. Let none through. Smash them on your shields!'

Reverberating horn blasts greeted the declaration, and the dwarf warriors cheered.

'They come now,' Skengi said calmly, hefting his forging hammer.

The earth was trembling. From out of the glittering host there arose a terrible thunder. Heavy-armoured dragon knights surged from the elven centre, their silver helmed kinsmen galloping in their wake. Either side of the lancehead there rumbled vast squadrons of war chariots, scythed wheels shimmering dangerously in the light as they raced. Several of the machines were crushed by boulders flung from the dwarf mangonels. The missiles rolled through them or ploughed into the earth to create immovable reefs upon which several chariots were dashed. But there were simply too many to hope the stone throwers could stop them all.

As the elven cavalry closed, hurtling along the open ground, the elven infantry regiments closed the gap in the line behind them and followed on swiftly. Mere feet from the dwarfs, the elven knights lowered their lances for the final charge.

'Raise shields,' roared Haggar, the tumult of galloping steeds filling his ears as the wall of iron and bronze went up. 'Give 'em nothing!'

BAGRIK SAT PENSIVELY upon his war shield watching the battle slowly unfold. The aged king, grown more ancient in these last few months than all of his one hundred and eighty-six winters, felt a sharp twinge in his side from where the Norscan had stabbed him. Gritting his teeth he forced the pain caused by the poison in his dying body to the back of his mind. He only needed to stay alive long enough to exact his revenge. Nothing else mattered anymore.

The initial advance had gone well. The dwarf centre and both its flanks had reached the standing point, making their shield walls in front of the enemy. Volleys from the stone throwers had all but destroyed the elven reapers, though their archers were still taking a heavy toll. Bagrik was all but ready to order the master engineer to concentrate on them when a war cry echoed to the king's far right. Out of a small cluster of trees emerged a mounted group of reavers, the horsemasters of Ellyrion, loosing arrows and javelins. Two dwarf crewmen slumped dead over their machine already, the remaining journeyman and sighter taking cover behind the stone thrower's carriage.

Another shout rang out, though this time it was followed by dwarf curses, as a concealed band of rangers burst from their hiding places amongst a dense thicket of scrub. Bagrik had learned his lesson against the northmen. He'd deployed these reserves purposely to protect his machineries and dissuade ambitious saboteurs. The dwarf king would not be outflanked by skirmishers so easily again.

Thrown axes thudded into the foremost reavers as the rangers attacked, the elven steeds panicked by the sudden ambush. The elves rallied quickly though, making a feigned flight to draw out their attackers before regrouping and driving at them again. Though slow, the dwarf rangers unslung crossbows and soon had the horsemasters pinned. A second harass of steeds with heavier-armoured, spear-wielding reavers undid their well-employed strategy.

Unable to handle both groups of reavers, the rangers were forced into retreat whilst the elves ran rampant amongst the dwarf war machines. Bagrik scowled at the carnage just a hundred feet from his vantage point, as his devastating stone thrower barrage was brought to an abrupt halt. Though the dwarf crews put up stern resistance, showing no signs of being overrun, they were locked at an impasse with the elves.

Bellowing for quarrellers, the dwarf king was determined to break it.

MOREK WATCHED THE mass of elven cavalry break away from their main battle-line, only for the gap to be filled a moment later by onrushing units of spearmen and bolstered by a smaller regiment of sword masters. The hearth guard captain's foes were closing too, though at a much slower rate than the knights. Another large block of elven spears was coming Morek's way, with more sword masters too. He counted one of the mages amongst their ranks, a silver-haired elf that seemed to radiate power. The dwarf looked askance down the line, to where Hurbad waited silently with a regiment of longbeards. Stroking the talisman around his neck, Morek hoped the runesmith would be able to staunch the elf's sorcery long enough for him to remove the mage's silver-maned head from his shoulders.

Swinging his rune axe in readiness, Morek's attention went back to the dwarf centre and Haggar's clan warriors. The elf knights had passed through the gauntlet lain down by the war machines and quarrellers,

who were now curiously silent. They struck the shield wall in an avalanche of steel and armoured horseflesh. Morek felt the ripple of the
elves' charge all the way down his own flank.

'Hold them, lad,' he muttered to himself. 'Stand your ground, Haggar.'

HAGGAR'S SHIELD WALL crumpled. Driven by the impetus of their onrushing steeds and the will of the elf noble leading them, the charge of
the dragon knights was irresistible. Burnished red armour flew by in
a furious blur and the clatter of steel and the discord of screams filled
the thane's ears. The gradually widening hole torn in the dwarf centre
was further exploited by the immediate wave of silver helms that followed. The dwarf warriors were afforded no time to recover and more
were trampled, or spit on sharpened lances as the elven knights ripped
through them.

Haggar was nearly pitched off his feet in the initial assault.
Staggering, he managed to steady himself and level his shield before
the chariots hit. The war machines ground through the dwarfs, only
the hardiest or the fortunate spared death or maiming beneath their
steel-shod wheels and razor-sharp scythes. The elves aboard the chariots loosed arrows or lunged with spears as they raced past, adding
further to the death toll.

Devastated in the wake of the cavalry charge, the dwarf centre rocked,
like a pugilist put on his heels by a body blow, and began to falter.

'Hold,' cried Haggar. 'Hold!' The command was voiced in desperation
as the thane thrust the banner of Karak Ungor into the air.

'Skengi Granitehand, are you still alive?' called Haggar through the
chaos when he thought the immediate moment of crisis had passed.

'Aye,' bawled the runesmith. 'Just.' A savage gash across the dwarf's
forehead was leaking blood down the side of his face, and Skengi held
his hammer-wielding arm close to his chest.

Haggar nodded, before shouting, 'Close ranks!'

Looking behind him, he saw the elves had punched right through
with few losses. The noble at the elves' head must have been a skilled
rider. He had managed to maintain the knights' impetus and angled
their approach so that they tore out of the dwarfs' flank, into a regiment
from the second throng, and then clean through into the open ground.

Haggar watched through a sea of bobbing helmets, axe blades and
banners as the elf cavalry cantered swiftly along the dwarf rear, bolts
and quarrels whipping by harmlessly as they kept out of bowshot.
Using their momentum, the noble led the knights around to the dwarf
right flank, darting audaciously in-between the two separate throngs.
Distant clan warriors reacted to the sudden threat, urgently sounding
trumpets to signal the change in formation. The dwarfs showed their
shields to the elves prowling alongside them, but were ignored. The
dragon knights were coming around for a second charge at Haggar's

still regrouping throng. It seemed the noble at the fore wanted to claim the banner of Karak Ungor for himself.

'You'll have to prise it from my cold dead hand,' Haggar muttered as the dwarf warriors drew in around him.

The dragon knights were building up speed. They were coming, only this time the elven infantry would be right behind them.

Haggar closed his grip even tighter on the banner and made an oath to Grungni that he would not let it fall.

'Here they come again! Dwarfs of Karak Ungor, dig in and stay with me,' he roared.

The adrenaline rush as the dragon knights bore down on the dwarfs was almost overwhelming. The hoofbeats from their armoured steeds hammered the ground like deafening thunder.

Skengi the runesmith stepped forward from the shield wall when the elves were just a few feet away. Haggar shouted out to him but his cry was lost in the bellowed avowal of rune rites as Skengi rammed his staff into the ground. The sigils inscribed down its shaft blazed into life and a moment later the earth shook as if with the footsteps of giants.

The dragon knights ran straight into the tremor as it rippled from Skengi's staff, their surefooting lost as the ground trembled beneath them. Elves were unhorsed in the quake, crushed as they struck the unyielding plain, or trampled by the steeds of oncoming knights. Others were driven into comrades alongside them, careening dangerously out of control, only to clatter against dwarf shields acting as breakers.

Suddenly the cavalry charge had faltered. Some, like the elven noble at the head, kept their balance and drove on with lances levelled, but the attack had paled in its power and ferocity. Even the chariots were undone, few getting through, most crashing to a halt or upended and destroyed against the stalwart dwarf warriors. Within the morass of iron and bronze, the elven knights found themselves mired.

No glorious charges to win the day. No lightning attacks to rend the foe asunder. This was the grind. Now it got ugly.

HIGH ABOVE THE battlefield, Ithalred gazed down at the struggle below. He soared through the grey heavens on Awari's back, the wind whipping against his face and whistling loudly through the curves of his ornate hawk-helm.

Bursts of magic erupted in the dust-filled chaos beneath him, just ephemeral sparks of lightning or spits of flame such was Ithalred's altitude. The enemy seemed equal to the elves' sorcerous barrage as bolts rebounded against iridescent shields and fiery conflagrations withered into smoke with the dwarfs' counter-magic.

Pinnacle of the glittering host, the elven cavalry led by the dragon knights had become trapped amongst the dwarf infantry. Ithalred watched with displeasure as a silver helm was dragged from his saddle and slain. He considered intervening to try and break the deadlock when elven battle horns announced the arrival of a massive block of spearmen and sword masters following up after the horse. Arcing back on himself, the elf prince turned his attention elsewhere.

A dense patch of cloud loomed in front of him. Ithalred leaned down in the saddle and whispered into Awari's ear. The great eagle pushed with his wings as they surged through it. Wisps of grey-black cumulonimbus tugged at the elf prince's armour, and peeled in misty tendrils from Awari's wings, as they broke free. The great eagle's rookery brothers gave chase and emerged seconds later. The dark vapour still clinging tenaciously to their magnificent bodies dissipated into ether as Ithalred plunged Awari into a sharp dive.

Skarhir and Urouke followed him, maintaining close aerial formation. The great eagles' beaks were dipped like down-thrusting arrows, their wings pinned back, before Ithalred let out a sharp screech and they arrested their descent, wings fanned and claws outstretched in front of them. Buoyed by warm currents of air, the eagles were content to glide as their master surveyed the carnage.

Directly below him, Ithalred saw a stricken band of reavers battling against a group of rangers and the sweating crewmen of the infernal dwarf catapults. Reaching over his left shoulder the elf prince pulled out his longbow, an exquisite weapon forged in the temples of Vaul at Caledor. He swiftly nocked an arrow and loosed. Ithalred smiled darkly as one of the dwarfs, an engineer clad in gilded armour and wielding an immense warhammer, fell dead with a shaft protruding from his neck. The elf prince's enjoyment at the deed was fleeting as he took another arrow and let fly. This time he aimed at the rangers. As the missile flew it broke into many pointed shafts and hammered against the dwarfs in a barrage, who fell in their droves.

Ithalred didn't wait to see what would happen next, his gaze was locked on the still struggling reavers, now being pin-cushioned by dwarf quarrellers. Against the relentless volley fire, the elf cavalry fled. Already the surviving dwarf crews were back toiling at their war machines, preparing to resume their assault. Ithalred narrowed his eyes and trilled aggressively through clenched teeth.

Here is where my sword will fall hardest, he thought as the great eagles dove earthward. The dwarf stone throwers were doomed.

MOREK WINCED AS a surging column of fire flared and then died before his eyes. No sooner had Hurbad dispelled the magicks, the silver-haired elf mage had conjured a luminous golden spear. Concentration etched on his face, the elf lunged with it at the runesmith. Hurbad cried out in agony as the enchanted weapon pierced his gromril armour and dug deep into his thigh.

He fell as the weapon was removed. Morek stepped in its path before silver-mane could finish Hurbad for good. Eldritch sparks danced and spat from the two blades as the hearth guard captain parried another thrust with his rune axe.

'Get him back!' he yelled, and saw two dwarfs come forward and pull the injured runesmith from the fighting rank and out of his eye-line.

'Hold 'em!' cried Morek, as he aimed to cleave the elf mage's neck but was thwarted by the gilded shaft of his magically summoned spear.

Morek's order was easier said than done. The hearth guard were hard-pressed, the warrior-scholars of the elven sword masters weaving about them, cutting and hewing in whirlwinds of deadly steel. Several dwarfs were already dead, no match for the elegant killers.

Kandor was holding his own, though the dwarf merchant was fortunate to be facing off against spearmen rather than the elven sword masters. Morek had deployed him farther down the line when he'd seen the enemy's approach. Kandor was an ufdi, yes, but he deserved a fighting chance at survival and redemption all the same.

'You'll live longer this way,' Morek had joked, calling out to him just before the elves had hit.

Kandor hadn't answered. His eyes had been fixed on the charging elves, knuckles white as he'd gripped his axe. The time for talking had ended.

Landing a punch in silver-mane's midriff, Morek was rewarded with a grunt of pain from his duelling partner. As he drove home the blow, he saw a dwarf cast a throwing axe at one of the sword masters, only to see it rebounded by a spinning arc of silver. The hearth guard fell dead, his own weapon lodged in his neck. Morek found he was still able to force a grave smile. Silver-mane had lost his golden spear. It evaporated into iridescent yellow dust in his spidery fingers.

'You'll lose a lot more than that,' Morek promised then felt his bravura ebb as the mage retreated, allowing two sword masters to take his place.

The dwarf's reaction was terse.

'Bugger...'

DEATH... DEATH WAS everywhere. It was the reek on the breeze. It was the screaming in his ears. It was the hot red haze in his eyes. Death was redolent. It permeated everything, soaked every pore. Death revelled with the savage ecstasy that filled Haggar's thumping heart as he killed.

The elf knights were pinned and had lost the advantage of the charge, but they were still fearsome foes. Well-armoured, high up on their steeds, they would be no pushovers. Even still, Haggar dragged one from his saddle by the boot and applied the death blow with his axe. One of the beasts rammed its muscled flank into him, but it obviously hadn't reckoned on dwarf tenacity and Haggar pushed back with his armoured shoulder, making the steed rear up and unhorsing its rider. Skengi, fighting just ahead of the thane, was quick to dispatch the fallen elf with a blow from his hammer.

It was hard fighting. Probably the hardest that Haggar had ever fought. The elves were skilled, disciplined and phenomenally fast. Dragon knights jabbed down with swords and lances in a crimson blur, piercing dwarf armour with their accurate blade thrusts. Steeds kicked and trampled. It could go either way.

Though the dwarfs fought for all they were worth, the arrival of the spearmen and limb-reaping sword masters had dented their resolve, pushing them to the edge. Haggar could feel the warriors hanging on the brink of retreat. Only the banner of Karak Ungor, the shame of fleeing from it and allowing it to be taken by the enemy, held them... at least for now.

'I'll be damned if I see you put us to flight,' Haggar snarled under his breath at the nearest elf in his eye-line.

With some satisfaction, he watched as the dragon knight was brought down. Another figure loomed out of the battle haze behind him, cutting at either flank with his shimmering, gore-slicked blade. Carving a path through a band of clan warriors, he found the dwarf he was looking for. The noble, he who had led the charge of the dragon knights with such ferocity and skill, levelled his long sword at Haggar. A ruby of blood peeled along the edge and fell ominously onto the ground in front of him.

The dwarf thane roared a challenge, thumping his chestplate and then brandishing the banner of Karak Ungor meaningfully.

'Try and take it you pointy-eared swine,' he cursed. 'I dare you.'

Haggar recognised the warrior. A black mane issued from beneath his stylised dragon helm. He even maintained the cocky swagger in the way he approached the dwarf on his steed. This was the raven-haired blademaster, the elf called Lethralmir.

A shrieking war cry tore from the noble's lips, sounding tinny through his helmet. Lethralmir stirred his barded horse and charged. Though it was only a short distance through the melee, Lethralmir's first blow struck with all the force of an avalanche. At least that's how it felt to Haggar, as he was battered, barely able to turn the blade aside from his neck.

The smallest of gaps had developed in the bloody struggle for the centre. It was through this that the elf noble brought his steed around for a second pass. Though he couldn't see the elf's face hidden by the snarling visage of his dragon helm, Haggar was sure he would be smiling.

Bastard, step down off that bloody horse and we'll see what's what, he thought, working the tension out of his axe-arm where Lethralmir had managed to strike him on the pauldron.

Three short strides and Lethralmir was upon him again, angling his blade in a vicious downward thrust intended to find the gap between the dwarf's gorget and battle helm. But Haggar was equal to it. He fended off the elf's attack, turning the sword with the flat blade of his rune axe. The impact jarred Lethralmir's arm, forcing the elf to take a tighter rein on his steed. As he pulled up, Haggar was able to stay on his feet and whirled his axe around, raking it down the beast's barded flank as it sped past. Armour chinks cascaded like red rain and the dwarf was rewarded with a whinny of pain from the elven horse. Haggar looked down at the freshly reddened edge to his axe blade and smiled.

Lethralmir's steed staggered and nearly fell. The ragged wound in its side was making its barding and armoured rider an intolerable burden. Even so, the elf hauled on its reins to bring it around. Despite loud protests, the steed obeyed. Blood was running freely down its flank now, the enforced exertions tearing its wound ever wider. Suddenly its forelegs bunched beneath it, fetlocks collapsing under the weight it could no longer bear, and Lethralmir was dumped onto the ground in front of it.

The elf blade-master rose swiftly, in spite of his heavy armour, dispatching a pair of clan warriors that came at him out of the melee, axes swinging. Two expert blows, the first whilst he was still on one knee striking the groin and the second rising to his full height, preceded by a deft pirouette that made the dwarf's axe strike seem slow and clumsy, followed by a brutal arcing slash that took the warrior's helmeted head from his shoulders.

Haggar blanched when he saw it – the elf's long sword had sheared straight through the decapitated dwarf's chainmail coif.

'You'll find me a sterner test,' he promised, growling beneath his breath as the elf stalked towards him.

RIDING ON AWARI'S back, Prince Ithalred bolted from the sky like a spear of lightning. With a wicked swipe, he cut the head from the shoulders of a dwarf loader, the stone he was lumbering over to the catapult thudding at his feet before his body toppled back. An engineer brought a mechanised crossbow up, only for Ithalred to swat the weapon aside, sending the quarrel off harmlessly to impact into the war machine's wooden carriage, before impaling the dwarf through the throat with a second blade. Awari raked a third crewman with his talons, ripping apart the dwarf's leather apron like damp parchment. Skarhir and Urouke dove down a moment later, rending with beak and claw. In the few short seconds since the descent of the great eagles, the entrenched stone thrower battery had become something more akin to an open air abattoir.

As he butchered the hapless dwarfs, Ithalred gazed further up the hill and saw King Bagrik glaring at him. The dwarf was stood with a small retinue of warriors and the ancient runesmith of his hold. It would be a simple matter for Ithalred to take flight with his eagles and kill the dwarf lord where he sat upon his war shield. For Bagrik to leave himself so exposed smacked of arrogance, or perhaps it was merely grief that had blotted out his caution and sense. It mattered not. Here was Ithalred's chance to slay the enemy general and win this fight in one clean stroke.

Acutely aware of the dwarf quarrellers beneath him, about to draw a bead at any moment, the elf prince was poised to order the attack when Bagrik raised the faceplate of his battle helm and smiled. Ithalred followed his gaze, to a cluster of large wicker baskets above the stone throwers, further up the hill.

The elf prince had seen them briefly as he'd dove to attack the war machines, but assumed they were filled with ammunition, rock carved from the mountainside in readiness to fling from the launching arms of the catapults, and gave them no further thought. When the lids of the baskets were thrown off and the front and sides fell away to reveal a second battery of war machines, heavy dwarf ballista with bolts primed, Ithalred's words caught in his throat.

The elf shrieked the order to ascend but the dwarf machineries had already loosed. Skarhir got two feet off the ground before his left wing was shredded and he crashed down again. Vindictive quarrellers pinioned him with crossbow bolts until the great eagle ceased floundering. Urouke fared no better and was struck through the neck, the triumphant whoop of the dwarf engineers drowning out the noble beast's death scream.

Awari took to the air with panicked urgency. A missile from one of the ballista grazed his side eliciting a squawk of pain but the great eagle kept on rising. Ithalred felt a crossbow bolt *thunk* into his armour, and knew that some of the volley must have struck his mount too. Already Awari was flagging, doing his best to duck and weave as he sought altitude and the relative safety of the clouds. Weakened though, and losing blood, the great eagle was unable to dodge a bolt that raked across his wing and sent him dipping towards the ground.

Ithalred roared, impelling his beloved mount onwards. They only need reach the safety of the walls of Tor Eorfith…

Awari drew deep on his reserves of strength, managing to put some distance between them and their attackers. But even gliding was painful, every feather ruffled by the wind sending daggers of agony through the proud beast. Ithalred could feel Awari's heart beating faster and faster as he pressed close to the great eagle's body and whispered encouragement. They pitched lower as a strong gust of wind almost sent them crashing earthward, but Awari held on. The white walls were close and the battle seemed dull and distant behind them. Ithalred urged his great eagle for one last effort as he struggled for loft, the high battlements their only remaining obstacle. Spiralling madly, elf prince and great eagle clawed their way over and plunged headlong into the courtyard below. As he fell, Ithalred thought he heard the distant clarion of horns…

* * *

TO THE EAST, dwarf battle horns echoed through the mountains as another force erupted from the hidden caves and crags on the elven left flank. Grikk, captain of the ironbreakers was at their head with a vast and heavily-armoured host. Travelling through the subterranean ungdrin, the dwarfs had been able to move unnoticed and arrive at the standing point where the elves were currently embroiled in fierce fighting against the main dwarf army. They struck up pipe and drum, and raised banners in salute of the king, who watched grimly from his distant vantage point.

Grikk's flanking force made the ground between them and their foes quickly and fell like a gromril wave upon the already embattled elves, massive cohorts of ironbreakers and stern-faced clan miners hewing and rending with axe and pick.

Outflanked, outnumbered and with their general already fled, the elves sounded the retreat.

HAGGAR HEARD THE bellowing horns of Grikk's battle company and breathed an inward sigh of relief. He and the elf blade-master merely stared at each other, still within striking distance, as the elves began disengaging. To their credit, the enemy retreated in good order, raising shields and adopting a defensive stance as they fell back. For their part, the dwarfs were content to let them go and consolidate their own position. It would be dishonourable to stab a foe in the back, even an elf.

As they slowly withdrew, Haggar's attention was suddenly drawn by one of the many small battles still petering out in the wake of the mass elven retreat.

Arthelas was fighting alongside a band of sword masters. He watched her rise up on a pillar of coruscating fire, eyes ablaze with white lightning. She was... magnificent, and for a split second Haggar took his eye off the foe. It was like he and she were the only ones upon the field.

Haggar shook away the glamour quickly.

'I'll see you aga–' he began. The blade in his chest prevented Haggar from finishing his threat.

Mere feet away, Lethralmir's eyes flashed behind his dragon helm with murderous satisfaction.

Sudden shock paralysed the dwarf as a warm sensation spread across his lower body. He felt the wound with his hand and brought up blood on his armoured fingers. It was pooling in his boot.

Lethralmir twisted the blade then yanked it free, before drifting away like a wraith.

Haggar spat blood onto the underside of his faceplate and gagged for air. His vision was fading. The blade had gone right through, piercing his armour as if it were nothing. He wanted to scream out, find strength in wrath but his mouth felt like it was stuffed with ash.

Instead, with the last of his life's blood oozing from his body, Haggar rammed the banner of Karak Ungor deep into the earth so that it would not fall. As the world broke away and darkness smothered him, he thought he could hear singing, like from the old days in the ancient hearth holds of his ancestors...

SKENGI FOUND HAGGAR slumped against the battle standard. It stood proudly like a spire of rock, the dragon banner snapping defiantly in the wind. The thane had not allowed it to fall. The honour of the Skengdrang clan was intact. It had cost Haggar his life.

CHAPTER TWENTY

Tighten the Noose

HAGGAR'S DEATH HIT Morek hardest. The young thane had been one of his charges. He had taught him axe-craft and taken him under his wing. Now he was dead, and there was nothing Morek could do to change that fact. At least he had kept his clan's honour. Another of the Skengdrangs had been chosen to carry the banner of Karak Ungor in Haggar's stead. It was small cause for joy.

So, the captain of the hearth guard was more sullen and morose than ever as he stood at the king's table in his war tent. The elves would pay in blood for all the dwarf lives they'd taken. Morek had seen the dragon-helmed noble at the head of the elven knights. He knew it was the raven-haired blade-master that had fought and killed Haggar. When the elves had retreated the hearth guard captain had lost sight of Lethralmir in the crowd, but he knew in his heart they'd meet again. The slaying of Haggar was ignoble, and the raven-haired elf had a reckoning coming his way for that and more. Such a thing could not stand and Morek promised the young thane vengeance. Even if he could no longer claim it himself, Morek would do it in his name.

Morek's growing canker was further unleavened by the fact that Bagrik seemed now to favour Skarbrag Ironback for war counsel. Skarbrag was old and wise for sure, but the great beard had long since succumbed to senility and hadn't fought on the battlefield for over a hundred years, let alone taken command of one. The king's sudden magnanimity upon finding Brunvilda in Morek's arms had obviously been feigned. Either that or Bagrik had found time to brood upon it during the battle and chose now to exact his grudge against the hearth guard captain.

'The elves are fragile,' stated Skarbrag. 'Their towers and walls will crumble swiftly beneath a determined assault.'

Bagrik nodded sagely, pipe cinched between his lips and gestured towards his war table.

'Here,' he announced to the assembled throng of thanes, captains and masters in his presence. 'This is where the fighting will be hardest.' Bagrik wheezed as he spoke, and had grown more ashen in these last few hours than in all the days he had been at Karak Ungor since being wounded by the poison blade. Many amongst the war council exchanged grave glances with one another at the king's condition, but dared not voice their concern. Bagrik was not to be denied. His will would ensure he would see the course.

The king had pointed to the elven gatehouse. The entire structure of Tor Eorfith was rendered in finely carved blocks of stone and set out upon a map of the battleground drawn by Bagrik's cartographers.

Since the fight outside the elven city the dwarfs had pushed up, bringing their camp with them, and laid siege to Eyrie Rock. Even as the dwarf lords debated their tactics, work crews could be heard through the walls of the tent constructing rams and ladders, gathering rope for grapnels and digging trenches. Rangers had already been sent to the nearby forests to hew more wood. Stone was being carved from the mountain and rocky escarpments of the land then collected in baskets for the stone throwers.

Smoke drifted through the tent flaps redolent with the aroma of iron, bronze and gromril as it was tempered in white-hot forges and bent to the dwarfs' will. All metal workings fell under the iron-hard gaze of Agrin Oakenheart and his apprentices – Morek had been glad to learn that Hurbad had survived his wounding by the silver-maned elf mage, though the runesmith now walked with a pronounced limp.

Racks of quarrels and thick-shafted bolts appeared by the hour and were stacked in makeshift armoury tents before being distributed amongst the dwarf crossbowmen and ballista crews. Piquets had gone up almost immediately, surrounding the elf city, all roads in and out watched by heavily-armoured patrols of hearth guard and longbeards. None could enter; none would be allowed to leave.

'I would not wish to be stationed there,' muttered Kandor beneath his breath, though Morek caught the gist of his words and couldn't help but agree. Taking the gate was a brutal task; certainly elven resistance would be at its fiercest before the gatehouse. Leading such an assault would be something of a death sentence. A pity the slayers could not do it, but no self-respecting dwarf with a death oath would ever cower beneath the mantlet of a battering ram. That was not their fight.

'High walls,' said Kozdokk, guildmaster of the miners. He stroked his chin as he spoke, as if pondering a solution. 'We'll need siege towers,' he added.

Morek was about to answer when Grikk Ironspike chipped in ahead of him. 'We could undermine the walls. I doubt the foundations are deep.'

Bagrik nodded his approval as did Kozdokk, the guildmaster's eyes narrowing with respect for the ironbreaker captain.

Morek cursed under his breath. He had been about to suggest the very same thing in the hope of trying to get back into Bagrik's good graces, but here Grikk had beaten him to the punch. It was galling.

'The elven towers present a problem, also,' growled Skarbrag. 'I saw thrice-cursed sorcery in the windows. They are a haven for elgi wizards.'

'Our stone throwers will put paid to them,' declared Bagrik, followed by a bout of coughing. Once recovered, wiping away the blood from his mouth on his sleeve, the king fixed them all with his steely gaze and announced the deployments for the siege. He came to Morek last of all.

'You'll be here,' he told his captain of the hearth guard in a snarl, 'at the gate.'

THE NIGHT WAS many hours old by the time Rugnir was moving through the camp. He had fought at Grikk's side in the flanking force, assisting the captain of the ironbreakers in negotiating the ungdrin caverns in order to ambush the elves swiftly, and was glad of the chance to fight. But still he wanted more. Nagrim was like a brother to him, one he loved dearly. Only he amongst all the dwarfs of Karak Ungor had been there at his death. It was a bitter memory, made harder to bear by the fact of his enforced sobriety, and one he planned to assuage with elven blood.

Rugnir was not the only dwarf awake and abroad that night. Few could sleep, it seemed, as the final preparations were being made for the siege of Tor Eorfith. The ex-miner walked solemnly past the numerous tents and workshops. To the east he saw the distant elven city. Lantern light glowed dully in the windows and along the parapets and battlements where patrolling spearmen paced back and forth in syncopated rhythm. Both elf and dwarf launched ranging shots into the darkness with their war machines but these were not intended to hit home, merely prepare the field for the following day and ensure the maximum amount of slaughter would be reaped on both sides.

Rugnir felt a strange empathy for the obvious anxiety felt by the elves. He felt it too and decided that he hated being sober, but hated the elves even more. Perhaps when all this was over, when he had sated the latter; he could indulge the former. Memories of Kraggin Goldmaster, Rugnir's father, sprang unbidden into the dwarf's mind as he walked. Rugnir gripped his father's rune pick in his hand. It was an heirloom, borne by Buldrin, his grandfather, and his grandfather before that. Remarkable that Rugnir had not hocked it already, that the entropic dwarf hadn't drunk or gambled it away. It was called Skrun-duraz, or *Stone Hewer*, and it had seen much better days. The pick blade itself was badly tarnished, encrusted by age and a thick patina of rust and grime. The gilded shaft no longer glimmered in the torchlight; rather it was dull and smeared by years of disuse. Rugnir wrenched his eyes away from the forlorn-looking weapon and pressed on with a heavy heart.

When he reached the metalsmith's forge, at the middle of the dwarf camp, Rugnir stopped. Stepping before the hot coals of the furnace, having been given the metalsmith's blessing, he beat away the rust and the age-tarnished sheath around Skrun-duraz. Sweating over the blazing forge, Rugnir hammered and chipped and honed for several hours. When he was done, he cooled the rune pick in a large metal water basin and let the steam from it wash over his face. It was like being reborn – just like Skrun-duraz had been reforged, so too was Rugnir.

Only when he retrieved the venerable weapon did he notice Agrin watching him from the shadows. The runelord was sitting on an upturned rock, studying Rugnir silently under his gimlet gaze. The ex-miner nodded at the aging dwarf, who may have reciprocated. It was impossible to tell. The older a dwarf became, the less pronounced his gestures were. And Agrin Oakenheart was amongst the eldest of all dwarfs.

Moving on, Rugnir had one more errand before he could retire for the night. As he left the forge, though, he felt as if someone was watching him. It wasn't Agrin. It was something else. Rugnir decided to ignore it, chalking up his paranoia to the fact that he hadn't had a drink in months. Right on cue, his dwarf stomach groaned in sympathy.

RUGNIR HEARD KING Bagrik before he saw him. The sound of a hacking, phlegmy cough rattled from his war tent as the dwarf approached. Rugnir was about to enter when another dwarf stepped out of the king's abode and into his path. Hetga was the matriarch of the priestesses of Valaya, and her old but handsome face was grave as she regarded Rugnir. Clearly she had been ministering to the king and, judging by her expression, to little avail.

'Don't keep him long,' she warned brusquely. 'He needs his rest. Though I dare say the cantankerous old bugger will be awake all night anyway.' The matriarch shuffled past him and was gone into the dark.

'Come then,' growled the voice of the king as Rugnir stood outside, wary of entering Bagrik's presence all of a sudden. Swallowing deeply, Rugnir went inside. 'Morek, if you've come to protest over the–' the king began. 'Oh, it's you,' he said, scowling when he saw Rugnir.

Bagrik was sat on his throne, a thick blanket draped over his knees and another across his shoulders. He looked smaller and somehow diminished since Rugnir had seen him last, and now he was divested of his armour. The king had been poring over the 'dead lists' when the other dwarf had entered. His face was fixed in a scowl and his foul mood was obvious. The dead lists were the records of all the slain, all those who would be returning to Karak Ungor beneath a tarp to be then entombed forever with their ancestors in the vaults. A great many leaves of parchment littered the area around Bagrik's throne and upon his lap. The death toll during the battle against the elves had been high and costly it seemed. Rugnir also noticed that Grumkaz Grimbrow was sitting in one corner of the room, stooped over the book of grudges transcribing all the recent edicts of the king.

'Ignore him,' snapped the king, when he'd followed Rugnir's errant gaze. 'He has much to occupy him and cannot hear us. What do you want at this hour, Goldmaster?'

'I have heard that we plan to undermine the walls of the elf city,' he said. 'And that you'll need expert tunnellers for the excavation.'

'What are you proposing, Rugnir?' asked the king shrewdly.

'That I lead the dig,' he answered boldly. 'There are none better than I, no dwarf as fast,' he reasoned.

In his heyday, Rugnir and the Goldmaster clan were peerless miners and excavators. Lodemasters all, they excelled in the business of digging. It was how their clan had prospered so quickly in the first place. Bagrik knew all this, just as he had known Kraggin and Buldrin, Rugnir's sires. This was a changed dwarf before him – no longer raucous and ebullient, nor frivolous or leeching.

'You loved my son – you loved Nagrim?' asked the king softly, seemingly older in that moment.

'Like he was my own kin,' Rugnir vowed, chin upraised proudly. 'He was hard as grimazul, your boy, but with courage and heart.'

Bagrik appraised the dwarf for a spell, judging him, making his decision.

'You'll lead the dig,' he told Rugnir. 'Bring that wall down for me. Bring it down for Nagrim,' he added, and the bitterness in his voice returned.

When Rugnir had gone, Bagrik sagged in his throne.

'Just a little longer…' he breathed, looking at the statue of Grungni set up in his war tent. The Ancestor God was depicted holding aloft a huge chunk of rock veined with silver. 'I'll need your strength,' said Bagrik as he met Grungni eye-to-eye.

The link was broken when Bagrik got the feeling he was being watched. A quick glance at Grumkaz showed him the grudgemaster was still engrossed. Other than that, he was alone.

Must be getting old… he thought, and went back to the grim business of the dead lists.

Bagrik didn't see the shadow figure retreating from the confines of his war tent. None noticed it slipping quietly through the camp and back into the foothills.

* * *

FIVE DAYS THE dwarfs had pounded the city of Tor Eorfith. Five days they had flung rock, rammed the gates and assaulted the walls. Still the elves would not yield. Even when their towers had been toppled by stone and lightning, they didn't give in. Even when their warriors died in droves and the dwarfs pressed relentlessly, they would not capitulate. The foundations of Eyrie Rock had been proven strong. They matched the will of its inhabitants. The elves, despite the dwarfs' earlier confidence, would not be easy to break.

'Loose!'

Morek heard the gruff voice of Master Engineer Lodkin as he shouted for another volley. Over a dozen hunks of mountain rock idled through the air from the stone thrower battery on the ridge above, seemingly in slow motion, before crashing against Tor Eorfith's walls in showers of marble and granite.

The hearth guard captain followed their trajectory with some satisfaction as the elves patrolling the parapets were crushed or fled before the barrage. Sat upon a small rise with his cohort of fifty hearth guard, Morek was glad of the view and the respite from ramming the gates. It seemed nothing, not even the gromril-headed battering ram forged by Agrin Oakenheart, could break down the door to the elven city. After their latest attempts had yielded little, Morek had been ordered back from the siege lines to protect the dwarf war engines whilst they loosed in concerted volleys.

Occasionally the chunks of spinning stone would be blasted apart by the elf mages on the battlements casting fireballs or lightning arcs, and the air would be filled with shards of falling rock. A few hundred feet in front of the stone throwers, Morek and his warriors raised shields as another granite shower rained down on their heads.

When it was over, Morek returned his attention to the elven city walls and saw a banner upraised. From behind a line of spearmen there emerged a host of elf archers. Immediately they began pouring arrows in a steel-fanged torrent towards the stone throwers. Even at extreme long range, the sweaty dwarf crews were forced into cover by the elven volleys. As they retreated and the stone thrower barrage abated, another banner went up. It was followed by the peal of horns.

'Valaya's golden cups!' Morek spat the pipe he was smoking out of his mouth then hurried to his feet and took up his axe.

The gates to Tor Eorfith were opening.

Morek was already shouting orders, rallying his hearth guard into defensive positions. Drummers rattled out the formation in sharp staccato beats as the dwarfs moved in front of the entrenched war machines and into the path of the elven knights hammering out of the city. The dwarf trenches and abatis were nigh on empty. Most of the troops were away from the battleline preparing for the next big push whilst the war machines tried to soften the hardy nut the warriors needed to crack. Only

Morek and his hearth guard stood between the elven sortie and the anni-hilation of the stone throwers.

'Shields together,' he cried as soon as the hearth guard were ready and in position. Unwillingly, Morek's mind returned to the earlier battle on the plain. He had seen what the elven dragon knights could do. He stroked the talisman around his neck without thinking then took a firmer grip on his rune axe and shield.

RUGNIR HEARD THUNDER through the many layers of earth between him and the surface. Though the din of the drilling engine was loud, the sound from above carried well and the miner felt it as much as heard it. It had taken five days to get to this point. Sweating at the rock face, digging deep into the bowels of the world, Rugnir had brought the dwarf excavators to within a hundred feet or so of the foundations to Tor Eorfith. He expected to hit rock in the next hour. From there they would undermine the walls and send them crumbling to the ground for King Bagrik's reserve forces to exploit.

'Hard work eh, ufdi?' Rugnir remarked to Kandor with some of his old cheek.

The dwarf merchant had offered to join the mining expedition almost as soon as it was mooted. He had long since stripped out of his fin-ery and adopted more practical attire of course garments and a rugged miner's helmet.

'You look almost like a proper dwarf,' he joked with good humour.

'We Silverbeards know gold,' Kandor said by way of explanation, 'and we know tunnelling also. It is long past due that I got my hands dirty again,' he added humbly.

Kozdokk, head of the Miners' Guild, smacked Rugnir on the back before he could reply. Rugnir was stripped down to tabard and breeches, a black pot helmet on his head with numerous candles affixed to it by their waxy emissions. He was sweating profusely and wiped a swathe of dirt across his forehead as he turned to the guildmaster.

'Not far,' Rugnir cried above the crushing of rock and the churning of earth.

Kozdokk nodded, chewing on a hunk of stonebread as he watched the work of his miners keenly. The guildmaster had brought the drilling engine all the way from Karak Ungor. A solid metal chassis supported an iron plated cage that ran on large, broad wheels. At the end was a grom-ril drill, tipped with diamond. A series of mechanical cranks and roped pulleys drove the engine itself, pure dwarf sweat and hard labour needed to turn it in order to build momentum. Teams of sappers worked either side of it, hauling back chunks of discarded rock to the waiting strings of mules that were led from the tunnel fully-laden and to the waiting baskets of engineers that supplied the stone throwers and shored up the dwarf entrenchments. Other miners worked with pick and shovel in tandem with the machine. Under Rugnir's expert guidance, progress was swift.

The large cohort of ironbreakers behind them, with Grikk Ironspike at their lead, would not have long to wait.

MOREK FELT THE ground trembling beneath him as the elven knights charged. The hearth guard had locked shields, anchoring themselves around the captain, their lynchpin. As Morek peered through the gap between shields, he saw the warrior leading the dragon knights.

'Lethralmir,' he spat beneath his breath. 'I hope you're watching this, Haggar…'

The elves rammed against the dwarf defence like a hammer hitting an anvil. Despite the power of their driven lances and the fury of their sudden attack, the dwarfs would not yield before them.

'You…' Morek cried, stepping out of the shield wall to level his axe in Lethralmir's direction as dragon knights and hearth guard cut each other down around him.

The raven-haired elf turned in the dwarf thane's direction and his eyes narrowed in the shadowed confines of his helmet.

'Face me!' the captain of the hearth guard roared.

Lethralmir dispatched a dwarf warrior impudently with his longsword in what might have been a gesture of acceptance. He called out a curt command to his knights and they backed away.

'Hold!' bellowed Morek in turn and the hearth guard disengaged, glowering hatefully at the enemy as they withdrew.

The warriors of both races knew a challenge when they saw it. Martial honour dictated that it be observed and that none other than challenger and challenged would fight. No one could intervene until one of the duellists was dead.

Morek was banking on the elf's arrogance to deliver him into the vicinity of his rune axe. When Lethralmir reared up on his steed and came at him, it seemed the dwarf's gambit had paid off.

The elf's first blow was swift and it glanced off Morek's shield with a loud *prang*. A second thrust was aimed at his neck, but the dwarf blocked that too, this time with his axe blade. Aloft on his steed's saddle, Lethralmir tried to press his height advantage. A low swipe arced over the dwarf's head. As he ducked only then did Morek make his move, ramming his shield into the horse's armoured chest. The beast neighed in pain and surprise, buckling onto its fetlocks. Lethralmir had no choice but to go with it. As he hung forward in his saddle, Morek severed the elf's neck as he scrabbled desperately for the reins.

Lethralmir's head fell from his shoulders to bounce over by Morek's feet. The expression on the dead elf's face as it rolled from his helmet was one of profound disbelief.

'I can fight dirty too,' muttered Morek, spitting on the decapitated head before smacking Lethralmir's half-panicked steed on the rump, sending it barging through the other knights and back towards the gates. At the sight of their leader so ignominiously dispatched, his headless body lolling in the saddle as his steed galloped away, the resolve of the dragon knights failed them. They fled, the sounds of jeering dwarfs dogging them all the way back to the city.

The attack on the war machines had failed. One of their nobles was dead and soon the tunnellers would reach the walls.

Slowly, the dwarfs tightened the noose.

CHAPTER TWENTY-ONE

Siege of Blood

DUST MOTES DRIFTED from the ceiling, covering Ithalred's pauldrons in a grey patina. The elf prince's armour was dented, his body bruised since his flight over the walls on Awari's back. Alas, the great eagle had not survived the fall and died in Ithalred's arms shortly after. Awari had been ancient, older than Ithalred, who himself had enjoyed a long life. The elf prince stumbled as a tremor ran beneath his feet. The barrage was unrelenting. The arcing foundation stones shook with the dwarfs' anger. Even through rock, Ithalred could hear the pleas of the dying and the clamour of battle from above. It was a constant reminder of his plight. So desperate was it that it had brought him here, to the lowest depths of Tor Eorfith, the nadir of Eyrie Rock itself.

The elf prince was not alone in the half-dark. Commander Valorian, warden of Tor Eorfith in Ithalred's absence, had joined him.

'He is lost to Khaine,' the elf commander muttered darkly. Resplendent in his silver ithilmar armour, chased with gold and with the lower half of the breastplate rendered in the image of a surging phoenix, he looked distinctly incongruous. Swathed in shadows, Valorian was standing next to his prince outside a prison chamber.

Shining a silver lantern into the depths of the gaol, Valorian revealed a ragged-looking elf in the lamplight. His eyes were bloodshot behind a hungry, desperate mask. His once beauteous silvern mane was now lank and wretched. Strips of cloth lay all about him on the floor where he squatted; they were the shreds of his robes, ripped from his body in a maddened rage. Long gashes throbbed angrily from where the elf had raked his skin with his nails.

Ithalred stepped towards the bars of the cage and regarded the feral creature before him without emotion.

'Still no sign of Korhvale?' he asked quietly with his back to Valorian.

'None my prince, though I have searched the city as best I can. For whatever it is worth, I do not believe a White Lion would ever abandon his post. A Chracian would rather die first.'

'That is what I'm afraid of,' Ithalred whispered to the dark.

Valorian didn't hear him and continued with his report.

'The last of the towers have now fallen, my lord, and I do not think the gates will endure much longer.'

Another tremor added credence to the commander's remarks.

'Arthelas?' asked the prince, without even acknowledging the slow disintegration of his city.

'She is hidden away from the fighting as you ordered. Though, I have not seen her since before the siege began...' replied Valorian, pausing a beat, before saying, 'perhaps the seeress was distraught at the news of Lord Lethralmir's death.'

Ithalred grunted dismissively.

'The hour draws near when we must make our final stand against the dwarfs,' said Valorian.

'Then we'll need every sword, won't we, commander?'

Ithalred's gaze was fixed upon the caged elf.

'Are you ready to fight, Malbeth?' he asked.

The elf ambassador nodded slowly and showed Ithalred his manacled wrists.

'Release him,' Ithalred said to his commander, 'and when the dwarfs break through here... give him his swords.'

THE GATE WAS down. And silver-mane was long dead. Morek had felt a measure of satisfaction upon seeing the mage plunge to his demise.

Recompense for Hurbad's limp, he thought grimly.

Weathering the fusillade from the elven reapers, Morek charged into the levelled spears of the elves that had now moved in front of it. His mouth described a battle cry as he and his warriors barrelled forward. A dwarf charge was a rare thing, likened to a boulder rolling down a steep hill – slow at first but with enough momentum, it could shatter any barrier. Only the elf spearmen stood between them and the city. This close, the captain of the hearth guard was not about to be denied.

Morek smashed one spear aside with his shield, hacked another in two with his rune axe before launching himself at the enemy proper. Dwarfs were impaled on the forest of spikes, twitching in their armour as the elves stabbed and lunged, but it wasn't enough. Inspired by their captain, the hearth guard trampled the well-ordered elf defence with brutality and sheer fury.

Morek could smell blood in his nostrils as he killed, when the spearmen's resolve finally broke and they ran. The dwarfs' momentum carried them further into the city. They wrecked the twin reaper bolt throwers, hacking them to kindling with their axes and dispatching any crew that lingered behind without mercy.

'Sound the horn,' cried Morek to his musician, 'the elgi gate has fallen!'

BAGRIK WAS ALREADY moving down the ridge when the signal that the gatehouse was taken pealed through the air.

A foothold in Eyrie Rock, thought Bagrik darkly, now all we have to do is keep it.

As he rocked from side to side with the march of his shield bearers, biting back every twinge of pain and clinging to his fading strength, Bagrik watched the battlefield roll by.

A storm was already brewing in the darkling sky when the hearth guard rear rankers stormed through the broken gate. Rain drizzled in sheets, tinkling against armour and soaking cloth. Sporadic lightning flashes illuminated the elf archers hunkered down either side of the gatehouse on ruined spurs of parapet, loosing arrows in desperation. It was but a feeble shower to the determined dwarfs, no more deterrent than the rain.

Further warriors surged from trenches and behind abatis, swarming towards the open gate in their hundreds to support the hearth guard.

Across the walls, lines of stout siege towers were locked in position and disgorged warriors into the hard-pressed elf spearmen atop the battlements. Alongside them were racks of ladders with further hordes of armoured dwarfs climbing resolutely to back their kin.

Overhead, the barrage from the stone throwers and ballista had abated. So too had the volleys from the quarrellers below them. Together they loosed sporadically, picking off isolated pockets of resistance, as across the entire battlefield the dwarfs made the final push.

At the south wall, Bagrik's reserves waited patiently. Five cohorts of one hundred clan warriors, plus all the hold's longbeards led by Skarbrag Ironback, bided for Rugnir's sappers to collapse the wall and open up Tor Eorfith completely.

Much to the king's annoyance, and despite the fact that the walls were overrun in places and their gate was now largely ornate tinder, the elves remained steadfast and refused to capitulate. Such tenacity would be laudable had the king not sworn an oath to bring the city down and slay its potentate. The dwarfs needed that south wall down, and soon.

BELOW THE EARTH, the dwarf sappers were nearing their goal. Rugnir had ordered the drilling engine removed from the tunnel. He and the miners would finish the job with picks and shovels.

'A few more feet,' he said to Kandor, digging alongside him. The merchant thane only nodded, intent on the rock face. Kandor had proven his worth during the excavation, not moaning once and unrelenting in his labour. Rugnir sensed he was not the only one trying to make up for past mistakes.

'Bring up the *zharrum*,' added the miner, and waited for a small group of engineers to make their way forward. They had fat satchels slung across their backs. Within were clay fire casks, roughly spherical pots filled with oil and other flammable materials that the dwarfs would use to burn the foundations of the city. Zharrum, or fire drums, generated incredible amounts of heat and cracked stone in minutes, burned down wood in seconds. They were the last element of the dwarf sabotage and would ensure the collapse of the south wall.

'We're almost through,' Rugnir announced. Flecks of ambient light were visible in the fragile earth wall that stood between them and their goal.

'Ironbreakers, prepare for battle!' cried Grikk Ironspike, the captain having only just returned from making his report to King Bagrik and already marshalling his troops. The dwarfs were expecting resistance.

They were not to be disappointed.

As the earth wall crumbled a flurry of arrows spat through the ragged hole leading into the bowels of the elf city. Several miners, unprepared for the sudden attack, were felled instantly.

Pushing past the sappers – Rugnir, Kandor and a few of the others dragging back the dead and wounded – Grikk and his ironbreakers made a shield wall. More elf arrows rained from the gap, breaking harmlessly against Grikk's gromril bulwark. The dwarf veterans stomped forward as one and bellowed, 'Khazuk!'

The elf archers loosed again, now just visible behind the curtain of earth dust and falling rock.

Arrows rebounding off their shields, the ironbreakers took another step.

'Khazuk!'

A third brought them level with the breach.

'Khazuk!'

Retreating swiftly, the elf archers made way for their second line of defence.

Rugnir saw a flash of silver at first then heard a tinny scream as one of the ironbreakers was spun around, nigh on bifurcated in his armour.

Weaving their web of steel, a group of elven sword masters forced the ironbreakers back, their deadly blades carving red ruin in the dwarfs' serried ranks.

Iron-shod boots dragging furrows into the earth at their feet, the ironbreakers had little choice but to give ground against the elven onslaught.

Grikk duelled with one of the elven bladelords – the cloak and plumed helmet he wore marked him out as the leader – but was getting the worst of it, battered into a desperate defence.

The elves had more. From out of the sword masters' ranks there emerged a maelstrom of bloody death. Naked from the waist up, a feral creature, an elf with twin blades, cut and hewed and killed. In the few short moments in which he had stormed into the tunnel, the possessed elf had slain a dozen ironbreakers. Blood rained across his body, criss-crossed by arterial spray, as he revelled in the slaughter.

'Miners to arms!' shouted Rugnir when he realised the sword masters, courtesy of their rampant slayer, would break through.

THE DWARFS WERE on the brink of victory.

Above, in the courtyard of Tor Eorfith's gatehouse, Morek and his hearth guard drove onward. He heard the tramp of booted feet behind him, the clamour of dwarf voices, and knew the rest of the army were following.

'Hold the gatehouse,' he cried to his warriors, 'keep the way open for King Bagrik!'

The hearth guard ground to a halt and stood firm with shields ready.

Across the flat stone of the courtyard, elves were storming from arches and alcoves to repel the dwarf invaders. Amongst them was a band of deadly sword masters. Prince Ithalred was leading them.

Stroking the talisman around his neck, Morek offered a pledge to Grungni that he would not been found wanting.

ITHALRED FOUGHT IN a blur. Every blow was precise; each and every strike was measured. It was as if the elf prince had choreographed the entire fight and already knew the outcome. In the few short moments it had taken Ithalred to parry Morek's first clumsy attack, and riposte with a shimmering arc, slicing the dwarf's forearm and opening him up completely as he dropped his shield, Morek knew he was outmatched.

The hearth guard couldn't even get close.

Ithalred killed them, coldly and efficiently, where they stood. The elf prince betrayed no arrogance in his skill, there was no flourish or swagger, no raw and murderous aggression like with the late Lethralmir; he was something else entirely – a very near perfect warrior.

'Grimnir's teeth!' Morek cursed, barely managing to fend off a searching lunge by the elf prince. Had it fallen, the blow would have impaled the hearth guard captain and it would all be over.

'Rally to me, rally to me!' the dwarf cried, acutely aware that his warriors were bearing the brunt of a serious battering. Morek backed off for a moment, unwilling to step into Ithalred's death arc just yet, and used the time to catch his breath. Clan warriors were forcing their way across the moat and in through the gate. Though in their wake, the elves had filled the gap left by the victorious hearth guard with spearmen. Even now, Morek knew his dwindling cohort were surrounded, that the elves had allowed them to get inside the courtyard so they could butcher them. As he cast about, he thought he saw a flash of armour, a lone warrior upon a sparsely guarded section of wall. It was only a glimpse out the corner of his eye, and with no time to look further Morek dismissed it as nothing.

Deeming he'd had long enough to gather his wits, Ithalred came at Morek again. The hearth guard captain was breathing heavily; he nursed a raft of small cuts and his armour felt hot and heavy. The elf had barely broken a sweat.

Morek blocked left then right, more by instinct and sheer desperation than through any strategy. Ithalred shaped for an overhead strike and the dwarf thought he had the drop on him at last.

No one's that good, he thought, already dodging to the side and preparing to counter with an axe blow to the prince's exposed back. Ithalred's attack never came, at least not the one the dwarf was expecting. Instead, he brought his sword around to lash at Morek's side, a second short blade seemingly emerging from nowhere to stab into the dwarf's opposite flank.

Morek felt the hot metal pierce armour, skin and flesh. Searing agony gave way to a sudden numbness and the hearth guard captain fell, his rune axe clattering to the ground after him.

With their leader down, the stubborn resolve of the hearth guard fractured and the unthinkable happened.

They fled. The sight of the veteran dwarf warriors abandoning the fight and running for their lives sent waves of panic rippling through the dwarf army. The elf spearmen at the gate parted, allowing the fleeing dwarfs through who stumbled into the pressing clan warriors and swept them up into the chaotic stampede.

Dwarfs fell screaming from the bridge into the molten silver moat as the broken warriors pushed their way out. Weighed down by their armour, they sank like bronze stones. In a matter of moments, one decisive act had turned the tide of the battle against the dwarfs and to the elves' favour. Hearth guard and clan warriors fled together and in their droves.

BAGRIK ROARED FROM atop his war shield. The wrathful dwarf king was only scant feet away from the abject retreat.

'Turn, Grimnir damn you! Turn back and face the foe!' Bagrik scoured the faces of the panicked warriors, making a mental note of every single one. They would be remembered forever in infamy in the pages of the book of grudges. Grumkaz Grimbrow was nearby, clasping the mighty tome. As Bagrik called out each name, the grudgemaster wrote it down. But it did no good, the dwarfs kept on running.

From his vantage point, Bagrik could see his lines were suddenly in danger of fragmenting. He wanted this over quickly. A defeat, like the one the dwarfs were close to, would only galvanise the elves. Bagrik had no desire to re-fight the siege again. In his heart, he knew he would not last out a protracted battle. Even raging at his fleeing warriors sapped at his strength – the poison had nearly done for him. He was about to order in his reserves, in spite of the fact that the south wall still stood, when a horn rang out into the blood-hazed night. Its pitch climbed above the thunder, clear as the first hammer strike against the anvil. Bagrik followed its source all the way to the top of the elven battlements.

'Not possible…' he breathed, as tears filled the old king's eyes.

MOREK THOUGHT HE was dead. All around him the clamour of voices drifted in and out. Peering through a dense fog, his gaze went to elven battlements directly above him. When he saw who stood there, shimmering in his ancestral armour, the hearth guard captain knew he was but a breath away from Gazul's Gate.

'Nagrim…' he rasped through bloodied teeth, and passed out.

'NAGRIM!' THE CRY went up from one of the fleeing hearth guard as he pointed to the battlements. In the frantic press to win the battle in the courtyard, the walls had all but been abandoned. The prince of Ungor stood there alone, the corpses of elf sentries slumped around him.

Other dwarfs took up the chorus swiftly and it built to a powerful crescendo as all those close enough to see gazed upon the slain hero of Karak Ungor in fear and awe. The legacy of the hold, personified in iron and gromril, had come back from the dead to fight alongside his kin in their hour of need. In one hand, Nagrim held his battle horn; in the other, a warhammer. Raising the weapon aloft, it was a rallying cry the dwarfs sorely needed and they cheered as one.

The effect was miraculous.

Drums sounded, pipes rang out and the warriors of Karak Ungor held up their banners once more and returned to the fight. The hearth guard found their courage at last, and turned, thundering back to the gate even as their hero descended the battlement steps to meet the foe.

BAGRIK WAS STUNNED into silence. He did not even notice the slowing of his shield bearers as the apparition of his dead son disappeared from sight.

'Not possible,' he muttered again, when he'd found his voice. It wore Nagrim's armour. Bagrik's warriors had cried his name. But…

The king's face darkened abruptly as he remembered how 'Nagrim' had cradled the battle horn. He hadn't noticed it at first. He had been too shocked by what he thought he had seen. The hand that gripped around that horn was crooked, Bagrik recognised it even beneath the dwarf's armoured gauntlet.

'*Lothvar*…' he snarled, face creasing into a scowl.

Brunvilda had defied him again.

Bagrik was close enough to the gate now to see over the heads of his clamouring warriors and the elven force within. Through a gap between banners, he recognised Ithalred. The elf prince was battling furiously, slaying dwarfs with every stroke. Lothvar had descended into that melee. It could be him falling beneath that sword next.

'Lothvar,' Bagrik said again, though this time his tone was urgent. 'Get me through the gate,' the dwarf king raged at his shield bearers suddenly. 'Do it now!'

IN THE TUNNELS, the miners and ironbreakers were taking a severe beating. Dwarf corpses littered the ground, for precious little reply. Alone, the sword masters were few and eminently defeatable, but with the half-naked elf blade-master they had the edge.

Rugnir ducked the swipe of an elf greatsword, before ramming the head of his pick into the startled sword master's chest. He wrenched it out, the wound spitting gore, and stepped over the still-cooling body into another fight.

'Stay with me, ufdi,' he said to Kandor, who fought at the other dwarf's back and was just trying to stay alive. Old Kozdokk was already dead, skewered by a flurry of elven silver. Rugnir tried to keep the guildmaster's bloody carcass out of his eye-line.

Kandor nodded, too tired to speak as he heaved enough breath into his lungs to fight.

Somewhere in the madness, Grikk and his ironbreakers were struggling. Rugnir had lost track of the ebb and flow of the battle almost immediately.

Tunnel fighting was chaotic at best. Sound resonated in the blackened confines of the subterranean; it echoed off the walls and fell away abruptly to nothing. In the gloom, shadows became real and foes became as shadows. The stench of blood and death was intensified. The effect was disconcerting. Hard enough to fight grobi in the dark places under the earth; battling a foe like the elves and their murderous talisman was proving almost impossible.

And then there he was… a crimson phantom, his blood-slicked body shimmering like red oil. Eyes white with crazed fury bored into Rugnir like daggers and the dwarf felt his courage draining.

'Name of Valaya,' he whispered at the spectre of death stalking towards him.

Salvation came from an unlikely source. Kandor appeared at Rugnir's side and one word from his lips saved them both.

'Malbeth?'

The feral elf stalled and recognition dawned upon his face.

'Kandor…'

Anger bled away, supplanted by anguish. Malbeth lowered his blades and let his arms drop to his sides.

'*End it,*' he mouthed to his erstwhile friend and shut his eyes.

A half dozen dwarf axes fell upon the elf, cutting him down at last. Kandor's had been the first. The merchant thane was sobbing by the time it was done. Rugnir gathered the other dwarf to him, putting a meaty arm around his shoulder, and let the miners and ironbreakers past him – now freed with the death of Malbeth – to finish the sword masters. Advantage had swung back into the dwarfs' favour. The elves were few, and though skilled, could not last long.

It was over in a matter of minutes. The tunnel was theirs. Engineers with the zharrum were rallied swiftly. Now, the south wall would crumble.

BAGRIK HAD GAINED the gate when the south wall of Tor Eorfith came down. Trumpets sounded loudly in the chaos as the dwarf reserves piled through the breach. The dwarf king did not need to see it to know that the elves' doom was now sealed. Strangely, it gave him no pleasure. Though he had tried, Bagrik could find no sign of Lothvar amongst the fighting or the fallen. He hoped that Grungni favoured him in all the ways that he had not. There was but one more thing left for Bagrik to do. Across the courtyard, he saw Prince Ithalred. The elf was tiring now. No warrior, however skilled, could reap a tally like he had and not feel fatigue. Bagrik's own malady evened the scales. The king was glad it would at least be a fair fight.

Cutting through a regiment of spearmen, the remaining hearth guard having gathered around their king as soon as he had arrived, Bagrik at last found himself face-to-face with his true nemesis.

There was no need to bellow a challenge this time, no pithy words or caustic insults. The elf prince knew this was coming and faced the dwarf king with dignity, offering a salute with his blade which Bagrik did not reciprocate.

The old king unclasped the faceplate from his helmet and let it fall to the ground. He wanted the elf to be able to see his face when he killed him.

Pleasantries over, Ithalred fell upon Bagrik. Blows came and went in a flurry, elven deftness and speed versus dwarf strength and aggression. Ithalred lunged, thrust, cut and sliced as his sword flashed like silver lightning. Bagrik weathered the barrage with typical dwarf obstinance, using his haft and blade to parry, getting in swings between the elf's blindingly fast attacks. The shield bearers did not intervene; they merely kept their king aloft while he fought.

Ithalred tried to open up Bagrik's defences by crafting an intricate array of attacks, but the dwarf king was equal to it. He replied with a forceful assault of his own. Such was the dwarf's fury that Ithalred felt every bone-rattling strike like a hammer blow.

Bagrik knew the elf's endurance was waning. No creature alive could match a dwarf for tenacity. As Bagrik pounded him, raining blow after heavy blow against Ithalred's improvised defence, the elf began to flag and sought a swift end to the duel. Waiting for a gap in the dwarf king's relentless assault, Ithalred lunged aiming for Bagrik's exposed neck. It was the moment of recklessness that the dwarf king had been waiting for. Feigning loss of balance, Bagrik allowed the elf to stretch and lead with the point of his sword. At the last moment, though, he twisted and brought the flat of his axe down on Ithalred's unprotected grip. The sudden blow forced the elf's sword aside. It grazed Bagrik's gorget before Ithalred dropped it from his nerveless fingers. Fashioning a return strike, Bagrik first caught the elf's wrist, as he went in from the dwarf king's blind side with his short sword, and snapped it. Ithalred suppressed a scream of agony when his wrist broke. He gasped blood when Bagrik finished the move, bringing his rune axe down onto the elf's exposed shoulder, cleaving through his armour and embedding bone.

Ithalred was breathing hard, the rune axe still lodged in his clavicle and his broken wrist limp in the dwarf king's iron grip.

Spitting blood, he rasped, 'Allow me a warrior's death.'

Bagrik's eyes were cold and lifeless.

'You killed my son,' he replied. Bagrik ripped out his rune axe with both hands and roared as he beheaded Prince Ithalred.

'Behold,' yelled Bagrik, once he had caught his breath, pointing down to the decapitated elf at his feet, 'your lord is dead!'

Nearby a few of the elves and dwarfs stopped fighting to look.

'Behold, Prince Ithalred is slain,' declared the king, as more and more warriors turned to face him. 'Cease now... Cease!' he cried. 'It is over. You elgi are defeated.' Across the length and breadth of Tor Eorfith, throughout the battlefield mire beyond, in the lowest depths of the city's foundations as the sound of Bagrik's declaration carried, elves and dwarfs together lowered their weapons and stopped fighting.

RUGNIR HAD EMERGED into the courtyard with Kandor, Grikk and the other survivors of the tunnel battle in tow. It had stopped raining and night was fading, giving way to a rising sun in the east. His warrior band was not far from the king, and he saw the pained expression on Bagrik's face as he spoke, knew that the poison ravaging the king's body was all but done with him as he mustered a final effort before the dawn.

'Leave this place,' shouted the king, his voice echoing around the courtyard. 'Go back to your island in shame. Your treachery has blighted any friendship, any accord with us dawi. You are no longer welcome in the Karaz Ankor.'

* * *

THE DAMNING WORDS of the dwarf king fell harder than any blow. Valorian, the sole surviving elf noble issued a clipped command in his native tongue and his warriors sheathed their swords and shouldered their weapons. There were precious few left in any case to make any kind of last stand. Though, truthfully, the elves had lost heart. Valorian had not been aware of their betrayal at first; he was not party to Ithalred's desperate plan to garner the dwarfs' martial might.

He knew it now, he had known since before the siege and it had sat ill with him even then, just, he suspected, as it had with Korhvale. It was his greatest regret that the Chracian had not been found. Elven horns sounded mournfully and the survivors of Tor Eorfith gathered into a bedraggled column with Commander Valorian at the front. The noble marched his warriors out, together with all who remained of the elven colony. They would head for their ships still at dock along the river to the east and from there back across the Great Ocean to Ulthuan.

'SET ME DOWN,' Bagrik growled, grateful for an end to the rocking of his war shield. He took off his helmet, watching the dwarfs in front of the gate parting to let the elves through. Reaching over without looking, he took a fistful of earth in his hand and clenched it tightly. Letting his rune axe slip from his fingers, Bagrik closed his eyes and exhaled a lingering breath. It was to be his last.

EPILOGUE

All Hail the Queen

KARAK UNGOR WAS silent as a tomb. The workshops were quiet. No clatter of hammers or ringing upon anvils could be heard. No voices called out, no murmuring of longbeards, no scrape and clash of picks on stone. No clank of armour as warriors patrolled. Even the gold counters were stilled. The hold had simply stopped so that all within could bear remembrance to their king, Bagrik Boarbrow. Such a thing was unprecedented. Never in all the days of the Delving Hold had utter quietude descended, but descend it had and like a bitter black veil.

In the days since the siege at Tor Eorfith, Bagrik had been returned to his hold. Grikk found him sat upon his shield, slate-grey eyes glaring sternly forever more, a fistful of earth in his leathery grasp.

The king is dead. The solemn pronouncement had rung around the battlefield like a mournful bell.

The king is dead.

As Bagrik's body was taken up by his shield bearers, a tearful Morek had led a slow procession from the city all the way to the camp and from there to Karak Ungor. In his wake, the miners and engineers had descended, smashing rock and hewing stone, finishing what the siege engines started and leaving Tor Eorfith a ruin.

Upon the dwarfs' return, Bagrik was entombed with Nagrim. There was a palpable wave of relief at the sight of the slain prince. There had been those who swore they had seen him battle the elves, even fought by his side, but none could remember what happened to him after the siege. He had simply been lost from sight.

Some, the overly superstitious or gullible, suggested Nagrim's body might not be in the temple of Valaya when the dwarfs came back, that he had somehow taken leave of his own death. It was not so. Rangers had scoured the battlefield afterwards, and the crags beyond, but no sign could be found of Nagrim or his apparent spectre. There was just his suit of armour left inexplicably in a shadowy alcove, laid out with reverence and respect. It too was taken back to the hold and entombed in the vaults.

Only Brunvilda knew the truth of it, and she would not say.

In time, missives would be sent by the High King Gotrek Starbreaker of Karaz-a-Karak pledging his support and expressing his grief. A new liege lord of Karak Ungor would be chosen by the elders, but for now it was Brunvilda who ruled. Addressing her throng in the wake of her husband's death was her first royal act as matriarch.

'We dawi stand alone,' the queen began.

She too was alone, stood before the throne of Ungor in the Great Hall.

Brunvilda was glorious. Clad in her ancestral armour, the shimmering crown set upon her brow flashed like a star of fire. Bedecked in jewels, clasped with vambrace and greave, she was every bit the warrior queen. A short cloak hung heavily from her shoulders; heavy like the dour mood that pervaded throughout the hold. In her hand, stone head held down-ward to the floor, was Brunvilda's rune hammer.

The vast chamber that stretched in front of her was teeming with dwarfs. They stood shoulder-to-shoulder like a mighty iron sea. All the clans were present; all the longbeards, the veterans, the craftguilds, mas-ters, artisans and merchants. No dwarf that day, save for the gate guards – and even they had their heads bowed and their bodies still – wasn't present for the queen's address.

Such was the magnitude of the gathering that the huge double doors to the Great Hall were thrown open wide and the dwarfs trailed back down the long corridor beyond for as far as the eye could see.

Flickering torches cast a weak and sombre light on the scene in the Great Hall. Even the statues of kings appeared bowed and subdued.

'Like the mountains we stand alone,' Brunvilda said, 'and like the mountains we will endure. We are rocks, you and I. Neither man nor elgi, nor grobi, nor any other creature of the world that looks upon our domain with jealous eyes will ever break us... ever!' Her voice echoed loudly through the massive chamber, resonating in all those present.

'They will find us resolute and belligerent. They will find a wall of iron and bronze, rooted in the bedrock of the very earth. Such things do not yield to force.' Brunvilda paused. Looking around the room, her gaze was as hard as her words, as hard as iron.

'Dark days are ahead, make no mistake about that,' she warned. 'We must look to ourselves for salvation. When the enemies of the Karaz Ankor come, and mark me they will... we will not bow to them, nor will we be put asunder. We are dawi! By all the Ancestor Gods, we will smash our foes to dust should they come to our walls. We are steadfast. Together, we will never be defeated. Never! So says, Brunvilda, Queen of Karak Ungor!'

She thrust her rune hammer into the air and the throng roared in affirmation.

The sound was deafening. It shook the walls and made the earth tremble. The dwarfs were defiant; their anger and their bitterness gave them strength and solidarity. But dark days *were* coming, and they were closer than anyone could have known...

Tor Eorfith was like a skeleton of shattered rock and broken spires. The former glory of the elven city had been smashed utterly from the face of the world. The miners and sappers led by Rugnir had set about their task with extreme prejudice.

Within the shadows of the bowels of a ruined tower, Lothvar awoke and found he was trussed to a slab of fallen stone. He remembered only snatches of how he came to be here. Like his mother had told him in the Temple of Valaya, he had found the battlesite by following the trail of his kinsdwarfs and fought with his father against the elves. His heart had sung, unshackled for the first time, exultation filling the dwarf prince as his kin had cheered. It did not matter that they shouted his brother's name; all that mattered was that he was there and had rallied the army. Lothvar had never been happier in all his miserable, mistreated life.

A presence in the hollowed-out tower got his attention and wrenched his thoughts back to his predicament. Once the battle was over, Lothvar had slipped away. He had wanted desperately to stay, but his mother had forbid it. Lothvar didn't really understand her reasons as she had explained them, but he did not wish to bring shame to his father by exposing the lie of his existence, so he had disappeared.

It had not been difficult; all eyes had been upon his father when he had retreated back over the wall. Once on the other side, he had hiked away from the battlefield. Both armies were spent, and none had the strength or inclination to follow him. Once out of sight, Lothvar had removed his ancestral armour, and placed it carefully out of the way where he knew it would eventually be found. Moving quickly, a hand before his eyes to ward off the painful light of the rising sun, Lothvar had tracked his way through the crags using scent and sound to guide him. There within a shallow gulley, beneath the shadow of a rocky promontory, he found the knapsack he had secreted before the siege began. There was a hooded cloak, which he had donned at once drawing the cowl to fend off the bright sun, food and weapons. He slung the crossbow over his back and cinched the hand axe to his belt. Then he began to make his way into the mountains.

Recollection became hazy after that. Lothvar had kept off the path, using seldom trodden ways and keeping to the shadows. It was within a copse of scattered pine, in the lee of an overhanging rock that he heard the crunch of stone. Something had moved in the gloom around him. He had reached for his hand axe, sensing danger, but all too quickly the shadows became warriors and the warriors subdued him. He had woken here, alone in the cold and merciless ruins of Tor Eorfith.

ONCE PAST THE dwarf piquets, Arthelas had found her followers quickly. In the confusion of the coming siege, she had slipped away from the citadel and beyond the city's walls. Using sorcery, she had adopted the form of Craggen the dwarf hermit, the guise with which she had duped Rugnir so easily. Unleashing him at precisely the right moment to bring about discord and war amongst the elves and dwarfs had been easy too.

The cave where she had held, and ministered, to him was found and secured by her followers already at large in the Old World. Magically transporting herself from Tor Eorfith to the cave for Craggen's appearances had been taxing, but not impossible, and vital to her lie.

Foolish Ithalred – he had no concept of her true ability. Now, it no longer mattered.

Swathed in purple robes, Arthelas stood at the apex of a triangle of three. Her two acolytes were standing silently at the opposite points. Between them, at the nexus of the triangle, was the dwarf sacrifice.

'With this blade, I invoke Hekarti,' she said in the sibilant tongue of dark magic. 'By the Cytharai, by Ereth Khial and all the fell gods of the Underworld, I beseech her power. Let blood seal the pact.'

Arthelas cried out, throwing her head back. Her face was twisted into a howl of pure malice. In her outstretched hand she clasped a jagged dagger. It was not so dissimilar from the one used to stab Bagrik and poison the dwarf king.

LOTHVAR'S EYES SNAPPED wide open when the blade went in, when it pierced his pale naked skin and entered flesh. A warm cascade flowed across his body at first, before it cooled and chilling numbness took hold. As he slipped away, his life blood pooling below the slab, Lothvar hoped he would see his father and brother in the Halls...

HER FACE WAS dashed with blood. Arthelas left it that way, staring wild eyed at the slain dwarf beneath her. She felt empowered, her mind awash with visions of war. Malekith would be pleased. She and her small coven had sown dissension between Karak Ungor and the elves of Ulthuan. Though in truth, Ithalred had been an easy dupe. His arrogance and desperation had led him down the path; Arthelas had only to show him the way. Lethralmir was an easy pawn in that regard. Love-sick and amorous, the blade-master had bent all too effortlessly to her will. Atharti, underworld goddess of pleasure, was well sated by their lustful desires.

It was all just the beginning of a much larger plan. Arthelas was wise enough to realise the small significance of her part in it. For she knew that all across the Old World her dark kin were making ready to ensure any lasting peace between elves and dwarfs would be fleeting. Malekith had willed it.

GRUDGELORE

A history of grudges and the great realm of the dwarfs

INTRODUCTION

Dwarfish lore and law have been both a passion and an indulgence of mine for most of my life. From my earliest years I have been fascinated by these folk, the closest of our allies, ever since a dwarf by the name of Grondik Knarkson befriended me whilst I attended Blackthorn College in Nuln. Though he is reticent by nature, the little I gleaned from my conversations with this doughty librarian was enough to set a fire in my mind that has smouldered for many years. Long I have yearned to study better the ways of these people, and by chance, or perhaps the guiding hand of Verena, I have been able to do so these past twelve years. This fire consumed me for that long time and I hope that the reader shares with me the excitement of discovery and scholarly pursuit that this tome represents.

It was an auspicious moment when a group of adventurous souls entered my shop of books and scribewares. They proffered to me an ancient dwarf tome, much scarred, which they claimed to have recovered from an ancient dwarf hall beneath the Worlds Edge Mountains. I examined the book and was delighted to authenticate their claim, for I held one of the books of grudges of the ancient dwarf hold of Karak Eight Peaks. It cost my entire savings to procure it from these mercenaries, for they had some inkling of its rarity and value and were hard bargainers, but it was worth every crown and shilling. By examining the book's contents, I have been able to study the dwarf mind, the culture of their civilisation and the history of their empire as never before. For these last dozen years I have spoken to many colleagues, both human and dwarf, and the volume you now hold is the result.

To understand the nature of the grudge is to be given rare insight into the dwarfish mind. On casual contact, one might mistake the dwarfs as capricious, yet not altogether unlike ourselves. However, as I reveal in this book, the dwarf mind and the human mind are as truly unalike as that of men and elves or even foul orcs. One must also come to appreciate how much of our own custom and tradition has been inspired and influenced by the traditions of the dwarfs, and how little our own culture has impacted upon them. Though some dwell in our towns and cities, and for many of us urban folk the sight of dwarfs is not uncommon, we must forever be of mind that they are a race apart. It is through good nature and conduct on our part that the dwarfs choose us as allies, but there are lessons to be learnt from the information I have gathered herein. Let it not be forgotten – never wrong a dwarf!

A grudge is, at face value, a simple thing. It is a record of a misdeed done to a dwarf, or the race of dwarfs, so that the wrong might not be forgotten. In this regard, it is not so dissimilar to the vendettas common in Tilea, or the concept of revenge with which we are all familiar. Yet a grudge is something much more than a simple call for vengeance. It forms a major part of dwarf law; it is an account of a dwarf's honour; it is a ledger of oaths and fealty. The diligence with which a dwarf trader totals his invoice is as nothing compared to the detail and gravitas placed upon the scribing of a grudge. Grudges are contracts and history. Before the scribing of a grudge, the grudges of ancient times are consulted, the old records brought forth to see what the wisdom of the ancestors can teach the kings of today. Through precedent and judgement, the weight of debt is measured, so that the deeds of all dwarfs, and their allies and enemies, can be properly reckoned.

A great part of dwarf society and endeavour is solely geared towards the recording and avenging of grudges, giving rise to the learned grudgemasters and loremasters, and the creation of the sinister reckoners. All dwarfs record their grudges, but it is the greatest of grudges that concern us here. Armed with the information in the volume I have in my possession, I am able to examine the grudges of kings.

Each king maintains a book of grudges, recorded in blood – several volumes, in fact. Some grudges are of a personal nature, some relate to his clan and his hold. Largest and most sacred of these is the Dammaz Kron, currently held by Thorgrim Grudgebearer, the High King of the dwarfs and lord of Karaz-a-Karak. In the Dammaz Kron are recorded all of the grudges of dwarfkind. Twice in every century the Day of Grudgement is held. All of the dwarf kings travel to Karaz-a-Karak and relate their new grudges together with grudges that have been settled, so that the Dammaz Kron can be kept accurately. In these dark times, this 'Day' of Grudgement now lasts for several weeks. When the dwarf empire is called to war, the Dammaz Kron is brought forth. From his Throne of Power, a gilded, rune-etched chair borne aloft by four sturdy dwarf warriors, Thorgrim leads his army, reading out aloud those grudges perpetrated by the enemy and not yet atoned for. Such is the power of the Dammaz Kron, it is said to drive the dwarfs into a fighting madness as their minds fill with the insults and wrongs of ages past.

Dwarf grudges can take many literary forms. Some are very formal, dictated by a grudgemaster for the king to inscribe properly. Others are simple histories, while some are elaborate tales. Some of the greatest and most popular dwarf sagas were first recorded as grudges, and some entries in this volume have a particularly poetic quality. The preferences of the king, the importance of the grudge and historical styles have all influenced different types of wording over the many centuries since the first grudge was recorded.

Once written, a grudge can neither be erased nor struck through until it has been settled. This might occur through the death of the perpetrator, material recompense, apology or punishment. Over centuries the grudges recorded by the king's predecessors and his peers form the basis of dwarfen law, so that the debt of a grudge in distant times and places forms the basis of judgement for the reckoning of grudges. The grudgemasters research long and hard for guidance to give their king, providing him with recommendations of suitable recompense taken from other grudges. Likewise, in matters of grudges against fellow dwarfs, a dwarf against whom a grudge is pending will employ his own grudgemaster to present other previous grudges that are similar in nature, with the aim of garnering leniency.

While a grudge still stands it is a burden to be carried by the king, an unavenged wrong that the dwarfs believe will weigh him down and be used in judgement against him come the time of his passing into the Halls of the Ancestors. Even those that have been settled, of which there are pitifully few in comparison to the many thousands recorded, are still held in permanent record should the need arise to refer to them. Grudges can also be recorded against a person after their death. In this regard, the descendants of the recorded transgressor are liable for making amends. A dwarf so grudged against will carry his grudges in the Halls of the Ancestors until suitable reparation is made, and will be so weighed down by the grudge that he will not be able to sit at Grungni's table.

Thus, the grudges are also one of the greatest histories of the dwarfen people, and through their study distant times and strange lands are laid before us. So, join me now, as we delve into tales of honour and deceit, of war and betrayal, of craftsmanship and beer.

Heinrich Altendorfer

Heinrich Altendorfer, 2519

CHAPTER ONE

The Greenskin Grudge

The Atrocities of Gorfang

There are many grudges that record the dwarfs' hatred of the greenskin, dating back thousands of years. One of the most recent and bitter events that has further fuelled this loathing is the attack of Gorfang Rotgut on Karak Azul.

Grobkul in the Upper Hall of the Third Deep

BE IT KNOWN that on this day King Kazador of Karak Azul bears witness to a grudge declared against the Red Sun grobi. This grudge be declared on behalf of Thorki Borrisson who broke his ankle whilst giving chase to grobi in the Third Deep east of the Upper Hall. This grudge names the Red Sun tribe as particularly poor sport. Today's grobkul[1] organised by King Kazador resulted in only a handful of green vermin being found. It is to be noted that the Red Sun tribe are of a particularly cowardly temperament, even more prone to running than normal grobi scum. This grudge shall be recompensed upon the annihilation of the Red Sun tribe and the fullest reclamation of the Third Deep east of the Upper Hall.

Be it known that King Kazador of Karak Azul has this day declared grudge against a grobi of the Crooked Claw tribe. The greenskin offered little entertainment to the king

---

1. Literally, 'the art of stalking goblins in caves', a common diversion of the dwarfs. See 'Dwarf Pastimes' for further details.

upon this day's hunt by dint of narrowly ducking a cross-bow bolt fired by King Kazador. Our king is most displeased at such selfish behaviour though it is to be expected from goblin filth. Said grobi avoided death at the expense of King Kazador slaying his one hundredth goblin in a single calendar year. This feat was achieved by the former king but has yet to be equalled or bettered by King Kazador and as such our thane-king's disappointment is great this day. The grobi can be identified by a large wart on the left side of its nose. It also has a broken tooth in its lower left jaw and a squint in its right eye. Its most defining feature is likely to be a fresh groove-like scar across the top of the head from front to back. King Kazador has offered twenty gold pieces as recompense to the individual who locates this grobi and presents it to him for a second shot.

The Greenskins of Black Crag

ON THIS GRAVE day let it be written that King Kazador of Karak Azul records a great grudge against the urks of Black Crag. One hundred and twenty-three dwarfs have lost their lives this day in battle against the greenskin menace. All fought hard and valiantly. Amongst the dead are four to be especially missed for their deeds during the fighting.

Thane Henkist of the Dwirrar clan was killed by a rock hurled by a crude war machine. He was leading the Dwirrar Longbeards on an attack against the urk left flank and had already accounted personally for some score or more of their number. Whilst fighting against a brutal and ugly urk warrior of some height and girth, Thane Henkist was momentarily laid upon his back. He was forced into this supine position by the fact of his opponent falling on top of him once its knees had been severed by a well-timed axe blow. From this predicament Thane Henkist was unable to extricate himself for several moments during which the crew of the aforementioned war machine loosed their engine against the longbeards. Most managed to evade the impact of the shot but Thane Henkist was crushed immediately as was his nephew Grodi who was attempting to assist Thane Henkist in freeing himself. Thane Henkist Will Be Remembered, Grodi Wirrar Will Be Remembered. Despite the loss of their Thane, the Dwirrar Longbeards continued to press the enemy and routed many of their number from the field.

The third death marked out for especial grudge is that of Gobrik Bannag of Clan Bannag. Gobrik Bannag gave his life in defence of King Kazador of Karak Azul. The brave beardling of only forty-three winters interposed himself between his liege-lord and the mace of a large and vicious boar-riding urk. Gobrik Bannag was carried from the field with his skull broken and despite the attentions of the priestesses of Valaya died from the injury before he reached the hold. Gobrik Bannag Will Be Remembered.

Engineer Baruurm Tubak is also especially mourned for his self-sacrifice. Fast-moving wolf riders had flanked the main force and were in the process of preparing to charge the war machine battery. In the skies aboard his gyrocopter, Engineer Tubak saw the threat posed by this development and acted in a manner that will see him lauded in the Halls of the Ancestors. Engineer Tubak expended the remaining ammunition in his Windlass-propelled Rotating Automated Handgun[2] but due to buffeting winds was unable to direct the greater part of his shot at the wolf riders. These cowardly raiders were moments from reaching the cannon on the outermost right flank when Engineer Tubak pushed his gyrocopter into a steep dive and crash-landed in their midst. Though many foul greenskins were killed by this heroic act, Engineer Tubak ensured the destruction of the flanking force in its entirety by the selfless detonation of the distilled alcohol burner powering the engine of his gyrocopter. The resultant explosion slew many of the stinking grobi and caused the few survivors to flee thus saving the cannon and other war engines. Engineer Baruum Tubak Will Be Remembered.

King Kazador of Karak Azul wishes his anger of the day to be particularly noted. Though long there has been a thrice-cursed greenskin presence in Black Crag, the orcs have of late been especially bold. Today they had crossed the Dearding Stream and marauded as far as the Fourth Tower. It was such reckless advance that arose the wrath of King Kazador and forced the throng of Karak Azul to march forth and do battle. The one hundred and twenty-three deaths of the warriors of the hold this day are laid solely upon the orcs of Black Crag. King Kazador demands that vengeance be swift lest the growing strength and boldness of these foul urks is not stemmed. The reclamation in full of Black Crag and the outlying outposts is already subject to many grudges. King Kazador wishes it to be known that recompense for this grudge is counted only by the death of the ruling warlord of the orcs of Black Crag. This brutal greenskin leader must be identified and dealt with in a speedy and forthright manner.

2. A somewhat revolutionary weapon frowned upon by the Engineers' Guild at the time.

IN THIS YEAR does the foul grobi chieftain, Gorfang Rotgut commit a heinous raft of wrongs against Azul and its noble lord, Kazador of the Donarkhun clan.[3]

By means of a tunnel lost in the dust of ages, does the grobi, squatter king of the once glorious Karak Drazh,[4] sneak into the hold. With low cunning, as befits its filthy breed, does the urk choose his time to attack with great Thane-King Kazador away from his realm at a grobkul. Many of his clan-kin are with him.

A horde of great urk, warriors of Rotgut's conspirator Morglum,[5] and grobi follow the squatter king. At the threshold to Azul, Badarin Stonehand and Kurgrin Cragbrow fall, the black shafts of grobi crossbow bolts embedded in their backs. *True grobi courage that! An arrow in the back as is their wont.* The blood of a hundred grobi each for their passing. Their names will be etched in blood in the kron.[6]

Rotgut and his foul kin reach the ale store of the Third Deep.[7] Brewmaster Thengeln, resting his eyes, is slain. A rusted blade through the heart as he is in repose. *Thagi!* Thengeln's blood still warm, the grobi befoul the many casks and firkins with their dung. Thengeln's Golden Preserve, a brew grown old by a century of fermentation is amongst those lost forever, much like his art. A great gorog takes place. In the aftermath, nought remains but dreg and grog. *Our vengeance shall be exacted in grobi blood of equal measure for every drop of grizdal spilled!*

The Hall of Kazgar runs thick with dwarfen blood. Black urks – with armour thick and blades broad – attack quickly and it is barely a battle. The clan warriors of Azul, slain in their sleep! More grobi treachery! A fight is made by those able but the grobi are many. No khrum is sounded in the deep and so

3. See 'Karak Azul – A Clan Record'.
4. Karak Drazh was one of the great holds of the dwarf realm. Indeed, it was one of the largest and possessed rich veins of metal ore and deposits of gemstones and jewels. It fell many hundreds of years ago to the orc warlord, Dork. In modern times it is known as Black Crag, now a formidable orc fortress ruled over by the warlord Gorfang Rotgut.
5. Some historical sources suggest that the infamous warlord Morglum Necksnapper was present at this battle. I am undecided on that theory, but it may be the case that only his black orcs were involved as part of some fragile treaty with Gorfang Rotgut.
6. Khazalid for book or historical record. Here, I believe, it is referring to the hold's book of grudges. See my introduction to this volume for further expansion on the subject of grudges.
7. Dwarf holds are arranged in a series of subterranean levels referred to as 'deeps'. See 'Anatomy of a Hold' for a more discursive discourse on this subject.

the chamber falls and Rotgut is left to commit further affronts. Statues, remembrances of the ancestors of Azul, are beheaded and made wrong. *Krut sores upon the grobi filth!* They smear their dung upon the walls. Its stench shall stain the hall for many years. *Uzkul take them!* This grobkaz is not the end of it. The Karak Zharr, its heart has burned since the thane-king was a beardling,[8] is extinguished. A mound of grobi dung befouls it. *A thousand woes that can only be dulled by blood!*

The urk force their way into the vaults in search of galaz, gorl and rhun. The lesser chambers are breached, their guardians slain by urk arrows. Grunak Bardikson is alerted by the commotion and rouses the vault warden and a band of clan warriors. They fight the grobi in the feasting hall[9] of the Fourth Deep. None so far have opposed the squatter king. Hallar Halgakrin is the only survivor of this battle. He tells of Grunak's rage at the debauchery of the urk. They make merry in the hall, gorging themselves on meat and ale as Grunak bellows a challenge to Rotgut. The dawi meets the horde with steel and grom, shields locked fiercely.

Rotgut is broad and thick of muscle.

His red blade carves a ruin in Grunak's kin.

Grobi blood is spilled, yet it is not enough.

Grunak and his warriors are encircled.

The shield wall thins.

It is a runk.

Grunak himself is slain by an urk crossbow as he fights to get to Rotgut. His beard is sheared and worn like a pelt at the squatter king's waist. *Rutz upon him until his bowels run loose!* The wounded and dying are left and Rotgut is free to plunder the vaults. Mercy of Valaya, the thindrongol[10] is not discovered. Urks do not possess the wit or cunning to bypass the concealed rhun seals.

Kazrik, son of Thane-King Kazador, rouses from slumber, ever vigilant in his father's stead. Together with his personal hammerers, Kazrik enters the feast hall of the Fourth Deep and finds the dwarf dead. A small group of urk, torturing

---

8. Beardlings are what the dwarfs call their youth. The name refers to the infancy of their beard growth – suggesting a lack of age and wisdom, but is also an indicator of a dwarf's mental maturity. Given their longer lifespans, beardlings are only regarded as adults once their beards have grown to a requisite length, despite the fact their bodies might already be fully developed. This can take several decades, making them much older than human children and adolescents.

9. See 'Dwarf Pastimes'.

10. Khazalid for a secret vault in which treasure or ale is kept. I believe in this instance, it is likely referring to a gold vault.

the wounded with coarse blade and flame, are quickly felled. Hallar Halgakrin, son of Fengast Halgakrin, tells the heir of Azul of the urk treachery, the besmirching of dwarf honour and of pillage most foul. It is his final breath. His name shall be etched in the book of remembering.[11] Upon sight of Grunak, Kazrik weeps openly. A great loremaster,[12] proud of tromm was Grunak. His wisdom will be missed. A thousand grobi swine shall perish in his name!

Karag blood in his veins,[13] Kazrik, with axe in hand, marches from the feast hall, hammerers in tow. Galin Thunderheart is the first to see the vaults. The doors are smashed with urk clubs, rhuns broken. Scattered gorl is in evidence, much of it has been stolen. In its wake is a grinning effigy of the urk gods, wrought in foul-smelling dung. Kazrik smashes it with his axe.

Tunnels lay thick with urkish dung. The grobi stench hangs in the air like a cankerous pall. The statue of Razek Forgehand, the first rune-maker of Azul, lies in ruins. An urk cleaver has split it in twain and remains stuck fast in the stone. Kazrik follows the trail of sacrilege to the Hearth Hall of Azul[14] in the Fifth Deep. It is dark within, all torches extinguished, the hearth slumbering. In the light of glowstones,[15] a figure is revealed at the back of the chamber. It is Thordrik Greymane, known as Thordrik the Venerable, longbeard of the Donarkhun clan and Kazrik's uncle. He is bloodied and broken. Urk chains bind his beard, hands and feet. The heir of Azul rushes, heedless, into

11. The book of remembering is a huge tome that simply lists all of the dwarf dead for a given clan and hold, much like a memorial plaque. In it is recorded the name of the deceased, their deeds and the manner in which they died. Particularly important or wealthy dwarfs are afforded an epithet from the king or hold loremaster.

12. Dwarfs that display a particular aptitude for learning and remembering things are often interned as loremasters. It is the solemn duty of the loremaster to scribe all of the deeds of his clan and indeed his hold, so that they might never be forgotten. A king will have a personal loremaster to record his life and his deeds, and on occasion I have read that they even transcribe grudges as dictated by the king himself. They hold a much-revered position in dwarf society as they are custodians of knowledge, something dwarfs place much stock and respect in. It is not uncommon for longbeards to be found amongst the ranks of these dwarf chroniclers. Their beards are a sure indicator of their tenure and they carry with them the wisdom of ages. Lesser loremasters, mere apprentices in the art, are known as lorekeepers.

13. Literally this means 'blood of the fire mountain'. I propose that this refers to lava and therefore suggest it relates to Kazrik's building fury and fire.

14. Dwarf recreational activities are often conducted in hearth and feast halls. My treatise on 'Dwarf Pastimes' sheds further light on this matter.

15. Glowstones are used by the dwarfs to illuminate subterranean passageways and tunnels. Dwarf understanding of geology is unfathomable to us; even the engineers of Nuln and the wizards of the Gold College are unable to unlock these secrets. A very rare glowstone is called brynduraz – meaning brightstone. It was mined solely from Mount Gunbad, which fell in -1457 (IC), sacked by night goblins.

the chamber intent on bringing vengeance to the grobi who committed such an act.

Thordrik mouths a silent warning at Kazrik's approach, but it is too late. Torches flare to life and to his horror Kazrik finds the heathen urk infesting the Great Throne Hall. The squatter king laughs upon the throne of Azul's ancestors, the corpses of dawi slain all about him, beards hewn for trophies.[16] In black urk chains are the rest of the Kazador clan bound, together with many others taken by Rotgut. Thordrik's tongue has been removed in an act of callousness. A thousand grobi shall be slain for this affront alone!

Kazrik's hammerer bodyguard surround him, even as the grobi close. Twenty dawi stand shoulder-to-shoulder against a hundred or more grobi. Kazrik, enraged beyond word or deed, shatters the shackles of Thordrik and vows vengeance paid in urkish blood. Bellowing a war cry in his heathen tongue, Gorfang orders the attack. In an orgy of bloodshed the first wave of urks are repulsed, skulls cracked by hammer and shield. Grim-faced, the hammerers press forward with Kazrik at their centre, their oathstone,[17] urk bodies trampled by dwarfen boot. The urk come again, this time buoyed by a flurry of black-shafted crossbow bolts. The stout armour of the hammerers repels the worst of it but Duric and Burdrakk are slain. Their Names Will Not Be Forgotten. Five-hundred grobi skulls shall mark their deeds.

The urks crash against the shield wall of the dawi in earnest. Once again, they are repelled. Bitter fighting ensues. These urk are Rotgut's personal warriors, much larger and brutish than their grobi brethren. Helgar, Rinnik, Dane and Fundrin are slain. In the Halls of the Ancestors do they now sit. Grobi dead piled to the height of Azul will avenge them.

Kazrik lays about him with fury. Iron and stone rend in the deep. The son of Kazador wields both grund and az. The urk are brought low. There are but ten hammerers now at the heir of Azul's side. Kalgar, Azlak, Zorin and Oleg will not see another feast nor feel the stone of the Karak at their feet. Grungni holds them to his breast. *May his wrath smite the grobi and bury their cursed race beneath the earth.*

16. A shorn beard is a mark of shame and a serious affront to any dwarf. Admission into certain guilds and the application of royal taxes, as well as overall status is affected by beard length. It is a documented punishment of the dwarfs to clip beards, thus undoing years of training in order to become an apprentice to a well-respected craft guild or to be deemed worthy to marry a dwarf female of status.
17. See 'Dwarf Battle Tactics'.

Rotgut joins the battle and Kazrik hews a path to him. The squatter king is huge and he smites the heir of Azul down with a blow from his red blade. Kazrik is undone. Those hammerers that remain are disarmed or dead. Rotgut orders them bound in urk chains. Kazrik is defeated and shamed.

The urks bellow and hoot, no better than beasts. Thordrik, in the wake of Kazrik's shaming, crawls to the Thunderhorn, heirloom of Azul. The grobi pay little heed to the venerable dawi. Though without tongue, without speech, breath remains in Thordrik still. Taking up the mighty war horn of Kazador, he blows a long and loud note. Ever mournful is its report. The deeps of Azul shake. The throng of the karak are already amassing and head for the bellow of the horn.

At the sound of dawi thunder, the grobi quail and snarl. Thordrik is struck by a crossbow bolt. The horn is ended. Booted feet, the scrape of klad, is heard in the deeps. Gorfang roars at the cowering grobi. Khrum rumbles from above. The king is returned! A panic fills the grobi scum as the great doors to the hearth hall are thrown open and the warriors of Azul charge, a red rage upon them. Rotgut and his warriors are put to flight. *Pah! Urk have little stomach for a battle face-to-face, one dawi for every three grobi.*

Kazador reaches the Great Throne Hall. Rotgut and his brood are gone. Driven out by steel and courage.

Azul is defiled.

Heirlooms are lost.

Treasures stolen.

No less than fifty dawi are taken, many the thane-king's kith and kin.

Freygar, priestess of Valaya, is gone.

Karagin, weaponmaster[18], is gone.

Varganson Ironmaster[19] is taken.

Hurl Badrikk is led away in chains.

Orgrin Stonebeater is gone.

Malrik Morbad is taken.

Kreln Kromson is gone.

Morga, queen of Kazador, mother of Kazrik, is abducted by the grobi – For this, does Thane-King Kazador swear particular vengeance – Kazador's clan all. A bitter blow. They are taken to

18. Weaponmasters are amongst the many craftguilds of the dwarfs, a highly respected position in dwarfen society. For Karak Azul in particular I have unearthed copious amounts of information relating to its abundant weapon shops and so the role of weaponmaster is lauded even more highly at this hold.

19. Much like weaponmasters, ironmasters are well respected members of dwarf society and part of one of the prestigious craft guilds.

Black Crag, formerly Karak Drazh. There they dwell with many others. Thordrik Greymane is dead. Kazrik is shamed. *By the blood of Grungni, the urk and the grobi shall pay. By hearth and hold, by wrath and ruin, by oath honour it is sworn!*

The Shaming of Kazrik

The deeds of the squatter king, Gorfang Rotgut, are fell indeed and Kazador was deeply wounded by the creature's trespass. Kazrik's fate, though, was worst of all and was separately recorded. It is likely that such detailed testimony came from Kazrik himself, in what brief snatches of lucidity the dwarf was able to muster.

BLOODIED AND BATTERED, Kazrik is taken by the urk lord, Gorfang. Dragged by his beard, Kazrik is thrust upon the throne of his thane-king. He struggles, held in place by no less than four of the urk. Kazrik's defiance is cut short, a blow from the hilt of Gorfang's red blade silencing him. His wrists are held in place by thick urk claws. A stout nail is driven into each. Kazrik does not scream. Rotgut is displeased. He takes a crude blade, blunted by use, dark with blood and shears Kazrik's beard. Kazrik is silent throughout. The urk then shaves the hair from his head. It is rough work and Kazrik suffers many wounds, his once proud beard juts in clumps. His head purpled by bruise, is a cross-hatch of cuts. Upon the heir of Azul's bald pate Gorfang sears a crude glyph, a mark of their heathen gods and a brand of ownership. There is he left, the rest of his kin taken, as a gesture of contempt.

Too late does the thane-king return. Into the Great Throne Hall, Kazador comes. At his seat does he find his son, Kazrik. Noble Kazador can barely bring himself to look at him. He weeps openly at this sacrilege. Then does his mood grow very dark. Vengeance must be wrought for this deed. *Dreng tromm! Dreng tromm!*[20]

Kazrik is removed from the throne. Days, weeks, years forth the wounds inflicted by Gorfang will not heal. Kazrik is not whole – his father's son no longer. Mind broken by the tortures of Gorfang, he is like zaki[21] now. No cure can be found for it.

---

20. The literal translation of the Khazalid is 'slay beard'. Judging by my own observances of the dwarfs, this is likely referring to the act of a dwarf tearing at his own beard – in my experience, a very serious lament.

21. I surmise from various testimony I have read, that Kazrik's torture and subsequent shaming at the hands of Gorfang left him in a delirious state, fraught with terrible nightmares, forever blighting the line of Kazador.

Forever has the hold of Karak Azul been stained this day. Forever will the grobi known as Gorfang Rotgut be the subject of our ire. Forever will he be hunted. Curse the grobi and all their foul kin. Curse them for eternity. May Grimnir's wrath take them. No mercy shall be given. No blood spilled will be enough. Never shall this grudge be struck out. Always will it be remembered. *Uzkul urk! Dreng urk!*

Kazador's Decree

THOUGH CONSIDERED GENIAL and welcoming before the attack on Karak Azul, Kazador's demeanour has become grim since the shaming of his son.

On this most dismal of days King Kazador has pronounced grudgement on Thane Begrid as doorwarden of the Fourth Level Eastern Portal.[22] Be it known by this grudge that it has come to light that Thane Begrid failed in his duties as doorwarden and by omission of action did allow the vile orc warlord Gorfang Rotgut to intrude upon the hold. An ancient tunnel with a hidden doorway was lost in the records of the Begrid clan and thus it was overlooked as a means of entry by the greenskin scum. By dint of failing to provide proper sentries Thane Begrid endangered the hold. Thane Begrid did further compound this error by the untimely celebration of his daughter's marriage that left the Fourth Level Eastern Portal unguarded by sober individuals. This action was key to the intrusion of Gorfang Rotgut and led directly to the calamities already recorded. Thane Begrid died whilst defending the Fourth Level Eastern Portal and thus recompense is named as that being the adjudication of his peers within the Halls of the Ancestors. King Kazador wishes it be known that when he finally goes to the Halls of the Ancestors himself, he shall seek out Thane Begrid for a full account of his failures.

On this day further grudge is sworn by King Kazador of Karak Azul against the orc warlord Gorfang Rotgut and the greenskins of Black Crag. In a brave attempt to recover their captured kin, the dwarfs of Karak Azul did the day before last invest the tower of Black Crag and attempt forceful entry. This expedition met with uncharacteristic resistance that led to the deaths of forty-seven dwarfs of the hold and the serious wounding of seventeen others whose future health is as yet uncertain. Though King Kazador led the throng of Karak Azul

22. See 'Anatomy of a Hold – Dwarfs and the Surface'.

through the hidden passages of the Underway to surprise the urks no ingress into Black Crag was found. It is believed that the gateway collapsed several years earlier and thus a grudge is also accounted against the Engineers' Guild of Karak Azul for improper maintenance, to the extent that sturdy wutroth pillars had splintered, and failing to report this turn of events to King Kazador before the expedition left. Their main course of entry thus thwarted, the throng of Karak Azul was forced to seek overground route to Black Crag during which they were severely harassed by grobi wolfriders and intermittent long range war-machine attack. With the element of surprise thus diminished, King Kazador wishes it to be known that no grudge is to be recorded against the warriors of the throng. The dwarfs of Karak Azul acquitted themselves with bravery and tenacity and it was upon King Kazador's own orders that the siege was lifted in its second day to prevent further unwarranted loss of life.

The Reward of Kazador

Years of war and the pressures of recovering from the orc attack meant that Kazador was only able to launch one assault to reclaim his captured kin. Since then, he has offered a grand reward for any thane or other adventurers who succeed in doing so. One half of his hoard he has promised to any dwarf who brings back his kin alive, and one third to any non-dwarf who does the same. A quarter of his gathered treasure is set aside for anybody who can return their bodies for proper burial. Any who bring King Kazador Gorfang's body are to have their pick of the king's riches. Although the exact amounts are not known and King Kazador's hoard has been oft-used lately, it is likely that these sums would be worth all of the gold of Altdorf and more. The following are just a selection of the many grudges recorded on behalf of those who have attempted to claim the reward.

KING KAZADOR WISHES to record grudge against Gorfang Rotgut for the death of Kurdat Brinngarda and his warriors whilst attempting to rescue the hostages of Black Crag or otherwise return their bodies if they be dead.

King Kazador wishes to record grudge against Gorfang Rotgut for the death of Killan Broadshoulder and his warriors whilst attempting to rescue the hostages of Black Crag or otherwise return their bodies if they be dead.

King Kazador wishes to record grudge against Gorfang Rotgut for the death of Snarlin Delmhut and his warriors whilst attempting to rescue the hostages of Black Crag or otherwise return their bodies if they be dead.

King Kazador wishes to record grudge against Gorfang Rotgut for the death of the manling of the Empire Leopald Hurstwencker and his warriors whilst attempting to rescue the hostages of Black Crag or otherwise return their bodies if they be dead.[23]

King Kazador wishes to record grudge against Gorfang Rotgut for the death of Zar Fundabar and his warriors whilst attempting to rescue the hostages of Black Crag or otherwise return their bodies if they be dead.

King Kazador wishes to record grudge against Gorfang Rotgut for the death of Yorri Borkodin and his warriors whilst attempting to rescue the hostages of Black Crag or otherwise return their bodies if they be dead.

King Kazador this day is displeased and thus bears witness to grudge against Thane Fredi of the Rikstak clan. Thane Fredi accompanied King Kazador upon a campaign against the grobi of the Broken Leg tribe. In the decisive engagement that took part four days ago Thane Fredi failed to pursue thoroughly the routed enemy and thus allowed a considerable number of the grobi filth to escape. Upon passing this judgement, King Kazador accepts that the warriors of clan Rikstak were tired from several weeks of military campaign. King Kazador lets it be known that no blame is to be placed upon Clan Rikstak for failing to catch the fleeing grobi but that Thane Fredi failed the hold by not ordering the pursuit and thus allowing the grobi to evade retribution for many ancient wrongs recorded in this tome. Upon hearing of his king's displeasure Thane Fredi has taken the slayer vow and so recompense of this grudge is to be considered exacted from Thane Fredi upon his noble death in battle as a slayer.

23. It is rare for non-dwarfs to be recognised in grudges. Hurstwencker was a notorious mercenary and brigand in the Empire at the time, so I expect honour was the least of his concerns.

CHAPTER TWO

The Dragon Grudge

The Ravages of Mordrak

The savage saga of the beast known only as Mordrak is a chilling
tale and one that resulted in a number of grudges over a long period,
spanning generations. It is typical of many such confrontations
between the dwarfs and one of their oldest foes – dragons.

Dwarfs and Dragons

Dragons are an ancient race, older perhaps than even the dwarfs.
The two have much in common, despite their obvious differences, and
this has led to a bitter history between them, fraught with death and
destruction. Dragons, or 'drakk' as they are known in the Khazalid,
make their lairs deep in the mountains, near the heart of the world
where it is warm and dry. As is their wont, dwarfs will ever dig deep
into the earth and there have been many occasions when the lair of
a dragon has been discovered and the inevitable vying for territory
begins.

Much like dwarfs, dragons covet gold and hoard it, making
their nests of it. The dwarf hunger for gold is well documented and
this has led many an expedition into the domain of such a beast
in search of treasure and riches. As they are such formidable and
deadly creatures, dragons are often sought out by devotees of the

Slayer Cult in their quest to meet a worthy end. I have come across numerous accounts of such dwarfs being granted their wish when undertaking this perilous task.

So old is the enmity between dwarfs and dragons, and the frequency with which the two races have clashed bloodily, that runesmiths have devised many magic runes to slay, and protect against, dragons. The Master Rune of Dragon Slaying was forged long ago and since legend purports that one of Grimnir's axes bore it, only one of the ancestor gods could have first inscribed it. There are many others, such as the Rune of the Furnace, which offers proof against the ravages of dragon fire – all arcane mysteries that baffle even the scholars of the Colleges of Magic.

Slaying a dragon is a great and mighty achievement. Few have done it. In my studies, I have unearthed several instances though. The Karaz-a-Karak Book of Days recounts the tale of Dorin Heldour and how he slew the dragon, Fyskar. Its skin was taken to High King Finn Sourscowl, who had his runesmith, Heganbor, fashion it into a runic cloak. After the great city of Karak Azgal – then Karak Izril – fell it became inhabited by the dragon, Graug the Terrible. The creature was the spawn of the fearsome Skaladrak the Incarnadine that once tormented the northern hold of Karak Kadrín. After many failed attempts by the knights of Bretonnia, Graug was slain by Skalf Dragonslayer who assumed kingship of Karak Azgal, now Dragon Crag, but Skalf made no effort to resettle it and instead established a small town in its foothills. If you believe rumour, it is still inhabited by a dragon to this day, one of Graug the Terrible's offspring that Skalf overlooked. Legend holds that Mordrak, despoiler of Karak Azul, was imprisoned by Kurik Kaznagar and this account is related in a transcription by your humble scribe from the Karak Azul Book of Grudges in this very tome.

Over the years, dwarfs have learned to make a great many things from the slain carcasses of dragons. They do so proudly and such items are a measure of the dwarfs' defiance towards the beasts. Drongnel, a form of thick stew; dragon-scale shields and cloaks; bone helmets and even dragon-tooth necklaces are all fashioned from dead dragons.

Kruzdil's Lament

LET IT BE known in this year that the overground farms at Kragvarn, Brakkzhuf and Gakzorn suffered ruination by fire. Herdmaster Kruzdil reports the loss of two score hruk and three fields of crops including wheat, barley and parsnips, rendered to ash. Of the goatherds, Jorli, Rukinn and Vagrik no sign could be found. A grudge is hereby entered against all three and the line of their clan is summarily besmirched until recompense is made for this negligence. Grobi are suspected of starting the fire. Kruzdil adds in his testimony that he did lead an expedition into the outlying lands, beyond the shadow of the karak, and discovered a small tribe of greenskins encamped in caves to the south of Brakkzhuf. A grudge is hereby lodged against the Yellow Fang tribe. Kuzril vows to return with clan warriors to exact summary vengeance.

On this day does Kruzdil discover an entire herd of hruk bone carcasses at Kragvarn. A throng of warriors from Thane Burrdrik's clan accompanies Kruzdil. *This act satisfies an old debt incurred for a spate of hruk bothering by the thane's kin.* The Yellow Fangs are suspected of the slaughter but upon approaching their lair are the grobi's corpses discovered, similarly bereft of flesh and meat. The grobi are burned. *The aforementioned grudge against the Yellow Fangs passes to the Red Tooth tribe, known associates of the Yellow Fangs.* Thane Burrdrik hereby lodges a grudge against Kruzdil and his clan for the needless expense of boot leather and an outbreak of kruti amongst his kin. Fifty pieces of izor[24] are entered into the reckoners' log.

Collapse at Grunspire

LET IT BE known that on this day the northern mines of Grunspire collapse. Lodewarden Borri Threkksson records the loss of several rich veins of ore and no less than four tunnels. Kraggi Svengeln, Dorki Baddrikson, Vorlkin Kakki, Drenk Fykison and Yorik Varnskan are all slain. May Grungni watch over them. A grudge is lodged against prospector Svengeln by the Threkksson clan on account of braces described by the accuser as 'umgak' and their failure to shore up the tunnels. Recompense is set at two hundred pieces of silven. The Svengeln clan lodge a counter-grudge against the Threkksson clan on behalf of their departed kinsman, Kraggi, for wrongful besmirchment of honour in referring to previous works as 'umgak'. Recompense is unset until the veracity of the claim can be upheld.

---

24. From the Khazalid, meaning 'copper'.

Besmirchment of the Svengeln Clan

UPON THE CLEARANCE of the tunnels at Grunspire, Thane-King Kazgar's clan engineer, Fydor Ungulfson, accompanied by a throng of ironbreakers, does conclude that the braces used by the Svengeln were made of stout wutroth, but weakened by aggressive gnawing. The Svengeln clan's (hereby referred to as the 'wronged') grudge against the Threkkson's is hereby upheld and thusly the wronged are awarded two hundred pieces of izor and two hundred pieces of silven as recompense for the aforementioned besmirchment by the Threkkson clan. Thane-King Kazgar hereby records a grudge against the rat-kin, clear instigators of the tunnel collapse at Grunspire. Fifty rat-kin tails for each of the slain is set as the promise price as recompense for this fell deed.

Retribution for Grunspire

UNGAZ IRONHAMMER, IRONBEARD of the Ironhammer clan does lead a throng of ironbreakers and warriors into the re-established tunnels at Grunspire. A dishevelled horde of rat-kin is discovered easily, whilst harvesting frongol in one of the larger caverns. A great battle erupts as many more of the filthy vermin emerge from hidden Ungdrin tunnels. Badrikk Stoneheart and a group of tunnel fighters of his clan do slay over thirty of the ratkin, pressing the creatures back with their broad-shield and long-mattocks Alas, Badrikk is slain whilst reloading his pistol, in a frenzied attack by the vermin. He Will Be Remembered. A hundred rat-tails for his passing.

Ungaz accounts for thirteen of the wretched rat things himself, whilst a tally of sixty-three tails is reaped in all, for a loss of three more warriors. Kurik, Badin and Ilfrik Will All Be Remembered. Thirty tails each as recompense for this act. Ungaz notes that the creatures are 'petrified' at the appearance his warriors, their fur 'scorched' as if by fire. A further foray into the hidden tunnels from where the vermin launched their ambush reveals rat-kin bone carcasses, at least four-hundred and thirty-one by the count of Loremaster Ruzik.

Calamity at the Cave of Mordrak

ENGINEER GODRIKSON AND a party of miners and sappers do venture forth into the tunnels around Grunspire. Many miles into the earth do the dawi dig, many blessings to Morgrim, leading to the discovery of an ancient, long forgotten Ungdrin road. Godrikson describes a mighty girt with walls ground smooth, first believed as if by the frequent passage of some large drilling engine or other such device but clearly not of dwarf manufacture as the tunnel is crudely made and seemingly without function. A mile further and the truth of the girt is revealed upon discovery of a cavern some ten-thousand beard spans, filled with rhun and gorl and galaz.

A grudge is lodged against Rittik Halfhand and Beldour Krunnson, rendered insensible by sudden gorl fever, by the Halfhand and Krunnson clans. Rittik falls foul of a sulphur pool, hidden behind a vast treasure pile. Plunging head first into the foul smelling liquid, all that remains of Rittik are his stout boots; both his armour and rhun-pick – an heirloom of the clan – are lost. Beldour, churning through a vast pit of ghalaz, disturbs a mighty mound of gold and is crushed to death as it falls upon him, ignorant of the warnings of Godrikson, so intent is he upon the treasure hoard.

Overcoming their own gold lust, Godrikson and his party explore the great cave. The engineer provides the following testimony as to what was found there.

'Grungni's oath, never had these old eyes beheld such a horde: gorl, galaz, grenzil, silven and izor piled higher than the magnificent columned halls of Karaz-a-Karak. Rhun was everywhere; heirlooms of a dozen or more clans, so old the memory of them was lost to me. Such a prize could not be uncoveted and true as the wisdom of Valaya I saw a great many skulls and scattered uzkul: dawi, manling and elgi all in klad, their weapons clutched in bone fingers. Lesser beings, their remains chewed and bit, tarnished the cavern too: grobi, urk and more of the rat-kin.

'With a prayer to Smednir, great shaper of ore, I felt the rock of the cavern. Twas warm; the blood of the mountain was close. The stench of gold was thick but so too was a rank odour emanating from the many pools throughout the cave – brave Rittik lost his life to one. I was forced into wielding my hammer to drum the gorl lust from the rest of my kith and kin.

'Crags, worn and scratched by the tooth and claw of some mighty drakk – for now I had no doubt this was the lair of such a beast – rose up out of the hoard like the many spiked peaks of the mountain. Several more tunnels stretched out from the cavern, all of them wrought smooth by the passing of the creature.

'We did not linger, not for lack of courage, but out of urgency at bringing such dire news to the king.'

Edict of Kazgar

THIS DAY DOES Kazgar, Thane-King of Azul declare the drakk, discovered by Godrikson, be found and slain, and the stolen treasures of its horde brought back to the vault of the king. A grudge is also made against Engineer Godrikson for failing to return the treasure hoard to the karak. The shame of this deed is set at the worth of four of Godrikson's finest cannon.

Thane-King Kazgar does name the beast Mordrak for it is surely a mighty creature, and old beyond reckoning, given the evidence of its hoard and the size of its lair. An expedition of the clan's mightiest warriors is gathered immediately to avenge the deaths of those dawi slain by Mordrak and a grudge is hereby entered against it and all its kind for this fell deed.

By the reckoning of ancient Runelord Varic Forgehand 'tis the very same beast that caused much damage to the former realm of Eight Peaks and a further grudge is lodged against the creature on behalf of the Eight Peaks clans. As such, Thane-King Kazgar has deemed it fitting that warriors representing the wronged clans of Eight Peaks be allowed to join the expedition.

Dreng Tromm! A horn is sounded in the deep this most bleak of days for the loss of twenty-five warriors of the Silvenback, Stonecutter and Stoutpeak clans of Karak Eight Peaks; seven slayers of Kadrin; thirty-one brave dawi of Karak Azul from the Dunrakin, Firehand and Ironfinger clans; and for Thane Durik Kaznagar whose oath it was to slay the dragon, Mordrak. None returned from the expedition. Their fates are unrecorded. May Grungni watch over them and Gazul guide them back to the Halls of the Ancestors. A grudge is writ against the beast for the loss of all. *May its foul flesh adorn the walls of the Hearth Hall of Azul and its skull be mounted above the great Zhar!*

Let it be known that upon this day, Thane Kaznagar is entered into the great kron for failing to uphold his oath to slay the beast. May the weight of this deed and the shame of his failure be passed down to his kin and the oath be fulfilled before he may sit at the grand feast table of Grungni.

On this day does Thane-King Kazgar order a second expedition into the Ungdrin to discover the fate of Thane Kaznagar and his warriors. Thane Borri Brakkson and some thirty of his most veteran warriors venture into the unknown deeps, together with twenty ironbreakers of the Ironbeard clan and engineers from Clan Flinthand who bring with them an organ cannon drawn by six stout lode ponies. A mere twenty-five winters, Kaznagar's only son, Kurik, was made to stay behind by King Kazgar himself in an effort to becalm the wailing of the long-departed thane's maiden-queen. The journal of Norgrin Nagsson, a lorekeeper[25] who had joined the expeditionary force and submitted for consideration, makes for grim reading.

'We followed the route scribed upon Godrikson's[26] map to the cavern of the beast and the last known destination of Kaznagar thane and his clansdwarfs. As the Ungdrin opened wide before us the air became thick with the stench of sulphur and soot, the walls black and fire-scorched. Lodefinder[27] Ungafel muttered an oath to Grungni, remarking on the condition of some of the rocks around us as if the very blood of the mountain had flowed here and cooled. In places there were great furrows ripped out of the stone – claw marks of the drakk – as long as a hammer haft and as broad as a hammer head, with space enough between for a great axe blade.

We reached the edge of the cavern at last – a deep, glow bathing the wall from the gold lustre within. Here, the stink of the drakk was at its strongest – the creature had returned.

Stood upon the threshold of its lair, I saw the beast and muttered oaths to Valaya, Grungni and Grimnir. Ancient evil flowed from eyes as black as tar pits. Its gnarled and thorny hide was like the razor crags of the karak, red and luminous as the blood of the mountain with thick lines run through it like veins of black ore. Claws the length of swords, twice thick, scraped the ground, pulling the glittering hoard in piles of hundreds. Seeing us, the beast reared up on its haunches; its bloated gut, filled with dawi dead, was yellow and barrel-ribbed.

25 An apprentice loremaster.
26. Why the engineer does not accompany the mission, or the reason that his fate is not recorded, is not known to me. Though it is likely, based on my rudimentary understanding of dwarf culture, due to his failure to return the treasure hoard, he was ejected from the Engineers' Guild of which he was undoubtedly a member. It is also possible to suppose that Godrikson was subjected to one of the many punitive expulsion rituals practised by the guild of which I submit the following examples: The Trouser Legs Ritual – an archaic practice of which little is known, save for the name; Cogging – in which the punished is stripped naked and must heft a chain of heavy cogs around the entirety of the hold's workshops; Blackbearding – in which the punished must use his beard to wipe down oily or soot-stained machinery, resulting in an extremely unkempt beard (hence the name) and abject humiliation; Quaffing – in which the punished must consume several gallons of oil (something only made possible by the stoutness of dwarfen constitution as you or I would be killed by such an act) and in so doing the dwarf suffers a long, painful bellyache and is unable to taste or enjoy ale or food of any description.
27. A lodefinder is a very experienced miner. I have come across many such names, all describing the same thing, which vary from clan to clan and from hold to hold. Such conventions, therefore, should not be treated as prescriptive.

'Thane Borri bellowed orders, with Grimnir's courage. Ten of the Ironbeard clan came forward and made a thick wall with stout shields. The Flinthand clan dragged the mighty organ cannon into position behind them – for the ponies drawing it had long since slipped their bonds and fled, doubtless spooked by the presence of the drakk[28] – and more warriors moved left and right. Some wavered, the lure of gorl filling their senses but Borri's voice was a hammer strike and their purpose was renewed. The shield wall came forward, locked tight like the Great Grimgrong,[29] advancing upon the drakk. The beast gave no ground but spread its tattered and torn wings, great spikes curving from each. At once the sulphur stink of its breath was no more and the air was sucked away. Its bloated gut filled. Thane Borri cried out a warning but his voice was crushed by a roar of flame. Those of the Ironbeard clan were engulfed. Black-red fire surged through them and once it had abated the Ironbreakers were no more, their flesh flayed, muscles cooked and bones turned to powder within the smoking husks of their fire-scorched armour.

'Without delay, the beast came down onto four legs, and a tremor wracked the cavern. It roared a challenge, assailing us with its sulphur breath but no fire came this time. It was enough for the Flinthand clan, Grungni curse them. They fled their war engine with not a shot fired, scattering from the cavern. May their beards be hewn and kruti afflict their nethers!

'Borri and his veterans would not be denied and charged the beast. Three of the Brakkson clan were crushed immediately beneath the drakk's claws, another three swept away by its tail. Borri barked orders and slowly the beast was encircled. Dawi blades fell against drakk hide but oft rebounded such was its thickness.

'For an hour did they battle the beast, Borri and his kin, but it was to no avail. I watched as the last of the clan warriors was bitten in two and only Thane Borri remained, his armour dented, the great rhun helm of the Brakkson clan no longer upon his head. Borri bade me flee, take word back to the Thane-King, "I have failed, send others to avenge me!" At that the beast lunged at Borri, but he dodged aside and struck a mighty blow, the blade of his rhun axe tasting flesh as it

28. It is interesting to note here that the dwarfs would rather drag a hefty war machine, despite the loss of the draught animals, rather than leave it behind.
29. From the Khazalid this literally translates as, 'Unyielding Anvil' and I believe could be referring to one of the great gates that guard the way into Karak Azul. See 'Anatomy of a Hold' for more details about great gates.

carved out the drakk's eye. A geyser of black blood erupted from the wound and for a moment, I thought Thane Borri had at last the besting of the creature. But it turned quickly, with a deafening roar of pain, and Thane Borri was unbalanced and undone. He fell, his axe clattering far from his grasp. The beast blew an inferno from its broad nostrils and Borri was no more. I fled, heat searing my eyes, the stink of burning meat in my nose. The drakk did not follow – I shall honour Valaya for that.'

A grudge against the beast, Mordrak for the slaying of no less than fifty-one dwarfs of the clans Ironbeard and Brakkson. A lament is sung in the Third Deep for the passing of Thane Borri Brakkson. For the loss of an organ cannon, the Engineers' Guild does hereby demand five hundred pieces of gorl and two hundred of izor from the Flinthand clan. A further grudge is lodged by the Flinthands against the dwarfs of Grey Mountains and the Goldhoarder clan for the supply of weak-willed lode ponies. Recompense for this deed is set at five hundred pieces of izor and a grudge by the Engineers' Guild, formerly the responsibility of the Flinthand clan, deferred to the Goldhoarder's for the loss of the aforementioned organ cannon.

Kurik makes his Oath

KURIK KAZNAGAR DOES on this day take the slayer's vow and swear to avenge the death of his thane and father by vanquishing the beast, Mordrak, and fulfilling well-remembered oaths. He is joined at the shrine of Grimnir by dwarfs of the Flinthand clan as penance for their lack of courage when facing the drakk.

Thane King Kazgar does agree to an expedition, led by Kurik, into the Ungdrin beneath the karak to at last destroy the beast. After meeting with the council of elders, it is decided that the rhun vaults of the karak be opened. Venerable Rune Lord Ganngrim Ironforge awakens the fabled Drakkaz-treng,[30] and invoking the favour of Thungni does present it to Kurik. *May it taste dragon-flesh again!*

30. From what sources I have been able to gather on this artefact, Drakkaz-treng literally translates as 'Slayer of Dragons' and is a rune axe of some age and reverence. Its significance to the Donarkhun clan and its previous history are lost, but to reopen a vault to 'awaken' (the meaning of this is unclear, but studies into the runic magic of the dwarfs suggests that some, particularly venerable, artefacts require re-imbuing by a powerful rune lord to make the ancient runes forged upon them potent again) such a treasure, one whose value to the dwarfs is greater than the wealth of some entire clans, denotes the seriousness in which the Karak Azal dwarfs took the presence of the dragon, Mordrak.

CHAPTER THREE

The Elf Grudge

The War of the Elves and Dwarfs

The first of the grudges presented here is typical of those that concern the entire dwarf race. So great is the wrong presented here that it is written in the words of the High King himself; Gotrek Starbreaker at the time. It takes the form of a letter to the kings of all the holds, which each painstakingly transcribed into his own book of grudges, with his own blood, so that all accounts of this momentous event are the same across the dwarf empire.

As can be seen by the contents of the letter, it provides a summary and appraisal of events spanning many years. During this period, the Karak Eight Peaks Book of Grudges records such instances as were pertinent to the hold and its clans, as one assumes do all of the books of grudges of the other holds. However, the issuing of this letter and the grudge it represents stands out as marking the beginning of one of the most important events in history, not only in the annals of the dwarfs but of all the people that dwell in the Old World. Thus, it seems a most suitable place with which to begin the tale of how the dwarfs and elves came to wage war upon each other.

The War of Vengeance, as the dwarfs record it, was a turning point in the history of these lands. For centuries the dwarfs and elves had lived in relative peace, their empires covering what is now The

Empire, Bretonnia and further afield. By the power of their armies were the dark beasts, the greenskins and the savage hordes kept at bay. Though perhaps we men played little part in these great affairs, it was through the diligence of these two races that we were, perhaps without conscious purpose, kept safe from the greatest harms. When both civilisations exhausted themselves in this war, the creatures of the woods and the orc tribes preyed upon us as they had never done before, and we were most beset as a people. Yet also, with the retreat of the dwarfish and elven armies, man was able to grow and prosper under his own strength and inherit the lands that we now hold. From then, history trod its inevitable path until the coming of great Sigmar and the Time of Men.

The War of Vengeance

Be it known that a most grim and worrisome event has taken place, which threatens the prosperity of our realms and the lives of our peoples. We hereby lay down this decree so that the truth be known to all our folk, for all time to come.[31]

Some years ago[32] our merchants were hindered most foully during the lawful conduction of their affairs. Knowing that the lands are perilous and many dangers confront our warriors daily, it is not unusual that we should not hear frequently from those of our subjects who labour far from our hearths and halls. Indeed, were it not for the risks undertaken by our brave subjects, our realms would not delve so deeply, stretch so widely and glitter so brightly as they do.

As we have sworn, we offer our protection to the furthest lands, and stretch our arm long indeed to guarantee the safety of our loyal subjects. Thus it was that upon being worried by the loss of communication with the caravan of Gungran Axebearer, may the Ancestors welcome him, four weeks out of Karak Azgal bound for Tor Alessi of the elves, we despatched such scouts and forces as were necessary to obtain information regarding their fate.

Our messengers brought back dire news, news that will shake our empire like the fiercest earthquake, and will light a fire in the hearts of our people hotter than the raging furnaces of all the smelteries of Karaz-a-Karak. Our folk were slain. Not by grobi misdeed did they fall, nor by beast of the woods, nor dark warrior of the north. Arrows were found piercing their bodies – many arrows. An ambush, wicked and unannounced, had caught them unprepared and they had been slaughtered. These arrows, these hated weapons that so callously ended the lives of our noble kin, were fashioned by the hands of elves.

Faced with such news, we were much distressed. Long and bountiful has been our relationship with the folk from beyond the sea. Much they crave our wares, and for our part we have always accorded ourselves with honour and good graces. Though they are a strange race, much given to odd ways and outlandish customs, we welcomed them into our holds. We offered the hand of friendship and they grasped it. In our own chambers have we hosted banquets in due ceremony for their lords, and lavished upon them all the hospitality of our people. We have ignored the slights and ill-manners for the sake of prosperity and peace. We have shared the spoils of our hard labours and divided the lands. Yet it seems that these misguided elves care not for the respect of alliance,

31. Note that elven chronicles differ widely from the events as outlined here.
32. Eight years, by other accounts.

and have dealt us an underhand blow that we deem beyond countenance.

For all our anguish, we listened to the counsel of our wisest advisors and cooled by their words, as the steam cools the newly-forged blade, we did not act rashly. Tempered by this wise advice, we despatched more of our kin to ascertain the extent of the elvish treachery, hoping perhaps that this incident was isolated and disavowed by those who rule the elves. Our hopes were to be dashed. Missing parties from all holds were found slain, some of them with their remains despoiled in a callous manner, their chins left naked so that their spirits will wander the dungeons beneath the Halls of the Ancestors wailing and weeping in eternal shame. This was no petty act of spite, but a concerted and deliberate attack upon our people by those we had called comrades.[33]

Still counselled for caution, and believing the elves perhaps had some shred of dignity remaining, we sent them word of our anger and gave them opportunity to account for their actions and offer just restitution for the offences they had committed against our people. We offer here a portion of the response we received to this diplomatic request, so that all might judge for themselves the character of the elves:

'We are unconcerned with your baseless threats. That you seek to treat with us as equals under the guise of allies whilst contemplating violence against us is proof that you offer no guarantees as to the good conduct of your people. The glorious and mighty Phoenix King of Ulthuan does not answer to the demands of a king of gravel, muck and coal. We, unlike the people of the mountains, are not uncouth, and the Phoenix King is happy to receive any pleas for assistance made with due reverence, polite language and humble civility.'[34]

They attack our people and speak of civility! Less twisted is the axle that warps in the mould! The provocative and untrustworthy nature of their king was revealed, and yet we would not be remembered as a warmonger and lover of slaughter. Again we offered opportunity to make right what had been done, and to recompense our peoples for the slights of the king's reply.

Word was sent and embassy was made to the Phoenix King, who speaks for all the elven princes. Undemanding were our questions. We

---

33. Or possibly not. Dwarfs and elves have never been that friendly as a whole, even during their greatest period of cooperation.

34. The exact wording here is doubtful, having been translated twice – from elvish to dwarfen to Reikspiel. Much of the original meaning and subtlety may have been lost. In addition, the original translation from the elvish must be considered suspect, and perhaps 'massaged' by the High King for propaganda purposes.

sought the truth; to know whether the bonds that have tied our peoples together were to be truly cut. It is not in our nature to seek bloodshed when peace will profit us greater, and so it was with the elves.

Such civility went unrewarded. No, not unrewarded, openly mocked! In the arrogance of their kind, the elves deigned not to answer our earnest and honest inquiries. Not content with besmirching our honour with this petty rebuke, the Phoenix King added injury to insult in the most dire manner possible. They shaved our ambassador and cast him from the court! He has since sworn the oath of Grimnir and seeks the solace of the slayer's death. This is a deed that cannot go unpunished. The slaughter of our folk and the embarrassment of our representatives is nothing less than the most calculated attack, designed to undermine our strength and humiliate our authority. They shall find our resolve not so easily shaken!

It is thus my grave duty to announce that we must wage war upon the elves. We must wage a war to reclaim our honour, and if that debt must be paid in the blood of elves, then so be it!

From the greatest king to the doughtiest smith and hard-working miner, we owe our glory and wealth to all who fight and work under the banner of our empire. Now a time has come that we might all be so sorely tested that we doubt the right tunnel to follow. Heed our words and know that we are right. We shall lay low the white towers, and we shall burn the fields, and we shall hew the trees, until the elves bend their knee and offer us that which they owe. They are a weak people, with no stomach for hardship! We shall see what becomes of the arrogance of elves when their cities burn and their sons are heaped upon a pyre of their own making!

There is strength in these mountains that has weathered the elements for untold years. We are from the mountains hewn. Our hearts must be as rock, our arms as untiring as the mountain stream, our backs as sturdy as any ridge, if we are to bear this burden. The elves are weak, and like wayward cousins must be taught that they are in error, and punished so that they will learn the lesson well.[35]

Stoke the furnaces, oil your armour and sharpen your axes, for war most bloody is upon us!

High King Gotrek Starbreaker, Bearer of the Dammaz Kron, Karaz-a-Karak

35. Most dwarfen punishments are mental and spiritual rather than physical in nature, due to the dwarfs' sturdy constitution, so the High King's analogy may be mis-translated.

SOME 1,335 GRUDGES are recorded in total concerning the elves and the War of Vengeance. Those that follow are just a few of the most interesting, the first few pages of which detail the first mustering of the throng of Karak Eight Peaks

Gadri Borrisson is reprimanded for failing to provide six hundred hogshead of pickled eggs required for the provisioning of the throng by the time of the throng's mustering, by a shortfall of some twenty-eight hogsheads. He will make up the difference and transport them to the throng at his own expense.[36]

An unknown elf who spied upon our workings this morning was shot by our sentries. We took his mail coat and it is has been smelted down and will be worked into belt buckles to be presented to the sentries for their due diligence.[37]

Urk of the Badlands bearing the symbol of a jagged fang waylaid the vanguard of the throng, near to the silver mines of Ghazak-kan in the workings of Barak Varr. The king is most perturbed that he cannot prosecute his vengeance against these vile greenskins, for such action will cause delay that will hinder our arrival at Tor Alessi and imperil the High King's throng awaiting us there. The Jagged Fang tribe will be dealt with once the matter with the elves is resolved.

There are several water-stained pages followed by this entry:

I, Grudgemaster Goldbrow, do humbly apologise to the king and his ancestors, may they feast forever in their Halls, for dropping the book of grudges into the water whilst the crossing of Blood River was made. By atonement I am to escort the mule train until I learn from them how to carry my burden with due consideration and care.

Thane Hangist Grobkul of Barak Varr is to pay for the damage done to the king's shield caused by Thane Hangist during his clumsy inspection thereof.[38]

Dammin Cloudy-eye is to make recompense for the loss of four wagons, lost in a storm as we cross the Vaults, for failing to secure them properly in camp.

A party of some fifty elves have harried the rearguard for six days, causing the deaths of eighteen dwarfs. Our rangers have yet to locate them, for which they humbly apologise.

36. Note that each clan and guild equips and feeds its warriors for the throng, for which the king covers part of the expense.
37 Note that Dwarfs do not take trophies directly, although they are not above taking precious metals and gems and reworking them into designs they find more pleasing or practical.
38. Reports from Barak Varr, unconfirmed, suggest that the thane in question dropped the king's shield into a firepit and was forced to quickly retrieve it with his bare hands.

We took to hewing the trees of the forest to make fires, and horrid spirits of the woods attacked our logging parties. Unnatural creatures in the form of walking trees attacked our camp and firepots were used to drive them back. In retaliation, Thane Ungrim Shaftcleaver built a great pyre and burnt many trees. A great shrieking has echoed through the night and all in the throng are eager to move on at dawn and leave this haunted place. The king has bid us to quit these dour trees and camp on the meadows.

Messengers from the High King are to offer full apology and three locks of beard for their impolite urging of the king to speed our progress. Kargun Stormfist, Brin Frongáltromm and Zaki Rockbearer are to return to the High King and convey the king's regards to the High King and his understanding of the need for urgency.

The First Siege of Tor Alessi

THE CITY OF Tor Alessi is garrisoned by some twenty thousand elves, and Kundi Firebeard has taken the oath of Grimnir for his woeful underestimation of the enemy forces in his reports to the king. Upon the walls the elves mustered many archers, the arrows of whom were as a steel-tipped storm upon our throng. By the western gate we mustered our crossbows and engines of war. Fifteen hundred stones inscribed with runes of vengeance and wall-breaking we hurled at the walls of the citadel, all the while under the attention of the elven archers and bolt throwers, which took a heavy toll of our crews and quarrellers.

Three times the elves sallied forth from the gate to attack our engineworks and saps, and their knights pierced many of our throng with their lances and then retreated swiftly to safety beneath the bows of their kin, before retiring within the walls once more. Thane Dumbrin, herafter taking the name Thane Wazzokrik as ordered by the king, lead an ill-judged pursuit after the retreating elves during which a full quarter of his clan were slain or seriously injured to the point of being unable to fight, for no gain on our part. Thane Wazzokrik[39] has been despatched to liaise with the mule train for the future provisioning of the throng.

On the second day the king has ordered the beginning of three mineworkings, to undermine the towers of the gatehouse. He has named them Thom, Grik and Ari.

Work proceeds well, concealed from the view and arrows of the elves by pavises made of sturdy wutroth brought from the Grey Mountains to the east.

---

39. Literal translation – King of Fools

On the sixth day magical fire has blasted the workings of Grik and forced a collapse. A sally led by an elven prince destroyed many of the workings of Thom, though we captured the prince before he could retreat. He names himself Prince Alyr of Eataine, and we have sent word and ransom to the commander of the garrison in Tor Alessi. Alyr has asked for no parole and we have offered none. He is currently caged with the mules, while his warriors have been set to work gathering wood for the furnaces.

The king has ordered work on Thom and Grik to be halted and all efforts to be concentrated on Ari.

Under covering bombardment of enchanted bolt and rune-carved boulder, we set the fires in Ari beneath the right-most tower of the western gatehouse. The tower, elf-made and weak, collapsed within minutes, crushing a great number of elves and opening a breach for us to attack. At the forefront strode the ironbreakers and a great skrund erupted in the debris as elven spears met the axes and hammers of our kin. The footing was unstable and our folk laboured badly to effect entrance, but were successful for a few hours to hold back the elves. In doing so, we have drawn forces that would have fought the High King's assault on the eastern gate in the last hours of light. We were forced to withdraw at dusk having lit many fires in the city, which now illuminate the night sky like day.

Word has reached us from the High King that an elven fleet has been sighted several miles off the coast, heading west and south. We are to lift the siege lest our forces become trapped between this newly arrived host and the walls of the elven city.

The elves rose a great jeering and clamour as we departed, yet they were soon silenced as we sent back Prince Alyr to his people, his head removed and packed in a pickling firkin to accompany the corpse. A great many engines have been abandoned on the field, for the elven reinforcements have landed and we must swiftly seek the sanctuary of the mountains while we judge their number and keenness for battle.

Some fourteen days past, the warriors of this hold did wage honourable war in the seeking of righteous compensation for the wrongs done to us by the fickle elves. Hereafter entered the names of those who did lay down their lives for the prosecution of our endeavours and the protection of the king and High King.[40]

It has come to the attention of the king that the frivolous elves are referring to this great and bloody conflict as the War of the Beard. This facetiousness is typical of the disdainful manner with which the elves view us, and another example of their facile and inappropriate humour.

40. Thus ends the first siege of Tor Alessi.

The Longest War

Dwarfs and elves are both long-lived folk and so it is no surprise that the war of vengeance lasted over many generations, for hundreds of years. The ending of the first siege of Tor Alessi marked the end of the opening dwarf offensive and the two sides continued to build their forces, the elves centred upon Tor Alessi, the dwarfs mustering at Karaz-a-Karak and Karak Kadrin in the north. A period of some twenty-three years passes between the last grudge I have included here and the next. This time saw sporadic fighting in many parts of the dwarfish and elven realms, and two more sieges of Tor Alessi, as well as an attack on Karak Azul by the elves. In total, I have calculated that the dwarfs of Karak Eight Peaks lost some eighteen thousand warriors in the fighting.

The next grudge is another letter written by the High King and delineates a new phase of the war. The personal loss of the High King certainly invigorated the war effort of the dwarfs, and for the next generation, the dwarfs launched offensive after offensive against the cities of the elves. However, this eventually exhausted even the resources of the dwarfs and the momentum could not be maintained. The elves swiftly retook what lands had been lost and launched a counter-attack that lasted for some one hundred and fifty years.

Many have been our brave and honourable warriors who had laid their lives upon the altar of battle and joined our ancestors in their hallowed Halls, may their flagstones never weather. Each will be remembered for their valour and steadfastness. Each shall be avenged upon the elves. Yet none is such a loss as that of our own blood, our son and heir, Snorri Halfhand.

Upon the bloodied heath at Angaz Baragdum, the vain Phoenix King, Caledor the Oathbreaker, took the field for the first time. The craven lord of the elves cowered behind his host while elf and dwarf died for his conceit. The noble Snorri, in whose veins the richest blood of kings flowed, saw that perhaps the darkness that has descended upon our realms might be ended. With due form and tradition, Snorri issued a personal challenge to the Phoenix King, so that this matter might be settled. Displaying integrity and bravery beyond all call, Snorri deigned to offer the Phoenix

King an honourable means by which this devastating war might be brought to proper conclusion. For his part, the Phoenix King accepted, with words full of pride and arrogance, dismissive of the skill at arms of our kin. Yet his was not the choice of honour but of fear, for the army of the elves was sorely beset and surrounded by our folk.

As Snorri observed the proper preparations for single combat, the despotic Caledor struck him a mighty blow with his spear, breaking apart Snorri's helm and casting him to the ground. Though dazed and confounded, Snorri ably used his shield to fend off the vicious blows of Caledor to regain his feet. Then, undoubtedly bewitched by the subtle sorceries of Ulthuan, Snorri's guard failed and the Phoenix King's spear found its mark once more, piercing Snorri's thigh and pinning him to the bloodied dirt. Drawing his sword, Caledor cleaved open the gromril breastplate of our son's armour and opened up his chest with a great spilling of blood. Though the victory was clearly his, the Phoenix King did not relent with his assault, and did strike the arm from Snorri.[41] Lifting it as a trophy, Caledor pranced pompously in front of his host holding aloft the severed limb. It was Snorri's guard who intervened lest more ruin be laid upon the remains of our son, and Caledor withdrew, casting the arm of our beloved heir into a deep pool from which it has not yet been recovered. Snorri's shade will wander the corridors of the Halls of the Ancestors in torment, with no axe arm with which to bear his weapon, and ashamed he will be swallowed by the mists of time. Be it known that the wealth and debt of the High King is pledged to our subject who slays Caledor and revenges us against the vile Phoenix King of Ulthuan. Long may his shade rot in the Cellars of Indignity.

41. Before the War of Vengeance, the nobles of both races dealt with each other in more civilised fashion and in military disputes clemency had usually been shown and ransoms exchanged for hostages. As the war progressed it became ever more bitter, and by the end prisoners on both sides were generally slain without second thought.

The Doom of Imladrik

There are more battles for the next six years, during which Karaz-a-Karak itself was assailed twice, though the armies of the elves were beaten back with heavy cost in lives. The next event of note was a major victory for the Dwarfs.

PRINCE IMLADRIK, BROTHER to Caledor II, is slain and his dishonour revoked. At Oeragor, in the foothills west of Karak Izril, the High King's cousin, Morgrim Elgidum, led a victorious throng against the hosts of Saphery and Yvresse.[42] For the ills done to our people, Morgrim exacted a bloody vengeance. Five thousand elves paid with their lives for their hubris. With bravery uncharacteristic of an elf, Imladrik led a charge against the shieldwall of Morgrim, and slew many of our finest warriors with his gleaming blade. Yet for all his valour, Imladrik is of the blood of the Phoenix King and of equal blame for the woes that have beset our people. With one blow of his rune axe, Morgrim beheaded the griffon on which Imladrik rode, He has sent this head to the High King as a gift, mounted on the elven prince's shield. Imladrik's sword could not break the warding runes laid upon Morgrim's armour by the great Ranuld Silverthumb, and Morgrim dealt the elf princeling a deadly blow to the head. Though great was the temptation to despoil the body in the same manner ignobly heaped upon that of Snorri Halfhand, Morgrim satisfied himself with the simple removal of the elf's nose, and then allowed the prince's retainers to remove the remains for whatever fawning burial ceremony awaits them.

A messenger was brought down by rangers near to the workings at Gotdrek-bin-Gazan, carrying missives from the Phoenix King for the elven army camped upon the banks of the Shadowmere. It offers the hand in marriage of Caledor's sister Alaine to whomsoever brings him the beard of Morgrim Elgidum. Caledor will be brought to answer for this heinous commission of vile assassination intended to humiliate the lords of our folk.[43]

42. Two princedoms of the elven isle of Ulthuan, one assumes identified by heraldry upon shields and banners.
43. Some 437 grudges in total are recorded against Caledor II.

The Destruction of Athel Maraya

As the war drags on for another twenty years, there are numerous grudges pertaining to poor supplies, lack of weapons and ammunition, and further battles with the elves. The tide truly began to turn after the dwarfs' assault on the fortress at Athel Maraya.

In defiance of the law of the High King, the elves of Athel Maraya refused to return the lands they have usurped these past two hundred years. Now their usurpation has been eradicated, along with the towers and halls that they built upon the lands of our people. A great train of war machines, brought together from Karak Eight Peaks, Karaz-a-Karak, Karaz Azul, Karak Varn and Karak Kadrin, has laid waste to the city of Athel Maraya. The elves of the city refused free passage offered them, foolishly believing us as weak-willed as themselves. They were slain by hammer and crossbow bolt for their folly.

The orchards have been burned and the fields razed. The meadows have been ploughed and salted, and the stones of the buildings ground to gravel to pave the Undgrin Ankor. The statues of marble have been broken and their pieces used in the privy tanks at the new brewery in Karak Kadrin. The keystone of the great gate has been taken by the masons to fashion into an oathstone for King Grundin. No small amount of gold was reclaimed from the vaults and has been cast afresh as proper coin. Many gems were found, some ground to dust for they contained elvish enchantments, the others now adorn the skydome of King Hrallson's chambers in Karak Azul. Here in Karak Eight Peaks, the door to the Engineers' Guild now proudly displays a badge of honour, fashioned in the likeness of Grungni, may his candle never dim, cast from the tips of two thousand elven spears taken from the bodies of the dead.

The Final Siege of Tor Alessi

Another 346 years pass and Caledor II arrives in the Old World to supervise the fighting having become frustrated with his generals. Being neither particularly willing to listen to others nor a sound strategist, this brings disaster upon the elves, although the dwarfs were not without their losses.

As a smith beats upon his anvil, our armies have hammered at the resolve of the elves, and now the task is done. At Tor Alessi we once again tested our mettle against the pernicious elves, this last and fourteenth time at the city on the coast, may its foundations shatter and plunge it into the waves. High King Gotrek, Axe of the Elves, the Starbreaker,[44] led the throng and

---

44. I am unsure where this honorific comes from, though it predates the War of Vengeance.

brought the despicable Caledor to battle. Upon a dragon red of scale and fiery of breath, hoarder of gold and despoiler of our lands, the so-called Pheonix King led his army. Great were the sorceries unleashed by the conjurers of Saphery, so that fireballs and lightning wreaked havoc upon our engines and filled the eye with multi-coloured light brighter than the star-lanterns of Karak Eight Peaks. The ground was rent with fissures that opened beneath the bolt throwers, plunging our crews into jagged chasms, which then sealed tighter than a king's vault.

With a glitter that pales only to the shining waters of the Okzhuf-a-Azgal, the elven arrows rained down upon the helmets of our throng, white-flighted and deadly. Thane Burakson was slain by a shaft that pieced his stokktromm[45] and a great grievance settled upon our hearts. As the turning of the wheel in the stream that drives the mill, our axes were unrelenting in their work and hewed a great many elves. Three of the Anvils of Doom had been brought forth, and their runes burned with power and the striking of the Runelords. Trommi Ironfriend swore that the shades of the fallen of the thirteen earlier battles of Tor Alessi rose from the Halls of the Ancestors, may their walls be hung with golden banners.

Thrice the host of Caledor the Coward sallied forth, in arrogance trusting to their spears and not their walls. Thrice they were hurled back by the throng of the High King leaving behind a carpet of their fallen. On a fourth assault the Phoenix King took the field himself, and our bolts and quarrels tore the wing from his mount as he charged the High King's position. The Starbreaker, Lord of the Mountains, Hammer of the Ancestors, was swift and unyielding in the prosecution of his duties. He cut his way through the elves that rushed to aid Caledor the Friendless, and hefted the Axe of Grimnir as mightily as the great Ancestor, may his beard ever grow. He smote the neck of the Phoenix King and the edge of the axe cut as smoothly as a hotly forged blade through kruchufi.[46]

From the severed head of the elf king Gotrek took the golden crown of Ulthuan, in payment of the debts incurred to our people for the past centuries. The elves, upon seeing their pitiful leader cut in twain like a sawed log, allowed the High King to withdraw with his just recompense, and thus the war has ended.

45. Note literal translation means 'beard that protects'. I am unsure to what this refers.
46. 'Goat-fat' – perhaps some kind of lard or cheese?

The War Ends

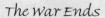

Just as with the start of the war, the High King himself marked its conclusion with a letter to every hold and fastness in the dwarf empire.

> **Due price has been levied for the wrongs done against our people. Let it not be said that we were of failing heart or of bending back under the burdens laid upon us. Through the hard work of all our subjects and the axe blade in our own hand, Caledor the Irredeemable lies dead and his crown taken as gild for our immense pains and expense. The three towers of Tor Alessi have been cast down and with the stones we shall build a vault to house our prize. We can retire in peace to our lands, to rebuild our families and homes, to lay aside our axes and shields and look to the future with hope. If the elves fail to accept the graciousness of this final act of mercy, we stand prepared to repel their assaults and cut down each and every one of them.**

The Elves Leave the Old World

With the death of Caledor II and the taking of the Phoenix Crown, the dwarfs believed that balance had been restored and the wrongs of the elves rectified. With their prize in hand, the dwarfs marched back to their holds, prepared to continue their lives as though the last few hundred years had not passed.

It is reported that the elves had different plans. Insulted by the capture of the Phoenix Crown, and what they saw as the murder of their king, the princes of the elves gathered together what forces remained for an assault on Karaz-a-Karak. Perhaps fortunately for the elves, the attack never took place. Had it done so, it is hard to see what end other than the slaughter of the elves could have occurred.

As it was, some unknown disaster befell the elven homeland and a proclamation from Caledor's successor halted the assault before it began. The elven armies embarked upon their ships and left these shores to return to Ulthuan to address whatever problems were occurring there. That was the last of the elves of the Phoenix King to be seen in the Old World for some four thousand years, until the time of their return shortly before the Great War Against Chaos.

CHAPTER FOUR

The Undead Grudge

The Depravities of Konrad

Dwarfs revere their dead above all things, for they are the mortal remains of their ancestors. Dwarf funerals are long affairs concerned with the remembrance of the deceased's deeds. Necromancy and the undead fill dwarfs with a particular loathing and horror, and to disturb the remains of the dead or interfere with souls in the Halls of the Ancestors is one of the gravest crimes in dwarf law.

Here follows a selection of grudges pertaining to the undead and, notably for scholars of the Empire, the dwarfs' involvement in the dreadful wars of the vampire counts.

Dealings with the Undead

AN UNKNOWN MANLING was chased from the second lower burial tiers in the west reaches, having gained access via an undiscovered crack in the sub-sub-vaults of the funerary cellars. He is being tracked and shall be brought to justice.

Implements of ghost-bothering[47] were found, including a receptacle of what appears to be goat's or chicken's blood, a small number of ironwood nails, a painting brush made with human hair and a silver mirror of ancient design and patina. Various scrapings on the protective runes of Thane

---

47. Literal translation, one assumes necromancy.

Furginnson's sepulchre reveal that the manling was attempting some vile incantation. Runesmith Bakkar Greyhammer inspected the runes and was satisfied that their wardings were still intact.

Grievous news has arrived from Zhufbar. The king's cousin Goghbad, betrothed to the daughter of King Barrin of Zhufbar, is dead.[48] Whilst visiting his bride-to-be, Goghbad joined the throng of Zhufbar investigating recent destruction wrought upon the barley fields west of the hold. Accompanying a contingent of rangers[49] knowledgeable of the area, Goghbad travelled to the trading outpost of Duraz Urbazund to ensure the safety of his kin-to-be. Duraz Urbazund was found to be ransacked and desolate, and not a body found. At first suspecting vile grobi, Goghbad sent word to Zhufbar for a hunting expedition to be mustered. Before greater numbers of warriors could arrive, Duraz Urbazund was attacked once more. A great and unnatural storm befell the hillside, obscuring all light and bathing the mountains in eerie twilight. Flocks of gigantic bats fell upon the outpost and with flaming brands and burning quarrels Goghbad and the rangers drove back the swirling cloud of fell bats without loss.

Those who had taken the folk of Duraz Urbazund then returned. It was not greenskins, but a host of the restless dead, led by a monstrous 'blood-drinker'.[50] Amongst the unliving throng stood the bodies of the folk of Duraz Urbazund. Incensed beyond imagining, Goghbad attacked and attempted to fight his way to the blood-drinker in order to strike its head from its body and destroy its remains. The attack stalled swiftly, and to avoid being surrounded by the uncountable horde, Goghbad and his warriors retired to the fortifications of Duraz Urbazund. Here they mounted a staunch defence, and were able to hold the walls for many hours, despite the never-ending tide of undead that assailed them. However, upon the fall of true night, the blood-drinker itself led the next wave of unliving creatures, and none of Goghbad's throng could stand before its strength and speed. Goghbad met this unnatural beast with rune axe and shield in hand, and dealt it a mighty blow to the chest. The creature fought on despite the gaping

48. The king's family, like many others, extends to most of the surviving holds, as can be seen in the summarised genealogical chart included elsewhere in this volume.
49. Rangers are dwarfs who spend the majority of their lives above ground. They are the first line of defence against attack, and knowledgeable of the surrounding area. Frequently they are used as scouts and ambushers, to stall an enemy advance or to attack enemy supplies.
50. 'Zanguzaz' – literal translation, presumably a vampire.

wound in its torso, and tore the throat from Goghbad with its fangs. Goghbad's companions fought hard but could not rescue the body of the king's cousin, and his fate is unknown. This is as related by those few rangers who escaped the massacre. The king has ordered the thanes to muster warriors for a march north, for a reckoning with the blood-drinker, and has sent emissaries to Zhufbar announcing his intent.

Word has arrived from Zhufbar that all is not well in the lands of the Empire. For many centuries strife has riven their accord, and our folk have been content to leave them to their own affairs. Our merchants have dealt with all factions and claimants to the throne without bias or favour, and much profit has been made. Though it be at the expense of the woes of the manlings, it is not our place to judge their internal problems.[51] Yet now it has become a matter for our kings, for a new claimant to the throne of the Emperor has declared himself. Count Vlad von Carstein of Sylvania, bordering on the realms of Zhufbar, is revealed as a blood-drinker, and a powerful one at that. The king is convinced that it is this Vlad, or one of his infernal get, that was responsible for the slaying of his cousin Goghbad, and has redoubled his efforts to mount an expedition to the north to battle this monstrosity.

The Rise of the Blood Count

THE KING IS fraught with wrath, for the accursed Vlad is slain, outside the walls of the manling town of Altdorf. Who now shall be held in account for the marauding of Duraz Urbazund and the disappearance of Goghbad?

A new creature has arisen to lead the thrice-cursed coven of blood-drinkers ruling Sylvania. Konrad is his name, and by all reports he is a mad and violent beast. The king passes on the debt of Vlad to Konrad, and will hold him to full account with flame and axe.

The king has razed the village of Gratelsperg on the borders of Hunger Wood. Seeking shelter and wares for his throng, he took sanctuary near to the manling hovels. As custom dictates, the king and a small retinue of hammerers announced themselves to the leader of the settlement, a strange manling named Kharl Vennegheist. At first all was well and the welcome,

51. Though the Time of the Three Emperors was a trying one for the Empire, the dwarfs profited highly. Without favour, they sold weapons and dwarf-made items to any and all nobles willing to pay their prices, which were considerable even by dwarf standards. Black powder made by the dwarfs, in particular, was much sought after and the greater efficiency of firearms from this period onward no doubt led to increasingly bloody battles.

though sparse due to the destitute nature of Gratelsperg and the depredations of the undead, was warm and good-natured. The hostelry of the village was put at our king's disposal, and a bed chamber in the master's own house was offered up for use.

As the king slumbered after sampling a great deal of the local brew, which by all accounts was fair for manling drink,[52] a cabal of villagers sneaked into the chambers and bound the king with sheets and gagged him with a pillow case. Thus restrained, the king was unable to raise the alarm and was carried to a dung cart outside and hidden underneath its malodorous contents before being conveyed to the ruins of an ancient tower on the outskirts of the village.

By this time, by dint of the king's observance of strict tradition and routine, his chief victualler Hynthyng Goldenspoon arrived at the king's resting place to enquire as to his appetite for a midnight supper. Upon finding the inn deserted and the king missing, Hynthyng bore these grave tidings to Thane Garbarak, who roused the throng and set about a search of the village and surrounds. They came upon the ruins of the tower where the king was concealed and were set upon by a great horde of filthy, bloodstained manlings, naked but for loincloths and feral in manner.[53] Smeared with blood as these debased creatures were, Thane Garbarak feared the worst had befallen the king and stormed the ruins with haste.

Within the dungeons they found a long hall, decked out in macabre fashion, in dark parody of a banquet. A monstrous vampire,[54] fully thrice the height of a sturdy dwarf warrior, officiated over the bleak proceedings from a high-backed chair at one end of a table lit by candles made of human fat. Our king lay trussed with twine, a withered apple placed in his mouth, upon a tarnished silver platter at the centre of the table, while villagers laboured at a firepit, over which a roasting spit was built. The beast fled the wrath of Thane Garbarak, disappearing by hidden ways, and its tracks vanished with the coming of dawn. The king was gratefully freed from his bonds.

The cannibalistic villagers were hunted. Those that resisted were cut down and a great pit was dug for their bodies, a dozen score of them at least though none of us had the stomach

52. Beers of Sylvania are considered near-undrinkable by most folk, so whether this place was remarkable or the observations of the king merely royal courtesy is debatable.

53. Crypt ghouls as known to men. The dwarfs have no equivalent in their language and are utterly abhorred by the concept of cannibalism.

54. I have read several corroborated reports of such creatures, sometimes called varghulfs, or the Beasts of Strigos.

to count for sure. The rest were bound and transported to Delverzheim six miles to the south, and handed into the custody of Captain Valgin of the army of Stirland. Searches have been conducted for the whereabouts of Kharl Vennegheist but he as yet remains at large and unaccounted for. The village was destroyed with fire and black powder, and the ruins of the tower consecrated by a human priest[55] as well as Runesmith Jarlbik.

Hunger Wood

THIS DAY WE remark upon the frailties of the manlings, and in particular their lack of honour. But also let us recognise their courage, for not all of the children of men are cowards and oathless.

Let us start with the former, for today the alliance in which our king has participated was shattered by the weaknesses of the manlings. Our partners upon this bloodied field were three: the leaders of the Empire lands of Reikland, Talabecland and the Wasteland.[56] An assassin struck, no doubt sent by Konrad von Carstein to sow disorder amongst this fragile coalition, for surely not even a manling would be so beardless as to slay his allies on the very eve of a battle against the hateful undead. The assassin or assassins struck at the Countess of Talabecland; her throat was slit from ear to ear.[57] Much aggrieved were her people, and much afeared too that their self-declared Empress would be raised from her death by the minions of the blood-drinker. Though we offered to prepare the body by the means that protect our ancestors, may their beer forever froth, such distraught and black thoughts had clouded the manlings' hearts that they simply hacked apart the unfortunate body and buried the separate pieces. Such disrespect is so typical of the manlings, for whom death is something to be greatly feared. Perhaps it is because they do not have our surety that their lives have been spent in honourable and noble pursuits, and thus they forever doubt that they will be accepted by their ancestors.

The death of the countess started a veritable rikigraz[58] of accusations and counter-accusations. All this took place whilst the hosts of Konrad the Blood Count were gathered for the

55. It is likely that this was a priest of Morr.
56. More specifically, Marienburg – all rivals to the Imperial throne at the time.
57. Some accounts back the claim that the Count of Reikland employed the assassin, and perhaps it is merely dwarfen disbelief at such treachery that disputes this.
58. A cave-in or landslide that swiftly gathers momentum.

attack. The fleshless dead of ancient wars marched upon us with green-slicked bronze shields and swords, while formless wailing things of terror beset our throng with their chilling touch and disconcerting shrieks. Whilst the armies of men fought amongst themselves, it was to the axes and shoulders of our throng that the burden of battle fell. If not for the courage of all of our kin, the battle was sure to have been lost, for the manlings were as eager to spill each other's blood as to hack at the foe.[59]

Come the end of the fighting, after a day's long and weary war work, it was the courage and strength of men that was to be credited. Helmar of Marienburg in the Wasteland, son of Helmut and orphaned by the hand of the Blood Count, did avenge his father, in a way most honourable and fitting. Aided by the doughty Grufbad, who himself owed debt of blood for a father's death, Helmar dealt the fatal blow to Konrad von Carstein. Grufbad twice cut upon the beast with axe blows that would have felled trees. Upon seeing the creature rise from these grievous wounds, Grufbad pinned the blood-drinker to the ground. Let it be known for posterity that he did not, despite some unflattering accounts of the manlings, sit upon Count Konrad to restrain him.[60] With his runefang, heirloom of his position, forged many centuries past by the genius of Alaric the Mad, Helmar decapitated Konrad von Carstein and thus ended his reign of terror,[61] and Helmar did even the score for the day's earlier tribulations. The king is satisfied that retribution has been made for the death of Goghbad.

59. A few regiments did not participate in the infighting and assisted the dwarfs, including several war machine crews who had spent time with dwarf engineers the previous night preparing range markers and receiving technical advice on their guns.
60. It is unknown what source this is disputing.
61. The end of the Wars of the Vampire Counts saw many dwarfs remain in the Empire, the second of three general waves of expatriation to the Empire. The first was during the time of Sigmar, may he forever protect us, following the Battle of Black Fire Pass. The latest was directly after the Great War Against Chaos. In particular, dwarfs of fallen holds sometimes prefer not to live in another hold, for fear of some nameless shame, and instead create new lives for themselves in the lands of men. As a result dwarf quarters in many cities are sizeable and their tradecraft more readily available here than in other lands.

CHAPTER FIVE

The Rat-kin Grudge

The Fall of Karak Eight Peaks

One of the longest and most bitterly felt grudges of the dwarf empire is that of the destruction of Karak Eight Peaks. So heinous was this act that several enemies of the dwarfs are implicated in the great hold's fall. The grudge you see transcribed below details the actions of the first of these enemies, what the dwarfs term 'thaggoraki', a strange race of rat-like beasts.

Dwarfs and the Rat-kin:

Rumours persist even within the Empire of rats the size of men that walk on two legs (though I have yet to witness such a creature, personally). The dwarf legends and books of grudges make mention of rat-kin or thaggoraki, though I doubt such things are related to the so-called skaven that allegedly plague the Empire in secret.

My research has revealed to me that the history between the dwarfs and the rat-kin is long indeed. Several entries in the Karak Eight Peaks Book of Grudges speak of protracted tunnel battles against these creatures, of the poisoning of wells, and of the 'dark technologies' that they possessed. Further entries are evident in extracts from the Karak Azul Book of Grudges in the discovery of the dragon, Mordrak, and from the reports reaching Karak Azul of the fall of Karak Varn and the rat-like things that emerged from the depths to claim it. Most infamous is the period when the Black Plague swept the Old World and the thaggoraki emerged from their burrows to attack the dwarf realms en masse. Entire chapters in the books of grudges of many holds are devoted to it.

Save for these testimonies, little is known to this scholar about the existence of such creatures and the veracity of claims that something akin to them walk beneath the very streets of the Empire itself! It would appear that the rat-kin have a labyrinthine tunnel network that spans the Old World, intersecting the dwarfen undgrin road at several points, even completely subsuming it at others. What is apparent though is the growing rancour of the dwarfs towards this race of intelligent rat mutants.

Rat-kin Warrens are discovered in the Fifth Deep

ON THIS DAY miners of the Grimstone clan, excavating a lucrative seam of gold, break through into a vast warren of tunnels. Upon closer inspection, the tunnels are revealed to be of thaggoraki[62] manufacture, crude and foul of stench as is the rat-kin's mark. Prospector Henkil does report the tunnels are impossible to map and stretch for many miles.

A war party of rat-kin broke through into the undgrin and did slay Zorbin Firehelm and sixteen miners of his clan. Clan warriors are mustered but the thaggoraki flee into the warrens and pursuit is impossible. A grudge is hereby lodged against Henkil Grimstone, and the Grimstone clan, for failure to shore up the breach discovered by them in the undgrin. Fifty rat-tails each is demanded as recompense against the rat-kin for the deaths of Zorbin and his kin.

Karag Zilfin Mines Destroyed

THE ATTACKS OF the rat-kin grows daily in frequency. The vermin are emboldened by their increasing numbers. They appear oft without warning, striking from their tunnel warrens. Grungni's lament, as three mines at Karag Zilfin[63] fall.

At Varkund, clan dwarfs of the Copperback, Flinthand and Bronzefist are slain, fifty in all, as a great poison cloud engulfs them, wrought by a band of rat-kin with strange contrivances strapped to their flea-infested muzzles and clutching globes of greenish gas. Lodemaster Ankmar Bronzefist shoots one with his

---

62. The literal translation is 'Assassin' or 'Footpad', but it also appears to refer to the rat creatures. See 'Dwarfs and the Rat-kin'.
63. Meaning 'Windswept Mountain'.

crossbow and quickly musters quarrellers to slay the others. In their wake come scores of rat-kin, led by a bigger, black-furred warrior wielding a broad-bladed halberd and clad in thick armour. The mine is overrun. Sappers collapse the tunnels at the behest of Lodemaster Ankmar, the vermin kept at bay by quarrellers, and the mine is abandoned to the hated foe. *Teeth of Valaya!*

At Runkarn the very mine workings themselves are attacked. Wooden supports are rendered to ash by a fire-throwing engine of the rat-kin, as are numerous dwarfs of the Ironback clan, and the mine itself collapses, burying all but a scant few survivors. Those that do escape to tell of these deeds most foul die quickly afterwards. *By Grungni's oath, such crude machineries are an affront to any dwarf!*

At Undkar black-garbed skaven do fall upon the prospectors there with poison blade. The cowards attack from the shadows and slay a great many dawi before any retaliation can be meted out. With typical vermin courage, the rat-kin flee as soon as they are met by stern dwarf resistance but not before poisoning a great many wells. Immediately after the attack, the underground river beneath Undkar is inspected, the prospectors discovering shards of green-black glowing rock – the pure stuff of Chaos! In short order, blasting charges[64] are set for a mile long stretch beneath Undkar and both mine and river are buried beneath rock. A thousand rat-tails for this deed!

This day does Rikti Ironback, sole survivor of the Ironback clan, take the slayer vow. After consuming a great many firkins of Duric's Best, the dawi slept through his shift at the Runkarn mine in the clan hold and thus avoided the fate of his kinsmen. He wanders into the long dark of the underway and is never seen again.

The Citadel of Eight Peaks is Lost

WITH THE EYES of the hold upon the vermin beneath, the grobi horde of the mountains grows unchecked. The horn at the East Gate[65] is sounded across the peaks as the surface citadel of the hold is attacked by a vast greenskin horde. Over a

---

64. See 'Miners'. Note that some records I have read suggest that blackpowder was not discovered by the dwarfs until around a hundred years later. These 'charges' were most likely alcohol-based and designed to remove 'key stones' placed through the hold to collapse specific tunnels and gateways in the event of invasion.

65. The East Gate is one of the main approaches into Karak Eight Peaks and can be reached through Death Pass. It is still guarded to this day by a stout watchtower, recently reinforced by King Belegar and his kin. The gate itself is vast and impressive as is all dwarfen architecture, though it too has recently been repaired and refortified with additional towers and the inclusion of static war engines.

hundred grobi perish as the first attack is repulsed, but not without the deaths of twenty-one clan warriors. King Lunn hereby declares a grudge against the greenskin tribes of the Snarling Sun and the Howling Moon for this latest wrong.

The royal hammerers of the king reinforce the citadel but it is for nought as the garrison is forced to give up the outer wall to the greenskins. Over a hundred dawi fall in this latest attack alone. Their names are scribed in the book of remembering.

Attacks from the rat-kin below continue unabated and no further troops can be spared to bolster the citadel. Many of the outer buildings of the city are abandoned: ale stores, drinking halls, brewhouses and clan halls that have stood for ages are ruined, the art of their former creators lost forever. *Dreng tromm!*

The grobi employ crude war machines and gather a great band of trolls to launch rocks at the citadel keep. Though their aim is poor, such is the amount of missiles levelled that great destruction is wrought, including the tower-mounted bolt throwers and grudge throwers.[66] Thane Halkenhaf Stonebeard, Citadel Gate Keeper[67] is slain, eaten by a troll, and the inner curtain almost falls. King Lunn hereby declares a grudge against the creature and all its foul kind.

The grobi assaults against the inner curtain wall are unrelenting and the tunnels of the upper deeps are also attacked. With a heavy heart, King Lunn declares all efforts to hold the great wall be abandoned. All remaining defenders are brought back into the citadel keep as a full retreat is ordered. King Lunn redoubles the defenders below at the Gate of Jewels. Reports reach the king's chambers that the rat-kin attacks intensify. All routes to the lower deeps of the hold are sealed.

Varkund Avenged

RUNNING BATTLES WITH the rat-kin are now becoming an every day occurrence. On this day, a large nest north of Varkund is discovered by an ironbreaker patrol. Master Engineer Finbold Finkson orders charges set by sappers at every exit. It is slow work but achieved without notice of the rat-kin. In the ensuing explosion, several birthing chambers and a great many burrows are destroyed as the nest cavern is collapsed. Varkund is denied to the vermin and small measure of vengeance is wrought, so decrees King Lunn!

---

66. The citadel of Eight Peaks was well protected, heavily garrisoned and bore several war machine emplacements at key points around it. These defensive measures were to prove in vain, however, as the goblins and skaven attacked through tunnels.

67. In this instance, as the citadel of Eight Peaks was above ground, the gate keeper had the dual responsibility of ward of the king's chambers and the citadel gate.

Eight Peaks is Torn Asunder

NUMEROUS EARTHQUAKES RAVAGE Vala-Azrilungol.[68] *Wrath of Grungni!* Deep chasms open up in the earth and the vaulted halls of Eight Peaks come crashing down throughout the hold. Karag Zilfin is completely overrun as thaggoraki and grobi inundate the tunnels in uncountable numbers, great clefts rent into the walls of the hold allowing them passage. The ironbreaker patrols are insufficient to keep them at bay and a desperate rearguard is ordered by the king. Dawi numbers are thinned by the cataclysm and Zilfin falls.

Karag Yar[69] is lost this day. Reports are scant as to the nature of its demise. What few survivors emerge from the peak speak of an 'ancient evil' that has awoke from beneath the mountain. King Lunn orders all routes into the karag magically rhun-sealed.

Further quakes are visited upon the hold and Karag Mhonar[70] bears the brunt. In the lower deeps, great rivers of lava consume entire mines as well as numerous workshops and forges. Word has reached the hold from Karak Drazh and Karak Azul that both Karag Dron and Karag Haraz[71] have erupted. Lava pits and chasms of fire make much of the peak impassable and hordes of skaven and grobi infest it. King Lunn orders the peak abandoned until the rat-kin and greenskins can be purged, and the extent of the damage wrought determined. Furthermore, a grudge against the rat-kin and the grobi is hereby entered into the kron for this latest sacrilege.

Karagril,[72] Karag Lhune,[73] Karag Rhyn[74] and Karag Nar[75] fall. *Dreng Tromm!* Much of the lower deeps of Karagril is swept away by flood, its upper deeps are beset by urk. A great mass of trolls assaults Karag Lhune through one of the many giant fissures wrought by the earthquakes devastating the hold. The rat-kin

68. Literally meaning 'Queen of the Silver Depths'.
69. Meaning 'Sunset Mountain'.
70. Meaning 'Shadow Mountain'.
71. Meaning 'Thunder Mountain' and 'Fire Mountain', respectively. Dwarfs have long learned to understand the dangers of volcanoes and how to yoke their power for benefit. It is reputed in the studies of some of my contemporaries (so take this information with a pinch of salt) that some engineers' guilds have managed to tap into the energy produced by a volcano, creating an elaborate system of fans and copper pipes to funnel it into the hold, thus heating it. Furthermore, it is noted that dwarfs like nothing better than to spit-roast over the molten rock produced by a volcano, maintaining there is no better way to cook meat.
72. Meaning 'Silverhorn'. Note that all the peaks up to Silverhorn guard the eastern approach to the city, whilst the remaining four peaks guard the west.
73. Meaning 'Crescent Mountain'.
74. Meaning 'Mount Redstone'.
75. Meaning 'Sunrise Mountain'.

attack from below, tainting wells and burning feast halls. The clan warriors of the hold fight in the tunnels and vaults of the peak but to no avail. At Karag Rhyn there are reports of a fearsome troll terrorising the deeps, goaded by beastmasters of the rat-kin. Rumours reach Kvinn-Wyr[76] of 'a beast, chunks of glowing rock hammered into its flesh, larger and more terrible than any troll of old,' so ancient and deadly that no dawi can stand against it. It is the last message from Karag Rhyn. Nar is overrun by thaggoraki, their wizard-weapons burning and slaying as dawi fights grobi and rat-kin on two fronts. Poison gas fills the Undgrin, the stout armour of the weaponshops of Eight Peaks is no protection against it! *Thagi!* No quarter is given lightly but the defenders are overwhelmed. They Will Be Remembered. King Lunn's lament is recorded here as are grudges against the entire grobi and rat-kin race for the loss of the seven peaks. Now only Kvinn-Wyr remains.[77]

Kvinn-Wyr is attacked by a vast horde of ratmen from below and greenskins continue to assault the citadel from above, with still more attacking through unguarded tunnels. The lower deeps fall quickly, the forges and mines destroyed with little resistance. A grudge against both grobi and rat-kin for this fell deed! Steadily, the hold is lost chamber by chamber but every foot is paid for in rat-kin and grobi blood. A last stand is mustered at the Gate of Jewels but the rat-kin are many. Their war engines wreak a terrible havoc, their ranks buoyed by mutated rat beasts and other monstrosities. The Gate of Jewels falls and the way is laid open to the East Stair of Eight Peaks and the heart of the hold. With deep shame and regret does King Lunn order a retreat, realising that with such few numbers resistance against the grobi and the rat-kin cannot be sustained. All the treasures of the hold that can be carried are gathered together. Yet several runic artefacts are not accounted for. The shrines and tombs of the ancestors are sealed with rhun in the hope the enemy will not be able to enter. The route into the deeps is blocked.

King Lunn gathers the remnants of Eight Peaks in the King's Hall of the citadel. What follows is the personal journal of the king himself.

---

76. The eighth and final peak, meaning 'White Lady'. It is here in this snow-capped mountain that the temple of Valaya resides.

77. Note the frequency and terseness of these grudge records, suggesting a very rapid decline and usurpation of the hold. It isn't clear from my readings which of the holds fell first but fall they did and hard. It is known that the White Lady, at the time the sole bastion of King Lunn, was the last to fall signalling the end of Karak Eight Peaks.

Kvinn-Wyr has fallen, and with it goes the last hopes of the Eight Peaks. From below the rat-kin have infested the lower deeps. Grimnir take their eyes! Above, the grobi tribes gather. Their stench has become a palpable fug staining the very air of the King's Hall. I can barely stand to breathe another breath of it. I beseech the forgiveness of Grungni, for we can no longer endure in this place of dark echoes and lost glories.

This day I did muster all of the clans, even as our very walls were attacked by grobi. As I beheld the dour expressions of my kin I realised the debt in blood paid by the dawi of Eight Peaks in fighting for their hold – scarcely a thousand dwarfs remained. But proud were they still, clutching az and grund, ready for one last battle. So armed, the clans gathered in skor and sakdon.[78] I did then declare the great gates of the upper citadel opened.

In surged the grobi, wailing and hooting. Dreng Tromm – that we should abandon the hold to such filth! Their foul ranks broke upon our shields and the advance was ordered. Steadily, though the press of grobi bodies was great, did the last throng of Eight Peaks march from her hallowed halls. We gained the citadel courtyard quickly and I wept as I slew, grobi blood bathing my beard in gore. Not for the grobi did I weep, but for those we leave behind us. The fighting was fiercest beyond the curtain wall, for here had most of the grobi tribes gathered. But with the way to Eight Peaks open, many lost the will to fight and the ruins of the citadel was soon cleared.

In the end, seventy-four clan brothers lay dead, their names etched in my own blood – a grudge debt for every one of them. Our path was southward to the hearth-hold of noble Kazgar, King of Azul; a journey undertook with a heavy heart. Eight Peaks has fallen, the jewel of the Karak Ankor is lost. Are these the last days of Vala-Azrilungol?[79]

---

78. See 'Khazalid – The Language of the Dwarfs' and 'Klinkarhun'. Based upon my knowledge of the dwarf counting system, skor refers to groups of twenty, while sakdon literally translates as five ten, meaning fifty.

79. Eight Peaks fell at the end of the period known as the Goblin Wars.

After a thousand years of resistance, once Karak Eight Peaks fell the dwarfs lost three strongholds in fifty short years. Indeed, from my research, it seems that Vala-Azrilungol' was the key to the defeat of all the southern holds in -469, barring Karak Azul. First Karak Izil, known now as Karak Azgal or 'Dragon Crag', was despoiled by the dragon, Graug the Terrible, then came the destruction of Karak Drazh, known now as Black Crag. Of course Karak Drazh was eventually to become the lair of the orc warchief, Gorfang Rotgut. For further enlightenments as to Gorfang's deeds and the grudge borne against him by the King of Karak Azul, Kazador of the Donarkhun clan, see Chapter One.

THE GREENSKIN GRUDGE

Part Two

The Impudence of Skarsnik

This grudge details the second of the dwarfs' enemies that they hold most to account over the destruction and subsequent defilement of Karak Eight Peaks. The name Skarsnik appears to live long in the memories of the dwarfs, a greenskin for whom they reserve particular ire.

Dwarfs and Greenskins

Ancient is the hatred felt by the dwarfs towards the race of greenskins. It dates back many hundreds of years to the time of the Goblin Wars. During this period, after the Karak Ankor had suffered the ruination of earthquakes and floods, orcs and goblins emerged from the dark beneath the world, sacking and claiming many of the lost holds. The dwarfs felt this bitterly and the war against the goblins lasted for over a thousand years, until even the dwarfs were forced to eventually admit several defeats. It is a cause of much enmity, one felt most keenly by the dwarfs who reserve particular ire for these creatures.

Karak Ungor was the first of the holds to fall, nearly four thousand years ago. It was taken over by night goblins and renamed Red Eye Mountain. It was followed by several others. Karak Drazh, now called Black Crag; Karak Varn; Karak Azgal, or Dragon Crag, all

729

fell, as did Karak Eight Peaks for a time. My records suggest it was not just the race of greenskins that caused the destruction of many of the dwarf holds, but they were certainly instrumental and that, together with many deeds perpetrated since and etched in blood in books of grudges, has ensured that the hatred felt by the dwarfs towards orcs and goblins will be everlasting.

The Clan Angrund Royal Book of Grudges of King Beregar Ironhammer, Lord of the Eight Peaks

Battle at the Citadel

THIS DAY DOES King Belegar Ironhammer of the Angrund clan[80] reclaim the citadel of Vala-Azrilungol.[81]

King Belegar, with an army mustered from Karaz-a-Karak, takes the northern route to the hold. Foul grobi totems befoul the edge of the road, the skulls of brave dawi adventurers adorning them. Belegar hereby declares a grudge against the night goblin tribes for perpetrating such a deed and for the filth their years of occupation has clearly wrought.

A thousand woes, as the citadel is sighted but in a state of ruination, proud dawi craftsmanship tainted by crude grobi structures. *A heavy toll of blood for this despolation!* Grobi, bedecked in tattered robe and hood, are seen amongst the rubble and a discordant horn sounds. Battle is joined at the citadel gate. Grobi wielding ball and chain, crazed beyond reason, inflict tremendous damage upon the Grim Brotherhood. In anger do King Belegar's quarrellers dispatch the filthy grobi with crossbow bolts.

More grobi cowardice as the throng is assailed by missiles flung by ramshackle machineries from the watch towers of the curtain wall and boulders launched down the narrow defile in which the citadel lies. Dawi deaths are many at this latest treachery. Their Names Will Be Remembered. *A curse upon the grobi and all their kind!*

Belegar does advance to the citadel walls, a great trail of greenskin dead in his wake. He and his loyal warriors do carve a red ruin in the grobi ranks, slaughtering every foul one as

80. See 'Karak Azul – A Clan Record'.
81. It took many years for the dwarfs to mount a successful expedition into Karak Eight Peaks. At its fall, and until Belegar's occupation, the hold was disputed by 'rat-kin' and greenskins, neither possessing the strength to drive the other out. A stalemate was reached and steadily more and more creatures took up residence in the deeps. Many adventurers from the other holds, and indeed the Empire, mounted expeditions to rescue the treasures still housed within but little is known of what, if anything, was recovered during this time.

they gain the keep itself. After many long years of greenskin occupation, the citadel is at last cleared and the taint upon it vanquished utterly as no grobi are allowed to escape or live.

Hastily, does King Belegar order the citadel refortified and all but one of the tunnels sealed. Ironbreakers are sent into the first deeps and treasures thought lost are recovered. Let it be known on this day, in the name of King Lunn, a blow was struck against the greenskin usurpers of Vala-Azrilungol. All hail Belegar, lord of the Eight Peaks!

The Way into the Lower Deeps is Shut

OF THREE PATROLS sent into the lower deeps this day, only one returns with word that grobi and rat-kin dwell there in abundance. King Belegar hereby lodges a grudge against the murderers of Badri Grimson, Krudd Ironspike, Gorim Jorgson, Finbul Stoneback, Skalli Trollbiter, Vragni Yorrison and Mundri Skalfinnson. Their names are forever etched in the kron.

Attacks against the surface city are growing daily and King Belegar hereby decrees that the tunnels to the Second Deep be sealed. Much of the First Deep is now in our possession, honour to Valaya, but further raids into the lower tombs are now increasingly rare.

Belegar allows Passage into the Deeps by Outsiders

ON THIS DAY does King Belegar allow a band of men from the Empire, honouring the debt of ages past, to venture beyond the Barak Khatûl[82] in search of the lost fortunes of Eight Peaks. A toll of one-tenth of any treasure recovered is set as the promise price and agreed by oath. None of the adventurers return and the Barak Khatûl is shut.

On this day does Faragrim of Eight Peaks[83] enter the deeps to quest for the lost treasures of the hold.

Faragrim returns from the lower deeps, having ventured farther than any before him, with word of an ancient treasure and

82. Literally meaning 'Gate to Lurking Dangers' this door is the only route from what is known as the Explorer's Hall, or audience chamber, to the unclaimed areas of Eight Peaks. I have read accounts of the door being made of steel, barred and reinforced with protective rune wards.

83. Some sources I have read suggest that Faragrim acted as Belegar's guide in finding a route through to the citadel and surface city of Eight Peaks, and that his knowledge of the tunnels and vaults of the deeps resulted in the recovery of several long lost treasures. I issue a warning however... such reports should be treated with caution, related second-hand from their original source: the poet and adventurer, Felix Jaeger – a wanted outlaw in Altdorf.

brooding evil at large in the dark beneath the world. Upon hearing of his deeds many others come to Eight Peaks, all seeking the gold and jewels of King Lunn. Many are never seen again.

Let it be known that on this day Gotrek, son of Gurni, with several men of the Empire in tow, is granted permission by King Belegar to venture beyond the Barak Khatûl and into the lower deeps of the Eight Peaks.

Gotrek, son of Gurni does return from the depths of Eight Peaks having slain a mighty troll, with one other survivor. The manling, hereby referred to as Felix Jaegar, recovers a magical blade of his ancestors. King Belegar hereby gives Felix Jaeger permission to take the sword without taxation in recognition of Gotrek, son of Gurni's, deeds and of old oaths sworn by High King Kurgan Ironbeard.[84]

The Citadel is Besieged

URK AND GROBI swell about the city walls of Eight Peaks in vast numbers. At the behest of Queen Kemma does King Belegar order a missive sent immediately to Karaz-a-Karak to petition for aid.[85] He sends a small force of rangers, may Grungni guide and protect them, through a hidden tunnel that leads out onto the western slopes where the greenskin hordes are at their thinnest.

84. Referring to the rescue of the high king by our lord Sigmar in ages past and the forging of strong relations between men of the Empire and Dwarfs. It is possible to suppose that as the blade was of Imperial origin, King Belegar was willing to part with it.

85. I have transcribed Belegar's missive to Duregar on the following page.

To his most venerable Lord Duregar,

I trust this message meets you strong in mind and wide in girth.

Tis a welcome change that I may send you news of our fortune, yet rejoice not early as though the message I send is of great tidings, the time of celebration has yet to pass. I will remind you of our last communication though I know I need not do so. My clan had spent many years gathering strength in preparation to march south. It was with high spirits that we set forth on the ancient pass. Once again the kinsfolk of Lunn were eager to feel the soil of our homeland beneath our boots. Far too many centuries had passed since Dwarf eyes have fallen upon Vala-Azrilungol.

The journey was swift and neither grobi nor gronti barred our way. We entered the basin where once the city stood proud and tall, via the pass that winds its way around Kvinn-Wyr. The sight of the fortifications, though they lay in ruinous form, stirred each warrior's heart with a passion that even I have never felt before.

A murmur grew up from the army and could not be quelled.

I wish I could claim that our route down the northern approach to the Kazad was met with the same joy, but the vile grobi totems of poor hapless adventurers brought down our spirits. Their skulls now hailed our arrival and brought swift reminder of the dangers we faced.

As we passed through the ruins of the north gate, a tide of black-robed night goblins poured from the walls and amassed before us. Forming into solid shieldwalls, my warriors prepared for the onslaught. Crazed fanatics fuelled by toxic fungi took a heavy toll of many of my kinsfolk, as did the vicious cave squigs whose huge teeth tore through even our strongest armour. Huge boulders crashed down upon our ranks and great spears were launched into our midst, yet with stout courage did the proud army hold fast.

We met the charge of the vile grobi whose numbers tripled that of our small band. Wave after wave of gibbering greenskins sallied from the ruins, but in our hearts we knew vengeance was at hand. With the names of our fallen forefathers on our lips each Dwarf amongst our clan took revenge. By evening there was not one greenskin who could draw breath remaining within the city walls.

As I write this message, my warriors and engineers are hastily constructing a barricade around the inner wall. Once word has spread, you can be sure as gold shines and elves lie that many more grobi will gather to try to retake what is not theirs to possess. Already my sentries have spied movement amongst the debris that litters what was once the outer walls.

If we are to stand any chance of holding our position within the city then we will need reinforcements. The time to reclaim the southern Holds is at hand but lies not within my power alone to do so.

My kin already owe you more than we can ever repay for your generous hospitality in letting us take refuge in Karaz-a-Karak. If you could send any help to aid us in this time of need then I can but dream that one day the proud city of Karak Eight Peaks will repay your friendship.

Honourably yours,
Belegar

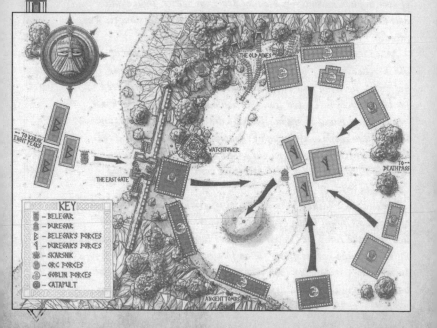

The Clan Akrund Book of Grudges, of Duregar Hammerfist, Lord of Karaz-a-Karak

Battle of the Jaws

LORD DUREGAR HAMMERFIST and a throng of his kin are attacked this day at the western entrance to Varag Kadrin.[89] The king is travelling south from Karaz-a-Karak, word reaching him that his clan brother King Belegar is besieged at Eight Peaks.

Grobi riding wolves do engage the rear lines of the dwarf column and some stragglers are slain. Their names will be writ in the book of remembering. Quickly does Lord Duregar marshal his forces as a vast army of urk emerge from tunnels in the steep-sided valley. Runesmith Hurgar the Black does smite two skor greenskins with his hammer. A band of slayers led by Dorin Badaxe destroys a large group of urk and stone trolls. Wolfriders harrying the flanks of the throng are brought down by quarrellers. A charge of some thirty clan warriors, led by Lord Duregar himself, breaks the back of the grobi horde who are sent fleeing into the rocky hills of the valley. The rest of the way eastward along the pass is made without further incident.

Duregar reaches the East Gate

LEAVING VARAG KADRIN behind and travelling southwards, Lord Duregar does reach the East Gate of Karak Eight Peaks at the end of Uzkul Kadrin[86] and is ambushed.[87] Showing unnatural cunning, the grobi and urk encircle the lord. What follows is a detailed account of the battle, as transcribed from Lord Duregar's personal journal.

The Clan Angrund Royal Book of Grudges of King Belegar Ironhammer, Lord of the Eight Peaks

The rescue of Duregar Hammerfist

ON THIS DAY, a great victory was won by King Belegar of the Eight Peaks and Lord Duregar Hammerfist against the grobi swine of Skarsnik. What follows is a record of the battle as writ by our noble king in his memoirs:

---

86. Translated as Mad Dog Pass. This route goes through the Worlds Edge Mountains to the north of the Black Mountains and east of Averland.
87. Translates as Death Pass, a route along the Old Dwarf Road, the likeliest means by which Duregar and his kin reached the East Gate.

From the high towers of the citadel did our warriors espy clan brother Duregar heading into the grobi's trap. Thagi! Had I the means to forewarn him, I would have. Instead, I mustered the dawi of the Eight Peaks and went stealthily to the East Gate. The cave grobi had placed a rearguard there, but it was swiftly and mercilessly vanquished before any warning could be given to the rest of their foul breed.

Dragging aside the stinking corpses of the enemy, engineers and sappers quickly set about rigging the great east gate with black powder. The grobi would feel the fury of Grungni at their backs soon enough!

Though the gate was thick and broad, and it did cause me much lamentation to destroy it, the sounds of battle could be heard. No longer could I bear it and, our forces making ready with old grudges upon our lips, I did order the powder lit.

A great explosion rocked the very peaks and into battle did the dawi of Eight Peaks sally forth once more. All around us the grobi were in disarray and I sung the songs of Valaya, Grimnir and Grungni as I slew. Across a sea of greenskin blood did Belegar and Duregar unite at last, and well met it was! Now formed into a mighty square of dawi steel,[88] we began the slow advance back through the East Gate and from there to the safety of the city. Arrows fell amongst my kin as the grobi regrouped, the coward-warlord Skarsnik, an ever-present thorn in my side, screeching his orders from a lofty vantage point atop the valley. A frenzied pack of cave beasts, round and red with gaping maws full of fangs, did assail us but were repelled by slayers. Many of the Cult of Grimnir fulfilled their oaths in that brutal clash. Some small measure of atonement for previous misdeeds, no doubt.

The fire of the ancestors in our hearts, none could slow us now, the thickness of our klad repelling the worst of the grobi arrows, and we headed west. Harried all the while, we reached the citadel and the safety of Eight Peaks at last.[89]

88. I believe this to be the 'anvil' formation as described in brief in 'Dwarf Battle Tactics'.
89. See attached map on page 730 describing the Battle of East Gate.

Eight Peaks is reinforced

ON THIS DAY is the muster of Eight Peaks bolstered with the return of Lord Duregar Hammerfist. *Praise to Grungni!* Though it is a moot celebration, for our numbers are few and the grobi warlord Skarsnik, curse his name, does still control much of the Eight Peaks. Belegar, liege-lord of Vala-Azrilungol, does now occupy the entire ground level of the city and of the First Deep, the King's Chambers, the Great Hall and a number of foundries and clan halls have all been reclaimed. Lament of Valaya, as the mines do remain sealed, the rat-kin and other, fouler, creatures an ever-present threat to our safety and freedom.

In the Great Hall a mighty throng is gathered, the Grimgar Miner's Chorus and the Baldrikksson Brewers in attendance, as *The Fall of the Southern Holds* does resonate about Eight Peaks once more.[90]

The forces of Eight Peaks are again bolstered today by clans, once of Eight Peaks in ages past, from Karak Azul, Karaz-a-Karak and the umgdawi.[91] King Belegar does hereby strike out grudges against the Dourback, Craghand, Guttrik, Ironfinger and Flintheart clans. The return to Eight Peaks is deemed as fair recompense for the early transgressions of their ancestors in abandoning the hold.[92]

The Underway is Reopened

AT LAST THE Undgrin road to our brothers in the south at Karak Azul is reopened after several successful ironbreaker expeditions to thin out the grobi and rat-kin nested there. A mighty gorog takes place in the Great Hall and it is a day of rare celebration in these bleak times. Alas, the way to the north, and Karak Drazh, is still not safe and remains sealed.

Ambush at Death Pass

THREE SHIPMENTS OF gold, kindly donated by the High King of Everpeak, fail to arrive this day and concerns grow as to what has become of the dawi escorting them. I, King Belegar, dare not risk an expedition of rangers into the pass for fear of them sharing the same fate.[93]

90. This solemn lament is sung upon the anniversary of the eve of the fall of Eight Peaks every year. See 'Dwarf Pastimes' for more details about dwarf choirs.

91. The name given to ex-patriot dwarfs living in the Empire. In order to reinforce the hold and bolster its survival prospects, Belegar welcomed all.

92. Many clans of Karak Eight Peaks, at the time of its fall, made their way to Karak Azul to seek solace there and as such the books of grudges of both holds bear much crossover as the fell deeds that befell each were subsumed together.

93. In an effort to supplement the hold's gold supplies, the High King Thorgrim Grudgebearer organised many such shipments but with varying success.

Grim times are these. Our allies lessen as our enemies become ever bolder. There are no more warriors and our gold is all but exhausted. No more settlers come to our halls. We are alone. Each day is a bitter struggle to survive. We must contest these halls, fight for them until we have given the last of our breath. We must prevail – for if not us then who? The light is growing ever darker though, I fear it will soon be eclipsed utterly...

APPENDIX

Dwarf Battle Tactics

In battle, a dwarf army is intractable. We of the Empire have fought at their sides many times and are grateful of this tenacity. Each clan brother fights together, supporting each other; the dwarfs are the finest exponents of the irresistible shield wall in the Old World. In his Incunabulum, the scholar Old Weirde notes that it is a misconception that dwarfs are slow in battle; the contrary is true. Dwarfs march quickly and resolutely, without need for rest. They can shoulder great burdens and so make the extensive use of baggage trains and other cumbersome war paraphernalia unnecessary. This often means that dwarfs advance far quicker than their enemies suppose, able to adopt the most favourable battlefield positions such as natural strong points like hills or narrow ravines. They also make use of rangers and miners who are able to move ahead of the main throng and attack enemy weak points or engage in flanking manoeuvres. Once the foe is engaged, a dwarf throng will seek to withstand its initial assault and reply with a devastating counter-blow.

MILITARY THEORISTS OF the Empire have identified several commonly used tactics adopted by dwarfs such as the Enduring Mountain, a defensive strong-point strategy and the Bear Trap, which is essentially a baiting manoeuvre. The Hammer is a rare, offensive tactic and the Anvil is a potent defensive formation, one that was adopted by King Belegar of Eight Peaks and Lord Duregar of Karaz-a-Karak at the Battle of the East Gate.

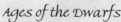

The dwarfs are an ancient race, far older than men, and their time upon the Old World can be broken down into distinct ages (note that all dates given adhere to the Imperial calendar used in honour of Emperor Karl Franz, praise his name). The following is translated from the runescript of the Karak Eight Peaks Book of Grudges.

The Time of the Ancestor Gods – Led by Grungni, Grimnir and Valaya, the slow colonisation of the Worlds Edge Mountains begins.

The Coming of Chaos – The end of the Time of the Ancestor Gods and the disappearance of Grimnir. The Chaos Gate is closed and the Old World is saved from certain destruction.

The Golden Age – Elves and dwarfs meet for the first time and establish trade to the mutual prosperity and benefit of both races. Many new holds are founded.

The War of Vengeance – The treachery of the elves signals an end to the Golden Age and the beginning of the War of Vengeance. The Phoenix King of the elves is slain and with that we are left to the Old World, but with our wealth and power much diminished.

The Time of Woes – Earthquakes ravage the land, destroying many holds and leaving them vulnerable to the predations of goblins and the creatures of Chaos. Many holds are lost, never to be reclaimed, and the lustre of the Everlasting Realm is dimmed further.

The Goblin Wars – The struggle for the Karaz Ankor is fought over a thousand years against the greenskins and a host of other foul creatures. Dragons, disturbed from their ancient slumber, sack many holds and the southern holds all fall bar one. The Everlasting Realm is left despoiled and in ruins.

The Silver Age – Contact is made with the race of men. In this age did the human prince, Sigmar, rescue High King Kurgan Ironbeard and a lasting alliance is formed. A vast orc horde is defeated at Black Fire Pass and with the creation of the Empire, an age of relative peace and prosperity is ushered.

The Chaos Wars – Men are warned of the dangers of Chaos and dwarfs fight side by side with the Empire once more during The Great War Against Chaos.

Khazalid – Language of the Dwarfs

The ancient high language of the dwarfs is called Khazalid. I have spent much time poring over ancient scripts researching it and gleaned what I humbly describe as a rudimentary under-satanding of its form and rules. What is clear is that it is a deeply conservative language that has not changed noticeably in many thousands of years either in its spoken or written 'runic' form. The dwarfs, if the evidence garnered from those I have met is anything to go by, are very proud of their tongue, which they rarely speak in the company of other races and never teach to other creatures. This treatise, therefore, is a work of linguistic conjecture and nothing more. To most humans it is the 'secret tongue of the dwarfs', occasionally overheard, but never properly understood.

FROM MY STUDIES I have ascertained that the dwarf language includes very few words of obviously human or elvish origin. By contrast there are many loan words from Khazalid in the tongue of men. This is most obviously so in the case of words concerning the traditional dwarfish craftskills of masonry and smithying, skills which we learned from the dwarfs many centuries past. These loans from Khazalid mean that some dwarf words sound very similar to equivalent human words, and this has enabled me to propose the theory given below.

Of course, some Khazalid words are all too familiar to the dwarfs' enemies – namely the fearsome battle-cries, oaths and curses of the dwarfs at war. Of these the most famous is the cry of 'Khazukan Kazakit-ha' or its common shortened form of, 'Khazuk! Khazuk! Khazuk!' which I have translated to mean 'Look out! The dwarfs are on the warpath'. It is also usual for dwarfs to call upon their ancestor gods during battle. I have heard it said that the guttural sound of dwarfs bellowing Grungni's name is enough to make an elf's knees knock and a goblin turn a sickly shade of yellow!

The sound of Khazalid is not much like human speech and very unlike the melodious sound of Elvish. Comparisons have been drawn to the rumble of thunder. All dwarfs have very deep, resonant voices and a tendency to speak more loudly than is strictly necessary. This can make dwarfs sound rowdy and irascible – which for the most part is a fair reflection of dwarfish temperament. Khazalid vowel sounds in particular are uncompromisingly precise and heavily accented. Consonants are often spat aggressively or gargled at the back of the throat as if attempting to dislodge a recalcitrant gobbet of phlegm. A drinking hall full of loud, drunken dwarfs sounds like a frightening place even when fists aren't flying – which isn't often.

From what I can gather in my studies, the vocabulary of Khazalid ably reflects the unique preoccupations of the dwarf race. There are hundreds of words for different kinds of rock, for passages and tunnels, and most of all for precious metals. Indeed, there are hundreds of words for gold alone.

In their dealings with others, the dwarfs choose their words carefully. A dwarf will not venture an opinion on anything that he has not considered deeply, and once his mind is made up you can be sure his view will be as immovable as a mountain. Dwarfs don't change their opinions except in the face of overwhelming necessity – and not always then. Many would rather die stubbornly than admit to a mistake that costs them their life! For this reason dwarfs take oaths and promises very seriously indeed, and this extends to their business affairs, even those with other races. In all the dwarf language, the word unbaraki is the most condemning of all – it means 'oathbreaker'. I had the misfortune of mentioning said word in dwarf company and still have cause to regret it to this very day.

Given how seriously dwarfs treat words, I have found their sense of humour tends to be especially unnerving. A common jest takes the form whereby two or more dwarfs conspire to make another feel deeply uncomfortable by pretending to know something about his circumstances, state of health, or past life that in reality they do not. This can go on for hours, days, or many years and is generally reckoned to be very funny indeed. More commonly a dwarf might make some provocative statement, wait for another to take offence, and then start a fight. Surprisingly these things tend to end in good humour, much back-slapping and mutual congratulations, with honour considered to have been satisfied all round.

The Runic Script

DELVING INTO WHAT ancient lore I have been able to procure, most of which came from the Karak Eight Peaks Book of Grudges now in my possession, dwarf runes were invented for carving Khazalid onto stone, hence the letters are formed from straight lines which can be easily cut with a chisel. The script consists of a core alphabetic structure, which I believe can be used to express any words, and additional individual runes, each of which is a shorthand sign that represents a single word, idea or name. This means that many words can be written in two forms – though this is only commonly seen with the names of people and places. Magical runes always take this second individual form and, for this reason, all non-alphabetic runes are regarded as having special significance or power.

From what I can gather, runes are usually carved from left to right, but can also be carved in alternate rows starting from left to right, the second row right to left, the third left to right and so on. Runes can also be carved vertically from top to bottom, this being a common form for monuments and important carvings. Written forms generally go left to right horizontally.

Klinkarhun

THE CORE ALPHABETIC runes are called klinkarhun, which means 'chisel runes', and these are the most commonly used and easily recognised. Although the sound of Khazalid does not exactly match the sounds of human speech, the chart shown on the next page gives the closest approximations. The sounds should be pronounced with force and the 'r' and 'kh' sound in particular are made as if enthusiastically clearing the throat, whilst 'z' is always given extra emphasis as in 'buzz'.

In addition to alphabetical runes, the Klinkarhun also includes a numeric series as shown below. The dwarf words for numbers are different depending on what it is they are counting – which can be very confusing – but it all makes sense to the dwarfs and serves to baffle other races. Dwarfs also count many things in twelves or dozens multiplying up to a gross (twelve twelves or one hundred and forty four), and other things in twenties or scores, as well as counting things in tens in a more conventional manner. There are no words for thirty, forty or so forth, rather a dwarf will say 'six tens and five' and 'three score and seven' – or 'sizdonun sak' and 'dweskorun set'.

Y	A OR I
ꑭ	AK
▷	AZ
ꔆ	B
ꔉ	D
ꑞ	DR OR TR
ꓮ	E
ꓝ	F OR V
ꓟ	G
ꓩ	H
K	K OR KH
M	KAR
ꑰ	L OR UL
ꓧ	M
ꓞ	N
Λ	NG
ꑬ	O
ꓣ	R
ꔤ	T
ꓩ	TH
Ƴ	W OR U
ꑄ	Z OR ZH

I	1	ONG
II	2	TUK
III	3	DWE
IIII	4	FUT
꒐	5	SAK
꒐ I	6	SIZ
꒐ II	7	SET
꒐ III	8	ODRO
꒐ IIII	9	NUK
ꔤ	10	DON
Iꔤ	12	DUZ
ꔤꔤ	20	SKOR
◇	100	KANTUZ
⊘	144	GROZ
⬡	1000	MILLUZ

WHILST KHAZALID UNDOUBTEDLY has a formal grammatical structure, as an outsider I have found it very hard to discover what it might be. I theorise that, in general, Khazalid places the subject before the verb and the object afterwards, but I also maintain that emphasis of pronunciation alone can sometimes determine a word's position within the structure of a sentence. In other cases, the importance of a particular word can demand that it be placed first in the sentence. Such words are often placed first out of respect and then again in their proper place later on, for example, 'the king – I went to see the king.' When repeated words are written or carved, they commonly appear as individual runes at the start of a sentence and klinkarhun elsewhere.

The first principle of the dwarf tongue is that almost all of its words represent solid physical things. There are surprisingly few specific words for abstract concepts. As a result many words double up as both a physical thing and an abstract concept strongly associated with that thing. For example, the root word for 'big-stone' is kar and the most common word for a mountain is karaz – the 'az' ending denoting a single material thing or specific place. The same root word, kar, is also used to mean enduring in the form 'karak' – the 'ak' ending denoting an abstract concept. Thus Karaz-a-Karak, the name of the dwarf capital, means 'enduring mountain' or literally 'big stony stone place', though the name is more attractively rendered into human speech as Everpeak.

Curiously the dwarf word for the race of men is umgi, whilst its abstract form of umgak means 'shoddy' – the dwarf word being equivalent to 'man-made'. This demonstrates just how important it is to look at the end of dwarf words – for it is these special 'signifiers' which usually tell you what the word actually means. There are many types of signifiers, some of which are given below, and by combining the different signifiers with root words it is possible to expand the basic Khazalid lexicon given in this book.

Although root words are often used on their own, many Khazalid words consist of a root word followed by one or more signifiers. So for example:

Root word	Signifier (1)	Signifier (2)
Kar-	-az	-i
Big stone	place	race, person, trade
Karazi a	Mountain	tribe/tribesman/ mountaineer

Some root words don't exist in a separate form at all. If a root word consists entirely of consonants it is usually written with an extra 'a' at the end but this is dropped when a signifier is added. For example, 'Ska-' is the root for 'thief', 'theft' and 'to steal'.

Ska - az	Skaz =	thief in general – 'a thief'
Ska - azi	Skazi =	a specific thief – 'the thief'
Ska - ak	Skak =	theft
Ska - it	Skit =	steal

As in the example above – verb signifiers usually appear at the end of words. In Khazalid almost every noun has a verb form which is usually denoted by '-it'. In the present tense and '–ed' in the past. Tenses other than the simple present and past are denoted by additional words before the verb rather than by different endings – the equivalent to 'will steal' (an skit) in the simple future tense. Although separate words these are often written together as shown.

Skit	steal
Sked	stole
Anskit	will steal
Adsked	had stolen
Anadsked	will have stole

Common Signifiers

IN THE CASE of all signifiers, a 'g' or 'k' can be added immediately before the signifier if the preceding root or signifier is a vowel or weak consonant such as 'l' or 'r'. This avoids placing two vowels together – which is something Khazalid strenuously avoids. However there are no rules for this, and in many cases one of the vowels is simply missed out especially if it is the weaker vowel 'a' or 'i' (which are almost the same sound in Khazalid and the same rune in klinkarhun).

-az   This is a very important and common signifier and it means the word represents a specific physical thing or place – a particular mountain not mountains in general. It is usually placed directly after the root before any other signifiers. That much is easy – unfortunately there are many things that the dwarfs regard as so real and solid that the -az signifier is used even though they are talking about something which is neither a place or a material object! For example 'galaz' which means 'fearless'. In this case the -az refers to the 'real essence' of the idea. So, from the root 'dur' which means 'stone that can be riven' comes duraz which means a stone slab but also durak which means 'hard like a stone slab'. Although it is perfectly right to describe a tough dwarf as durak (rock hard) it would also be correct to describe him as duraz (literally stone).

-ak This is the other major common signifier and means that the word represents a concept, something abstract such as honour, courage or fortitude. Of course, dwarfs being dwarfs, really important abstract concepts are accorded the status of real things, so 'a grudge to be avenged' is dammaz, not dammak, but dammak still stands for the general concept of outstanding grudges.

-ar This signifies something that continues indefinitely over time – usually an activity such as trade (urbar) but also an experience such as chronic pain (urtar) and natural forces such as the movement of the sun (zonstrollar – sun-walk-ing).

-en This signifies something that is currently ongoing but not indefinite such as journey-ing (strollen), marching (gotten) or carrying a heavy burden (hunken).

-i The signifier 'i' shows that the word refers to an individual person, or a profession, or race. In general it is most easily thought of as representing the definite article 'the' or even 'that person just there'. Many personal names end with this signifier too.

-al The signifier 'al' shows that the word refers to a group or band of people or creatures – rather like a collective noun. So, whilst the word for both the race of men and 'the man' is umgi a band of men is umgal. It is also used to encompass a person's kinsfolk in the form Grummal – Grumm's people often translated as Grummlings.

-it or -git This signifier when applied to a noun indicates something small or trivial. It is also used for a present tense verb – but dwarfs

	are used to such things and rarely let it confuse them.
-ul or-kul	This is a common word ending for dwarf words and not always a signifier but often means 'the art of, understanding of, or master of', for example grungkul the art of mining, and kazakul the art of battle or generalship.
-ha	This signifier always appears at the end of a word and is the equivalent to an exclamation mark. It is pronounced very abruptly and can be read as 'so there' or 'so watch it' – definitely fighting talk.

Useful Elements

FROM MY STUDIES, I believe the following useful words are the dwarf equivalent of conjunctions, relative pronouns and other common grammatical elements. Although words in their own right, they are often appended directly before other words to form new compound words such as 'okrik' which means usurper king (literally: why-king) and aguz which means 'replete' (literally: with-food). I have listed these words below.

A	Of, with, within, to
Ad	Did, done, (preceding a verb)
Af	They, you (plural)
Ai, I, Ap and Ip	All forms of yes
An	Will/shall/am going to/with purpose (preceding a verb)
Anad	Will have done or shall have done
Bin	In, on, beside
Anu	Soon, very soon, any minute now!
Bar	But, bear in mind, except for (also the word for a fortified gate)
Ek	He, she, it, you (singular)
Nai, Na or Nuf	All forms of no, not and never
Nu	Now, at this time
Ok	Why, how
Or	I, me, myself
Sar	May, could, might (preceding a verb)
Um	Them, those, these
Un	And
Ut	Us, we, ourselves
Wanrag	Where
Wanrak	When (preceding a verb),

Magic Runes

Weapons

꜀ Rune of Snorri Spangelhelm
Ⴟ Master Rune of Skalf Blackhammer
▣ Master Rune of Alaric the Mad
↑ Master Rune of Death
✦ Master Rune of Swiftness
Ӽ Master Rune of Daemon Slaying
Ⴟ Master Rune of Dragon Slaying
ξ Master Rune of Banishment
Ⱳ Master Rune of Flight
Δ Master Rune of Breaking
⊘ Master Rune of Kragg the Grim
◁ Rune of Cleaving
⟨ Curse Rune
∨ Rune of Cutting
⟩ Rune of Fire
Ⱶ Rune of Fate
Ᵽ Rune of Fury
Ӝ Rune of Might
⟩ Rune of Parrying
◁ Master Rune of Smiting
∑ Rune of Striking
✸ Grudge Rune
Λ Rune of Speed

Armour

⅂ Master Rune of Steel
A Master Rune of Adamant
Ꮆ Master Rune of Gromril
Ᵽ Rune of Resistence
≺ Rune of Shielding
◊ Rune of Preservation
ℨ Rune of Stone
I Rune of Iron
Ᵽ Rune of Fortitude

Protection

⅄ Master Rune of Stromni Redbeard
Ӿ Master Rune of Groth One-Eye
Ӝ Master Rune of Valaya
✿ Master Rune of Grungni

(Talismanic column — Weapons right side)

↓ Rune of Guarding
Ⱥ Rune of Stoicism
⧣ Rune of Determination
Ⴟ Strollaz's Rune
φ Rune of Battle
Ɛ Rune of Courage
Ⱳ Rune of Sanctuary
⅃ Master Rune of Fear
Ħ Rune of Slowness
Ⰿ Ancestor Rune

Engineering

Ӎ Master Rune of Defence
Ᵽ Master Rune of Skewering
⧈ Rune of Accuracy
⚡ Rune of Burning
Π Master Rune of Disguise
Ħ Rune of Forging
∇ Rune of Reloading
∡ Valiant Rune
Ⱶ Rune of Fortune
Ⱶ Master Rune of Immolation
⬦ Rune of Penetrating
Ⱶ Flakkson's Rune of Seeking
▵ Stalwart Rune

Talismanic

↑ Master Rune of Balance
⩜ Master Rune of Spellbinding
Ӎ Master Rune of Dismay
Ӎ Master Rune of Kingship
ⱡ Master Rune of Spite
↝ Master Rune of Challenge
Ӎ Rune of the Furnace
∨ Rune of Luck
⧊ Rune of Passage
ⵝ Rune of Spellbreaking
Ⴟ Spelleater Rune
Ᵽ Rune of Fate
◁ Rune of Warding

Khazalid Lexicon

This lexicon has been the result of almost two decades of diligent research and primary resource gathering. In the guest quarters of the hold of Karak Norn I spent many, many long hours with dwarfs of numerous clans, listening to their dialect, asking questions when appropriate and garnering as much as I could of the words and phrases of the Khazalid language. Doubtless, the extent of the Khazalid 'dictionary' is far greater than the sum of these few words and the meanings I have proposed are derived from well-informed supposition.

A

Agrul	Stone carving; lines in face of very old dwarf.
Angaz	Ironwork.
Ankor	Domain or realm.
Arm	The Khazalid irregular verb to be (present tense *arm* – past tense *urz*).
Az	War axe.
Azgal	Treasure hoard.
Azul	Metal of any kind; dependable; a sturdy dwarf.

B

Bak	Fist, punch.
Bar	A fortified gateway or door.
Barag	War machine.
Baraz	A bond or promise.
Boga	A candle which blows out unexpectedly plunging the tunnel into darkness.
Bok	Banging your head on the roof of a low tunnel; characteristic scar on forehead caused by same!
Boki	Slang word for dwarf miners.
Bolg	Large, fat belly. Also a state of extreme wealth, age and contentment.
Bozdok	Unhinged as a result of constantly banging one's head on low roofs and pit-props – 'crosseyed'.
Bran	Clever, alert, mentally sharp.
Brodag	An annual brewing festival of Grungni.
Bryn	Gold that shines strikingly in the sunlight; anything shiny or brilliant.

Bugrit	An invocation against ill-luck uttered by a dwarf who has banged his head, hit his thumb, stubbed his toe or some other minor misfortune. Usually repeated three times for luck.

C

Chuf	Piece of very old cheese a dwarf miner keeps under his hat for emergencies.

D

Dal	Old, good.
Dammaz	A grievance, grudge or insult to be avenged.
Dammaz Kron	The Book of Grudges.
Dar	A challenge or bet.
Dawi	Dwarfs.
Dawr	As good as something can get without it being proven over time and hard use. Most dwarf words for 'good' imply age and reliability too but dawr simply means 'looks like it might be good'. It literally translates as 'like dwarf'.
Deb	New, untried, raw.
Dibnin	The act of tinkering with something that already works perfectly, out of a belief that it can still be improved – hence *Dibna*, a dwarf who engages in dibnin.
Doh	Stupid, slow-witted, gullable.
Dok	Watch, observe, see, the eye.
Dongliz	The parts of a dwarf's body impossible for him to scratch.
Dork	Giant, tall, unstable.
Drakk	Dragon.
Drek	Far, a great distance; great ambition or enterprise.
Dreng	Slay in combat.
Drengi	Slayer, one of the cult of Slayers.
Drongnel	Dragon stew with cave mushrooms marinated in strong ale.
Drung	To defeat, vanquish.
Duk	Low, narrow tunnel.
Dum	Doom or darkness.
Dunkin	Annual bath traditionally taken whether needed or not.

Durak	Hard.
Duraz	Stone or slab.

E

Ekrund	A stairway descending beneath the ground.
Elgi	Elves.
Elgram	Weak, enfeebled, thin.
Elgraz	Construction that looks as if it is about to collapse.
Endrinkuli	An engineer or mechanic (generally a dwarf engineer).

F

Fleg	Banner, standard.
Frongol	Mushrooms that grow at the back of a cave.

G

Galaz	Gold of particular ornamental value.
Gand	Find, discover.
Garaz	Fearless, rebellious.
Gazan	Plains, wasteland.
Gibal	Fragments of food enmeshed in a dwarf's beard.
Ginit	Small stone which works its way into your boot causing discomfort.
Girt	Broad tunnel with plenty of headroom.
Git	The Khazalid irregular verb to go (present tense *git* – past tense *ged*) the word is related to got (ibid).
Gnol	Old, reliable, proven, wise.
Gnollengrom	Respect due to a dwarf who has a longer and more spectacular beard.
Gnorl	An especially bright and obvious boil or similar blemish on the end of the nose.
Gor	Wild beast.
Gorak	Great cunning, uncanny.
Gorl	Gold that is especially soft and yellow; the colour yellow.
Gorog	Ale; high spirits; a drinking binge.
Got	March or travel quickly and with purpose.
Gov	Thane.
Gozunda	Practically anything kept under the bed 'for emergencies'.

Grik	Pain in the neck caused by continually stooping in low tunnels.
Grim	Harsh, unyielding.
Grimaz	Barren place.
Grindal	Long flaxen plaits worn by dwarf maidens.
Grint	Waste rock or spoil left by miners' excavations.
Grizal	Poor meat.
Grizdal	Ale that has been fermented for at least a century.
Grob	The colour green, also goblins and orcs – literally greenies.
Grobi	Goblins.
Grobkaz	Goblin work, evil deeds.
Grobkul	Art of stalking goblins in caves.
Grog	Inferior or watered ale; mannish brew.
Grom	Brave or defiant.
Gromdal	An ancient artefact.
Gromthi	Ancestor.
Grong	Anvil.
Gronit	The Khazalid irregular verb to do (present tense *gronit* – past tense *gird*).
Gronti	Giant (as in the creature).
Grumbak	A short measure of ale; trivial complaint or grumble.
Grumbaki	A grumbler or whiner.
Grund	Hammer (also sometimes called 'rikkaz').
Grung	A mine.
Grungnaz	Making or smithying.
Grungni	Dwarf ancestor, god of mines and smiths.
Grungron	A forge.
Gruntaz	Strip of cloth worn round the loins and supposedly eaten in extreme emergencies hence, 'down to his gruntaz'.
Gruntitrogg	Secret coming of age ritual practiced amongst dwarfkind – details of this are amongst the most closely kept of all dwarf secrets.
Guz	To consume food or drink.
Guzzen	Feed, insert, push.

H

Hazkal	Ale brewed recently; a fiery young warrior.
Hunk	Carry heavy rocks or other burden.
Hruki	Breed of mountain goat.

I

Ik   Putting your hand in something slimy and unpleasant in the darkness.

Irkul   Pillared vault hewn in rock.

J

Jifful   Process of careful and precise adjustment to fit – especially in respect of engineering or stonemasonry.

K

Kadrin   Mountain pass.

Kalan   Clan.

Karag   Volcano or barren mountain.

Karak   Enduring.

Karaz   Mountain.

Karin   Shield, temporary protection.

Kazad   Fortress.

Kazak   War or battle.

Khaz   An underground hall.

Khazhunki   Knight, cavalry, rider. Lit. 'carried warrior'.

Khazukan   Dwarfs – literally hall-dwellers.

Khrum   War drum.

Klad   Armour.

Klinka   Chisel.

Klinkarhun   Common runes.

Kol   Black stone, the colour black, sombre.

Konk   Gold that is ruddy in colour; large and bulbous nose.

Krink   Bad back due to continual stooping.

Kro   Crow, raven, dark bird.

Kron   Book, record or history.

Kruk   A seemingly promising vein of ore which gives out suddenly; an unexpected disappointment; a venture which comes to nothing.

Krunk   Underground rockfall; a disaster!

Krut   A discomforting disease contracted from mountain goats.

Kruti   A dwarf suffering from krut; a goatherd; an insult.

Kulgur   The art of cooking troll.

Kuri   Meat stew boiled up by travelling dwarfs from whatever ingredients are at hand. Traditionally spiced with wild berries.

L

Lok — Highly embellished or intricate; praiseworthy.

M

Makaz — Weapon or tool.

Mingol — Tall watchtower built on lowland.

N

Naggrund — An area of great upheaval, devastation, or industry.

Narwangli — A dung collector or dwarf who smells strongly of dung.

Nogarung — Drinking tankard made from a troll's skull.

Nubungki — A dwarf child deformed at birth, shunned by its clan and exiled. A great shame to the clan and the hold.

O

Ogri — Ogre.

Ok — Cunning or skilful.

Okri — Craftsman – a common personal name.

Onk — Comradely accretion of dirt and grime on a company of dwarfs who have spent many days underground.

R

Ragarin — Coarse and uncomfortable clothing made from a troll's hide.

Rhun — Rune, word or power.

Rhunki — Runesmith.

Rik — King or lord.

Rikkazen — Crush, to beat to a pulp, to turn to rubble.

Rikkit — A small stone that falls on your head as you walk down a tunnel.

Ril — Gold ore that shines brightly in rock.

Rink — Command, to give orders, to lead.

Rinn — A lady dwarf or king's consort.

Rogwak — An improvised team game played underground and using anything to hand as a ball – often a rock, preferably a goblin's head, or even a whole goblin.

Rorkaz	Informal shouting contest.
Ruf	A large underground dome either natural or constructed.
Runk	A one-sided fight; a sound thrashing!
Rutz	Slackness of bowels caused by drinking too much ale.

S

Skarrenruf	The colour bright blue, the day time sky.
Skaz	Thief.
Skof	A cold meal eaten underground.
Skrat	To search for gold amongst rock debris or stream bed; scavenge; sparse living.
Skrati	Poor prospector.
Skree	Loose rock on a mountainside.
Skruff	A scrawny beard; an outrageous insult!
Skrund	To hew rock; to get stuck in!
Skuf	A drunken brawl or skirmish.
Slotch	The sodden mix of water, mud and pulverised stone found at the bottom of a mineworking.
Smak	Punish physically.
Stok	To hit or strike.
Strol	Walk or travel leisurely.
Stromez	Stream.

T

Thag	Slay by act of treachery.
Thagi	Murderous traitor.
Thaggoraki	Skaven, assassin, footpad.
Thindrongol	Secret vault in which ale or treasure is hidden.
Thingaz	Dense forest.
Throng	Army; huge assembly of dwarfs; a clan.
Thrund	A hand gun.
Trogg	A feast or heavy drinking bout.
Troll	Troll.
Tromm	Beard; respect due to age or experience.
Tusk	Tooth.

U

Ufdi	A dwarf overfond of preening and decorating his beard; a vain dwarf; a dwarf who cannot be trusted to fight.
Umanar	Roughly or approximately, and also indecision or vacillation.
Umgak	Shoddy, poorly made.
Umgi	Men.
Unbak	Break permanently.
Unbaraki	An oathbreaker – there is nothing worse in dwarf estimation.
Und	A watchpost carved into the mountainside.
Ungdrin	Ankor Underway, the ancient underground roadway of the dwarfs.
Ungor	Cavern.
Ungrim	A dwarf who has not yet fulfilled an important oath; an untrustworthy dwarf.
Urbar	Trade.
Urbaz	A trading post or market.
Urk	Orc or enemy (also fear, to be afraid of, to retreat).
Uzkul	Bones or death.
Uzkular	Undead.

V

Valdahaz	Brewery.
Varf	Wolf, hound.
Varn	Mountain lake.
Vongal	Raiding band.
Vorn	A farm.

W

Wan	On its own at the start of a phrase, wan shows the phrase is a question. It's the dwarf equivalent of a question mark. This is usually missed off where a standard wan – question word is used instead (wanrag, wanrak, wanrum). Wan – is also used immediately before another word to frame a question (ek wangit? 'are you going' literally 'you go?', wandar 'is it good?' literally 'good?').
Wanaz	A disreputable dwarf with an unkempt beard; an insult.

Wattock	An unsuccessful dwarf prospector; a down-at-heel dwarf; an insult.
Wazzok	A dwarf who has exchanged gold or some other valuable item for something of little or no worth; a foolish or gullible dwarf; an insult.
Werit	A dwarf who has forgotten where he placed his tankard of ale; a state of befuddlement.
Wutroth	Wood from ancient mountain oak.

Z

Zak	An isolated hut in the mountains.
Zaki	A crazed dwarf who wanders in the mountains.
Zan	Blood, the colour red.
Zanen	A bleeding wound.
Zanguzaz	Vampire.
Zank	Cleave, cut, divide.
Zharr	Fire.
Zhuf	Waterfall or rapidly flowing river.
Zint	The metal tin – hence *zinti*, a tinsmith or tinker.
Zorn	Upland plateau or high meadow.
Zon	Sun.

KARAK AZUL – A CLAN RECORD

*Gathered from the partial and fragmented records of the
Karak Eight Peaks Book of Grudges.*

Karak Azul

Donarkhun Clan (royalty)
Bael (ancestor)
Kazgar (ancestor – father of Kazador)
Hilga of Karak Azul (ancestor – wife of Kazgar, mother of Kazador)
Kazador of Karak Azul (King)
Kazrik (thane – son of Kazador)
Thordrik Greymane (living ancestor – Kazrik's uncle)
Morga of Karak Azul (Queen)
Freygar (Priestess of Valaya)
Vargansson (Ironmaster)
Malrik Morbad (hammerer)
Kreln Kromsson (hammerer)

Redbeard Clan (runesmiths)
Stromni
Forgehand Clan (runesmiths)
Razek (ancestor – Runelord)
Varik (ancestor – Runelord)
Karagin (Runesmith and weaponmaster)
Stoutgirth Clan (brewers)
Thengeln (Brewmaster)
Dunrakin Clan (brewers)

Stonebeater Clan (masons)
Orgrin (Stonemaster)
Flinthand Clan (engineers)
Ironforge Clan (runesmiths)
Ganngrim (ancestor – Runelord)
Ironbrow Clan (runesmiths)
Thorek (Runelord and Master of the Weapons Shops)

Stonehand Clan (masons)
Cragbrow Clan (miners)
Thunderheart Clan (jewel smiths)
Badrikk Clan (metal smiths)
Burrdrik Clan (metal smiths)
Ironhammer Clan (metal smiths)
Stoneheart Clan (masons)
Silvenback Clan (jewel smiths)
Stonecutter Clan (masons)
Firehand Clan (metal smiths)
Ironfinger Clan (metal smiths)
Kaznagar Clan (jewel smiths)

Halgakrin Clan (carpenters)
Threkkson Clan (lode wardens)
Svengeln Clan (prospectors)
Kakki Clan (miners)
Varnskan Clan (miners)
Stoutpeak Clan (carpenters)

(Note that many clans of Eight Peaks migrated to Karak Azul after its fall and so became subsumed into the clan history of the hold.)

Karak Eight Peaks

Angrund Clan (royalty)
Lunn Ironhammer (ancestor – King)
Belegar Ironhammer of Karak Eight Peaks (King)
Kemma Ironhammer (Queen of Belegar)
Duregar Hammerfist (lord)

Stonebeard Clan (engineers)
Dourback Clan (brewers)

Stoneback Clan (masons)
Ironfinger Clan (metal smiths)
Flintheart Clan (metal smiths)

Grimstone Clan (prospector)
Firehelm Clan (miners)
Copperback Clan (miners)
Flinthand Clan (miners – not to be confused with the Karak Azul Flinthands)
Bronzefist Clan (lode wardens)
Ironback Clan (miners)
Ironspike Clan (carpenters)
Craghand Clan (miners)

Guttrik Clan (rope-makers)

Anatomy of a Hold

Dwarfs and the Surface

THOUGH THE DWARFS live for much of their life underground, and the greater part of their realm is beneath the rock, they do not shun the surface altogether. Indeed, as much as one third of a king's domains may be above ground and far afield.

Such surface structures include not only the gates and gatehouses into the hold, but also a network of other delvings that may only be connected to the hold by overground routes. These incorporate all manner of mines, lookout towers, goat-herding stations, trading posts, breweries, farms, gyrocopter landing stages and ranger outposts.

All of these are considered part of the hold, and regular contact is maintained with them when possible. However, some of these outlying realms may be cut off by war, weather or other circumstance for decades, if not centuries. In these times, expeditions are sent to re-establish communications, often several generations later. Some of these isolated settlements may have been wiped out, others will have grown and will seek nominal independence from their hold; for an appropriate severance payment to the ruling king, of course.

The most obvious outward signs of a dwarf hold are the bastions and skybridges. Walls and watch towers jut from the snowy rock, manned every hour of the day and night, with beacon fires ready to be lit. Often these are linked by covered walkways, reinforced trenches and roads with parapets, so that forces can be moved safely from one place to another. Some are linked by tunnels that never connect with the hold, allowing warriors to redeploy secretly from one tower to the next, yet at no time risk the security of the hold should they be overrun.

The skybridges vary enormously. Some are thin and have no parapet, barely wide enough for a single traveller to cross. Others are broad enough for three carts to move abreast, with high towers along their length. No skybridge has been built for over four thousand years, for they were constructed when dwarf power was at its height, before the Time of Woes. Many were destroyed in the eruptions and earthquakes, others have been abandoned and have all but collapsed. Those that survive are impressive indeed, soaring from peak to peak across the mountains, spanning valleys many miles wide, some as high as the clouds themselves.

Beneath the Earth

BELOW ITS SURFACE, a dwarf hold is divided into a series of descending levels called 'deeps'. These deeps are most usually linked by long stairways, subterranean tunnels and shafts, invariably brazier lit, expertly crafted and adorned with dwarfen mosaics and runic insignia.

Through what materials I have been able to procure, assorted maps and my own experiences, I propose a rough organisational structure of a typical hold, including the deeps, halls, chambers etcetera that they each contain. It is worth noting that the rooms, temples and so on, along with their conjoined tunnels and passageways, are often vast and of staggering stature, despite the shortness of the occupants.

DWARF HOLDS POSSESS many gates. The so-called 'Great Gate', singularly the largest of a given hold and that which opens it to the world above, is the most important. I have seen the Great Gate of Karak Norn and it appeared to me much like a gargantuan slab of the mountainside, though ornately carved. I have unearthed several accounts by some traders admitted to certain holds that rituals exist whereby a much smaller ingress can be 'opened' within one of the great gates enabling small groups of visitors to enter the hold without the need to fully open the great gate and leave it vulnerable. My researches have revealed secondary entrances into the hold, usually through the subterranean Underway or occasionally on the opposite side of a peak, and these gates, much like the great gate, are well secured and guarded at all times.

Other, smaller (I say 'smaller', but in truth, the inner gates I have seen are still immense and awe-inspiring), but still well fortified and heavily guarded inner gates to a hold are found between deeps and bar open passage to rooms and areas of importance such as the king's chambers, great hall, guild halls and some particularly prestigious clan halls. Of course, dwarfs also erect protective barriers to guard their treasure vaults and ancestor tombs, many of which are hidden with magical runes and cunning geological trickery.

UPPER DEEP

This level is found immediately beyond the great gate to a hold and is used for receiving the troops of visiting dwarf lords and other visitors.

I   Entrance hall, barrack rooms, audience chamber and guardrooms.

LOWER DEEPS – IN ORDER OF DEPTH.

II   Merchant halls, clan halls, barracks (clan standards are kept here), armouries, the king's court, council chambers, throne room, galleries.

III   Great hall, guild halls (metal smiths, stone cutters and masons, carpenters, rope-wrights, candlemakers and miners), breweries, ale stores, kitchens, pantries, drinking and feast halls.

IIII   King's chambers, royal clan hall, esteemed guild halls (runesmiths, jewel smiths, gold smiths, brewmasters, engineers), loremaster's chambers, library, scribe's chambers, armouries, hammerer barrack room, trophy room, counting room, servant quarters, guard rooms.

IIIII   Armouries, foundries, forges, workshops and powder rooms.

IIIII I   Shrines and temples, hall of remembering and hall of deeds.

VAULTS

IIIII II   Treasure vaults, king's hoard room, ancestor chambers.

IIIII III   Tombs, burial chambers, preparation rooms.

IIIII IIII   Mines, barrack rooms, clan halls, refectories (smaller version of a drinking/feast hall).

UNDERDEEP

✝   Lowest levels of a hold, sometimes abandoned completely, dwarfs don't usually venture here...

Miners

AS ONE MIGHT expect from a race that dwells almost constantly underground, the role of the miner is a much valued and lauded one. The Miners' Guild in any hold is perhaps second only to the Engineers' Guild in prestige and influence, and sometimes up to half the adult dwarfs of a clan may be employed as miners, and some clans consist almost entirely of mining families.

While we may use the term 'miner' to describe these dwarfs, there are many, many subsets of this profession. Dwarf mining is highly complex, and the members of a mining team have specific roles; to the dwarfs it is much more than simply swinging a tool at a rock face. The proper preparation and maintenance of mineshafts is one area of expertise, the surveying and analysis of rock and its ore is another. There is much overlap with engineering, particularly as new tools such as blasting charges – black powder explosives used to shear off large parts of a face – and steam-driven hammers and drills become more common. Within each of these many areas, a dwarf will specialise in a particular type of ore or rock. Some are coal miners, others iron workers, others seek gems, while many are wholly dedicated to the pursuit of precious metals. The best ways to locate and extract these ores are often clan-held secrets, and no few grudges have been recorded on account of other clans attempting espionage to gain some insight into a particular clan's techniques.

As a beardling, a dwarf miner will begin to learn his trade by helping move the ore from the rock face to the smelteries, learning how to identify different types of rock in the process. He will then progress to shoring up mine shafts, and then working on the face itself, first with a pick but later with more sophisticated tools. Over many decades, a miner may move from one type of ore to another, and his knowledge will broaden as well as deepen. The guildmasters are venerable miners that can use smell, touch and hearing to identify hidden seams, and can operate mining machinery in almost total darkness.

The mines themselves make up the outermost regions of any hold. Rather than being abandoned as are the mines of other races, the mines of the dwarfs are turned into corridors, chambers and halls by mining teams and stone masons. Even the most glorious throne room or vault once started life as a simple mine! As the miners follow the seams of ore, the hold expands. This can seem haphazard to outsiders, as galleries and tunnels often follow convoluted paths. To aid navigation, the dwarfs have a well-established vocabulary to define the areas of a hold, as revealed elsewhere.

Dwarf Pastimes

ALTHOUGH COMMONLY RESERVED and reclusive amongst other
races, even downright distrustful in the case of elves, there
is evidence to suggest that dwarfs are a very sociable people
when amongst their own.

*Feasting – Dwarf pastimes are varied but usually revolve
around or culminate in feasting and drinking (in the
Khazalid, a rough translation is 'trogg' and 'gororg').
Feast halls, for instance, are fashioned with such a purpose in mind. Dwarf eating habits vary but their known
staples are red meat, stews, kuri and stone bread – a
granite-like victual that only a dwarf could chew, let
alone eat. (I once sampled a piece and it was not unlike
swallowing a stone.)*

*Feasting is an opportunity for the clans of the hold to
gather together, eat, drink and make merry, tell stories
and sing of great deeds. As such, feast halls are often
vast, enabling several hundred dwarfs to sit together at
one time. Seating etiquette is strict and proximity to the
royal table is an indication of status. During these occasions the king will be attended by his chief victualer,
who is a chef, brewmaster and head taster in equal measure – it is his responsibility to ensure that the royal
table wants for nothing for the duration of the feast.*

*Drinking – Drinking is the natural accompaniment
to feasting and dwarfs take even greater pleasure in
this than the actual feast itself. Indeed, such drinking
binges or 'gorog', give rise to all manner of contestation
and trials of dwarfen constitution and alcoholic endurance. After the ale has been flowing for many hours and
thoughts turn to days gone by, ancient deeds and grudges
unreckoned, a sombre mood descends and the bawdy,
light-hearted atmosphere is replaced by dour lamentation.*

*Singing and story telling – Singing and the recounting
of great poetic sagas is very much a part of dwarfen feast
culture. Drinking hymns are popular, so much so that it
is not uncommon for the Brewers' Guild to have its own
chorus line. Four-and-twenty Firkins is one recorded
anthem – though I have yet to try to sing it – as are The*

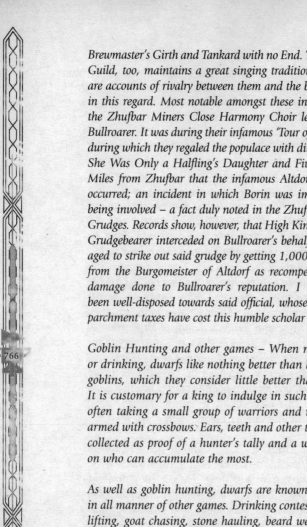

Brewmaster's Girth and Tankard with no End. The Miners' Guild, too, maintains a great singing tradition and there are accounts of rivalry between them and the brewmasters in this regard. Most notable amongst these institutions is the Zhufbar Miners Close Harmony Choir led by Borin Bullroarer. It was during their infamous 'Tour of Reikland', during which they regaled the populace with ditties such as She Was Only a Halfling's Daughter and Five Hundred Miles from Zhufbar that the infamous Altdorf stampede occurred; an incident in which Borin was implicated as being involved – a fact duly noted in the Zhufbar Book of Grudges. Records show, however, that High King Thorgrim Grudgebearer interceded on Bullroarer's behalf and managed to strike out said grudge by getting 1,000 gold pieces from the Burgomeister of Altdorf as recompense for the damage done to Bullroarer's reputation. I have never been well-disposed towards said official, whose outrageous parchment taxes have cost this humble scholar much.

Goblin Hunting and other games – When not feasting or drinking, dwarfs like nothing better than hunting for goblins, which they consider little better than vermin. It is customary for a king to indulge in such a pastime, often taking a small group of warriors and rangers, all armed with crossbows. Ears, teeth and other trophies are collected as proof of a hunter's tally and a wager made on who can accumulate the most.

As well as goblin hunting, dwarfs are known to indulge in all manner of other games. Drinking contests aside: ox lifting, goat chasing, stone hauling, beard weaving, bellowing, axe throwing, hammer tossing and anvil heaving are all particular favourites.

Gold counting – A dwarf, particularly a king, likes nothing better than counting the vast amounts of gold in his treasure hoard (I have known money lenders and pawn brokers with a similar predilection). The process can take several hours, even days, but it is done with painstaking accuracy and deliberation so as to derive as much pleasure from the experience as possible.

MORE FROM GAV THORPE
AND NICK KYME

ABOUT THE AUTHORS

Nick Kyme is a writer and editor. He lives in Nottingham where he began a career at Games Workshop on *White Dwarf* magazine. Now Black Library's Senior Range Editor, Nick's writing credits include the Warhammer 40,000 Tome of Fire trilogy featuring the Salamanders, his Warhammer Fantasy-based dwarf novels and several short stories. Read his blog at *www.nickkyme.com*

Prior to becoming a freelance writer, **Gav Thorpe** worked for Games Workshop as lead background designer, overseeing and contributing to the Warhammer and Warhammer 40,000 worlds. He has written numerous novels and short stories set in the fictional worlds of Games Workshop, including the Time of Legends 'The Sundering' series, the seminal Dark Angels novel *Angels of Darkness*, and the Eldar Path trilogy. He lives in Nottingham, UK, with his mechanical hamster, Dennis.

MORE FROM GAV THORPE
AND NICK KYME